ON VACATION

~

Also by Tina Day/Tina Knight

~

The Kastle Fortunes Series
The Courtship of Princess and Pirate
A Soul Lost at Sea
A Pirate's Promise
The Heart of a Woman

The Watching Trilogy
Watching
Wanting
Willing

Other Novels
Sweet Revenge

ON VACATION

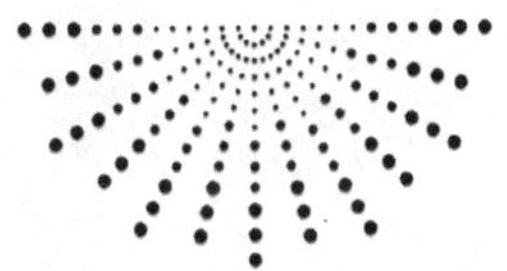

TINA KNIGHT

Day and Knight
Romance
Publications

For all of the incredible medical professionals I have worked with through the years, thank you for devoting yourselves to helping others. Your sacrifices are appreciated more than you could ever know.

1

WHEN LIFE GIVES YOU LEMONS

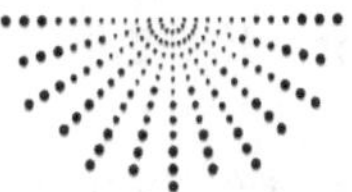

Hunter Gregory downshifted the gear of his sleek, silver Porsche, hearing the engine rev as it worked to climb the steep incline. "I can't believe I'm doing this," he muttered to himself. "I can't believe Will actually talked me into this."

Hunter controlled an involuntary cringe, hating this feeling of weakness. Especially now, with his Porsche nagging at him while scaling the final sharp roads toward Blissful Blue Retreat, he questioned the necessity of this journey. No matter what Dr. William Rand thought, this mountainous trip couldn't possibly fix the deficits in Hunter's life.

"Blissful Blue is simply a place for relaxation," Will had informed him a month ago, as he'd handed Hunter a beer and flipped on the television, turning his eyes to the basketball game. "It's gorgeous there. Just a bunch of log cabins in the middle of the Blue Ridge Mountains. So quiet and peaceful. You're the CEO of Gregory Global, Hunter, yet you never take a vacation. I think you're allowed the same benefits as any of your employees."

As he'd slumped down beside Will on the couch, Hunter shook his head. "This wouldn't be a vacation, though. It's a *psychiatric* retreat."

Will looked at him with his dark, knowing eyes, and sighed. "Call it whatever you need to, Hunter. You don't have to talk to another soul for the whole three weeks if you don't want to. But, if you choose, there are group meetings and get-togethers, with working people just like you."

"You mean patients like me, *Doctor*."

"You're not my patient, and don't call me *doctor*. You always look like you're going to vomit when you say that word. You're the one who sought my advice, so I'll give it to you. Take three weeks off of work – I promise the company will survive that long without you – and spend it up at Blissful Blue."

"You actually think I need to be trapped in the mountains for three weeks with a bunch of psychiatric patients? Isn't that the premise of a horror film?"

Will chuckled. "You can't do it, can you?"

"Can't do what?"

"You can't let go. Not even for a handful of days."

"Yes, I can let go. That's not what this is about. I just don't think I need this kind of intensive therapy."

"Well, if you don't need therapy, then sit in your goddamn log cabin for three weeks and don't talk to anyone. That's fine, as long as you're away from here. Because you need that, whether you want to admit it or not."

"You're wrong, Will. I don't need that. And I can let go."

"Whatever, man."

Hunter remembered sitting there in Will's living room, staring at the basketball game on his friend's big screen, fuming over the dare Will had issued him. Yes, Will was his friend and not his doctor, but that didn't change the fact that William Rand was one of the most respected psychiatrists in Richmond. And Hunter did ask for his advice, and Blissful Blue was Will's answer.

Hunter huffed. "Okay, fine. I'll go."

"Maybe you shouldn't."

"I'm going, damn it!"

"Hey, if you want to go, then go," Will said, raising his hands in mock surrender. "I won't stop you." He laughed and Hunter shook his head, since they both knew Will had won the round.

Will didn't always win in the boxing ring at their gym, where they'd been beating the shit out of each other for nearly a decade, but he often won when it came to personal dares. Hunter knew theirs was a unique relationship, more brothers than friends, and he trusted Will with his life. But taking this partic-ular vacation made Hunter feel like he was putting his life in a stranger's hands, and he wasn't sure if he could. Even if Will was the one asking him to do it.

That conversation with Will had taken place a month ago, yet it still rang fresh in Hunter's mind. Especially now, while his Porsche growled on its way up the mountain toward Blissful Blue. He'd spent the past month rearranging his appointments at Gregory Global, ensuring the continuity of long-brewing business deals, as he'd planned this *vacation*. He'd also spent the month continually questioning the sanity of his decision and wondering what kind of world awaited him.

While Hunter drove farther into the trees, he worked to cope with the insane amount of green surrounding him. He wasn't paying nearly enough attention to the road. Not until a squirrel darted out from the wooded underbrush, diving in front of his bumper.

He cursed and swerved, trying like hell to avoid hitting the critter. He ran the Porsche's back tire into the gravel at the edge of the road and listened with dread to the ensuing explosion. While the squirrel flitted safely across the street, Hunter tapped his brakes and pulled the car over.

Due to the unbalanced skew of his windshield, he could admit he'd blown a tire. What he didn't want to admit was how badly this decision was already playing out. He didn't believe in Fate – being fully capable of holding his life in his own hands – but it did seem as if someone was trying to tell him something.

Running a hand roughly through his short brown hair, Hunter stared briefly at his reflection in the rearview mirror. His blue eyes looked weathered, their edges marked with subtle wrinkles that supposedly gave a man 'character'. His mouth was currently drawn, his lips pressed into a fixed frown, his teeth rigidly clenched as his jaw muscle twitched beneath his well-groomed stubble.

Was this the same face he'd seen in the mirror for thirty-four years? Were these the classically Roman features capable of both closing business deals and seducing women with little to no effort? It couldn't be. This face looked worn. And weary.

Hunter forced himself to breathe. He glanced out to the road beyond his windshield, still canopied by large boughs of excessive evergreens, and reminded himself he was supposed to be on vacation. "Just fix the tire, Gregory," he grumbled, shoving the car door open.

Early October made the air crisp and clean as he stepped outside. This was definitely not Richmond, even though he was still in Virginia and only a few hours away from home. But there were no exhaust fumes or skyscrapers here. There were only trees, and trees, and then some more goddamn trees, with no other vehicles in sight.

Hunter knew this place existed on a map. After all, he'd looked it up with morbid curiosity a month ago, and every day since. Yet the barely paved road seemed to originate from nowhere and continue steeply upward to nowhere. And he was stuck exactly in the middle.

The slam of his car door reverberated eerily off the surrounding tree trunks while he made his way around the bumper to view the damage. The back tire's tread lay slumped to one side, showcasing a shining metal rim. He sighed as he popped open the trunk, digging beneath the mat for a jack and a wrench. Within moments, he crouched low to the ground – the crisp white sleeves of his thick cotton shirt rolled above his elbows, the shine of his Italian leather loafers scuffed with dirt and gravel – as he set to work on his onerous task.

Although hours at the gym had made him physically powerful, not to mention hours of sparring with Doctor-Rand-of-the-massive-biceps, Hunter discovered the tire didn't give a fuck about how strong he was. He cursed a filthy stream of repulsive words as he damned the lug nuts for their tenacity, thinking they were indeed lugs in the most derogatory sense of the term. Then again, maybe he was the lug. And probably nuts, too, for even being here right now.

With a growl of effort, he loosened the last nut. "Amazing!" he shouted, feeling as if something was finally going his way.

"Thank God for tiny miracles," an airy voice sang from behind him.

The light, unexpected sound startled him into dropping his wrench. The tool missed pummeling his foot by centimeters, at best. Hunter stood and spun simultaneously, facing the intruder who'd nearly cost him a toe. He stood fully prepared to give the culprit a lecture on the atrocities of sneaking up on people, until he caught sight of the offender.

When he zeroed in on her, all words left him but one.

Stunning.

She was positively stunning. He didn't know if she struck him so deeply because she'd materialized out of nowhere, or because she looked like she should be on the cover of a magazine. By the way she was dressed, it would be some sort of jungle-safari magazine, but she'd still deserve the cover.

A cropped, navy tank top and khaki shorts hugged her feminine curves and showcased a flat, bared midriff of flawless, cream skin. Her eyes were a bright, emerald green, her full lips were painted dark pink, and her smile was radiant and gorgeous. Loose black curls framed her face, reflecting the sunlight originating directly behind her. She was the perfect combination of adorable and sexy, and that sounded like the worst pick-up line he'd ever heard, but he'd be damned if it wasn't true.

Hunter barely took note of the obscenely large camera hanging around her neck – the lens of which would make any normal phallic symbol green with envy – or the rugged brown climbing boots laced around her slender ankles. No one could possibly care about such manly footwear with legs like those above them. Legs that went on forever. Legs he could easily picture wrapped around him.

He considered, for the first time ever, that this vacation might not be a complete waste after all.

"I'm sorry if I startled you," she spoke again, her voice soft and warm and infinitely appealing.

Hunter blinked his vision into focus and settled his eyes on hers. "Oh, no, don't worry about it. It's no problem."

"Well, that's good. But can I ask what's amazing?"

"Amazing?"

"As I stepped out of the forest, you yelled the word *amazing*."

For the life of him, Hunter couldn't recall what had been so amazing – not with such a woman standing before him. He glanced to her left ring finger. No ring. Potentially available. Although why someone wouldn't have snatched her up long ago was a baffling mystery.

"Was it something to do with the tire?" she prompted in his moment of awkward, gawking silence.

"The tire?" he echoed, just now recalling the tenacious lug nuts. "Oh, yes. It was the tire."

"Then I would have to agree."

"About what?"

"About tires being amazing. They're so *round*. I mean, who really thought of that first, anyway? So even and shiny and smooth, spinning around and around and around. You stare at a tire long enough and it becomes rather hypnotic, don't you think?"

Hunter frowned. Now he knew why she was single. She was crazy.

Well, what did he expect? After all, he was moments away from a psychotherapeutic vacation spot. At least, he hoped he was moments away, because his hobbled Porsche wouldn't make it much farther.

"Is Blissful Blue Retreat up ahead?" he asked, pretty damn certain she would have the answer.

"Yes, it is. The information cabin is a quarter mile up this road to your left, and the guest cabins start after that toward the right. You can't miss it; there's nothing else up here, really."

"So, you're staying at Blissful Blue, I take it?"

"I am." She grinned at him, her bright eyes wide. "Cabin 10."

"And you're, um, on vacation?" he prodded, not sure if it was appropriate to ask a perfect stranger about their psychological status.

"Actually," she replied as she glided toward him, "I'm a freelance nature reporter, working on a piece for *National Geographic* magazine."

"Really?"

"Yes. I'm trying to photograph a rare bird."

Wait – she's a nature reporter and not a psychiatric patient?

Hunter relaxed his guard somewhat, watching as she approached him with her dark hair moving softly around her shoulders. Damn, she really was beautiful. "Working for *National Geographic* is impressive," he considered. "What's the name of your rare bird?"

She stopped when she stood just a few feet in front of him. She studied him for a long moment as she bit her lower lip in her teeth. Hunter made every effort to not stare at her mouth, since he couldn't be held responsible for what he might imagine doing with that mouth, and he still hadn't decided if this woman was crazy or not.

She helped him make his decision the moment she shouted, "The yellow-crowned purple fantini!" with unearthly giddiness.

His eyebrows rose. "That is an actual thing?"

"Oh, yes! One of the most beautiful birds in the world! It's found only here, in the Blue Ridge Mountains. It has a deep purple body and a large, bright yellow cap of feathers that rise above its head when angry. Like this...."

Hunter watched with censured amazement, and no small amount of fear, as she raised her hands up, spread her fingers out above her head, and wriggled them in the air. Then she smiled, her eyes full of mirth and excitement, as if she'd imparted him with miraculous knowledge.

His face contorted. He had no idea what sort of horrific expression currently consumed his features, but it must have been pretty ridiculous, because she dropped her hands back to her sides and started laughing.

"Wow. I guess you don't like impressions?"

"Um..." was all he managed to say.

"Oh, I know! How about this one?"

Hunter remained frozen in place as she started flapping her arms, wiggling her fingers, twisting her hips, and clapping, over and over again. She giggled like a winsome child, and he had no earthly idea what to say, so he just stood there. He observed her with wide eyes and held breath, returning to his previous, apparently astute, assessment.

This woman is crazy. Totally, utterly, completely crazy.

Finally, after several rounds of the bizarre behavior, she threw her hands up. "Oh, come on! Seriously? I don't get a laugh for that? It's the Chicken Dance! Everyone laughs at the Chicken Dance! I thought it was physically impossible to watch someone do the Chicken Dance and *not* laugh. Apparently, I was wrong."

Hunter cleared his throat. "Well, um, it's probably just that I'm in the middle of something important," he offered, keeping his voice low and even, afraid to make any sudden moves. "In fact, I should get back to it...I mean, get back to the tire. It's a shame I can't watch more of your, uh, dance, but duty calls."

She made no move to leave, so he reached down very slowly and picked up the wrench. He held it out in front of him, presenting proof of his predicament. She stared at the tool in his hand before peering around him to the heap of tread on the ground. Her lips puckered as she whistled softly. "Golly, that tire really blew."

"Yes. Yes, it sure did."

"What on earth happened?" she asked, her eyes lively with intrigue.

Hunter resisted the urge to think she was delightful. "It was a squirrel. Darted right out in front of me."

Good Lord, how long is she going to stay?

The bird woman nodded. "Ah yes, the ever-darting squirrel. Did you know squirrels are the fastest land mammals?"

"No, I wasn't aware of that."

Apparently, she's going to stay for a while.

Hunter wondered what would happen right now if he made the effort to stand really, really still. Perhaps she might think he'd turned into a statue, then get bored and wander off. On second thought, that was probably a terrible idea. After all, birds just fucking loved statues, didn't they? It was some sort of inexplicable opposites-attract thing. And the statues always came out on the worse end of that particular relationship.

She continued to stare at him, for seconds that turned to minutes that turned to hours, studying him as if searching for something she couldn't quite find. She licked her pink lips and he focused on her luscious mouth again. Not because he wanted to, but because he was a man. And because she was still as gorgeous now as she had been the minute she'd stepped out of the forest, even despite all the wacky dancing.

Hunter shifted his stance from one leg to the next, fighting between the urge to dart away faster than a squirrel and the urge to pull her to him and lick those sweet, sexy lips for himself.

Damn male desires. Damn the crazy woman with the beautiful body. Damn me straight to hell for even having these thoughts about her.

He closed his eyes for a moment and concentrated on breathing. When he reopened them, she still stared at him. He didn't know what to do, so he just stared back.

She finally broke the loaded silence with a single word. "Scarlet."

"Scarlet?" Hunter echoed. *Good God, am I blushing right now? That can't be true. I haven't blushed since I was twelve.*

She extended her hand. "Scarlet," she repeated. "Scarlet Tracey, pleased to meet you."

"Oh. Um, hello."

"Hello. Do you have a name?"

"I'm Hunter," he replied, taking her hand in a simple introduction that felt, at this point, almost bizarre.

He gripped her fingers with a powerful handshake, perfected over a thousand board meetings. He tried not to notice how deliciously soft her skin felt. As he attempted to let go of her, she held on.

"Do you like lemonade, Hunter?"

He didn't know if he liked lemonade. He didn't know much of anything at this moment. "Yes," he replied, still unable to extract his hand from her grip, although not trying overzealously to do so.

"Good. You'll come visit me, then. I make it fresh-squeezed. Lots of cute little yellow lemons. You'll love it." She finally released her hold on him. "You know, I'd offer to call someone to fix your tire, but there's no cell service up here. I don't even bother to carry my phone with me. And besides, the nearest mechanic is all the way back at the bottom of the mountain and is closed on weekends anyway."

"Of course," Hunter said, since that all made perfect sense right now.

"Is there something I can do to help you fix it?"

He had a sudden vision of her crouched down beside him, her ebony hair tickling his arms and her little tank top riding up her back, as she bent over to hold onto...something. "No, thank you. I appreciate the offer, but I'll manage just fine on my own."

Scarlet shrugged. "Okay, well, I'm sorry I'm not more helpful. When you swing by my cabin, I promise I'll make it up to you." With those words she grinned exuberantly, causing him to wonder how she planned to make it up to him. A smile that dazzling probably involved more than just the sharing of squished fruit.

She finally turned to leave, her hefty hiking boots thumping on the pavement while she marched up the steep hill. "See you soon, Hunter," she sang, looking back only once to give him a wink.

When Scarlet had moved a safe enough distance away, his gaze slipped down to her bottom: a perfect, reverse-heart-shaped ass that made his fingers twitch at his sides. "No," he muttered to himself. "No touching. She's not a normal person. Definitely not normal."

As he sank back to the ground, he could still feel her skin against his fingers. "Focus on the tire, Hunter. There will be no lemonade, or anything else. She is out of the question."

Deep inside, he knew that with certainty.

~

He spent nearly an hour mounting the spare tire. Not because it was exceptionally difficult, or because he hadn't done it before, but because his treacherous thoughts ran elsewhere. To Freebird Scarlet, with eyes like the forest and a backside he wanted to eat dinner off of.

While Hunter steered his hobbled Porsche back onto the road, he reminded himself there could be no touching. Touching led to kissing and kissing led to the bedroom and the bedroom led to relationships. Not that he was opposed to relationships. In truth, he'd been trying to make a relationship work – with one woman or another – for as long as he could recall. But he generally renounced relationships with crazy women, especially ones he knew were crazy right off the bat.

The information cabin appeared to his left almost immediately, just as Scarlet said. A worn wooden entry marker greeted him: *Welcome to Blissful Blue Retreat*. Hunter drove the Porsche into a roughly marked parking space, eased the keys from the ignition, and opened his briefcase, extracting his reservation paperwork.

He dragged himself out of the car and up the steps of the log cabin before his sound judgment could attempt to shake reason into him again. The thick, mahogany door creaked when he eased it open. A powerful odor of cinnamon and pine struck him in the face as he stepped inside the sparsely lit dwelling that reminded him of an overgrown tree house. Heat seeped beneath his skin, generated by a steadily glowing fireplace to his right. Immediately before him lay a smattering of log benches with plaid cushions. Beyond that, an oak counter grew up from the ground, housing deer antlers above it and a stout little man behind it.

"Hello, there!" the man called out. "Welcome to Blissful Blue. I'm Pete Jackson, the caretaker."

Hunter approached the counter, noting offhandedly that Pete's round pink cheeks and twinkling blue eyes, combined with his plaid shirt and red flannel vest, gave him the striking appearance of a garden gnome.

"Nice to meet you, Mr. Jackson," Hunter offered the pleasantry along with his hand. "Hunter Gregory, checking in."

Pete gave a firm handshake and an easy smile. "You've picked a great place to stay, Mr. Gregory," he assured, his aged voice soothing in a Grandfather Time sort of way. "Plenty of rest and relaxation up here."

"That's wonderful," Hunter forced himself to reply, even while his stomach clenched at the idea of wasted time and inertia. He reminded himself of Will's advice. "This is just what I need."

Hunter handed his reservation to Pete, watching as the man produced a page with detailed listings of Blissful Blue offerings: daily counseling sessions, both group and individual; biweekly Retreat Socials; Spa appointments available with a phone call; and gourmet meal delivery services. Apparently, Hunter had arrived at *Lifestyles of the Rich and Famous – Deeply Wooded and A Little Crazy.*

"Here's everything you need," Pete offered, handing Hunter a packet of information, complete with an electronic door card. "You're in Cabin 9, up the hill to the right."

Cabin 9? Freebird Scarlet is in 10. How close will we be?

"Thank you for your assistance, Mr. Jackson," Hunter stated, stuffing the card into his pocket.

"Sure thing. If you need anything while you're here, I'm your guy."

"I'll remember that. I assume there's Wi-Fi in the rooms?"

Pete chuckled. "Nope. Mountains don't care much for that stuff."

"You mean there's no internet access at all? That can't be true. I know I read online that access was available."

"Well, you can have one of them cords if you want to."

"A cord?" *What is this, the Dark Ages?*

"Yep, but I don't recommend using it," the caretaker added.

"Why not? Will I be struck by lightning? Burn the cabin down?"

Mr. Jackson shook his head and rose from his chair, bending over to fumble beneath the counter. When he stood back up, he handed Hunter an internet connection cable with more than a little dust on it. "Here you go, Mr. Gregory. But can I offer you a piece of advice?"

Hunter's brow rose, but he nodded.

"Don't use this," Pete said, tapping the cord with his stubby fingers. "You need to disconnect from all that hullabaloo and reconnect to what's really important."

Hullabaloo? Did he actually say hullabaloo? Hunter grabbed the cord and mustered a smile. "I appreciate the advice, Mr. Jackson."

"You call me Pete, now. You're not in the big city anymore. Things'll be different around here. It'll be good for you. You'll see."

With those words, Hunter experienced a bout of sheer panic. A serious, palm-sweating, heart-pounding, gut-churning bout of absolute fucking *panic.* "Thanks," he barked, pushing the word from his throat to cover the quaver in his voice. "I'm sure it will be."

The man's kindly eyes bored into him as Hunter exited swiftly through the door.

~

HE COULD HAVE BOLTED, of course. He could have driven his wounded car right out of these woods and back to civilization. He wanted to. Damn, how he wanted to. But this was a matter of pride.

Dr. William Rand had given Hunter a dare – a double dog dare, to recall the insipid terminology of his forgone youth – and if he cowered away, he could never live it down. Even if his parents believed he was on vacation in Cozumel with friends from the office, and his office believed he was mountain climbing in Washington with his parents, Will would know the truth. He would look at Hunter with his unerringly perceptive eyes, and shake his head slowly, acknowledging the fact that he couldn't do this one little thing he'd asked of him. No matter what, Hunter could not face that.

Cabins 4 and 5 passed idly by as he drove higher up the mountain. He could almost hear Will's voice in his mind. *Try to relax, Hunter.*

Normally, he would never consider leaving a decision like this up to anyone other than himself. His parents had raised him to be strong and independent, a confident adult capable of assuming the reigns of the massively successful family business his grandfather had built from the ground up. But when Hunter finally acknowledged that his life wasn't progressing as planned, and that he had no clue how to fix it, and that he required input from someone who gave advice as a profession, he'd managed to ask his friend for help.

Will had always offered him advice, on countless occasions through their years of friendship, in wise little sentences that Hunter could either take at face value or read the world into, as he saw fit. But he'd never before asked for his friend's assistance. Not until a month ago.

Nothing specific had brought the question into play, really. They'd just been sitting in Will's living room, getting ready to watch a game, when Hunter caught sight of a photo of Will and his wife, Maggie, on their wedding day. The pair looked blissfully happy together, and in that moment, he decided to ask Will what he could do to make his life better.

Thankfully, Will hadn't looked at him like he was crazy. He didn't tell him to make an appointment at his office. He simply started talking about Blissful Blue, and before Hunter knew it, he found himself rearranging his entire life to come here. Still, he hadn't told another soul about this place.

The Porsche made it all the way to his cabin without any further misadventure. Cabin 9 appeared rather roomy. At least, that's what he assumed as he visually inspected the exterior of his home-away-from-home. Parking a few yards from the front porch steps, Hunter pulled his briefcase from the seat and exited the Porsche, slamming his door shut before moving to the trunk to grab his suitcase. He locked up the car, sucked in a deep breath, and walked the gravel driveway to the stairs.

The entire structure was made of logs, each one the definition of knotty excellence. Several large windows hung above the railings of the wrapped porch, inside which a weather-beaten rocking chair swayed softly in the October breeze. Trees canopied the dwelling on all sides, the only way in or out being the gravel road that brought him here. With all this suffocating nature, Hunter could barely believe a modernized key-card entry system opened the door. Yet, as he crossed the threshold, he realized nothing else here would bear any resemblance to the real world...or life as he knew it.

The living room was large, although smaller than his. What his spacious apartment in the city did not have to offer, apparently, was the all-log construction of everything he saw before him: the couch, the chairs, the desk, the kitchen counters, the doors, the floors, the walls, the ceiling. *Hell, is anyone here aware that other building materials exist?*

Closing the front door behind him, Hunter set his suitcase aside and carried his briefcase to the desk, holding his breath as he searched for a lifeline. "Yes!" he celebrated when he located the wall outlet.

Removing his laptop and situating it with great care on the desk, he pulled out the cord Pete had given him and plugged it in. Hunter sat on the red-and-green plaid cushion of the log chair, listening to the calming whirr as the computer sprang to life, promising to keep him connected to the real world. That promise enabled him to search the remainder of the cabin, and even unpack his things, without any further panic symptoms.

Night invaded quickly. Hunter made himself as at-home as possible, placing all his personal items with great care into the log dresser, on the log countertops, in the log closets. He'd been amused to discover the bathroom had a normal, ceramic sink and toilet, although the deer-antler towel rack made up for that in spades.

Hunter huffed at the log-ness of it all. He wondered offhandedly if *logness* was a word, and if there had been any sightings of a Logness Monster. Up here, right now, he could see it happening.

After lining his toiletries up properly in order of usage – deodorant, toothpaste, toothbrush, razor, comb and cologne – he returned to his computer and delved into his work email. The world had not forgotten him. Far from it. Office business continued on as usual: items needing his approval, people requiring his assessment skills, functions begging his control. He found it easy to spend several hours at these tasks, achieving almost mindless simpatico with his keyboard and his thoughts.

"I might not know how to make a relationship last," he mumbled in the darkness of his cabin, "but this I can do."

He had to shake his head, since Will always told him work was his comfort zone, and that sure as hell was the truth. Hunter thought – when he'd first begun seeing Clarissa so long ago – he could change that. In the end, he'd only proven it beyond the shadow of a doubt. In the end, Clarissa hated his work. Yet she'd still wanted to marry him.

Clarissa Hill had been perfect from day one. Physically striking, socially alluring, intellectually stimulating: she was everything he categorized as suitable in a partner. And she said she loved him, so why couldn't he agree? He wasn't upset she'd proposed instead of him. But when he looked at her, truly looked at her, she just wasn't the person he imagined standing beside him forever.

It was a crippling realization – having Clarissa fit perfectly into his cookie-cutter mold of a wife and still not being able to make it work – and it finally forced him to acknowledge that the problem resided with him.

He was thirty-four, after all. He was CEO of Gregory Global. He was financially desirable, physically attractive, and passably amusing. He should be married with 2.3 kids, or whatever. He shouldn't be sitting in a deserted cabin, wondering if he was crazy, or worse...wondering if a crazy person would beat down his door at any moment.

Scarlet.

The name sprang to his mind of its own volition. Freebird Forest Scarlet, with the gorgeous lips and the soft hands and the fantastic ass, existed just one cabin over. Hunter remembered too easily how she'd smiled at him – with unnerving beauty and more than a little mischief – when she'd invited him over for lemonade to make up for not assisting with his tire repair. He had no idea what her "make-up" would entail, but there were parts of his body that wanted to sprint to her cabin right now and pound on her door like a certifiable madman until he found out.

Will had often advised Hunter to be more adventurous in his choice of a partner. He'd urged him to consider that the person he would truly fall in love with might not meet his preset ideals, but that wouldn't matter, because they would just fit. Hunter wanted to believe that. He wanted more than anything to find the person who fit him. But he was ninety-nine percent certain crazy Scarlet was not that person. After all, the woman thought tires were hypnotizing. She performed chicken-dances in front of complete strangers. And she spouted random knowledge about squirrels.

Did you know squirrels are the fastest land mammals?

He stilled as her disarmingly charming voice filled his mind. That's what she'd said to him, with her emerald eyes sparkling. She'd had him thrown so off-balance at the time that he hadn't even thought to question her. But there was just no way that information could be true.

Turning back to his computer, Hunter exited his email in order to search "fastest land mammal". The results came quickly: the cheetah could sprint the fastest at 70 miles per hour; the Pronghorn antelope could sustain 60 miles per hour over long distances; and the squirrel could manage a mere 12 miles per hour. It *was* faster than a chicken, at least.

Leaning back in his log chair, Hunter stared blankly at the screen. Why did Scarlet lie to him? Did she truly believe squirrels were the fastest mammals? Did she fabricate it for the sake of conversation? Or did she just enjoy lying? And if so, did she only lie to him, or to everyone?

Knowing he couldn't possibly have the answers to those questions, and certain he should never ask, Hunter shut down his laptop and prepared for sleep. He found the bed exceedingly comfortable, its patchwork quilt a soft, warm cover.

Sleep readily overtook him, accompanied by wild, weird dreams. Dreams of tires spinning idly in the air. And forest fairies with emerald eyes and ebony hair, buzzing around his head. And squirrels zooming past him, stopping only long enough to tell him he needed to get a life.

2

LEMONADE

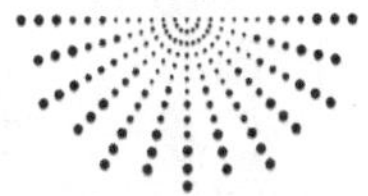

The next morning started the same as any morning in Hunter's life – a hundred pushups, a hundred sit-ups, a shower, and then a sensible breakfast. The only difference here at Blissful Blue, if he overlooked all the logs and antlers, was that breakfast was gourmet, delivered to his doorstep by a young man in a red hoodie, who nodded and grinned but didn't say a word. The breakfast tray also held an itinerary.

As Hunter sat on his log couch, he scrutinized the list of daily Blue programs. Several group psychotherapy sessions were available, addressing various addictive personalities such as overeaters, smokers, alcoholics, and workaholics. As if that wasn't enough, individual appointments could be made with a mere phone call to Pete-the-gnome caretaker. The call to Pete would need to be placed on the old-fashioned landline phone – situated prominently on the log coffee table – because, of course, there wasn't any cell service up here.

Hunter scoffed as he read the final offering of the day: *5 p.m...Retreat Social in the common cabin, number 13. Casual wear. All guests invited. Please attend.*

He instantly envisioned a group of overweight chain-smokers passing around liquor bottles and handing out business cards. An involuntary shudder ran the long length of his spine. Did he really want to get himself into that? And what if Scarlet was there, toting a basket of lemons and performing random bird dances?

Hunter set the paper aside, finished eating, and placed the empty food tray back on the porch for pickup. *No, thanks,* he thought to himself while planning a day of solitude with his computer.

You're not opening yourself to new possibilities, Will lectured.

Just not today, Hunter responded to the disembodied voice in his head before settling down in front of his laptop.

Hours later, after managing every possible office decision of which he was capable at this distance, after eating a healthy lunch and making his dinner selections, and after staring at a particularly odd knot of pine on the wall that somehow resembled his tenth-grade algebra teacher, Hunter could still hear William Rand's voice.

Go to the Social. No one will bite you. They're just people. People like you, overworked and in need of relaxation and companionship. Go.

"Nope," Hunter replied aloud, standing from the plaid-cushioned chair to stretch his legs. He walked around the cabin, examining the interior in more detail. He opened all the drawers in the kitchen. Pushed all the buttons on the stove and the microwave. Marched into the bedroom to straighten the clothes he'd placed in the drawers. Proceeded into the hallway and opened the closet.

Hunter paused while staring into the hall closet. He'd expected to find some linens and maybe some extra rolls of toilet paper. Instead, he saw stacks and stacks of board games sitting on the shelves. Monopoly, Life, Risk, Twister, Sorry, Scrabble...the list went on. He stood there and looked at the games for the longest time. Until he realized every one of them was intended for at least two people to play.

"There's not even a deck of cards for Solitaire," he grumbled.

That's because you're not supposed to sit all alone in your cabin, Will's voice insisted. *Go to the damn Social, asshole.*

"God, okay, Will," he grunted, unsure if his friend had ever called him an asshole before. "But just once, and if I don't like it, I'll leave."

Hunter pulled on his shoes, grabbed his car keys, and walked out to the front porch. "I don't have to stay if I don't want to," he reiterated. The words comforted him for approximately two seconds, at which point he saw his Porsche, with its pitiful spare tire, sitting on the gravel driveway. That darting squirrel had definitely been trying to tell him something yesterday. With a sigh, he decided to walk rather than force the car to endure any further humiliation.

Scenic perfection surrounded him as he strode to the main road to scale the steep incline toward Cabin 13, yet he barely noticed the woodsy beauty. A heightened level of anxiety sprang to his chest when Hunter realized he had to pass Cabin 10 on the way. Scarlet's driveway came closer with each step he took, making his footing falter.

Would she be there? Standing by the roadside, shouting some ritualistic birdcall? Or perhaps squatting down, waiting to catch a glimpse of the hypnotizing revolutions of passing car tires?

His pulse surged, equal parts fear and anticipation, when the entrance to her cabin emerged on his right. He risked a lightning-fast glance down her gravel pathway while he passed by.

No crazy Scarlet. No bird dances. No ebony hair and emerald eyes.

Hunter continued walking, moving on toward Cabin 13, yet his footsteps slowed. Something welled inside his chest. He couldn't quite identify the emotion, but it resembled...disappointment.

Good Lord, was I really hoping to see the certifiable woman again?

No. It couldn't be true. He knew better.

Yet here he stood, apparently disappointed that she hadn't been waiting for him by the side of the road, chickens and all.

Why in the hell am I disappointed? That doesn't make any damn sense. I mean, unless it's about her lying to me. Yes, that has to be it. Her lying to me is an injustice, plain and simple.

He grit his teeth as he begrudgingly acknowledged that her act of dishonesty had lodged itself inside his brain, pestering him, inciting him to see her again.

I shouldn't. I shouldn't turn around and march back down this road, straight to her cabin, and bang my fist on her door until she has no choice but to open it. I shouldn't give her the good, stern lecture she has coming. Definitely not. I should stay away from her – far, far away.

Except he couldn't. It wouldn't be right to stay away from her, since she obviously needed his help. She needed to understand what she'd done wrong, and it was up to him to tell her, because really, who else would do it? Certainly not Pete-the-caretaker. After all, a gentle geezer garden gnome would never tell a beautiful bounding bird to settle down and be more practical.

"Ridiculous!" Hunter shouted out loud as he came to a halt shortly after passing Cabin 11. "This is ridiculous!"

Scarlet lied to me! Blatantly lied to me! About squirrels, no less!

"You okay, buddy?" a deep voice spoke from behind him.

Hunter spun toward the sound, focusing on the dark-haired, athletically built man emerging from Cabin 11's driveway.

What's the goddamn deal with people here sneaking up on me?

"Is there something I can help you with?" the man asked, looking at Hunter with noticeable pity in his eyes.

Oh, hell. This man thinks I'm the crazy one.

"No, no," Hunter reassured the stranger. "I'm just...I'm fine."

"Okay." The man offered a boyish grin. "Tyler Hensen," he said, extending his hand. "I'm heading to the Social. Are you?"

Hunter gave Tyler his best commanding handshake, even as he inwardly seethed at Scarlet. "Hunter Gregory. Pleased to meet you, Tyler. I am heading to the Social, but realized I forgot to do something. Don't you hate it when that happens? It feels ridiculous, right?"

He hoped his words would disguise the morbid display of frustration he'd shown by shouting to himself on the side of a deserted road, but the man still observed him with wary concern.

"Things do feel ridiculous sometimes," Tyler placated, reaching out to pat Hunter on the shoulder. "But try to take it easy while you're up here, okay?"

"Yeah, I sure will," he replied through tight lips, forcing a smile as Tyler nodded and moved up the road. Inside, Hunter's gut roiled.

My God! That man thinks I'm insane! And it's all Scarlet's fault! She made me look like an idiot! She needs to understand that lying to people isn't right! You can't tell lies and live with a clear conscience!

The next thing he knew, his feet stomped down the road, leading him toward Cabin 10 before he could overcome the urge. A moment later, the gravel of her driveway crunched beneath his shoes as her cabin rushed toward him. He noted offhandedly that Scarlet's cabin was much bigger than his and even had an attached garage. He wondered if Pete gave her the bigger place because the little gnome harbored some sort of freaky fetish for bird-women. Then Hunter shook his head, because that was a fucking ridiculous thought. Which was, once again, all her fault.

Holy hell, why did she chicken-dance in front of a complete stranger? Why did she tell me she's a National Geographic reporter when she's obviously a patient, just like me? And what about the squirrels? How could she smile so sweetly while lying about something so ridiculous?

Hunter reached the front porch of her cabin and bounded up the stairs. He lifted his hand to knock, poised to hold her accountable for her egregious crimes. But the door opened before he had the chance to bang out his anger on the wood.

And there she stood – Frolicking Freebird Scarlet – in all her glory.

A few seconds slipped by as he decided whether to offer a haughty greeting first, or just dive right into her well-deserved scolding. Then he took a look at her, a really long look, and said absolutely nothing. Damn, he'd forgotten just how remarkable she was.

"Oh, good, Hunter. I hoped it was you," Scarlet chirped, smiling vibrantly into his eyes, her entire body humming with energy. "I must say, that gravel driveway is the best alarm system ever created. Not that there's anything to be alarmed about up here."

Another lie, he thought. She was more alarming than ever: from the loose black curls eased behind her bare shoulders, to the curves of her breasts outlined with sensuous detail by the green satin camisole that matched her eyes, to the slim, sculpted legs easing from her ivory capris down to her bare feet and pink painted toenails. The sight of her set off so many alarm bells in his head that he barely heard his own thoughts.

"Well, don't stand outside all day, Mr. Talkative," she directed, reaching up to take hold of the hand he'd apparently left suspended in midair. "Come in, come in." She drew him inside, pulling his body into her cabin and kicking the door closed behind them, all while keeping her fingers tangled with his.

Scarlet tugged on him until he stood before her in the middle of her spacious log living room, holding her hand and staring into her eyes like a love-struck schoolboy on a playground. "I know just why you're here," she said. "This is about what I said to you yesterday, isn't it?"

His brow rose. *Is she talking about the squirrel comment? Does she feel guilty now? Is she actually going to apologize for lying to me?*

He observed her expression. She didn't look the least bit remorseful. She looked entrancing. And frisky. And mischievous.

Damn it. He'd forgotten about the make-up session she'd promised him for not helping to fix his tire. What exactly would that entail? Based on the gleam in her eyes, it could be anything.

His body reacted compulsively, stimulated by the thought of her feeling indebted to him. *No, Hunter. No touching.* Except for holding hands – since he hadn't yet brought himself to extricate his large fingers from her dainty ones.

Scarlet stepped closer, even though mere inches separated them. Her breasts brushed lightly against his chest. "No one can resist, you know."

Her lips were candy pink and beyond temptation. He stared at them, absorbing the contours, imagining how softly those lips would mold beneath his, how warm and inviting she would taste if he could just slip his tongue....

Hunter reared back, redirecting his vision to her eyes.

Scarlet wasn't smiling anymore. She studied him, and he knew she knew exactly what he'd been thinking. She licked her lips, which rendered him completely and utterly mute.

It occurred to him then that he hadn't managed to say a goddamn word since he'd arrived. He had no idea what she thought of the silent, skulking stranger standing in front of her.

A long minute passed before she grinned again. "I'm talking about the lemonade, of course. I'm sure that's why you came." She finally released his hand. "You've never had any better, I can assure you. Just make yourself at home and I promise you'll be in heaven in no time."

Heaven, he considered. Or perhaps hell. It would depend on his point of view. Watching her well-sculpted backside swish away to the kitchen, he considered some heavenly possibilities. Too many to count.

Hunter cleared his throat along with his mind, working to refocus on the reality of her – the sheer and utter craziness factor – the bird dances and squirrelly lies. That should be enough to keep his animalistic desires in check, to remind him of why he'd come here. Once he'd said his piece, Frivolous Forest Scarlet would certainly not be tempted to lie again with such recklessness.

Straightening to his impressive height, he folded his muscular arms across his broad chest and tried to glare formidably at her. He'd had years of practice glaring, whenever he'd needed to get a business point across, or to tell his parents they should take more care in choosing their retirement activities. But somehow, while he watched her, he couldn't muster up the necessary glaring-gumption.

Scarlet was dancing again, but it wasn't the Chicken Dance. She wriggled her hips melodically instead, humming a delightful tune as she opened the refrigerator and pulled out a full gallon pitcher of yellow liquid. She rested the jug on the counter and spun around, still moving giddily to her own music, twirling over to a cabinet from which she pulled two glasses. Her flourished sliding maneuver back to the freezer for ice was nearly his undoing. He shut his eyes for a moment, needing to complete his mission before she sidetracked him further.

"You were mistaken, you know," Hunter barked as he looked back to her. He sounded like an asshole, even to himself.

Scarlet didn't stop dancing. "No, I wasn't," she sang, pouring the opaque concoction into the glasses. "This really is the best lemonade you've ever had."

Damn it, I'm not talking about the lemonade.

He opened his mouth to correct her, but found it watering instead – with the sight of her bottom as she bent over to put the pitcher back into the fridge. Fuck, that was definitely the best ass he'd ever seen.

For the love of all that's good, Hunter, control yourself!

He struggled to breathe when she turned toward him. She hoisted the stately glasses and sauntered forward. The next instant, she stood before him, her arm outstretched with her sunshine-yellow offering.

"Thank you," he managed to say as he accepted the glass. He raised his drink to his lips and took a huge gulp while mentally preparing the proper and thorough reprimand she required.

But then everything came to a screeching halt.

Good God, this isn't lemonade!

For a split second, Hunter thought she'd poisoned him. His taste buds screamed when he realized what he'd just ingested. He nearly spit the entire mouthful out on the floor. The sour affront of straight lemon juice stabbed his tongue, causing a gag reflex that could only be subdued by smacking his lips together like an elderly man missing his dentures. His saliva fermented while he swallowed again and again, attempting to cleanse his shocked palate.

"Holy hell, Scarlet!" he hollered, fisting the glass in his hand. "This is pure lemon juice! Pure, undiluted lemon juice!"

"I know! It really wakes the mouth up, doesn't it?"

Hunter stared in sheer disbelief as she lifted her glass to her lips, took a giant swallow of the foul liquid, stilled for an instant, then shook gleefully while a shiver ran the length of her body. "Hoo-wee!" she squealed. "That is wild! Everything feels so *alive*, right?"

She watched him expectantly, obviously desiring some validation of her own giddiness, yet all he could think was that she'd deceived him. Again. Not even her adorable button nose could save her this time.

"You lied to me," he snapped, his voice deep and stern as he willed away the sour pangs in the back of his throat. "And not just now, with the lemonade, but also yesterday by the road. You told me squirrels are the fastest land mammals and that's not true at all. They aren't even close to the fastest. They only run 12 miles per hour."

Whatever he expected her reaction to be – sorrow, guilt, or shame – it wasn't. She simply looked into his eyes, staring deep inside him in the most unsettling way. At that moment, he had the bizarre sensation that she could see into his soul. The thought shook him hard. He didn't want anyone looking that far inside.

"Cheetahs are the fastest," he continued, suddenly feeling the need to fill the empty air. "Also, the Pronghorn antelope is quite fast."

She just kept staring.

Hunter felt himself backing down – an emotion as foreign and unsettling as any he could recall – yet he couldn't overcome the need to soothe her wounded ego, whether she required it or not. "Squirrels are, at least, faster than chickens," he added before he could stop himself.

Scarlet reached out to take the lecherous lemonade from his hand. She rested both glasses on the coffee table before pivoting back to him. Stepping forward, she closed the space between them until she filled his senses. She smelled of fresh soap and tiny flowers, her green eyes sparkled like jewels, and her lemony breath eased softly from her lips with every exhale.

As her arms drew toward him, he heard a shrill warning that sounded an awful lot like, "Run away now!" But he stayed very, very still.

Her small hands landed on his shoulders, resting firmly, as if she had every right in the world to touch his body. She stood toe-to-toe with him, looking into his eyes with a sweet smile plastered on her lips.

"Tell me something," she invited. "Who are you?"

The warmth of her fingers seeped through his shirt. He definitely should have run when he had the chance. "I'm...I'm Hunter."

"Mm-hmm." She studied him, waiting for something more.

Like what? What does she want to know?

"I'm the CEO of a very successful company," he added, even while reminding himself that he didn't owe her anything.

"Wow. The CEO, huh? I suppose that means you're the boss."

"Yes, I am."

"Like, the *boss* boss. The top dog. The head cheese."

"The head cheese? Really?"

"And being the *boss* boss means that a lot of people are counting on you to make the right decisions, all the time. It places a heavy burden on your shoulders." Her eyes drifted down as her fingers moved softly across the same shoulders she'd just mentioned.

"I can handle it," he insisted, unfamiliar with receiving this sort of response. Most women who met Hunter Gregory turned instantly predatory, with hungered looks and clawed fingers. They never looked at him like Scarlet did now, tilting her head and nibbling her lip, obviously concerned for his wellbeing.

"I'm sure you can handle it, Hunter. But even so, I imagine it creates a great deal of stress."

"It's fine. The job isn't a problem."

"What does the job entail, exactly?" she inquired, her hands easing slowly over his arms, tracing all the way down to his wrists.

Hunter's eyes shifted to her fingers, watching in fascination as she repeated the path of her touch – smoothing her hands up and down his arms – from his shoulders to his wrists and back again. Her fingers were slim, her nails painted purple, her skin warm and smooth and lulling.

"I'm, um, I'm the boss, like you said." He forced his gaze back to her face. "I keep everything in order. I keep everyone in order."

"I see. So, you make your living by telling other people what to do."

"Well, when you put it that way, it sounds..." He caught himself before he backpedaled. "Yes, that is one way to look at it."

Scarlet continued the slow, methodical movement of her hands as she met his determined stare. "Hmm. Well, you obviously have a commanding presence. And a deep, authoritative voice. And intense blue eyes. So, I imagine people do whatever you tell them. Willingly."

Her lips were too close. Too close and far too kissable. Just one kiss couldn't hurt, right? Just one touch of his mouth to hers. Just one tiny moan from her throat that would tell him how on fire she was, the same as him. He knew she would bend into him so easily, her breasts crushed to his chest, her arms wrapped around his neck, her fingers in his hair. She'd whimper and writhe as his fingers ran down her back, all the way down, so he could grab two handfuls of her perfect...

Hunter blinked. "I'm damn good at my job, if that's what you're asking."

"No, actually, I'm asking something completely different. And you still haven't answered."

"Answered what?"

"The question."

"Which is?"

"Who are you?"

"I told you."

"No, you didn't. You told me your name, and what you do for a living, but you didn't tell me who you are." The calming path of her hands continued, up and down his arms, over and over.

Hunter realized her touch felt somehow familiar.

"I know you don't like lies," she continued in her gentle tone. "And you don't like lemon juice. But I don't know who you are, not entirely."

"I think everyone dislikes lies and lemon juice."

Good Lord, I know why her touch feels familiar! This woman is petting me right now! She's petting me like I'm an animal! Why in the hell is she doing that? And why am I letting her?

"No, not everyone dislikes lies and lemon juice." Still staring into him, Scarlet seemed to consider a thousand possibilities in the span of seconds. "You really don't know who you are, do you?"

He opened his mouth to protest. She continued speaking before he had the chance. "It's okay. A lot of people don't know who they are. You should come with me sometime, into the woods. It's wonderfully peaceful there. Great for reflection. It might help you figure yourself out. I imagine that's why you came to Blissful Blue in the first place."

Stop petting me.

"No, that's not why I came at all."

And of course I know who I am.

"Then why did you come here?"

"I...I..."

"Yes, Hunter?"

He exhaled heavily. "It was a dare, okay?" he admitted, knowing the truth made him sound ridiculous, but refusing to lie to her.

Her face lit with a brilliant smile. "You came here on a dare?"

"Basically."

"Was it, like, a game of Truth or Dare?"

"No, it wasn't a game. It was a suggestion from a friend."

"Must be a really good friend, I take it."

"The best."

"Wow. A best friend who can convince you to do something you really, really don't want to do. That's impressive."

"He is impressive, so I asked his opinion, and he gave it to me, and now I'm here. End of story."

"Actually, I think that's just the beginning of the story. But, I must admit, I'm curious as to why you trust this particular friend so much."

"Because he's a psychiatrist. A damn good one."

"Really? Does he have a name?"

"Dr. William Rand."

Her eyes widened. "You're Will Rand's best friend?"

Hunter's gaze narrowed. "Do you know Will?"

"I do. He comes up here to Blissful Blue sometimes, to provide counseling. He stays for a few weeks at a time and sees patients."

Patients like you, Hunter realized. *Hell, had Will treated her before?*

"How often do you come up here, Scarlet?"

"Often enough," she said, shrugging. "But this is your first time, and you need to get as much out of it as possible. I'm afraid Will won't be able to convince you to come back again, and that would be a shame."

"Why would that be a shame?"

"Because you could really use the therapy here."

His jaw dropped at the insinuation that he was the one in need of counseling, when she stood here before him, knee-deep in all her crazy, squirrely, lemonade lies. "I don't need therapy. That's not why I'm here. I'm just...I'm on vacation."

"On vacation," she echoed.

The strangest thing happened then. With those two little words, her entire demeanor changed. Her hands dropped from his arms to lie limply at her sides. Her jeweled eyes lost their spark. Her beautiful lips turned down at the edges. "I'm on vacation, too," she whispered, her normally exuberant voice now edged with distress.

Hunter froze, hardly believing what his eyes and ears told him. Was Scarlet sad? Was she having a normal human emotion, like regret?

What the hell?

She pulled away from him, picking up the lemonade glasses and moving back to the kitchen with her head hung.

"You're on vacation?" he questioned, following eagerly on her heels, wanting to see how long this moment of lucidity might last her. "I thought you were on assignment for *National Geographic.*"

Scarlet stopped in her tracks. She set the glasses down on the kitchen counter and let out a high-pitched squeal. "The yellow-crowned purple fantini!" She spun around to face him, giddy joy filling her eyes once more. "That bird and I have a date with destiny!"

The next instant, she laughed, jumped up and down, and wiggled, dancing in front of him as if shaking troubled thoughts from her body.

Hunter knew precisely what he should do at this moment. He should run away. He should bolt like lightning in the opposite direction, since she'd turned back into Freebird Forest Scarlet faster than he could blink.

But he didn't run. He ignored everything in his brain in order to move toward her. He focused on her face, wishing to see Solemnly Sedate Scarlet for one more second, to know he hadn't imagined her.

Her eyes rose to his when he came to a stop mere inches away. "I wish you'd come with me," she said, excitement oozing from every pore. "I go out in the mornings and sit quietly in the woods, waiting to see him and all his cute, colorful feathers. Would you like to come?"

Hunter stared hard, hoping to catch a glimpse of that other woman inside her. The one who looked sullen and serious. The one who was far more in touch with reality. But all he saw was a flitting fairy, chicken-dancing by the side of the road.

He chose to take a step back.

"No, thanks," he answered, able to regain his control now that she wasn't touching him anymore. "Actually, I had best be going."

"So soon?"

"Yes. I have...things to do."

"Oh. Of course."

She took a step toward him and he retreated. He hurried to the door, afraid of having her too close as she followed on his heels. When he reached for the handle, her hand covered his. She stood by his side, smiling up at him.

"Come back anytime, Hunter. My door is always open to you."

"I appreciate that," he said, even though he knew he should never return. "Goodnight, Scarlet. And good luck with...the bird."

When his hand slipped from under hers, he felt instantly cold.

3

TWISTER

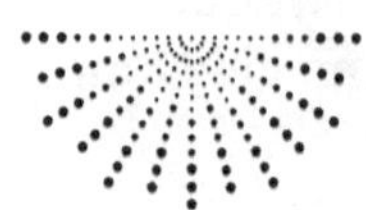

Hunter slept poorly. He didn't attempt to go to the Social after leaving Scarlet's cabin, since she'd been enough new territory for one evening. Or for one lifetime. He'd also had no desire to see Tyler Hensen again, after the man witnessed him shouting to himself like a homeless person.

Honestly, the entire situation last night had gotten completely out of control. All Hunter intended to do was to find the little forest fairy, hold her accountable for the grievous wrongs she'd perpetrated against him, and come away from her cabin feeling the victor. Instead, he'd merely stood there while she petted him and toyed with him, and then he'd hastily retreated with his tail tucked between his legs.

Hunter regretted the previous night's events the instant he woke. He tried not to think about Scarlet as he did his push-ups and sit-ups, took his shower, and accepted his breakfast from the silent delivery driver in the red hoodie. Unfortunately, he couldn't quiet the vexing memories.

He should never have allowed her to sidetrack him. He should never have allowed her to think he didn't know who he was. And he should never have allowed her touch him.

God, she'd just kept touching him, over and over. But he hadn't moved away. He hadn't told her to stop. If anything, he stayed right where he was, so she could keep touching him. He'd wanted her to touch him. He wanted it then. He wanted it now.

Hunter stared at the expertly prepared eggs benedict on his tray, willing himself to shovel food into his churning stomach. *Damn it, why can't I stop thinking about her? What is wrong with me?*

He'd certainly desired women before. And he'd enjoyed many, in carefully manipulated instants. The women were beautiful, the pleasure mutual. But they didn't occupy his thoughts incessantly. They certainly didn't dominate his mind while he slept. Not like Scarlet did last night.

He wasn't sure why he'd dreamt about her. Maybe it was because she was the last person he'd spoken to before bed. Maybe it was the heavy, decadent dinner he'd savored after the lemon-mouth fiasco. Or maybe it was because he hadn't been with a woman in a long time, having only allowed himself one brief affair since he and Clarissa separated over a year ago.

Hunter honestly didn't know the reason. He only knew Scarlet's tempting body cemented itself in his brain for the entire night. Hell, he'd needed ten minutes this morning to calm himself enough to pee.

Everything about the little fairy distracted him. Everything about her haunted him. His reaction to her was insane, and what he needed more than anything was to find a way to regain control of his senses.

After taking a few bites of his breakfast, Hunter walked back to his bedroom, threw on a T-shirt and shorts, grabbed his room card, and headed out to Blissful Blue's gym. As he marched up his driveway, he thanked the heavens the gym facilities were to the left in Cabin 6, and not to the right toward Scarlet's 10. He just couldn't be held responsible for how his mind and body responded whenever he was near her.

Starting down the main paved road toward the gym, he forced several deep breaths into his lungs. The air was crisp, and probably cleaner than he'd ever experienced, even on all his youthful outings with his mother and father. The evergreen boughs shaded his steps, allowing the sun to peek out for seconds at best. It was beautiful, he considered, knowing anyone on the planet would reach that conclusion. Still, he was grateful when he arrived at the gym, eager for the kempt air.

A few people were already in the thick of morning workouts as he used his room card to gain entry to the facility. Rather larger than he'd expected, the gym held nearly every type of cardio and weight training equipment he'd grown accustomed to at the Richmond gym where he'd met Will almost a decade ago. He wished Will could be here now, so they could use each other as punching bags. Hunter wanted nothing more than to expend some of his body's Scarlet-driven excess energy.

The mere consideration of her name brought instant images of her dark curls and bright eyes to mind. He shook his head, frustrated by his inability to scrub her from his thoughts. Stepping to a treadmill in the corner, he began a slow jog that escalated quickly into a full run.

The other occupants of the gym smiled at him in passing as he worked out. Hunter nodded back cordially, wondering if he would have met any of them at the Social. No one appeared to be an overweight, chain-smoking, boozing workaholic, but gym attire didn't lend itself to business cards, either. Even so, he had to admit that these people – psychiatric patients though they must all be – just looked like *people*.

Maybe he wasn't the only sane one, surrounded by lunatics. Maybe they were all sane. Or maybe he blended in nicely as one of the lunatics.

While the treadmill shook under the weight of his body, he watched in mortification when the door opened and Tyler Hensen stepped inside. "Oh, shit," Hunter mumbled, hoping Tyler would ignore him so he wouldn't have to revisit the embarrassing encounter from the night before. But, of course, Tyler saw him immediately and waved. Hunter returned the gesture, trying to look as normal and lucid as possible, secretly hoping the man wouldn't feel the need to talk to him.

The next instant, Tyler made a beeline for Hunter's treadmill. He didn't stop until he stood beside him, glancing at his workout timer. "I've never understood why they have treadmills in here," Tyler noted, crinkling his eyebrows as if contemplating a mystery of the universe. "There are miles and miles of road outside to run on. I think that would be much more refreshing."

Hunter shook his head as he ran. "I don't do nature."

"Yeah, it does get pretty easy to forget nature exists when you're hard at work." Tyler smiled. "I realized after we met last night that your name is Hunter *Gregory*. Are you the CEO of Gregory Global?"

He slowed to a trot. "Yeah, that's me."

"I've heard a lot about you. You're doing an amazing job."

"I have my family to thank for making the company what it is," he admitted. "You're Tyler *Hensen*. Would that be Hensen Incorporated?"

Tyler's blue eyes twinkled beneath his dark brows. "Yep, that's us."

"You operate out of New York, right?"

"The main offices are there, where my father works. But I plan to head up the new Richmond branch we're looking into."

"A Richmond branch? We'll be neighbors, then. You'll have to give me a call when you get into town."

"Yeah, I'll do that. But we shouldn't discuss it here."

"No? Why not?"

"Because this is Blissful Blue. This is the only place in the world where I don't have to talk about business."

Hunter's footsteps slowed even further. "Did you actually fly all the way from New York just to come here?"

"Absolutely. I come here as often as possible. Three or four times a year, if I'm able. I take it this is your first time?"

"How did you guess?"

"Well, no offense, but you looked pretty wound up last night. It reminded me of how I looked the first time I came here. It took me a while to realize what was missing from my life."

That statement made Hunter stop running entirely. Tyler was roughly his age and build, jovial, personable, and an executive, also. If Tyler had found what was missing from his life, then perhaps he'd actually solved one of the mysteries of the universe.

Hunter looked the man straight in the eye. "What was missing?"

"Appreciation. I know it sounds cliché, but it's really the little things that matter. You get so involved in business dealings and mundane day-to-day tasks, you forget to appreciate all the tiny things that make life so damn spectacular."

Tyler flashed a perfectly straight, sparkly-toothed grin. Hunter stared in utter disbelief, unable to fathom how this man could look so goddamn happy while leading basically the same life that had him questioning everything. *Appreciation. Bah, humbug.*

"How about you get off that contraption and join me in a little one-on-one?" Tyler goaded, retrieving a basketball from a nearby bin and spinning it on the tip of his finger. "I promise I'll take it easy on you."

Hunter huffed. "Don't you dare. I can hold my own."

"Oh, we'll see about that," Tyler promised, leading him outside of the gym facility to the waiting basketball court.

Within moments of hitting the blacktop, Hunter knew he'd found a friend. Tyler was fun, uncomplicated, and easy to talk to. On top of that, he was a fairly decent basketball player. Although Hunter had no intention of letting him win.

He blocked one of his shots, watching while Tyler faked a foot injury before sneaking behind him to steal the ball, dribbling it niftily between his legs. "That's how you pull a one-two fake-out," Tyler announced, grinning as he took a shot and missed. "It's a lot more effective, however, if you actually make the basket."

"Sure, I can see that." Hunter chuckled, rebounding the ball and dribbling around the man's back. From the corner of his eye, he saw a bleached-blond woman emerge from the gym. She moved to the bench next to the court to stretch her toned legs. She wore a fitted purple jacket, black shorts that barely covered her butt, and a wicked smile.

The blond observed their game for a moment before Hunter met her eyes. She bent forward to touch her toes, causing her miniscule shorts to rise up even higher, offering him a rather tempting view. He turned his attentions back to the basket, shooting the ball with expert precision.

"The score is tied," Tyler announced, catching the ball after it dropped through the net. "And we're being watched," he added under his breath.

"I noticed that." Hunter glanced back to her. Their onlooker was exceedingly attractive, and his entire body should have been deftly attuned to her twisty-pretzel stretches. Yet he couldn't have cared less.

"How about the next shot is winner-take-all?" Tyler suggested.

"Sounds good," Hunter said, focusing as his new friend took a shot.

Hunter deflected it easily, catching the ball and dribbling back toward the basket. He wasn't about to let this bendy woman distract him from winning a game of hoops, even if it was just a friendly competition. She would have to be far more alluring to deter him from his mission. She'd have to be...well, she'd have to be Scarlet. Frolicking Freebird Scarlet, with the gorgeous smile and the mouth-watering ass and the eyes that looked straight through him.

Hunter's fingers twitched with the unbidden images of his forest fairy. The ball wobbled out of his hands. Tyler picked it up and shot perfectly. As Hunter watched the ball sink through the hoop, he cursed his mutinous mind. "That was a damn fine shot, Tyler. Well done."

"Thanks, but I feel a little guilty. You would have beaten me fair and square if you hadn't been distracted by our lovely spectator."

Hunter ran a hand through his hair. *God help me, she wasn't the woman who distracted me.* "Maybe you could give me a chance to redeem myself sometime?"

Tyler grinned. "Love to," he agreed, motioning his head toward the limber blond. "I met this lady at the Social last night. She's the CFO of a weapons development company in California. She's smart, beautiful, and a little scary... the whole package. Come on, I'll introduce you."

Not wanting to appear rude, Hunter followed Tyler toward the bench where the woman manipulated her body with stretches that didn't seem quite human. She straightened as they approached. "Hello again, Tyler. Nice game," she offered with a piercing stare.

He took her hand and kissed it. "A pleasure, as always, Jocelyn."

She shifted her intent gaze to Hunter. "Who is your friend?"

"Hunter Gregory – this is Jocelyn Greenfield."

"Pleased to meet you, Hunter," she purred, offering him her fingers.

"And you," he replied, shaking her hand with utmost brevity.

"Sorry I distracted you from your game. I certainly didn't mean to make you fumble the ball. I was only stretching before my run."

Hunter gave her a tight smile. "No need to apologize."

"Well, I'd best be on my way. You want to join me on the trails?"

"Yes!" Tyler leapt on the invitation before turning expectant eyes to Hunter.

"No, thanks," he insisted. "I've already had my run today."

Tyler's brow rose. "You sure, buddy?"

Hunter got the strangest sensation that the man was asking his permission to pursue the beguiling blond. "I am absolutely sure."

When Jocelyn began running toward the trails, Tyler gave him a wink, obviously intending to go after her in more ways than one. "I'll see you again?" he asked while jogging backwards.

"Oh, yes. I will have my revenge," Hunter chided, watching while Tyler turned to run after her.

Jocelyn's shorts revealed more flesh with every bounce, yet Hunter stared after her with no reaction to the quivering of her exposed skin. He wondered, for the second time today, what was wrong with him. Jocelyn was certainly attractive enough – the flowing hair, the fit body, the freakish flexibility – and knowing Tyler was interested should make her even more attractive, if only for the challenge of the game. But as Hunter watched her leave, he felt absolutely nothing.

The most amazing thought occurred to him then: Jocelyn reminded him of Clarissa. Clarissa, the woman he'd spent years learning about and being intimate with. The woman he'd almost married.

Yet here he stood, with another Clarissa in arms' reach, and he couldn't drum up interest if he tried. Clarissa had been cookie-cutter perfect, and Jocelyn might be also. But Hunter didn't want that. He didn't want the flawlessly formed confection – not today. Today, he was in the mood for a lump of dough with a ton of sprinkles on top.

"Damn it," he grumbled, wondering when in the hell half-baked became appealing to him.

Then again, he already knew the answer to that question.

~

MORNING WAS over by the time Hunter returned to his cabin. He sighed in relief when he saw his empty front porch. After Scarlet's invitation last evening, he feared she'd be waiting at his door, demanding he accompany her into the woods for...whatever she did in the woods.

Did he want to know what she did in the woods? *Maybe.*

No. He did not want to know. He needed to keep up his resolve.

Stay away from her.

He showered again. He dressed business-casual in a short-sleeve navy polo and khakis. He ate his lunch. He turned on his computer.

Several emails awaited him, although surprisingly less than the day before. Diving in headfirst, he sought out further company issues to occupy his time. He worked until night began to fall and the familiar sound of the food truck's wheels crunched onto his gravel driveway.

Best alarm system in the world.

Hunter opened his front door before the delivery guy had a chance to knock. "Thanks," he said to the young man in the red hoodie.

The boy handed over the tray with a stiff smile and a nod before he pivoted and marched off the steps, striding back to his truck.

"He's not a big talker," Hunter mumbled to himself as he brought the tray in and set it on the coffee table. He sunk down onto the plaid couch cushions to admire his feast: glazed lamb with roasted potatoes and vegetables in a thick béarnaise sauce, complemented by a bottle of red wine. He would definitely have to work out again tomorrow.

Taking a bite of potatoes, he reached for the itinerary accompanying his meal. *Blissful Blue events for tomorrow: 8 a.m...Breakfast gathering in Cabin 13. 10 a.m...Group therapy session: "How to Find Your Inner Calm" by Dr. Adrien Abbott. 1-6 p.m...Individual therapy sessions. Please contact Pete Jackson at the front desk for registration.*

Hunter sighed as he set the paper down beside him. He didn't need this amount of therapy. He only came here because Will asked him, not because he needed it. This was a dare rather than a desire, and he'd be damned if this place was going to make him question himself.

You really don't know who you are, do you? It's okay. A lot of people don't know who they are.

Hunter harrumphed at the sound of Scarlet's voice in his brain. Of course he knew who he was. She was just...she was just....

What was she doing, anyway? Challenging him? Seeing if he would buckle beneath her insults to his psyche? If he would accept her lying to him? If he would drink pure lemon juice out of her hand and do nothing about it?

Rising from the couch, Hunter began pacing. "What else is there to do in this godforsaken place? Is there anything *not* related to therapy?"

He could go see Tyler in Cabin 11, he supposed. He could walk there. But Jocelyn might be there, and Hunter didn't want to interrupt.

"Lemon juice!" he hollered into his empty cabin. "Scarlet had me drink pure lemon juice! She outright challenged me and I did nothing but cower away!"

He understood now what had happened between them last night. They were gunslingers – standing on opposite sides of a corral with tumbleweeds rolling by – waiting for someone to make a move. She shot first, and he took one right in the gut. *Literally*, his gut reminded him.

Hunter stilled as he stared out the window at the blackening sky. Scarlet had gotten the better of him, plain and simple. His entire body clenched, revolting against the thought of being conquered so easily. Especially in a war he hadn't realized she'd waged.

"Holy hell. I'm going back, aren't I? I'm going to see her again."

Only this time, he would be prepared. She was not the all-knowing, powerful Oz. She was nothing to be frightened of, or to hide from. He was the CEO of a Fortune-500 company, for crying out loud. He could take whatever she dished out and dish his own right back.

After all, she'd shown him a vulnerable side yesterday.

It was only a tiny glimpse, but he saw it.

Hunter flew out of his front door before he could second-guess his decision. He didn't even see the outrageous amount of trees surrounding him as he strode, since all he could see was the flash of vulnerability he'd witnessed in his forest fairy last night: the far-off look in her eyes that suggested she might have an inner sane person.

What had he said to make her act normally, even for those brief seconds? Simply that he was *on vacation*. Yet she'd repeated the words almost reverently, turning away from him for the very first time.

Nothing about that moment made sense. Why did those two little words reach her in such a way? Why did she care about that simple thought, when him calling her a liar was a footnote on a thousand pages?

His feet crunched down her driveway as he considered the fact that he had actually called her a liar. That was rude, he supposed, even if it were true. Most people would get angry and defensive. But not Scarlet.

"She's not going to beat me this time," Hunter assured himself when her cabin loomed closer. "I'm on to her game. I will stand my ground."

His foot slipped on the gravel before he bounded up her front porch steps. Hunter corrected his balance quickly and poised himself to knock. The door opened before he had the chance. And there she stood.

Her dark hair was pulled back into a messy bun, with a few defiant strands hanging down to her shoulders. Her shirt was pale pink with a deep V that showcased more skin than he should have seen. The shirt did cover her midriff, at least, being tucked into a little pair of jeans that hugged her perfectly. Tonight, her toenails were painted red.

Do you change your toenail polish every day?

He didn't have the chance to ask his question. Not before she grabbed his hand and pulled him inside. Scarlet kicked the door shut and stepped closer, fully invading his personal space.

"Thank God you're here," she breathed with nervous energy, her fingers trembling as they gripped his. "I desperately need your help."

His heart banged against his ribcage. *Is she in trouble? Having some sort of delusional episode? Why did I come here again?*

"Is everything okay, Scarlet?"

"It's better than okay! Just look!"

Hunter followed the line of her pointing finger, drawing his attention to the opposite side of the living room. She'd hung a new picture on the wall, a picture of a tree. "Um, wow," he offered, unsure of the response she desired. "Did you take that photo?"

"Yes! Yes!" She nodded violently, tugging him toward it. "What do you think? Is it straight? I feel like I've been staring at it for hours, trying to decide if it's straight or not. You can't gauge anything by the knots in these log walls."

He smiled despite himself when they came to a stop in front of her photograph. "The walls are a problem," he agreed, glancing to her face. He watched her stare up at him with worry-filled eyes and he completely forgot every thought he'd had before this moment. The only thing he wanted was for her to be happy.

Hunter used his free hand – the one not tangled up in her fingers – to reach to the wall. He shifted the frame a millimeter to the left. "There," he assured. "It's absolutely straight now."

"Oh, thank you." She sighed as if the weight of the world had lifted from her shoulders. "Sometimes you just need someone else's help."

He nodded. "I suppose everyone does, at some point."

Scarlet gazed sweetly up to his face. The impulse to wrap her in his arms nearly overwhelmed him. Nearly.

How could she manage to look so damn innocent when he knew for a fact that she was a spitfire? It was only a picture of a tree. But she was a picture, too. Unlike anything he'd ever seen.

"Do you like the view?" she asked in a soft whisper.

Hell, yes. How could he not? Looking at her could be a hobby of his.

Despite her personality, or perhaps because of it, he could find no fault in anything he saw before him. "I love the view," he admitted.

"So, you see the bird, then?"

"The bird?" *Do you have a bird tattoo? Where is it? Can I see it?*

"In the picture! The yellow-crowned purple fantini! I took the photo just this morning!"

Hunter spent a moment registering her words before turning back to the wall. Feeling sheepish for thinking she'd been asking about her own appearance, he released his hold on her hand to approach the portrait. He stared hard at the image, but all he saw was a tree. And even that wasn't really in focus. Good Lord, she was a bad photographer.

"Um..." he stalled, hoping he could discern something else.

"It's right there!" She moved up to his side again, pointing to a spot in the photo that appeared to be a concentration of sunshine reflecting off a blob of leaves. "I know it's not exactly in focus, but I got so excited! I was shaking the camera from sheer nerves!"

Hunter concentrated harder. He wanted to see the bird. He truly wanted to see it. But there was nothing but blurs of green and yellow. He cleared his throat. "The picture is...it's really something, Scarlet."

"Thank you. Thank you so much." She grinned luminously as she stood at his shoulder and gazed into his eyes. "I wish you'd been there. The forest was amazing this morning, just full of life. So still and calm at times, yet other times the noises fill your ears to bursting. Did you know there are over 400 species of trees in the Blue Ridge Mountains?"

The warmth of her breath tickled his skin. "No, I didn't know that."

"You should come with me tomorrow. I'd be happy to pick you up, bright and early, so we can walk my little path together. I know the exact spot I was in when I took this picture. Maybe, if we're lucky, the fantini will return and I can snap a photo without shaking like a child!"

Her exhilarated giggles infected him. She hopped up and down, her breast brushing his arm. He wanted to turn to her and crush her to his chest, to kiss that adorable, silly grin right off her lips. He wanted it so badly it scared him. The intensity of his fear finally sobered his mind.

Hunter made himself look away. He stood frozen beside her, staring at the photo frame nailed to the wall. He willed away his freakish desire for her, a desire that took hold of him against his better judgment, against *any* judgment, threatening to overtake his semblance of calm.

He could be calm around her. That would be the only way he could even begin to participate in this war of wills, a war she'd mastered so skillfully that he'd barely even noticed it taking place. Squirrels. Lemon Juice. Questioning his psyche. He would not let her win again.

Hunter stared at the photo – no bird. He stared at the frame – nailed to the wall. Then it struck him.

"Scarlet," he growled, looking back to her, "you have nailed this photo to the wall."

"Yes, of course. How else do you expect it to stay up there?"

"But this is private property. You don't own this cabin, do you?"

"No, I don't own it."

"Good God, woman! You can't just go around nailing your own photos into walls that aren't yours! Did you ask permission to do this?"

Scarlet held his icy gaze for a long minute before grasping both his hands in her own. She turned his body to face hers. "Hunter, are you actually telling me you think one little nail hole could possibly matter in a wall that has more knots, holes, and twists than a minefield?"

"That's not the point," he stated, wishing for his own peace of mind that she wasn't holding his hands, or standing so close. "This is about principle. You're on private property and you've defaced it."

"Will you be happy if I say I'll buy wood spackle before I leave?"

"I don't know. Will you buy wood spackle before you leave?"

"No. I just wonder if the thought of me fixing the hole will make you happy."

"Not if you're lying to me, it won't."

Scarlet sighed, her shoulders falling, and Hunter instantly regretted his words. He'd called her a liar. Again. Certainly, she'd be upset by it this time. There was no way around it. She might even slap him.

She didn't slap him. She simply stared into his eyes, stared and stared, until he shifted his feet. She was looking into him again, in that harrowing way she had, and he feared what she saw. She didn't need to know more about him than he did.

"Hmm," she murmured after several minutes. "There is something about you, Hunter, something..."

"What?"

Scrunching her nose, she looked like she was about to sneeze when instead she said, "Closed."

He arched an eyebrow. "What's closed?"

"You are. You're just...closed."

"I am not closed."

"Yes, you are. Do you know why you're closed?"

His mind reached back sixteen years. He forced the memory down. "I'm not closed."

"No? How is your relationship with your parents, then?"

Hunter choked out a laugh. "What is this? Are you learning some psycho babble being encased up here at Chez Nutjob?"

Scarlet shook her head. "No need to get defensive. If you have nothing to hide, simply answer the question."

"Mom and Dad are great," he stated, refusing to let her gain the upper hand. "We have a wonderful relationship, they have an amazing marriage, and I love them both dearly. They raised me with every advantage."

"And where are they now?"

"Mountain climbing in Washington State."

"Mountain climbing? Really? How old are they?"

"Just turned sixty. Their birthdays are only two days apart. The trip was a gift to each other."

"That's amazing. I hope I'll still be climbing mountains when I'm sixty." Scarlet smiled radiantly for a moment. Then her brow furrowed. "But you're not, are you?"

"I'm not what?"

"Climbing mountains with your parents."

"No, I'm here."

"Why?"

"Because I don't like climbing mountains."

"Well, if you think about it, you climbed a mountain to get here."

"No, I drove a car to get here."

"I know why you climbed a mountain to get here, Hunter."

"Oh, really? This should be good."

"You climbed your way here because you're closed…"

"I am *not* closed."

"…and you realize you would rather be open."

"And are you going to open me, then, Scarlet?" He drilled the question into her eyes, wondering how she would recover from his purposefully tempting suggestion. But as he pinned her beneath a steely gaze, he realized he hadn't ruffled her feathers in the slightest.

She wasn't flummoxed or flustered. She wasn't anything he expected anyone to be. Honestly, he had no fucking clue what to expect from her, and it unnerved him on every level. When she stepped closer, he held his breath, waiting to see what she would do next.

The little forest fairy extracted one of her hands from his and reached up to his face. She touched him, her fingers smoothing slowly across his jaw, and he had to actively resist the urge to close his eyes and sigh into her soft skin. Her hand trailed down, over his neck and onto his shoulder, before she began tracing another one of her rhythmic, methodical paths up and down his bare arm.

Dear Lord, she's petting me again. And I'm letting her. Again.

"Do you play Twister, Hunter?"

He watched her for a lingering minute, working to register her words through the warm, plying touch of her fingers. "What?"

"Twister, the game. You know: spin the arrow, right hand on blue, left foot on yellow. Twister."

Hunter was at a loss, but for only a moment. He knew what was happening right now. Scarlet was challenging him, attempting to throw him off-kilter with her little flight-of-ideas superiority. But she wouldn't conquer him so easily.

"Yes, I play Twister quite well. You'd be hard pressed to beat me."

She grinned up at him. "Well, that's the spirit! Where does your competitive nature originate, I wonder?"

"Four years of football in high school, with a very militant coach."

Scarlet finally pulled her hands from his body to walk toward the hall. He ignored the fact that he could still feel her fingers on his skin.

Her closet-muffled voice reached his ears even when she'd stepped out of sight. "Did you play football in college, too?"

Hunter winced. Thankfully, she didn't see his momentary display of weakness. "No, I didn't," he dismissed. "So, where's this Twister?"

"Here!" she hollered, raising the box triumphantly in her hands when she reappeared in the hall doorway. "I love all the board games they put in these cabins. It's just good, basic fun, you know?"

Once she'd sauntered back into the living room, Hunter pushed the coffee table out of the way so she could unfold the plastic game mat and shake it out over the throw rug. He huffed at the familiar sight from his youth. He couldn't believe he was about to play Twister with Frolicking Freebird Scarlet.

He watched intently as she knelt down to straighten each corner of the mat, crawling on her knees and stretching her body to achieve the perfect symmetry of plastic against the rug. Her pink T-shirt pulled up from the waist of her jeans while she moved, revealing an inch of flawless skin across her low back. As Hunter watched her bend and wriggle, he had to clear his throat for some reason. Actually, he knew the reason. He just didn't want to acknowledge it.

Finally finished with her task, Scarlet sat back on her heels. She peered up at him from the ground with one eyebrow raised. Then she simply waited for him to read her mind.

"What?" he grumbled, wondering what ridiculous thing she wanted him to do next.

"Um, I was hoping you could take off your shoes?"

"Oh. Yeah, of course." He kicked off the offending loafers.

"Thank you, Hunter. It's just that you're quite a bit bigger than me, and I would really hate to have my toes crushed. Especially since I just painted my toenails today."

"They're adorable." *Damn it, I didn't mean to say that out loud.*

Scarlet beamed at him, her cheeks flushing. "I'm glad you like them." She looked back to the mat, focusing on the colorful circles beneath her crouched body. "I'm so excited we're going to play this. I haven't played since I was a child. Do you want to spin or should I?"

God, does it matter? The whole room is spinning, isn't it?

Hunter fisted his hands, frustrated by how ferociously he wanted to touch her. Even though he felt certain he shouldn't touch her. Except for the fact that they were about to play a game that would require him to touch her, over and over again. It would require him to constantly feel the warmth of her body against his and not lose his mind.

"You can spin," he offered, steeling himself for what was about to happen.

"Yay!" she squealed before giving the little plastic arrow a thorough beating. He watched her body quiver with anticipation as the arrow finally pointed to *right hand – blue.* She waited patiently until he knelt down and placed his hand in the middle of the blue dots. Her hand came down immediately next to his.

Scarlet spun again. *Left hand – green.* They complied, their bodies side by side as they spread their arms to accommodate their instructions.

Right foot – blue.

Hunter immediately placed his right foot next to his right hand, but because Scarlet had chosen the blue circle beside his she was now left with little option. She could twist her body to get her right leg over to the blue dot on her left...or she could straddle him.

She chose the latter.

Hoisting her leg over his back, she reached the very edge of the next blue circle with the tip of her big toe, stretching fully to maintain her hand placement. He lay encased beneath her, her chest and stomach resting against his back. Her breathing pattern changed, her heightened inhales and exhales causing her breasts to rub against his spine.

She felt warm and soft, and Hunter closed his eyes as the sweet smell of fresh soap and tiny flowers enveloped him. He breathed in deeply, trying to capture her scent, but the motion only made her chest come into fuller contact with his back. He groaned under his breath, unsure of how long he could maintain this position before parts of his body responded aggressively to her proximity.

Relax, he commanded. He was not prepared to lose another battle of wills with her. He quieted his mind and waited for her to spin again. He waited a while.

"Um…" she finally spoke after stretched seconds traipsed across his back. "I'm so sorry, Hunter, but I can't reach the spinner thingy."

"Would you like me to get that for you?"

"If you would be so kind," she answered, her tone quite noble, considering she required only a saddle to be officially riding him.

He reached his fingers out and spun, returning quickly to his previous position as he saw *right hand – red.*

They lunged simultaneously, her chest plopping down on his back, collapsing them both to the mat. Her body thudded on top of his and he instantly flipped over beneath her straddling legs. Scarlet didn't bother to move away. She merely situated herself more comfortably on his lap.

He eased up on his elbows to look her in the eyes. "I won," he announced, trying to ignore the fact that she'd perched herself on top of him and didn't appear to have any plans to fly away.

"You won? How do you figure that? You hit the mat first."

"Only because you made me. I would have kept my balance if you'd kept yours."

"I disagree."

"Me, too."

"Hmm," she considered, her thighs still pinned around his waist. "I guess this calls for a rematch, then."

"You're on."

"Yes, I am." She glanced down to his chest. "But I'll get off of you now. There's work to be done."

She smiled sweetly, her body rubbing against his as she rose. Hunter encouraged himself to breathe slowly, in and out. He didn't know what work she referred to, but he wasn't going to be putty in her hands, no matter how fucking adorable and gorgeous and sexy she was. Or how often she planned to use him as her personal hobbyhorse.

Unfortunately, his goal proved difficult to achieve.

Scarlet threw herself across him in every game. Again and again, no matter how quickly he moved or how he contorted his body, she finagled herself between his arms, through his legs, and over his back. He found himself mere inches from her chest on multiple occasions, with the deep V of her top gaping down to showcase the ivory lace bra that barely contained her breasts. He had to rest his head on her tiny bared stomach once, to reach his hand to green, and tried like hell not to notice how close his teeth came to the button on her jeans.

The worst part, however, wasn't how her closeness affected him. The worst part was how blatantly *his* closeness affected *her*. Having to listen to the little pants escaping her throat when their bodies aligned perfectly together, having to witness the dilation of her pupils when his face came flush with hers, and having to hear her whimper when his arm *accidentally* brushed across her breasts, was absolute torture.

But Hunter forged through. Scarlet would not crack him. She would not open him. No matter how much work she thought she had to do.

Eventually, they collapsed together while reaching their right feet for red. Utterly exhausted, Hunter rested his back against the mat and let his head drop onto the rug. Scarlet lay sideways across him, their stomachs pressed together, but he couldn't muster the energy or desire to move.

Turning her face to his, she moaned. "I'm so sore."

"Me, too."

A disheveled hair, falling from her barely contained bun, covered part of her mouth. She blew out a breath, attempting to dislodge the loose curl. "How long were we at that?"

"Hours," he answered. Unthinking, he raised a sore arm to ease the hair from her lips. He brushed his fingers against her cheek, absorbing the heat of her skin, before tucking the wandering curl behind her ear.

Her eyes closed with his touch, her lips parting on a contented sigh.

Hunter yanked his hand away. "Time to get up now," he ordered himself, willing his tired limbs to escape the easy pleasure of her body.

"Okay," she murmured, finally crawling off of him to rest back against the couch frame. He sat next to her on the plastic mat, although still several feet away, slumping against the logs.

"Did one of us win, Hunter?"

"I don't think so."

"That's too bad."

"Yeah, it really is."

They rested in silence for several minutes. He used the respite to catch his breath and calm his racing pulse. Then, from his peripheral vision, he saw her grin wickedly.

"May I offer you some lemonade?"

He desperately fought the urge to roll his eyes. *Goddamn lemonade!*

"Yes, Scarlet. I would *love* some."

"Wonderful! Wait right here."

He watched her jump up, heard her rustle in the kitchen, listened to the refrigerator door open and ice clank into glasses, and grimaced as her footsteps returned. She plopped down on the floor again, the sickly yellow liquid sloshing in the glasses and dribbling onto the Twister dots beneath them. She offered him one and he accepted.

Hunter stared down at the opaque swill, wondering if drinking an entire serving could harm something of vital importance inside his body.

Is this going to destroy my pancreas? Or my spleen? Good Lord, what does a spleen do, anyway? Can I survive without it?

He inhaled steeply and brought the rim of the glass to his lips.

"Wait." Scarlet held up her hand. "I need to know something first."

Hunter sighed in relief. "Yes?"

"What's your last name?"

"Haven't I told you?"

"No, you haven't."

"Oh. Well, it's Gregory. Hunter Gregory."

Her jaw unhinged. "You don't mean *the* Hunter Gregory, do you?"

"I think I do."

"You're the CEO of Gregory Global in Richmond?"

He watched the stark curiosity shift over her face. "That's me. How do you know about Gregory Global?"

She nibbled her lip. "Well, um, who wouldn't know about Gregory Global? My goodness, you're the head of a Fortune-500 company."

"Yes, I am." A part of him felt proud she'd heard of his family's company. Another part feared her next reaction: the hungered looks and clawed fingers he'd come to expect from any woman who realized who he was. He held his breath until she spoke again.

"Wow, Hunter. You too, huh?"

"Me too, what?"

"You have two first names. It stinks, doesn't it?"

He ogled her for a minute. "I only have one first name."

"Yes, but no one would know that if you didn't tell them. You could be Hunter Gregory or Gregory Hunter. Who's to say?"

"And you could be Scarlet Tracey or Tracey Scarlet," he replied, unsure if he was more excited about her lack of a predatory response, or with the realization that he could now follow her wandering thoughts.

"Exactly!" she shouted, her lemonade sluicing over the glass rim.

He suppressed the groan that leapt into his throat as he imagined licking her fingers clean. "Do you plan to change your name, then?"

She shook her head. "Oh, no, I've had it for thirty-two years, so it would be far too much paperwork to change it now. I just wish my parents would've made my first name sound like a last name, so I could have both. Maybe something like Scarlet...son. Scarletson Tracey."

"And then people would call you Tracey?"

"Or Scarletson. I'd be good with either one."

He chuckled. "Hmm. But then you'd only have one name."

"Lots of rock stars do it," she defended, wiggling her toes on the plastic. "Although, if I went full-on rock star, I'd probably have to buy more clothes with sequins and glitter on them. But maybe that's a good thing, since my sequins-and-glitter collection is sorely lacking."

She gave him a broad, bubbly smile. Hunter returned it, fully aware that she was joking. He could tell that much now, a feat he wasn't capable of yesterday. He was starting to see inside her, to glimpse the fantastical world inside her brain, and found it strangely appealing.

"Well, as beautiful as I'm sure you'll look in sequins and glitter, I think I'll still call you Scarlet. I like Scarlet."

"You can call me whatever makes you happy, Hunter. I like it when you're happy."

He squeezed onto the glass while watching her bright green eyes sparkle. She was so close to him. Close enough that he could reach out and grab her. He could take her in his arms, lay her down on this Twister-floor, and kiss every inch of her. He knew by the way she gazed at him now, and by the way her body had pulled toward his this entire evening, that she would let him do whatever he wanted to do with her. For the love of all things holy, he wanted to do everything.

Drinking an entire glass of straight lemon juice suddenly sounded quite reasonable, since he desperately needed to force his mind back to reality. He looked down to the disgusting liquid filth in his hand and raised his cup. "Cheers, Scarlet."

She clinked her glass with his. "Cheers, Hunter."

She straightened and stared him down. He matched her determined gaze with his own. They were two gunslingers standing across a corral. With tumbleweeds drifting past. Or it could have just been lint.

They threw their glasses to their lips simultaneously, tipping them back to force the lemon juice swiftly down their throats. The acidic fluid burned all the way down. Hunter tried to imagine this was beer – attempting to trick his mind into thinking he was drinking something other than horse piss – but it didn't work. Yet he still swallowed every last drop, not releasing the glass until he'd finished.

They slammed their empty cups to the floor at the same moment, staring at each other with tears in their eyes.

"Shit," he choked out. "Did you ever drink a whole glass before?"

Scarlet sucked in her cheeks as shivers rocked her shoulders. "No. Never. God, it's so awful."

Hunter tried not to laugh. He truly did. He tried not to think of how stupid they were acting, or how silly this entire night had been, but he couldn't help himself. As he watched her body quake beneath the onslaught of pure lemon juice, he chuckled. Softly at first, but then louder and harder.

Scarlet joined him, her giggles a lively, glittering sound filling his ears and running straight to his chest. The more she laughed, the more he followed, until they were both in near fits on the floor. Hunter couldn't remember ever laughing this hard in his life. It drained every semblance of obstinate reality from his body, for these few precious moments, and he loved that she was here beside him through it all.

When he finally managed to calm down, he continued absorbing the blissful giggles still erupting from her throat. Hunter realized, quite clearly, that she had won the night. Whatever game they were playing, he'd come away feeling changed. Yet she was still just...Scarlet.

That realization, although not sad, was enough to encourage him to leave. He wasn't on stable ground when he was around her. He didn't know if he ever would be. But nothing else could happen between them tonight. He'd allowed too much to happen already.

"Scarlet, I should...I should really be going."

A twinge of sadness darkened her eyes. "Okay. If you must."

He started to rise when her hand landed on his knee, gently preventing his escape. He stilled and looked back to her.

"Hunter, before you go, can I ask you something?"

He settled down beside her again. "Sure."

She scooted closer, her thigh pressing against his. "Did you like playing football in high school?"

Of all the things he thought she might ask him, that question was definitely not on the list. "Yes. I loved it, actually."

"I'll bet you were good at it, too."

"Yeah, I was."

"And you were Hunter Gregory."

He huffed out a laugh. "I'm pretty sure I still am."

"Yes, but back then you were *the* Hunter Gregory – the youthful, gorgeous, athletic son of ridiculously wealthy parents. I can only imagine what that must have been like for you, having the whole world at your feet. I suppose you were deliriously happy, all the time."

He stared at her, wondering what point she was trying to make. He wasn't entirely sure, but he was bitterly aware of an undeniable truth. "Actually, Scarlet, I was a complete asshole."

She gulped. "An...an asshole?"

"Yup. A total dick. I mean, don't get me wrong; I was charming. I could charm the pants off of anyone. And I often did."

Her cheeks flushed. "You had a lot of women, I guess."

"More than my fair share. Not that I was faithful to any of them. I was too busy partying to care how they felt. Too busy making sure I had the most fun I could. I didn't really give a shit about anything, except football. Once, I even keyed a cop car."

"Wow. Seriously?"

Hunter hung his head. "Hell, I haven't thought about that in so many years. It feels like a lifetime ago."

Scarlet's fingers, which had been resting on his knee this entire time, began rubbing softly up and down his thigh. He knew she was petting him again, but he was used to it now. And honestly, he liked it.

"So, what happened then, Hunter?"

His eyes drew back to hers. "What do you mean?"

"Well, that's not who you are anymore, is it? The happy-go-lucky boy, with a line of girls chasing him, isn't the man sitting with me now."

He smiled despite himself. "No, I suppose not."

"Then what happened to change him?"

Hunter stared at her. She stared back. He had that feeling again, like she was looking farther into him than possible, and definitely farther than he wanted. Yet here he sat, letting her do it, because he really didn't want to leave this cabin tonight. He didn't want to be alone again, no matter what she saw inside him.

Scarlet leaned closer, even though she was already far too close. Despite his desperate desire to remain right here with her, Hunter knew he shouldn't. "You know, I just...I grew up," he answered. It wasn't entirely the truth, but it was close enough for him to not feel guilty about lying. "And now, I really should be going."

He stood swiftly, disconnecting from her body. He wanted to leave before she had the chance to mesmerize him again with the lulling sound of her voice and the perfect touch of her skin. He should have taken the opportunity to escape and stepped away instantly. But instead, he looked back down. Her gentle eyes gazed up at him, and before he could stop himself, he held out his hand for her. Scarlet took the offering, settling her fingers into his palm and pulling herself up to stand in front of him.

The Twister mat crinkled beneath her feet as she reached to his face. She slipped her fingers across his jaw, exploring for lengthy moments, before her hand dropped to his chest to press against his shirt. Hunter's breath hitched, responding to her proximity, to the warmth of her body, to her sweet scent of flowers drifting into his nostrils. He looked to her mouth, watching in pained wonder as she wet her lips. When he could tear his gaze away from that maddening sight, he fisted his hands at his sides and refocused on her eyes.

Her palm still rested on his chest. But not just anywhere. Her hand lay over his heart, as if she wanted to physically reach inside and take hold. She was so comfortable touching him, so goddamn comfortable, and he wanted nothing more than to touch her back.

Oddly, even though they'd spent the entire night draped across each other, Hunter felt nervous to touch her now. Probably because she'd always been the one to touch him. She was the one who held his hand, who petted him, who reached for his heart. The only time he'd even touched her face was when he'd eased her stray hair from her mouth earlier, and that tiny touch of his fingers to her skin left him scorched.

Anxiety infused his body, yet it wasn't enough to prevent him from doing what he wanted. Reaching out, he placed his hand on her shoulder. This simple action seemed safe, until he felt the heat of her skin beneath the fabric of her shirt, and had to watch as she sighed and leaned closer.

Damn, she was just beautiful. So happy and gentle and perfect. His hand wandered up, first to the side of her neck and then to her face, exploring the contours of her skin as his heart hammered inside his chest. Her mouth was still wet from the touch of her tongue and he eased his thumb to her lower lip, dragging it across that smooth, moist warmth. She let out a little whimper as he cupped her cheek in his hand.

"God, I want to kiss you," Hunter confessed, not even realizing he'd said the words out loud until her breath caught in her throat.

Scarlet trembled beneath his touch. "I want that, too," she said, her gaze falling to his chest. She focused on her fingers as she fiddled with a button on his shirt. "It's a funny thing, isn't it? Attraction, I mean. You meet a hundred people – a thousand, even – and you may find a few of them attractive. But then, out of the blue, you see one. Just one. And that person feels so different, and makes you feel open and connected to the entire world. At that moment, you know you're just...alive." Her eyes moved back to his. "But, in truth, attraction is nothing more than a simple chemical reaction that takes place in the human body."

"Is it?" he questioned. Part of him knew it was. The other part of him didn't give a fuck what it was, because he just wanted to feel the warmth of her lips melting beneath his.

"It is," she confirmed. "So, it's probably not a good idea for us to do anything about it."

"You're right. It's probably not a good idea at all. It's probably the worst idea ever." His hand slid up her cheek, pushing into her hair to ground her in place.

Scarlet wet her lips again. "Y-yes. The worst idea ever."

She didn't try to pull away. She just kept playing her fingers against his shirt as her gaze drifted from his eyes to his lips and back. Hunter knew all he had to do was lean down. All he had to do was move a little closer and she would do the rest, since she obviously didn't give a fuck about what chemicals were in play here, either.

He wound his fingers into the curls at the nape of her neck. He inhaled deeply, silently acknowledging the strength of his desire for this woman. Hell, right this minute, he'd give up all he owned just to learn what sound she'd make when his tongue parted her lips for the first time.

But was that really the best thing for either of them? This wasn't exactly a normal vacation, and they weren't exactly a normal couple. Scarlet could very well be crazy. Or she could be perfectly sane, which meant he was the crazy one.

Hunter couldn't be sure which of those were true, but he did know two things for certain. The first was that his forest fairy planned to open him, and probably could, and he didn't know if he was ready for it. The second was that if he started kissing her, he wouldn't want to stop. He wouldn't want to stop for the rest of the night, right on into the morning.

That last thought sobered him. Given how easily and clearly he could picture himself waking naked in bed beside her, he knew he needed to leave before he did something they might both regret.

Hunter finally found the strength to straighten his spine. Releasing his hold on her hair, he pulled away entirely. "Well, then. I suppose I should say goodnight now, Scarlet."

She closed her eyes, taking a moment to settle, before nodding.

He stepped off the plastic mat, thrusting his feet into his shoes and striding toward the front door before he changed his mind. He yanked open the handle, turning to see her close behind him as he stepped outside. She looked as lovely as ever – especially with tiny ebony hairs sticking out from her tousled bun – and he had to assure his disgruntled body that leaving her now was the right thing to do.

When he'd made it safely onto the porch, Scarlet leaned against the door-frame. "Which cabin are you staying in, Hunter?"

Don't answer! "Cabin 9."

"I'll pick you up at 8 a.m.," she confirmed, as if he'd agreed to her plans long ago. "I'll show you my woods as they're meant to be seen."

Hunter absorbed the sight of her body haloed by the light from inside the cabin. "Okay," he decided without an ounce of regret, just wanting to see where this thing took him. After all, he was already floundering out in the middle of nowhere. There had to be a logical conclusion to all of this. He only wished it didn't feel like she already knew what it was.

Scarlet smiled. "I'll see you tomorrow."

"Tomorrow," he echoed, stepping off the porch and onto the gravel. Hunter felt her bright eyes on his back, all the way down her driveway. When he finally made it to the main road, he congratulated himself for not spinning on his heels and sprinting back for that kiss.

4

SOOTHING THE SAVAGE BEAST

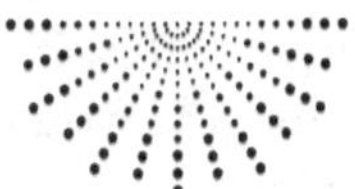

Hunter's alarm woke him at 7 a.m. He jumped out of bed. Scarlet would be here soon, to flutter her way into his world and drag him off to the woods, and he needed time to prepare. Today held too many unknowns, and he had to keep his wits about him.

He proceeded with his usual morning routine, completing his sit-ups and push-ups before hopping in the shower. He tried not to think about Frolicking Freebird Scarlet as he washed, but he couldn't prevent his mind from drifting to the previous night. Their entire evening in her cabin felt like a test, with her engaging him in one contest after the next, just to see who would call *Uncle* first.

Scarlet obviously wanted to open him. But Hunter wanted to open her, too. His little fairy had layers – a hell of a lot of layers – and he wanted to see beneath them all.

He closed his eyes under the hot running water, picturing the look on her face two nights ago when he'd said he was on vacation. The mere mention of those two words had thrown her into a moment of lucidity bordering on normalcy. Why? If she wasn't silly, frivolous, devil-may-care-and-I'll-nail-this-picture-to-the-wall-if-I-want-to Scarlet, then who was she? Could he ever possibly find out?

Hunter shook his head while stepping out of the shower. Wrapping his towel around his waist, he stared at his personal care items on the sink, lined up in order of usage: deodorant, toothpaste, toothbrush, razor, comb and cologne. He always kept them like that, having enacted his morning routine exactly the same way for as long as he could recall.

He wondered if Scarlet had a routine. She probably didn't. She probably had to search for where she left her perfume. She probably forgot to brush her hair sometimes, too. Did that make her crazy? Or did it just make him obsessive?

Hunter stared at his lineup of products on the bathroom counter. He moved his deodorant to the end of the line. He smiled.

There. See? I can do things differently. I can be adventurous.

Scarlet would not throw him off-kilter. He would simply choose to be off-kilter, and beat her at her own game. He would show her that he could put his deodorant on after his cologne, damn it.

Hunter exited the bathroom with a sense of accomplishment. He would have to go into the woods this morning – into all that disgruntling nature – but he would do it with a smile on his face. He had no earthly desire to see the 400 species of trees Scarlet told him were out there, but she didn't have to know that.

After pulling on a black T-shirt and tan cargo pants, Hunter moved hurriedly to his laptop. He took a seat, knowing only minutes remained for him to check on work. But as he waited for the computer to connect him to the real world, a sickly sensation crawled into his gut.

His fingers twitched against the keyboard. *Are there really 400 species of trees in the Blue Ridge Mountains? That sounds like a lot of fucking trees. Did she do it again? After I called her out about the squirrels, did she look me in the face and lie about trees?*

Hunter grit his teeth as he typed *Blue Ridge Mountain trees* into the search engine. The information appeared swiftly. The Blue Ridge held 1,400 herbaceous plants, 34 types of salamanders, and 158 species of trees.

"158 species of trees," he seethed.

Why? Why couldn't she be honest with him? Who the hell cared how many trees were in the Blue Ridge? She could have simply said *a lot*. That wouldn't have been a lie.

Hunter leaned back in the log chair and stared up at the log ceiling.

"Why does she keep doing this?" he wondered aloud.

Admittedly, at first, he thought the lies were just part of the craziness of her. But now, as he looked back on each little deception, he didn't believe that anymore. Her deceits were too precise and well-placed, each one exaggerated enough to become obvious the moment he thought about it. Which probably meant it all had some purpose in her mind. But what the hell could that be?

Hunter didn't know what to think about her. He didn't know what to do with her. She'd lied to him repeatedly, about silly things like squirrels and lemonade and trees. But he also believed she'd lied about a much more fundamental thing, since he didn't believe for a second that she was a freelance nature reporter.

Scarlet was a patient, just like him, and he wanted nothing more than for her to admit it. Not because he wanted to expose her flaws, but because he didn't care that she was a patient. It didn't matter to him that she needed help. After all, as much as he'd fought the admission, the fact remained that he needed help, too.

Shutting his computer down, he pressed his fingers into his eyelids. *Scarlet.* How could one tiny woman manage to crawl so far under his skin in such a short period of time? She'd worked her way inside him, not just with her ridiculous lies, but with her kindness and beauty.

God, she was beautiful. He wanted to touch her, both her heart and her body, even though he knew he shouldn't. The conversation they'd had last night was good. They'd agreed not to act on their attraction to each other, and that was for the best.

He appreciated her being the voice of reason after he'd blurted out his desire to kiss her. After all, he was 90% certain he shouldn't kiss her. Or peel her clothes off. Or push himself inside her skin, like she was already inside his. That would all be a terrible mistake, right?

Tire wheels crunched against his gravel driveway.

Hunter's head popped up at the sound. He sprang out of his chair and ran for the door, hoping to catch the red-hooded deliveryman before he scurried silently away. Hunter reached the door handle and jerked it open, but instead of finding the stealthy delivery boy, he found Scarlet.

His little fairy stood perched on the porch, holding his food tray in both hands. "Breakfast at your service," she sang with a curtsey.

Hunter barely registered how delectable she looked in her matching heather gray yoga pants and zippered jacket before he saw the delivery guy returning to his truck.

"Have a nice day, Scarlet!" the young man hollered beneath his red hood as he eased into the driver's seat.

"You too, Colin!" she yelled back.

Hunter's brow arched. "The meal delivery guy talks to you?"

Her head tilted. "Yeah. Doesn't he talk to you?"

"No. He's never said a word to me."

"Oh, well, he's just a little shy. Once he gets used to you, he'll talk your ear off." Scarlet smiled as she fluttered into his cabin, her manly hiking boots barely making a sound against the log floor.

Hunter closed the door behind her, wondering just how much time she'd spent up at Blissful Blue. Enough time for red-hooded Colin to get used to her. Enough time for her to be comfortable traipsing through the woods. Enough time for her to know Will in an official capacity. Did she come here every chance she could, like Tyler? Was she also a stressed-out executive who'd found peace here in these mountains?

Scarlet delivered his food to the coffee table and plopped down on his plaid couch cushions. She stole the croissant from his tray, breaking off a flaky piece and popping it in her mouth. She gave him a silly grin as she proceeded to eat his breakfast, and Hunter focused on the upturn of her bright pink lips. Looking at her right this moment, he honestly couldn't imagine Freebird Forest Scarlet ever being stressed out.

"You want some?" she asked, holding the partially devoured croissant up in the air. "I mean, it's yours, of course. You really should eat something before we head out. The food here is amazing, right?"

He joined her on the couch, although he sat at the opposite end. He pivoted toward her as she held the croissant out to him. He took it, careful not to touch her in the process, and shoved a bite into his mouth.

"Did you sleep well, Hunter?"

He nodded while swallowing. "I did."

"Oh, good. Honestly, I hoped you'd still be asleep when I got here, so I could serve you breakfast in bed. But I don't imagine you want to go lay back down now. You don't seem like someone who takes naps."

He stared at her with his brow cocked, trying to decide which thing she'd said was the most worrisome: the fact that she'd planned to break into his cabin while he slept; her use of the word *honestly*; the thought of seeing her smiling down at him when he first woke; or the suggestion that he wasn't capable of napping. And no, he never took naps, but she didn't need to know that.

Hunter chewed thoughtfully on the last bite of his croissant, working to pinpoint which troublesome topic he should address first. He grabbed his orange juice and took a big swallow before locking onto her eyes. "Well, Scarlet, we do have to head out into the woods this morning. But we should definitely plan on having breakfast in bed another day."

He watched in shameless anticipation as the words reached her ears.

Then it came: the sweet blush of pink he knew would light her cheeks the instant she understood his suggestion. He loved the subtle widening of her eyes and the way her tongue peeked out between her lips. Damn, he could kiss her so easily right now. He could press her into these couch cushions and do a hundred different things to her. Things that would make her whimper and gasp and moan.

But that wasn't an option, was it? Hadn't they agreed last night that nothing should happen between them? And since that was a perfectly sensible agreement, why in hell were they discussing breakfast in bed?

Scarlet leaned toward him, easing her hand onto his face. Her fingers trembled as she ran them across his jaw. Then she wiped a piece of croissant from his chin stubble and grinned. "You're right, Hunter. We have things to do today. Breakfast in bed will have to wait."

She took his glass out of his hand, drank the rest of his orange juice, and set the cup down before bounding toward the door. His eager eyes followed her, dragging unapologetically across her body. Her heather-gray yoga pants outlined her scrumptious ass with expert attention to detail. The fact that he could see a tiny shadow of black thong panties beneath her cropped jacket was simply the icing on the cake.

Scarlet opened the door. "Are you coming?"

"Mm-hmm," he said, dragging his eyes back up. "Coming."

She waited as he gathered his mostly-full food tray, walked it onto the porch, and set it down. She pulled the door shut behind them and reached out. "Hold my hand, Hunter?"

He didn't hesitate. He took her hand in his, threading their fingers together. He sighed with her soft warmth just before she guided him down the steps and into the forest behind his cabin.

~

SCARLET STEERED him through the trees and underbrush, with no trail or path in sight, seemingly knowing exactly where she was going. He followed her with utmost trust, but still said a silent prayer that they would be able to find their way back out one day. He had no desire for an unsuspecting hiker to trip over his half-eaten body in a week.

"I take it you know where we are?" Hunter finally asked, much to his dismay. He'd wanted to mimic her startlingly nonchalant attitude for the entire day, but the idea of various and sundry forest creatures had simply gotten the better of him. There were 34 types of goddamn salamanders out here, for fuck's sake.

She squeezed his hand. "Don't worry. I'll take good care of you."

"I'm not worried," he protested to the back of her head. "But everything looks the same around here and I know you don't have GPS or any..."

Scarlet stopped cold in her tracks. The rapid, unexpected action caused him to bump into her backside. Hunter reached for her waist, gripping both her hips in his hands to keep her from toppling over.

"Mmm," she hummed, resting back against his chest, allowing him to support some of her weight. "Thanks for steadying me."

She fit onto him perfectly. "No problem. Forgive my clumsiness."

"Oh, it was my fault," she insisted, patting his hands before stepping aside to stare at a nearby tree. Hunter would have been more amazed by the fact that she'd just accepted responsibility for something, had he not been dejected by the absence of her warm body.

Scarlet stood quietly for several minutes, just gazing up at the tree's branches, until he started shuffling his feet. "So, we're here now," he announced, anxious to proceed with this bird watching of hers and retreat from these woods as quickly as possible. "What do we do?"

"Patience, Hunter. I have to make sure this is the right tree." She fingered the knots of the oak in front of her, and then circled the trunk entirely, before returning to her exact spot of origin. "Yes, I believe this is the one. The picture I took looks exactly like this."

Hunter surveyed the oak, wondering how she could possibly know that this one tree – in an entire forest of them – was the one she searched for. "Okay. If you think so."

Scarlet glanced back to him. "Will you give me your hand again?"

Holy hell, how many times is she going to ask me to touch her?

He held his hand out, palm up. She smiled as she grasped him by the wrist and yanked him forward. His chest bumped up onto her back again when she placed his hand on the trunk, trapping herself between him and the tree.

The roughness of the bark scratched at his palm, but he barely registered the sensation. All he could think of was how much he loved having her pressed against him. And how cold he would be if she left.

"Do you feel that?" she asked, her gaze fastened on the oak.

She took a deep breath in, causing her back to shift against his chest. Hunter closed his eyes so he could relish her scent, that intoxicatingly sweet mix of fresh soap and tiny flowers. He allowed his body to lean heavier into hers. "What do you want me to feel?"

"The tree, Hunter. All the little cracks and crevices in the bark." She moved his hand against the trunk while she spoke, her fingers on top of his as she reverently traced the indentations. "Can you feel them? How they each have their own path, and how they all wind together?"

He opened his eyes to stare at the top of her head, battling the urge to press his lips into her hair. "It's just a tree, Scarlet."

"No, it's not. It's alive," she insisted, twisting inside the shelter of his arms to meet his eyes. "Everything here is alive. Can't you feel it?"

God, he didn't know. He only knew how she felt: soft and warm and perfect. "It's just a tree," he repeated, wanting to see the spark of indignation that would certainly light her eyes. She didn't disappoint.

"Oh, Hunter," she groaned, yet her lips still eased into a smile. She reached to his face, placing her hand on his cheek before she stepped away.

He wanted to grab hold of her. To pull her back onto him. To press her up against this tree trunk and...

She fell down.

"Scarlet!" he shouted, attempting to catch her as she landed on the ground at his feet with a decided thud.

"What are you doing?" she asked, staring at his outstretched arms.

"I'm...I'm trying to help you get back up."

"Why?"

"Because you fell."

"No. I sat."

"You sat?"

"Yes. And now I'm going to lay."

He watched in pure dread as she eased herself back to rest on the forest floor, stretching out her legs and gazing serenely up at him.

She doesn't actually think I'm going to join her, does she?

"Hunter Gregory! Come on down!" she shouted in a *The Price Is Right* voice.

"No, thanks. I'm fine right here," he insisted, crossing his arms over his chest. He was not about to lie on the ground. Who knows what had pooped there.

A tug against his clothes made his eyes wander down. Scarlet's fingers wrapped around one leg of his pants, yanking on the material over and over. "I imagine this will irritate you sooner or later, Hunter."

Sooner.

"Please come lay next to me," she urged. "You're blocking my view and I don't want to miss anything." She gave him a sweet smile before adding, "I promise I won't bite."

Hunter glared up at the tree branches. He silently admitted he'd be more inclined to lie beside her if she said she would bite him. But that was another issue altogether.

His pants' leg jiggled for the twentieth time and he sighed. *Okay, okay. You win, Scarlet. Again.* But he wasn't about to let her know it.

Slumping onto the dirt floor beside her, Hunter settled down on his back.

He pretended the ground wasn't hard as a rock and covered in 400 species of animal droppings. "Yes, this does give a much better view," he offered instead, struggling to sound interested.

He didn't have to look at her to know she still smiled.

Time passed in bizarre silence. He initially attempted to discern birds in the trees, to possibly even see this purple fantini she was so obsessed with, but gave up quickly when he realized everything here looked exactly the same. One big blur of green and brown, punctuated by an occasional noise that made him wonder what sort of beady eyes were fastened on his prone form. He was simply not prepared for a squirrel attack at this juncture.

Good Lord, will she find this bird of hers soon? Or is she planning to wait for my entire body to go numb on this freezing cold ground? Why won't she just take some damn pictures and be done with this?

Realization hit him like a fist to his chest.

"Scarlet," he began, working to keep his voice from rising, "if we hiked this whole way so you can take another picture of your fantini bird, then why don't you have your *camera* with you?"

"Oh, well. I really don't think he'll come back today. That would be like lightning striking twice on the same tree."

Hunter's head whipped toward hers. "But if we're not looking for the bird, then why the hell are we lying on the ground, staring at trees?"

Scarlet matched his intent gaze. "Because you need to be here."

"What? No, I don't."

She sighed, looking back up to the sky. "Yes, you do."

Hunter harrumphed and turned his gaze back up, too. "No, I don't," he muttered under his breath, not caring if she heard.

Time continued on, but he didn't say another word. He lay stiff and rigid beside her, carefully eyeing the tree branches, with every muscle on full alert. At one point, an acorn dropped beside his head and he nearly jumped from his skin. Hell, if that pointy little thing had landed six inches to the right, it could have easily poked his eye out.

"Tell me something," Scarlet eventually said, her airy voice a welcome intrusion in the creepy silence. "Why do you hate nature?"

"I don't hate nature," Hunter insisted, inwardly cursing the pinecone currently burrowing into his left butt cheek.

"Then why aren't you mountain climbing with your parents?"

"I told you. I don't like mountain climbing."

"And why aren't you enjoying the forest right now?"

"It's because I just...I find it overrated."

"Overrated? What about all the wonder around you? The delicate, beautiful shapes of original, irreplaceable living things?"

He resisted his body's pull toward her childlike appreciation. "The forest is uncontrolled, Scarlet. It's dangerous. You have no idea what is going to happen out here. We could be eaten by something big and hairy at any moment."

"Hmm. What upsets you is the safety issue, then?"

"I suppose."

"The fact that you can't control what happens?"

"I am not a control freak."

"I didn't say you were. But you did inform me that you tell people what to do for a living."

"I didn't put it that way. You did."

"But it's true."

He exhaled. "Yes, it's true."

"What about your parents? Did you encourage them to go on their trip?"

"No, I wasn't crazy about the idea."

"Because they might get hurt?"

"I think it would be fairly easy for two sixty-year-olds to fall off the side of a mountain."

"But what about the thrill of it? What about them being able to hold onto that experience for the rest of their lives?"

"What about them breaking their necks and ending their lives?"

Scarlet paused, her fingers playing over the dried leaves beneath her hands. "I suppose you tried to stop them."

"Yes, I did."

"And what did they say?"

"They just asked me to come along."

"So, they know about your little problem."

Hunter glared up at the sky. "*What* little problem?"

"The fact that you like to tell people how to live their lives."

"I like to help people understand what's *best* for them, if that's what you mean."

"No, that's not what I mean," she hummed. The next instant, her hand eased over to him. Her fingers settled on his forearm, warm and gentle against his skin. Then she started doing it again – the petting – that slow, lulling movement he'd come to know as hers.

He wanted to be angry right now. He wanted to growl and glower. But if he wanted to do all that, he'd have to stop her petting him.

Hunter didn't stop her. He didn't move at all. He lay entirely still, absorbing her touch. She stroked his skin, easy and languid, and he actually felt his heart rate slow with the soothing motion.

"Scarlet?" he mumbled, his speech thicker than before.

"Yes?"

"Are you petting me right now?"

Her fingers halted on his arm. "Does it feel like I'm petting you?"

"Pretty much."

"Sorry. I really don't mean for it to feel that way. Do you want me to stop?"

Hunter looked down, concentrating on the sight of her hand resting on his skin. "No, I don't want you to stop."

She restarted the leisurely movement instantly, trailing her fingers up and down. "I'm glad you don't want me to stop. I like touching you."

He had to close his eyes to let that information soak in properly. "I like it, too. But it's very methodical, like petting."

"Hmm. I guess I can see that. It's called therapeutic touch."

"Therapeutic touch?"

"Yes. Touch is an incredible means of communication, you know. It's a way to relax muscles, lower blood pressure, and calm anxiety. The skin is the body's largest organ, so touching the skin can touch the heart, the mind, and the soul." She looked to him with a tender smile on her lips. "Essentially, therapeutic touch can soothe the savage beast."

His brow quirked. *Did she just call me a savage beast?* "So, is this more of the psychological drivel you've learned up at Blue?"

"Actually, your best friend gave a lecture on it a few years back."

"Will Rand gave a lecture here on therapeutic touch?"

"He did."

"That's odd."

"Why?"

"Because the only touch I get from Will is when he's beating the shit out of me in the boxing ring at our gym."

Scarlet laughed. "Well, for big, growly men like the two of you, perhaps punching is a form of therapeutic touch."

Hunter glanced down at her hand against his arm, watching the movement accompanying the serene feeling. His entire body settled as her dainty fingers shifted across his skin. "I like your version better."

"I'm glad," she said. "Although I am sorry it feels like petting. I only started doing it because I thought you might need it."

"Why would you think I need it?"

"Because it seems like you haven't been touched in a while."

"Damn," he cursed, hating just how true her statement was. "You're right about that. I haven't been touched in a really long time."

She looked to him, a flash of sadness dimming her bright eyes.

Hunter studied her as she rested on the forest floor. Just now, he could see a deep, unsettling loneliness inside her. It was something he'd never seen before, and his fingers clenched against the ground. "What about you, Scarlet? Has it been a while since you've been touched?"

She turned her gaze back to the sky. "Sometimes it feels like it's been forever."

His chest constricted with her words. His muscles stiffened as the breeze ruffled her hair. He knew he shouldn't touch her. He knew it.

Don't do it. Change the subject. Talk about anything else.

"Will made me the godfather of his daughter, Evelyn," Hunter told her, desperate for any other topic of conversation.

He wasn't quite sure why that particular sentence popped out of his mouth. But when Scarlet smiled and said, "I'm sure he was happy that you accepted," he knew exactly why he'd told her. He simply wanted her to see him as more. More than the savage beast.

"I'll bet you're an amazing godfather," she added.

He cringed despite the soothing motion of her fingers. "Actually, I'm not. I've never even held baby Evie. Not once."

"No? Why not?"

"I don't know. She's so small. Innocent. I might break her."

Scarlet's hand grasped onto his arm. "Evie doesn't need you to be perfect, though. She just needs you to be there for her."

"But I don't know if I'll be any good at that. Honestly, I don't know why Will picked me."

"It sounds like he picked you because you're his best friend and he loves you."

"Yeah, he does love me. I'm just...I'm not sure why."

Her fingers started their slow sway across his arm again. "It's because you're very loveable, Hunter Gregory."

Loveable?

He turned onto his side, shifting up on his elbow to get a better look at his forest fairy. He moved slowly, not wanting to break the contact of her hand on his arm, while he inched closer. He gazed down at her soft features as she lay on the hard earth.

No woman had ever called him *loveable* like Scarlet just did. He'd been called *handsome* many, many times. He'd been called *skilled* by women he'd slept with. And there was that one time he'd walked off the Gregory Global elevator on the wrong floor and overheard a group of women in an employee lounge refer to him as *infinitely fuckable*. It hadn't been the worst moment of his life.

But nothing could hold a candle to this: feeling Scarlet's touch as she smiled into the tree-shaded sunshine and called him *loveable*.

Hunter wanted to touch her. He needed to touch her. But he knew where that would lead, since he could readily envision her naked and moaning beneath him. She wanted his touch as badly as he wanted hers, but adding a physical element to this already bizarre relationship would only complicate the shit out of it. He couldn't do that. Could he?

No, I can't. Not when she keeps lying to me. Absolutely not.

But what if that changes? What if she admits she lied? What if she takes responsibility for her actions? I could touch her then, couldn't I?

Hope swelled in his chest, even as nerves coiled in his gut. "Scarlet, I need to tell you something," he began. "I...I know you lied to me last night. Again."

"Did I? About what?"

"About the trees here. You told me there are over 400 species."

She didn't respond. She just looked up into the sky.

"There aren't," he continued. "There are only 158 species."

Hunter wanted her to admit she'd been caught. He wanted her to look guilty, for once. But she didn't. Not at all.

That fact should have made him mad. He should have been completely pissed off at her and want to run full force in the opposite direction. Only he didn't want to run. He wanted to stay here beside her. He wanted her to keep touching him. And he wanted to touch her back.

"You've told me some pretty absurd lies, you know. I'd just really like to know why you said them."

Her hand stilled against his arm. "You're right, Hunter. I did lie to you. And I'm sorry."

The lead weight on his chest finally lifted. "Thank you for that."

She smiled softly before resuming the peaceful path of her fingers.

He focused on her face. "Can you tell me why you lied to me?"

"Yes, I can. But I don't think you'll like my answer."

"Try me, please."

"Well, sometimes you have to light a powder keg's fuse, and have it blow up in front of you, in order to see what's inside."

Did she just call me a powder keg? What's she going to call me next? "Just so we're clear, I did not blow up in front of you."

"No, but you did get growly and broody, like a big old grizzly bear."

Apparently, she's going to call me a grizzly bear next.

"Let me get this straight, Scarlet. You're saying you thought I was a big, growly grizzly bear, so you figured it would be fun to poke me with a stick?"

She burst out laughing. "My goodness. When you put it that way, it sounds like a pretty dumb thing to do."

"You're damn right it was a dumb thing to do, and you don't strike me as a dumb person. I think you might actually be a fucking genius, so I really don't understand why you did that. If you thought I was a grizzly bear, how could you possibly know I wouldn't hurt you?"

Scarlet shrugged. "You're a good man with a good heart. You would never hurt me."

"But you just met me. How could you know that?"

"I just do," she said, closing her eyes again.

Hunter stared down at her tiny prone form, haloed in leaves and twigs. She looked so fragile right now. So small and innocent. He couldn't stand the thought of her lighting any more powder kegs. He hated to think of the pain he might see behind her luminous green eyes if any of those bombs blew up in her face.

"Um, Scarlet?"

"Yes?"

"Please don't poke any more bears. I don't want you to get hurt."

She looked back to him with a tender smile. "Your concern is so sweet. But I assure you, I'm tougher than I look."

I already know you're tough. And I know you're sunny and bright and joyous. But that's exactly the kind of person the world can break.

He wanted to demand that she never poke another bear again, as long as she lived. Unfortunately, she'd never agree to it. She was going to do what she wanted, and live on the edge, like the freebird she was.

"So, everything between us these past days – all the lies and all the games – it's all just been a way for you to challenge me. Is that right?"

"Yes," she admitted. "I suppose I have been challenging you."

"But why? Other than the powder keg thing."

"I guess I just...I needed to know you'd fight back."

"Why did you need me to fight back?"

"To know for sure that you hadn't given up."

"Given up on what?"

Scarlet held him with her eyes. "On life, Hunter."

His shoulders deflated.

Life. She was obsessed with it. Drinking lemon juice made her feel alive. Tree trunks made her feel alive. And the attraction between them – that made her feel alive, too.

He watched her for a long minute. He watched the sunlight reflect off her eyes. He watched the breeze brush her dark hair across the earth. He watched the tiny tremble that moved over her pink lips as she waited for his assurance.

Hunter couldn't hold himself back from her any longer. Reaching out, he slipped his hand onto her cheek. He eased over her warm skin before pushing his fingers into her hair.

Her response to him was immediate. A tender whimper slipped from her throat as she leaned into his touch, already melting against him. Tangling his fingers up in her loose curls, he spoke without question. "I haven't given up on life, Scarlet."

He thought she'd been relaxed before, lying here on her bed of leaves. But that was nothing compared to now. With his assurance, her entire body sank into the dirt floor. "Thank you," she breathed. Her eyes fluttered shut, her dark lashes resting on her flushed cheeks.

Hunter couldn't stop staring. She looked like an angel, sent to him straight from the heavens, and all he wanted was to make her happy. He moved his fingers, massaging her scalp, listening to her purr in response. Then he trailed his hand down, out of the ebony softness and onto her shoulder, stroking her sleeve all the way to her hand.

Scarlet exhaled on a blissful sigh and he couldn't stop the swell of pride in his chest. He could perform therapeutic touch just as well as she could, it seemed. Although he wasn't sure which of them was getting the therapy here. Touching her felt like a reward for something, and he didn't know if he deserved such a medal, but it was shiny and sparkly and he wanted to hold onto it for as long as he could.

Easing his hand back up her arm, he stilled as he watched her heartbeat pulse in the hollow of her throat. His fingers sought out that tiny motion of their own accord, marveling at the life beneath her skin. Hunter listened intently to the little mewling sound she made as he stroked from the base of her throat up to her chin and back again.

"My God, that feels so good," she breathed, biting her lip.

He smiled, knowing she hadn't meant to say the words out loud. "Talk to me," he urged, painfully aware of how much he missed hearing her voice, her thoughts. "Tell me something about yourself."

"What do you want to know?"

"Anything. Tell me about your parents."

"My parents?" she echoed. "Wow, is this some psycho babble you're learning up here at Blue?"

Hunter couldn't help chuckling. "I suppose it is," he said, easing his fingers back over her cheek and into her hair.

"Hmm. Let's see, then. I'm an only child. My mother is a very free-spirited woman. She sculpts and paints and soul searches, and is quite formidable in her own way. My father was a cardiac surgeon."

"Was?"

"He died two years ago."

"Oh. May I ask how?"

She inhaled deeply, her eyelids fluttering, before she answered. "He was a workaholic. Day and night he was at the hospital, or at his office. He had a massive coronary one night while working late. It wasn't abnormal for him to fall asleep in his office, so we didn't question where he was. No one found him until the staff came in the next morning."

"I'm...I'm sorry," Hunter mumbled, pulling his hand away from her.

Her eyelids popped open. "Don't stop touching me. Please."

He returned to her immediately, half because she asked it of him, half because he felt a sizeable ache the moment his skin lost contact with hers. Witnessing the dulled pain of her memories, he brushed the long strands of her hair gently down her arm. Scarlet settled further into the ground as he petted her, her body definitively at home in the earth.

"I guess you take after your mother," he surmised.

"Hell, I used to think she was crazy. Can you believe that?"

Hunter chuckled, knowing he'd thought the same of his forest fairy. But he could see now that she simply took after her mother – free-spirited and formidable. "When did you change your mind about her?"

"Oh, you know how it is when you grow up," Scarlet answered. "You start to look at life differently."

"And you didn't want to be a workaholic like your father?"

"Well, life is short. I can see my mom's point of view now. I want to appreciate all the little things in life, to appreciate every moment for what it has to offer. Every laugh. Every sigh. Every tree. Every bird."

"Every tire."

Scarlet grinned. "Yes, the car tires, too. It's all about appreciation."

Appreciation. He'd heard that word before. From Tyler Hensen.

Hunter stiffened. *Does she know Tyler? Has she allowed him to touch her this way? Is this where Tyler learned how to be so happy?*

He couldn't stomach the thought. "You're not seeing anyone, are you?" Hunter asked, even though he knew it was a stupid question. She'd just confessed that it had been forever since someone touched her, and if she had a man in her life, he knew that lucky bastard would be all over her from morning until night.

"No, I'm not seeing anyone, Hunter. I meant what I said to you earlier. I haven't been touched in a very long time."

"Good. I mean, good about the not-seeing-anyone part, not the haven't-been-touched part."

She grinned wider at his fumbled reply. "Are you seeing anyone?"

"No, I'm not."

"Good," she said, letting her eyes flutter shut again.

As the sun lit her face and she turned toward the light over the trees, Hunter wondered what colors popped up behind her closed eyelids. He swore she was more beautiful right now than ever before, just basking in the bright warmth, so he gave himself entirely over to his need to touch. Slipping his hands to her forehead, he traced the outline of her hair before drawing his fingers down her neck. When he arrived at the curve of her shoulder, he stared at her little zippered jacket. He wished she wasn't wearing so many clothes. Not that he wanted to undress her entirely, right here and now, on the forest floor – of course he didn't want that. He merely wanted a little more skin to touch.

Hunter reached for the zipper pull at the base of her throat. He told himself he would only grant access to a tiny bit more of her. Just a tiny bit. Grasping the metal between his fingertips, he drew the zipper down a few inches. When Scarlet's breath caught, he stopped.

He saw nothing but smooth skin beneath the section of jacket he'd opened. Tracing the edge of the material, he slid it toward her shoulder, slipping his fingers underneath to explore the straight line of her collarbone. The moment he pushed his hand under the heather gray edge, she moaned out loud.

His eyes flew to hers, curious to see if she would be embarrassed by the rather bold noise she'd made. But her lids remained closed, and her face looked just as serene as ever. He decided to test his boundaries, moving his hand lower to massage across her upper chest.

"Mmm, you're a magician," she mumbled, her body turning into his.

Hunter shifted closer, silently offering refuge. The moment her forehead came into contact with his bicep, Scarlet curled entirely into him. Her fingers gripped the skin on his lower arm as his hand continued exploring beneath her jacket. Hunter glanced down to her chest, where her taut nipples strained against the thin material. He grit his teeth, trying to maintain his composure while she emitted needy noises with every stroke of his fingers on her bare skin.

Scarlet's thighs shifted, her knees pressing together, making him swallow hard. He knew he couldn't keep these touches of skin on skin chaste for much longer. For his own sanity, he pulled his fingers out from beneath her jacket and returned to the familiarity of petting her sleeve. But she seemed to enjoy that touch just as much, snuggling her forehead even farther into the crook of his arm.

He dropped his nose into her hair, inhaling steeply, filling his lungs with her sweet scent. Scarlet clutched tighter to his forearm the moment he breathed her in. His hand slipped off of its normal, safe path, taking a detour down to her waist.

Hunter lifted his head just enough to watch his fingers find the little indentation of her hipbone. Gripping onto that perfectly formed handle, he pulled forward, edging her whole body onto his. She practically laid beneath him now, her hot, wispy breaths on his skin driving him mad.

His gaze drifted up, from her slender waist to her perfect breasts to her full lips. He stared hard at her mouth. The desire to kiss her burned through his veins, lighting his entire being on fire. He had to do something, to say something, to get his mind off this damnable craving.

"Scarlet, please," he begged, the huskiness of his voice an outright betrayal of his thoughts. "Talk to me. Tell me more about you."

She reached to his chest, balling the fabric of his shirt into her fist. "Wh-what do you want to know?"

"Anything," he said, drawing his fingers slowly back up her body, all the way to her face. "Anything you want to tell me."

"Well, I, um..."

Hunter eased his hand to her jaw, his fingers skimming dangerously close to her mouth.

"I don't know what to say," she mumbled, her lower lip brushing against his thumb. He groaned and Scarlet gathered more of his shirt inside her fingers. "I'm...I'm, um...I'm allergic...to latex."

For a few seconds, they each froze in place. Neither of them dared move a muscle. Then her eyes popped open, round as saucers, and she sat bolt upright. "And peanuts! I'm allergic to peanuts, too!"

Hunter continued to lie on the ground, briefly stunned by the rapidity of her withdrawal. He followed her to a sitting position, facing her as she stared at him with cheeks bright as cherries. He wanted to curse the fact that they weren't touching anymore, but his mind was too preoccupied by what she'd just said. "You're allergic to latex?"

"And peanuts," Scarlet reiterated, clasping her hands tightly together in her lap. "I have a funny story about it, actually. Well, not so much funny as sad. It was my freshman year of college and I wandered into this fraternity party and I had a few of those Kool-Aid things – you know the ones they mix up in the big bins with the Kool-Aid and some unknown form of alcohol –

and I wasn't used to drinking, and then they passed around this tray of brownies, which I really thought was Betty Crocker or something, and my mother always told me to stay away from peanuts because I got a rash once when I was a kid, not that I need to carry an Epi-pen with me or anything, so anyway I stayed away from peanuts, but I'd had a bit to drink, as I said, and I didn't notice the peanuts were in the brownie, although I didn't know the pot was in there either, and the next thing I knew my eyelids swelled up and my lips got really big, but I didn't even care because, well, because of the pot, I assume, although I can assure you, I've never done drugs on purpose, and that was just a really unfortunate night."

Hunter blinked a few times. He wasn't sure if he'd ever heard a longer run-on sentence in his life. But that wasn't what interested him at the moment. "Why did you tell me you're allergic to latex, Scarlet?"

Her fingers twisted around each other. "I don't know. You said you wanted to know something about me."

He pinned her eyes, having no intention of letting her off the hook so easily. "But why did you tell me about latex, specifically?"

She slumped back against the tree. "Oh, God. It's because you were touching me, and it felt amazing, and I was thinking about condoms."

There it is. Hunter shifted toward her. "So, what you're telling me is we won't be able to use condoms when we're together."

Scarlet shook her head. "I'm so sorry. I know I said last night that it would be a mistake to act on this thing between us, and I shouldn't have brought it up again, but your touch is so incredible and I just..."

"I want you, too," he assured, because for some unimaginable reason he didn't think she knew he wanted her. Or, at least, she didn't know how fiercely he did.

"You want me? I mean, you just said you do, so that's...yeah, that's fantastic. And I want you. Obviously. Like, I know it's really obvious, and I feel kind of bad about that, but rest assured, I am disease-free."

She paused her speech as her eyebrows shot to her hairline.

"Holy hell, Hunter! I don't know why I just said that to you! Except I just told you I'm allergic to latex, and I don't want you to think I'm asking you to do something reckless, because I'm not. I'm really not asking you to have unprotected sex with me, although I guess I just did, and there are certain types of condoms I can use, but I didn't bring any with me, since I wasn't expecting to have this kind of situation at Blue, and I don't think Pete Jackson would stock the kind of condoms I need, and good heavens, I can't even imagine asking sweet old Pete for condoms, so I'm totally unprepared, but I really am disease-free, and I imagine you are, too, although I didn't bring any medical paperwork with me, and I also promise I'm on birth control, I'll even show you the pills, since I have no desire to be a single mother, not that there's anything wrong with being a single mother, I'm just not interested in that, although I'll never say never, but even if I want to be a single mother, they have sperm banks for that sort of thing, and..."

"Scarlet!"

She gulped. "Y-yes?"

"Take a breath, please."

He watched her register his words. She nodded, inhaling and exhaling. Hunter shifted on the ground. Undeniably, he'd pressed her on the latex thing, but he'd only wanted her to admit the truth of why she'd said it. He had no earthly idea it was going to send her into this kind of tailspin.

When her fingers finally unclenched, he found he could breathe easier, too. "Are you okay now?"

"I'm just kind of...mortified," she admitted. "I don't suppose we could both agree that the last five minutes never happened?"

"Sorry, but no. I can't agree because there's nothing for you to be embarrassed about. You wanted to have the safe sex discussion, and honestly, I appreciate it. Of course, you chose a really interesting way to have that particular conversation, but I would expect nothing less. And yes, I am disease-free, although I don't have any medical paperwork with me, either. And no, we don't need to use condoms when we're together, as long as you're comfortable with that."

"Oh," she said. "Okay."

Hunter watched her worry her lower lip in her teeth. "Are you feeling better about everything?"

Her shoulders finally eased away from the level of her ears. "Yes, thank you. Although I'm really sorry about the nervous-talking thing I just did. I actually haven't done that in years."

"You used to do that often?"

"All the time. Especially as a kid. My mind would just run away from me, and I couldn't stop my mouth from following. But I haven't done that since I got therapy for it in college."

"I take it you've enjoyed therapy ever since college, then."

"Well, it truly helped me. It's been so long since I've spoken like that. I thought I'd completely conquered it. So, that's weird."

"What's weird?"

"It's just, it must be you. There's something about you that affects me really differently. You're so unexpected, Hunter."

He stared blankly at her, with his brow raised and his jaw unhinged, certain he'd witnessed the ultimate pot-calling-the-kettle-black.

"Or maybe it's because I've never done this before," she added.

"Never done what?"

"This," she repeated, motioning from him to her and back again.

"Do you mean you've never taken a lover before?"

"Lover? My goodness. That's a word I never thought I'd use up here."

"Hell, me neither," Hunter admitted. "But I assume you've had lovers before, since you know you can't use latex condoms. Also, you're incredibly beautiful, and I can't imagine men haven't lined up for the chance to be with you."

Another flush of pink climbed from her neck to her face, like an artist's canvas coming to life, as he watched in complete fascination.

"I've been with a few men," she conceded. "Although I can assure you no one has ever formed a line. But this – whatever this is between us – it's unusual, and I don't know how to handle it. I don't feel like I'm standing on even ground here."

"Believe me, I know the feeling."

Scarlet smiled. "Part of me wants to say we're both on vacation, and we're both adults, and we can do what we want. Another part of me..."

"Thinks it might be the worst idea ever?" he finished for her.

"Exactly. What do you think?"

Hunter knew what he thought. He wanted her, plain and simple. He wanted to hold her, to taste her, to push himself inside her. Then again, something told him there would be nothing plain or simple about it.

She was absolutely right, though. Whatever existed between them was unusual. Honestly, this whole situation was absolutely bizarre, and he only knew one thing for certain: he couldn't tolerate her lying to him. As much as he wanted to throw caution to the wind, as much as he wanted to pretend the dishonesty didn't exist, he just couldn't do it.

"I'll tell you what I think, Scarlet. You've lied to me. Repeatedly. And even though you've worked it out in your mind that your lies were somehow helpful to me, I can't be with you if you're still lying. So, before we go any further, what I want from you is the truth."

She cocked her head, as if she couldn't quite grasp his meaning. Then her gaze drifted down to the dirt floor between them. "The truth is I've lied to you about more than squirrels and trees, Hunter."

I know that. He knew exactly what she'd lied about, too. She wasn't a nature photographer. She was a patient here, just like him. At least, he hoped she wasn't a photographer, because the picture she'd taken of her bird was truly terrible. And today, she didn't even bring her camera. If Scarlet was on assignment, she was officially the worst reporter ever.

In a way, he didn't blame her for lying about being a patient. She didn't know anything about him when she'd found him crouched down and growling beside his blown tire. Even if she truly believed he was a good man from that very first moment, she probably hadn't wanted to admit her weaknesses in front of a complete stranger. But they weren't strangers anymore.

"Please tell me what else you've lied about," he urged, keeping his voice low and even. "I want complete honesty. About everything."

Scarlet clenched her hands. "It's...it's complicated."

"Then un-complicate it. Be honest with me."

"I can't give you complete honesty."

"You can't or you won't?"

She looked to the forest floor in silence. He watched as she dropped her hands back into her lap, and as her hair fell across her shoulders. Then he saw it. A little red leaf, with tiny green veins threaded through it, clung to her loose curls. It had wound into her dark strands while she'd been lying on the ground and now refused to leave.

Hunter stared at the leaf. He wanted to take it out for her. But he didn't just want to take it out. He wanted to run his fingers through her hair again. He wanted to feel the softness of her skin on his own. He wanted to hear her moan and sigh and pant with the sensations, knowing his touch was the reason for the change in her breathing.

He knew he could have her right now, if he let himself. He could lift her off of this cold, hard ground and pin her up against this damn oak tree and fuck her as hard as he desired, until she felt alive. Until they both felt completely alive, even if only for a few moments.

Scarlet wanted to feel alive. He could give her that. He wanted to give her that. Just not like this. Not with these lies between them.

"So? What's it going to be?" he snapped.

She finally matched his stern glare. He saw nothing but sadness and regret in her dull green eyes. Hunter huffed with the sight of this new person sitting in front of him. He had her back – Solemnly Sedate Scarlet – the woman he'd met briefly that first night.

He recognized this person so easily now. This was the woman who lamented being on vacation. This was the woman who appeared lucid and normal and deeply unhappy. He'd managed to bring her back again, and judging by the look on her face, this Scarlet wasn't willing to give him anything. She was nothing like his Frolicking Freebird Scarlet, who would give him everything.

Right now, he wasn't sure which Scarlet he wanted to be with. He only knew he needed them both to be honest with him.

Hunter studied her sad eyes for another minute before realizing what her silence meant. "You're not going to tell me the truth, are you?"

She shook her head slowly.

"Okay," he said through gritted teeth. "Then we should head back."

He stood swiftly, separating himself from her body, shaking the dirt from his clothes. Scarlet picked herself up off the ground, brushing at her pants before looking to his face. "I'll take you to your cabin now."

"I'd appreciate that," he replied, keeping his tone stiff and formal.

She turned away, leading him on her unbeaten path through the trees and underbrush. Hunter followed behind, trying desperately to not look at the tiny leaf still holding strong in her hair. But he just couldn't help himself. He watched the way the little red-and-green culprit moved inside her ebony waves. He watched how it clung to her, not wanting to ever let go, and he understood that feeling all too well.

By some miracle, Scarlet found her way out of the forest and back to his cabin. He'd never been so happy to see so many logs. Stepping onto the first stair of his porch, a wave of relief passed through him.

"Um, Hunter?"

His footsteps froze with her singsong voice. He pivoted, holding steady on his porch steps as he looked down at her. "Yes?"

Scarlet shifted her feet on his gravel driveway. "I know I probably don't have the right, but could I ask you a favor? As my friend?"

"Your friend?"

"Yes. My friend."

He saw the hope in her eyes, tempered by a healthy dose of sorrow, and felt himself soften. "You can ask."

She grasped her hands in front of her stomach, her fingers working hard against each other. "Will you please attend some of the therapy sessions while you're here? It doesn't matter which doctor you choose; they're all good. I just need to know, in case I don't see you again, that you'll talk to someone."

In case I don't see you again. Those words left a sick, bitter taste in his mouth. Worse than pure lemon juice.

He wanted to deny her request, to tell her she had no right to ask him for any favors. But as he stood here, watching her twist her fingers and nibble her lip, his shoulders fell. "I promise I'll think about it."

"Thank you," she breathed, gazing up at him. "Goodbye, Hunter."

He didn't respond. He stood entirely still as she turned away, listening to the crunch of her boots while she moved up the driveway. She was almost out of sight before he called out to her. "Scarlet?"

She spun around immediately. "Yes?"

Even at this distance, he could see the fresh light in her eyes. "It's just...you just..." He balled his fists. "You have a leaf in your hair."

"Oh." She reached her hands up to find it.

Hunter watched her comb her fingers through her curls.

He swallowed hard.

Scarlet finally found the tiny freeloader, pulling it out to rest it inside her palm. "Hmm. He's a handsome little fellow. I'll set him on my kitchen counter, so I can see him every day." Her eyes moved back to his, although the light inside had dimmed. "Thank you. Again."

"Yeah. Sure."

She spun in her boots and strode up the driveway, twirling the leaf's stem between her fingertips.

"You're doing the right thing," Hunter muttered.

He stood stiffly on his porch, watching her walk away from him. He fucking hated the sight. But there was nothing else he could do.

5

IMAGINARY FRIENDS

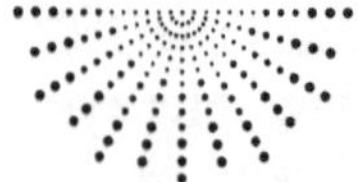

After Hunter watched Scarlet walk away from him, after he grumbled and grunted as he marched up the steps of his porch, after he forced his way inside his cabin and kicked the door shut behind him, he stood in the middle of his log living room and stared into space.

He hated the fact that she wasn't here anymore. He hated that he'd pushed her away. He hated the havoc it created inside his brain and his body, making his mind reel and his heart ache. He was alone again now, utterly alone, yet he could see his forest fairy standing before him.

It was an ethereal image, this Scarlet he created. She looked like a ghost, a sparkling spirit, too bright and celestial to be real. Hunter knew he couldn't touch this vision of her. He couldn't feel her skin beneath his fingers, or hear her infectious laughter. But he still wanted to look.

At first, this otherworldly woman gave him a vibrant smile, her body bouncing with childlike joy as she held her hand out to him. He knew this Scarlet very well. This was his Frolicking Freebird, and he wanted to wrap her in his arms and dance, even though he never danced.

Within seconds, the image changed. His little bird transformed in front of him. Her smile fell and her fingers clenched. She regarded him with intelligent, knowing eyes – eyes that held such loneliness and pain – eyes that looked straight through all of his bullshit and right into his soul. He knew this woman, too, although not as well as the other one. This was Solemnly Sedate Scarlet, and he wanted to sit with her and talk with her and soothe her pain.

Hunter looked away. Shoving his hands through his hair, he averted his gaze from the separate, yet equally unsettling, visions he'd conjured. There were definitely two different people living inside of his forest fairy. He had no fucking clue how she fit both of those women in that tiny body of hers, but they were there. In truth, he didn't know which one of them he preferred. He only knew he should stay away from both.

"Goddamnit," he groaned, stripping off his clothes on the way to the bathroom. He needed to get in the shower again, to wash off whatever remnants of nature might still be clinging to him. He also needed to get the smell of her fresh soap and tiny flowers off of his body and out of his brain. Scarlet was simply everywhere and he needed her gone.

Once he stood under the pummeling water, he scrubbed his skin until he was nearly raw. Afterwards, he braced his hands against the wall, dropping his head to let the spray pour over his back. He tried not to think about what happened between them in the woods this morning. But it was too fresh, and too frightening, and he couldn't stop himself.

"Scarlet," he whispered, afraid if he spoke her name too loud she might appear out of thin air. "What is it about you that I can't control?"

He'd told her things he'd never told anyone, like what an asshole he'd been in high school, and how he'd never held his goddaughter, and how he didn't understand why his best friend loved him. He didn't know why he'd said those things to her, except for the fact that he trusted her. Despite all her lies, he still trusted her, and he just wanted her to trust him the same way. He needed her to be honest. He needed her to be open. He needed her laid out in front of him, completely bare. Literally and figuratively.

Running a hand across his aching chest, Hunter grimaced. He'd been more vulnerable with her today than he'd been with anyone in his entire life. It left him feeling raw and exposed, and it hurt like hell.

Why can't you be vulnerable with me, too? he questioned the vision of his forest fairy. But his imaginary Scarlet simply smiled at him, and danced in a circle, and didn't say a word.

"Fuck," Hunter growled. "Fuck all of this."

He jumped out of the shower, dried off, dressed in a fresh T-shirt and shorts, and grabbed his key card. He ran through his living room and yanked open the front door, slamming it shut before rushing up the driveway. He needed the gym right now. Exercise would clear his head and work the frustrations out of his body, sexual and otherwise.

As he arrived at Cabin 6, he still had hope that he could turn this day around. Stepping inside and taking a huge breath of the kempt air, he honestly believed he could remove Scarlet from his head. But two hours on the treadmill still didn't do the trick. She was with him the entire time, like a colorful bird perched on his back, sitting on one of his branches and pecking at all the cracks and crevices in his bark.

After the treadmill, he moved to a weight machine and continued torturing his body. His muscles still hurt from Twister-stretching the night before, and now they strained against the load he forced on them. But he didn't stop. He didn't give in. He kept going, kept pushing, until he truly had nothing left and his only choice was to admit defeat.

When Hunter finally exited the gym and started back up the road, his hands trembled. It was almost dinnertime and he hadn't eaten anything all day, except for part of a croissant and half a glass of orange juice. Still, he didn't think starvation was the actual problem. He just didn't want to go back to his cabin. He didn't want to be alone again.

Hope came in the form of whistling, drifting over the hill before him. Hunter smiled when he heard the sound. "Hey there, Tyler!"

Tyler Henson ambled down the road with a spring in his step. "Hey, Hunter! Good to see you, man. I missed you this morning at the gym. I thought we could have a rematch of hoops."

Hunter came to a stop in front of his friend. "Yeah, that would have been an easy, fun way to spend the morning. What are you up to now? I was just at the gym, but I could head back for a game."

"Oh, sorry. I'm heading to dinner with Jocelyn down in Cabin 4."

Well, shit. "No problem. Perhaps another time."

"How about a rematch in the morning?"

"Yes. Definitely."

"Fantastic. Are you coming to the Social tomorrow evening? It's a great chance to meet everyone. Especially the *ladies*," Tyler sang, wiggling his eyebrows in a ridiculously cartoonish display.

Hunter laughed, not at his friend's silliness, but at the irony of the suggestion. The last thing he needed was to meet another woman up here. "Probably not, but I'll take you up on the basketball game."

"Gym. 9 a.m. I'll change your mind about the Social then."

"See you in the morning."

With a goofy grin, Tyler proceeded past him, whistling his way down the mountain as if he didn't have a care in the world. Hunter stood and watched him for a few moments. He honestly couldn't recall the last time he'd felt that carefree. Definitely not when he was with Clarissa, who supposedly loved him. Hell, he probably hadn't been *that* happy since high school, which was a stupid, uncaring sort of happiness. It wasn't what he searched for now. It wasn't what he needed.

Hunter started back up the steep road to his cabin. He thought about

Clarissa, and about the simplistic perfection that was their life together, until the day he put a stop to it. In the end, he hadn't wanted that life. In the end, he'd pushed her away. At the time, he truly didn't know why. But now, he saw the light.

He'd pushed Clarissa away because she didn't challenge him. His cookie-cutter mold of a girlfriend never challenged him in the slightest. In stark-raving contrast, all his forest fairy ever did was challenge him. He'd pushed Scarlet away today because the challenge was too much.

Hunter huffed while climbing the steep road. Squirrels. Lemonade. Trees. She'd told him in the forest that she'd lied to him for his own good, to make sure he would fight back. "I haven't given up on life, Scarlet," he repeated the words he'd said this morning, knowing the reassurance had been as much for her as for him. It may have even been *more* for her, which confused the living shit out of him.

"God, Will, where are you when I need you?" Hunter grumbled while striding down his driveway, wishing his best friend would simply appear before him. If Will were here, he would offer a smile before heaving a sigh of frustration. Hunter wouldn't care, though, since Will would then sit down with him, pop open a beer, and listen to his questions and fears. He'd look at him with his dark, perceptive eyes and tell him exactly what he should do, which would be perfect, since not knowing what to do was a really horrible fucking feeling.

When Hunter reached the first step of his porch, he heard the meal truck wheels grumbling down the driveway. Pivoting on his heels, he waited for red-hooded Colin to steer the vehicle to a stop beside Hunter's pathetically wounded Porsche. He watched as the near-silent delivery boy jumped out of the driver's seat, opened the rear of the truck, and pulled out his dinner tray.

"Hello," Hunter offered while Colin approached him.

Colin nodded stiffly and held out the tray.

Hunter took it. "Colin? Your name is Colin, right?"

The young man cleared his throat. "Yes, Mr. Gregory."

"Call me Hunter, please."

"Okay. Do you need something from me? Other than your tray?"

"Yeah, actually. When you bring my dinner tomorrow, could you also bring me a six-pack of beer? I don't really care what kind."

"Um, well, are you an alcoholic, Mr. Gre....Hunter?"

"Why do you ask?"

Colin grimaced. "It's just that I'm not supposed to deliver alcohol to alco-holics. Company rules, and all. But you've only ordered one bottle of wine since you got here, so I suppose you're not."

"And what makes you think I'd actually admit to being an alcoholic? I mean, it would be pretty easy for me to lie."

"Yeah, but what good would that do you? The first step to recovery is always admitting you need help. Everyone knows that."

Hunter couldn't help chuckling. *Does everybody up here practice their own odd little form of psychotherapy?*

"Do you mind waiting here for a minute, Colin?"

The boy shrugged beneath his hoodie. "Sure."

Hunter stepped into his cabin, setting his dinner tray on the table before moving to his bedroom. He pulled his wallet from the closet safe and took out a hundred dollar bill. Then he walked back to the porch.

"Here," he said, extending the money in his hand. "I promise I'm not an alcoholic. I'd just like a beer or two."

Colin raised an eyebrow as he stared at the bill. "I can't take that."

"Why not?"

"Well, first of all, everything you order goes on your tab. Second, I don't know where you call home, but around here a six-pack of beer doesn't cost a hundred dollars."

"Consider it a tip, please. You are allowed to accept tips, right?"

Colin took the bill and shoved it into the pocket of his jeans. "Thanks. I'll put it in my savings fund," he said, turning back toward the truck. "I'll have your beer for you tomorrow."

Hunter nodded. "See you tomorrow."

The young man smiled at him before driving back up the gravel.

Feeling as if he had something to look forward to, Hunter stepped back into the cabin with a lighter heart. First, he collapsed on the couch and devoured every last morsel of his meal. Next, he moved to the desk.

Opening his laptop, he watched his home screen burst to life. His body eased with the sights and sounds of the real world, even as he heard Will growl, pissed off that he'd chosen to bury his head in work yet again. But tonight, Hunter didn't have a choice. He needed this.

Much to his disappointment, he found Gregory Global functioning perfectly well without him. He knew he should be proud of his well-oiled machine, especially since he'd spent a month ensuring all GG business deals would progress smoothly in his absence. But right now, he just needed something to occupy his attention. He needed to keep his mind off of Scarlet long enough for exhaustion to overtake him.

Not having actual work to do, Hunter chose the most mundane task he could think of, which was to look over the quarterly financial statements. This realm of the company usually fell to the Gregorys' long-time family friend, their CFO, Ken Feng. Hunter already knew the statements would be in perfect order, because Ken was a professional, and a perfectionist, and someone Hunter could trust implicitly. It meant that reviewing the financial records would be the most boring, draining, and coma-inducing activity of all time, which was perfect.

Sure enough, hours and hours later, his eyelids drooped and his shoulders sagged. Finally, he dragged himself to bed. Then he tossed and turned all night.

~

HUNTER AWOKE to sunshine lying across his patchwork quilt. *Awoke* was too strong a word, though, since he'd never really been asleep. He'd spent the entire night trapped between rest and wakefulness, forcing him to acknowledge that the only good night of sleep he'd had since he arrived here was the night when he knew he would see Scarlet in the morning. Which didn't make any sense, since she was all tornadoes and wildfires and floods. None of that should make him feel peaceful at all, and yet it did. He tried not to think about what that meant.

Forcing himself out of bed, he trudged into the bathroom. He made the decision to skip his sit-ups and push-ups this morning, since he still ached from his ridiculously aggressive workout yesterday. And he decided to postpone his shower, since he was going back to the gym for basketball and would need to shower when he returned. He also ignored his lineup of personal care items in the bathroom, saving that regimen for later. Although he did put on his deodorant, for Tyler's sake.

Hunter exited his cabin, ambling down the driveway to the road. As he walked, he thought of how unusual this morning felt, having not completed any of his typical routine. He figured Scarlet would be proud of him for it. If she knew how he'd veered off of his normal course, his Frolicking Freebird would probably grin up at him, bounce around a bit, and then put her hand over his heart and tell him he'd done a good job.

He wished he could see her right now. He wished she would just appear by the side of the road, so he could tell her how differently he'd acted today. Of course, he was still mad at her. And he needed her to be completely honest with him. But at the same time, he also wanted her to know how much progress he'd made with some of his control issues.

When he reached the main road, Hunter glanced to his right, toward her Cabin 10. Nearly an entire day had passed since he'd seen her smiling face. He wanted her to be here. He wanted her to flutter down this road, so he could tell her how well he'd done this morning.

It wouldn't be all sunshine and roses between them, unfortunately, since he would still have to glare and growl at her. He would also have to insist on lengthy, tiring discussions over her bizarre need to lie to him. But after that, he would be able to let go. He'd be able to sit with her, absorbing the sensation of her fingertips as she petted him. He'd be able to look into her sparkling emerald eyes and forget everything else in the world, even if only for those few moments.

Hunter stood entirely still, looking toward Cabin 10. As much as he hated to admit it, he knew she wouldn't appear here. After all, he never saw her on this road. He never saw her at the gym. He never saw her anywhere in public. He only saw her when they were alone.

His brow furrowed as he turned to his left and continued down the pavement. He considered every moment he'd been with his forest fairy: first when she'd stepped out of the forest; twice when he went to her cabin; once at his own cabin; and then in the woods yesterday morning. Each time, they were always alone.

Hunter laughed, a bit maniacally, as the strangest thought crept into his brain. *What if she doesn't actually exist? What if I'm so stressed out that I made her up? What if that's the reason we're always alone?*

He stopped walking. The V in his brow deepened while a shiver ran the length of his spine. He shoved his hands through his hair with enough force to be painful. "I'm going bat-shit crazy on this mountain," he groaned, not because he actually believed he'd made Scarlet up, but because he even considered the possibility that he might have.

"Good Lord, of course she's real," he assured himself, shaking his head as he resumed walking. After all, he distinctly remembered touching her in the forest yesterday. He remembered the warmth of her skin beneath his fingertips. He remembered the sound of her whimpers when he slipped his hand inside her jacket. He remembered her whole body curling into his as she balled his shirt up in her fierce little fist.

But then again, if he was crazy, he probably could have made up that stuff, too. Honestly, touching her felt too good to be true, so maybe it was. Maybe Blissful Blue had dug beneath his skin, snatched reality right out of his brain, and made him imagine every last tiny bit of her.

His footsteps halted again. Hunter forced himself to breathe.

"No, goddamnit. I did not fabricate her out of thin air. Scarlet is real, because if I wanted to create a fantasy woman, it sure as hell wouldn't be one who lies to me constantly. That makes no fucking sense at all."

He wanted to start walking again. Purposefully. To the gym. But he couldn't, because he felt too shaken by his thoughts. Too shaken by his bizarre-yet-delicious imaginary friend. Too shaken by the idea of losing what was left of his mind.

"Wait a minute!" he shouted, remembering something wonderful. "Colin saw her! He talked to her yesterday morning at my cabin! And she talked back to him!"

Hunter's shoulders dropped. "Oh, thank God," he muttered, his feet finally resuming their steady pace. He wasn't crazy. She was definitely real, because Colin saw her, too.

Unless I also made Colin up.

"For the love of the heavens, Hunter, go to the gym. Stop thinking about her. Make the decision to stop thinking about her, then just stop."

MAKING the decision to stop thinking about Scarlet was really easy.

Actually stopping turned out to be difficult as hell.

Even hours later, with Tyler beside him the entire time, Hunter could barely focus. Tyler rambled on and on about his night with Jocelyn, about how they'd eaten a romantic dinner together and gone for a walk under the stars, but Hunter hardly heard a word. Every time he saw another person walk out of the gym, or jog by the basketball court, he looked to see if it was Scarlet. Yet it never was.

When he missed his tenth basket in a row, Tyler caught hold of the ball and stood, staring him down. "What's up with you today, man? You're completely off your game. I'm starting to worry."

"Man, I'm sorry about that. My mind is...elsewhere."

"Do you want to talk about it?"

Hunter shook his head. "No, thanks."

"It's okay, buddy. I understand. You're not a big talker and that's fine. However, I do expect you to come to the Social tonight. You can let everyone else talk. Believe me, they love to do that."

"I just...I don't know if I'm up to it."

"Well, if I make this basket, you'll come," Tyler said before tossing the ball effortlessly above his head and watching it swish through the rim. "There you go. It has been decided by a power greater than you."

"And that would be?"

"The power of the basketball gods. They will not be denied."

Hunter chuckled. As much as he wanted to refuse this Social outing, he also couldn't imagine spending another night alone, poring over financial spreadsheets. "Okay, I suppose it'll be fun."

"Yes, it will." Tyler winked and tossed him the ball.

~

BY THE TIME Hunter returned to his cabin, lunch was already sitting on his porch. He took the tray inside, ate his meal and put the tray back out, then jumped in the shower. When he finished drying off, he wrapped the towel around his waist and stood in front of the mirror in his bedroom. Although working out made his body physically powerful, his face still looked as worn and weary as the day he'd arrived here. Not that he ever really thought Blissful Blue would change him. But this place had certainly made him doubt himself today.

Stepping away from the mirror, Hunter carefully chose his clothes for the Social. The itinerary said dress was business casual, so he decided on a long-sleeved ivory button-down shirt with dark gray slacks and a matching sport coat. Donning office attire made him feel more at home in his skin, and his confidence returned a bit as he strode from the bedroom to the desk. Sitting down on the red-and-green plaid cushion, he waited patiently for his laptop to connect. He knew there wouldn't be much in the way of business matters to attend, but he needed to make the hours pass until he left for the Social.

The moment his search engine popped up, his fingers froze against the keyboard. He meant to go straight to his company website, but he didn't. He stared at the screen instead, recalling all the things he'd typed into here, like *fastest land mammal* and *Blue Ridge Mountain trees.*

His computer always revealed Scarlet's lies so easily. But there was one truth he hadn't searched for yet: the yellow-crowned purple fantini. He typed in the words now, his fingers hovering over the enter key. All he had to do was press down, and he would know for certain that there was no bird. He would know for certain that she was no photographer.

Hunter sat, barely breathing, for painful seconds. Then he reached to the delete key and pressed down hard, until the name was fully erased. God help him, he didn't want to find out this way. He wanted *her* to tell him there was no bird. He wanted Scarlet to tell him there was no *National Geographic* arti-cle. He wanted to hear, from her own gorgeous mouth, that she was here because she needed help. And he wanted her to tell him willingly, because he needed that vulnerability from her.

Rubbing the back of his stiff neck, he opened the Gregory Global home-page. He logged in and went immediately to the financial records he'd been scouring the night before. Within moments of accessing the data, an instant message popped up on his screen.

Ken Feng: Hello, Hunter. How are you?

Hunter stared at the IM, finding it strange to know another person was on the other end of his computer, back in the real world. He smiled, imagining Ken's kind eyes through the words on the screen. Ken wasn't just a coworker to him. He was more like a second father, and Hunter missed the older man's comforting presence.

Hunter Gregory: I'm fine, Ken. How are you?

Ken Feng: I'm well, thank you. Just curious if something is wrong?

Hunter Gregory: Why would anything be wrong?

Ken Feng: I saw that you looked over the quarterly financial records for hours last night, and now you're back, looking over them again. Is there a problem I need to know about?

Hunter cringed, having never considered that his CFO would know he'd been knee-deep in financial records while supposedly on vacation.

Hunter Gregory: No, Ken. No problem. I didn't mean to alarm you. I was just trying to fill up some free time.

Ken Feng: Oh? Aren't you mountain climbing with your parents?

Hunter's heart stopped dead in his chest. His entire body shook as those words soaked into his skin. Ken thought he was on vacation with his parents in Washington. Everyone at work thought that. And his parents thought he was in Cozumel with friends from the office. None of them knew where he really was. Because he'd lied.

"Holy shit. I lied to everyone," Hunter breathed. "And then I sat on that forest floor with Scarlet, insisting she tell me the truth. I demanded complete honesty from her, while here I am, lying to all my coworkers and my parents. My God, I'm such a hypocrite. I'm the biggest fucking hypocrite in the whole goddamn world."

His fingers shook as he pressed them against his eyelids. When he managed to control their tremors, he looked back to his computer and typed: *Thanks for all your work on the financials, Ken. They're perfect, as always. I won't be in contact again until I get home. See you then.*

Hunter shut his laptop. Reaching around the side of the machine, he yanked the internet cord out of the wall. He shoved the computer back in his briefcase and stood from the empty desk.

He paced his living room floor for as long as he could bear to stay inside. Then he exited his cabin and slumped down on the porch steps, waiting for Colin to bring his dinner. And his beer.

While Hunter sat, he wondered again if he'd actually made Scarlet up in his mind. He wondered if he'd fabricated a beautiful little liar to teach him how awful it felt to be lied to by someone he cared about. Every muscle he owned stiffened against the log steps. "No. Don't go there again, Hunter. That is a ridiculous idea."

Scarlet couldn't be a figment of his imagination. She wasn't an Ebenezer Scrooge, you-will-be-visited-by-three-ghosts spirit, sent to show him what he was doing wrong in his life. She absolutely could not be a stress-induced hallucination of insane proportions, because that was a fucking maniacal thought.

Hunter twisted his fingers together. He chuckled softly as he sat on the porch and continued to wait. He had no earthly idea how long he sat there. He just knew how relieved he felt when the meal delivery truck finally came down his driveway.

Colin parked a few feet from the porch steps and hopped out of the driver's seat. He nodded before retrieving a tray from the back. Hunter held his breath until he saw the six-pack in the young man's other hand.

"You brought it," he sighed, accepting the beer the moment Colin approached. "Thank you so much."

"Sure thing." The boy set the tray down and turned toward his truck.

Hunter watched him walk away. "Um, Colin?"

He looked back as he reached the driver's door. "Yes?"

"I don't suppose you'd like to have a beer with me?"

"Um, I'd like to, but I can't. Because I have to drive the truck."

"Oh, right. That was a stupid suggestion. Sorry."

"It's no problem. I just can't drink beer while I'm on duty," he said, observing Hunter for a moment. "But I could sit with you, if you want."

"That would be great. If you have the time."

The boy walked back over, settling down beside him on the steps. They both looked out to the surrounding trees. Hunter grabbed a beer from the pack, popped the cap off the bottle, and took a long drink.

At first, neither of them said a word. It was a peaceful silence, but Hunter needed more right now. Fiddling with the label on his bottle, he cleared his throat. "So, Colin, what are you saving for?"

"I'm sorry?"

"Yesterday, when I gave you the hundred, you said you were going to put it in your savings fund."

"Oh, that." His gaze dropped to the gravel under his sneakers. "I, um, I have a year left of college. I'm saving up to go back."

"Did you have to stop for some reason?"

"Kind of a lot of reasons."

Hunter heard a note of distress in the boy's voice. "What reasons?"

Colin rubbed his hands together. "The summer after my third year of college, my folks were in a car accident. They both died. I couldn't go back to college then, not just because I didn't have the money, but because I was struggling to keep my head up."

Hunter clutched his beer bottle. "God, I'm sorry. Are you okay?"

"*Okay* is a strong word, but I'm making it. I like it up at Blue. It's peaceful and it feels like a home, at least until I get back on my feet."

"I'm sorry I asked. I mean, I'm not sorry I asked, but I'm sorry if it hurts you to talk about it."

Colin smiled. "You know, if I'm learning anything here, it's that it gets a little easier, and just a little bit better, every time I say it out loud."

Hunter watched him for another minute before looking out to the trees. He gripped his bottle so tightly that he feared it might burst. "Well, I'm glad this place can give you what you need for now."

"Thanks."

"Yeah," he offered halfheartedly, unable to imagine being an orphan. His parents were his strength, especially as a young man. He took another drink of his beer and fell back into silence.

"So, what about you?" Colin asked.

"What about me?"

"Is Blissful Blue giving you what you need for now?"

"I don't know. Maybe." *But only because of her. Only because of my forest fairy.* "Can I, um, can I ask you another question?"

"Sure."

"Can you tell me about Scarlet?"

Colin turned to him. "Are you asking me an art question?"

"What?"

"Are you asking me about the color red?"

Hunter huffed out a laugh. "No, I'm not asking about art. I'm asking about the person, Scarlet. The woman who was here yesterday morning when you delivered my breakfast."

Colin chuckled. "I'm glad you're not asking about art, since I'm not any good with that. Although I'm afraid I won't be much help with the other Scarlet, either."

Hunter's heart tripped. "No? Why not?"

Please don't say she's not real. Anything but that.

"Well, as much as I'd like to help you out, I'm not supposed to talk about the other guests up here. Because of discretion and all."

"Oh. I understand, Colin. Completely. It's just...she was here, right? I mean, you saw her here?"

The boy's head tilted. "Yeah, she was here."

Hunter shut his eyes and sighed. "Thank you. Truly. Thank you."

"Sure thing."

They relapsed into silence. Hunter knew he should be mortified right now, for having even asked. Yet he was too relieved to care.

"It's really nice sitting here with you," Colin told him after another long while, "but I should get going, before the other dinners turn cold."

"Yeah, of course. I appreciate the beer. And the talk."

"I'm here to talk anytime," he assured as he stood and stepped down onto the driveway.

"Me, too," Hunter called out when the young man reached his truck. "I'm available to talk, if you ever need it."

"Thanks," Colin said, climbing into the driver's seat and waving.

Hunter waved back, waiting until the truck drove off before grabbing his dinner tray and returning to his cabin. He sat on the log couch and picked at his food. He had little appetite, even though Colin had brought him steak tonight, which was his favorite.

As Hunter pushed the meat around his plate, he thought about the red-hooded young man with no parents. He thought about his own parents, and how supportive they'd always been. He thought about the things that happened when he was a teenager, things he couldn't have gotten through without Mom and Dad. He thought about how he'd lied to both of them about coming here to Blue. And he thought about how he'd looked into Scarlet's eyes yesterday and demanded complete honesty from her, when he could barely be honest with himself.

Hunter set his fork down. The living room had darkened, although he'd scarcely noticed the sun setting. Glancing to the clock on the wall, he realized the Social had started a while ago and he would be more than fashionably late. That was okay, though, since he didn't really want to go anyway. But he would still keep his promise to Tyler.

Pulling himself up off the couch, Hunter pocketed his key card in his sport coat and carried the food tray back to the porch. Easing the door shut behind him, he walked off the steps and up the gravel drive. When he reached the main road, he turned to the right and forced himself to stare straight ahead. He worked hard to maintain his composure, but his heart still thumped harder with every step he took toward Cabin 10.

He meant to pass by her cabin without even a sidelong glance. He meant to move by without thinking about her at all. He couldn't.

Hunter stopped at the top of Scarlet's driveway and stared down the tree-lined path. He wanted so badly to take that road. He wanted to run to the very end, to watch her open her door to him, to see the smile on her pink lips and the sparkle in her emerald eyes.

He stood, frozen in place. He told himself the reason he didn't sprint toward her at full speed was because he'd promised to go to the Social. That was a lie, though. He didn't go to her because he still needed her to be honest with him, despite having told so many lies of his own. He didn't go to her because he needed her to be vulnerable with him and she wouldn't. He didn't go to her because he knew she could open him and he didn't know if he could ever open her. And he didn't go to her because going to her was the one thing he wanted to do most in the entire world and it absolutely terrified him.

Hunter dragged himself away from her path. He kept his feet going, watching every step he took, his designer shoes highlighted by the moonlight bursting sporadically through the overhanging branches. He didn't exhale fully until he heard the din of music coming from ahead.

Cabin 13 was brightly lit, with wide windows revealing multiple people inside the large, open rooms. This cabin was three times the size of the residential ones, and he knew by the raucous sound of voices that the party was in full swing. Stepping onto the front porch and grasping the door handle, he straightened his shoulders and lifted his chin.

The door opened to a rush of scents and sounds. Thick odors of wine and beer accosted his nostrils, along with pervasive scents of perfume and cologne. Thumping beats of music vibrated beneath rampant, blaring conversations. Closing the door quietly behind him, Hunter took a good look around at the horde of people.

They were all dressed like he was: business casual, leaning toward formal. The women were beautiful, many sporting diamond jewelry and cosmetically enhanced chests. The men were like him, well groomed and obviously affluent. Hunter couldn't help but chuckle, since this felt like any business function he'd ever been to in his life.

What had Will told him about the patients up here at Blue? *They're working people, just like you, Hunter.* And they were. All these people looked like the ones he already knew. They were the same people he'd been with nearly every day of his life. Right this minute, he wasn't sure if that made him happy or sad.

"Hey there, friend!" A tall, thin man in a black suit stepped up to greet him. "My name is Grant."

"Hunter," he replied, shaking the man's hand. "Nice to meet you."

"Are you an alcoholic, Hunter?"

God, do I look like an alcoholic? "Um, no. Should I be?"

A deep laugh emanated from Grant's reedy chest. "Good one, good one. Anyway...the beer and wine is over on the back table. Help yourself. Non-alcoholic refreshments are this way, if you'd rather."

"Thanks, Grant."

The greeter nodded and stepped away, leaving Hunter to search the other faces. He spotted Tyler by the spirits table, talking to Jocelyn and another woman. Hunter advanced through the crowd, returning the smiles he received along the way, until he stood before his friend.

"You did come!" Tyler announced on his arrival. "I'm damn glad, Hunter. You remember Jocelyn?"

"Yes, of course. How are you, Jocelyn?"

"I am doing well, thank you. This is my friend, Mitzi Fisher."

Hunter glanced to the woman on Jocelyn's left. She was just as beautiful as Jocelyn, with bright blond hair and big brown eyes. Her bone structure was perfect, her height in heels nearly six feet, since she stood only a couple inches shorter than him.

"Pleasure to meet you, Hunter," Mitzi said, glancing down to his chest and back to his eyes before flashing an approving smile. "Tyler was just telling us what a wonderful basketball player you are."

Hunter ran a hand across his tight neck. "Oh, I don't know about that. He beat up on me pretty good today."

"Only because you were distracted," Tyler interjected. "Otherwise, your form was perfect."

"What were you distracted by?" Jocelyn questioned.

"Just...things. I'm a little preoccupied, I suppose."

Tyler patted him on the shoulder. "Aren't we all? That's why most of us are here. We just need to let everything go and enjoy ourselves."

"Have you been to see Dr. Abbott yet, Hunter?" Mitzi asked.

"Um, no. I can't say that I have."

"Oh, you really should. He's the resident psychiatrist. The guest physicians come and go, but Dr. Abbott is always here, sturdy and stable. He gave a great talk this week about finding your inner calm."

"Yes, he's truly a genius," Jocelyn added. "I always feel like I have a new perspective after listening to him."

"I enjoyed that talk as well," Tyler agreed.

The three of them chatted about Dr. Abbott's admirable qualities as Hunter stood and listened, amazed by how openly everyone discussed psychotherapy, as if it was the norm. Then again, it was the norm here.

"So, Hunter, what do you do for a living?" Mitzi asked, stepping over on her high heels to come stand by his side.

"Mitzi!" Tyler barked. "You know we don't talk business here!"

"It's okay," Hunter conceded, since business was the easiest thing for him to talk about. "I run my family's company, Gregory Global."

Mitzi's eyes widened instantly before narrowing to near slits. "You mean you're Hunter Gregory? The CEO of Gregory Global?"

He forced a smile. "That would be me."

She wound her hand around his bicep, curling her fingers into his jacket. "That's impressive. Your company is Fortune-500, isn't it?"

Hunter nodded as she slithered closer.

"Amazing job you're doing," she said, fastening her gaze on his lips.

He wanted to laugh. Even on this crazy-ass mountain, he couldn't get away from the typical reaction of any woman who found out who he was. Hungered looks? *Check*. Clawed fingers? *Check*.

"Thanks," he sighed.

Mitzi didn't release his arm or move an inch from his side.

"Ugh," Tyler grunted. "No more business talk. Let's go dance." He pulled Jocelyn into the next room filled with gyrating bodies.

Hunter stilled as he watched the couple move to the pounding music.

Mitzi's grasp on his bicep tightened. "Do you dance, Hunter?"

"No, I don't. But tonight, I will drink."

"Okay, then. Wine or beer?"

"I'll start with wine," he decided, reaching for a pre-filled glass from the refreshment table and downing the entirety of the contents in one long gulp. He set the glass down and picked up another.

Mitzi took a wine glass for herself and sipped. "I'll talk business with you, if that makes you happy. I'm actually the COO of a pharmaceuticals company in Florida, myself."

"Oh, really?" he asked, trying hard to sound interested.

"Yes. We can talk about business, or anything else you like."

A smile pulled at her darkly painted lips, making his stomach roil. "Well, I will listen to anything you want to say."

She squeezed his arm. "You're such a gentleman. And since you're being so good, I'll be good as well, and not talk business. Those are Tyler's rules, after all. Would you like to hear about my childhood?"

Hunter said, "Yes," even though it was a complete and utter lie. He brought the second glass of wine to his lips and drank it dry.

"I was born in Miami, close to where my company's home base is now. My father owned a chain of convenience stores and my mother..."

He watched Mitzi's mouth move, wishing this alcohol would kick in already. Normally, he would never drink like this. Drinking dampened control, and that wasn't a sensation he enjoyed. But right now, he definitely needed to numb his racing mind.

Hunter grabbed a third glass of wine and forced it down as she kept talking, laughing at her own jokes while continuously caressing his arm. He chuckled at one point, not because he found her funny, but because he realized her touch on his body wasn't at all therapeutic. When the alcohol finally began scrambling his senses, he focused on her left eye, since he figured it would make him look interested. That worked for a while, but then something else caught his attention.

His gaze darted to the dance floor. From behind, he saw a woman with long, loose black hair. His entire body latched to the sight as he watched her dance. A light of hope swelled in his chest, until his eyes drifted down to the woman's bottom.

Damn it. That wasn't his forest fairy's backside. He would know Scarlet's perfect ass anywhere, and that definitely wasn't it.

Hunter looked to Mitzi again. Her thin lips still spewed a lot of words. He sighed, his gaze falling to her shoes. She wore tan high heels. He wondered if Scarlet ever wore heels. He'd only seen her in hiking boots, or in bare feet with adorable little painted toenails.

Even with heels on, Scarlet wouldn't come close to his height. She was a tiny fairy, and he would have to bend down when he kissed her. Or he could just lift her. He could grab hold of her perfect ass and lift her onto him, feeling every inch of her body pressed against his, her arms clutching his neck, her breasts crushed against his chest, her thighs gripping his waist...

"Don't you agree, Hunter?"

Mitzi's question yanked him from his fantasy. He refocused on the left eyeball. "Yes," he said, not entirely sure what he'd agreed to.

"I feel the same way," she cooed, dragging her hand down his arm in order to clutch onto his. Her touch was cold, her fingers thin.

Hunter reached for a fourth glass of wine when her constant speech restarted. Mitzi stepped closer, rubbing up against him, and he knew his jacket was going to smell like her. The thought of having her heavy, pungent perfume on his clothes repulsed him. The only scents he wanted on him were his forest fairy's fresh soap and tiny flowers.

Mitzi squeezed his hand again.

Shit. He didn't want her to touch him. He wanted Scarlet to touch him. He didn't even care which Scarlet did the touching – Frolicking Freebird or Solemnly Sedate – he wanted both, but he would take either.

"...and then, when I was sixteen, my brother went off to college, which I believe was a real sense of loss for me..."

Hunter stared at the woman beside him as she droned on. Mitzi's hair didn't shine quite like Scarlet's. It didn't move like Scarlet's, as if it had a mind of its own, or make him ache with the need to touch it.

"...but I was able to see my brother on school breaks, at which point I realized I could still have him in my life..."

Her lips weren't nearly as full as Scarlet's, and nowhere near as kissable. They didn't mesmerize him while she spoke. They didn't captivate him when she smiled.

"...and then my friend Sandra, the one with the golden retriever I told you about earlier, came over and we both gave my brother advice on his new girlfriend..."

Her voice didn't sing like Scarlet's. Her words didn't crawl under his skin, making him question everything. Her laugh didn't stir his soul.

"...years later, he ended up marrying that girl, and I began to feel like I should consider settling down, too. Especially since I'd developed so much of my career and nearly nothing of my personal life..."

Hunter heard those words. This was a thing he actually had in common with the woman currently draping her body onto his. The career he could handle. It was the personal life he stunk at managing.

Right now, standing here with this blandly ambitious creature, Hunter finally understood what he'd been doing wrong this entire time. Women like this one didn't challenge him at all, yet this was precisely the type he'd spent his whole life seeking out. She was just like Clarissa, just like Jocelyn, just like so many others he'd known.

"I'm staying in Cabin 27," Mitzi said. "If you'd care to walk me back to my place, I have a lovely bottle of Merlot we could share."

Hunter choked on his drink. The buzz in his head wasn't loud enough to mute her intentions. He could have this woman if he wanted, even though he'd spoken less than twenty sentences through the course of the evening. He could take her to bed, offer pleasure and accept it, and be on his way.

How many times had he found himself in this same situation? How many times had he stood in a crowd at a business party, with some unfamiliar woman hanging on his arm, letting him know in no uncertain terms that she would be his in an instant? The women were always intelligent, wealthy, and beautiful. Just like this one.

Everything seemed to be in perfect order, as it should be. This night was turning out precisely like any other night of his life. This gathering was exactly like any other business gathering he'd ever been to.

Except Hunter wasn't even present in the room.

He surveyed the polished bodies surrounding him, currently unable to fathom this idea of perfection he'd tried to achieve for so long. Nothing about this situation felt remotely real. This room wasn't his home. These people weren't his family. They were mannequins in a storefront, chattering at him until he couldn't hear anything else, when the only person he truly wanted to listen to was his Scarlet.

Right at this moment, Hunter couldn't believe he ever thought she might not be real. Standing here now, enclosed by all these fake bodies and fake smiles, his little forest fairy was the only real thing he knew.

"Earth to Hunter," Mitzi prodded. "Did you even hear what I said?"

"Yes, I heard you. Unfortunately, I have a previous engagement," he lied, knowing he would crawl out of his skin if he remained beside her for one more second. "You'll have to excuse me."

He didn't wait for a response. Hunter extracted himself from her icy grip and rushed through the crowd to the front door. He pushed his way out into the night, down the stairs, and off the porch. When the fresh mountain air struck his face, he sucked a deep breath into his lungs.

"Hey, where are you headed?" Tyler's voice came from behind.

Hunter whirled around on the gravel to see his friend standing at the door. "I'm sorry, Tyler. Thanks for inviting me, but I need to leave."

"Why? It seemed like you and Mitzi were getting pretty friendly."

"Mitzi?" Hunter echoed, having trouble recalling her face. "Sure, I guess. I just...I think I've had too much to drink."

"But that leaves two beautiful women here and only one of me. Not that I'm complaining. At all," Tyler said, grinning ear to ear.

Hunter's head cocked to the side as he regarded his friend. From the expression on Tyler's face, it was obvious he planned to pursue both women at once. Hunter wasn't sure what to think about that. He opened his mouth, prepared to impart a healthy, brotherly lecture, when he realized a simple truth and had to clamp his jaw shut again.

The simple truth was he couldn't fault Tyler for wanting two women at once. After all, Hunter also wanted two women at once. It just so happened that the two women he wanted both resided in the same body.

"I – I really need to go now," he managed to say as he backed away.

"Okay, buddy. You gonna make it back to your cabin?"

"I'll be fine."

"Then I'll catch you on the basketball court in the morning?"

"Yeah, in the morning," he agreed, turning toward the main road.

"Goodnight!" Tyler shouted.

Hunter waved his hand in the air while he walked. He strode down Cabin 13's driveway with purpose and determination, finally knowing exactly where he was going. He was headed to Cabin 10 and to the little fairy who lived inside.

6

TO TOUCH OR NOT TO TOUCH

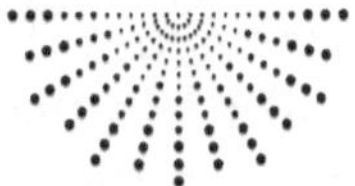

Hunter kept walking down the driveway, away from the Social and toward the main road. When he finally stepped off the gravel and onto the pavement, he turned toward Cabin 10. Toward *her*.

He and Scarlet still had issues – a lot of issues. Honestly, he didn't know if it was humanly possible to work through them all. But he had to at least try, since he couldn't bear to hold himself back from her any longer, and he sure as hell didn't want to push her away.

Striding farther down the moonlit path toward her cabin, Hunter thought about how he'd had her beside him on that frigid forest floor yesterday, resting in a bed of leaves with the most serene smile on her face. He thought about how soft her skin felt beneath his fingertips and how his entire body begged to know hers. He thought about the lies she'd told him to make him fight back, to make him fight for *something*.

He knew his little bird was trying to help him. It was a weird kind of help, yet it was apparently just what he needed, since her lying to him made him want to be honest with her. Maybe that was always her intention. Maybe this was all some well-constructed, elaborate plan to open him. Maybe she was actually the evil mastermind of Blissful Blue.

Except that couldn't be true. Scarlet wasn't evil. And as brilliant as she obviously was, at times she was innocent and unsure and vulnerable.

Vulnerable. That's what Hunter wanted her to be. He wanted vulnerability. He'd pushed her away yesterday because he thought she wouldn't give it to him, but now he could see just how wrong he'd been.

Hadn't she already exposed a million weaknesses? She'd admitted she hadn't been touched in forever and showed him how much she craved his touch. She'd looked into him with worried eyes and confessed her fear that he'd given up on life. She'd spoken with such nervousness about sex that her anxiety reached out of her body and into his own. And she'd shown him the two sides of herself: the frolicking, frivolous side and the solemn, serious side. He didn't know if she'd meant to reveal all of that, but did it really matter?

"Hell, she practically cut herself open in front of me yesterday," he realized, listening intently to his own words drifting in the cool night air. "She bled out in front of my eyes, and I had the gall to think she wasn't being vulnerable. Do I really need her to say the words? Yes, she lied to me about being a patient, but didn't I lie about the same thing? I didn't come here on a dare. I came because I need help with my life. Maybe not as much as she needs, but I still need it. I asked Will for help and he told me to come here and that's why I'm here. And I lied to everyone about it, and then called Scarlet a liar for not telling me the complete truth."

Hunter stopped walking, his heart clawing so hard at his chest that he thought it would tear its way out. He wanted to tell her all of this. He wanted to lay himself out in front of her, to be real and honest with her, and pray to God she would listen and understand. Then maybe, if they worked together, they could reach some sort of compromise.

With renewed determination, he began moving again. The alcohol still ran through his veins, so he marched faster to push it out. He wanted his head clear when she opened her door to him, allowing him entry into her world again. He needed to be inside her world right now – deep inside, with her standing right beside him.

But what did Scarlet need?

He shook his head, afraid of not being able to help her the way she helped him. He didn't know if he was capable of giving her any sage advice. He probably couldn't solve whatever problems existed in her life. But there was one thing he could do for her. He could touch her.

Touch was one of the things Scarlet said she needed. His touch. She wanted his touch so she could feel alive, and he could give that to her. He wouldn't deny how much he wanted to give that to her. He wanted to wrap her in his arms, to kiss her everywhere, to hear his name on her lips as he made her come harder than she ever had in her life.

Hunter knew he could accomplish those goals, not just because of his extensive history with women, but also because of her innocence. Scarlet told him she'd had lovers before, yet he doubted that she'd ever truly let herself go.

Her own touches were too pure, her hesitance too genuine, to be the actions of a sexually seasoned woman.

He could become whatever kind of lover she needed. He could find countless ways to please her. After all, he'd never lacked skill in that arena. What he'd lacked, with every woman before now, was the desire to be inside her. Not just physically, but in every possible way.

Hunter wanted to be inside of Scarlet. He wanted all of her.

When his foot finally hit the entrance to her driveway, his pulse sputtered. The alcohol was nearly gone, and his nerves were fried. A day and a half had passed since he'd last seen her, and right now thirty-six hours felt like a goddamn eternity.

He stared straight ahead as he crunched down the gravel path, waiting for her cabin to come into view. When he finally saw a dim light glowing from her living room window, his body eased. She was inside. She was in that light. He was so close.

His anticipation skyrocketed as he approached her porch. He knew, any second now, she would appear. She would hear the gravel alarm system, yank open her door, grab hold of his hand, tug him inside, and gaze deliriously up at him while bouncing on the balls of her bare feet.

He could barely contain his excitement at the thought of seeing her again. His entire body tensed when he came to the noisy end of her driveway. Any second now...any second...

Hunter stood there, waiting and waiting, yet nothing happened. Her door didn't automatically open. She didn't simply materialize before him, like she always had before. He ogled her cabin steps, unsure if he should actually use them.

The moment he felt brave enough, he stomped up her porch stairs, banging his feet against the wood slats. When the boisterous sounds he'd made finished echoing off the log walls, he stood and stared at her closed door. And still, nothing happened.

Reaching out a tentative hand, Hunter knocked once. He waited even longer. The door didn't budge an inch, so he moved closer and knocked again. "Scarlet?" he called. "It's me, Hunter."

Nothing. He heard absolutely nothing from behind the logs, although he was positive she stood on the other side of them. He swore he could feel her warm body even through the thick wood.

He knocked harder. "Scarlet. Open the door. Please."

Hunter froze entirely this time, determined to hear her breathing on the other side. He held his own breath and shut his eyes. Yet he heard nothing but the hooting of an owl and the cool wind swishing the trees.

Goddamnit. She's not going to let me in.

Slumping forward, he dropped his forehead onto the hard slab of wood. His shoulders sagged as he reached out to trace his fingers over the cracks and crevices in the logs. He knew what was happening right now. He knew why the door wouldn't open, because he knew exactly who stood behind it. Solemnly Sedate Scarlet stood there, and she would never let him inside. She was far too practical for that.

What else did you expect, asshole?

Hunter huffed at himself, knowing he was the one who'd conjured her. Yesterday in the forest – when he'd called Scarlet a liar and demanded total honesty from her – he'd dragged this somber person right out of his forest fairy's body. Apparently, she hadn't left.

He shook his head back and forth against the cold, unforgiving wood. He needed to get inside, despite the fact that the serious, solemn woman standing on the other side of these logs wouldn't open the damn door. However, maybe the *other* woman would.

What was the other woman's name? He knew her name. She'd told him the night they'd played Twister. It was Scarlet...something.

"Scarletson," he whispered.

Hunter fisted his hand and banged it against the wood. He cringed when the sound reverberated through his forehead. "Scarletson!" he echoed, louder this time. "Please let me in."

There was another long moment of silence. Finally, the lock on the other side clicked. He straightened, the air catching in his throat as he stared at the dark wood. A moment later, the door creaked open slightly.

She hadn't materialized in front of him, but she had given him silent permission to come inside. Hunter didn't hesitate. He pushed through the doorway, his eyes searching the dimly lit cabin until he saw her.

Scarlet stood in her living room with her back turned, busily tugging a robe over her nightgown and fastening the tie around her waist. He hadn't even considered the hour. "I'm sorry I'm here so late," he apologized, closing the door behind him before taking another step inside. "Were you trying to sleep?"

She turned to face him, cinching the fabric belt tighter over her stomach. His eyes dropped to her hands, watching her fingers fumble against the ends of the silky tie. Her robe was hunter green satin, with a matching gown peeking out beneath the deep V of the opening. Neither of the short, shimmery pieces came past her mid-thigh, and his gaze trailed leisurely down her bare legs to her tiny painted toenails.

"I wasn't asleep yet," she said, the soft stroke of her voice pulling his focus back to her eyes. "I was having a glass of wine before bed."

"Oh," he replied, giving her a gentle smile before glancing to the subdued light coming from the kitchen. She'd set a few candles on the counter, which were already burning down to the ends. There was an open bottle of red wine, and a half-full glass, next to the flickering lights. There was also that little red-and-green leaf – the tiny culprit he'd wanted to pull from her hair yesterday – sitting proudly on the countertop. Hunter stared at it before turning his eyes back to hers.

Solemnly Sedate Scarlet observed him wearily. He figured he must look like hell. He must look threadbare and beaten, after the past thirty-six hours. Yet he could tell she hadn't fared much better.

Not that she wasn't beautiful. She was more gorgeous than ever, with her soft ebony curls draped loosely around her shoulders and the luminous green satin skimming over her skin. But her eyes looked tired and sad, and Hunter wanted nothing more than to take her pain away.

"Are you okay?" she asked while she studied him.

"Kind of," he answered as honestly as possible. "You?"

Scarlet shrugged. "Kind of," she offered, shuffling her feet against the floor. "So, to what do I owe the pleasure of your visit tonight?"

"I was at the Social." *And all I could think of was being inside you.*

"Really? I imagine you met all sorts of interesting people there."

"I suppose."

"Lots of beautiful women, I'm sure," she said, clenching her fingers. "It seems like this place is a haven for supermodels sometimes."

Hunter shook his head. "None of them could hold a candle to you."

She gave him a tiny smile. "Thank you for that. But still, there are some really good people up on this mountain. Some wonderful people. You should spend time with them, and give them a chance to…"

"I don't care about those people right now, Scarlet. The only person I care about is you. The only person I want to be with is you."

Her eyes widened with his words. The column of her throat shifted on a hard swallow. Her hands trembled against the ties of her robe.

He huffed out a laugh. "I know what you're thinking, but I didn't come here for sex," he assured. The next instant, he cocked his head and amended his statement. "Well, I didn't come here *just* for sex."

Hunter could hear her tiny gasp, even at this distance, but he refused to break eye contact. He needed Scarlet fully focused on him right now, because sooner or later he was going to move toward her. He was going to walk across this floor, take her in his arms, crush her body against his, kiss the hell out of her, and then press his face into her hair and simply breathe her in. And he needed her consent to do all of that.

The thought of filling his lungs with her scent made him loathe the dense, perfumed odor still clinging to his jacket. He grasped the lapels in his hands, shrugged the material off his shoulders, and laid the coat across the back of the couch. He took another step toward her.

Scarlet took a step back. "Have you been drinking tonight, Hunter?"

"Yes, I have. But the alcohol has pretty much worn off at this point. You can trust me on that."

"I do trust you. I just want to make sure you know what you're saying right now. I want to make sure you know what you're *doing*, because I don't want you to regret anything tomorrow."

"I'm not drunk, Scarlet. I want to be here. Please believe me when I tell you I desperately want to be here."

She chewed on her lip along with his words. "Well, your alcohol may have worn off, but I feel like I need some. If you don't mind."

He motioned his hand toward the kitchen. "Help yourself."

She took her eyes off of his for the first time since he'd arrived, keeping her distance while maneuvering around the far end of the couch to make her way into the kitchen. When she arrived at the counter, she leaned heavily against it, her satin-covered stomach propped against the wood. She grabbed the stem of her glass and took a long drink before setting it back down. "Can I offer you some wine?" she asked.

"No, thank you. Honestly, I don't like the feeling of alcohol."

"Yeah, I didn't think you would. Too uncontrolled, right?"

"That's exactly right," he confirmed, knowing how often she'd tried to get him to admit that fact. He didn't see any reason to hide it now. "I like being in control, Scarlet."

"I know, Hunter."

She stood entirely still, observing him from across the room, as the candle-light played with her hair and licked her skin, just like he wanted to. It was all he could do to remain motionless, when the desire to have her in his arms burned through his veins, threatening to render him senseless. But he couldn't succumb to that. Not yet. Not until they'd cleared the air.

"You and I, we need to talk."

"About what?"

"About you lying to me."

Scarlet sighed. "I thought we settled this in the woods yesterday."

"I thought we did, too. But then I spent thirty-six hours away from you, and I honestly felt like I was going crazy."

She reached her hand out to him, willing him to come closer. But then she stopped herself, settling her palm against the counter instead. "What happened since I last saw you?"

He shrugged. "Nothing, really. But all I've done, since the minute you walked away from me, is think. And I've realized a few things."

"Yeah? Like what?"

"Like I don't care about any of the lies you've told me before now."

Her jaw unhinged. "No. *No.* You do care, and I understand why. It was wrong of me to lie. I'm not even trying to make excuses, I just..."

"Scarlet." He cut off her words, waiting patiently until she pressed her lips together and refocused. "I honestly don't care about any lie you've told me *before now.*"

"Before now?"

"That's right. I know I pressed you unfairly in the woods yesterday. I pushed you to tell me the truth about everything, and that was a shitty thing to do, because nobody tells the truth about everything. I just...I wanted to know you. I wanted you to confide in me, to tell me why you came to Blue. But I realize now that it doesn't matter why you came here. Whatever your reasons, I think you're brave for choosing to get help. I think you're brave for accepting therapy with such open arms."

Hunter paused to watch how his words affected her. He watched the sorrow move through her eyes, watched the quiver of her lips, watched her fingers twist into the countertop. A new fear overtook him, right here and now: the fear of doing more harm than good.

"I don't want to hurt you," he told her, his voice raw and strained. "I don't know why you came to Blue, and I don't know what problems exist in your life that made you look to therapy for help, but I do know I never want to hurt you. So, if my actions here tonight are in any way detrimental to you, just tell me. Tell me and I will leave this instant."

She gave him a tremulous smile. "Oh, Hunter. You aren't hurting me. Not at all. Quite the opposite, actually."

It was his turn to smile. "I'm really glad to hear that, because I want to be as helpful to you as I can be. You've helped me so much already, you know. Seeing how brave you are, how you embrace this place with utter joy, it amazes me. Especially since I wasn't brave at all. I wasn't able to admit to anyone that I came here for help."

Scarlet's hand inched closer to him against the countertop. "What are you saying? Are you telling me you didn't come here on a dare?"

He looked down to her fingers, his own twitching with the need to touch. "No, I didn't come here on a dare. I lied and said I did, because I couldn't even admit to myself that I need help. And I dreaded coming here. I thought I was going to absolutely hate this place. But then you found me, and everything changed. My whole world changed."

Hunter started walking toward her, just putting one foot in front of the other. "I love your company, Scarlet. I love hearing your voice. I love listening to your thoughts. I love it when you touch me. And God, I really love touching you. But I don't expect you to tell me why you came to Blue. Not if you don't want to. I only want the chance to be with you – to keep watching you and listening to you and learning from you – for the rest of the time we're up on this mountain. Because I honestly can't imagine making it through this vacation without you."

He stopped walking when he reached the other side of the counter, looking across the smooth log surface to where she stood. "I just need to ask you for one little thing," he continued. "Just one small favor, before we go any further."

Her breaths came in short, uneven bursts. "Wh-what favor is that?"

"I want you to stop lying to me, as of now. From this point forward, I want to know that every word coming out of your ungodly gorgeous mouth is the truth."

Scarlet reached up to touch her lips. "But I've...I've already told you so many lies, Hunter."

"I don't care about that. I honestly don't. What I do care about is knowing you won't lie to me anymore."

"But what if you ask me something I don't want to answer?"

"Then tell me you don't want to answer. I'll accept that. Just don't lie. Please."

She whimpered with his request.

Hunter rested his hands against the countertop, voraciously aware that only a few feet separated her body from his. "You know, when you stood in my driveway yesterday, you told me I am your friend."

Scarlet nodded without hesitation. "Yes. You are my friend."

"Good, because you're my friend, too, and I want that. I really want to be your friend. Of course, I want to be your lover, also. But right now, I just need to know we can reach this compromise together. I need your promise that every word you say to me, from this moment on, is the truth. Will you give me that? Will you promise to be honest with me?"

Hunter held his breath as he waited for her response, until he thought he would collapse right here on the floor. Then he saw her nod. She nodded and said, "I promise," and all the air rushed back to his lungs.

His body slumped against the countertop. He hadn't even realized how much stress he held in his muscles until she freed him. As far as he was concerned, Scarlet had removed all barriers between them. As far as he was concerned, nothing prevented him from being with her now, in any way he desired.

At this moment, Hunter wanted to say he felt like his old self again. But that wasn't true, because this was even better. This was his new self, the one who could be here with his forest fairy, openly and honestly. He liked being this person. He loved being this person.

He looked into Scarlet's eyes, fully aware of the absurdly giddy grin now plastered onto his mouth. Yet she still appeared as solemn and fearful as when he'd first stepped inside this cabin tonight. He didn't want that for her. He wanted her to feel as free and alive as he did.

Straightening to his full height, Hunter began moving toward her around the countertop. He knew she hadn't actually agreed to anything more than honest friendship yet, but it was a damn good start. Scarlet glued her eyes onto him, gripping the edge of the wood in her fingertips.

Hunter glanced down as he walked, noting that the height of the counter came right to his waist. It was the perfect level to sit her on, so he could fuck her. Hard and wild. He wouldn't do that tonight, though.

Tonight, he would make love to her in her bed. He would lay her down in the red sheets – he figured the sheets would be red, since he could picture them making love in red sheets, and since everything up here was either red or green, which was kind of ironic, considering this was Blissful Blue – and he would treasure every second she allowed him to be inside her. However, at some point before he returned home, he would have to fuck her on this countertop. That was simply a necessity.

Hunter watched her fingers grip tighter and tighter to the edge of the wood as he wound his way around the counter. By the time he arrived at her back, her knuckles were blanched white. He stood behind her, trying to regulate his breathing, as the scents he'd been aching for – her fresh soap and tiny flowers – filled his mind. Those scents would be all over him soon. They would remain with him tonight, tomorrow, the next day, and the next, because he intended to be with her for every second he could, in every imaginable way.

Staring down at her shoulders, Hunter watched them move unsteadily beneath her robe. He wanted to touch the silky material, and since he'd decided nothing should keep him away from her anymore, he did as he desired. Reaching out, he rested his hands on her shoulders.

The moment he touched her, Scarlet took a shuddering breath in. He smiled to himself, achingly aware of how responsive her body was to his. His eager cock swelled in his pants, testing the limitations of his zipper, leaving no doubt as to how his body responded to hers.

Hunter smoothed his palms down her arms, from her shoulders all the way to her wrists. He covered her hands with his own, sliding across them again and again, until she finally released her fierce grip on the counter. The moment she did, he threaded their fingers together and rested his chin against her shoulder.

"Mmm," he hummed in contentment. "You know, now that we're such good friends, I really think we should consider becoming lovers."

Scarlet's fingers tightened inside his.

"I'd like to take this opportunity to say I think it's a fantastic idea," he continued. "I actually think it's the best idea in the whole goddamn world, so if you still want to talk about it, I'm all for it."

She made a little choking noise in the back of her throat. "It's...it's probably not a good idea, Hunter."

"Really? I don't see why not. After all, we already decided in the woods yesterday that this would be safe sex."

"No, what we decided was that we didn't need to use condoms."

He sighed, well aware of what she meant. Nothing about this felt safe at all. In fact, touching her felt downright fucking dangerous.

Yet even with the alarm bells clanging diligently inside his brain, Hunter couldn't bring himself to care. He straightened, unthreading his fingers from hers in order to drag them back up her sleeves. He dropped his forehead into her hair and closed his eyes.

"I like being your friend," he whispered into her loose waves.

Scarlet shifted on her bare feet. "I like being your friend, too."

"Good," he replied, his hands massaging across the satin on her shoulders, working their way closer to her neck. "But I'm not going to lie to you. I want to be more than your friend. I just want...more."

His fingers found the neckline of her robe, curling beneath the fabric, pulling it gently across her skin until it came to her upper arms. He pressed his face beside hers, resting his stubbly cheek against her soft one. "I'm going to take your robe off now, Scarlet. I want it off so I can touch more of you. But you can stop me, if you honestly want to."

He waited for lengthy, baited seconds to see if she would protest. When she didn't, he pulled the silky fabric all the way down. Her arms fell to her sides, allowing the material slip off the tips of her fingers. Hunter reached both hands to her waist, digging into the knot at the front of her robe. When he finished untying the thin belt, the fabric pooled entirely at their feet.

He flattened both his palms on her nightgown, directly over her belly, and pulled her back against his body. His prominent erection pressed into one supple cheek of her ass. Scarlet groaned and grabbed onto the countertop again, clinging ferociously to the wood.

Hunter smoothed his hands across her waist, down to the tops of her thighs. This little slip of a gown was even shorter than her robe, and it barely covered her panties. He wanted to know what kind she wore, so he moved his fingers to the sides of her legs, then up further still, inch by inch, raising the little slip until it rested at her hipbones.

She whimpered when he ran his hands over the tiny straps of her underwear, slipping his fingers across the edge until they met at the center of her stomach. Her bellybutton lay beneath his fingertips and he traced that tiny circle as he explored the smooth edge of what he now knew to be a thong. It needed to come off soon. Just as soon as she agreed to be more than friends.

Hunter slipped one finger beneath the front edge of her panties. Scarlet mewled and leaned back against him, which made his aching shaft jut harder into her flesh. He was terribly, horribly aware that her tiny thong left her ass cheeks bare, and that his pants' button and zipper were the only things separating them at this point.

He groaned with the sinful knowledge, sinking his head down onto her shoulder. Her skin was there, directly beneath his lips, so he pressed his mouth to it. He kissed her exposed flesh, and licked it, and nipped at it. Scarlet shifted against him, instinctively rubbing her backside up and down his hard length. His finger wandered even further below the scrap of fabric that was her underwear.

"Uh, H-Hunter," she panted when he reached a little too far down.

He forced himself to withdraw. Pulling his hands out from under her satiny clothes, he placed them back on her shoulders. He told himself this was safer for now, to touch her arms and only her arms. But in reality, it didn't matter which part of her he touched. It was all softness and warmth and delight. It was all her, and he wanted every bit of it.

Hunter shook his head, not able to comprehend why his pull to her was so damn strong. Was it just that neither of them had been touched in so long? Was this merely two lonely people looking for someone to touch? Or was it only a simple chemical reaction happening inside his body? Was it both? Or perhaps something else entirely?

He honestly didn't know the cause. He only knew that touching her was heaven – truly unearthly – and he couldn't imagine stopping. But he would have to, if that was what she wanted.

Holy hell, that isn't really what she wants, is it?

"Come here," he demanded, pulling her away from the counter and spinning her body to face him. "I need you to tell me what you want, Scarlet. I need you to tell me now. Do you want us to only be friends? Because I can stop touching you, if that's what you want. I can spend the rest of this vacation seeing you every day, talking to you every day, and enjoying every minute I get to spend as your friend. And I'll love every second of it, even though my entire body will *ache* with the need to touch you."

Tears sprang to her eyes. "Please don't say things like that to me."

"Why not?"

"Because that...*that* hurts."

He sighed, shoulders falling. "It doesn't have to. I'll do whatever you want. If you don't want me to touch you anymore, just tell me."

She matched his intent gaze. "You know I can't tell you that."

"Why not?"

"Because I just promised to be honest with you, and if I said I didn't want your touch, it would be an incredibly preposterous lie."

Hunter couldn't help smiling. He drew both hands down her arms. "You love it when I touch you. Don't you?"

She moaned shamelessly. "God, yes."

"I love it, too. But it's not just therapeutic touch, is it? There's something electric beneath my skin when I feel you."

"Yes. Undeniably."

He absorbed her admission as his hands slipped back up her arms. "You talked about this attraction the night we played Twister. You said it was a simple chemical reaction that takes place in the human body."

She gazed at him with her eyelids at half-mast. "I did say that."

He moved one hand to her cheek, smoothing his fingers across her face. "And do you still believe it? Because this doesn't feel like a simple thing to me."

"No, this doesn't feel simple at all."

He ran his thumb across her lower lip. "Is it still the worst idea ever, then? To act on this attraction?"

"Probably."

"Why? Why would it be so bad?"

"Because this – this whole place, everything up here, everything between you and me – is unusual, Hunter. It's not reality."

"I don't know; this feels pretty goddamn real to me. And I promise I understand what you're saying, but you also said in the woods yesterday that we're both adults and we're both on vacation. I think we can agree that vacation is time off from reality. Much needed time off. When you're on vacation, you do things you normally wouldn't do."

She swallowed, the movement causing her lip to shift against his thumb.

Her next words came out in a hoarse whisper. "Sometimes you make really bad decisions on vacation. Then, when you go back to reality, you regret those decisions."

"Sometimes you regret them. Sometimes you don't." He reached to her waist, pulling her forward to bring her entire body flush with his. Bending down, he skimmed his lips across her cheek before pressing the tip of his nose to hers. "Which do you think this will be, Scarlet?"

She whimpered against his mouth. "Good Lord, I have no idea."

"Neither do I. But I'm more than willing to find out. Are you?"

He waited, feeling every breath that left her body and every one that entered his own. He waited for her consent, knowing he would have to step away if she refused. He waited, his heart grinding to a near stop.

She wrapped her arms around his neck. "Yes, Hunter. I'm willing."

All the air whooshed from his lungs. He reared back, grabbing her face in both hands, grounding her to him. "Are you sure?" he asked, his fingers shifting over her cheeks as he stared into her eyes.

Hunter allowed her time to respond. He needed to know she meant what she'd said. He needed her to be happy and without regret. He needed her to leave this solemn woman behind, just for a while, so his frolicking freebird could come out to play with him here and now.

After forever, Scarlet nodded. "I'm sure. I promise."

The moment he heard those words, Hunter gave her the silliest grin he could. "Well, geez. Thank goodness for that."

His Scarlet smiled then – really smiled – for the first time tonight. It was joyous and bubbly, and he laughed when he saw it. He shifted his hands to her hair, running his fingers through her smooth curls. She tilted her chin up and sighed, as if feeling sunshine on her face for the very first time. An instant later, she rested her hand over his heart.

"I'm so happy you're here with me," she sang.

His smile turned painful. "I'm happy I'm here with you, too."

Her eyes sparkled when she draped her arms over his shoulders. Hunter slipped his hands down her back, flattening his palms onto her spine to pull her further against him. His heart banged riotously in his chest as he gazed at his forest fairy. Just now, this very second, he finally, *finally*, felt like he had the right to kiss her. So, he did.

The first touch of his lips to hers created an explosion of sensation, a pulsing current that surged straight through his body. He pressed his mouth to hers, hard and strong, despite the quaking waves. When he pulled back, only after lengthy, lingering minutes spent savoring her lips, he worked to catch his breath.

Scarlet trembled and gasped against him, curling her fingers into his shirt collar. Hunter wrapped his hands tighter around her back. He wanted more of her. He wanted so much more.

He took it.

The second kiss blended seamlessly into the third, the fourth, and the fifth. He lost count at some point, lost track of everything except the soothing warmth of her skin and the smooth wetness of her tongue and the perfect sound of her tender moans. Her fingers clung to the fabric of his shirt while his hands moved restlessly up and down her satin-covered spine, but his mouth never left hers.

He kissed her every way he could think of. Softly. Aggressively. Sweetly. Hungrily. Leisurely. Urgently. Lovingly. Desperately.

Hunter tasted her tongue over and over, tangling it into his own, learning the rhythm of her movements and the pattern of her responses. He nibbled her lip, as he'd seen her do many times, pulling the delicate skin into his mouth before letting go so he could start another kiss. One time, he pushed so hard into her that their teeth clashed, and he merely smiled against her mouth while she giggled. He did everything he wanted to do, everything he'd wanted to do since the moment she first appeared before him by the side of the road, and it felt amazing and unbelievable and so very, very freeing.

When he finally eased back, he watched a slow grin pull up the corners of her mouth. Her lips were dark pink and a little swollen and it was all he could do to not devour them again. Scarlet kept her eyes closed for the longest time. Her body swayed against his, her fingers gripping ferociously to his shirt.

Hunter knew she'd probably collapse if he took a step away. "I'm not going anywhere," he assured in a gentle whisper.

The instant she heard his words, her fists uncurled and her body sank forward. She sighed heavily, letting him take her weight into his arms. He banded her against him, accustoming himself to the feel of her breasts pushed into his chest. He wasn't sure if he would ever get used to that sensation, but he sure as hell wanted to give it a try.

Scarlet let her face fall onto his shoulder, snuggling her forehead into his neck. Her fingers played with buttons on his shirt. "My heavens, you're certainly good at that," she breathed, the warm air of her hushed words brushing against his skin and raising goose bumps on his arms.

Hunter couldn't recall the last time that had happened. Hell, he was thirty-four years old. He wasn't supposed to get goose bumps anymore. "What exactly am I good at?"

"Oh my God, everything."

His hand traced up the length of her spine before pushing into her hair.

"Do you have a particular favorite kiss?" he wondered, intent to repeat whatever she liked the most.

Scarlet pulled at one of his buttons. "Um, all of them?"

He chuckled. She was going to be so easy to please. No matter how many lovers she'd had in her life, his forest fairy had a sexual innocence that made him feel simultaneously protective and predatory.

Hunter didn't even know how the coexistence of those two emotions was possible. All he knew was that part of him wanted to shelter her, and only make love to her in the dark, with the two of them cocooned inside warm, soft sheets. The other part of him wanted to teach her everything he knew, to fuck her on every surface of this cabin and in every possible way, so she would understand every imaginable sensation he could give her. Then she could tell him exactly how and where she wanted his mouth and tongue and fingers and body.

The thought of all the ways he could have her caused his thick erection to twitch into the softness of her belly. Scarlet moaned against his neck. The goose bumps crawled higher up his arms.

"What do you want to do right now?" he asked, not because he couldn't think of anything he wanted to do, but because he could think of everything he wanted to do, and the limitlessness of his imagination made it difficult to decide.

"Hmm. Can I, um, can I get this shirt off of you?"

She raised her head as she asked her tentative question. Her eyes twinkled with giddy anticipation. Hunter cupped her cheek, absorbing the excitement written in that emerald green. He made his decision then.

I'm going to make love to her tonight. Gentle and tender and sweet. Everything else can wait. At least until tomorrow.

"You can definitely take my shirt off. Would you like my help?"

Scarlet shook her head. "Nope. Uh-uh. Want to do this myself," she announced with a smile. Then she attempted to focus, her dreamy gaze drifting to his chest. She took her time unfastening each and every button, being careful with the expensive material as she worked slowly from his collar all the way down to his abdomen. When she reached his waist, she stilled and gulped, her eyes focused solely on his pants.

Sorry about the absurdly massive erection, he thought. But he didn't say it out loud, since it would've been a lie. He wasn't sorry at all.

"Everything okay?" he offered instead.

She dragged her eyes back up to his. "Um, yup," she replied, licking her lips. "I'm going to take your shirt off now, but I have to, you know, pull it out of your pants for that, so..."

"Do whatever you want to do. I'm not going to stop you."

"Okay." She kept her focus on his face as her fingers curled into the material and pulled it all the way up.

The sensation of the soft fabric sliding over his stiff length caused his breath to catch in his throat.

"Sorry," she offered.

"God, don't be sorry."

Scarlet grinned with his assurance. She looked back down, to where her fingers now rested against his bare stomach. Slowly and surely, she watched her hands move upward, tracing over the small strip of flesh his unbuttoned shirt revealed. Her fingers finally eased beneath the fabric, smoothing it over his shoulders before pulling it all the way down his arms. She'd forgotten to unbutton his sleeves, so the material caught on his wrists, effectively pinning his arms at his sides.

Hunter thought she would realize her mistake now and free his hands, but she just stood in place, staring at his bared chest. He wasn't sure if she even breathed. He didn't relax at all until she finally made a whimpering sound, assuring him that she was getting some air, at least.

"Scarlet? Is everything still okay?"

"Good Lord, Hunter. You're..." She motioned to his body with her fingers, over and over again. "You're quite, um...intimidating."

"Intimidating?"

Her eyes darted to his. "Oh, I didn't mean that in a, 'Grrr, I'm a big man who's going to be all growly with you,' way. I meant it in a, 'Holy crap, each one of your muscles looks like it's been cut by steel and I'm totally intimidated to be naked in front of you,' way."

He burst out laughing, his whole body shaking until he regained his voice. "You're gorgeous, you know. Every inch of you is gorgeous."

"How can you say that? You haven't even seen every inch of me."

"No, but I intend to. I intend to touch every inch, and taste every inch. And I already know I'm going to love every tiny piece of you."

Scarlet bit into her lip.

Hunter pulled against the constraint of his sleeves. "Dear God, please get this shirt off of me. I really need to use my hands now."

"Oh. Right." She looked down to the cuffs fisted in his fingers. "I suppose I should help with that."

"I would appreciate it," he growled through clenched teeth.

She refocused on his arm, working to find the opening of one sleeve. She'd pulled the fabric so far down that it hung to the ground, and she had to fish and fumble to find his skin. When she did, she wrestled with the tiny double buttons at his wrist, utterly fixated on her task while making curious little noises of consternation.

Her tongue slipped over her lips as she concentrated. He stared at the wet trail she'd left behind and nearly popped open his zipper.

"Scarlet. Hurry, please. I desperately need to touch you."

"Saying that doesn't help me focus at all, you know. Where in the heck was this shirt made? A magician's workshop? I feel like I need a special degree to get these buttons undone."

"Here, just...let me do it." Hunter stepped back to try to reach his hands in front of him, but the material wouldn't budge. After ten whole seconds of struggling, he gave up and yanked his arms out of the cuffs, ripping the fabric across both wrists before shoving the tenacious material to the floor. When he looked back to Scarlet, her mouth gaped.

"Oh my God! You tore it! How much did that shirt even cost?"

"I don't know, maybe a few hundred. I don't really give a shit right now."

"Well, you should! Although we can probably get it repaired. I know a good tailor in the town at the bottom of the mountain who..."

He shut her up with his mouth. Stepping into her body, he slipped his tongue past her lips and pressed her backside against the countertop. She whimpered and clung to his shoulders. The feel of her silky satin gown on his bare chest made him growl with want and desire and crazy fucking *need*. He reached down, grabbing each cheek of her ass in one of his hands, palms flush to her soft, exposed skin.

Hunter massaged her flesh as his fingers traveled closer and closer to her soft center seam. Eventually, he felt the edge of her thong panties against his fingertips. He knew this flimsy scrap of fabric was the only thing keeping him from touching her properly, and at this moment, he hated her underwear. Reaching both hands to her hips, he threaded his fingers around the dainty straps and gave a quick tug. The material snapped easily, dropping instantly to the floor.

He listened instantly as Scarlet gasped beside his ear. "I'm sorry," he offered, palming the flawless, bare flesh of her ass. "I didn't mean to tear them off."

"It's...it's okay," she panted.

Hunter pulled her harder against him, burying his face in her hair and breathing in deep, loving the fact that he could touch her freely now. That realization made him smile, but only for a second.

"Damn it," he groaned.

Scarlet pulled back to search his eyes. "What's wrong?"

"Nothing. Except I think our honesty agreement needs to go both ways, so

I have to tell you I just lied to you."

"You did?"

"I did. I'm not sorry I ripped off your panties. I'm not sorry at all. I've wanted to do that ever since I saw the tiny black triangle of your thong beneath your yoga pants yesterday morning."

"You saw my underwear through my pants yesterday? Well, that's embarrassing. I probably shouldn't wear those pants anymore."

Hunter chuckled. "I think you're missing the point, here. I didn't tell you to embarrass you. I told you because you should know I've wanted to get my hands on you for what feels like forever, and now that I've finally got you here, I want to touch you everywhere."

A strangled moan slipped past her lips.

His fingers twitched against her bottom. "It's okay for me to touch you wherever I want, right?"

"Lord, yes," Scarlet breathed, sinking against his chest and winding her arms tighter around his neck. "Feel free to do whatever you like."

It was Hunter's turn to moan. He'd never been given such an open invitation. By anyone. Ever. For anything. Yet now, his little forest fairy stood before him, smiling bright as the sun, offering him all of her.

He dropped his mouth onto hers. She tilted her head up when he pushed his tongue inside, opening herself to him without reservation. She was so trusting. She had so much faith in him. He wanted to deserve it. Wanted to make her feel cherished and needed and desired. Wanted to satisfy her in every possible way. Wanted to make her come so hard she wouldn't even remember her own name.

Hunter growled into her, sucking on her tongue as he pressed the rigid length of his erection into the softness of her belly. He allowed his hands to roam toward the center of her bottom, tracing her soft seam all the way down to the juncture of her thighs. Scarlet parted her legs, granting him the access he desired. He explored further, smoothing his fingers in from behind, seeking out what he hoped would be the very wet entrance to her sex. *Fuck*, he wasn't disappointed. She was soaking wet – even her thighs were damp – and he pressed one finger gently inside, pushing all the way into her warmth.

Scarlet moaned and shifted beneath the tender invasion, her satiny gown rubbing against him. Rolling her forehead onto his shoulder, she pressed her mouth to his chest. Her tongue peeked out over his collarbone and she hummed with the sensation, her lips pulling into a smile he could feel against his skin. Hunter pushed a second finger inside her, delving even deeper into her body.

"Mmm," she murmured, pressing down into his hand. He pulled his fingers out and then surged back in, again and again, listening attentively to the changes in her breathing. She placed more open-mouthed kisses on his chest while his other hand grasped one of her ass cheeks, pulling up to spread her further apart, granting him easier, smoother access. His fingers were coated fully in her wetness now, cocooned in her tight sheath, as his mind struggled in vain to maintain his body's composure.

Scarlet mewled and panted against his skin and Hunter dropped his head into her dark curls and shut his eyes tight. He wasn't going to last much longer like this. He needed to be inside her, and he knew this was the point where he should pick her up and carry her into the bedroom. He should place her carefully onto a plush mattress, and make soft, slow, sweet love to her, over and over, right up until morning.

But when her mouth covered his nipple, and her tongue darted out to tease, he nearly went mad. Pulling his fingers from the heat of her sex, he grasped her hips in both hands and pinned her back against the counter. "Damn it, Scarlet. I changed my mind."

She raised her face from his chest, her body turning stiff in his arms. "Are you...are you saying you don't want me anymore?"

Hunter's eyes flew to hers. "What? No! *Hell no*, that's not what I'm saying at all. I want you so goddamn badly. You have *no idea*."

"Well, geez. Thank goodness for that," she teased, relaxing back onto him. "But then what did you change your mind about?"

He squeezed tighter to her hips. "Honestly, I thought I was going to carry you into your bedroom tonight. I thought I was going to lay you down in your sheets and make love to you properly, like a gentleman. And I still have every intention of doing that, at some point before we leave this mountain. But at this very minute, I just want to fuck the hell out of you, right here on this countertop."

Scarlet's eyes widened exponentially.

Hunter smiled. "Is that okay with you?"

She didn't say a word in response. But she did nod her head so vigorously and violently that he feared she might give herself whiplash. Leaning down, he bit into her lip again, listening to her breath catch.

"Good," he whispered against her mouth.

He looked to the counter, taking a moment to move the wine bottle and glass over to the left, next to the flickering candles and the little red-and-green leaf. Then he reached down, re-grabbed his two favorite handfuls of her ass, and lifted her up to place her into the freshly cleared space. The instant she sat on the hard wood surface, he stepped between her legs. "How is this, Scarlet? You're not too cold, are you?"

"Cold? Goodness, no. I'm on fire."

Hunter reached up to trace the pulse point in her throat. "You are, aren't you?" he realized, leaning forward to kiss a path from her jaw down to her collarbone. "I love that. I love how warm you are."

She sighed and draped her arms across his back. He kissed his way to her shoulder, licking and sucking the entire time. When he reached the tiny green strap of her gown, he glared at it. "I don't want this here anymore. I want it off."

"Oh. Okay. Would you like me to…"

"I want to do it," he insisted, moving as close to the counter as his stiff length allowed, parting her thighs further. "Lift your arms, please."

She complied, reaching her fingers toward the ceiling. He took his time gathering the hem of green satin inside his palms before raising the unwanted fabric above her head. The moment he removed the gown and let it drop to the floor, Scarlet lowered her arms and looked to his face.

Hunter knew she feared his reaction to her body, but he honestly didn't understand why. Reaching to her neck, he eased his hand slowly down the smooth center of her chest, between the round, soft firmness of her breasts, and across her tiny belly. He skimmed over the juncture of her thighs last, his eyes feasting on every inch along the way.

His gaze eventually returned to hers. "Damn, you're perfect."

Scarlet smiled so brightly that it lit her entire face. She positively glowed, making him realize it wouldn't have mattered what she looked like beneath her clothes. It wouldn't have mattered if her whole body were covered in scars. She would still be absolutely beautiful.

"Do you mean it, Hunter?"

He couldn't believe she ever doubted the fact. For whatever reason, this stunning creature before him wasn't comfortable in her own skin. He wasn't sure why, except that there were definitely two women inside her. Perhaps she simply didn't know which woman truly belonged.

He took her face in both his hands. "Scarlet, trust me. You are perfect. Just as you are now, or in any way you choose to be."

Tears sprang to her eyes that instant. "Kiss me, please," she begged. They were the sweetest words he'd ever heard.

Her arms encased him the moment his lips touched hers. She opened herself entirely to his tongue and his taste and his touch. Her fingers curled into his hair, urging him closer and closer.

Hunter kissed her long and hard and forever, until the sound of her panting broke through the haze in his brain. He realized how hard her body arched against his, pleading to be filled. Scarlet moaned as her thighs hitched up on either side of his waist.

"Need to be inside you now," he mumbled against her mouth, trying to speak while pressing tiny, constant kisses across her lips.

"Yes, please. Pretty please with a cherry on top and lots of sugar."

"Mm-hmm, sugar," Hunter echoed, not exactly sure what he was even saying at this point.

Taking a step back, he reached to undo his pants. His hand brushed against his thick, swollen length and just the feel of his own fingers nearly unraveled him. He shook his head as he popped open the button.

"I'm sorry this first time isn't going to last as long as I'd like," he apologized in advance, knowing he didn't have much willpower left. He pulled down his zipper, freeing the erection that was so hard and painful it nearly required medical attention. "But I promise you, I will make you come."

Scarlet gave him a soft smile. "Don't worry; I shouldn't take long."

"You that close already?"

"Oh, yes. It'll only take a good, stiff wind to send me over the edge. Or maybe even a gentle breeze."

"Gentle breeze?" Hunter echoed as he moved back to the counter. "I think I can do a bit better than that."

He briefly considered removing his pants and boxers entirely, but that would mean too much precious time away from her, so he decided it wasn't necessary. He shoved the material roughly down to his thighs instead. Grasping fully onto her hipbones, he pulled her forward until she sat balanced on the very edge.

Scarlet steadied herself with her hands on his shoulders, bringing their bodies even closer. The head of his cock jutted up against her sex and her lips parted on a gasp. His fingers dug into her skin.

"Wrap your legs around me," he instructed, waiting in tense anticipation until she complied. The moment her warm thighs encased his waist, he rested his forehead on hers and took another deep breath. He filled his lungs with the smell of her soap and flowers, mixed now with the intoxicating scent of her arousal. "Are you ready for me?"

"Yes. Yes. I'm ready for you."

Hunter clearly heard the desperation in her voice, so he allowed himself to push slowly inside her, inch by sweet inch, savoring every moment until he was buried to the hilt in her wet heat. She was so tight, so soft, so incredibly perfect. She surrounded him, fully and completely, the overpowering sensation making him struggle to even breathe.

He clamped his eyes shut and pressed his forehead into her shoulder. A stream of curses ran through his mind as he struggled to keep control.

"Oh. My. God. Having you inside me feels *amazing*, Hunter."

"Scarlet, please. Don't say things like that to me right now. I'm barely holding on as it is."

She whimpered in response to his pained request, her arms banding around his neck. She pressed her face beside his cheek, the little puffs of her sighs infusing his skin. Wrapping her legs tighter around his waist, she linked her feet together in the middle of his back. He'd never felt anything better.

Hunter tried to move, even a little bit. He wanted to give her some friction, to give her something. But the moment he did, a surge of electricity shot down his spine and he nearly emptied himself inside her.

"Damn it," he breathed. "I'm so sorry."

She pressed her lips into his hair. "Why are you sorry?"

He lifted his head. "I can't seem to get control over myself. I'm trying to give you an earth-shattering experience, yet I can barely keep from coming this instant, simply from the warmth of your body. I feel like some fumbling teenager. You'd think I'd never had sex before."

"Oh, no, I don't think that at all," she said with a firm shake of her head. "I can tell you're experienced. Like really, really experienced."

Scarlet grinned at him after she made her comment. The happy glow on her face was rapidly overcome by sheer terror.

"No, wait!" she yelped. "I didn't mean to suggest you have that much experience. I'm not saying you've slept with every woman on the East Coast, or any number remotely near that. I just remember you telling me you'd been with a lot of women in high school, and now that you're an adult – with this body and those eyes and that smile – I figure you've had a lot more since. But I don't mean that in a negative way. Not at all. I'm not saying you're a scoundrel or anything. I was actually trying to reassure you that you're incredibly good at this whole thing. Which I now realize I probably did not succeed in doing."

Hunter waited patiently for her speech to run its course.

"Scoundrel?" he questioned. "Did you just call me a scoundrel?"

"No, I said you aren't a scoundrel. But I am sorry about the word choice. Did you ever see that scene in *The Empire Strikes Back*, when Han Solo is about to kiss Princess Leia, and she calls him a scoundrel?"

"Yes, I saw it."

"Well, I always thought that was pretty sexy, so..."

"Are you actually thinking about *Star Wars* right now?"

"Oh, well, I'm not actively thinking about *Star Wars*, like with the flying spaceships and all that. It was more just the sexy scene part, if that helps. I don't know. Does that help?"

Scarlet cringed and bit into her lip.

He reached up to pull her lip from her teeth, running his thumb across the indentations she'd made. "You know, oddly enough, it helps," he said, pulling the full length of his erection slowly out of her warmth before sinking entirely back inside her again.

Hunter watched her eyelids flutter in response. He was grateful to be back in control of his body. The scoundrel conversation was truly helpful, not because it lessened his desire for her, but because it renewed his determination to make her enjoy this moment as much as he would.

"Kiss me," he demanded, needing to pull his frolicking freebird back to him. He needed to have her present and aware and ready. After all, he had every intention of proving what a scoundrel could do for her.

She leaned forward, tentatively slipping her lips over his. He smiled at the shyness of her actions, given that he was currently buried deep inside her body. The next instant, he took control.

Hunter devoured her, tangling his tongue with hers while digging his fingers into the flesh of her hips. He gripped her body for leverage, so he could drive inside her with expert precision. He found an exceptional rhythm, thrusting in and out of her slick walls so easily, as her arms tightened further around his shoulders with each passing second.

The sweetest, sexiest little pants escaped her throat with every lunge he made. He forced himself to slow down after a while, resting his forehead onto hers so he could savor the delicate, delightful sounds. While he listened, his gaze slipped down to her chest. Her breasts shook with each one of his full, determined thrusts, making his mouth water. The luscious sight forced Hunter to stop moving altogether.

Scarlet whimpered in distress. "Wh-why did you stop?"

"Because I need you to lean back on the counter. Now, please."

She didn't hesitate, resting back on her arms and spreading her fingers out on the wood. "How is this? Is it good?"

"It's perfect," he assured, taking the weight of her breast in his hand. He dipped his head to center his lips over her nipple and sucked in hard.

"Great...hell...damn," she breathed, her nonsensical curse making him smile against her chest. Hunter supported her low back with his other hand, keeping her close while he feasted. He restarted his rhythmic thrusts, trying to keep them measured and deliberate so he would have ample time to enjoy her body.

Her skin tasted both sweet and salty on his tongue, the effect more intoxicating than any alcohol. He dragged his mouth from one breast to the other, although he didn't recall making that decision. He only knew he wanted more of her. He wanted everything she would give.

When his teeth grazed her nipple, turning the pink bud hard and jutting beneath his tongue, Scarlet gasped and squealed. She wrenched one hand into his hair, mumbling unintelligible words that sounded like curses and prayers rolled together. He kept driving his stiff shaft into her sex, again and again, while sliding his tongue over her skin.

As the candles beside them burned down to the quick, her fingers clamped painfully against his scalp with every thrust. Hunter didn't care about the pain. In truth, he enjoyed it. But it did cause a fevered rush of sensation, making his whole body throb.

He knew he didn't have much time left. He picked up his pace, anchoring her hips at the edge of the counter so he could lunge harder and faster. "Oh… oh…Hunter," she moaned, her hot, panted breaths slipping from her lips each and every time he drove inside.

When her entire body contracted around his, with all her muscles strung tight as a bow, he lifted his head and reached one hand to her face. He pulled her back to him, planting his lips on hers, desperate to be with her at the end.

The moment he pushed his tongue into her mouth, she exploded around him. The inner walls of her sex tightened fiercely, milking his cock until he saw stars. Hunter let himself go, spilling deep inside her, since he didn't have any other choice. They screamed out in unison, their carnal shouts echoing off the log floors, log walls, and log ceiling.

"Holy fuck," he groaned against her lips, his entire body lit on fire.

"Yes, yes, that," she chanted, clutching his hair like a lifeline.

He supported her as best he could in the haze of his delirium. His arms encased her, hands spanning her back while he emptied himself completely inside her slick, clenched sheath. His head collapsed onto her shoulder, his face pressing fully into her sweat-dampened skin.

Scarlet sagged against him, her cheek flopping against his hair. He wanted to lift her up, to raise her body higher, but he was incapable of movement. He could only wait for the air to return to his lungs and his pulse to resume a normal pace.

That all took time. A lot of time. He didn't know how long.

When his wild heart rate finally slowed, Hunter still didn't move. He refused to release her. He refused to leave her body, even though he was utterly spent and should most definitely withdraw.

He just didn't want to let her go. Hell, if he could be hard again this instant, he would stay here indefinitely. He would never leave.

"Wow," Scarlet whispered beside his ear. "That was just…wow."

He dragged his head up so he could witness the jeweled gleam in her eyes. "Am I still a scoundrel?"

She giggled. "I said you aren't a scoundrel."

"Well, give me a few more chances. You might change your mind."

"Oh, no, I won't ever change my mind. Never, ever. You're not a scoundrel, Hunter. You're lovely and kind and giving and wonderful. Everything about you is simply wonderful."

Scarlet ran her fingers back into his hair, smoothing the tufts she'd created moments ago. She gazed on him with glassy eyes and a silly grin, looking absolutely drunk with pleasure. He didn't know if he'd ever seen anything more beautiful in his entire life.

His arms tightened around her of their own volition. He clung to her – just *clung* to her. In this moment, he accepted an obvious truth: he needed this woman. For these few days of his life, for every second he remained up here on this mountain, he needed her with him. He needed her more than he needed food or water or air.

He accepted that fact because it was undeniable.

But it still scared the living hell out of him.

Scarlet traced her fingers down his face, looking into him with the most adoring eyes. Hunter's heart pounded frantically against his ribcage as he watched her. His palms dampened. His throat tightened. She was so close. She was too close. He blinked and straightened his spine, suddenly desperate to fight this unyielding hold she had on him.

Untangling himself from the cocoon of her limbs, he mumbled, "I...I need to be excused. To go to the restroom. For a minute."

Scarlet's head tilted before she dropped her hands back down on the countertop. "Of course. It's right down the hall."

When Hunter pulled out of her body, a sense of profound loss descended on him, bringing with it a shit-storm of pain. He turned away from her, yanking his pants back up and grabbing his torn shirt from the floor. He strode swiftly down the hall and into the bathroom.

The instant he stepped inside, he shut the door, dropped his shirt over the edge of the tub, pivoted toward the sink, and shoved the faucet on. He stuck his hands beneath the cold mountain water, bending down to splash the icy liquid over his burning face. It was fucking freezing, stunning him for a moment before forcing him to suck air into his lungs.

He concentrated on the task of breathing for several minutes. When he could manage it without conscious thought, he shut off the water and grabbed a towel from the antler rack, running the soft fabric across his face and neck. After drying his cooled skin, he stood at the sink and stared into the mirror.

Hunter didn't know who stared back at him. He didn't know what was happening here. He only knew what he felt tonight wasn't normal. That wasn't just sex. That wasn't just a good fuck against a countertop. He honestly didn't know what it was. And he really didn't know where to go from here, or how to even find a path forward.

"What the hell are you thinking?" he questioned his reflection. He didn't have any sort of answer, so all he could do was sigh and shake his head. At a loss for explanations, he gave up trying to figure anything out right now. Instead, he hung the towel up and turned to grab his shirt.

When he shifted toward the bathtub, his eyes fastened to the side of the sink. His entire body stilled while he stared at the strangest sight – the perfectly ordered set of personal care items sitting there on the ledge. All of Scarlet's things, her deodorant, toothpaste, toothbrush, makeup, hairbrush, and perfume, sat distinctly arranged in an immaculate pattern.

Hunter's jaw fell open. He gawked at each product in turn, not quite sure if his eyes deceived him. He stood frozen in place for several more seconds. Then he laughed out loud.

"Good Lord, is she a frolicking freebird at all?" he questioned. "Does happy, carefree Scarlet even exist? Or is the real Scarlet just like me, a stressed-out executive trying desperately to make life better?"

Hunter still didn't have any answers. But he did grab hold of her deodorant and move it to the end of the product line. That made him smile. It was a wicked smile, honestly. But it was still a smile.

When he could tear his eyes away from that peculiar view, he picked his shirt up off the edge of the bathtub. As he pushed his arms through his torn sleeves, his eyes drifted over her bear-claw-footed soaking tub. He instantly pictured his freebird perched inside the porcelain basin, with candles glowing on the ledge behind her and bubbles clinging to her gorgeously naked body.

"Fuck, yes," he assured himself, unquestionably certain that he needed to have her in this tub with him at some point. He'd never be able to leave this mountain with any sense of accomplishment unless he did that.

Holding onto the perfect image of wet, naked Scarlet in his mind, Hunter buttoned his shirt and rolled the torn sleeves up to his elbows. In truth, he thought his shirt looked better this way – more relaxed. He smiled before opening the door, having successfully quelled his panic attack and wanting nothing more than to see her again. He needed to get back to his forest fairy, or whoever she was at the moment.

When he came around the corner of the hallway, he saw her standing in the kitchen with her back leaning against the counter. She'd pulled her robe on, tightened the ties around her stomach, and now stared at the floor while chewing on her thumbnail. Her shoulders were tight as a drum and he could sense her anxiety from across the room. His stomach sank to his feet.

Damn you, Hunter. You did this to her.

He took a tentative step toward her. "Hey there, beautiful."

Scarlet's head popped up with the sound of his voice, her arms falling to her sides. He moved forward until they stood face to face. Hunter looked into her jeweled eyes, now dull with fear.

"Do you regret it already?" she whispered, blinking back tears.

He wanted to grab hold of his chest in a vain attempt to control the sharp, stabbing pain inside. Instead, he grabbed hold of her face. "I don't regret anything, Scarlet. I never will."

With his assurance, a tiny smile pulled up the edges of her lips.

Hunter returned her smile as best he could. "Do you want me to stay the night?" he asked, unable to bear the thought of her feeling alone.

Part of him wanted her to say yes, so he could carry her into the bedroom and make love to her now. But the other part of him needed her to say no, because this was all too much, too soon, and he had to keep some walls intact.

Scarlet observed him for a long while before shaking her head. "No, you shouldn't stay. You should go home and get some rest."

"Oh. Okay. Only if you're sure."

"I'm sure," she said, reaching up to run her fingers across his jaw. "I'd like you to come back for dinner tomorrow, though. If you want."

"Yes," he accepted without hesitation. "I would love that."

"Wonderful. What's your favorite food?"

"Steak."

"That's what we'll eat, then. I'll have Colin bring your dinner here."

"Fantastic. I'll see you back here tomorrow night."

The moment he promised Scarlet a tomorrow, all the tension eased from her body. She grinned up at him, bouncing on the balls of her feet.

"Kiss me one more time, Hunter?"

He matched her grin while leaning down to press his lips to hers. As he started to pull away, he went back in and claimed her mouth again. "That was two kisses," he announced when he straightened. "I'm a scoundrel like that."

She laughed, running her fingers down his arm to squeeze his hand.

"Goodnight, Scarlet."

He stepped away, not letting go of her hand until he had no choice. After retrieving his jacket from the couch, he headed to the door.

"Goodnight, Hunter."

He looked back, absorbing her gorgeous smile, before stepping outside into the cold night air.

7

GREEN AND RED

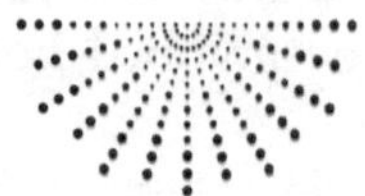

Hunter's alarm didn't wake him the next morning.

Probably because he hadn't set an alarm.

He woke instead to a bird chirping outside his bedroom window. It was a soothing sound, working its way into his mind to pull him slowly from the bliss of his dreams. Except they weren't just dreams...they were memories. Memories of last night. Memories of Scarlet. Of holding her, of kissing her, of being inside her.

A smile curved his lips before he even opened his eyes. He could still smell her tiny flowers and fresh soap, most likely because he'd worn his shirt, complete with torn sleeves, to bed. Or maybe he could still smell her because she was here with him even when she wasn't.

Hunter sat up in bed, placing his feet on the hard wood floor. He rested his elbows on his knees and stared at the log wall. He recalled staring into the mirror in Scarlet's bathroom last night, not knowing exactly what had happened between them or what he'd been thinking.

Honestly, he still didn't know what he'd been thinking. Well, except for the obvious thought. He'd wanted her, plain and simple.

Hunter pressed his fingers into his eyelids as he thought of what he'd truly done last night. He'd desired nothing more in the entire world than to be inside of Scarlet, so he made it happen. Of course, he'd given her a choice in the matter. But had he really given her that much of a choice? His little bird was sexually innocent, yet he'd come on stronger than he ever had with any woman in his life. He'd used every bit of charm and charisma he possessed to convince her to let him in.

Looking back on his actions in the cold light of day, Hunter realized it wasn't very fair of him. The moment she'd agreed to be honest with him, he knew he'd won. She obviously desired his touch and couldn't lie to say she didn't. So, he'd pushed her – with his words and with his body – until he had her right where he wanted her. Then he simply took what he wanted.

Dropping his hands onto the mattress, Hunter shook his head. Scarlet had asked him last night if he regretted being with her. But the real question was whether or not she would regret being with him.

He sucked in a painful breath and stood. Stepping to the dresser, he peeled off his old clothes and grabbed a T-shirt and shorts. He tried not to think about what his freebird might be doing this morning, especially if she was busy drowning in regret. He tried not to think about anything at all as he retrieved his breakfast tray from the porch and settled down on his green-and-red plaid couch cushions. But as Hunter shoved a bite of croissant into his mouth, he couldn't help imagining Scarlet lying in bed beside him now, feeding him breakfast.

He would have liked the chance to wake up beside her this morning. To be honest, he would have absolutely relished the opportunity to curl his body around hers, and bury his face in her hair, and catch a glimpse of her smile in the early light of dawn. Still, he knew it was best for both of them that he'd left when he did last night. He'd needed time to recoup from that particular encounter. Scarlet probably needed time, too. He figured that was the reason she'd encouraged him to leave.

But none of that mattered now. Today was a new day, and Hunter had a chance to set everything right. In just a few hours, they would see each other again. This evening, they would share a normal, peaceful dinner together. He would sit across a candlelit table from her, eat his favorite food with her, talk with her, and laugh with her. And when they finished their meal, he would take her into her bedroom and make love to her – slowly and gently and sweetly. Then, tomorrow morning, he would wake with his little bird in his arms.

Blissfully certain of how this day would play out, Hunter finished his food with a smile plastered to his lips. When he stood from the couch, his eyes darted to the empty desk in the corner of the room. His trusted computer sat in its case on the floor, where he'd shoved it yesterday afternoon. The internet cord Pete had given him hung out of the side.

Hunter walked to the desk and grabbed the cord. He wound it up and shoved it in the pocket of his gym shorts. Then he returned his food tray to the porch, locked the door, and started up the gravel driveway.

While he walked, he felt the cord jostle against his leg. The thought of giving up this lifeline made him feel a bit nauseous, but he needed to finally take the advice Pete had given him his first day at Blue: to disconnect from the real world for as long as he was on this mountain. Hunter could do that now. He didn't need to cling to his work anymore, because he'd found another lifeline. He could cling to Scarlet.

In truth, he didn't have a choice in the matter. He had to cling to her. Thankfully, his frolicking freebird would give him anything he needed. Knowing for certain that Scarlet would willingly be his lifeline soothed him, for the most part. But it was also the reason he had a slight panic attack after they were together last night. Relying on someone that much – especially someone he'd just met – was terrifying, at best.

Hunter was used to his independence. He was used to being in control and wasn't sure if he could ever give it up. Not even for her.

~

Hunter jumped up off the blacktop and shot at the basket. He watched the basketball bounce off the rim into Tyler's waiting hands. Again.

Tyler cocked his head. "Damn, man. No offense, but your playing sucks today. Are you okay?"

Hunter blinked. "What?"

"I'm just wondering what's going on with you right now," Tyler continued, stuffing the ball under his arm. "Yesterday you were distracted, and this morning you're in another world."

"I'm...I'm sorry."

"Don't be. I just want to help. Are you thinking about Mitzi?"

"Who?"

"Mitzi Fisher? The incredibly gorgeous woman you talked to for hours at the Social last night?"

"Mitzi. Right," Hunter recalled. "No, I'm not thinking about her."

"I see. I guess." Tyler studied him for a moment before his eyebrows shot up. "Oh, shit. I really do see. Hell, I'm sorry, buddy. I swear I didn't know. But now that I do, I won't push it anymore."

"What are you talking about?"

"I just – I didn't realize you're gay. But now that I know, I promise I'll stop. I won't keep trying to push women at you over and over."

"Tyler, I'm not gay."

"Hey, it's okay with me if you are. I'm not one of those people who will judge you because of who you love. I've actually tried being gay a few times myself. Or more bisexual, I guess."

Hunter smiled. "Okay, I won't judge, either. But I'm not gay. And as much as I appreciate your friendship, I actually don't need your help with the ladies."

"No? Why not?"

The words were on the tip of his tongue, but Hunter bit them back. Lord help him, he didn't want Tyler to know about Scarlet. He'd seen the man operate too many times to feel comfortable giving him her name. "It's nothing. No reason."

Tyler grinned wildly. "It's a woman, isn't it? You met someone."

Hunter reached out to knock the basketball from his friend's slack arm. He dribbled toward the net. "Why would you think that?"

"It's the only thing that makes sense. You're totally preoccupied, one minute you look confused as hell, then the next minute you've got a dopey smile on your face. Only a woman can drive a man that crazy."

Hunter jumped up and slammed the ball through the hoop. Dropping back to the ground, he turned and tossed it to his friend. "Yes, she can drive you crazy, but she can also make you feel like..."

"Like LeBron James, apparently."

"Yeah. Just like that."

Tyler dribbled toward the basket. "So, are you planning to share the name of this mystery woman with me?"

"Sorry," Hunter said, knocking the ball from his hands. "I don't kiss and tell."

"*Kiss* and tell?"

He clenched his fingers around the basketball to keep from fumbling. "Well, that's just an expression, it's not..."

"I know exactly what it is. Damn, you're blushing! You were with Mitzi half the night. How'd you hook up with another lady so quickly?"

"Hey, it's not that quick. I mean, I didn't go out after the Social and pick up a complete stranger. I've known this woman for a while now."

"Yeah? How long is a while?"

His heartbeat tripped. Tyler was asking him to define something he hadn't had the chance to define for himself. Not that he could define it, even if he tried his damnedest. "Six days. I've known her for six days."

"Six whole days, huh? Wow, that is a while. When's the wedding?"

Hunter huffed out a laugh. "Okay, okay, I get your point. I haven't known her forever. But does that even matter up here at Blue? It's not like we're dating. She and I are...we're both just...on vacation."

As the words left his mouth, Hunter's stomach churned. Still, he'd spoken the truth. This thing with Scarlet wasn't permanent. They were just two people who'd found each other for a brief period of time. They were just two people holding onto each other at the top of a mountain.

"You're sure that's all it is?" Tyler questioned. "Because you look awfully involved for a guy who is only having a little fling on vacation."

"Yes, I'm sure. That's all it is."

After all, it's not like I'm going to take Frolicking Freebird Scarlet home to meet my parents. I mean...I'm not going to do that. Am I?

"She and I are both just on vacation," Hunter reiterated, although he wasn't exactly sure which of them he was trying to convince.

"Well, okay, then. Good luck with that, buddy." Tyler knocked the ball out of his hand, dribbled up to the basket, and dunked it in.

Hunter stood there and stared.

∼

AN HOUR LATER, Hunter left his friend at the gym and started walking down the road toward the information cabin. He was still rattled by their conversation on the basketball court, but the more he walked, the more his head cleared. He didn't have to define this thing with Scarlet. She certainly wasn't asking him to define it. They were both adults. Both on vacation. Both in need of someone to touch. That was all this was. That was all it needed to be.

Hunter knew Blissful Blue wasn't reality. They were here because they needed a break from reality, and he wanted to give her that. He wanted to help his little bird, even if only for these few days.

The information cabin came into view straight ahead, redirecting his mind to the purpose of his afternoon journey. He continued down the driveway and up the porch stairs to the thick mahogany door. Turning the handle, he stepped into the overgrown tree house.

Inside the large front room, the fireplace still sparked and glowed, the cinnamon and pine scents still accosted his nostrils, and the deer antlers still hung over the oak desk, just as they had the day he'd arrived. Only now, he didn't panic at the sight. In fact, as he watched Pete look up from his crossword puzzle, Hunter felt a smile spread his lips. He imagined Scarlet standing in front of the little gnome caretaker, wringing her hands while asking for non-latex condoms. The image of her adorably scrunched brow sent a shot of warmth through his body.

"Hey there, Mr. Jackson," he offered while moving up to the desk.

"Aw, I told you to call me Pete, Mr. Gregory."

"I remember. And I'd like for you to call me Hunter, please."

The kindly old man grinned as he peered over the top of his bifocals. "Now, that is something I can do," he agreed, setting his crossword puzzle down. "It's been a busy day today. I don't normally get so many visitors. What can I do for you? Maybe schedule a therapy session?"

"No, thanks. I just wanted to bring you this." Hunter reached into his pocket and pulled out the internet cable. He set the cord on the desk.

"Well, finally," the gnome sighed. "You held onto it a lot longer than most first-timers. Ever been told you're a bit tenacious, Hunter?"

He chuckled. "Maybe once or twice."

"Good for you, for bringing it back," Pete praised, grabbing the cord in his stubby fingers and shoving it under the desk. "Since you're here, let me give you an updated list of the doctors on staff this week."

"No, I'm...I'm really not here to schedule a therapy session."

"I know you're not." He laid the paper out on the desktop. "But it's always good to have the information, in case you change your mind."

Hunter glanced down at the list. His eyes shifted over the names of the various physicians, but he only recognized one: Adrien Abbott. He ran his finger across the printed letters.

"Dr. Abbott," Pete observed. "Have you seen him around?"

"I just heard some guests talking about him at the Social last night."

"He'd be a good fit for you, I think. Abbott is very no-nonsense. Usually does well with the hard-working types, like yourself."

Hunter looked to Pete's gentle blue eyes. "I appreciate the advice, but I think I'm good."

"Well, you take that paper on home with you, anyway. If you do change your mind, just give me a call."

"Okay," Hunter agreed, not wanting to disappoint the little gnome. "Thanks, Pete."

"Anytime, Hunter."

He grabbed the list of names and walked back out of the cabin.

~

A MILLION HOURS passed before dinnertime. That might have been a slight exaggeration. Still, it felt pretty close to real time.

Hunter stood by the window of his living room, waiting for the sun to set. He'd returned from the information cabin a lifetime ago, showered and dressed, and paced the log floors until his feet hurt. Colin would be delivering his meal to Scarlet's tonight, so he couldn't even distract himself by talking to the red-hooded young man.

Having to wait this long to see her was torture. Hunter stood in front of his mirror more than once, trying to find the right outfit. Eventually, he chose khakis and a black button-down shirt, thinking he looked formal enough for a nice dinner, despite his short sleeves. He just didn't want Scarlet to have to deal with any buttons on his wrists tonight.

When dusk finally came, he flew out of his door, barely getting it shut behind him. Frigid air surrounded him as he strode away from his cabin up to the paved road. He probably should have worn a jacket, but the heated blood rushing through his veins made the chill bearable. He told himself to act calm and casual, knowing he shouldn't make more of this relationship with Scarlet than what it was. Yet his pulse still raced when he arrived at the entrance to her driveway.

Taking a step onto her gravel, listening to it crunch under his shoes as he hurried forward, Hunter wondered how his forest fairy would feel now, after what they'd done last night. Would she be excited to see him again, bouncing through her cabin with giddy smiles and laughter? Would she be shy in his presence, fumbling with her words and her fingers? Would his little bird be all-aflutter? Or demure? Or regretful?

Please don't let her be regretful. I can handle anything but that.

He didn't want Scarlet to regret anything, even though he'd basically seduced her into letting him fuck her on a countertop. But he would make up for that. Tonight, he'd be a perfect gentleman. He'd make love to her the right way. And in the morning, it would all be okay.

When her cabin came into view, a smile lit his face. That smile only lasted for a second. Once he took a good look, his footsteps faltered.

Scarlet's cabin was completely dark. There was no light coming from the windows at all. It was pitch black inside.

For a moment, Hunter's vision blurred. The only thing he could imagine was that she'd left. After everything they'd shared these past days, even after last night, she'd simply packed up her things and gone.

That thought stabbed like a knife in his chest.

He started running. "Scarlet?" he called out when he was within a few feet of the cabin. "Are you there?"

An instant later, Hunter bounded up onto her porch. "Scarlet!" he yelled, raising his hand to pound ferociously on the thick wood door. Before he had the chance, it opened. A blast of scorching hot air struck him in the face.

His utter relief that she hadn't abandoned him transformed into fear of the sweltering heat roiling toward him from inside her cabin. He hesitated, unsure if he should cross the dark, infernal threshold. "Damn, why is it so hot in there? Did you start a fire?"

"Nothing is on fire this minute," Scarlet spoke from behind the door.

"Was there a fire before? And can you please turn on a light?"

"Nope, no fire. And no lights. Just step inside."

"What?"

"I want you to step into the living room, please."

Hunter sucked in one last lungful of cool mountain air before doing as she asked. He moved a couple feet into the boiling cabin, trying in vain to discern the log shapes in the darkness. As soon as he entered, the door snapped shut behind him and the lock clicked into place.

"Can you please tell me what's going on here?" he asked, trying to quell the lingering panic in his voice. "When I saw all the lights off in your cabin, it worried me sick."

"Everything is fine," Scarlet assured, her melodic voice coming from over his shoulder. As he turned toward her, her hand wrapped around his forearm, gently restraining his actions. "Don't move, please. I need you to stand very still right now."

"Why?"

She eased her fingers up over his bicep. "Do you trust me, Hunter?"

"Yes," he answered without hesitation.

"Good, because I want us to do something a bit unusual tonight."

"Unusual? How unusual?"

"Do you feel this?" she asked, running a soft fabric across his hand.

Hunter clenched the material in his fist. "It's silky."

"It is. It's a silk scarf. I would like to blindfold you with it."

"*Blindfold me*? Why in the hell do you want to do that?"

"Because I've never done it before, and I've always had a fantasy about blindfolding a man before I have sex with him. I thought tonight could be the perfect opportunity, if you're willing."

Hunter nearly swallowed his tongue. *Did she just say what I think she said? And why is it so dark in here? And so hot? And holy shit, did she just say what I think she said?*

"Are you being serious right now, Scarlet?"

"I am," she answered, dragging the fluid fabric away from his hand and up his arm. "I'd like to do this very much. Provided you'll let me."

"I...I..." Hunter began a thought, not knowing how to finish. His mind scattered in a hundred directions as his pants grew uncomfortably tight. "I just need a minute to process all this. If that's okay with you."

"It's perfectly fine."

"Good, because I'm not exactly sure what's happening right now. I thought I was coming over here for a nice dinner, but instead, it's pitch black and crazy hot and you're trying to wrap a scarf around my head. And you also mentioned having sex, which I'm definitely not opposed to, but it's a little difficult to absorb so much information at once..."

His voice trailed off, his head tilting in her general direction. "Wait a minute, here. Have you honestly never blindfolded a man before?"

"That's the thing you want to focus on?"

"To start with, yes."

"No," she sighed. "I've never blindfolded a man before."

"But you have a fantasy about it."

"I do. I'll admit I'm curious about a few things, and I really want to try this. With you, specifically, if that helps."

Hunter inhaled sharply when she stroked his arm, concentrating on the feel of her petting him. God, he'd missed that today. He'd missed her touch. He'd missed her voice. He'd missed every damn thing about her. He'd even missed all the surprises that came with her. In fact, he'd probably missed them most of all.

"Okay, then," he acquiesced, wanting to make her smile, even if he wouldn't be able to see it. "If this is what you want, if it'll make you happy, go ahead."

Her hand stilled against his. "Are you sure?"

"Yes, I'm sure. You can blindfold me."

Scarlet laughed. It was a luminous sound, like sunshine bursting through the pitch black room. Hunter held very still when she moved to stand behind him. Her hands brushed his hair while she wrapped the silky material over his eyes and tied it behind his head. She didn't pull too hard, but she did make sure the blindfold was secure.

"How is it, Hunter? Not too tight?"

"It's fine."

"And you can't see anything through it, right?"

"I don't think so. But I'm not sure, since it's dark as hell in here."

"Oh, yeah, sorry." She moved away from him, bustling about a few feet ahead. "I'm going to fix that now."

A distinct snap filled his ears. Hunter saw a haze of color from behind the silk scarf. "Are you lighting candles?"

"I set a few on the coffee table. But you can't see me, can you?"

"No. Just a faint yellow glow."

"Good."

The blur that was her body straightened before him. He huffed at his inability to see her face. "Scarlet, please tell me what's happening here tonight. I really thought we were going to have a nice dinner together."

"We are having dinner. I won't let you go hungry."

"But what's with the blindfold? And the darkness? And the heat?"

"Don't worry. I promise there wasn't a fire in here earlier. It's only this hot because I turned the thermostat all the way up."

"You did this on purpose? Can I ask why?"

"Because I don't want you to get cold when you're naked."

Hunter coughed. "And when, exactly, am I going to be naked?"

"Right now is good for me. I'd like for you to undress, please."

"You want me to undress here? In the middle of your living room?"

"Mm-hmm. I want to see all of you."

"But I can't see any of you."

"Yeah, it's funny how those blindfolds work, isn't it?"

Scarlet laughed again, the sparkling sound seeping deep into his skin. Hunter fisted his hands, tempted to reach up and snatch this scarf off of his face so he could reclaim a modicum of control. But then her fingers slipped down his arm again, petting him perfectly, and he sighed.

"You're really happy right now, aren't you?" he asked, not because he didn't know the answer, but because he wanted her to acknowledge the smile that must be lighting her whole face.

"Yes, I am. I'm blissfully happy."

The bashfulness in her voice shot fresh warmth through his body. He imagined how lively and gleaming her eyes would be, if he could only see them. He imagined how her body would thrum with excitement for this sexual venture, if he could only touch her. "I'm glad you're doing so well."

"I am doing well. But how are you, Hunter?"

He knew exactly how he was. He was whipped. Right this minute, he couldn't possibly deny her anything. "I'm actually doing pretty well myself. And, apparently, I'm going to get undressed now."

"Oh my gosh! Are you really? That's fantastic!"

Scarlet clapped then. She actually clapped.

Hunter chuckled as he reached for his shirt. "I don't think I've ever had anyone clap for me while I undress." He undid the front buttons and pulled the material open across his chest.

She made a choking sound when his shirt hit the floor. "Well, that's ridiculous. You should definitely be applauded for undressing. Have you seen you?"

He smiled as he kicked off his shoes and socks. "I'm much more interested in seeing you," he insisted, popping open the button on his pants. She made another odd sound, like a gulping squeak.

Hunter could feel her eyes glued to his every move, which made his cock grow harder as he stripped. When he undid his zipper, his jutting length forced its way out. He shoved his pants and boxers to the floor so he could stand before her, naked as a jaybird, with his entire body erect.

"Okay, Scarlet. You've got me blindfolded and naked. What on earth are you going to do with me now?"

"Well...I just...uh..."

He wasn't certain what had her brain muddled at this moment. He hoped it was the sight of his overly eager cock begging for her attention. But he couldn't be sure, not with this goddamn scarf covering his eyes.

"I, um, I actually want to try something else unusual, Hunter."

"Yeah? What's that?"

He held very still, listening as her footsteps padded across the floor. Her body circled around his. She came to a stop behind him.

"Will you put your hands behind your back?" she asked. "Please?"

Hunter placed both hands behind him.

She set another thing inside his palms. "Do you feel that?"

"What am I feeling now? Is that...is that a *rope*?"

"It is."

His fingers clenched around the hard twine. "Good God, woman! What has gotten into you tonight?"

She laughed again, even brighter than before, and he knew exactly what had gotten into her tonight. This was Frolicking Freebird Scarlet at her finest. She was with him now, in all her glory, and he probably didn't stand a chance against whatever she had planned.

That thought should terrify him. Yet it didn't. At least, not entirely.

"Honestly, I just want to try some things that are entirely new for me," she explained, stepping closer but still not touching him. "And in that spirit of adventure, I'd like to use this rope to tie you up a bit."

"A bit? What exactly does *a bit* mean?"

"It means I'd like to tie your hands behind your back. Just your hands. I'm sorry the rope is scratchy. I only packed one scarf."

"But you also packed *rope*?"

"No, I didn't pack rope."

"Then how did you get it?"

"If you must know, I got it from Pete earlier today."

"Pete? Seriously? You told me you'd feel nervous asking him for *condoms*, yet you felt perfectly comfortable asking him for *rope*?"

"I guess that does sound odd."

"Yes, it does. I can't believe you asked sweet old Pete for a rope and he just gave it to you."

"Well, I've known Pete for a long time. He trusts me."

"Yeah, but still. Nearly deserted mountains, a bunch of psychiatric patients, and a rope, don't exactly add up to the best combination. Did he at least ask you what it was for?"

"He did. And I did not tell him I planned to tie you up for sex, if that's what you're worried about."

"Well, thank God for that. But what *did* you tell him?"

"*Hunter*," she breathed, leaning forward to press her body against his spine – her tantalizingly, maddeningly, utterly naked body. "Do you really want to stand here and discuss Pete right now?"

Her tight nipples grazed across his back. Her soft lips pressed against his shoulder blade. Her bare tummy pressed into his hands, which he still held behind him. Even with the rope between them, he could trace the smooth outline of her bellybutton with his fingertips.

"You're, um...you're naked," he mastered the obvious.

"Yes, I am."

"Have you been naked this whole time?"

"I have. Which is why the lights were out when you came in, since I wanted it to be a surprise. It's also the reason it's so hot in here, because I didn't want to freeze to death while waiting for you."

"Were you naked when Colin delivered our dinners?"

Her forehead collapsed onto his shoulder as her body shook with laughter. "No. *No.* Definitely not. Now, can we please get back to the rope thing?" She straightened, her body losing all contact with his. She even let the rope drop from his hands, so he could return his arms to his sides. "If you don't want me to tie you up, I promise I'll understand."

"I didn't say that," Hunter protested. After all, this wasn't his first venture into kinky sex. He'd been tied up by women before. He'd also been the one to do the tying. But with Scarlet, he didn't think kinkiness was the real reason she wanted this, and not knowing her true motive was far more disturbing than her being a closeted dominatrix. "Before I agree, I'd just like to know *why* you want to tie me up."

"That's fair," she granted, although he could hear the hesitance in her voice. "To be honest, I don't have a very active sex-fantasy life. At least, not compared to other people I've met. But I do have a few fantasies, and this is one I've always wanted to try. Also, aside from the novelty, I think it could be a really good bonding experience. Which sounds funny, since it's both literal and figurative."

"You think tying me up is going to be a bonding experience for us?"

"I think it could be."

"Why?"

"Because it's unplanned."

Hunter huffed. "Well, we both know that's not true. You've planned this all day, at least. Unless...did you plan this before today? Damn, how long ago did you plan this?"

"Just today, I promise. I got the idea last night, when your arms were pinned to your sides by your shirtsleeves. And yes, I did plan all this, but that's not the point. The point is that *you* didn't plan it."

"Why is that the point?"

"Because I think everything in your life is planned. Completely and utterly planned, in exceptional detail, by you. Am I wrong?"

This from the woman who lines up her toiletries the same way I do.

"Just so you know, Scarlet, I do some things very spontaneously."

"You do? Like what?"

"Um..." He tried to think of an answer, but it was difficult. First, because he rarely did anything spontaneously. Second, because having her naked body so close to his warped his mind. "Well, I came up here for vacation, didn't I?"

"And how long did it take you to get your affairs in order first?"

Hunter's shoulders fell. "A month," he grumbled.

"Wow. That's a lot of planning for a spontaneous vacation."

"Okay, okay. I'm a planner. It's not a crime."

"No, it's not. But I'm asking you, just once, to let that go. I'm asking you to trust me. Let me be in control tonight. Please."

Fuck. He didn't want to do this. He didn't want to hand over the reins, even though he knew it was the fair thing to do. He hadn't let Scarlet be in control of anything last night. He'd done exactly what *he* wanted to do their first time together, and she'd given him everything he'd asked for. Now, it was only right for him to reciprocate.

"So, you've never blindfolded a man," he said, testing the waters of this new world she'd created. "And you've also never tied a man up."

"Nope. Neither one. I'd really like you to be my first."

He put one hand behind his back. "Let me feel the rope?" he asked, not because he needed to feel *it*, but because he needed to feel *her*.

When she rested her hand inside of his, Hunter smiled to himself. Her dainty fingers trembled around the twine, and he knew his fierce little fairy was nervous. He didn't want her to feel anxious, not with him, not when he was perfectly willing to be her alternative to reality.

"Well, then," he said, playing the rope between his fingers. "How can I possibly say no to being your first?"

"Really? Oh, Hunter, that's wonderful! But only if you want to. I mean, only if it's not going to cause you any harm. You told me last night that you don't want to hurt me, and I don't want to hurt you, either. I really want to try this with you, but if my actions are in any way detrimental to you, just tell me and I will stop."

"You won't hurt me," he assured, drawing his other hand behind his back and pressing his wrists together. "Go ahead. Tie me up."

"Are you sure?" Scarlet asked, the excitement returning to her voice.

"Positive. You know what? I want you to do it. Please tie me up. Pretty please with a cherry on top and lots of sugar."

Wafts of air shifted over his back, making him grin with the realization that she now bounced up and down behind him. "You're really sure? Absolutely?"

"Yes, I'm sure. Seriously. Do your worst."

Scarlet slipped the rope around his wrists, working the twine around his skin. "Let me know if it's too tight."

"It'll be fine," he told her, certain he'd be able to undo whatever knot she tied. She'd never tied anyone up before, so he figured she'd be timid about it. Still, he would pretend she'd done a good job, and hold his hands together as long as he could, just to make her happy.

She giggled as she wound the rope in and out between his hands, whipping it around and over. Hunter's eyes narrowed behind his blindfold. "What is that you're tying?" he asked. "Is it a sailor's knot?"

Scarlet performed several more maneuvers before answering. "I did a couple of those. I also did a figure eight and a timber hitch, too."

What the actual fuck? "That's, um, that's very impressive. Where did you learn to tie knots like this?"

"Oh. I used to be a Girl Scout."

"A Girl Scout?"

"Mm-hmm," she confirmed, tugging on the rope to secure it. "I spent a lot of time traipsing through the woods as a kid, camping with my troop. Along the way, I learned a few things about tying knots."

Hunter huffed. He should have known she was a Girl Scout. He could envision a tinier Scarlet crawling around campgrounds on scraped hands and knees, talking to plants.

He tried not to panic when he pulled against the rope at his wrists. He definitely wasn't getting out of these knots without her help, unless he used some sort of shiv. Which he didn't have on him, because he was naked. Not that he'd ever had a shiv on him, that he could recall.

"I think I'm done with the knots now. How does it feel?"

Hunter pulled on the ropes again. "Tight."

"Too tight?"

"No, it's just very secure."

"Not bad for my first try, then?"

"Nope. You are an expert already."

"Gosh, this is fun. I'm having so much fun! Are you having fun?"

"I...I think so."

"Well, that didn't sound too certain. But have no fear, because I'm going to make sure you enjoy yourself tonight. I swear it."

His ears perked up. "Yeah? What did you have planned next? I mean, after you blindfolded me, had me strip naked, and tied me up?"

She curled her fingers around his bicep. "Well, I told you I would feed you dinner, so that's what I'll do. Now take a few steps forward."

He cringed behind the scarf, resisting her pull on his arm.

"What's wrong, Hunter?"

"I don't feel comfortable with this. Everything here is made of logs. I have no desire to trip and fall on my face."

"I promise I won't let you fall."

"And I appreciate the reassurance, but I think I need to move a bit to the left because of where the table usually is."

Scarlet stepped in front of him. Her nipples grazed his chest, making his jaw clench. "Don't think, please. Not right now. Tonight isn't about thinking. It's about feeling. I want you to just *feel*."

He did feel. He felt hot. And blind.

She pressed her lips to his jaw. "Come on, you can do this for me."

Hunter leaned down to capture her lips with his. She immediately pushed her bare chest into his and swept her tongue inside his mouth. He groaned, needing to use his hands now more than ever. All he wanted was to touch her everywhere, and kiss her forever, and fuck her deep and hard, and then make slow, sweet love to her, again and again.

After several minutes, Scarlet eased back. "Mmm. We should stop all this kissing, or we'll never get to dinner. I'm sure you're starving."

"You're right. I am starving. In so many ways."

Her fingers traced his face. "I know you are, and I'll try to fix as many of them as I can. Now step forward. I promise to keep you safe."

She tugged on his arm again. This time he followed, though his steps remained cautious. She led him forward several paces before pressing him back a bit, until he could feel the log couch frame against his calves.

"You can sit now, Hunter."

"Okay," he agreed, lowering himself down. The couch fabric felt soft against his bare butt as his arms pressed back into the cushions. The twine at his wrist scraped his lower spine, but he could cope with that.

"There you go. See? I didn't let anything bad happen to you. Now just sit tight for a minute while I get everything ready."

Hunter listened as her footsteps padded away to the kitchen. He frowned and twisted the rope, hating her being so far away. The moment she returned, his hands eased again. "Did you bring back our dinner, Scarlet? Is it steak?"

"There is steak, as promised."

"What is that sound? What are you doing now?"

"Try to relax, please. I'm only setting the tray beside you. Also, try not to move around too much, since I don't want anything to spill."

"I'll do my best to sit still. But where will you sit?"

"Right here," she said, placing her knee beside his hip. The next instant, she straddled him entirely, plopping gently down onto his lap. "You are going to be my seat for dinner this evening, Mr. Gregory."

The tray shifted on the cushion beside them as she settled, but Hunter barely noticed the sound of rattling dishes. Frolicking Freebird Scarlet sat naked on top of him, with her soft, shapely bottom pressed into his hard thighs. It was the best sensation he could ever recall.

"Fuck, I love your ass," he mumbled, the words popping out of his mouth before he could even think to censor them.

"What was that? I didn't hear you."

"Nothing. It was nothing."

She leaned in closer, pressing her face beside his. He felt her smile against his cheek before she pulled his earlobe between her teeth. She bit down a little, then ran her tongue over the indentations she'd made.

"Mmm. You *have* to tell me what you said, Hunter."

The goose bumps she'd given him last night returned with a vengeance, flitting down his arms and scurrying beneath the rope. He knew his forest fairy felt quite empowered at the moment. But he also knew he wasn't entirely helpless in this scenario of hers.

"If you must know, my exact words were, 'Fuck, I love your ass.'"

"Oh. Well, um..." She sat up, gripping his shoulders. "Really?"

"Absolutely. I'm pretty sure it's the best ass I've ever seen. It's definitely the best one I've ever had my hands on. I'd like to have my hands on it again. Right now, if possible. Actually, if you'd be so kind as to untie me, I will lay you down on this couch and run my hands over every inch of your body. Then I'll flip you over onto your stomach and eat my steak dinner directly off your backside. And after that, I will…"

He let his words trail off purposefully, just to hear the tiny puffs of air escaping erratically from her throat.

"Do you want to know what I'll do after that, Scarlet?"

"Y-yes. Yes, please."

"Mmm. Once I've finished eating my dinner off your backside, and licked your skin clean, I will pay thorough attention to your ass cheeks. I'll worship them with my hands and fingers and mouth, for as long as you like. Afterwards, I'll use my tongue exhaustively to explore you in unmentionable places – unless, of course, you'd like me to mention them. And, since I'm being brutally honest, I should warn you I might bite a little. But I promise it won't be too painful. It'll just be painful enough to make you come exceptionally hard. Because I am very eager to learn how you will taste when you come in my mouth."

Hunter stopped talking then. Scarlet's fingertips quivered against his skin, making him grin rather wickedly. Even blindfolded with his hands tied behind his back, he could still be in control of *some* things.

She shifted against him, spreading her legs farther apart. When she settled back down on his lap, the wet entrance of her sex pressed into his thigh. Wild fucking desire shot through his body, and all he could do was grit his teeth and fist his fingers in response.

"I – I don't, uh," Scarlet fumbled, her unsteady hands slipping down to his chest. "I don't think those things are in the plans. Not tonight."

"It's a good thing we have a few more days together, then."

"Yes. It's such a good thing. My God, Hunter. You're lethal."

"Lethal?"

"To women, I mean. You have everything. Intoxicating words, an earth-shattering smile, a crazy-sexy voice, gorgeous blue eyes, and a body to drool over. Honestly, I can't figure out why some lucky lady hasn't snatched you up already. I imagine you could have any woman you want, with all of this," she said, jostling against him.

"Just so you know, I can't actually see anything you're doing."

"Oh, right. Well, I'm gesturing toward *all* of you."

He chuckled. "Yeah, that's what I figured."

"So, why aren't you married? I mean, unless it's not something you want. Maybe you prefer having a variety of women. Maybe you…"

"No," he insisted, unable to bear the thought of her seeing him in that light. "That's not me. That hasn't been me for a long time. I want to get married. I want the house and the kids and the dog and all of it."

"You do?"

"Yes. Very much."

"Then why don't you already have that?"

Hunter sighed, his shoulders collapsing back against the cushion. "Damn, I wish I knew. I guess I haven't found the right woman."

"I see," she said, her fingers curling into his chest, directly over his heart. "Well, I'm sure she exists. You just have to keep searching until you find her. Keep putting yourself out there until you find the one."

He tugged against the rope. "Scarlet?"

"Hmm?"

"Can we please stop talking about other women? I'm quite fixated on one woman at the moment, and I'd like to keep my focus on her."

"Oh, yes, of course. I'm sorry. I shouldn't talk about other women while I'm sitting naked on your lap. It's just that my mind runs away from me sometimes, and I want so much for you to be happy."

"It's okay. I appreciate you wanting me to be happy. But I assure you, I am truly, blissfully happy right this minute."

"Really? Even with your hands tied?"

"Yup. Even with my hands tied."

She slipped her fingers over his shoulders before running them down his arms. Her movements stopped when she came in contact with the couch cushions. He leaned forward so she could continue petting him, easing his chin onto her shoulder, enjoying the tickling of her hair on his face as she traced the knots at his wrists.

"How is this rope treating you, Hunter?"

"It's okay," he answered, grasping onto her fingers. He wished the hazy blur of yellow candlelight flickering behind this scarf would clear, so he'd be able to look into her eyes. He didn't have any hold on the multitude of emotions coursing through his veins right now, and he desperately wished he could see what was happening inside her.

"You know," she said, her breath warming his cheek as her fingers laced between his, "after this experience, I'm thinking rope may be one of the two handiest things on earth. I mean, along with silly putty."

He tried to grip onto her, but she slipped away. "Silly putty?"

"Absolutely." She drew her hands back up to his shoulders. "What else can you squish between your fingers *and* copy a cartoon with?"

Hunter's empty hands fisted. "You do make a fine point. But you forget duct tape. Duct tape is the finest, all-purpose thing on earth."

"You're a duct tape guy? What would you do if you had it now?"

"God, I could think of several things."

"Hmm, I bet you can. You have a really filthy mind. I mean, in a totally good way. I thoroughly enjoy your filthy thoughts. A lot."

"Well, I'm certainly happy about that. And I love talking to you about silly putty and duct tape and filthy thoughts. I really do. But you did promise me dinner, right?"

"Oh. Yes, you're right. I did."

Hunter smiled so hard it hurt, adoring the fact that he had to remind her to keep her seduction on track. She shifted against his lap as she fiddled with something on the tray. "Do I get my steak now, Scarlet?"

"In a moment. First, there's an appetizer."

"Yeah? What's that?"

She sat up straight on him again. "Open your mouth for me."

He did as she asked, even if he was a little scared. When his lips parted, Hunter felt warm a warm, thick liquid drip onto his tongue and chin. He closed his mouth and tasted. "Chocolate?"

"It's a chocolate fondue. I have strawberries to dip in it, if you like. Although I do have other plans for the strawberries, for later."

"It's okay. I don't want strawberries now. I want more chocolate."

"Well, good. Just open up your mouth again."

"No. Not that way. I want to eat the chocolate off of you."

"Off of me? Which part of me?"

"I literally do not care in the slightest. I just want to lick it off of some part of your body, so I can taste your skin on my tongue. You see, as good as this chocolate is, I know you'll taste even better."

Scarlet wriggled on his thighs. He knew, if he could see her eyes, her emerald green would look nearly black.

"Hunter, I don't...I don't know which part of me to offer you. I can imagine a thousand places I want you to lick me. Except, do I even have a thousand places on my body? I guess I do, if we count skin pores, or individual hair follicles. God, I don't even know what I'm saying. You turn my brain to mush sometimes."

"You do the same to me. And I definitely want to lick all the thousand places on your body. But for now, why don't you just put the chocolate on your finger? I think that might be a good place to start."

"Okay, yes. I can do that."

He waited impatiently, his mouth open, as she shifted on his lap.

"Here you go," she said finally, placing her finger against his tongue.

Hunter took the offering. He sucked the sweet flavor off of her, just to get rid of it. Then he swirled his tongue around her skin. He smelled her fresh soap and tiny flowers, and tasted a hint of saltiness beneath the lingering chocolate. But mostly, he felt her warmth and softness in his mouth, at the same time he felt the wet heat of her sex against his thigh.

He released her finger with a little popping sound, but he didn't let her go far. He pressed his lips into her hand, trailing his tongue down to her palm to bury his face in her skin. Scarlet giggled wildly.

Hunter raised his head. "I see you're ticklish. Am I bothering you?"

"Oh, no. I like this very much. I just had a funny thought."

"What thought is that?"

"At this moment, I have Hunter Gregory eating out of my hand."

He froze with her statement, since she had no idea how true it really was. "You most certainly do," he agreed, pressing his lips back into her palm to nip at her skin. He hated not being able to see or touch her in normal ways right now. The distortion of his senses made him thirsty and hungry and achy all over. Arching back, he strained to see her face. "I want more, Scarlet. More chocolate, more skin."

"I'm sure you do. But you can't have it."

"What do you mean I can't have it? Why not?"

She leaned over to kiss his lips. "Because. Life's not all chocolate." Scarlet reached for the tray again. He heard the dishes clank and felt her resituate on his lap. "Now open your mouth for me again, please."

Hunter squeezed his hands together, but still did as she asked. The next liquid she dropped on his tongue was thin and tart and sour as hell. He smacked his lips together. "Lemon juice? Seriously?"

"Chocolate and lemons. The best combination in the world."

"No, it's awful. It's like wanting beer and getting milk. Or wanting lobster and getting broccoli. What is it with you and lemons?"

"I love lemons! They're truly the cutest of all the fruits. And yes, that includes the clementine, which is also adorable. But I like lemons better because they're bright and happy on the outside, yet once you open them up, they have a sour kick that really catches you off guard."

"Wow. I can honestly say I've never given that much thought to fruit before. But it still doesn't make the taste of chocolate and lemons go together in any way, shape, or form."

"Oh, it can't be that bad." Scarlet traced her hand down his face, stopping when she reached his chin. "You have a little something right here," she whispered, bending forward to lick the spilled drop of chocolate from his stubble. "Mmm. I think this tastes quite good."

"That's because you only got the chocolate part," he grumbled, although his complaint was half-hearted. The feel of her shapely ass pressed to his thighs, and the wetness of her tongue on his skin, had him concentrating mostly on his huge erection wedged between his stomach and hers. "But I suppose you're right. Life's not all chocolate."

"No, but you can still make the best of it." When Scarlet finished speaking, she made a soft sucking noise. A shiver ran the length of her spine, jostling her body against his and making the dishes rattle.

Good Lord, did she just suck right out of a lemon?

"Kiss me," she begged, her tart breath tickling his nose.

Yup, she just sucked right out of a lemon.

Still, Hunter didn't hesitate. If she wanted him to kiss her, he was damn well going to do it. The moment his lips touched hers, she slipped her tongue into his mouth. The tart flavor assaulted his taste buds, but he only noticed for a second.

Scarlet settled further onto his chest, warm and pliant. He yanked on the rope, hating that he could only touch her passively. His mouth was his only weapon, so he used it. He deepened their kiss with intention, enticing her to melt into him, as each and every one of his nerve endings came alive beneath her body.

When she pulled away, he nearly screamed for her to come back. The only satisfaction he had now was the quaver in her voice. "Uh, Hu-Hunter, that'll be enough of that. You still haven't had your dinner."

I don't fucking care, he thought, but didn't dare say it out loud. His forest fairy wanted to feed him, seduce him, and have him at her mercy. He was determined to give her that experience, even if it killed him.

She wriggled against his thighs when she turned back to the tray. He heard the drag of a fork against a plate. "Smell this," she instructed.

He breathed in deep. "That is my steak, I believe."

"Not just steak, the choicest cut filet mignon. It's phenomenal. I had the chef prepare it for you." She slipped the morsel past his lips.

Hunter bit down, savoring the incredible flavor that burst on his tongue as he chewed and swallowed. "Damn, Scarlet, that is delicious."

"Good. I hoped you'd like it."

"You asked the chef to prepare it personally?"

"I did. After I saw Pete today, I went to see him. His name's Phil."

"And how long have you known Phil?"

Scarlet slipped another bite of steak into his mouth. "For a while now. I like to know people. I always have."

Hunter chewed on the meat and on her words. "So, you're one of those gregarious extroverts, I take it."

"Actually, I'm not. I prefer to know people on a more individual basis, so I can understand what makes them tick. A personality is like a mystery for me, and I think all mysteries should be solved."

He swallowed hard. "I would guess you're exceptionally good at solving people's mysteries."

"I daresay I am good at it. Although you are still a mystery to me."

"Really? I can't imagine I offer you any sort of mystery. Honestly, I feel like you know more about me than I do."

Scarlet placed another bite of meat on his tongue. "Oh, no, I don't think that's true at all. I have so much more to discover about you."

"Yeah? Like what?"

"Like the thing that happened to you."

"What thing?"

"The event that changed your life."

Hunter gulped his steak down. "I...I don't know what you mean."

She leaned closer, her hand drifting over his heart. "I think you do know. I'm pretty sure it happened when you were a teenager. I think it's the reason you stopped playing football after high school. It's the reason you transformed from a wild party boy into a staunch, stuffy executive with fierce control issues and a penchant for planning."

"I'm not stuffy," Hunter insisted, gripping hard to the rope as he struggled to think of a way to change the subject. "But I am thirsty. Do you have anything for me to drink?"

Scarlet sighed and reached for the tray. "I have some red wine. I know you don't care for alcohol, but is wine okay tonight?"

"Yes, it's fine."

She brought the glass to his lips. "Drink, Hunter."

He did as instructed, taking quenching gulps while she tipped the cup toward him. When he'd finished, he licked his lips. "Thank you."

"Of course," she said, replacing the glass on the tray and her hand on his heart. "I always want to give you what you need."

"I know," he confirmed, certain it was true. But he still wasn't ready to answer her, even though he knew precisely what had transformed him all those years ago. "I just don't want you unraveling all my mysteries."

"Why not?"

"Just...because."

"Hmm. Well, I suppose I could fill in the gaps with my imagination. I like imagining things about you. You're so interesting. So colorful."

"Colorful?" he questioned, wondering if he'd heard her correctly. "Do you really think I'm colorful?"

"I do. Why do you sound surprised?"

"I guess I don't think my life lends itself to much color."

"Oh, it does. I know it does. One color in particular, actually."

"What color is that?"

"Green. You're a forest's green, profound and lush and full of life."

"Green?" he repeated, trying to accustom himself to the thought, since none of that sounded like him at all.

"Yes. You're a forest's green, just like the sturdy, mighty trees outside. But you're also a hunter's green, as your name suggests. Skillful and intelligent. Even predatory, when necessary."

She ran her fingers across the stubble on his jaw. Hunter absorbed her touch at the same time he absorbed her words. He loved how she saw him. He loved the person he could be when he was with her.

He smiled, very much enjoying this little game of hers. "I can play along with this, too, Scarlet. Your name is also a color, and it's the perfect color I'd use to describe you. A bright, beautiful red."

Hunter expected her to giggle wildly. Or to bounce up and down on his lap. Or to press her lips to his with feverish intent. He expected a huge, wonderful reaction from her. He couldn't have been more wrong.

Scarlet's body turned rigid against him. Her hands dropped to his shoulders, her fingernails digging into his skin. "Red? No. No, no, *no*. Please not *red*. Red is a *horrible* color. It's so angry – it's angry and it's violent and it's blood – and I *hate* the sight of blood."

His gut lurched from the agony in her voice. He had no fucking clue why the simple mention of a color had set her off so fiercely. He tried in vain to wrench his wrists apart, desperate to hold her.

"Will you pick a different color for me, Hunter? Please? *Please?*"

She trembled all over now. Her sudden, unexpected terror carved deep into his skin, and he wanted to simply give in, to pick a different color and repress her rising panic. But he couldn't surrender in the face of her fear. Somehow, he knew that wouldn't do her any good.

"No, Scarlet. Your color is definitely red. But I need you to hear me out, because you're not seeing it the way I do."

She inhaled sharply, her hands still clamped onto his shoulders. She counted backwards, "5...4...3...2...1." Then she exhaled fully and eased her severe grip on him. "Okay, then. I'm listening."

He tried to see her through the blindfold, concentrating on the shape of her face haloed by the candlelight. "Your color is red because it's deep, and vibrant, and promising. It's the color of fire, the kind that burns right down into your soul. It's the color of your heart, pumping faithfully every moment to keep you surging with life. It's the color of your blush, as you gaze into your lover's eyes and experience desire like you've never known before. And it's the color of the morning sky, the glorious red that tells you, in no uncertain terms, that the sun is going to come out – it's going to burst from the earth and fill your life with such warmth and joy, if you just stand still and open yourself up to let it in."

Hunter held his breath when he finished. He sat as quietly as he could, not knowing what she would say or do. Then he heard her sniffle and felt a drop of wetness fall onto his chest.

"Scarlet? Are you okay?"

"Mm-hmm."

God, he hated not being able to see her right now. He leaned forward, pressing his face beside hers, verifying what he already knew. The tears on her skin slipped over his cheek and he sighed.

"You're not okay. You're crying."

"Yes, I am crying."

He stiffened, yanking against the goddamn rope that prevented him from touching her. "Please don't. Please. I can't bear for you to cry, especially when I can't even hold you."

She ran her hand across his cheek, wiping her tears from his skin. "It's okay. It's a good kind of crying."

"Is there such a thing?"

"Oh, yes. They're definitely happy tears."

Scarlet leaned forward, pressing her bare chest to his. She eased soft little kisses onto his lips. He still felt the wetness on her cheek, and tasted the salt on her skin, but he relished having her this close again.

"You just did the most amazing thing, Hunter. Do you realize that? It might be the most amazing thing anyone has ever done for me."

"What did I do?"

"You gave me back a color. A *color*. My God, it's not every day of your life that you get a color back. It's a truly incredible day, and I'm so grateful for it. I'm so grateful for you."

"And I'm so grateful for you. You have to know that."

"I do know," she assured, wrapping her arms around his neck and pressing her bottom down on his thighs. "I love being this close to you."

He sought out her mouth again, savoring the tart lemony taste that lingered on her tongue. "I love it, too. I love it so damn much."

Pushing farther into him, she pressed her breasts to his chest and wound her fingers in his hair. She arched her hips, pinning his shaft between their stomachs. His little bird grasped him with her entire body, holding onto him in every possible way. "Let me be closer," she urged in a frantic whisper. "I want to be even closer to you."

He pressed his eyes shut behind the blindfold. He wasn't entirely sure what she meant. He just wanted whatever she wanted. "Yes. Yes. Closer," he breathed, his mouth finding hers again.

"Tell me, please," she panted between his kisses. "I have to know."

He blinked in the darkness. "What do you have to know?"

Scarlet pressed her forehead against his. "I have to know the thing that happened to you...the thing that changed you forever."

Hunter's breath hitched. He lifted his head, struggling to put a little distance between them. But Scarlet didn't stop.

"I can picture you so easily," she breathed. "Back in high school. So young, so beautiful, so alive. I picture you playing football, striving to be the best, challenging everyone around you. I see you being driven, like you are now, but also vibrant and excited and adventurous. I see you smiling and laughing and making the most of your life."

She smoothed her fingers up his jaw, grounding his face in both hands. "I can still see that person inside of you, Hunter, here and now. You let him out sometimes and I catch a glimpse of him. I just want to know, I *have* to know, what made you lock him away so deep inside."

"I...I don't..."

"You don't have to tell me tonight. In fact, I think it's best you don't tell me tonight. But I would like to ask you for a promise."

"What promise?"

"I want you to promise you'll share this with me. Sometime before we leave this mountain, I want you to tell me about this turning point in your life. I want you to let me see inside you. Will you give me that?"

Hunter shook his head, terribly aware of what he should say. He should say *fuck, no*. He should push her away. He should *force* her away. But he couldn't. He couldn't risk her abandoning him. He couldn't bear to be on this mountain for one single second without her, so he said, "Yes, I promise," and waited for his chest to explode from the pressure.

Scarlet remained with him, her body pressed fully against his, holding him together. "Thank you," she sighed over his lips, relaxing entirely before easing her mouth onto his.

Her kiss was gentle and tender and timid. Hunter couldn't let it go on that way. He took over, claiming her by the only means currently available to him. He kissed her as deep and hard as he could, winding his tongue in hers, luring her to him so he could drink her in.

She sank onto his chest, so willingly, arching her back and moaning into his mouth. He pushed closer as she balled her fingers into his hair, rocking her bottom against his thighs in a sinfully perfect rhythm. The harder he kissed her, the more she picked up her pace, bucking into his lap while his rigid erection strained into her soft belly.

Hunter finally tore his mouth away, which took more effort than anything ever, and gasped for air. "Scarlet. I need to be inside you."

"Mmm, what?"

"I need to fuck you. Please. Let me fuck you."

Her fingers tightened against his scalp. "But, but I…"

"Damn it, *please*."

"But I have so many other plans for us tonight."

"Plans? What plans?"

"I have dessert for you. It's strawberries and whipped cream. To be honest, I'd planned to do filthy things with the whipped cream. I planned to smear it over your chest, and lick it off with my tongue, all the way down to your…your cock. Then I planned to take you in my mouth, and wrap my lips around you, and suck on you until…"

"Goddamnit, stop talking. I need to be inside you."

"But don't you want any of that?"

"Holy hell, I want *all* of that. But right now, I need you the way I need you. Just promise me we can do all those things another time."

She smiled against his lips. "I promise."

"Good. Now lift your hips toward me and let me fuck you."

"Uh, um…"

"Now, Scarlet. *Now*."

She set her hands on his shoulders. "No."

"What?"

Her fingers traced down his arms, stopping just shy of the rope tied to his wrists – the rope he currently tugged so hard against that he could very well be bleeding on the couch cushions. She slipped her hands over the knots, soothing his skin, before straightening on his lap. "No," she defended. "You're not in control tonight, remember?"

"But…but…"

"You must realize you're taking control of this situation. And I understand it's your way, but tonight isn't about that. Tonight is about feeling. I want you to let me be in control, and I want you to feel."

"Good Lord! I get it, okay? I understand tonight is about me giving up control. But you don't understand how much I need you right now."

"I do understand, since I need you just as much. I'm going to give you what you want, but I'm going to do it *my* way, and I need you to let me."

Damn! Fuck! Shit! God Bless America! "Alright. Fine."

"Hunter."

He exhaled heavily, releasing his strain on the rope. "Okay, okay. I'll let you do anything you want. You know that, right? Hell, if you didn't know before tonight, you must know now. I am at your mercy. I will give you anything in the whole, entire world."

"Well, that's...wow. I actually did not know that." She grasped his shoulders as she shifted her hips up off his thighs. "But now I do."

Scarlet reached one hand down between them, wrapping her fingers around his throbbing erection. His eyes rolled back in his head with the feel of her warm, gentle grip. She lined the tip of his cock up with the soaking wet entrance of her sex. Then she returned her hand to his shoulder, steadying herself above him.

"Are you ready for me, Hunter?"

"Yes. *Yes.*"

She sank down, slow and steady, her slick flesh sliding over his, squeezing around him as she took her sweet time to join them fully.

Fuck, fuck, fuck, fuck, he chanted in his head. Or perhaps out loud.

Once she'd lowered herself all the way down, her fingers dug into his shoulders and a harsh moan left her throat. Hunter balled his hands, not knowing if that was a good moan or a bad moan. He hated not being able to read the answer in her eyes.

"Scarlet? That wasn't a sound of pain, was it?"

She rested her cheek against his. "Oh, no," she hummed into his ear. "That definitely didn't come from pain. I'm sorry I'm noisy. It's just that you're so big and hard. I love the first moment when you slide all the way inside me. I love the way you fill me up, the way you..."

"God, stop, please. I need you to stop talking."

"But...why? Don't you like my voice? I mean, last night you said you liked it, but tonight you've asked me to stop talking twice."

Hunter shook his head. "You don't understand. I don't just *like* your voice. I fucking *love* it. I could listen to you talk all day, every day, for the rest of my life. But it's difficult for me to hear you say those things and maintain my restraint."

"Oh." She raised herself up, drawing him almost entirely out of her, before she sank down again. "I didn't realize you loved my voice that much. I thought what you really loved was my ass."

She repeated her unhurried actions, gliding all the way up his shaft. Hunter had to unclench his jaw to speak. "I do love your ass."

"Mmm," Scarlet hummed, her hot, wet sheath tightening around his length as she slid all the way back down.

He groaned deep in his throat, his next words falling out in a heated rush. "You must know I meant everything I said to you last night. I love your voice, and your thoughts, and your touch. And yes, I love your ass, too. But there's so much more. I love your eyes and your smile. I love your mind and your strength. I love your warmth and your heart. I just...I love everything about you."

Scarlet stopped moving entirely, fixating in place on top of him.

Hunter's fingers twisted into the rope. *Oh, shit. I went too far.*

He wondered if she would bolt away from him now. He wondered if she would leave him right here on this couch, bound and helpless. But then she leaned forward and peppered soft kisses across his face.

"I love everything about you, too, Hunter."

The sound of those words rang through his entire body before settling firmly inside his chest. He didn't respond to her. He couldn't.

She began moving again. Up and down, raising her hips leisurely off his thighs before sinking onto him again. She repeated her actions over and over, riding him slowly and smoothly, with her fingers clinging to his shoulders and her breaths coming rapid and shallow to her chest.

When she pressed her mouth to his, Hunter kissed her for all he was worth. He tasted her warmth and sucked on her tongue and pulled her lip between his teeth, trying to be as close to her as humanly possible. His overwhelming need to touch her turned into a longing that grew into a desire that morphed into a frenzied, hungered craving, clawing at his insides.

"Untie me, Scarlet. You *have* to untie me. *Now.*"

"Not...not yet."

"Good God, please," he begged, bucking his hips off the couch.

"Easy, Hunter. Let me do the work. Just feel. I need you to feel."

"Damn it, I can't feel any more than I already do. I swear I can't. I need you to go faster. Please. *Please.* Go faster."

She held tight to his shoulders, her panted air shifting over his face in tiny bursts. "Okay," she agreed, lifting up and pushing down again.

Scarlet picked up her speed, filling herself with him over and over. She sighed every time her body came flush with his, every time her ass landed against his thighs. The sound of flesh hitting flesh filled his ears. The sensation of her hot, wet sex tightening around him drove him to madness. Her sighs turned to moans that escalated to barely contained screams. Hunter clenched his jaw, trying to hold on as long as he could.

All he could hear was her – all he wanted to hear was her – so he missed the rattling of silverware as their dinner tray headed off the side of the couch. When it fell to floor, the dishes crashed wildly, shattering into bits and pieces. Shards of glass sprinkled over his ankles and feet.

He honestly didn't give a shit about it. But she did.

"Oh," she breathed, ceasing all her movements. "Oh, no."

"Leave it, Scarlet."

"But, Hunter, I forgot to..."

"Honey, just leave it. Stay with me. Keep fucking me. I need you to come. I need to feel you come apart around me."

Her hips bucked with his words. "Mmm, please say that again."

"Which part?"

"Any of it. All of it. Especially the *honey* part."

He leaned forward, capturing her mouth with his. "Honey," he breathed against her lips, "I need you to come for me. Please."

Scarlet whimpered. She restarted her movements, just as rapid and certain as before the crash. She fucked him thoroughly, with utter determination, impaling herself on his cock, not hesitating for a moment. "My God, you feel so good," she gasped. "I can feel you *everywhere.*"

He strained against the ropes. "I know what you mean. Believe me, I know. Move faster for me now. *Faster.*"

She did as instructed. She moaned and panted while increasing her pace, her fingernails clawing into his skin, the flesh of her ass pounding against his thighs. "Hunter...Hunter...*Hunter*!" she screamed. He nearly bit through his tongue.

Scarlet came hard, crying out her release, grasping onto his body with her arms, her hands, her thighs, and her tightly clenched, pulsing sex. He didn't last another second. He growled when he joined her, emptying himself inside her fiery hot walls. She moaned while she continued to move, disjointedly now, milking his erection.

"Fuck, you're amazing," Hunter groaned, his orgasm going on and on with her inner muscles contracting around him. For a minute, he thought he might never stop. Then Scarlet collapsed, her head dropping into his neck and her chest flopping against his.

Her body melted into him, but her arms still clung to his shoulders, desperately grasping him to her. He understood that desire all too well. "I'm here. I'm right here with you," he whispered beside her ear, waiting patiently until she sighed and released her ferocious grip.

Hunter closed his eyes, letting his face fall against her curls while sinking his spine into the cushions. He allowed himself to simply feel her. To feel her softness. To feel her warmth. To feel the joy and peace radiating off her skin.

He tried to absorb it all. He tried to absorb all of her and hold it to him. But he couldn't, since he still couldn't touch her with his hands or see her with his eyes. That inability killed him now more than ever.

Somehow, Scarlet knew. Maybe she had some sort of sixth sense. Or maybe she could actually feel the pain in his chest as she lay against him. He didn't know how. He only knew that her hands drifted down to his wrists, to untie the bindings he could no longer tolerate.

Hunter leaned forward slightly, maintaining her position on his chest while giving her better access to the rope. She tugged lazily on the knots she'd tied so thoroughly. It took her forever to get them undone.

The second his binds came loose – the instant Hunter could pull himself free – he reached for her. He banded her so tightly in his arms that he forced the air from her lungs. He honestly feared he might hurt her, but she merely giggled and smiled into his neck.

The next moment, he ripped the scarf off his face and threw it to the ground. He blinked his eyes, adjusting his vision to the dim candlelight that was far brighter than what he'd endured throughout the night. He wrenched Scarlet's body fully onto his and stood straight up off the couch. Doing his best to avoid the broken glass on the ground, he pivoted on his heels with his forest fairy still firmly attached to him. Then he laid her down against the cushions and covered her body with his own, all in one smooth, continuous motion.

Once Hunter had her beneath him, he grabbed her face in both hands and stared down into her. His little bird gazed up at him with a soft, satiated smile. Her eyes were glossed and gleaming. Her cheeks were bright and rosy. Her curls were tussled and unruly.

He couldn't believe he'd been inside her twice now and yet this was the first time he'd felt her lying beneath him. Her body was so soft in all the right places, like a Scarlet-shaped pillow made just for him. At this moment, he knew he'd be perfectly happy to never leave this spot again.

Hunter studied her face, seeing the same drunk pleasure written across her skin as she'd had on the countertop last night. Her smile was easy and joyful and so goddamn beautiful that it hurt like hell. He pressed his lips to hers, simply because he could.

"Hmm," she hummed against his mouth. "Thank you."

He looked to her bright eyes. "For what?"

"For everything."

Hunter shook his head. "I should be the one thanking you, since that was truly incredible. But I have to admit, I feel a little shell-shocked. What was all of this? The blindfold? The rope? Where did this come from?"

Scarlet shrugged. "I don't know. It was you, I think. When I'm with you, I feel free. Really, truly free. Is that okay?"

"God, yes. You can be whatever you want to be when you're with me. You know that, right?"

Moisture sprang to the corners of her eyes. "I do. I know."

Hunter reached for the first tear that fell down her cheek, tracing its path with his fingertip. "More tears. Why so many tears tonight?"

"I already told you. They're happy tears."

He nodded, even though he didn't entirely understand her. Tears were tears. They hurt.

"Will you come with me to the woods in the morning?" she asked, pleading with her eyes as well as her voice. "I want to see the red things again. I want to see *all* the colors. To see them and to appreciate them."

"If that's what you want, then I'll be right there beside you."

"Good," she said as another tear ran down her cheek. "You know, before tonight, I'd really been trying to like red again. I paint my toenails red. I drink red wine. And for the past few days, I've been staring at that little red leaf – the one that wound its way into my hair the day we were in the forest. I wanted so badly to see the beauty in that leaf, to see the beauty in the color red. But I couldn't."

Scarlet took a shaky breath in. "Then tonight, you just...you just said a few words to me. A few of the most beautiful words I've ever heard. And now, all of a sudden, I have red back again."

She held his intent gaze, the look on her face no less than sheer, utter adoration. "My Hunter is a poet."

He wrapped both arms around her, holding on as tight as he could. She'd said *my* Hunter, and it was undeniably true. This person he was, right here and now, belonged to her. He'd never been this person before her, and he didn't know if he could ever be this person again after. He only knew how proud he felt for giving the color red back to her.

He just wished it had never left her to begin with.

"What happened to you?" he whispered, afraid to speak too loudly for fear of disturbing her peace. "What took the color red away?"

Scarlet stiffened instantly, all her muscles hardening beneath him. He watched in dread as her head shook back and forth, over and over. Her tears returned, swift and numerous, cascading down her cheeks.

"Oh, no, *shh*..." Hunter soothed, slipping his hand up her face to run his fingers over her wet skin. "*Shh*, it's okay."

He rubbed her nose with his and pressed tiny kisses to her parted lips, listening as she sucked ragged breaths into her lungs. "You don't have to tell me, honey. Just please don't cry. I never want you to cry."

She inhaled and exhaled, her breaths turning slower and steadier as time passed. "It's okay, Hunter. Sometimes you need to cry."

He looked back to her eyes, his mind creating so many horrific images of things that could make her hate the sight of blood. He swallowed hard against the lump in his throat. "Scarlet, you don't have to tell me what happened to you right now. But I really need to know one thing. Can you please tell me if you were physically hurt? Can you just say yes or no?"

She gave him the tiniest smile. "No. I wasn't physically hurt."

He nodded, a little of the tension leaving his shoulders. "And mentally? What about mentally?"

"Mentally, I'm...I'm working out some issues."

Hunter closed his eyes, letting the kempt air leave his body. "Okay," he said, since he could accept that answer. She was being honest with him, and she'd admitted she needed help, and that was enough for now.

"But I hope you know," her voice returned, drawing his eyes back to hers, "I am not mentally ill. I'm only trying to deal with a few things."

"Of course," he confirmed. "I know that."

"Do you really? Because I'm pretty sure, when you first met me by the side of the road, you thought I was mentally unstable."

Hunter cringed. "Was it that obvious?"

"God, it was so obvious. You should have seen your face."

"I'm sorry. I'm truly sorry I questioned your sanity back then."

He ran his fingers across her cheek, absorbing the warmth of her skin. He remembered how much he'd wanted to touch her, from that very first moment. And why he thought he'd never get the chance.

"In my defense, Scarlet, you confused the hell out of me that day. I mean, I'd barely even laid eyes on you before you performed an angry bird impression followed swiftly by a chicken dance."

"Well, in my defense, I was trying really hard to get you to laugh. You looked like you hadn't truly laughed in years."

Hunter huffed. "Hell, I probably hadn't."

She eased her hands up to his face, smoothing her fingers across his jaw. "I love it when you laugh."

"I love it when you laugh with me, honey."

"Mmm. I also really love it when you call me honey."

"Then I'll keep doing it. *Honey.*"

Scarlet smiled, the sheer joy of it sparkling in her eyes. He did nothing but watch her, since he hadn't gotten the chance all night and he'd missed it so badly. He'd missed her emerald eyes and her rose lips and her ebony hair. He'd missed all of her colors.

She explored his face with her fingertips, tracing a path across his forehead, down his nose, and over his mouth. "You've been so good tonight, Hunter. You let me be in control, in spite of how difficult I know it was for you. So now, I'll give control back to you. The rest of the evening is in your hands. What would you like to do with it?"

Her fingers still caressed his lips. He nipped at her skin, causing giggles to erupt from her throat. She looked so happy, so innocent, so perfect. Hunter's heart clenched at the sight. "Honestly, I just want to lay here with you, and touch you, and kiss you. How does that sound?"

Scarlet gazed dreamily up at him. "That sounds pretty incredible."

"It does," he agreed, smiling all the way to her mouth.

8

VULNERABILITY

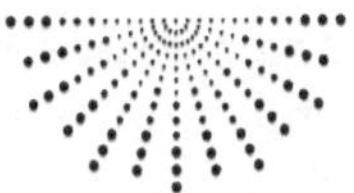

Hunter sat on the steps of his porch, looking out into the surrounding trees. The evergreens seemed darker this early in the morning, without the full sunlight shining on them, but they were still beautiful. He understood that everything at Blue was beautiful, but he wasn't sitting here right now to see all the nature. He only wanted to see Scarlet.

It's probably best that you sleep in your own bed, to get some rest.

Those were the words she'd said to him last night, just before she planted a kiss on his lips and scooted him out of her cabin. At the time, Hunter didn't protest. A lot had happened between them over the course of the evening, so it made sense they would both need time to process.

Still, that logic didn't make it any easier to be without her when he opened his eyes. He didn't stay in his cold, empty bed for a single second longer after waking. He leapt up, took a quick shower, threw on his clothes, and made his way outside to wait for her.

Scarlet wanted to go into the woods today, to see all the colors. She especially wanted to see red, since he'd given that color back to her last night. He'd given her something she'd been searching for, something she'd needed, and he loved being able to change her life for the better.

As he sat on his frigid porch stair, Hunter scrubbed his hands across his face. He swore he could still feel his little bird's skin against his. He could still smell her sweet scents. He could still feel the warmth of her body and her heart. All he wanted was to have his hands on her again. He just wanted her with him in every possible way.

The strength of his desire overwhelmed him. Nothing about it made sense. His pull to her was so strong – his ache for her so potent – that it couldn't be normal. God, he'd been so caught up in her last night that he'd told her he loved everything about her. He'd told her he was at her mercy. He'd told her he'd give her anything in the whole, entire world.

At the time, he meant every bit of it.

That wasn't the problem, though. Saying preposterous things to Scarlet in the heat of passion wasn't the issue here. After all, everyone knew passion-induced declarations weren't often based in reality. The problem wasn't the ridiculous feelings he'd confessed to her last night. The problem was that now, in the stark light of morning, he still meant every single word he'd said.

"Goddamnit, Hunter," he chastised himself. "What is wrong with you? It's only been a week. You've known this woman for a *week*. And you spent half that week thinking she was crazy."

Of course, he didn't believe that anymore. Especially not after last night. He knew now that something terrible had happened to his little bird. Something angry and violent and bloody. Something that didn't hurt her physically, but sure as hell fucked her up mentally.

Hunter wanted her to tell him what it was. He wanted her to lean on him and use his strength. He wanted to give her that much, at least. He'd tried last night. He'd honestly tried to give her everything he could. After she'd untied the rope and allowed him to resume control, he'd laid on the couch with her forever, kissing her lips and playing with her hair and touching her face. He'd wanted to be whatever she needed.

His actions weren't entirely selfless, obviously. He loved touching her. He loved feeling her skin beneath his. He'd spent a ridiculous amount of the evening with his ear pressed to her bare chest, listening to the steady pulsation of her heart. That rhythmic thumping sang to him, and lulled him, and he hadn't wanted to leave that spot, ever.

To be perfectly honest, this unrelenting hunger absolutely terrified him. He felt trapped between the desire to cling to Scarlet for the rest of his life and the desire to run screaming from this mountain right now, retreating to the shelter of the tedious, dreary life he knew so well. He should probably do just that. He should probably put an end to this overwhelming relationship. He should probably tell her it wasn't a good idea for them to see each other anymore and then simply walk away.

Hunter shifted against the wood staircase. He dropped his hands to his thighs and fisted his fingers. The mere consideration of saying those words to her made his lungs seize and his gut roil.

He'd already tried being up here at Blue without her. He'd barely made it thirty-six hours without losing his mind. He couldn't walk away from her now, because he didn't want to, and because he wasn't able to.

He simply needed his forest fairy, and since he had no choice but to remain by her side, he also had no choice but to fulfill the promise he'd made to her last night. She wanted to know the thing that altered his life when he was a teenager, and he had to tell her. He had to tell her *today*, because he had to get it over with.

Hunter needed to get all of that mess out of the way. He needed to just say the words and lay the memories quickly back to rest. He needed to put it all behind him again, so he could concentrate solely on her for the few days they had left.

After all, the two of them had no future beyond these moments. Whatever happened up here at Blue would stay here. When he went back to reality, he never had to think about this place, or her, ever again.

That knowledge should make him ecstatic. Yet right now, it only made him want to vomit. He simply couldn't imagine any future in which he didn't want to wrap his arms around his little bird and hold on as tight as he could.

The grating sound of tires crunching on gravel accosted his ears. His eyes shot up to watch the food truck shimmy down the driveway and park beside his hobbled Porsche. Colin dropped out of the front seat, pulled a tray from the back, and walked up to the porch.

He stood as far away as possible. He didn't make eye contact. He just said, "Hey," and handed over the tray.

"Hey," Hunter replied, taking the food he couldn't fathom eating right now and setting it behind him. He turned back to the boy. "If you don't mind me saying, Colin, you don't look so good today."

"Well, you don't look so good yourself."

"Yeah, that sounds about right. You want to sit for a minute?"

The young man didn't move at all for a long moment. Then he shrugged and stepped up to sit on the wood stairs.

Hunter sighed as Colin settled in beside him. "So, I guess we're both having a bad start to the day."

"Yeah, I guess so."

"I'll tell you mine if you tell me yours."

The boy smiled, although it didn't reach his eyes. "You first."

"Okay," Hunter agreed, rubbing his hand together. "I really just need to ask you a question, if you don't mind."

"Sure. Go ahead."

"Do you, um, do you ever see patients get together up here?"

Colin's brow rose. "What do you mean by 'get together'?"

"Together, romantically. Do you ever see people on this mountain try to start relationships with each other?"

"Oh, that. Yeah, I suppose I do. Sometimes."

"Does it ever work out? After they leave here, do they stay together?"

"Well, I don't really know, because I don't see anyone when they go home. But I do see some of them return to Blue, and I've never known anyone to still be with the same person from the time before."

Hunter looked out to the surrounding forest. "And why do you think that is? Why don't romantic relationships last beyond this mountain?"

"Probably because it's not the real world up here. This place is too different, and I would think reality changes everything."

Hunter's shoulders sagged. "Yeah, I can see that. Thanks, Colin."

"I don't know why you're thanking me. I can't imagine that was what you wanted to hear."

"You're right, it wasn't. Still, I appreciate your honesty."

"Then you're welcome, I guess."

Hunter glanced at the boy and forced a smile. "It's your turn now. Why are you having a bad morning?"

Colin flinched as he stared out into the evergreens. "Today is my mother's birthday. Well, it *was* my mother's birthday."

All the air left Hunter's lungs. "Fuck, man. Don't let me sit here and talk about stupid shit when you're dealing with something like *that*."

"It's not stupid shit. Everyone deals with different issues. It's not a contest. It's all about figuring out a way to get through it. Besides, it's good to concentrate on someone else's problems for a while, to get your mind off your own."

"God, you're wise beyond your years. How did you manage that?"

"Oh, don't give me too much credit. Scarlet taught me that part about life not being a contest. She's taught me a lot of things."

"Scarlet taught you?"

"Yeah."

"Did I hear my name?" she asked, stepping out of the grove of trees between her cabin and his. Her hiking boots crunched on the gravel when she left the underbrush to approach the two of them.

Hunter's heart pounded with the sight of his forest fairy. He stood from the porch stairs at the same time Colin did, and they both took a step toward her simultaneously. But then he glanced at Colin's stricken face and held himself back, allowing the young man to move forward.

Scarlet smiled at Hunter before turning her attention to the red-hooded boy. They stepped up to each other and she reached out to take his hands inside hers. Colin stilled the moment she touched him.

"It's a good day," Scarlet whispered, focused on his eyes. "She would be so proud of you. She *is* proud of you. You know that, right?"

Colin nodded as a single tear fell down his cheek. "I do. I know."

Scarlet threw her arms around him. He hugged her back just as hard.

Hunter stood with his breath held. He watched his little bird give her heart and soul to the bedraggled young man. His fingers twitched with the need to touch her, but he steadied himself, knowing she had more than enough love in that tiny body of hers to give to each of them.

When Colin finally extracted himself from her embrace, he swiped at the tears on his face. "Well, I should finish my route," he mumbled.

She gave him a soft smile. "You always know where to find me."

"Thanks, Scarlet." He straightened his spine and turned to Hunter. "And thank you. For listening."

"Anytime. Thank you for listening, too."

Colin nodded to him before pivoting back to his truck.

Hunter couldn't wait another second. Scarlet's eyes were still focused on Colin's retreating back as Hunter stepped toward her. It took him exactly three strides to reach her, grab her face in his hands, and press his lips to hers.

She returned his kiss without question, fully accepting the insistence of his mouth. Yet a mere moment later, she pulled back and placed her hand on his chest. Her eyes darted over to where Colin stood.

Hunter smiled when he realized the reason for her hesitation. "I don't think you need to be bashful about our relationship, Scarlet. I'm sure Colin understands. He is an adult."

"I didn't see anything!" the boy hollered when he jumped up into the driver's seat. "Not a damn thing!"

Hunter chuckled while the truck drove off down the gravel.

Scarlet looked back to him. "I take it Colin told you what today is?"

"Yeah, he told me."

"I'm glad you two can talk. You're both such wonderful people."

Hunter absorbed the admiration written across her face. He shook his head, not knowing exactly where she came from or how she came to be in his arms. "Damn, Scarlet. I missed you."

She rested her hand over his heart. "I missed you, too, honey."

"Hmm. I like it when you call me honey."

"It's nice, isn't it? I loved it when you called me that last night. Of course, that wasn't the only thing I loved about last night. It was all quite...lovely."

Hunter watched her cheeks flush pink with her memories. "I loved last night, too. Every blind and bound moment of it," he said, wanting to see her blush further. She didn't disappoint.

His gaze dropped, drawn to the thin black sweatshirt and yoga pants she wore. "Are you going to be warm enough in this outfit to go out into the woods? It's a bit chillier than usual this morning."

"I'll be fine," she assured, running her hand up the sleeve of the navy thermal shirt he wore. "How about you? Is this warm enough?"

"Yeah, I'm good. But I do want to get one thing before we go."

"What do you want to get?"

"I'll be right back," he assured, forcing himself away from her. He bounded into his cabin to grab the blanket he'd left on the couch. Once he closed the door behind him, he returned to her side. "Here it is."

Scarlet crinkled her nose. "What's that?"

"It's a nice, cozy blanket. I found it in the closet behind the games."

"I know what it is, but what is it for?"

"It's for lying on the ground beneath us when we sit. Or lay," he offered, still traumatized by the prospect of random animal droppings. "I realize I don't know all of your forest rules yet, but I hope using a blanket will still allow us to properly commune with nature."

"Okay, silly," she consented with a laugh. "Bring your blanket."

He smiled, tucking the fabric under one arm before reaching for her hand. Scarlet threaded their fingers together. "You ready?"

"Ready."

Hunter walked beside her today, through the trees and underbrush. She didn't have to pull him along like she did the first time. He still couldn't say he relished the experience, but he definitely wanted to be here with her. He even began to see things through her eyes.

Scarlet looked entranced by everything she witnessed. She gasped and squealed with every acorn that dropped on the ground and every bird that fluttered its wings. Hunter watched in awe as she bounced, giggled, and danced. He feared staring at her for too long, since his heart clawed at his ribcage with every glimpse of her innocent passion.

She wandered through the forest with no path in sight, just like last time, yet he recognized a few gnarled, rocky landmarks. He realized his fairy wasn't just flitting about here. She knew exactly where she was going. In truth, it seemed as if she always knew where she was going.

Hunter figured that must be because of the Girl Scout in her. The same Girl Scout who'd tied him up with sailor's knots and a timber hitch the night before. "So..." he began, watching the side of her face while they moved through the trees, "last night was really something, wasn't it? I'm still not quite over your latent dominatrix tendencies."

Scarlet nibbled her lip. "I really should say thank you. Again."

"What are you thanking me for now?"

"For letting me act out my fantasy. I certainly wouldn't do anything like that in my normal, everyday life."

"Well then, I'm glad I got to be there when you let yourself go."

"I did let myself go, since you allowed me that freedom." She glanced over at him. "You know, you were so good about everything I wanted to do last night, it would only be fair of me to reciprocate."

His brow rose. "What do you mean?"

"I mean, I could fulfill a fantasy of yours in return. If you want."

"Are you really asking me if I want you to fulfill a fantasy of mine?"

"I am."

"Good Lord. Yes, Scarlet. Hell, yes. I definitely want that."

"Okay, then. I hereby promise to fulfill any fantasy you desire, Hunter Gregory. At the time and place of your choosing."

He pinned her eyes. "But what if my fantasy is to tie you up?"

"I'll...I'll do whatever you want."

"Are you sure about that? You must know I would be a lot more aggressive with you. If I was the one in control."

"I do know," she said, her fingers squeezing onto his. "Do you think it makes me a bad person for wanting to tie you up first?"

"I don't think there's a force on earth that could make you a bad person," he insisted, amazed by her open acceptance of all his obvious issues. "Besides, you already know you can be completely free when you're with me. I'm here with you, for as long as you want."

Scarlet sighed. "That makes me so happy."

"I'm glad. It makes me happy, too."

She gave him a shy smile before glancing to the trees, her hand still firmly planted inside his as they strolled along together. His mind wandered to all the fantasies he wanted to fulfill with her, racing with a million different possibilities. He'd probably spend the whole next two weeks just trying to decide which one of them he desired most.

Multiple naked-Scarlet images swam blissfully through his brain when a rapid firing noise startled him from his daydreams. "Holy shit! What on earth was that?"

"Oh my goodness," she breathed, halting her footsteps.

"What? What is it?"

"*Shh*, Hunter, don't scare him. *Look*."

She pointed up into the boughs of a tall pine tree. He followed her finger to a black-and-white speckled bird with a red crest of feathers above its beady black eyes. The bird slammed its beak into the tree trunk, making the obnoxious hammering sound again.

"Damn," Hunter grunted. "He sure is noisy."

"He's a redheaded woodpecker. He's supposed to be noisy."

"Hmm. I take it you like him?"

"I love him. He's absolutely astonishing."

Hunter absorbed the sight of her face as she stood beside him and gazed up into the trees, the warmth of her body radiating through her thin clothing. Eventually, he heard the rustle of feathers from above. He knew the bird flew away, not because he watched it, but because he watched her. Sheer joy radiated from Scarlet's body as she stood enthralled by the woodpecker's flight, bringing a memory to the surface of his mind: the memory of a sweet little girl with dark blond hair, looking up to the sky and giggling whenever birds flew by.

"You know, Scarlet, sometimes you remind me of my sister."

Her eyes darted to his. "You have a sister?"

"Yeah. Her name is Maxine. She's ten years younger than me."

"Oh, wow. What's she like?"

"She's fun and bright and bubbly, like you."

"Are you close to her?"

"As close as I can be, with her living in Paris right now."

"Paris? How did she end up there?"

"She wanted to travel the world, so she took a position with our Gregory Global branch in France. She loves it over there."

"Hmm. You must hate having her so far away, out of your reach."

"You're right. I hate it."

Scarlet smiled, squeezed his hand, and resumed walking.

He kept pace beside her, the two of them in utter synchronicity. The reality of their perfectly matched steps made him ache for the future they would never have. "I think you and Maxine would get along so well, back in the real world," he admitted before he could stop himself.

Scarlet's fingers twitched inside his. "I'm sure we would," she mumbled, looking back to the trees.

Hunter knew he should drop this conversation. He just didn't want to. "You know, I had an interesting talk with Colin this morning."

"Yeah? What about?"

"About romantic relationships that start up here on this mountain."

Her footing faltered. Hunter held tighter to her hand.

"Oh? What did Colin have to say about that?"

"He said people don't usually stay together after they leave Blue. He said he's never seen a couple survive back in the real world."

"No, I don't believe they do. At least, not that I've ever seen."

"And why do you think that is?"

Scarlet fell silent for a long moment, just walking beside him, before she answered. "Have you ever seen the movie *Speed*? Where they have to keep the bus going above fifty miles per hour or it will blow up?"

"Yes, I've seen it. It's been a few years, though."

"Well, in that movie, Keanu Reeves tells Sandra Bullock that relationships based on intense experiences never work. I think it applies up here, too. Relationships that start on this mountain can't last."

"Do you often live your life based on Keanu Reeves movie quotes?"

"Okay, maybe that was a bad example. But you know what I mean."

Hunter wanted to say he didn't know. He wanted to say her *Speed* theory was utter nonsense and anyone could make anything work, if they just tried hard enough. But he couldn't say it, since it would be a lie.

"Yeah, I suppose I do know what you mean," he admitted, the words stabbing like a knife in his gut. He unthreaded their fingers and dropped his hold on her hand, but only because he needed her closer. Reaching his arm around her back, he pulled her hip flush with his.

Scarlet's fingers grasped the material of his shirt, balling up against his spine. She slipped into silence as they continued walking, which was a good thing, since he needed a few moments to process. The entire forest grew still around them while they moved forward, with Hunter's mind shifting fiercely from one thought to the next. He barely noticed her footsteps slowing. But he definitely felt her body start to tremble.

He turned toward her that instant. "Honey, are you okay?"

She stopped walking, her eyes wide as she stared straight ahead. He followed her line of sight to a slender brown tree in the distance, with hundreds of branches supporting a million bright red leaves. "Oh, look," she gasped. "This...this is a red maple. It's always been my favorite tree."

Scarlet stepped away from him, pulled toward the diverse shades of red. He let her go, knowing she needed to feel them. She reached up, running her hand reverently across a single stem before her fingers stilled against one small, crimson leaf.

"My God, it's beautiful," she whispered. "It's so beautiful."

When he heard the quaver in her voice, Hunter stepped up behind her. He wrapped his arms around her waist to pull her back against his chest, although he was very careful not to pull her away from her leaf. Her free hand slipped down to cover his, overlapping his fingers.

He dropped his head into her hair. The scent of her tiny flowers floated through his tumultuous brain, clearing his mind of everything but her. All he wanted was to be here, in this moment, with his little bird.

"Thank you so much for this, Hunter. I love having this tree back."

"You're welcome," he said, prouder than he'd ever been in his life.

She shivered and wrapped both her hands around his forearms, holding him tight to her body. He didn't know how long they stood like that, with her staring at the red leaves as he breathed into her soft curls. Eventually, she turned around inside his embrace and looked to his eyes. She pushed up on her tiptoes and pressed her lips to his.

Hunter kissed her, soft and slow. He kissed her until her body melded entirely with his. When she finally settled back down on her heels, she gave him a tender, satiated smile.

"Do you want to spread our blanket out here by the maple, Scarlet? Or do you want to go find your oak tree? I think we're close to it."

"We are close. Let's go there."

"Okay," he agreed, grateful for the respite of walking. He honestly didn't know what desperate acts he might commit if he had to continue witnessing the drunken look on her face after just one of his kisses.

Within minutes of leaving the maple, she guided him to the front of a large oak. "Here it is," she announced. Hunter laughed as soon as he saw it, since he was pretty sure it was the same tree from last time.

Scarlet reached for the blanket under his arm. He unfolded it and handed her a side, so they could lay it down together. She placed her half on the ground a few feet from the base of the oak as he knelt down to help her. Unfortunately, he wasn't all that helpful, since he was too memorized by watching her crawl around to straighten the material.

Seeing her on all fours like this reminded him of the night she'd spread the Twister mat out on her living room floor. He remembered how tempting it was to watch her then, too. Hunter wanted her just as much now as he had that night. Honestly, he probably wanted her even more now, since he already knew what it felt like to be inside her, and he wanted to experience that sensation again and again and again.

When Scarlet finished with her task, she perched herself on the green fabric and looked up to his eyes. "Are you going to come sit with me?"

"I am," he assured, settling down on the blanket.

"Do you mind if I take off my shoes?"

"Seriously? It's freezing out here. You'll get frostbite."

"It's not that cold." She began untying the laces of her hiking boots. "Besides, I told you the last time we were here, I'm tougher than I look."

Scarlet obviously believed those words. He wanted nothing more than to believe them, too. Especially since she'd told him how much she enjoyed blowing up powder kegs and poking grizzly bears, and he needed her to be strong enough to survive all of that.

She pulled off her boots and socks and set them beside the blanket. Then she sunk her bare feet onto the ground and curled her toes up in the dried, fallen leaves. Hunter noticed she'd painted her toenails red again.

"Do you actually enjoy having your feet in the dirt like that?"

"I do. Sometimes you need to dance around in the dirt, you know?"

He didn't know. But it made her happy. Which made him happy.

She flopped back onto the blanket, her dark hair spreading out like a halo around her head as she looked up to the sky. He followed her lead. Hunter lay down beside her, rested his arm next to hers, and looked up.

The tree branches went on and on above him, reaching all the way up to the vast blue sky. The morning sun eased through the leaves with tiny streaks of silver and gold. It was beautiful, and enormous.

He still wasn't sure how safe they were here. But then he felt Scarlet's hand move to his, her fingers stroking softly across the back of his own. She loved this place, so he would try to love it, too.

Hunter listened to the flutter of unseen birds, and to the occasional dropping of acorns, and worked to keep his body relaxed. Today, that feat proved even more difficult than the last time, since he couldn't simply lay here beside her. He had a promise to fulfill, to tell her what had happened to change his life back when he was a teenager.

He knew what the thing was. He didn't have to search his memory, or figure out what event she might be referring to. He knew the exact date and time and place, yet he still wanted to ignore its existence. He just didn't find it necessary to dredge the event from its resting place.

His muscles tensed against the blanket, even though he wasn't afraid to tell her what happened. Hunter didn't fear reciting the specifics of the incident itself. What he feared was what would inevitably come after.

Scarlet would never understand that he had, in fact, put it all behind him. She would react like his parents did at the time, trying to dissect his feelings, trying to force him to get help. But he hadn't wanted to deal with doctors, pills, and unrelenting psychoanalysis sixteen years ago, and he sure as hell didn't want to deal with it now.

After all, it wasn't as if this thing affected him anymore. Despite his parents begging him to seek counseling, he had managed – on his own – to put it in the past. It wasn't the reason he questioned his life now. It wasn't the reason he'd been unable to commit to Clarissa. It certainly wasn't the reason he'd let Will talk him into coming here.

Hunter simply preferred to keep the memory where it was: deeply buried, infrequently recalled, and definitely unshared. The only adults in his life who knew about that night were his parents. He'd long ago broken contact with anyone from high school, and his sister had been too young to truly remember. He never found it necessary to share the incident with any women over the years, either. Not even with Clarissa.

Yet here he was, having made a promise in a moment of sexually induced weakness. Now, he would have to share this dreaded memory. Now, he would be forced to leave himself open to Scarlet's examination, granting her the opportunity to dissect him like the psychological fodder he'd never wanted to become.

He definitely wasn't looking forward to any of this. But it was still best to get it over with. If he told her today, then he could continue with this vacation without ever having to think about it again. He could rebury it, where it had been for sixteen years now, and move along.

Hunter sucked in a deep breath.

He stared up at the trees and cleared his throat.

"Um, Scarlet?"

"Hmm?"

"I – I made you a promise last night. And I intend to keep it."

Her fingers stilled against his hand. Out of the corner of his eye, Hunter saw her turn to face him. He swallowed hard.

"Do you want to keep it?" she questioned.

"That doesn't matter. It was a promise."

"I know it was a promise. But let's face it, I pretty much coerced you into making it."

He chuckled. "I'm glad you can admit to that."

"I do admit it. I enjoyed exploring my feminine powers last night."

"They're quite exceptional."

"Why, thank you."

"You're welcome," he said, smiling at her gentle confidence before forcing himself to refocus. "Still, your feminine powers aren't the real issue here. I made a promise to you, so I'm obligated to keep it."

Scarlet quieted. He could feel her watching him. Finally, after forever, she exhaled. "Well, then. I release you from your promise."

His eyes shot to hers. "You do?"

"Yes, I do, because I got it unfairly. My only excuse is that I was emotionally overwhelmed last night. I mean, on top of allowing me to act out my fantasy, you gave me back a color. A *color*, Hunter. That just made me want to know even more about you. It made me desperate to see as far inside of you as I can. And honestly, I still want to do that. But I won't ask you to keep this promise. Not if you don't want to."

Holy hell. Is she really going to allow me to walk away from this?

Scarlet's offer certainly tempted him. He'd love to let sleeping dogs lie and forget this whole thing. Yet nothing about that felt right. Part of it was his guilt over backing out of a promise, but that wasn't all it was.

Hunter knew that the woman lying here beside him, gazing at him in pure, undiluted adoration, had already given him more than he could have ever hoped for here. He would leave this mountain a changed man, all because of her, yet she wanted nothing of real value in return. She'd asked nothing of him – nothing at all – except to be with him, and to see inside his heart. So maybe, just maybe, he actually wanted her to see.

"Hmm. That's odd," he considered.

"What's odd?"

"Well, it seems I still want to keep my promise, even though you've released me from it. Apparently, I do want to share this thing with you."

"That's wonderful, Hunter. But why is it so odd?"

"Because I haven't told anyone."

"In a long time?"

"No. I haven't told anyone. Ever."

Scarlet's eyes widened. He shifted his gaze up to the sky, refocusing on the nothingness. He didn't want her looking into him just yet. He didn't want her to see those deep, dark places until he was ready.

"This thing – this night – it happened a long time ago," Hunter began, steeling his determination as he struggled to find the words.

"When you were a teenager," Scarlet continued for him.

"Yes. I was eighteen. It was my senior year of high school. You already know I was...very popular."

"I do know. I also know you loved playing football."

"I did love it. I was the quarterback, and I was good. Really good. I already had a scholarship to play college ball. Not that I needed a scholarship, financially speaking, but it felt good to know I'd earned it myself. It was entirely mine."

Her hand smoothed over his. "You were happy."

"Yeah, I was. It was a foolish, childish sort of happiness, but at least I understood how much I'd been given. My parents were incredible, and they loved me without limits. I had all the money and all the things I could possibly desire. I had an amazing future before me. And it didn't hurt that I could have any girl I wanted. My life was full of promise."

His words trailed off while he concentrated on the feel of her fingers rising slowly up and down his forearm. Hunter closed his eyes with that sensation as visions of the past formed behind his eyelids. Scarlet's touch grounded him, and yet he was back there again, on that football field, throwing the pass that won the game.

"It was homecoming night," he heard his own words from a distance, "and we won. Coach named me MVP right on the field, and my teammates carried me off on their shoulders. I saw Mom and Dad and Maxine cheering in the stands, and I knew how proud they were of me. It was an incredible moment."

Hunter exhaled shakily. "My team crowded into the locker room, screaming and howling and slapping each other's backs. I don't know who saw her first, because it took a while for us to settle down. It took a moment for us all to stop yelling and to realize what had happened.

"A girl from our school hung from a rafter, with her feet dangling above a knocked-over bench. Her eyes were bugged out and her skin was mottled. She'd used the homecoming banner from the hallway to make a noose and she'd hung herself right there beside my locker.

"Our coach pushed past us as soon as he could and shouted for one of the guys to help him get her down. They started CPR, and they called for an ambulance, but she was already gone."

Hunter felt movement coming from beside him.

"Did you know this girl?"

He opened his eyes. Scarlet had shifted toward him and propped herself up on her forearm. She now gazed intently down at his face.

"No, I didn't know her. I didn't even recognize her at first. But she looked different, of course. The body hanging there...that wasn't who she was. Later on, I remembered her saying hello to me in the halls a few times. And that night, before the game, she'd wished me luck as I ran out onto the field – her and twenty other girls, hollering at me from the stands. The only reason I even remembered her being there was because she was normally so quiet. It seemed strange for her to stand in the middle of that crowd and shout along with everyone else."

"Did you know her name?"

"Not then," he answered with a shake of his head. "They ushered us all out of the locker room before we had a chance to change clothes. I remember riding home with my family that night. The car was so silent. My father didn't even turn the radio on, and he always had the radio on. But not that night.

"The rest of the evening was difficult. I couldn't sleep for thinking about the girl. I just couldn't fathom what had brought her to commit that act. She was so young, as young as I was, and I was so fortunate. I recognized all the happiness and potential in my life, and I couldn't understand how she didn't see the same things in her own. I mourned her that night, even though I never knew who she was."

Scarlet sniffled with his words. Hunter watched a tear stream down her cheek. He worked hard to steady himself, since he couldn't stand for her to cry. He'd seen his mother cry way too many times over him. He distinctly remembered how she'd sobbed the day he told her he was giving up his football scholarship.

Now, he had to watch the drops fall from Scarlet's beautiful eyes. Hunter could feel his own tears, salty and burning, behind his eyelids. But he refused to let them out, because they would not control him.

Scarlet inched closer, resting her head in the crook of his shoulder and placing her hand over his heart. "I'm so sorry, Hunter."

"There's more," he rasped, barely recognizing his own voice. "I went back the next day. They'd reopened the locker room and I needed to grab my things. A few other guys from my team were there, but no one had much to say. I stared briefly at the rafter she'd hung herself from, then reached for my locker. I didn't want to be there at all.

"I yanked open the door and stuffed my things into a bag. When I started to close the door, I noticed a small envelope taped to the inside. It wasn't addressed, but I knew it hadn't been there before the game.

"I sat down on the bench and opened it. It was a piece of paper with a girl's handwriting on it, very flowery and yet crooked in places. It had my name at the top, and when I looked down, I saw that it was from her. Samantha. The girl who'd hung herself. She'd left me this letter."

Hunter pressed his eyes shut tight. *Samantha Morris.* He hadn't thought her name in so long. He could still see the letter...the smudges made by her tears...the smudges that developed later with his own.

"She wrote that she'd been watching me for years," he continued, his tongue dry and thick. "She said she thought I was the most incredible person, and I had such a wonderful life, and she'd always wanted to be a part of it. She said she'd tried to write to me before, but never had the courage. Then she told me things in her life weren't very good. She was afraid when she was at home, and she didn't want to be there anymore. She told me she wished she could have been my girlfriend, because she knew I would have made her happy. She said if I had just wanted her, then maybe things would have been different.

"But she also said she didn't blame me. She said she'd always loved me. The last thing she did was wish me luck on my football game – that ridiculous, stupid fucking football game. Then she signed it: *Samantha*. I imagine she put it in my locker just before she took her life."

He opened his eyes to the blank sky. "I read it over and over again. It's been sixteen years, but I can still see her handwriting. I gave the letter to the police the next day, after I spent an entire night reading it, and after I worked up the nerve to show it to my parents. The police investigated her home and arrested her father. A report came out later that said he'd been abusing Samantha and her younger sister."

Hunter dragged in a breath. "I guess she'd just found her way out."

Scarlet raised her head from his shoulder to stare into his eyes. He didn't really see her at first. It took him time to acclimate to the present. When she finally spoke, he already knew the words. He'd certainly heard them before.

"You know this wasn't your fault. Samantha was clearly troubled, and she could have focused her needs on anyone. It didn't really have anything to do with you."

His jaw clenched.

Goddamnit. Here it comes. The psychological interrogation.

Hunter sat up. He pulled away from Scarlet's body to balance on the edge of the blanket. "Yeah, I know," he told her, staring out into the forest. He ran both hands across his thighs, working to control the trembling in his fingers.

Scarlet sat up beside him. She blew out an exasperated breath.

He fought the urge to comfort her. He was not about to be fodder for anyone. Not even his little bird.

"But you obviously don't know, Hunter. You blame yourself for Samantha's death as sure as if you took her life with your own hands."

He shivered with the sound of Samantha's name. He couldn't recall it ever being spoken aloud since high school. "I know I didn't take her life. That was a horrible night, and the next few months were stressful, but it's in the past. I've moved on."

Scarlet froze against the blanket. She turned so stiff that he couldn't prevent himself from glancing at her, just to make sure she still breathed. The instant he met her intent gaze, he regretted it. She looked mournful, and soulful, and impassioned, and he knew she'd only begun.

"Good Lord, you can't actually believe that. You don't really think this was some bothersome event you've moved on from, do you?"

"Yes, I do believe it, because that's exactly what it is," he insisted. "And you can stop with your psychoanalysis of me now, because I already know what you're going to say next."

"What am I going to say next?"

"That I felt a lot of guilt about it and it fucked with my head."

"So, did you?"

"Did I what?"

"Did you feel a lot of guilt about it?"

Hunter turned away from her to glare at the trees. "I told you I was an asshole back then. I just...I wish she'd picked someone else. I mean, I wish she wouldn't have done it at all, but if she had to pick someone, it shouldn't have been me. She shouldn't have seen me as her knight in shining armor."

Scarlet moved closer to him. She eased her fingers onto his arm.

He flinched with her touch. "Do you want to know what I did the morning of the homecoming game, Scarlet?"

"What did you do?"

"I fucked two girls. Not at the same time, but...one of them was my girlfriend. The other one was her twin sister."

Her hand moved tenderly across his forearm. He grit his teeth as his little bird pet him, feeling his gut churn while he recounted his actions. "I went to my girlfriend's house first thing in the morning and climbed the trellis outside her window and snuck into her bedroom. I woke her up and told her I needed her, so I could have luck for the big game. She smiled at me and opened her arms and let me fuck her. When I'd finished, I climbed back outside and shimmied across the trellis to the next window. That was her twin sister's bedroom. She was already waiting for me, since we'd been sleeping together behind my girlfriend's back for a while. I looked right at her and said I needed luck before the big game. Then I fucked her, too. That's what I did the day Samantha took her life."

"Hunter...you were just a boy. Those were the actions of a boy."

"No," he protested, fisting his hands against his thighs. "I was an asshole. I was a complete fucking asshole and she shouldn't have picked me. Samantha should never have picked me."

Scarlet drew her hand slowly up his arm to reach for his face. She curved her fingers around his jaw and pulled him toward her. When he finally worked up the nerve to meet her eyes, she smiled softly. "You have too much guilt over this. More than any innocent has a right to."

Innocent? He had no goddamn clue how she could use that word to describe him. He only knew he needed to bury all of this back down now, deep in the recesses of his mind, where it had settled so long ago.

"I'm sorry to have to say this, Scarlet, but you don't know what you're talking about. Yes, I felt guilty back then because of what I'd done that day, but whatever guilt I may have felt as a teenager..."

"You have carried with you each and every day of your life since."

Hunter glared at her. "You know, this is why I don't tell people. They always want to make an issue out of something long gone and forgotten. I didn't tell you so you could use your amateur psychology on me. You asked me a question and I answered it. That's all."

She watched him with eyes as concerned and compassionate as they were focused and determined. Hunter knew she wasn't done. He knew she was going to come at him now, with all of the psychological vomit she'd learned up here at Blue, and he couldn't bear the thought of it.

He pulled away, shifting over on the blanket to stare at the oak tree.

Scarlet followed him immediately. She sat up on her knees, pressing the side of her body onto his, encircling his upper arm with her hand.

"You did answer my question, Hunter. I asked you to tell me about the event that changed your life forever – the one that changed who you are as a person – and you told me. The thing is, even though you knew exactly what it was, you still don't acknowledge the significance of it. Or the fact that it completely transformed you."

"You don't know that," he muttered, rejecting his need to touch her, to breathe her in, to drown in the warmth of her body.

"Don't I?" she whispered, her soft breath fanning over his cheek. "Last night, you admitted you hadn't truly laughed in years. We both know you have fierce control issues. You plan everything you do in excruciating detail. You don't let anyone around you take risks, because you don't want them making mistakes. You spend your life telling people what to do, just to save them from themselves."

"You can't...you can't relate all of that to one incident."

"Yes, I can. But it's not all about that one night. It's about the years and years of pressure and pain that have built on top of it. You threw yourself into a job that gives you the power to tell people what's best for them. You chastise your parents for climbing mountains because they might get hurt. You hate that your sister lives so far away because you want her under your thumb. You deny yourself the joys of nature because of its inherent chaos. My God, Hunter. You have let this guilt rule you. You've let it rule your *entire life*. And you've been so busy trying to maintain control of everything and everyone that you didn't even realize you never had control. Because nobody does. Not really."

Hunter shook his head, over and over. Good Lord, this was even worse than he'd imagined. Scarlet spewed more Freudian waste than he'd thought possible. But at least he'd learned his lesson: he would definitely never tell this to anyone, ever again.

"Honey," she sighed, her soft body nestling closer to his side, "will you please answer another question for me?"

"It depends," he replied, staring out at the endless trees, wishing she had no effect on him at all.

"On what does it depend?"

"On what the question is. I'm not making any more promises."

"Fair enough. Will you tell me about the relationships you've had? Since you've been an adult, I mean."

"Relationships?"

"With women."

Hunter shrugged. "There's not much to tell. Just the normal stuff."

"But you told me you want to be married. You said you want the house and the kids and everything. I imagine you've known dozens of women who were more than willing to give you that."

"I...I did find a woman. Once."

"Yeah? Will you tell me about her?"

He didn't like where this was headed. But he knew Scarlet wouldn't stop until he told her, and *holy hell*, he just wanted this over with.

"Her name was Clarissa. We were together for three years. She was a financial planner."

"And what did you like about her?"

"I don't know. The normal things you like about someone, I guess. She was beautiful. Intelligent. Socially connected. It made sense."

"What made sense?"

"She did. Any man would be lucky to have a future with her."

"I see. Did the two of you discuss a future?"

"Yes."

"Did she want to get married?"

"Actually, she asked me."

"Really? Well, then. Why aren't you married?"

A harsh laugh forced itself from his throat. "I don't know why. Is that what you want from me? Do you want to hear that I don't have any goddamn idea why I said no to her?"

"I know you don't. But I do. I know exactly why you said no."

He turned to see her face, so close to his own. "Well, of course you know. Because, apparently, you have all the answers."

Scarlet's hand tightened on his arm. "I didn't say I have all the answers. But I do have this answer. Would you like to hear it?"

"Oh, sure. Why not?"

"Okay, here it is. You told me last night that you aren't married because you haven't found the right woman. But the real reason is that you aren't looking for the right kind of woman. You don't want a wife who simply makes sense. The real Hunter Gregory – the one you've kept buried since that night in high school – doesn't want a woman who checks off boxes on a list. He wants someone who challenges him. He wants someone he can argue with. He wants someone to explore the world with. He wants a woman who gives him everything, and takes everything, all at the same time. You are not a man who wants a boring, perfect little life. You think you do, because of all the years you've tortured yourself with guilt over Samantha. You think if you lead a picture-perfect existence, with a picture-perfect wife, then you will do her memory justice. You think it will prove her final beliefs weren't based on lies. Except you can't quite force yourself to go through with it, because deep down, it's not who you really are."

Hunter stared at her for stretched seconds before he could form words. "Good God. You realize everything you're saying is ludicrous, right? Samantha isn't the reason I can't make a relationship work."

Scarlet's shoulders dropped. Her eyes fell to the ground. He knew she was disappointed in him. Honestly, he hoped her frustration with his response meant she would finally give up on this absurd psychoanalysis of his life. But when her determined gaze fixated on him once again, he could tell she'd simply been gearing up for more.

"Okay, then. Let's look at another issue. What about your work?"

He huffed out a laugh. "What about it?"

"How many hours a week are you at your job?"

"What difference does that make?"

"I'm just curious. How many hours a week?"

"I don't know. Maybe seventy or eighty."

"That's almost every waking minute, you know."

"I'm the goddamn CEO, Scarlet."

"When was the last time you took a vacation before this one?"

"It's been a few years."

"A few?"

"It's been a while. I don't remember how long. Having a work ethic isn't a flaw. Those people – my employees – they rely on me."

"I know they do, and you give them everything. I can see that. I know you want to make their lives better. I know you want to be strong for them, so they'll have all they need to be happy. But you don't leave anything for yourself. You don't have anything to come home to."

Hunter's blood boiled in his veins, because a frolicking freebird would have no fucking clue what it meant to be responsible for the lives of so many people. "No offense, but you don't know what the hell you're talking about. I am officially done with this conversation now."

She held tighter to his arm. "You work so hard for everyone else, but you don't leave anything for yourself. And it's killing you."

"Stop. I don't want to talk about this anymore."

"You've been cowering in dread since that night in high school. You've never held your goddaughter, because you're afraid you'll break her. You can't even understand why your best friend loves you, because you don't realize how loveable you are."

"*Scarlet...*"

"I can't stand to see you suffer this way."

"*Stop*. I'm telling you to *stop*."

"Because you are, Hunter. You're suffering."

"Damn it, I said stop!"

"No. I need you to hear me. I need you to see. You've allowed this to suck the joy from your life. It's killing you, slowly but surely, and I can't bear to watch..."

"Then you don't have to!"

Hunter detached from her body and stood. He took several steps away, coming to a stop in front of the oak tree, with his back turned to her. Every muscle he owned tensed as his next words rushed out.

"We've already decided this thing between us isn't permanent. We both know we're only on vacation here. So, if you think I'm suffering and you can't bear to watch, then you should just *leave me*."

He stared at the oak's trunk, clenching his teeth so tight he thought his jaw would break. He listened as Scarlet heaved out a sigh. He heard the padding of her bare feet as she came to stand behind him.

"I don't want to leave you," she said, her voice like an angel's.

Hunter's heartbeat pounded in his ears while he stared at all of the cracks and crevices in the bark. "Then I won't give you a choice." He turned to face her, straightening to his full height and staring hard into her brimming eyes. "We've had a few fun days together, you and I. But that's all this was, so now we'll say goodbye. For good, this time."

A tear fell down her cheek.

His stomach ground against itself, pushing acid into his throat.

"But, Hunter..."

"I'm serious, Scarlet. Take me back to my cabin. I'm done here."

She brushed at her wet skin with the back of her hand. "Okay. If that's what you really want, I'll take you back. And we'll say goodbye."

He battled the stinging behind his eyelids. "That's what I want."

A hundred different emotions crawled over her face as she studied him. He made himself stand tall and take it all in. Eventually, she said, "Okay." He'd never felt more relieved or more sickened.

Hunter continued staring at her, waiting for her to move. He waited for her to turn and lead him out of this forest, back to some semblance of safety. He waited a thousand hours.

Then she smiled so softly and sweetly that it forced all the air from his lungs. "Before we go," she breathed, taking a step toward him, "can I ask you for one more thing?"

"Good Lord! What in the hell do you want now?"

She blinked with the harshness of his voice. "Will you please give me a hug goodbye? I promise I won't ask you for anything else. I just want to feel your touch one more time. Just once more."

Debilitating pain tore through his chest. He feared she'd broken something inside him, something that could never be fixed. But the thought of denying her this one last thing, as she looked up at him with the biggest, saddest eyes he'd ever seen, hurt a million times worse.

"*Fine*," he told her.

His entire body clenched, hard as stone, as he waited for her to come to him. She gazed into his eyes for an eternity. By the time she stepped up to him, and reached her hands to his waist, Hunter's muscles burned.

Scarlet wrapped her arms around him, curling her fingers into the back of his shirt. She rested her cheek against his chest, nuzzling her ear over his heart. She sighed and melted into him entirely.

Hunter remained stiff as a board.

He wanted to hold her. He *needed* to hold her. But he knew he couldn't. He forced himself to remain still, with his arms at his sides, knowing this was for the best. She needed to walk away from him. He needed to let her go. He *had* to.

He almost made it. He almost endured her entire embrace without breaking. He lasted until she started to pull away. But then he couldn't take it anymore.

As Scarlet straightened, as she eased her arms away from his body, he grabbed hold of her shoulders. She lifted her head from his chest, tilting her face up to see him. He leaned down to press his cheek against hers, feeling the softness of her skin against his scratchy stubble. His fingers squeezed into her arms as he breathed raggedly beside her ear.

She didn't move. She didn't twitch or squirm or pull away from the fierce grip of his hands. She did tremble, though.

He knew he should leave her alone. She was too good. Too pure. Too innocent. He should walk away. He should run away.

But he didn't. He just stood there, listening to the shallow breaths escaping her lips. He stood there as long as he could. Then he dragged his cheek across hers and sought out her mouth. The instant he pressed his lips to hers, he hauled her body closer, banding her so fiercely to his chest that she whimpered inside his merciless grip.

Hunter deepened the kiss, pushing himself fully inside her. Scarlet let him. She sank into his severe embrace, curling her arms around his shoulders and running her fingers into his hair.

He kissed her as hard as he could. In the back of his mind, he knew it was too hard. Too punishing. He wanted to stop, and he didn't want to stop. She just held him, caressed him, and let him do as he desired.

Hunter couldn't bear it. He couldn't accept this trust she willingly gave. He pulled back, tearing his mouth away and staring into her face.

Scarlet gazed up at him as serenely as ever. He didn't know why she still stood here, especially with her lips swollen from the callousness of his kiss. She was so childlike and so beautiful and so full of life and he'd never felt more like an animal than he did right now.

"You need to leave," Hunter growled.

"I'm not going anywhere."

"You need to *leave*," he demanded, not recognizing his own voice.

Scarlet shook her head, slow and steady.

Goddamnit, doesn't she know what's best for her?

He gripped tight to her shoulders. "If you stay here, I am going to do exactly what I want to do."

Hunter expected her to recoil from the feral look in his eyes.

She didn't. Her determination never wavered.

He decided to give her one last warning. "If you stay here, you will not touch me. I will do *all* the touching. I will be in control of *everything*. Do you understand?"

"Yes," she consented. "I understand."

Hunter groaned from the pain of her surrender.

"Lift your arms, Scarlet."

She complied. She didn't flinch or falter. She didn't take her eyes off of his. She raised her hands above her head and stilled.

He reached to the hem of her sweatshirt and gathered the fabric in his hands. His fingers scraped against the warm skin at her waist. She sucked in a breath but didn't move.

Hunter watched her closely as he raised the shirt up, all the way to the end of her fingertips, before letting it fall to the ground. He stared at her smooth skin. He knew the air was frigid. He knew she would start to shiver soon. But she still didn't move.

Reaching around her back, he undid the clasp of her bra. He lifted the black lace up and over her arms. He let it fall.

Hunter grabbed the hem of his own shirt and whipped it up over his head, tossing it next to her clothes in the dirt. Stepping into her body, he pressed his bare chest against hers. Her tight nipples pushed into his skin, and a little moan escaped her lips, but she still didn't move. Reaching down, he grabbed hold of her ass and lifted her.

"Wrap your legs around me," he demanded, waiting impatiently until she obeyed. When her thighs encased his waist, she lowered her hands onto his shoulders. Hunter winced at the tenderness of her touch.

He took the necessary steps to reach the blanket. Grasping her tightly, he lowered her onto the soft fabric. He covered her body with his, pressing her into the ground. Scarlet's hands eased into his hair.

"Put your arms back above your head. Now."

Her lashes fluttered for a moment, but she did as ordered. She placed her arms above her head, beside the halo of dark curls framing her face. Hunter stared down into her wide, trusting eyes.

He didn't want her to look at him. He couldn't bear for her to see. He let his forehead fall onto her chest, resting against her heart.

Her skin was warm and perfect and he pressed his lips to it. For a second, he tried to be gentle. It didn't work. He gave up and bit down.

Scarlet arched beneath him as he pulled her flesh between his teeth. He licked and nipped her skin, moving from one breast to the other, taking each nipple into his mouth in turn. He sucked in tight and hard until she cried out harshly into the cold air. Her thighs squeezed around his hips, holding him to her.

"Unwrap your legs. Put your feet on the ground," he commanded when he finally released her breast from his mouth. Her nipples were taut and jutting, still wet from his tongue. She moaned as she complied.

When Hunter felt her thighs spread open, he pressed his lips to her breastbone. He bit into her flesh again before dragging his mouth down the center of her body, purposefully scraping his rough chin stubble across her pale skin. When he reached the top of her pants, he nipped at her stomach while curling his fingers into the waistband.

He shifted back to sit up on his knees. "Lift your hips, Scarlet."

She submitted instantly, matching his stare as he pulled her pants down her thighs. He reached to one of her bare feet, bending her leg up so he could remove her pant leg. When that was done, he stripped the remaining material from her other leg and threw it to the side.

Scarlet lay before him then, in nothing but a tiny pair of black thong panties. He knew it was too goddamn cold out here for her to be naked, but she didn't say a word. She didn't protest anything. She just looked up at him, with her arms above her head, and waited.

Her fingers dug into the blanket beside her hair. Her chest shifted on shallow breaths, her taut, wet nipples pointed skyward. The skin from her neck to her belly was dark pink, marred by the coarse scruff on his chin. Red bite marks tarnished the cream color of her breasts and belly.

Hunter stared at the evidence of what he'd already done.

His little bird was so sweet and so trusting and he was going to devour her. She should care about that. She should possess the self-preservation to get the hell away from him. Obviously, she didn't.

I'm tougher than I look. She'd said those words to him more than once. But Hunter didn't know if she was tough enough to truly be with him. He didn't think anyone could be that strong.

Reaching to the straps at her hips, he ripped her underwear off. She gasped, but still didn't move. He let the torn material fall to the ground. Then he dropped down on the blanket, buried his face between her thighs, pressed his mouth to her sex, and drank her in.

Hunter heard her swift inhalation, and her shuddered moan, as he ran his tongue into her tender folds. He wrapped his arms around both her thighs, hitching her knees up over his shoulders to get a better grip on her body. He held her tightly in place while he dove in, licking and tasting and sucking and doing every damn thing he'd wanted to do since the moment she'd first walked out of the woods by the side of the road.

He wasn't playful with her. He wasn't gentle. He was determined and consuming and insistent and he didn't let up. Not for a second.

Scarlet didn't fight him. She stayed as still as possible while she groaned with every movement of his mouth and his tongue. The noisier she became, the harder he held her in place.

Hunter was so engrossed in her body, so engrossed in his ability to finally taste her sex, that he didn't notice her touch. He didn't notice her hands slipping onto his head. He didn't notice the soft ruffling of her fingers through his hair. Not at first.

But then he did. He felt her caress him during his invasion, and he sure as hell couldn't accept that tenderness right now. Snapping his head up, he looked to her face. Her eyes were slammed shut. Her teeth were clamped onto her lip, practically drawing blood.

"Scarlet. Look at me. Now."

Her eyelids popped open. She stared down at his face between her legs. Her lip eased free of her teeth when she drew a shaky breath in.

"Put. Your. Arms. Above. Your. Head."

She whimpered with his command.

"I told you before. You will *not* touch me."

Hunter waited forever for her to submit. Finally, she did. She gave in, returning her hands to the top of the blanket. Only then did he return to her wet, salty skin.

He buried his face between her thighs, buried his tongue deep inside her walls. She tasted like honey and wine and *her*, as intoxicating as any drug he could fathom. He worked her tender flesh over thoroughly with his mouth, drunk off the power and control.

Scarlet mewled and panted and wriggled. When he pulled one hand from her thigh to press his fingers inside her tight, soaking sheath, she shouted into the cold forest air. Her inner muscles squeezed around his fingers and he knew she was so close to the edge.

Hunter wanted her to come. He wanted her to come uncontrollably and violently against his tongue. He wanted to know she would give him everything, absolutely everything, without question. Even though that knowledge would torture him as much as it empowered him.

Her hips moved with sinful rhythm while he continued fucking her with his mouth and his fingers, over and over and over. He manipulated her flesh expertly, relishing the wetness he coaxed from deep inside her body, while he nipped and licked and sucked on her tight little circle of nerves. When Scarlet finally let herself go, when she gave into him entirely, she clamped her thighs against his neck and screamed.

Hunter's erection throbbed in his pants as he pressed his face into her folds and rode the crest of her orgasm. The insane, feral noises she made echoed off the trees and through his chest. *Goddamnit*, he needed to be inside her. He needed to fuck her. Hard. Untamed. Unrelenting.

Pulling his fingers back out of her, he grabbed hold of her thighs and pried them apart. He sat up, reached for his zipper, and freed his cock, all in an instant. He dropped forward on his arms and plunged himself inside her, driving deep and full into the warm walls of her sex. She inhaled sharply when his chest landed on hers.

Hunter found himself face-to-face with his little bird.

She looked up at him beneath heavy-lidded eyes. He knew she was still in the aftermath of her orgasm, since he could feel the waves of her inner muscles contracting around his thick length. But he still needed her to pay attention, so she could comprehend what he was about to do.

"Scarlet," he said, waiting until she could focus. "You need to keep your hands above your head. You understand that?"

She nodded slowly.

"I'm going to be rough," he confessed. He wasn't just talking about this moment. But it was the only warning he could get out.

Hunter forced himself to be still as he waited for her consent.

Or, more likely, her refusal.

He fully expected her to deny him, since he needed to use her right now. He needed to use her body for his own selfish purpose, and he didn't want her to allow it. He wanted her to shove him away. He wanted her to fight against him with all her might. He wanted her to tell him he was a goddamn monster and to get the fuck off of her.

Hunter lay still, buried inside of her, waiting for her rejection.

Except Scarlet didn't reject him. She didn't deny him anything. Instead, she gazed up at him in gentle acceptance, curled her fingers tighter into the blanket beneath her hair, and said, "I'm here."

That was her answer. *I'm here.*

He knew, without a single doubt, that he didn't deserve her.

Hunter began fucking her then. He fucked her as hard as he possibly could. He wasn't loving. He didn't kiss her. He dropped his head into her shoulder, desperate to not have to see her face, as he drove himself inside her over and over. He took it all out on her – all his frustration, all his pain, all those godforsaken, everlasting years of anger and fear and self-loathing. He took it all out on her with a relentless, frantic, pounding need.

Scarlet just allowed it, panting beside his ear as he lost himself inside the haven of her body. Hunter heard the wispy sounds that escaped her throat with every hammering thrust, her delicate little moans gripping like a vice around his heart. He didn't deserve her acceptance. He didn't deserve her understanding. He sure as hell didn't deserve her innocence. But he took it anyway. He took everything she offered, took every single tiny piece of her she gave him. And he still wanted more.

He kept fucking her, his forceful lunges into her body now turning stuttered and desperate. Yet Scarlet's hands remained exactly where they were. She lay utterly pliant and peaceful and willing beneath him.

At this moment, Hunter loved her, and hated himself, all at once.

He jerked fiercely into her several more times before his orgasm hit him like a freight train. He came inside her with a harsh, roaring growl. His whole body tensed and pulsed as he emptied himself entirely.

Scarlet wrapped her legs around his back, enveloping him while he took his release. Hunter collapsed on top of her, pressing her fully into the ground. He buried his forehead in her neck, struggling to draw air back into his lungs. She linked her feet together at the base of his spine, holding him to her more securely, although he honestly couldn't comprehend why.

As soon as he could, he used every ounce of strength remaining in his body to grab onto her. He wrapped his arms around her shoulders, gripping tighter and tighter while battling the sting of salt behind his eyelids. Wetness fell onto his cheek. For a moment, he thought the tears were his. Then he realized they weren't.

Hunter raised his head to see her. Tiny droplets streamed from her glassy green eyes. His stomach dropped to his feet.

"Oh, God, no," he breathed, grabbing her face in both hands. "Did I hurt you? I'm sorry, Scarlet. I'm so, so sorry. Please forgive me."

She shook her head and more tears fell, slipping down her cheeks and onto his fingers. "You didn't hurt me, Hunter. I need you to understand that. You're a good person. You're a good man."

He traced the outline of her face. "I don't...I don't understand how you can say that. You're crying. I must have hurt you."

"That's not why I'm crying. I swear you didn't hurt me."

"Then why are you crying?"

Her lips trembled. "I'm crying because I can't bear to lose you yet."

"Wh-what? What are you talking about?"

"You said you wanted to say goodbye to me."

All the air slammed out of his lungs. He hadn't even remembered saying those fucking idiotic words. "Scarlet, I..."

"No, wait. I need to apologize. I pushed you too hard. You confided in me, and I pushed you, and I'll understand if you don't want to see me anymore. But is there any chance at all that you might change your mind? If I promise not to say anything else about your past after we leave these woods today, could you possibly stay with me?"

"Good Lord, you don't have to ask me that. I have no desire to say goodbye to you, ever. Those were stupid, panicked words that I didn't mean and should never have said."

She gave him a tremulous smile. "So, we'll stay together while we're up on this mountain?"

"Of course. We'll stay together for as long as you want."

"Oh, thank goodness," she sighed, her fingers twisting in the blanket beside her hair. "Can I...can I please touch you now?"

"Only if you still want to."

She immediately raised her hands to his face, running her fingers across his jaw and into his hair. Hunter's heart came to a grinding halt as she smiled up at him with peaceful, tender affection.

"I'm sorry, Scarlet. I'm sorry. I'm sorry. I'm sorry," he echoed, knowing he could never say it enough. "I'm so sorry for what I did."

"You don't have to apologize. It's okay."

Hunter stared hard into her eyes. "No, it's not okay. I'm sorry for everything, and I need you to forgive me."

"But you didn't hurt me. I already told you that."

"I need you to forgive me."

Scarlet steadied his face in her hands. "I do forgive you."

His heart restarted, pounding wildly inside his chest. He shook his head again, over and over, because she didn't understand. She couldn't possibly understand. "No, not just for today. I need you to forgive me for everything. For *everything*."

Another tear fell down her cheek. "Hunter...you were just a boy."

He reached his fingers into her hair. "I need you to forgive me."

"Listen to me, honey. Really listen. You're a good person. You're strong and caring and passionate and so very, very loveable. The boy you were can't hurt the man you are now. Not if you don't let him."

He clenched her curls tighter in his hands. "I need you to forgive me. God, Scarlet, please. *Forgive me*."

She looked up at him with nothing but peaceful, certain acceptance. Raising her head from the blanket, she pressed her lips to his for one perfect moment. "I forgive you," she whispered. "You're forgiven."

Hunter listened to her. He listened to those gorgeous, amazing words before crumpling down onto her chest. His forehead fell against her shoulder as the tears he'd never wanted began spilling from his eyes.

The moment his tears landed on Scarlet's skin, her own fell without constraint. He held her as close as he could while tremors wracked her body. She held him back harder, clinging to him with all she possessed.

Hunter breathed her into his lungs and allowed himself to cry. He let himself feel everything all at once, until he sobbed beyond control. Yet somehow, Scarlet managed to keep him in one piece.

For the first time in as long as he could remember, Hunter didn't feel entirely broken. He felt raw and exposed and bare, but not broken. At this very moment, after sixteen long, miserable, lonely years, he thought maybe, just maybe, he could pull himself back together.

9

UNBREAKABLE

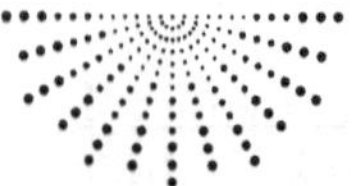

Hunter and Scarlet walked out of the forest together, hand in hand.

He looked to her constantly, trying to gauge her expression. She always gazed back at him the same way, with a kind smile and adoring eyes. It made his heart clench tighter in his chest.

Hunter wanted to grip onto her hand like a vice, to ensure she would never leave his side. But he knew he couldn't, since his little bird had the right to fly away from him at any moment. Instead, he held onto her gently, taking utmost care to not harm her in any way, shape, or form.

Scarlet led him from the woods directly to her cabin. He didn't question it. He simply trusted her to take him where he needed to go.

When they stepped through the front door into her living room, she arched up on her tiptoes to kiss his cheek. "Make yourself at home," she instructed before closing the door and disappearing down the hall.

Hunter stood stiffly, watching her retreating back. He wanted to do as she'd said, but he couldn't feel at home here without her. The instant she left his sight, his blood rushed furiously through his veins. He remained in place, raw and unnerved, until she returned.

The moment she reemerged from the hall, Hunter could breathe normally again. When Scarlet realized he hadn't moved from that one spot, she walked up to him and took his hand. "Come with me," she encouraged, guiding him to a chair at her kitchen table.

He absorbed the sight of his forest fairy while she urged him into a seat. She'd changed into a pink T-shirt and navy pajama bottoms, even though it was the middle of the day. He knew she'd had to put on a new outfit because of him, since he'd thrown her clothes in the dirt and torn off her underwear. And although she'd granted him unquestioning forgiveness for everything, he still hated himself for what he'd done.

Memories of what just happened between them in the woods accosted him. He clenched his jaw as he sat stiff as stone at her kitchen table. Scarlet regarded him for several moments before ruffling her fingers through his hair and kissing his forehead. "Please don't forget to breathe, Hunter. I really need you to breathe."

He did what she asked. He took a deep, ragged inhale and exhaled slowly, allowing his icy body to seek the heat of hers. She wrapped her arms around him, cradling his face to her chest. She secured him to her, but Hunter was afraid to hold her back. He was afraid to touch her at all.

Scarlet started petting him, stroking her fingers gently up and down his arms. He closed his eyes and sank into her embrace. Eventually, his body eased enough for him to lay his hands carefully against her hips. She placed another kiss on his forehead. "How about some lunch? Can you eat something for me?"

"Yes," he agreed, wanting to do something – anything – for her.

She left his side just long enough to gather the lunch tray from the porch and bring it to the table. Perching herself on the chair beside him, she picked up her sandwich, tore it in two, and handed him the larger portion. He didn't protest. He just took the offering, and chewed and swallowed, as he watched her.

Scarlet started talking as they ate. She talked about the redheaded woodpecker they'd seen in the woods this morning. Between bites of sandwich and long sips of tea, she told him about the bird's nesting habits and dietary needs and how woodpeckers had evolved special anatomical qualities to protect their brains from damage while they compulsively hammered their beaks into tree trunks.

Hunter heard a lot of what she said. But mostly he heard her voice. It was familiar and soothing and he could focus on it. Her voice settled him, and grounded him, and he began to feel comfortable touching her. Tenderly, of course. Reverently. He stroked her forearm with the tips of his fingers as she spoke, unendingly fascinated by the feel of her skin.

When they'd finished lunch, and she'd completed her oral report on woodpeckers, she asked if he wanted to play a board game. He agreed immediately. Honestly, he would do anything to be here with her.

He walked to the hall closet as Scarlet placed the empty tray on the porch. He stared at the games on the shelves for a long minute, then just picked the one on top. "How does Scrabble sound?" he asked while stepping back to the kitchen.

"Sounds great to me." She smiled as they settled onto the chairs around the table again. Hunter smiled back while opening the box.

Scarlet kicked his ass at Scrabble. He wanted to say it was because he took it easy on her, but that wasn't true at all. She was phenomenal at it, and he came to the realization that she was the one taking it easy on him. By the time they'd finished playing, the score was basically a bazillion to one. But at least he'd learned a few new words.

As she packed the game back into the box, he heard Colin's truck coming down her driveway. "I'll go get your dinner," Hunter offered.

"Thanks."

He stepped through the front door and down the porch steps, meeting Colin as he exited the driver's seat. The sun was setting, but even in the dim light, Hunter could tell the young man looked better now than he had this morning. "Hey, Colin. You hanging in there?"

The boy shrugged. "Yeah. I'm slowly realizing this isn't the worst day of my life. How about you?"

Hunter didn't know what today was, so he just said, "I'm still here."

"Good. I'm really glad you are." Colin reached into the back of the truck and pulled out two trays. "I brought your dinner over here. I figured, when you weren't at your cabin, you'd be with her."

Yes, I am with her. That much I do know.

"I appreciate you looking out for me."

"Sure. Happy to do it."

By the time Hunter stepped back inside, Scarlet had lit candles on the coffee table and set two chair cushions at the base of the couch. She looked up at him. "Do you mind if we sit on the floor for dinner?"

He nodded as he kicked the door shut behind him. "Sure. Colin brought my food over here, so there's plenty."

"Oh, wonderful. He's so thoughtful."

"Yeah, he is," Hunter agreed, setting the trays beside the candles.

They situated themselves on the floor cushions, eating in silence, except for when Scarlet hummed as she chewed. Or when she offered random remarks on the tastiness of the meal and how Phil-the-chef deserved some sort of award. Hunter simply nodded in agreement.

Once they'd finished eating, he pulled himself up onto the couch. "Come sit with me?" he asked, reaching his hand out to her.

"Love to," she answered, clasping onto his fingers and standing from the ground. The only light in the cabin came from her candles, since the world outside had turned to darkness. The golden glow of the flames haloed her body, and he'd never seen her look more angelic. He'd also never needed to have her in his arms more than he did right now.

Scarlet settled down beside him on the couch cushion.

"You're too far away from me," Hunter complained.

"Really? If I move any closer, I'll be in your lap."

"Yes, please."

She met his expectant eyes. Then she eased her legs across his and scooted over, settling her bottom onto his thighs. Hunter reached one arm around her back, supporting her as she sat sideways on top of him. His other hand slipped onto her legs, smoothing lightly across her pajama-clad thighs. Scarlet's head fell onto his chest and her hand came to rest over his heart, where it always found a home.

He finally relaxed, more than he had all day. She was here in his arms, real and warm and solid. She wouldn't fly away tonight.

"How is this?" she questioned as her fingers curled into his shirt.

"It's wonderful."

"What would you like to do for the rest of the night?"

Hunter stroked her legs. "I just want you to talk to me some more."

"Yeah? What do you want me to talk about?"

"Anything you want. Maybe you could tell me about Girl Scouts."

"Girl Scouts? My goodness, you have no idea what you're asking. I could talk about Girl Scouts for hours."

He pressed a kiss to the top of her head. "That sounds perfect."

Scarlet wasn't kidding. She talked about Girl Scouts for three entire hours. Hunter learned everything she knew about trees, birds, pitching tents, and tying knots. He listened to the many escapades she'd had with her best friend, Holly Stanton, and how they'd dreamed of exploring the world when they grew up.

Hunter paid rapt attention as Scarlet recalled how her mother came on some of the camping trips while her father was busy at work, and how Dianna Tracey would sit around the bonfire at night, teaching the girls to make animal shadows with their hands in the firelight. He heard every word Scarlet said to him, relishing the picture she painted. He could almost see the young woman she was, so joyful and openhearted, discovering her spirit while forging an unbeaten path through the woods.

He held her the entire time she spoke. He rubbed her back, caressed her arms, and smoothed over her hair, all while she leaned heavier against his chest. Her words continued on and on, until they slowly began to trail off, with longer pauses lingering in between. Eventually, her words stopped entirely.

Her whole body slumped onto his as her breathing assumed a steady, even pace.

Hunter knew she'd dozed off, but he didn't dare twitch a muscle for fear of disturbing her peace. Or his own. After several more minutes, tiny snores escaped her throat. Yet her fierce little fist still held tight over his heart.

He peered down at his forest fairy as her mouth hung open against his shirt and her curls spread out across his shoulder. This image of her struck deep, since he was intensely aware that he'd never felt her asleep in his arms before this moment. He'd never lain beside her in a bed. He'd never made love to her. Hell, what he'd done to her in the forest this morning was nearly the exact opposite of making love, and he needed to make up for his actions. His Scarlet was precious, and he wanted her safe and sound and happy. Always happy.

Today, he hadn't made her happy. He'd made her cry. She should have been crying because of how rough he'd been with her. Instead, she'd cried in fear of losing him...which, he now realized, meant the entire time he'd been using her body, she believed he would walk away from her when he'd finished. And still, despite all of that, she'd given herself to him without limitations.

He'd honestly never met anyone so generous or selfless in his whole life. He didn't know how his forest fairy even existed, let alone how she came to be here with him. He didn't know why she'd picked him, of all the men in the world, to share her love and joy and trust with.

Hunter sat very still as she snored and clung to his shirt, just feeling her in his arms. Then he glanced to the far wall, where she'd hung the photo of her bird. He remembered how excited she'd been the day she showed him the picture, how she'd fretted over whether it was straight and how she'd asked for his help aligning the frame on the knotty wall.

Scarlet had never mentioned the yellow-crowned purple fantini again. Not since the night she'd agreed to stop lying to him. He was more certain now than ever that the bird didn't exist, yet she'd still taken the photo and nailed the picture right into the wall. He couldn't help wondering what significance the blurry green-and-yellow image held for her. He wondered what she saw inside of it that he couldn't.

Hunter wanted to ask her that question. He wanted to ask her a million questions...especially what had stolen the color red away from her. But she'd promised him in the woods today to not push any further about his past, so he didn't want to push her, either. Instead, he wanted to be gentle and loving with her, allowing her to work out her problems with him beside her, supporting her in any way he could.

Scarlet went completely limp in his arms then. Her hand finally fell from his chest onto her lap. He was pretty sure she'd drooled on his shirt, but he still didn't want to move from this spot. He just wanted to stay here and keep holding her for as long as he could.

Unfortunately, when Clearly Comatose Scarlet began mumbling garbled words, Hunter begrudgingly admitted her need to sleep in a warm, cozy bed. Gathering her close to his heart, he lifted his little bird and stood from the couch. He took a moment to balance himself, since his legs were unsteady from sitting with her for so long and he didn't want to drop her. He would never forgive himself if he let her fall.

He carried her through the living room, down the hall, and into her bedroom. As he stepped through the doorway, he became acutely aware that this was the first time he'd ever been in her bedroom. He wished he'd gotten here under different circumstances.

The room was dimly lit by faint moonlight from the window as he stepped cautiously over to her mattress. He eased Scarlet down on the plaid comforter and watched her curl into a ball. Hunter wanted nothing more than to lie beside her, to be the big spoon to her small one, and wake in the morning with a sleepy fairy in his arms. But she hadn't actually invited him into her bedroom, and he didn't want the first night he spent here to be without her explicit knowledge or desire.

He covered her body with a blanket he found at the end of the bed, tucking the green fabric around her sides. He leaned down to press a kiss to her temple. Scarlet stirred with the movement but didn't open her eyes.

"Wi'you come dinner 'morrow?" she breathed.

Hunter smiled into her hair. "Yes, honey. I'll be here for dinner tomorrow. Now get some sleep, please."

"Hmm...'kay."

He watched her for another moment as she snuggled her face into the soft quilt beneath her cheek, then he turned and walked out of her bedroom. He strode through her living room, out her front door, and down her porch stairs. He marched up her gravel driveway, across the deserted main road, and down his own driveway.

When he reached his cabin, Hunter stepped inside and shut the door. He moved immediately over to the table where the landline phone sat. He picked up the receiver and dialed the front desk.

"This is Blissful Blue. How may I help you?"

He sighed in relief. "Oh, good. I'm glad it's you, Pete. I was worried you wouldn't be there, since it's so late."

"I'm always around, Hunter. You doing okay?"

"I just, I need to, um..." His voice trailed into silence. He could hear the little gnome breathing on the other end of the phone.

Pete cleared his throat. "You know, Dr. Abbott has an appointment available tomorrow at 1 p.m. How does that sound?"

"God, that...that actually sounds perfect."

"Okay. I've got you scheduled, then. Cabin 13, tomorrow at 1."

"Thank you, Pete."

"Of course. You get some rest, now."

"I will."

"'Night, Hunter."

"'Night."

Hunter hung up the phone. He only stared at the receiver for another second. Then he dragged himself to his bedroom, collapsed on top of the sheets, and fell instantly to sleep.

~

WHEN HUNTER WOKE the next morning, his first thought was of Scarlet. And his second. And his third. Pretty much every thought he had while laying in bed was of her, except for the few of his therapy appointment.

Hunter was ready to see the *doctor* today. The word didn't even make him nauseous, not like it normally would. He was truly ready now to start putting things back together.

Scarlet had given him that ability. She'd given him everything, and he had no idea if he'd given her anything, but he was going to try. For the next two weeks, he would try to be everything she needed. He could barely stomach the idea of walking away from Blue without her, but if he really had to, then he would damn well do right by her before he left.

After finally dragging himself out of bed, Hunter threw on his gym clothes and headed to see Tyler for their regular morning basketball game. He expected his friend to already be warming up on the court, but when Hunter arrived, the blacktop was empty. He scanned the courtyard, spotting Tyler on a bench near the woods behind the gym.

As Hunter approached, he noted the slump of his friend's shoulders and the shifting of his fingers. "Hey, buddy, how are you?"

Tyler lifted his head, his features drawn. "Oh, hey, Hunter. I wasn't sure you'd show today."

"Yeah, sorry I wasn't here yesterday. I had somewhere I needed to be. But I'm up for a game today, if you are."

"I, um, I don't know about that."

Hunter sat beside his friend on the thick log bench. "Why not?"

Tyler huffed. "Hell, you're gonna think I'm ridiculous if I tell you."

"I'm not going to think you're ridiculous. It's obvious something's upsetting you. I know I'm not a therapist, but you can still talk to me."

"I appreciate that, man. It's just...it's Jocelyn. She's gone home."

"Oh. I'm sorry."

"Yeah, me too, although it's not like I didn't know it was coming. I knew she only had a week left when I met her, but I still feel like dirt. The worst part is that it's my own fault. I get too attached to women when I'm up here. It's one of the pitfalls of this place, yet I still do it."

Hunter shuddered. "Don't be so hard on yourself. You can't always control your emotions. Sometimes you want things that aren't possible."

"Yeah, but I knew it wasn't possible from the beginning. I live in New York. She lives in California. I was never going to be able to convince her to move across the country after knowing me for a week."

Damn, I have no clue where Scarlet lives. She could be visiting here from Timbuktu, for all I know.

"Isn't there a way to see her after you leave, Tyler? Long distance relationships are tough, but you can probably make it work."

I have a company plane. I can fly to Timbuktu if need be.

"No, I can't. It's finished. I just have to accept it and move on."

"But maybe you don't."

"Thanks for the wishful thinking, buddy, but that's all it is. I need to deal with the fact that she's gone and keep moving forward."

Hunter gulped. "I guess that's the right answer. Relationships that start up here on this mountain aren't meant to last."

"That is the right answer," Tyler agreed, patting him on the back. "Thanks for bringing me back to reality."

"Yeah. Sure."

"Now, what about you?"

"What about me?"

"Why are you so upset today?"

"Do I look upset?"

"Right now you do."

"Oh, it's nothing, really." *God help me, I still don't want you to know about Scarlet.* "I just have a therapy appointment today."

"A therapy appointment? Well, you shouldn't be upset about that. I think it's great you're going to give it a try. You know, the doctors up here take turns giving group lectures. We could go to some together, if that makes it easier for you."

"I appreciate the offer, Tyler. Truly. But I think I need to start out by myself. I'm going to try some one on one."

"Who are you seeing?"

"Dr. Abbott."

"Nice choice. He's really good. Super strict, of course. He's the big boss up here at Blue. I've always wanted him to like me. Probably because of a latent desire for my father's approval that I transferred over to Abbott, because he's in charge."

Hunter chuckled. "That's a nice self-diagnosis."

"Eh, you get pretty good at that when you've been in therapy as long as I have. But I'm happy for you. I think it's great you're seeing him."

"Thanks."

"You're welcome. And thank you."

"What for?"

"For helping me realize I need to move on from Jocelyn. That's going to make things so much easier for me tonight."

"Yeah? What's tonight?"

"I have a date with Mitzi Fisher. You said you didn't want her, since you have another woman up here, so I figured I could date her?"

Hunter stared at his friend. "Oh. Well, sure, I guess. I mean, it's fine by me if you date Mitzi. I certainly have no interest there. But I just thought you were really upset about Jocelyn leaving."

"God, yes, I am. But what better way to get over one woman than to be with another woman?"

Holy hell, how can you even think that? I can't imagine being with any woman but Scarlet. Ever.

"Tyler, I don't know if that's a very healthy thought."

"Sure it is. We all have our coping mechanisms. This is mine. Now, how about some basketball?"

Hunter watched the man stand from the bench. He rose slowly to meet him. "Yeah, we can play some ball."

"Let's go. Time's wasting." Tyler stepped toward the blacktop.

"Coming," Hunter replied, putting one foot in front of the other.

⁓

AFTER PLAYING the worst game of basketball in the history of the sport, Hunter left a grinning Tyler and proceeded back to his cabin to shower and eat. At 12:45, he left to walk up the hill toward Cabin 13. When he passed by Cabin 10, his body veered toward Scarlet's driveway.

He had to drag himself away from her. After his talk with Tyler this morning, Hunter was blatantly aware of how attached he'd become to his forest fairy and how horrible it was going to be when she left him. Not that he hadn't already figured that out for himself, but seeing Tyler after Jocelyn's departure painted it in a much starker light.

Hunter fisted his fingers as he continued trudging up the mountain, certain beyond doubt that watching Scarlet walk away from him was going to tear a fucking hole in his heart. *Get it together, man. You have other things to focus on right now. Besides, you still have two weeks left with her. Well, more like thirteen days. But still...you have time.*

As he passed Tyler's driveway, Hunter focused on his footsteps. Eventually, he reached Cabin 13. He climbed the porch steps, grasped the handle of the front door, took a deep breath, and stepped inside.

The large cabin was just as he remembered it from the night of the Social, vast and open and strangely welcoming. A few people buzzed through the halls, nodding at him and offering warm greetings. An older, grey-haired woman in a white, high-collared blouse and a flowing red skirt approached him from an adjoining room.

"May I help you, dear?"

"Yes, please. I have an appointment with Dr. Abbott."

He watched the glint in the woman's pale eyes and the rosiness on her crinkled cheeks as she smiled up at him. "You must be Hunter. Pete told me you'd be here."

Hunter grinned when Mrs. Claus took him by the arm and led him into the next room. He wondered if Pete enjoyed more than just talking with her. A gnome and a Claus should have a lot in common.

She guided him down a long hallway, ending in a closed wood door. "Here's his office. You just head right in."

"Thank you so much. I'm sorry, I didn't catch your name?"

"It's Betsy."

"Nice to meet you, Betsy. Please say hello to Pete for me."

She gave his arm a squeeze. "Oh, I will. And you be sure to create a wonderful day for yourself, Hunter."

"Thanks. I'll try."

He waited until Betsy bustled away before turning to the door. He knocked as he entered, scanning the room while stepping forward.

"Come on in," a deep male voice instructed from within.

Hunter made his way into the brightly lit area and closed the door behind him. He looked first to the large office windows, focusing on the surrounding forest, before he turned to the man behind the proverbial curtain. Adrien

Abbott sat in a brown leather office chair, looking up across a neatly organized desk.

"Hello, Mr. Gregory."

He shook his head immediately. "Hunter. Please."

"Hunter," the doctor echoed, extending his hand over the desktop.

Hunter reciprocated the firm handshake, scanning the middle-aged man's angular features and discerning eyes before releasing him.

"You can call me Adrien, if you like," Abbott offered.

"I appreciate that. But...do you mind if I call you Dr. Abbott?"

"No, I don't mind."

"Good, because I think I need that. I've been resisting therapy for so long, and I want to embrace it now. I want to accept the fact that I'm talking to a physician because I need help."

"Okay. Why don't you sit down, so we can talk about helping you."

Hunter looked to the high-backed brown chair across from Abbott's desk. "Actually, I prefer to stand. If that's okay."

"This is for you, so do what you need to do to feel comfortable."

"Thanks," he sighed, walking over to the window. "You know, the guests I met at the Social all spoke very highly of you, Dr. Abbott."

"Well, that's good to hear. In truth, we have many talented doctors on staff. I'm just fortunate enough to call Blissful Blue my home, instead of coming and going."

"I imagine it would be nice to stay here a while," Hunter said, his eyes skimming the forest outside before shifting to the framed certificates on the wall. He examined the bold print of the closest document: *Dr. Adrien Abbott, Medical Director, Blissful Blue Retreat.*

Hunter turned back to the man. "So, you're the boss up here?"

Abbott shrugged. "In a way. I coordinate the traveling physicians, and make sure everything is in order for the guests. I like to think I run a fairly tight ship. What about you?"

"What about me?"

"I know you're CEO of Gregory Global. Do you run a tight ship?"

Hunter chuckled. "I do. Honestly, I'm a complete control freak."

"A control freak? I see. Would you like to talk about that?"

"I probably should," he admitted as he stepped toward the doctor. A photo on the desk caught his eye. "Are these your daughters?"

Abbott glanced at the two young women in the picture. "Yeah, that's Natalie and Naomi, my baby girls. They're both grown women now, much as I hate to admit it. Do you have children, Hunter?"

"No, I don't."

"Do you want them?"

"Yes, I very much do. But I'm not married yet. I want to be, but..."

"But what?"

Hunter's shoulders fell. "Apparently, I have some issues to work out first, before I can pursue what I truly want to have in my life."

"And what issues are those?"

"Well, something happened. It happened a long time ago, and I honestly believed I'd put it behind me, but I realize now that I haven't. I need to figure out how to work through it, so I can finally move on."

Abbott nodded. "Okay. I can help you figure out how to move on."

Hunter's legs buckled. He eased down in the chair opposite the doctor. "God, that's...that's wonderful."

HUNTER STOOD in his cabin several hours later, waiting for night to fall. Soon, he would get to see his forest fairy. He would gaze into her eyes, watch her smile at him, hold her gently in his arms, and be whole again.

In truth, he felt nearly whole now, except for the lack of her presence. His therapy session earlier had gone better than expected. It wasn't easy to recount the story of Samantha, but it was easier to repeat the words today, since he'd said them to Scarlet just yesterday.

He'd spoken to Dr. Abbott for hours. At the end of their session, Hunter asked one question. He asked the doctor if he thought a person like the one he'd been – a person who'd been so blind and so selfish – deserved a loving woman and children. He asked if a person like that deserved a family.

The doctor answered his question with another: *What do you think?*

Hunter shook his head as he looked out of his living room window. The doctor was right; he had to find his own answers to a lot of things. The good news was that Abbott would help him figure out how. He would help Hunter find the path to the life he'd been searching for.

Hope filled his chest, for the first time in so very long, and he knew it was all because of Scarlet. She'd shown him what he couldn't see. She'd helped him understand what was broken in his life.

Hunter could only pray he hadn't broken *her* in the process.

The thought of harming her in any way made his stomach knot. Dusk hadn't settled yet, but he still strode out of his front door. He bounded down the steps and up his driveway, well aware it was too early to show up at her cabin for dinner, but unable to wait any longer.

He just needed to see his little bird, and talk to her, and hold her. He had to be with her now. There was simply no other option.

At the end of his driveway, Hunter turned right onto the paved road, moving eagerly toward Cabin 10. Anticipation consumed his body, his fingers stretching with the mere thought of touching her again. His heart thumped faster, the zealous noise drowning out the sound of whistling from up ahead. When he finally did hear the whistling, his feet ground to a halt on the pavement. After all, he'd heard this tune before.

Hunter watched in horror as Tyler emerged from Scarlet's driveway before turning right toward his own Cabin 11. Tyler didn't look back, so he didn't see Hunter standing in shock a few yards down the hill. Which was a good thing, because if looks could kill, Tyler would be dead now. Like, *dead* dead. With knives and bullets in his chest.

Hunter's entire body shook as he watched the other man walk away from Scarlet's cabin. The words Tyler had uttered to him just a few hours ago rang in his ears: *What better way to get over one woman than to be with another woman?*

"Good God," Hunter grumbled to himself, "is Tyler trying to use Scarlet to get over Jocelyn?"

That had better not be the truth. Hunter couldn't be held responsible for what he would do to Tyler if he'd laid his hands on Scarlet. Even if she'd agreed to have Tyler's hands on her, which she actually had every right to do, since Hunter certainly didn't own her.

"Holy fuck," he swore out loud. His legs started working again then. Hunter ran the rest of the way up the paved road and down her gravel driveway. He told himself to calm the hell down as he rushed toward her, but it was difficult to hear rational thoughts over the pounding in his skull. When he reached her porch, he took the steps two at a time.

"Scarlet!" he hollered as he strode inside. "Where are you?"

Please don't walk out of the bedroom. And please be fully clothed.

"Hey there," she sang. "I'm so happy to see you."

His eyes darted toward the sound of her voice. She stood in the kitchen, directly in front of the counter. She looked absolutely beautiful, especially with all her clothes on.

Scarlet smiled when Hunter shut the door behind him. She held a large chef's knife in her hand, busily preparing food for their dinner. "I'm sorry I can't come over to kiss you right now," she apologized. "But you're here a bit early, and I'm still working on your meal. I was trying to do a little something to surprise you."

Hunter's shoulders fell from his ears as he stepped forward to glance over the countertop. Scarlet returned her attention to the partially carved steak in front of her. An ivory dinner plate sat beside it, already covered in several bite-size pieces of the juicy meat. The presentation of the filet was quite meticulous, and he could tell she'd been working on it for a while, which made his muscles relax further.

"Do you mind having another steak dinner, Hunter? You said it's your favorite, and you really didn't get a whole serving the other night, so I thought I'd fix that," she explained as she continued slicing the meat into smaller bites. "Although you weren't supposed to be here yet."

"Was Tyler Hensen supposed to be here?" he bit out.

Scarlet's brow rose while she stared at him from across the counter.

Hunter exhaled. "Sorry. It's...it's none of my business, I suppose."

"I guess you saw him leaving just now?"

"Yeah, I did. But he didn't see me."

She shifted on her feet. "I can assure you, I didn't invite Tyler over here. He only wanted to talk. I've known him for many years, so he feels comfortable around me. He was upset and needed an ear."

Hunter studied her eyes as she spoke, witnessing the truth of her words. Tyler needed Scarlet's friendship today, just like Colin needed her friendship the day before. They simply relied on her, and Hunter understood the feeling all too well. He understood it to the point of pain.

"Damn, I really am sorry," he relented. "It's obvious everyone trusts and depends on you, and I shouldn't have jumped to conclusions. My only excuse is I've spent time with Tyler, and learned how he operates, so I had trouble controlling my jealousy when I saw him leaving here."

"You felt jealous of Tyler and me? Seriously?"

"Yes, seriously. You're an incredible, loving, intelligent, beautiful woman. And I'm well aware we've only known each other for eight days, but I don't particularly want to share you with another man."

Scarlet laughed wildly with his words, her emerald eyes sparkling.

Hunter huffed. "I'm glad my jealousy amuses you."

"Oh, it doesn't, I promise. You just have no idea how funny that is. I mean, Tyler Hensen is not my type. Truly. Not in any way, shape, or form. I don't think I could ever explain to you how *not* my type he is."

"Okay, then. If Tyler isn't your type, who is?"

Scarlet set the knife down and stepped to the sink. "I really thought I'd made that obvious by now," she said as she washed and dried her hands. Resting the towel back on the counter, she squared her shoulders and pinned his eyes. "You are the only man I want to be with, Hunter."

Damn, those were the best words he'd ever heard. "Well, good. Because you are the only woman I want to be with, Scarlet."

"Well, good."

He knew she meant what she'd said. And he sure as hell meant what he'd said. Hunter raked a hand through his hair. "God, this is crazy."

Her head tilted. "What's crazy?"

"All of it. Everything. Does it ever freak you out?"

"Which part, exactly?"

He motioned between the two of them. "This? Us? Does this thing we have – this *attraction*, or whatever – ever freak you out?"

She chewed on her lip before nodding. "It did, especially at first. But since the night we decided to become lovers, I've tried to let my concerns go. I want to experience this. All of it. What we have here is unlike anything I've ever known, and yes, it's scary, but I want to feel that part, too. I want to feel everything I can, because when I'm with you, I know for certain that I'm alive. To be perfectly truthful, the closer we become, the happier I find myself."

The emotion in her words struck dead center in his chest. "Well, who knows? With as close as we've become in just one week, in another two weeks we might end up married."

Her face fell entirely, the light in her eyes dimming to a dull green.

Hunter instantly regretted his impulsiveness. "I'm sorry," he said. "I didn't mean to upset you. The marriage thing was just a joke."

"I know it was a joke. I'm not upset about that. I'm upset because I have something to tell you, something I really don't want to say."

"Just...just tell me."

She swallowed hard. "I only have six more days left on vacation."

Hunter's fists balled into knots. "What are you talking about? Don't people usually spend three weeks up here? Isn't that the standard stay?"

"Yes, it is. But I'd already been here for a week when we met."

His jaw slackened. *Well, shit.* That made perfect sense. She'd emerged from the woods that first day, which meant she'd already been here, communing with nature, long before he arrived.

Hunter's gaze fell to the floor. He worked to breathe. For a split second, he lost sight of everything. "Scarlet, I can't...I can't survive on this mountain without you."

His heart hammered against his ribcage as she eased around the counter. He focused on the sound of her bare padded footsteps. A moment later, he felt the warmth of her body pressing into his chest.

"Look at me," she whispered, waiting until he met her eyes. She smiled up at him with tender determination. "You *can* survive up here without me, because you're strong. You're one of the strongest people I've ever met. You can do anything you set your mind to. Anything."

Hunter reached for her, stroking his hands down her arms to thread her fingers in his own. He didn't want to admit to the things she'd given him credit for. Yet he also knew it wasn't fair to place the burden of his survival on her shoulders. "Yeah, I suppose you're right. I'll be okay."

"Are you sure?"

"I am. After all, I finally did something good for myself today."

"What did you do?"

"I went to see Dr. Abbott. For therapy."

Scarlet squeezed onto his hands, so hard it actually hurt. Her eyes filled with tears, gigantic brimming drops that made her emeralds glow. "Really? Did you really do that, Hunter?"

"I did. I told him about my past, and about Samantha. He's going to help me learn how to fix the things in my life that are broken."

Tears slipped down Scarlet's face. Her forehead fell onto his chest.

"Thank you," she breathed. "Thank you so much."

He extracted one hand from hers to run his fingers through her hair. "Why are you thanking me? I should be the one thanking you."

She raised her head up to see him. "I don't want you to take this the wrong way, but I'm just so proud of you."

"How could I take that the wrong way? I know you want the best for me. I think I've always known that, from the day you found me."

Scarlet threw her arms around his shoulders. "You're wonderful. Do you know that? Have I told you how wonderful you are?"

Hunter pressed his hands against her spine, pulling her closer. He wanted to hold her sweet words close to his chest – as close as he now held her body – but he couldn't. He'd hurt her just yesterday, and even though she'd forgiven him, he certainly didn't deserve her praise today.

Snuggling further into his arms, Scarlet tilted her chin up. She smiled before pressing her lips to his. He kissed her back, softly and lovingly, keeping his actions as gentle as possible.

She returned the easy pressure of his lips for a few moments. Then her body slid harder against his, her arms tightened around his neck, and her fingers knotted into his hair. She moaned rather indecently when she pushed her tongue into his mouth.

Hunter couldn't resist tasting her. He wound his tongue with hers, just for a moment, as his entire being begged for more. But he pulled back, forcing himself to ease his escalating grip on her body. He rested his forehead on hers and nudged the tip of her nose with his own.

"Mmm. Kiss me again," she urged in a heated whisper.

He complied, although only briefly and with utmost care.

Scarlet stilled inside his well-controlled embrace. She huffed out a laugh. "Okay, then. I think you need to leave now, Hunter."

"What? You actually want me to leave?"

Untangling herself from his arms, she stepped away. "Just for a few minutes. I meant what I said earlier; you showed up too soon tonight. I have a surprise for you, and I wasn't able to prepare it all before you arrived, so now you need to go outside while I finish getting it ready."

"But I don't need surprises. I only need you. I'll be perfectly happy sitting on the couch and holding you tonight, just like last night."

"Oh, no, that won't do at all. Last night, you listened to me ramble about Girl Scouts for hours, and then I fell asleep on you. Literally *on* you. Which I'm sorry about, by the way. I hope I didn't snore."

"You may have snored a bit."

"Dear Lord, that's horrible. I really did not need to know that."

"Then I probably shouldn't mention the drool."

"Holy hell."

Hunter grinned. "There's no need to worry about it. Honestly, I found it all quite adorable. In fact, I'd love a repeat performance."

Scarlet shook her head. "Nope. Nope, nope. Not going to happen. I have other plans for us tonight, so you need to go outside now."

"But, honey..."

"Outside! Please. Stand on the porch and I'll yell when I'm ready."

Hunter wanted to protest further, until she arched an eyebrow and stared him down. His shoulders fell. "Okay, I'll go wait on the porch."

"Good. Thank you."

He sighed as he turned and walked back to the door. Stepping into the cold night air, he pulled the latch shut behind him. Darkness had descended rapidly while he'd been inside her cabin. He took a few steps forward to look up past the treetops into the clear sky littered with stars.

Hunter rested his forearms on her porch railing, gazing up at the tiny twinkling lights and wondering what his forest fairy had planned for him. He hoped it wasn't anything too untamed. He was going to have enough trouble dialing back their physical relationship from boiling to a slow simmer, even without her being in latent-dominatrix mode.

Frolicking Freebird Scarlet may still want to explore her fantasies, but he didn't think he could indulge her after what happened in the woods yesterday. He wanted to treat her like the angel she was for every moment they had left, to show her how much he appreciated her. He wanted to prove he was more than the monster she'd witnessed.

"I'm ready!" Scarlet yelled from beyond the logs.

Hunter took one last long look at the stars. He filled his lungs with icy air before turning to the door and pushing it open. The first thing he noticed when he stepped back inside was the warmer temperature, which meant she'd turned the thermostat up. The next thing he noticed was how she'd turned the lights off and lit candles on multiple surfaces. He didn't see his little bird at first, but his eyes kept searching through the flickering yellow glow until he found her.

Scarlet lay on the couch. Belly down. Completely naked. With the ivory plate full of carved-up steak situated over the small of her back.

Hunter closed the door behind him. He remained where he stood, several feet away. He cleared his throat. "What, um...what is all this?"

She peered up at him over the log armrest. "Just a little something I thought you'd like. Do you remember the night I tied you up?"

"Honest to God, I will never forget that. Not as long as I live."

A perfectly wicked grin spread across her lips. "Well, that night you mentioned how you'd like to eat your dinner off my backside. So, I thought I'd provide you the opportunity to do that now."

Desire slammed into Hunter's chest, thick and hot and excruciating. His eager eyes traced down the slope of her bare spine, over the plate of painstakingly prepared steak, and onto her perfectly rounded ass. He licked his lips, and his fingers clenched, but he refused to move. "This isn't necessary, Scarlet. I appreciate the effort, but why don't we sit at the table and eat a nice meal together? I can go get your robe for you."

She rolled her eyes. "I don't want my robe. I want to be here on this couch, entirely naked, with you eating your dinner off of me. You said you wanted that, so I want it for you."

"But you don't have to do this."

"I know I don't have to. I want to. Now please come over here."

He stared in sheer pain at her naked body. He didn't know what to say to her, so he opted for the ugly truth. "I'd love to, but I can't. This is too tempting for me. It isn't safe, and I don't want to hurt you again."

"Hunter, you have never hurt me. Please stop feeling so guilty."

His jaw clenched. He wished he could say guilt wasn't the problem. But that would be an absolute lie, so he remained silent.

Scarlet studied him, looking deep inside, even in the dim light. "I know you still feel guilty about what happened in the woods yesterday."

"You're right," he admitted, knowing he couldn't hide from her, even if he wanted to. "I do feel guilty."

"Even though I swore you didn't hurt me?"

"It's...it's hard for me to accept that."

She sighed. "Do you even remember everything that happened between us yesterday morning? Do you remember how you tried to make me walk away from you, to leave you there in the woods alone?"

"I do remember. I told you to leave me. More than once."

"But I didn't. That was my choice. I wanted to be there with you."

"Dear God, why? Why on earth did you want to be there?"

Scarlet gave him a soft smile. "Because you needed me. Sixteen years is a hell of a long time to repress so many emotions. It's a lot of pain to feel all at once. You needed me in a very raw way, and I knew that. I also knew, without any sliver of doubt, that you wouldn't hurt me. You told me what you needed. You told me you were going to be rough. I accepted it. I consented to it."

"I know you did. I swear I would have stopped if you hadn't."

"I don't question that. I didn't question it then, nor do I now. And if you still feel like you're drowning under those emotions, and you still need to be rough with me, just let me know. I promise I will tell you to stop if I need it. I trust you, Hunter. I fully, completely trust you to stop yourself if I don't like something we're doing with each other."

He heard her words, but he still couldn't accept them. He shook his head as images from the forest flooded his mind. "Scarlet, what happened in those woods yesterday...it fucking terrified me."

"I know it did. It was scary. But I'm not afraid. I'm still here."

"Yes, you are. Although I honestly don't know why. I just want to prove to you that I can be different. I want to prove that I can change."

"But I don't want you to change. I don't want you to feel guilty about who you are, and I certainly don't want you to hide your nature. You're a sexually aggressive person. I've known that since the first time we were together. The things you make me feel are incredible, and I've never experienced anything like them before, and I love that you're able to give me so much. Honestly, that's only one item on the ridiculously long list of things I love about you. So, please just be yourself when you're with me, because that's the person I want."

Hunter stared at his freebird, looking into her earnest eyes, trying to comprehend her words. He stared at her forever, awed by her undiluted acceptance of both his strengths and his faults. He wanted nothing more than to believe her, to be real and honest with her in every way.

"Please, Hunter. I just want *you*."

Her words allowed him to release the kempt air from his lungs and to fully appreciate the sight before him. He absorbed her bare, luscious curves. He drank in her exquisite, enchanting smile. Slowly but surely, his muscles started to ease. "Do you really have a ridiculously long list of things you love about me?"

Scarlet nodded. "Oh, yes. I most certainly do."

"How ridiculous is it?"

"Like, ridiculously ridiculous."

"Hmm. I thought you'd come up with a more creative adverb than that, Scrabble Queen."

She rolled her eyes. "Well, damn. Now you're just frustrating me."

"Am I? Why is that?"

"Because you're chatting with me like I'm your Scrabble buddy – which I love being – but it doesn't mean I can't be more. A lot more. And also because I'm extremely frustrated that you haven't taken a single step toward me, even though I'm lying here naked. I am utterly, completely naked, yet you're still standing on the other side of the room. I know *exactly* what you're capable of making me feel when you touch me, and I do *not* want you treating me like a china doll."

"I'm not treating you like a china doll."

"Yes, you are! You've treated me like porcelain since we walked out of those woods yesterday! But I am not made of glass, and you will not break me! Now pick your damn feet up, get the hell over here, and eat your dinner off my ass like you said you wanted to!"

Hunter's brow shot up. The forcefulness of her words didn't begin to compare to the tenacity in her eyes. He wished he could defy her still, to prove to both of them that he could resist this entire glorious spectacle before him. But even with as much strength as Scarlet gave him credit for, he simply wasn't strong enough to stay away from her any longer.

Taking several steps forward, he came to a stop a few feet in front of her face. He reached to the collar of his shirt and slowly undid the buttons, all the way down to his waist. Her pupils dilated impossibly large in the candlelight as he proceeded to strip himself bare.

Hunter savored her reaction to his body. He grew impossibly hard as he watched her watching him. By the time he removed the last of his clothes, his forest fairy stared blatantly at his erection while licking her lips. The sight of her wet mouth made him ache with need. He forced himself to calm down, so he could focus on fulfilling this fantasy.

When he moved to the front of the couch, he saw a chair cushion on the floor, ready for him to kneel on. He wasn't surprised Scarlet had placed it there for him. The woman thought of everything.

Hunter sank to his knees on the green-and-red plaid fabric, right next to her lower back. He glanced down to her bare ass, appreciating the curves he knew would feel as soft as they looked, before dragging his eyes back up. "Do you truly want the real me?"

She turned her face to his, folding her arms beneath her head and resting her cheek against her hands. "I do. I always want the real you."

He reached for the plate. "Then I must tell you that I remember, in exact detail, what I said to you the night you tied me up."

"What did you say?"

Taking the plate of steak in his hand, he lifted it off her body. "I said I wanted to eat my dinner *directly* off your backside."

Hunter reached to the base of her spine, easing his fingers across her heated flesh. Scarlet moaned indecently with his touch. He traced up the smooth, straight line of her back, brushing her hair off to the side.

"Are you willing to let me eat directly off of you, Scarlet?"

"Dear Lord, yes. I'm more than willing."

He reached for the steak, taking one expertly dissected morsel between his fingertips. With great care, he placed the warm meat at the base of her spine. Her eyes closed on a sigh and his cock throbbed.

"Mmm. Don't worry, Hunter. I promise I've showered today."

"I honestly couldn't care in the least," he confessed, taking another portion of filet and laying it directly between her shoulder blades. He continued his placement, one piece after the other, across every section of her skin from her shoulders to her heart-shaped bottom. When finished, he set the plate on the floor and feasted his eyes on his creation. "You know, I think I missed my calling in life."

"Yeah?" she breathed. "What should you have been?"

"An artist. Although I'd only be inspired when you're my canvas."

Scarlet laughed and her body quaked, causing the meat to dance on her skin. He bent down and sucked one piece into his mouth, letting his teeth and lips linger, dragging his tongue over her flesh while slowly pulling away. He chewed and swallowed leisurely before looking back to her face. "Mmm. I have never tasted better steak in my life."

"Well, Phil does make a mean filet."

"Phil doesn't have a goddamn thing to do with it. It's because I get to eat it off of *you*."

She blushed wildly with his words. Hunter had never been more engrossed by the flush of her skin, especially since it wasn't just on her face anymore.

Scarlet blushed across her entire body, and his eyes followed the spread of the color as it moved all the way down to her perfect bottom. He reached his hand to the smooth seam separating her round cheeks. "Fuck, I love your ass. Have I already told you that?"

"Hmm. You may have mentioned it once or twice."

His fingers eased over that delicate seam, sliding down to the juncture of her thighs. Scarlet whimpered with the intimate touch, parting her legs for him. The motion shifted her body on the cushions.

Hunter's eyes darted to her back, where a sliver of meat tipped over with her movement. He dove down to catch it, his lips closing around her skin at the same time his hand found the wet opening to her sex. He bit into the steak while pressing one finger into the heat of her walls.

She moaned deep in her chest. The sensual sound rumbled against his lips and his erection jerked violently against the side of the couch. He added a second finger inside her, pushing in deep. Her legs spread further to accommodate him as he swallowed the second piece of steak.

When Hunter leaned over for another bite, this one between her shoulder blades, Scarlet shivered. He slid his fingers slowly out, and then back inside. "Is this bothering you?" he murmured against her skin.

"Yes, it's definitely bothering me. In the best possible way."

He pulled his hand completely out of her so he could trace up the seam of her ass. Her wetness coated his fingers, leaving a glistening trail behind. "Do you want me to keep going, then?"

"I do. Please."

A smile curved his lips when he bent over to suck another piece of meat from her flesh. He slid his fingers down her bottom and into her sex, where she felt even wetter now. Impossibly so. He pulled out again to follow the trail he'd started up the center of her ass cheeks, all the way to the base of her spine. While he chewed on his food, he watched his fingers glide back down into her tight, hot sheath.

"Holy hell, this is the best dinner I've ever had."

She gave him a drunken grin. "Is it really?"

"Absolutely. It just narrowly beats out the dinner I had when you tied me up. I only like this one better because I get to touch you any way I want to. Although I did enjoy you being on top of me that night."

"Do you want me to be on top again?"

Hunter dragged his fingers out of her heat and up her seam again, leaving a slick trail in his wake. "No, I don't want you on top tonight. After I finish my dinner, I want to fuck you from behind, just like this. Is that okay with you?"

He ran his fingers back down the center of her ass and into her sex.

Scarlet groaned. "Mmm...that's just...so good."

Hunter leaned down to suck another piece of meat from her skin. He repeated the path of his fingers, again and again, watching the journey his hand took as he chewed one morsel after another. His fingers transitioned even more smoothly now, from her hot sheath all the way to her lower back, having seamlessly lubricated the path.

His cock pulsed, thick and heavy, wanting to be inside of her in the worst possible way. He cursed the fact that she'd cut up so much steak for him, and yet he still appreciated it, since it forced him to enjoy every moment of this sweet torture. When he finally sucked the last bite into his mouth, he watched her lick her lips. He brought his other hand to her face, drawing her hair back from her cheek. "Damn, Scarlet, I really need to be inside you."

She smiled dreamily. "Good, because I really need you inside me."

Every muscle in his body tightened. He stood up at the side of the couch, gazing down at his little bird. The skin across her back was slightly pink from where he'd eaten off of her, but he'd left no lasting marks. A few spots where he'd licked her still glistened from the moisture of his tongue, but it was nothing compared to how the candlelight caught on the thoroughly wet seam of her ass.

"Spread your legs for me," he instructed, leaning down to brace his hands beside her shoulders on the cushion. Scarlet complied, drawing her thighs further apart. He climbed onto the couch, the wood groaning beneath his weight while he pressed his knees between hers. As he positioned himself behind her, his erection landed in the center of her ass. His hips jerked, quite involuntarily. Hunter stared at the sight of his rigid length resting between her wet cheeks.

"Are you doing okay?" Scarlet whispered.

"Yeah, I'm...I'm good."

"What are you thinking about?"

"Truthfully?"

"Please."

Hunter balanced himself on one arm so he could run his other hand over her skin. He touched the small of her back with his still-wet fingers. "I'm thinking about this little hollow at the bottom of your spine," he admitted, reverently tracing across the flawless dimple.

"What are you thinking about it?"

His hips arched again, running his cock against her damp seam. "I'm thinking the skin over your ass is really wet now, which is entirely my fault. And since it is so wet, I could fuck the seam between your ass cheeks and come into this perfect dimple in your back."

She made a tiny choking sound. "W-would you enjoy that?"

"Hell, yes," he admitted, outlining the indentation with his fingers.

"Then I want it, too."

Hunter's eyes shot up to her face. "No, Scarlet. I won't do that. You asked what I was thinking, and I was just being brutally honest."

"I love your honesty. I'm willing to try it. It sounds interesting."

His gaze fell back down the curve of her spine, to where his fingers rested. The head of his cock pulsed against her. He could picture himself coming right here, spurting out on her skin, and he knew he'd love every second of that scenario. But he wasn't sure she would, so it simply wasn't an option. "I appreciate you wanting to try it, honey. I really do. But right now, I just need to be inside you."

"Hmm. That sounds good, too."

"It sounds better than good. It sounds amazing."

Leaning back, Hunter distanced himself enough to grasp his stiff cock. He lined up the tip with the soaking entrance to her sex. She bit into her lip and he groaned. He lowered himself on both arms, easing his chest onto her back, so he could kiss the curve of her ear. Scarlet giggled and he began to push his way inside her while she still smiled.

She arched her back as he entered her, pressing her bottom up into his abs. He sunk all the way in, relishing the softness of her snug, slick walls. She drew her hands out from under her head to grip the side of the couch while her body sheathed his cock fully. Hunter saw her fingers grip the wood armrest before he rested his forehead on her hair.

"You doing okay?" he whispered into her loose curls.

"Mmm, yes. You just...you feel so good."

He shifted his hips, easing out and back inside her. "So do you."

"Do I really? Tell me."

"Tell you what?"

"Tell me how it feels to be inside me."

Hunter groaned, sliding out and sinking in again, focusing on the sensation as he searched for words. "It's hard to describe. You feel incredibly soft and so very, very wet. I love how wet you are. I love knowing your body aches for mine just like mine aches for yours."

He pulled out and lunged back in, listening as she whimpered. "You're so tight around me," he told her. "And so unbelievably warm. I swear I can't get enough of you, no matter how hard I try."

Pressing his nose to her ear, he nuzzled her earlobe while filling his lungs with the scent of tiny flowers. "Your turn, Scarlet."

"You want to know what you feel like to me?"

"Mm-hmm."

"Oh, Hunter, you feel miraculous," she began, digging her fingers into the armrest when he pushed himself in to the hilt. "You feel so big and thick, especially from behind like this."

His hips jerked with her words. "You like this position?"

"I love it. I love having your chest against my back, and your breath on my cheek. I just wish…"

"What do you wish?"

"I wish you would hold my hands."

He raised his arms instantly, covering her hands with his, entwining their fingers so they could grip the log armrest together. The full weight of his chest now rested on her spine, settling them both deeper into the cushions. "How is this for you? It's not too much pressure, is it?"

"Not at all. I'd like it even harder."

"You want me to fuck you harder?"

"Yes. Please."

"Mmm. If you insist." Hunter thrust himself deep inside her body. He panted into her neck as he drove into her over and over again. He tried to keep the pace slow, so he could last longer, but he was terribly aware of the wet seam of her ass pressing into his abs. That sensation made him tremble with a fierce, pounding need, a need he feared would claim him before he had the chance to satisfy her.

"Please tell me you're still enjoying this," he begged as he lunged forward, desperately wanting her with him.

"Oh, I am," she sighed. "Beyond words."

"Do you think you can come this way?"

"I…I don't know."

"I could use my hands to touch you, to make you come."

"No. I like your hands where they are, holding mine. It makes all of this so much more incredible than it already is. Your cock feels thicker from behind somehow, even though you always fill me up entirely. I love having you inside me, and on top of me, and all around me. You just fit me perfectly. It's like you're everywhere, all at once. I love it, Hunter. I love it when you fuck me."

Her words sent a pulse of electricity down his spine. He slammed his eyes shut and grit his teeth together. He gripped hard to her fingers, fighting the sensations as best he could. But then she arched her ass up even higher, drawing him further inside, and he lost the fight.

He came with a feral growl, dropping his forehead against her neck, gasping for air with his next stuttered, purely instinctive thrusts. Scarlet's shoulder blade lay beneath his lips, so he sucked on her skin while emptying himself entirely inside her sex. She moaned with the pulsations of his hips and cock, her fingers still entwined with his as she clamped down on the armrest and trembled beneath him.

When Hunter's body finally stopped thrumming, it took him several minutes to reopen his eyes. He worked to refocus and return to reality. The instant he did, he exhaled harshly. "Damn it, I'm so sorry."

"Why on earth are you sorry?"

"I came without you. Entirely without you."

"It wasn't entirely without me," she countered. "I was right here the whole time. And I really enjoyed it."

He lifted his head to see her face. "I'm glad you enjoyed it, but I'm still disappointed in myself that you didn't finish when I did."

Scarlet sighed against the cushion. "Well, I promise I'm just fine."

"What do you mean by that?"

"I mean I had a nice time. I don't need an orgasm to feel satisfied."

Hunter rose up on his forearms, trying to get a better look at her eyes. "Are you kidding me right now? Please tell me you're joking."

"I'm not joking."

"Good God. Did the boyfriends you had before me actually convince you of that shit?"

"Hunter, it's...it's okay."

"No, it's not okay. You're such a giving person, and I love that about you, but it doesn't mean you shouldn't get something in return."

She shook her head. "I don't need a reward."

"Well, you're getting a reward, whether you need it or not." He pulled out of her, instantly hating the loss of warmth, as he lifted his legs over hers. Planting his feet firmly beside the couch, he stood and looked down at his little bird. "I fully intend to give you an orgasm. I'm going to make you come extremely hard, and it will be better for you if you just accept that. However, I will need to join you on the couch to accomplish it, so I'll need you to turn on your side."

"But, it's really not..."

"Turn. On. Your. Side. Please."

She still didn't move.

Hunter glared at her. "In case you don't already know, Scarlet, I am at least as stubborn as you are, if not more. I will wait right here, buck-ass naked, for the next six days, if I have to."

His words etched a smile on her lips. Unfortunately, the smile faded nearly as soon as it appeared. When she finally exhaled and tilted over on her side, Scarlet looked up to his face in pained anticipation.

Hunter wanted to be happy she'd given in to the fact that he was going to please her, come hell or high water. He wanted to be ecstatic about it. But the moment she turned over, he saw them. He saw the fearsome, angry bite marks he'd left on her skin the day before.

All the air sucked out of the room.

His eyes fixated on her chest. The bruises were purple and mottled and he could see shadows of teeth marks against the cream of her skin. His whole body revolted against the sight, pushing acid into his throat.

"Dear Lord, honey..."

"They don't hurt," she whispered. "And I will heal just fine."

Hunter felt his knees go weak. He sank down on the couch, turning on his side so he could be face to face with his forest fairy. For tortured seconds, he could only see the bruises. Then he pulled his eyes up to hers and took her face in one hand. "Please tell me you weren't lying on your stomach because you were trying to hide this from me."

"No, I wasn't trying to hide it. At least, not forever. I knew you'd see them eventually, but I also knew you'd feel guilty, and I didn't want that tonight. I didn't want you treating me like something breakable. Because I'm not that easily broken. I swear I'm not."

She reached her hand to his chest, pressing her palm over his heart. "You're a wonderful man, you know. You give me so much. I really can't even tell you how much. I just couldn't bear to see this distressed look on your face tonight. I wanted to spend this evening with the real Hunter – the one who lives without guilt or regret."

He shut his eyes against the pain of her words. "I don't...I don't even know if that man exists anymore."

"He does, I promise. I can see him in there. You just need to let him live. You just need to let him breathe."

Hunter reopened his eyes. He gazed on her sweet face, watching a gentle smile grace her lips. He didn't understand how she could be with him like this, so open and loving, after witnessing him at his worst. His gaze fell to her chest, to the bruises littered across her skin.

Bending his head down, he eased his mouth onto her breast slowly and tentatively. He pressed his lips to the first purple mark he came to, taking care not to hurt her again. When his mouth met her skin, Scarlet dropped her face into his hair and moaned. Reaching one hand to her hip, he pulled her body closer to his as he moved on to the next bruise, and then the next. Hunter took his time, kissing each one in turn while she hummed her approval against his scalp.

His fingers drifted steadily across her skin as he attempted to kiss away the wounds he'd inflicted. She shifted beneath the touch of his lips and his hands, pressing her knees together on breathy whimpers. His touches became firmer, and farther-reaching, while he tried to mend what he'd nearly broken. He stroked all the way up her ribcage and then down again, across her waist and onto her thigh. He felt the goose bumps spread over her skin as he kissed from one breast to the other.

Scarlet groaned when his lips brushed the peak of her nipple. He worshiped the tiny bud with his tongue, causing her to mumble garbled words while twisting her fingers into his hair. Hunter ran his hand across her thigh and onto her softly rounded belly before moving further down, easing his fingers between her rigidly clenched legs. She arched into his touch even as she protested. "Hunter, you don't have to..."

He freed her nipple to look on her face. Her eyes were darkened, her cheeks flushed, her lips trembling. "Let me give you this, Scarlet."

"But you give me so much already."

"Then let me give you more. Please."

She searched his eyes. He didn't falter at all beneath her tender scrutiny. He waited patiently until she nodded.

Hunter felt her stiff legs relax, easing apart so he could run his fingers over the soft folds of her sex. Scarlet moaned the instant he touched her there, her mouth parting as her eyelids fluttered shut. She was beautiful – so incredibly beautiful – and he had to kiss her.

When he pressed his lips to hers, she immediately wrapped her arms around his neck and fell against his chest. Hunter tangled his tongue with hers while dipping his hand down further still. He discovered the opening of her body so easily, pressing two fingers inside her hot sheath.

Damn, Scarlet was so fucking wet right now. He knew it wasn't just from her, but also from him. He liked feeling his thicker liquid pooled deep within her walls. He liked knowing part of his body remained inside hers, even though he realized that was a ridiculously possessive, caveman-like thought. He just couldn't bring himself to care.

As Hunter dragged his fingers back out of her heat and up onto her tight bundle of nerves, she shuddered against him. His mouth left hers, only to move across her cheek and onto her neck. His fingers circled slowly around her fleshy, tender nub before easing back down through her folds and into her heat. "Damn, you feel so good," he rasped, running his tongue into the hollow of her throat.

"I...I do?"

"Yes, and your skin tastes perfect. Salty and sweet and amazing."

She moaned with his words, making him grin as he moved his mouth down to her chest. He found one nipple with his lips, running his tongue across the tight, eager peak. His fingers drove in and out of her sex while she yanked on his hair, whimpering and gasping with every thrust.

Scarlet shifted her hips up and down more furiously now, trying her damnedest to fuck his hand. He loved feeling how much she needed him. He loved knowing he could make her feel it. Pushing his fingers deeper inside her, he added his thumb to caress her taut little nerve bud.

"Damn, that's...*damn*."

Hunter smiled against her skin when he heard her breathy curse. "Come for me," he instructed, his breath hot against her wet breast while he worked her sensitive flesh harder and faster with his fingers. "I want you to come. I need you to."

"Um-hmm. Yes. *Yes*."

"Do it for me now, Scarlet. Let me hear you."

"I'm going to. I'm going...to...oh...oh...Hunter!"

Her arms tightened fiercely around his neck as her legs clamped around his hand. He latched his mouth on her breast and pulled her nipple onto his tongue. She screamed out, her entire body clenched and thrumming, as he continued moving his hand and tongue with the rhythm of her pulsing hips. He wanted to spend eternity feeling her inner muscles grip him as she moaned his name, yet barely a second passed before he heard a thud and a gruffly muttered, "Ouch."

Hunter lifted his eyes to her face.

Scarlet rubbed the back of her head. "I'm so sorry. I didn't mean to ruin the moment. I just banged my head on the arm of the couch."

"You didn't ruin anything. Is your head okay?"

"It's fine. I should know better than to thrash around with all this log furniture, but I completely forgot where I was for a minute."

"Well, I'm going to take that as a compliment."

"Oh, yes, do. Please do."

Hunter eased his fingers out of her, dragging them up and around her back. He used the new leverage to pull her closer, leaning down to press a kiss to her mouth. She responded to him instantly and completely.

He relished the taste of her tongue for lengthy moments, until he felt her collapse further into the cushions. Blissful with the knowledge that she felt utterly spent, he peered into her eyes with a confident grin. "Did you have a nice orgasm, Scarlet?"

"Heavens, yes. It was awesome."

"Good."

She beamed up at him. "How about you? Did you enjoy yourself tonight? I mean, with dinner, and what came afterward?"

"I don't think *enjoyed* is a strong enough word."

"That's wonderful. I'm so glad I was able to guess."

His brow arched. "What did you guess?"

"Your fantasy – the one I promised you when we were walking in the woods yesterday. I figured this would be the one you'd want most."

"Ah, yes. I do remember your promise to fulfill a fantasy of mine. And I have to admit, this was certainly amazing."

"Oh, good. I'm so glad I could make you happy."

"You do make me happy. Astoundingly happy." He wrapped his arms tighter around her back. "But I'd still like to discuss my fantasy."

Scarlet's forehead crinkled. "What are you talking about?"

"I'm talking about the fantasy you still owe me."

"But I just gave you your fantasy."

"You gave me *a* fantasy," he corrected, bending down to kiss the tip of her nose. "But you didn't give me *my* fantasy, which *I* get to choose. I do still get to choose my own fantasy, like you promised, don't I?"

The confused look on her face was priceless. Hunter fought back a laugh as she pondered his question. Eventually, she nodded.

"Of course, you still get to choose. That is what I promised you."

"Yes, it is," he confirmed with another kiss to her nose.

She giggled, shifting the soft contours of her body against the hardness of his. Hunter sighed in contentment. He loved laying here with her, naked and entangled on the couch, although he'd give anything to take her into her bedroom and curl up with her under her sheets.

"Scarlet, I have another question for you."

"Yeah? What's your question?"

"Do you like my arms?"

"Lord, yes. I most certainly do."

"Well, since you like my arms so much, I bet you'll like waking up in them."

She burst out laughing. "Wow. I think that's the corniest line I've ever heard."

"I'm pretty sure it's the corniest line I've ever said. But the fact remains that you and I have never slept in a bed together, and I'd really like to wake up tomorrow with you in my arms."

Her laughter died down. "That does sound nice. Unfortunately, we probably shouldn't. You saw Dr. Abbott for the first time today, and that is a huge thing. You need time and space to process it all."

Hunter's brain knew those words made perfect sense, yet his body rebelled fiercely against the thought of letting her go. "I guess I'll have to accept that. But only if I can have another promise from you."

"What promise is that?"

"I want you to promise me that I can sleep over for at least one of the next six days, and spend the entire night holding you in my arms."

"Very well, I promise. But I reserve the right to pick which night."

"Fair enough," he agreed, easing his hand onto her hip. "I don't suppose you'd change your mind and let it be tonight?"

"Sorry, but no. Not tonight."

"Well, you can't blame a guy for trying. Just so you know, I'm still going to lay here and hold you for a good, long while."

"Thank goodness for that. I'd be pissed off if you didn't."

His eyes caught hers. "Really? Do you even get pissed off?"

"Sure. Everyone gets pissed off sometimes."

"Yes, but I have trouble imagining it with you."

"Oh, but I do. I have a loud voice and everything."

"A loud voice, huh? I think I may have actually experienced that tonight. I mean, you did demand that I eat my dinner off your ass."

She smiled, the sight winding its way around his heart. "If you must know, that wasn't even close to my real loud voice. Also, when I'm super angry, I have been known to stomp my foot. From time to time."

"You stomp your foot? Yikes. I'll try to stay on your good side."

Scarlet laughed and he joined her, letting the sound lighten his soul. When his eyes drew to the bruises marring her skin, he quieted again. She reached her hands to his face, waiting patiently until he refocused on her. "Everything heals with time," she assured.

He listened and nodded, banding his arms tighter around her back. "Tell me something I can do for you, Scarlet. Tell me something I can give you. Please."

"Mmm. You give me so much already. But since you asked, I could definitely use more kisses. If it's not too much trouble."

Hunter leaned down, his mouth hovering over hers. "I'll give you anything you want," he promised against her lips.

Even if that means letting you go.

10

POSITIVE REINFORCEMENT

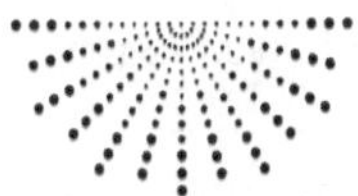

Two days. That's how long he had left with her. Scarlet would walk away from him the day after tomorrow.

Hunter's jaw clenched as he sat on the porch steps of his cabin, waiting for his little bird to flutter back into his life. It was already mid-morning. He'd already showered and dressed. Breakfast had already come and gone. But she still wasn't here yet.

The lack of her presence made his hands tremble. Hunter alternately stretched and squeezed his fingers as he waited on the cool wood stair, looking toward the clump of trees separating her cabin from his. He hated not knowing the exact moment he would see her again.

He wasn't quite sure how the time with his forest fairy had flown by so quickly. From the moment she'd told him she only had six days left on vacation, everything moved so fast. His life at Blue had adopted a strangely comforting pattern: morning basketball with Tyler, afternoon therapy with Dr. Abbott, and evening frolicking with Scarlet.

The morning basketball wasn't easy to go back to at first, knowing Tyler had been in Scarlet's cabin. But Hunter understood Tyler needed her support, so he continued their friendship. Still, he never brought up her name, needing to keep as much of her to himself as possible.

The afternoons were a bit better. Hunter embraced his time with Dr. Abbott. He bared his soul: the good, bad, and ugly. It was hard as hell, and emotionally exhausting, but at least he knew he was on the right road. He thanked the heavens that Scarlet had shown him the entrance.

The evenings were the best. Colin always brought two dinners to Scarlet's cabin. The red-hooded young man never questioned Hunter's constant presence in her life. Colin acted as if it was completely natural for the two of them to be together, and Hunter appreciated the unspoken approval more than he could say. After all, it did feel natural to be with her. It felt like the most natural thing ever, which he couldn't explain.

Of course, Scarlet didn't ask for explanations. She just sat beside him, gripping his hand and smiling with her whole body, gazing into his eyes like she'd discovered a new universe inside him. Every time she looked at him like that, Hunter wanted her more. Which was crazy, since he wanted her constantly... even despite having her every day.

The night after he'd eaten his steak dinner off her backside, they'd spent the evening playing Twister again. Only this time, it was a version Scarlet called "Kissing Twister", which meant they had to kiss whatever part of each other's body they were closest to at the end of their turn. They tried to make the game last as long as they could. They ended up ripping each other's clothes off – literally, in the case of her underwear – and having laughing, smiling, sweaty sex on top of the plastic mat.

The next night, after sharing a mostly platonic dinner on the couch, Hunter followed her into the kitchen to help clean up. He had every intention of making love to her in her bedroom that evening, but then Scarlet dropped a fork on the floor. When she bent over to pick it up, he lost his mind. That position made her ass look *holy damn wow*, so he grabbed her and fucked her up against the refrigerator door. At first she gasped in surprise, then she giggled, then she moaned, and then she screamed in pleasure. He couldn't bring himself to regret a second of it.

Last night, he truly tried to make everything romantic. They shared a charming meal by candlelight, sitting at an actual table. He spoke softly and sweetly to her, caressing her arm and holding her hand, bound and determined to be invited into her bedroom. But when they walked into the kitchen after dinner with their dirty dishes, Scarlet armed herself with the hose from the sink and started a water fight. By the time he finished retaliating, she sat with her bare ass on the wet countertop and another pair of torn panties on the floor. She didn't complain about losing more underwear, but she did laugh a lot. He also made sure she screamed a lot. Especially his name, as her eyes rolled back in her head.

Hunter didn't want to leave her cabin after the water fight last night, but his forest fairy hadn't given him a choice. She sent him out of her door with one last, long goodbye kiss. He left with a warm smile on his face despite the cold air seeping through his wet clothes, although only after he'd secured solid plans for today. He'd told her he wouldn't leave her porch unless she promised to spend this entire day with him.

Scarlet hemmed about it at first; she said he needed to have his time with Abbott. Hunter answered her with a promise to see the doctor tomorrow. Next, she explained how she really wanted to spend today in the woods. Hunter answered by offering to go with her.

He remained persistent despite all her protests and eventually she agreed to his terms. He exhaled in relief the moment she did, stealing one more kiss before rushing home to collapse into bed. He'd slept like the dead every night this week, probably from the emotional toll of therapy. Yet he still woke each morning with the clawing desire to see her — a desire that worsened every minute.

Now he sat on the cold wood of his porch steps, itching to spend the whole day with her. And wondering why she wasn't here yet. And why she still hadn't fulfilled her promise to spend an entire night in his arms. And why she never, ever spoke of a future between them, no matter how intimate and connected they became, emotionally and physically.

A rustling sound came from the trees beside his cabin then, followed by a loudly shouted, "Hunter!" He turned to see her running at him with a wild grin on her lips and loose curls flying around her face. He had just enough time to stand before she launched herself into his arms.

Scarlet knocked the wind out of him when he caught her to his chest. He stumbled back a few steps. "Oh my God," she breathed beside his ear, her arms tightening around his neck. "I'm so happy to see you."

"I'm happy to see you, too," he assured, supporting her weight as she pushed up on the toes of her boots to be closer. She shivered so hard and clung to him so fiercely that he wondered if something bad had happened. "Honey, are you..."

She halted his question by pressing her lips to his. Scarlet planted fast and furious kisses over his mouth, cheeks, and nose, before easing back to peer up at him. Her fingers fumbled with his shirt collar.

Hunter studied his forest fairy. Her eyes were wide and luminous. Her body hummed against his. She felt like a ball of nervous energy in his arms, reminding him of the night she'd hung the picture of her fantini bird on the wall. He wasn't sure what to make of it.

"Are you doing okay today?" he finished his previous question.

"Yeah, yeah. I'm okay."

He took her face in both hands. "I can tell you're not. Talk to me. Please."

She exhaled as she rested her fingers over his heart. "It's just...this is it, you know? This is my last day in the forest."

A surge of panic shot through his body. "No. This isn't your last day. We still have one more. You'll still be here tomorrow."

"Yes, I'll still be here, but I won't be able to go into the woods. I have to get ready to return to the real world. There's so much to get ready for. I have to pack, of course. And there's dinner. I'd love to have dinner with you one more time. You will come, right? I'll make it special. I'll talk to Phil to see if he'll make another steak for you. I mean, if that's okay. Is it okay? Or is it too much steak? I don't know if it's too much of a good thing. But that sounds ridiculous, right? Too much of a good thing? I've always found that an odd expression, so..."

"Scarlet. Take a breath. Please."

She stopped rambling, staring up at him as heated air came in little bursts from her lips. She blinked her eyes before nodding. "Sorry."

Hunter set his hands on her shoulders. "Don't be sorry. I just want to know for sure that you're okay. And I'll always come over for any sort of dinner, if it means I get to spend time with you. But..."

"But what?"

"Do you really want me to come into the woods with you today? If this is the last chance for you to be there, I don't want to interfere. If you need to be alone, I promise I'll understand."

Scarlet reached up to touch his cheek. "Thank you for that. But I don't want to be alone today. I've been alone in the woods every day – all morning while you play basketball with Tyler, and all afternoon while you have your talks with Dr. Abbott – and I just want to spend my last day in the forest with you by my side. If that's okay."

Hunter nodded full-force. "Yes. That is definitely okay."

She grinned and grasped for his hand. "Come on, then. Let's go."

～

THEY WALKED into the woods together. Well, *he* walked. She bounced. Through brambles and underbrush and snapped twigs, she bounced and sang and giggled. Hunter watched her in both amazement and apprehension. He honestly didn't know how she maintained this level of energy day after day, and he couldn't bear the thought of losing these precious moments from his life.

They found her red maple again. Scarlet stood before it, touching the leaves with uncensored awe, radiating more light than the sun shining down on her through the overhanging branches. After lengthy minutes in silence, she turned to him and asked, "Dance with me?"

"You mean here?"

She balanced on her tiptoes and pulled on his hands. "Right here."

"I'm sorry, but no. I don't dance."

"Yes, you do. I just haven't seen it on the outside yet."

Hunter tugged her onto his chest. "I don't dance, but I do kiss," he offered, pressing his lips to her mouth, cheek, and neck. Scarlet whimpered as he tasted her skin, her fingers curling around his biceps. He found that little spot behind her ear – the one that always made her giggle and squirm – and kissed her there. She did exactly what he expected, laughing and wriggling inside his arms.

He banded her tighter to his body, but his little bird was harder to hold onto than he'd imagined. As he nibbled against that tender spot, she twisted out of his arms and jumped several feet away. "You have to stop that!" she chastised with a giant, silly grin. "I'm ticklish there!"

"I know. That's why I do it. Now come back and I'll do it again."

"Uh-uh," she said, inching backwards. "You'll have to catch me."

"I can do that, you know."

Hunter wiggled his eyebrows and Scarlet cackled in near hysteria. She squealed and spun around to run through the trees. He smiled while watching her retreating form, giving her a head start since her cute little legs were no match for his long ones. He watched her hair brush across her back as she darted around branches, listening to the music of her giggles floating in the air.

Once he started after her, Hunter closed the distance between them with only a few long strides. He was quite preoccupied by the thought of catching her, wrapping her in his arms, and kissing her senseless. Consequently, she scared the hell out of him when she skidded to a halt and shrieked, "Oh my God! Look!"

Every muscle he owned stiffened as he followed her gaze down to the forest floor. "What? What am I looking at?"

"This!" she exclaimed, pointing to a little twig sticking up out of the dirt. "It's a baby pine tree!"

His brow rose while he stared at the tiny brown stem with patches of thin green needles dangling off of it. Scarlet turned to him and grinned. She clasped her fingers together, bouncing on the balls of her feet.

A vision entered his mind that instant: a vision of her holding a baby girl in her arms. A little girl with curly black hair and bright green eyes. A cherubic child who reached out to him with her tiny, chubby fingers.

Hunter's blood bounded through his veins. He scrubbed his fingers across his eyelids. He forced himself to breathe.

When he managed to refocus on Scarlet, he watched her head tilt.

"Are you okay, Hunter?"

"I'm...yeah. Sure. I'm okay."

"Then come see! Come see the baby!"

He nodded, schooling his features so he didn't have to explain where his mind just went. He didn't think he could explain it. Not right now.

She reached out to him with wriggling fingers. "Are you coming?"

He stepped up beside her and took her hand. She turned back to the tiny branch and sighed. Hunter could tell she needed to be closer to the baby pine, so he plopped onto the ground, pulling her down with him.

Scarlet yelped in surprise when they landed in the dirt. He chuckled and wrapped one arm around her back, tugging her into his side. She gazed over at him. "What are we doing down here?"

He brushed a wayward hair from her cheek. "We're appreciating the little tree. Although it's pretty much just a twig at this point."

"Well, right now he's just a twig, but one day he'll be as big as all the others. He'll have the traits of his parents, and yet he'll be his own tree, with his own trunk, own branches, and own cracks and crevices."

Hunter ran his fingers through her hair as he listened. She rested her head on his shoulder, sinking against him. Her constantly humming body finally began to calm while they sat in silence.

After a long while, her eyes drew back to his. "Who are you more like, Hunter? Your mother or your father?"

"I'm not entirely sure. I have my father's business skill, but my mother's fierce sense of family." He pulled Scarlet tighter into his side. "What about you? Are you more like your mother or your father?"

The look on her face shifted from peaceful to anxious the moment he asked. Her response didn't surprise him, since he knew it was a loaded question. She would have to choose between her deceased, workaholic father, or her wandering-but-not-lost mother. It was a choice between Solemnly Sedate Scarlet and Frolicking Freebird Scarlet, and as much as Hunter wanted the answer, he didn't know if she could give it to him.

His little bird stared at him for stretched seconds before answering. She looked back to the baby pine tree and said, "I honestly don't know. But I'm figuring it out, day by day."

Hunter nodded, knowing how truthful the statement was. He settled into the dirt, banding her to him as she stared at the little branch. He could feel the warmth of her body, and the steadiness of her breathing, and he smiled while they spent time together in the peaceful quiet.

The flapping of wings eventually broke the stillness and he glanced up to one of the tall oaks. "Hey, look. It's a redheaded woodpecker."

Scarlet's gaze followed his to the branches. "Oh my goodness, it is," she breathed, her body instantly humming once again.

He grinned with her enthusiastic response, proud of himself for both remembering the bird's name and for making her happy. He rubbed his hand across her back while they watched the woodpecker hop along the tree branches. Scarlet trembled beneath his fingers. At first, he thought it was an excited kind of trembling. But then she made a strangled sound. "Oh, no," she murmured.

Hunter turned his body toward hers, seeing tears well in the corners of her eyes. "Scarlet? What's wrong?"

Her head shook as she sniffled. "I...I lied to you."

"About what?"

"That isn't a redheaded woodpecker. It's a red *bellied* woodpecker."

"Really? The belly looks pretty white to me."

"I know. I used to think that was so weird when I was a kid. The actual redheaded woodpecker has a red head and mostly black wings, and this one's wings are striped. I remember my friend Holly and I joking that whoever named it 'red bellied' needed new binoculars, because this bird's belly is mostly white. I know that's a silly memory, but I thought I would never forget it. I thought I would never forget any of those things from my childhood. But I did. I forgot so many things, and then I lied to you."

Hunter's chest tightened as she looked to him with utter fear and panic in her eyes. He wrapped both his arms around her, encasing her completely. "You didn't lie to me, honey. You made a mistake."

The trembling of her body increased exponentially. "No, I lied to you. Even though I swore I wouldn't anymore. I *swore* it."

"You didn't remember the bird's name. It was an honest mistake."

She shook her head, over and over, as tears spilled down her cheeks. "You don't understand. I lied to you and I pushed you. I pushed you so hard, from the second we met. I forced you to look at things that maybe you weren't ready to see, and I hate knowing I did it against your will."

Hunter understood now. This was about the last time they were here in these woods, how she'd forced him to acknowledge the significance of what had happened with Samantha. That day had been so painful – and he'd reacted poorly, to say the least – but he knew Scarlet had only pushed him for his own good, so he could finally start moving in the right direction. In truth, he felt nothing but gratitude for her actions.

"Scarlet, you may have pushed me, but you have to know by now that my will is pretty damn strong. The things I've done up here at Blue have been of my own choosing, and you don't need to feel bad about anything that has ever happened between us on this mountain."

More tears fell from her eyes. "I'm sorry, Hunter."

"Please don't be."

"God, I'm so, so sorry."

The look of crumpled defeat on her face gutted him. "Come here," he demanded, pulling her whole body onto his lap. She immediately curled into a ball on his chest. He dropped his forehead into her hair, filling his lungs with her soft scent as she struggled to steady her breathing. He hoped his touch would reassure her, but she couldn't manage to settle down. Scarlet trembled and cried and quaked, unraveling at her seams and falling apart in his arms.

Hunter honestly didn't know how to hold her together. He only knew he had to try. "*Shh*. It's okay. Everything is going to be okay."

Her fingers twisted against his shirt, her words coming raw and pained from her throat. "I'm so sorry I pushed you. I thought I was doing the right thing, and I'm just...I'm so, so sorry."

He shook his head, not understanding the strength of her reaction. He didn't know what the hell to do for her. But then, as she continued to whisper the word *sorry* over and over, Hunter finally understood what she needed.

"I forgive you," he told her. "You're forgiven."

She sobbed. She gripped hard to his shirt and simply sobbed. He held her tighter, having no clue what she needed forgiveness for, but grateful to be able to give it. This was his forest fairy, his freebird, his Scarlet. She'd changed his whole world. She'd given everything to make him happier, and he didn't know if he'd given her anything. But he could give her this.

"You're forgiven. You're forgiven," he whispered, again and again.

Hunter didn't know how long they stayed like that. All he knew was he needed to hold her until she stopped crying and shaking. He offered her his forgiveness and his strength, and when she eventually collapsed in his arms, he silently thanked the heavens that he could be here for her.

Once her trembling finally stopped, and she'd dried her face with the back of her hands, and her breathing resumed an even pace, he still didn't move. Scarlet reached to his shirt and smoothed out the fabric beneath her cheek. A little laugh bubbled up from her throat.

"I completely soaked your shirt," she said, her voice nearly back to normal. "I think even worse than I did with the kitchen hose last night."

"My shirt and I will be fine. As long as you're okay."

She raised her head up to his. Her eyes were red around the edges. Hunter forced himself to smile, even though it killed him to see her so sad. "I'm okay," she assured, matching his smile. "I apologize for my colossal panic attack."

"You don't need to apologize. Do you want to talk about it?"

Her brow knitted. "Thanks, but no."

"Okay, well, do you want to go find your favorite oak tree now?"

"That sounds nice, but I just want to go back to my cabin."

"Are you sure? It's only early afternoon. We still have time left."

"Yeah, I know, but I think we should head back."

Hunter nodded as she stood. He jumped up, wrapped his arm around her waist, and pulled her next to him. Scarlet dropped her head against his shoulder as they walked slowly toward civilization. She didn't say anything. She barely moved, except for the drag of her feet, and he hated that she wasn't dancing.

"I have an idea," he offered, breaking the unbearable silence.

Scarlet looked up to his eyes. "What idea?"

"Do you want to play a game with me?"

"Which game?"

"Maybe hide-and-seek?"

It took her a moment to register his suggestion. When she did, she grinned from ear to ear. He felt that smile everywhere.

"Goodness, Hunter. I haven't played hide-and-seek in forever."

"Do you want to hide or should I?"

"Can I hide?"

"Sure. But you do realize I get to kiss you when I find you, right?"

"Ooh, I realize that now!" she squealed. She laughed and bounced in front of him, and his world made sense again. "Close your eyes and count to twenty."

He did as instructed. When he finished counting and reopened his eyes, he found her. Over and over. It never took very long to discover her hiding place, even when she managed to find a tree big enough to shield her entirely. He could always see her hot breath in the cool air, or hear her muffled giggles, or catch sight of her hair. He would sneak up behind her, startling her every time, at which point she shrieked and giggled and threw her arms around his neck.

Hunter knew his little fairy felt unnerved today, but playing with her made her happy for a while and he loved being able to give her that. The next time she hid, he snuck up and grabbed her, planting his lips against her mouth when she gasped. After a very thorough kiss, he met her eyes and smiled. "Gotcha," he said.

"Good heavens! How are you so amazing at this game?"

"I'll always be able to find you, Scarlet. You must know that."

He didn't mean it as a threat. He really didn't. It was a simple fact. And maybe even a promise. But when a flicker of fear passed through her eyes, he knew she didn't see it that way. He kissed the tip of her nose and changed the subject. "Want to race me back to your cabin?"

"I can't race you. You're like a stealthy ninja jet plane."

"Well, how about I give you a ridiculous head start?"

"But what if you lose sight of me and get lost?"

"I won't get lost," he assured her. "I know how to navigate this forest now. You taught me well."

Scarlet smiled brilliantly. She leaned in to kiss him, waited until his eyes closed, then shrieked and ran in the opposite direction. Hunter laughed as he watched her bound through the trees. He waited until she was almost out of sight before following. By the time she reached the back of her cabin, he'd caught up with her. He slowed to a jog, making sure she could round the porch and hop up onto the steps before him.

"Yes! I did it!" she cheered, jumping up and down in front of her door and pumping her fists in the air. "I beat you here! And I'm going to celebrate like crazy! Even though I know you totally let me win!"

He grinned as he walked up the stairs. "It was worth it to see you so happy."

"Thank you, Hunter. For everything. For this whole day."

"You're welcome."

She grabbed his hand and tugged. "Come inside," she encouraged, as if he wouldn't follow her anywhere.

When she turned to step into the living room, his eyes focused on the loose curls hanging down her back. Kicking the door shut, he stepped up behind her. "Scarlet, you have something in your hair."

"What? Where?"

"Here, let me." Hunter eased his fingers into her dark waves and pulled out a little green leaf.

"Oh!" she gasped as he handed it to her. "It's another one, just like the first time we went into the forest. It's as if they want to cling to me."

"Yeah. I know the feeling."

Scarlet's breath caught. "Well, I...I suppose I should put this one on the counter, right beside the other one."

Hunter watched her walk away to set this leaf next to the first. He stared at the two of them, lying side by side. The new leaf was mostly green with just a little red inside it, a reverse image of the first. Like yin and yang. He marveled at the sight before turning back to his freebird. "You know, I hate to say this, but the leaf proves it. You're dirty."

Her nose crinkled. "What? No, I'm not. We weren't in the forest that long, and I took a shower just this morning."

"Oh, but you are. You're so very, very dirty."

"Hunter! I am not dirty! Smell my hair! I shampooed it this..."

"Scarlet," he growled, grabbing her hips and pulling her against him. "Trust me, you are dirty. You need to take a bath in that big, bear-claw bathtub you have, and you need someone to wash you. Thoroughly."

"Oh." Her eyes widened. "*Oh*. I see now. You are entirely right. I'm so dirty. I'm actually filthy. It's disgusting, really. I don't even know how you can stand be in the same room with me." She stopped talking when he chuckled. "Sorry. I took it too far, didn't I?"

He leaned down to kiss her, since there was nothing else he could do. "It was perfect. Now let me get you clean."

"Ooh, yay," she sang, her face lighting up like Christmas.

Hunter grabbed her hand to pull her with him. When they entered the bathroom, his gaze wandered to the sink. All of her toiletries were still there, lined up in exact order. He catalogued them in his mind before shifting his attention to the large porcelain soaking tub. Releasing her hand, he reached down to plug the drain, turn on the water, and test the temperature. Then he looked to the wide tiled ledge connecting the tub to the wall, where several bottles rested.

"What things do you have here on the ledge?"

"It's bubble bath, shampoo and conditioner, and a cup to rinse my hair," she explained. "And candles and matches. I love candles."

"That sounds perfect." Hunter poured a healthy dose of bubble bath beneath the running water. The scent of vanilla filled the air as he lit the candles. When the tiny yellow lights began to flicker, he closed the door and flipped off the lights.

The windowless room darkened instantly, the candlelight now licking the curves of her body. "How do you like this, Scarlet?"

"It's amazing. Want to play another game?"

"What game?"

"The see-who-can-get-their-clothes-off-the-fastest game?"

"Oh, yes," he agreed. "I definitely want to play that."

"Ready, set, go!"

Scarlet grabbed the hem of her shirt, rushing to remove her outfit. She was still no match for him, though. Especially since she slowed herself down with near constant giggling. By the time she wore nothing but her underwear, Hunter stood completely naked and waiting.

"Hmm. I guess you didn't let me win this time," she said, reaching for her panties.

"Wait. Can I tear those off of you?"

"Again? Really? This would be the *fifth* pair."

Hunter gave her his best puppy-dog face. "Is that too many?"

"Hmm. You know what? If it makes you happy, go ahead."

He hooked his fingers into the straps on her hips and pulled. When her torn thong fell to the floor, he stepped up to her. "Man, that's fun."

She smiled into his kiss. It was the best feeling in the world.

"You ready to get in now, Scarlet?"

"Most definitely."

Hunter shut off the water, testing the temperature once more before stepping into the tub. He sat, pressing his spine against the high-topped wall opposite the faucet, and reached for her. Scarlet took his hand and eased her body beneath the clouds of bubbles. She sat inside his legs, with her back to his chest, and pushed her bottom between his thighs.

Wrapping both arms around her waist, he pulled her in closer. Her head dropped onto his shoulder while the ends of her hair soaked into the water. Hunter's eyes moved down to her chest. Even in the dim candlelight, he could still see the shadow of his teeth marks against her skin. The bruises didn't look nearly as angry as before, and he didn't feel the same levels of pain and guilt when he saw them, but it still amazed him to think of how much she'd given of herself in the few days they'd had together.

Scarlet sighed as the contours of her curves lined up perfectly in his arms. He felt the warmth of her skin despite the heat of the water, and he reached his hand to hers on the ledge of the tub, entranced by the way their fingers wound together. He would never be able to get enough of this, no matter how much time they spent together. And yet they basically had no time left at all.

Surviving his last week of vacation here alone was going to be hard as hell. But Hunter couldn't even imagine how horrifying it would be to go back to his actual home without this. Without her.

I don't want to let her go. I want her with me in the real world. I want to see her smiling face the first time she crosses through my front door. I want to know how it feels to sit beside her at my dining room table. I want to sleep with her in my arms, in my bed. I want to wake to the sight of her beside me. Again and again and again.

His fingers clenched onto hers. "God, I don't want to give this up," he admitted in a hoarse rasp. "Do you? Do you want to give this up?"

She stiffened against him, her muscles bracing beneath the water.

Hunter cringed when he felt her tension. He knew he shouldn't ruin these last hours they had together. But he couldn't help how he felt.

"I just can't imagine it, Scarlet. I can't imagine you leaving here the day after tomorrow. I can't imagine having to stand there, and kiss you for the last time, and watch you walk away from me."

His voice left him for a moment. He could only lay here with her in his arms. She didn't say anything. She just held his hand in her own.

Hunter sighed. "I know what you're thinking. You think we're on a speeding bus and we won't be able to stay together once we jump off."

"That is what I think," she admitted, her voice barely a whisper.

"But...there's not enough time left for us. There are still so many things I want to know about you, and there's just not enough time."

"Wh-what do you want to know?"

"I want to know where you'll go when you leave here. I want to know where you call home. And I want to know what you do for a living, since I'm pretty sure you're not a freelance nature reporter."

Scarlet's breath caught, confirming that he'd crossed a line.

"I'm sorry," Hunter offered, peering down at the side of her face to gauge her reaction. "I know I told you that you didn't have to share anything with me you didn't feel comfortable sharing. And I promise I don't want to put you in a position where you feel like you have to lie, since I appreciate your honesty more than I can say. I just want more of you. I want to know where you grew up. I want to know what side of the bed you sleep on. I want to know your favorite singer and your favorite food. I want you to tell me anything and everything."

"I – I understand your desires, and I can answer, but what difference will it make? Blue still isn't reality, and I'm still leaving in two days."

"I know you are, and I know Blue isn't the real world. But if it's a fantasy, then I want as much as I can have for as long as I can have it."

When he finished speaking, he held his breath. He stilled, waiting to see if she would allow this. To see if she would give him *more*.

Scarlet didn't respond at first. She lay rigidly against him, moving only when she breathed. After an eternity, she said, "Elvis."

A smile tugged at Hunter's lips as he watched the dark ends of her hair float in the bubbly water. "Why is Elvis your favorite singer?"

"Because my mother always played his songs when I was little and I fell in love with them. Also, the hip-swinging thing was pretty cool."

"It definitely was. And what's your favorite food?"

Her muscles eased a bit against his chest. "Twinkies."

"Twinkies? Really?"

"I can't help it. I love things that look a certain way on the outside, but once you get to the inside, it's a complete surprise. Like Twinkies. Oh, and corndogs. And lemons, of course – the adorable fruit with the surprising kick inside."

"Don't forget powder kegs," Hunter added.

Scarlet reached up behind her, finding his face with her hand and cradling his jaw in her fingertips. "Especially powder kegs."

He kissed the top of her head. Slipping his hand down to her elbow, he dragged his fingers along the underside of her arm. She laughed and squirmed, like he knew she would, since he'd discovered this ticklish spot just yesterday.

Hunter loved knowing her ticklish places. He loved knowing about Elvis, Twinkies, and lemons. Even if they merely scratched the surface.

"Will you answer something else for me, Scarlet?"

"What's that?"

"Do you like having your hair washed?"

"God, yes. I didn't know that was an option. Is that an option?"

"It's more than an option. It's a necessity."

"Why is it a necessity?"

"Well, even though I haven't spent nearly as much time at Blissful Blue as you have, and I'm nowhere near as good at this psychology stuff as you are, there is one theory I'm familiar with."

"Yeah? Which one?"

"Positive reinforcement," he said, reaching to the ledge to grab her shampoo bottle. "You confided in me just now, and I want you to know how much I appreciate it. Therefore, I'm going to reward you with something you like in an attempt to further said behavior."

"You know, I think positive reinforcement works better if you don't actually tell your subject you're going to use it on them."

"Yes, but I don't have a choice in the matter, since I know you'd figure it out on your own anyway. Now sit up, please."

She laughed while she complied, arching up and placing her hands on the sides of the tub. Hunter squeezed his thighs around her hips so she wouldn't drift too far away. He popped open the shampoo bottle and took a whiff. "This smells like you," he realized, pouring the shimmery liquid into his hands. "Like a field of tiny wildflowers."

The moment his fingers pushed into her hair, Scarlet groaned. Her knuckles whitened against the ledges, fighting to keep her body upright. "Good Lord, Hunter, that is just...mmm..."

He smiled as he continued, moving his fingers tenderly yet firmly across her scalp. The shampoo lathered into thick bubbles, releasing her scent all around them. She turned to mush under his hands, descending into a state of bliss that hypnotized him as much as it did her.

Hunter knew his positive reinforcement was working. At least, he hoped it was. He wanted more knowledge, more confidences, more *her*.

He used the cup from the wide tub ledge to rinse the shampoo from her hair. Then he restarted the whole process with her conditioner. Scarlet turned utterly boneless, her hands dropping into the water while she swayed and moaned with the movement of his fingers.

Damn, she was so *his* right now. It was probably wrong of him to use her body against her like this. But he did tell her he was going to do it, so that made him feel a bit less guilty.

Once he'd rinsed out the conditioner, and her hair lay slick beneath his fingers, he reached to her shoulders to pull her toward him. She flopped back onto his chest, sloshing the water around them as she collapsed. Hunter slid his hands down her arms and onto her hips, adjusting her between his legs so her perfectly rounded bottom came flush with his lower abs. Her head lolled onto his shoulder as he whispered into her ear. "How is this? Are you comfortable?"

"Mmm. Comfor'ble not good enough word."

He grinned with her almost-sentence, running his hands across her hips and over her belly. "I'm glad you enjoyed it."

"I did. So much. You deserve a shampooing award."

"I'll take it. I like awards."

"Who doesn't like awards?"

Hunter threaded their fingers. She sighed, a sound of utter contentment, and snuggled her face beside his. This moment was calm, and peaceful, and he hated having to take advantage of it. But he had no other choice. He was out of time.

"Have you ever gotten any awards, Scarlet?"

"Awards? Uh, sure. I mean, I got a lot in high school."

"What kind of awards?"

"Oh, you know. I won the State Science Fair. I was Valedictorian of my class. Things like that."

"Yeah, that sounds about right. You're a genius, aren't you?"

She shifted against his chest, but she didn't run. "Is this about me kicking your butt at Scrabble? Because I'm sure you would have given me a run for my money if you'd been in a different headspace."

"Actually, I don't think I could ever challenge you at Scrabble. But that's just the tip of the iceberg. I suspected the truth before, but when I think about everything I've seen you do and say, I realize just how much of a genius you are. Mensa-level, if I had to guess. Am I right?"

Her fingers clamped onto his. "Yes."

"You don't sound happy about it."

"I am happy. Intelligence is a gift."

"But?"

"But it comes with a lot of responsibility, and I don't know if I handled it well when I was younger. The older I got, the more seriously I took it. I drifted away from my mother's encouragement to be free and celebrate life, and leaned toward my father's goals of science and studies. I started to think all those things my mother believed in were silly and frivolous. I started to think I'd wasted my life gallivanting in the woods, watching the squirrels jump and the birds fly."

Scarlet paused to suck in a breath. She exhaled shakily.

"You're right, you know," she told him. "I'm not a nature reporter."

Hunter froze, his heart pounding. He didn't say a word for fear of ruining the moment. He listened intently, his entire body focused on hers, as she spoke again.

"When I was a kid, I always wanted to be a nature photographer. I used to fantasize about it on my Girl Scout campouts. When I decided to come on vacation up here at Blue this time, I brought my camera with me because it felt like it could be fun. It felt hopeful."

Scarlet eased her fingers out of his in order to draw them across his forearms. "Do you remember the picture I took, Hunter? The photo of the yellow-crowned purple fantini that I hung up in the living room?"

"Of course."

"Well, that...that bird doesn't exist. At least, nowhere but in my imagination. In the imagination of a young girl in the woods, a girl who believed everything her mother said about magic and miracles and being able to do anything you set your mind to. A girl who wanted to discover a new bird, to see something no one else had ever seen before."

"So, that's what the picture represents? It's your imagination?"

"It's everything I loved about my childhood. All the joy, all the excitement, all the limitless opportunities laid out before me. The day I took that photo, I actually thought I saw something in the tree. I swore I saw my bird. But looking back on it now, I realize it was just wishful thinking. I saw what I wanted to see, because I wanted to believe in excitement and possibility again."

Hunter banded her tighter to his chest.

"You said you wanted to know why I came to Blue," she whispered, the words sending chills down his spine. "The answer is I came here to reconnect with the joy I knew in my childhood, to begin a journey that would hopefully take me back to my roots. I came here to feel open and free and silly again. I'd been missing all of those things for so long, and I just wanted to see if they were still here, inside me."

"And did you...did you find what you wanted to find?"

Scarlet clung to his arms. "I got here the week before you did. I spent a lot of that week walking in the woods. I reminisced about the countless hours I'd wandered through the forest as a kid, looking for my fantini bird, and how I'd appreciated everything around me – every leaf on every tree. As the week went on, I realized being at Blue was helping me so much. I started to feel whole again, like I remembered what magic was. In truth, that would have been enough for me to call this vacation a success. Reconnecting to those feelings was all I'd wanted. But then the most amazing thing happened."

"What happened?"

She nestled her cheek against his shoulder. "One day, after I'd finished my walk in the woods, I stepped out of the forest and saw a man hunched over a blown tire, cursing and grumbling and being generally pissed off at life. A squirrel had darted out in front of his car, and it looked to be the last straw for him, because he obviously didn't want to be here in the first place. I decided, right then and there, that I was going to take him with me on my journey. I decided he needed the same journey I did, whether he wanted to admit it or not.

"I knew it wouldn't be easy to take him with me. I knew he would resist. But I believed I could pull him along, so I set about doing just that. I purposefully provoked him with silly lies. I did ridiculous things, like tricking him into drinking straight lemon juice. All because I wanted him to fight for his life the way I was trying to fight for my own.

"He reacted to my atrocious behavior as I hoped. He fought back, and I was happy about that, because I felt like he was traveling with me. But after a few days, he became fed up with my lies and pushed me away. That moment broke my heart, since I already knew what a wonderful man he was, and I worried he didn't see it in himself. And also, because I was alone on my journey again.

"After he pushed me away, I spent a day and a half without him. It felt like torture. Then, thank God, he came back to me. He looked as miserable as I felt, and he asked me to stop lying and just be with him. That night, we stopped fighting with each other. Ever since, we've been fighting *for* each other. We've been working together through all of this, yet I think he believes this journey was one-sided. I think he believes I helped him, and not the other way around."

Scarlet paused to take a breath, her body quaking in his arms. "You have no idea how much you've done for me, Hunter. I felt weak and beaten when I came up here to Blue. I don't feel that way anymore. I can go back to the real world now. I can go back to deal with all those problems. My confidence has returned, entirely because of you. Because the entire time I thought I was taking you on a journey, you were actually taking me on one. And I honestly don't have the words to tell you how grateful I am for everything you've given me."

When she finished, Hunter shook nearly as much as she did.

He had so many questions. He wanted to know what made her feel weak and beaten. He wanted to know what stole the color red away. He wanted to know what problems she had to face back in the real world.

Hunter had a hundred thousand bazillion questions, but she'd already said more than he ever thought he'd hear. He could tell by the trembling of her body that she'd given him as much as she could. Instead of pushing her, he pulled her into his chest and held onto her for dear life.

Scarlet sighed, melting into his arms. He gripped her even tighter. He wanted to grip her so tightly that they would simply meld into one person. He couldn't do that, of course. The choice to remain with him was hers. All he could do was hold her, and support her, and hope she realized this was where she truly belonged.

Time passed. Hunter didn't have any earthly idea how long they lay together in the warmth of the water. Eventually, her breathing evened out, making him wonder if she'd fallen asleep. She wasn't snoring yet, but her eyes were closed. He watched her softened face, loving how carefree she looked right now, especially after the day she'd had.

"You asleep?" he whispered.

"Not entirely. Although you do make a fine pillow, Mr. Gregory."

"Why don't you take a nap, then? I've got you."

"Mmm, I'd love to. Maybe you could nap with me? On second thought, that's probably a really bad idea. Drowning sounds like an awful way to go."

Hunter chuckled. "It's okay. I promise I won't fall asleep."

"Why not? Aren't you comfortable?"

"I'm incredibly comfortable. I just don't think it's nighttime yet."

"That's right. You don't take naps during the day, do you?"

"No."

"Too much wasted time?"

"Exactly."

Scarlet peeled her eyes open. "Well, if you aren't going to nap, then I won't either. I will stay wide, wide awake." She shifted inside his embrace, causing him to groan as her wet skin rubbed between his legs.

"Well, since you're wide awake," he said, staring down at her body beneath the scattered bubbles, "there is something else I'd like to do."

"Yeah? What's that?"

Reaching one arm to the wide ledge of the tub, he pushed the shampoo and conditioner toward the flickering candles. Hunter patted his hand on the freshly cleared tile surface. "I want you to sit up here."

"Why?"

"Because I want to press my face between your thighs and lick and suck on you until you come in my mouth."

A gasp escaped her throat. "Oh, wow. Really?"

"Yes, really."

"I see. That sounds, um, very good."

"I'm glad it does, since it serves two important purposes."

"What purposes are those?"

"The first is allowing me to taste you again, which I desperately want."

Scarlet moaned. "And the second purpose?"

"Well, as I mentioned, I'm a firm believer in positive reinforcement. You confided in me just now, and I know it wasn't easy for you, so I fully intend to reward you."

"You don't need to reward me for that. Besides, I'd say this reward is significantly more involved than a hair shampooing."

"Yes, but the more you confide in me, the bigger the rewards will become. Please do keep that in mind, Scarlet, because I sincerely mean it. Now sit up on the ledge, please. I have work to do."

Her hands reached to the edges of the tub, gripping onto the porcelain. She sat up, but hesitated. Hunter ran his fingers over her wet hair, tracing all the way down her back, before slipping over the indentation at the base of her spine. She whimpered with his touch.

"I want you to know I'm waiting very patiently for you to do as I've asked," he informed her. "There's a huge part of me that wants to grab you by the ass and set you on the ledge myself. But I won't do that just yet. I'll wait a bit longer, since I believe you'll obey me in this."

"Obey you?" She huffed out a laugh. "You certainly are pushy."

"Yes, I am. I'm demanding and controlling and domineering and lots of other similar adjectives." He gripped her hips in his fingers. "You already know that about me. You also know I'm working on my control issues. But you did tell me the other night that you want the real me when we're together. This is the real me, Scarlet. Now, I'd like for you to sit up on the ledge. I won't ask nicely again."

She drummed her fingernails on the tile ledge. "Well, I suppose you're right," she conceded after a long moment of deliberation. "I told you I want the real you, and I meant it. So, for tonight, I'll obey."

He watched in sheer hunger while she pushed herself up on her knees. She bent forward, bringing her ass to the level of his eyes. He stared hard at her flawlessly rounded cheeks as water droplets slid down her skin. His cock throbbed with need, instantly desperate and painful.

Hunter licked his lips when Scarlet finally shifted to the side of the tub. She lifted herself up to the ledge, sitting down on the hard tiles. Pressing her back firmly against the wall, she looked to his face.

He could see all of her from this position, even in the meager candlelight. His eyes dragged over her body, across the tight peaks of her nipples and onto the gentle curve of her belly. He stared at the faint, healing bruises on her chest, terribly aware that he'd made those marks right before the last time he'd pushed his face between her legs.

Hunter still wasn't sure why she accepted all of him with such an open heart. When he looked back to her face, it took him a minute to refocus on her eyes. He could see, so damn plainly, her utter adoration.

Before he had the chance to drown himself in an ocean of guilt, Scarlet smiled. "I'm looking forward to my positive reinforcement."

Her words hung in the air while she nibbled her lower lip. Hunter's hands fisted in the water, his entire being pulsing with the need to touch. He allowed his gaze to fall down her body, soaking in her lush curves before settling on her closed thighs. Reaching for her hips, he tugged her closer to the edge and centered himself in front of her knees.

He looked back to her face. "Spread your legs for me, Scarlet."

She did as instructed, her eyelids instantly falling to half-mast. He smiled before easing forward in the water and lowering his mouth to her stomach. Her thighs encased his chest when he began licking the skin over her belly. He played and nipped and teased, listening to the eruption of sweet giggles from her throat as he worked his tongue slowly and worshipfully across her flesh. Hunter knew this wasn't anything like it had been the first time in the woods, and he was grateful for that. He wanted her to know this could be different, and he could make her feel a million different things. He wanted her aching to know them all.

Once she stopped giggling and started moaning, once her thighs trembled and clamped against his ribcage, he knew she'd had enough teasing. He put them both out of their misery. He kissed his way down her stomach and onto her soft folds. Then he ran his tongue straight up the seam of her sex. She cried out, her fingers threading into his hair.

Hunter repeated his actions, licking up her folds and onto her tight nub of nerves. He tried to taste her – he wanted to taste her so badly – but realized quickly he couldn't. They'd been soaking in this tub too long. Her skin was perfumed by vanilla bubble bath and floral shampoo, and while he loved those scents on her, they weren't what he wanted.

He didn't want her skin wet because of this bathwater. He wanted to make her wet, to have it come from inside her, to have her body openly plead for his. Hunter took his time tonguing her. He sucked gently on her tender skin as she moaned and squirmed, dragging her feet in the water and lapping the warm liquid against his skin.

When he finally pushed his tongue deep inside her sex, Scarlet curled her fingers forcefully into his hair, imprisoning him between her thighs. He wanted to tell her it wasn't necessary to hold him here. He wanted to assure her the hounds of hell couldn't drag him away from his clawing need to taste her. But he didn't want to spend that much time away from her skin, since she was truly wet now. Her taste soaked his tongue when he curled it inside her. Her back arched and her muscles shook and her voice cracked as she chanted his name.

Hunter smiled against her salted skin, grasping her hips in his hands, edging her forward so he could get better leverage for his mouth. Her legs shifted rhythmically, rocking her into him while she whimpered. He could feel the tension tightening inside her. He quickened his movements, licking and sucking her sweet flesh over and over. Her hands fisted into his hair when she came apart. His stiff cock jerked as he drank her in – from her taste in his mouth, to the sound of her panted gasps, to the sensation of her warm, throbbing skin against his lips.

He didn't stop then. He continued running his tongue across her soft folds, just to keep feeling her tremble. He could have easily persisted until she came a second time, but then he heard a thud and an, "Ow."

Hunter looked up to find her holding onto the back of her head.

When Scarlet's glassy eyes met his, she let out a tiny laugh. "Sorry. Forgot where I was again. Banged my head against the wall."

"Come here. Let me kiss it and make it all better."

"More kissing? God, there's so much kissing."

He chuckled as he eased away, resuming his position against the wall of the tub, before holding his arms out to her. Scarlet sank into the bubbles, fitting her bottom between his thighs. Hunter urged her back onto his chest so he could cradle her head. "There," he said, pressing a kiss into her hair. "How's that?"

"It's perfect. I'm all better now."

"I'm glad, although I think we may need to get you a helmet or something.

You keep hitting your head when you orgasm, and we need to protect all these brains of yours."

She laughed wildly, which caused her whole body to shake against his, which made his thick, swollen cock twitch into her ass.

"Mmm," she moaned, grasping onto his thighs. "You're so hard."

"Do I need to apologize for being aroused by tasting you?"

"No, no. Don't ever apologize for that. Bless you for enjoying it."

"Oh, I definitely enjoy it."

Scarlet shifted against his throbbing erection. "And you're so good at it. I mean, I don't have much to compare it to, but I can't imagine it getting any better than that. You're really just magical."

Hunter wanted to dwell on her compliments, but he had difficulty focusing on anything except the movement of her hips. She'd pressed her ass firmly against his cock, and now rocked back onto him, her breaths coming in staccato pants. She was so damn eager for him, and her body's responsiveness ramped his desire to levels of lunacy.

He took her by the shoulders, stilling her actions in order to maintain his control. "Scarlet. Tell me what you want to do right now."

"I think you know. Don't you?"

"Yes, I'm pretty sure I know. But I'd like you to tell me exactly what you want."

She shook her head. "This probably seems silly, given all we've done with each other, but it still feels strange to say the words out loud."

Hunter ran his hands from her shoulders down to her wrists, dragging little drops of water with him, watching them caress her skin. "I don't want to make you feel uncomfortable. Ever. But if you can, I would love to hear you say what you want me to do to you."

"You would?"

"God, yes."

"Well, then. I want you inside me. Deep inside me. I want you to fuck me, Hunter. Here, in the water."

"How would you like me to fuck you? Do you want to face me? Or do you want me from behind? Fast or slow? Hard or gentle?"

"Um, from behind. Just like this. As for the rest, surprise me."

He smiled. "We should probably go slow, so we don't spill too much over the side of the tub. We made enough of a mess in the kitchen with the water fight yesterday."

"Oh my goodness! That water fight was so much fun!"

"It was. This is going to be fun, too," he promised, grasping onto her hips to lift her. Scarlet clutched the sides of the tub, using the leverage to tilt her ass higher. His cock found the entrance to her sex instantly, as if it had an internal homing beacon just for her. Right now, that peculiar idea made perfect sense, which made him laugh.

She turned her head to his. "Is something funny?"

Hunter watched her eyes darken while he pulled down on her hips, pushing himself slowly up inside her. She whimpered as their bodies joined. The moment he sat fully sheathed in her sex, he tugged her hands away from the side of the tub and wove his fingers into hers.

"Nothing's funny. It just amazes me how well we fit together."

She fell back against his chest, her head dropping on his shoulder. "Oh, I'm really glad you think so, too. I thought I was imagining it."

He shifted his hips, pulling out of her just a little before sinking back inside. "You're not imagining anything."

"Mmm. This feels so incredible."

"Yeah? I promise I'm going to make it feel even better."

"How is that even possible?"

"Easy. I'm going to make you come again."

Scarlet tensed, her fingers knotting into his.

Hunter's brow rose. "What's wrong?" he asked, baffled by her adverse reaction. "Don't you want to come again?"

"It's not that I don't want to, it's just..."

"Just what?"

"I, um, I haven't ever been able to do that before."

"Wait a minute. Are you telling me you've never had more than one orgasm during sex?"

"No, I haven't."

"*Goddamnit*," he growled. "Seriously, who are these men you dated before me? I fucking hate every single one of them."

"It's not all their fault. Trust me. I wasn't exactly open to trying new things. I wasn't like this, like I am with you."

"Well, I guess I'll take selfish pride in the fact that you're willing to try new things with me. But it's still an abomination that no one ever made you come twice. Honestly, I feel like an asshole for not giving you more before now."

"Please don't feel that way. I love what you give me when we're together. Besides, I think I'm fortunate to have one orgasm during sex. I mean, I've spoken to women who don't even get that, so..."

"Scarlet?"

"Yes?"

"You're going to have another orgasm now."

"But it's really not..."

"Honey, let me do this. You know I can."

"But what if it's not you? What if it's me?"

Hunter cringed at the fearful sound in her voice. It killed him to think she believed something might be wrong with her, just because she hadn't experienced more than minimally adequate lovers. Holding tight to her hands, he shifted his hips to push his cock deeper into her warmth.

"Do you even realize how sexy you are?" he questioned, pressing his lips to her shoulder as she shivered. "You are extraordinarily beautiful and so amazingly sexy. You have no idea how much I want you. I'm not even talking emotionally or intellectually right now. I'm speaking purely physically. My body aches for yours. I've told you that before and I meant it. If I could be inside you all fucking day long, I would. I want you constantly. You are gorgeous and perfect and I want you so badly it's painful."

She whimpered, her inner muscles contracting around his erection.

He kissed his way up her neck. "You always say you feel free when you're with me," he whispered beside her ear.

"Oh, I do. So free."

"Then be free with me now. Let everything else go. Be here with me and let me give you this. I want to. More than you can imagine."

She exhaled slowly, her tension finally easing. "Okay. I will."

He smiled in triumph against her skin.

"Um, Hunter?"

"Yes?"

"Just in case it doesn't work, thank you in advance for trying."

He released her hands to flatten his palms against her softly rounded belly. "You're welcome, in advance, for the next orgasm. Because it's going to happen."

Scarlet giggled, which may have been the best sound he'd ever heard. She reached one arm up behind her to thread her fingers into his hair, turning her face to his. When their mouths met, Hunter curled his body around hers and eased his tongue past her lips.

His hands slipped across the wet skin of her stomach before pushing further down to her hips. She spread her legs apart, as far as the porcelain walls allowed, and planted her feet against the bottom of the tub beside his knees. This new position gave her the leverage she needed to push herself up off his cock before sliding back down onto him. She moaned into his mouth and he kissed her again, matching her eager tongue with his own.

Hunter drew one hand up her body, taking the weight of her breast in his palm and running his thumb across the tight peak. When she sucked in a breath, he drew his other hand across to her inner thigh. She shifted up and down on his shaft as he parted the folds of her sex with his fingers, searching out the soft nub he'd spent so much time sucking on.

"Oh!" she yelped when he found his target. "That is, um…"

"Is this touch okay?" he questioned, running his fingers lightly over her skin. "You're not too tender from having my mouth here earlier?"

"I do feel a little tender, but in a good way."

"As long as it's good, I want you to put your hand on top of mine."

"On top?" she verified, keeping her fingers entangled in his hair as she looked down. She eased her other hand across his forearm until her palm rested against the back of his, directly over her sex. "Like this?"

"Just like this. I want you to guide me."

"You mean…guide you to touch me?"

"Yes. I want to learn how to touch you the way you touch yourself. You do touch yourself, right?"

"Oh, yes. I hadn't had a boyfriend in a while before you."

Hunter coughed, since the only thing he took from her statement was that she considered him her boyfriend. "Well, that's, um, that's perfect. Just move my hand the way you want it moved."

It took her a few seconds to do as he said, but she did. Her hand glided over his and he mimicked her touch, easing his fingers through her soft, slick folds. She focused his pressure around her nerve bud, circling and rubbing, shifting her hips to ride his erection.

He watched the few remaining bubbles break against her arms, watched her fingers as they directed his through the tender skin between her legs. While Scarlet hummed and purred, he added the rhythmic stroke of his other hand across her nipple. Her hand moved faster, her fingers pressing down harder against his.

Her body wound tighter and tighter as she impaled herself on his cock, teaching him to touch her in the most basic, instinctual way. Her fingers moved so quickly and desperately that she slipped a bit too far down, touching the base of his shaft where it joined with her sex.

Hunter inhaled sharply.

Scarlet stilled. "I'm…I'm sorry," she panted. "Did that hurt you?"

"Fuck, no. It didn't hurt."

"Did it feel good?"

"Yes," he admitted, his voice little more than a rasp. "Very good."

"Oh." Her fingers slipped down again, purposefully this time, smoothing across the only part of his stiff length that wasn't planted firmly inside her. Her touch sent a pulse of electricity shooting through his body. His eyes slammed shut on a feral growl.

The untamed noise he made only emboldened her. Scarlet reached farther down, smoothing across his balls before easing her fingers back up to the base of his cock. Hunter bit into his tongue, hoping the pain would keep him under control. She repeated the motion again and again while he played his fingers across her nipple and over her tender nub. Her breaths came in shallow spurts and he barely held himself together.

"Holy hell," he groaned. "You...you need to stop doing that. I don't want to come without you."

"I won't mind."

"Scarlet, you *will* have a second orgasm. Put your hand on mine."

"Oh, very well," she huffed, aligning their fingers together again.

"Now behave yourself, please. Remember this is about you. We're both going to touch you until you come."

"I want you to come, too."

"Good Lord, that won't be an issue. Just keep showing me how you like to be touched. I need to do this exactly the way you want it."

"But, Hunter...everything you do is exactly the way I want it."

His forehead fell into her hair. "Damn it, woman. Will you please stop being so adorable while I'm trying to fuck the hell out of you?"

Scarlet laughed. "Sorry. I promise I will take this more seriously."

He kissed her wet curls. "Good. Now move my hand again."

She obeyed, pressing down on his fingertips so they shifted in tiny circles across her nerve bud. She settled back against him, resting her head on his shoulder. Hunter watched the air heave from her chest as she used her legs to push up and down, riding his cock while they stroked her sex together. She managed to keep a solid rhythm for several moments, until her hand slipped off of his again, back down to where their bodies met.

Scarlet stilled on top of him. "God, that feels amazing," she sighed.

"What feels amazing?"

Her fingers eased apart around the base of his shaft. "You and me, joined together." She took hold of his hand, urging him to touch further down. "Feel this, Hunter. Feel this with me."

He did as she asked, spreading his fingers out through her folds and around his cock. He could feel himself, and her. He felt her soft skin where it opened so willingly to accept his hard length. He felt the slickness from inside her body coating each of them, even in the water.

"You're right," he groaned. "That feels amazing."

She pressed her face into his scratchy jaw as she pushed down on his palm, flattening it against her tender flesh. "Mmm...right there."

Her little circle of nerves jutted up against his palm. Hunter pressed down harder while she guided his touch. "Just like this?"

She gripped the ledge with her other hand to push herself up. Her fingers curled around his cock, right where it met the opening of her sex. She sank back down onto his erection with a shuddered exhale.

"God, yes. Just like this."

His palm shifted against her skin as she began moving up and down, over and over. He felt his thick shaft glide in and out of her body, directly against his fingertips. Hunter knew she felt it, too. The intimate connection was both erotic and overwhelming, and he fought the urge to run from it. He didn't want to run. He wanted to be right here, with her.

"Yes, yes, yes," Scarlet moaned, riding him faster and harder, pressing his palm into her skin, fucking both his cock and his hand.

Water sloshed violently around them, but he didn't give a damn about anything but her. Her muscles wound up to come apart around him, and he wanted that more than anything in the world. It was the only reason he held on as long as he did. It was the only reason he lasted until she breathed, "Oh, fuck," and her entire body shuddered.

The instant her inner walls contracted around his shaft, Hunter let himself feel everything at once. He screamed when he came. He screamed so loud he worried he would hurt her ears, so he bit into her shoulder to muffle the sound.

She cried out in pure ecstasy, thrashing in the water as she gasped and moaned. His eyes shut tight while his body poured inside hers. He couldn't think. He could barely breathe.

The instant her muscles stopped convulsing, she degenerated into an amorphous mass and fell back against his chest. He somehow had the presence of mind to grab her head and cradle it beside his, so she didn't hit the ledge of the tub. He might not be sure of exactly where he was at the moment, but he knew he didn't want her banging her big, beautiful brains on another hard surface.

When the side of her face slumped against his, Scarlet turned toward him and pressed her lips to his jaw. She licked and nipped at the stubble on his cheek as he wrapped both arms around her waist, pulling her even closer. They lay in silence for several minutes while Hunter focused on the sound of her slowly calming inhales and exhales.

Eventually, she stretched her back against his chest and sighed. "Wow. I, um, I don't really know what to say about all that."

"Neither do I. Maybe we just shouldn't say anything."

"That's probably best," she agreed, resting her hands over top of his. "Well, I mean, except thank you. I should definitely say thank you."

"You already thanked me. Before we even started."

"That was a thanks for trying. This is a thanks for truly succeeding."

He wound their fingers together. "Hmm. You're welcome, then."

Scarlet snuggled deeper into his arms. The next instant, she stiffened again. "Oh, damn it. Look what we did to the floor."

Hunter peeled one eyelid open. "Hmm. We spilled a little water."

"A little? It's practically a lake."

"Yeah, well. Shit happens."

She laughed. "It does, doesn't it? But I should clean it up now."

"Nope. I'm not letting you go yet."

"But the floor..."

"Will be fine for a little while longer."

"But I should..."

"Scarlet, I will only let you get out of this tub on one condition."

"What condition is that?"

"If you tell me I can stay the night in your bed."

Her fingers twitched over his. "I don't think that's a good idea."

"You did promise to spend a night in my arms before you left Blue."

"I know. Just not tonight."

"But that only leaves tomorrow night."

"Yes. Tomorrow."

"Okay," he agreed, since he didn't have a choice. Raising his leg, he moved his foot to the spigot and turned on the hot water with his big toe.

She watched the water pour into the tub. "What are you doing?"

"Replacing the water we spilled. And making it warmer for you."

"Aren't we getting out? I need to clean the floor."

"I can clean the floor later."

"But, Hunter..."

"We're not leaving here yet. I told you we could only get out on one condition, and you didn't meet that condition. So, now we stay."

"We've been soaking forever. We're going to turn into prunes."

He shrugged. "I like prunes. I mean, they're not as cute as lemons. In truth, they're just dry, wrinkly plums. Yet still admirable."

Scarlet shifted against his chest as the heat from the new water seeped in around them. "Well, even if we stay, I don't know what you expect us to do in here. I don't think I can have a third orgasm."

"Oh, you can. I can prove it to you, if you want. But that's not what I expect of you right this minute."

She tilted her face up to his. "What do you expect of me?"

Hunter met her searching gaze. "I expect you to take a nap."

"A nap?"

"I know it's been a long day for you."

"Yes, it has, but..."

He smoothed her damp hair from her face. "Please don't overthink it, honey. Let your mind rest for a while, and just be here with me."

"My goodness, that sounds heavenly. Although I still feel guilty, since you won't get anything out of this."

"That's not true at all. I'll get to feel you asleep in my arms again. I want that. I want to feel you at peace. And since I'm not allowed to lay with you in a bed right now, I'll have to settle for the bathtub."

The water filled back up to its original level and Hunter reached his toe to the faucet to turn it off.

Scarlet giggled. "You sure do have talented feet, Mr. Gregory."

"I'd like to think I have a lot of talented body parts."

"Oh, don't I know it," she agreed, tucking her forehead into his neck. "Are you really sure it's okay for me to nap on you?"

"Definitely."

"But what if you get tired, too?"

"I won't. Trust me, Scarlet. I've got you."

She rested her hand over his heart. "I know you do. Thank you."

He pressed another kiss to her hair. "Go to sleep, please."

"Hmm, 'kay," she sighed, her body already slumping further onto his. In just a few moments, her hand fell into the water.

When she started to snore, Hunter smiled against her damp hair.

"Don't worry, my little bird. I've always got you."

11

THE FIRST DATE

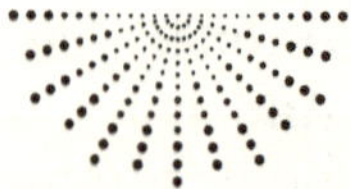

Hunter woke alone in his bed, as he always did at Blue. He'd grown used to his pattern here: morning basketball with Tyler, afternoon therapy sessions with Abbott, and dinner with Scarlet, followed by a lonely walk back to his cabin in the cold and dark. But it wouldn't be that way tonight, because his forest fairy would finally fulfill her promise. She would allow him to spend this entire night in her bed.

Hunter wanted to dwell on the perfect image his brain created: waking beside her in the morning, tangled up in her body, with her unruly hair draped across his face. He wanted to imagine how her scent would fill his lungs and his mind before he thought of anything else. But he did not want to imagine what would come next. He didn't want to even consider how he would be forced to get out of her bed, and kiss her goodbye, and watch her walk away from him. And then stand there, wondering how in the hell he could ever possibly reassemble his heart.

Opening his eyes, he stared at the ceiling. He couldn't believe this was their last day. He couldn't believe she would leave him tomorrow. Especially since he didn't even know where she called home.

I'll always be able to find you, Scarlet.

He'd said those words to her just yesterday, and they were true. How many women named Scarlet Tracey could there be in the world? If he couldn't find her with a simple Web search, he could assign someone else to find her. All he had to do was walk into the IT department of Gregory Global and grab his employee and friend, Clay Saunders, who was a genius at computers. Clay could definitely find her for him.

But what good would that do, if she didn't want to be found?

Scarlet obviously didn't want him coming after her once she left Blue. She believed they were on a speeding bus right now, and as much as Hunter wanted to deny her logic, he understood the analogy. After all, only two weeks had passed since they'd first met. Two weeks filled with overwhelming, sometimes brutal, emotions. He'd been more open with her than he'd ever been with anyone in his life, and she'd struggled with the two sides of herself right in front of him. They'd seen each other at their most vulnerable, and they'd clung to each other out of desperation. It wasn't exactly a normal relationship.

"God, maybe she's right," Hunter muttered to himself. A bond like theirs probably wasn't meant to last forever. It was too immediate, and too delicate, and to force it into a world of harsh realities would most likely shatter it into a million bitter pieces.

He stared off into space, trying to convince himself of those truths. Scarlet's reasoning was logical and practical: Blissful Blue was a break from life, far from reality. They were just two people who'd found each other for a brief moment in time, like a spark of something unexplained in the night sky. Trying to hold onto that would be foolish, at best.

She would walk away from him tomorrow, because that was the prudent, reasonable thing to do. She would walk away and it would be worse than the worst thing he could imagine. It would be sheer, utter hell, and Hunter didn't even want to think about it, let alone live it.

Of course, Scarlet had tried to warn him about this. From the second he said he wanted to kiss her, she told him it wasn't a good idea to act on their attraction. From the minute he convinced her to become his lover, she cautioned that they might come to regret indulging in this fantasy.

Bolting upright, Hunter swung his legs over the side of the bed to plant his feet on the hard floor. "Oh, shit. I understand now."

For the first time, he understood why she sent him away every night and why he woke alone in his cabin every morning. His little bird had been trying to protect him. She'd been trying to protect them both. She always knew they'd have to return to reality alone, and she'd wanted to save them from feeling the loss of something they never really had.

Scarlet couldn't allow either of them the luxury of dreaming about a future because they had no future. They would never go out on a date, or stroll through town together, or wake entangled in each other's arms on a lazy weekend morning. She knew those moments would never exist for them, so she'd separated this one thing – making love in a bed and falling asleep in each other's arms – in order to distance their relationship as much as possible from the real world.

Hunter understood why she did it. He knew she'd wanted to protect their hearts from such pointless pain, and he appreciated her trying. But she'd failed.

"Damn it," he grumbled, achingly aware that he'd lost his control with Scarlet. He'd lost control of so many things in the past two weeks, not the least of which were his emotions. To be honest, his attachment to her had scared him at first. It scared him so much that he'd nearly had a panic attack the first time they had sex. Yet his feelings for her had only grown wildly and exponentially since.

Hunter had become so used to these insane emotions that they didn't frighten him anymore. He loved how he felt with her. He loved who he was with her. He wanted to embrace these feelings, to ignore her prudent decision to part ways amicably, and to grab hold of this chance at happiness, however unlikely it may be.

But that obviously wasn't what Scarlet wanted.

He'd tried yesterday to tell her he didn't want to give up on them, yet she wouldn't bend. For whatever reason, whether it was the speeding bus or something else entirely, his forest fairy didn't believe they could stay together after Blue. Hunter simply couldn't comprehend why she refused to see their potential beyond these mountains.

"Good Lord, what the hell happened to me?" he questioned the crisp morning air. "When did I become the sunshine optimist here? At what point did I forgo logic and reason and choose to believe anything is possible? And why won't my freebird agree with me?"

Hunter stood to pace the floor in front of his bed. He balled his fists in frustration, knowing exactly what he should do: embrace the logical truth of the situation, accept his fate, and allow her to walk out of his life. But he didn't want to be logical anymore. Not when it came to her.

There were just too many things he still needed. He needed her to tell him where in the world she lived. He needed her to commit to seeing him again next week, and the next. He needed her to admit that they could make this relationship work, however long-distance it may be, if they both wanted it badly enough. He needed her to believe they could turn this fantasy into a reality, if they simply worked together.

Hunter huffed as he paced, knowing there was little to no chance of any of those things actually happening. His Scarlet was quite stubborn, so he probably couldn't convince her to change her mind about their fate. He probably couldn't talk her out of anything...but maybe he could *show* her a different path.

Halting in place, he forced his fingers roughly through his hair. He already knew what was expected of him today. He was supposed to play basketball with Tyler this morning, talk about his feelings with Abbott this afternoon, and wait patiently for sundown to see his little bird. But Hunter couldn't imagine doing any of that, since anything that kept him away from her sounded like a steaming pile of bullshit.

Scarlet only had one day left at Blue, and he needed every bit of it. He needed every single second to show her how perfect things could be for them as a real couple in the real world. He needed to spend this entire day romancing the hell out of her, so she'd never want to leave.

Hunter knew his earnest-yet-flimsy plan probably wouldn't work. She'd most likely dig in her heels and not budge an inch. But even if Scarlet refused to see reason – or more like the opposite of reason – at least he'd get to experience all he could with her in the few hours they had left. After all, his feelings ran way too deep now. Nothing in the world could make the thought of losing her tomorrow any less painful, so he didn't see the purpose of holding anything back.

Stripping off his clothes, Hunter rushed into the shower. He washed quickly, dried off even faster, yanked on pants and a shirt, and sprinted to the living room. He snagged his food tray from the porch, shoved a few bites in his mouth, and grabbed the phone to dial Cabin 13.

Mrs. Claus answered. "Blissful Blue Retreat, this is Betsy."

"Good morning, Betsy. This is Hunter Gregory."

"Oh, hello, Hunter! What can I help you with, dear?"

"I need to cancel my appointment with Dr. Abbott today."

"But you missed your appointment yesterday, too. Are you okay?"

"Yes, I'm fine. I just have something else I need to do. Can you please tell the doctor I'll be there tomorrow?"

"I will. You take care of yourself, and we'll see you tomorrow."

"Thanks, Betsy."

He dialed Cabin 11 next. Tyler didn't answer, so Hunter left a brief message saying he wouldn't be at the gym this morning. Dropping the receiver back in place, he reached for his shoes. He barely got the front door shut behind him before bounding up the gravel.

Anticipation built in his chest as he wound his way over the road and onto Scarlet's driveway – anticipation and *hope*. He honestly couldn't remember the last time he'd felt this hopeful. A week ago, he'd asked Dr. Abbott if a man with his selfish past even deserved to have a family. Yesterday, he'd imagined

Scarlet holding their baby girl in her arms. That image in his mind was so beautiful. Startling, but beautiful.

As he strode down her path, Hunter thought of how perfect their time together had been yesterday. Scarlet had played with him, leaned on him, and confided in him. She'd come apart for him in her bathtub. Twice. She'd taken a nap, wrapped in his arms in the warm water, before spending the rest of the evening cuddled up with him on her couch, grinning and laughing and pressing soft kisses all over his face.

Hunter needed today to be as wonderful as yesterday. He needed to prove to her that they could have this every day. Maybe then, she'd finally admit this shouldn't be their last day. It should be their first day.

He reached her porch in no time, flying up the stairs, hoping the door would burst open to reveal her smiling face. But he wasn't surprised when she didn't appear, since she wasn't expecting his early arrival. Grabbing the handle, Hunter knocked and entered simultaneously.

"Scarlet?" he called as he stepped inside her cabin.

Movement came from the back rooms, but she didn't reply. He closed the door and walked toward the hallway. "Scarlet? You home?"

"Hunter?" She emerged from the back of the cabin, halting when she saw him. "You're not supposed to be here yet. What's going on?"

She stilled in the doorway between the living room and the hall. Her ebony curls were pulled back into the confines of a tight, high ponytail. She wore crisp black slacks, a sensible blue blouse, and low-heeled dress shoes. Her stance was rigid and resolute. She didn't giggle, or bounce, or even smile as she stared him down from across the room.

Hunter's footing faltered. His heart sank to the floor, because he recognized this person immediately. This was Solemnly Sedate Scarlet.

He hadn't seen her very often, but he'd know her anywhere. This was the steadfast, unyielding woman who lived inside his forest fairy's body. She was serious and sober and strict. She didn't play any games, and wouldn't allow him any leeway, and he should probably tuck his tail between his legs and run. But he wasn't about to back down now.

Hunter matched her fixed gaze. "I came to spend the day with you."

Her brow arched. "You're not supposed to be here until tonight. You're supposed to see Tyler this morning, have your therapy session with Abbott this afternoon, and then come here for dinner. Later."

"Well, I decided to change those plans."

"But this isn't...hmm." She placed her hands on her hips and tapped her shoe against the floor. "You said if we spent the whole day together yesterday, you would go to therapy today. You *promised* me."

Scarlet's eyes flared with fire while she reprimanded him. In truth, Hunter couldn't have been happier about the fact that she was pissed off right now. He felt positively giddy about it, since he wanted to be under her skin as deeply as she was under his.

"I can see my doctor tomorrow," he assured when he resumed moving toward her, "and the next day, and the next." He only stopped walking once he stood directly in front of her. Scarlet had to crane her neck to look up at him while he smiled down into her eyes. "I can spend the rest of the week with him. But I only have today left with you."

She was struggling to stay mad at him – Hunter could tell by the way she forcibly furrowed her brow and pinched her lips together before huffing out a breath. He simply reached out, ran his hands down her arms, and caught her fingers in his own. "Please tell me you're happy to see me, Scarlet. Tell me I can spend the day with you."

Her legs swayed with his touch, so he tugged her closer. She licked her lips. He stared hungrily at the movement of her tongue.

Scarlet whimpered before placing one hand firmly on his chest. "I am happy to see you, but you can't be here yet." She spun on her heels, heading back down the hall. "I have too many things to do today."

He followed, stopping when he came to her bedroom door. A pile of clothes lay on her mattress beside her suitcase. "You're packing?"

Grabbing a shirt, Scarlet folded it with expert skill before laying it meticulously inside her luggage. "Yes, I'm packing."

Hunter forced himself to shrug, even as acid crept into his throat. "Okay, well, I can wait here until you're done."

She exhaled heavily while folding a pair of pants. "It doesn't make sense for you to wait here. I have a bunch of other things to do after this, so it would be easier if you came back later, like we planned."

He rested his shoulder against the doorframe. "What other things do you have to do?"

"I...I..." She glanced over at him. "Why don't you just come back for dinner? I'll make everything nice this evening. Besides, there isn't anything for you to do here today, and watching me pack will bore you."

Hunter shook his head. "Nothing you do ever bores me."

Scarlet glared at him before returning to her task. He absorbed the tautness of her muscles as she tended to each piece of her clothing with detailed attention. He'd never seen anyone pack luggage this precisely, but it made perfect sense for Solemnly Sedate Scarlet to do so.

After all, this was a meticulous woman. This was the woman he'd first seen the night his freebird handed him straight lemon juice. She was the woman who lamented being on vacation, lined up her toiletries in order of usage, and warned him about the perils of acting on the fantasy of this relationship. And she stood here with him now, preparing to return to all the problems of the real world.

There was a part of Hunter that wished she wasn't here, so he could spend today with Frolicking Freebird Scarlet. But the other part of him was pleased to see this stoic side of her again. Solemnly Sedate Scarlet was a huge, interwoven piece of the person he cared so deeply for, and if he had any chance of being with his forest fairy in the real world, he would have to work his way beneath this woman's hardened shell.

Hunter stood quietly in her doorway, watching her stiff, structured movements as she prepared her things to leave. He knew she was going to try to push him away now. But he had no intention of letting her.

Once she'd finished placing the last of her items inside her suitcase, Scarlet closed the top, zipped it, and began to lift the large bag. "Here, let me," he offered, stepping inside the room to reach for her luggage.

The moment his hand covered hers, her fingers tightened around the handle. "I'll be okay, Hunter. I can do this on my own."

"Yes, I'm quite certain you can do everything in the world on your own. But you don't have to."

She blinked while releasing her grip. "Well...thank you."

"You're welcome. Where would you like me to put it?"

"The living room is fine."

"Okay." He pulled the heavy case off the bed and carried it out into the front room. He set it down beside the couch before turning to watch her flutter into the kitchen. "What's next on your to-do list?"

"I have to clean out the refrigerator," she mumbled in reply, opening the door and burying her head inside the cooled shelves.

Hunter watched her pull out leftovers and throw them into the trash. Scarlet's gaze darted from the fridge to the trashcan, but never to him. Her movements became quicker and less efficient as she continued, emptying the entire fridge, until only one thing remained. The last item she pulled from the shelves was her lemonade. The cloudy liquid sloshed against the glass as she hoisted the pitcher onto the counter.

He stepped forward. "What are you doing with your lemonade?"

"It's time to let it go." The quaver in Scarlet's voice betrayed her. She wasn't holding herself together nearly as well as she wanted him to believe. She needed him now, whether she would admit it or not.

As she poured the liquid into the sink, Hunter moved steadily around the counter. He didn't stop until he reached her side, watching her eyes glass over while the lemon juice disappeared down the drain. Her fingers trembled, the air left her lips in little gasps, and she barely held back a sob. He couldn't bear to see her this way.

"Hey," he whispered, retrieving the now-empty pitcher from her unstable grip. He set it on the counter and then reached for her hands, entwining their fingers. "Relax. Take a breath. I need you to breathe."

She focused on his eyes as a shiver flitted down her spine. After a few seconds, she nodded stiffly. She forced herself to inhale and exhale.

Hunter offered her a soft smile. "I know you're getting ready to go back to the real world, Scarlet. And I know there are a lot of problems waiting for you there. But right now, you're still here with me and we still have one day left together. I want to spend it with you. Please."

It took a moment for his words to register. Then her shoulders fell and her fingers eased in his. "I want that, too. I'd love it, actually. But I have things to do."

"Like what?"

"Like I have to go into town."

"You mean the town at the bottom of the mountain?"

"Yes. I need to pick up a few items there."

"What items?"

"Well, I need new underwear, for one. I could pick some up when I get home, but life will be hectic there, especially at first, since I've been gone for so long. Also, there's a really cute women's boutique at the bottom of the mountain, and I could go there tomorrow on my way out, but tomorrow is Sunday, and it's closed on Sunday, so I really can't go tomorrow, which just leaves today."

Hunter grinned. "You know, the fact that you need new underwear is entirely my fault, so I should buy them for you."

"That's silly. I can certainly pay for my own underwear."

"I'm sure you can, but that's not the issue. I tore them off, therefore I should pay for them."

"But..."

"It's settled. I'm coming with you into town. I've actually got no choice in the matter, since I'm bound by honor to buy you new underwear. You wouldn't deny me my underwear honor, would you?"

"Underwear honor? Seriously?"

"Yes. That's a real thing, and I need to maintain it. Do you want me to drive? I can, although my car still has a spare tire and may not be the smoothest ride."

"Actually, I had planned to take my car."

"Great, we'll take your car. While we're in town, we can also grab a bite to eat, and walk around a bit, and..."

Scarlet set her hand on his chest, stopping him mid-sentence. Her fingers eased across his heart. "Hunter, what are you doing right now?"

"I'm making plans to take you out on a date – our first date."

A mixture of sadness and pain shifted across her face.

He worked to fill his lungs. "Please don't say it," he begged. "Don't say it will be our last date, too. I'd like to think of it as our first, even if it's just for today."

Scarlet searched his eyes forever. When she finally opened her mouth to speak, Hunter panicked. He knew her words would be in protest, and he didn't want to hear them, so he kissed her. He wrapped her in his arms, dragged her onto his body, and kissed her deeply and thoroughly.

It took a good, solid minute for her to surrender to him. But she did. She melted into his body as his tongue wound with hers. He explored her mouth rather mercilessly, until her knees buckled and she allowed him to take her full weight. Only then did he pull back to see her face.

Scarlet had trouble keeping her eyelids open. "Tell me I can spend the day with you," Hunter urged. "Tell me we can have our first date."

"O-Okay. We can have our first date."

"Perfect. Thank you."

"You're welcome," she said, trying to pull away. He only held her tighter. "You have to let me go now, you know. I need to get my keys."

Hunter frowned as he opened his arms, staring after her as she left the kitchen and walked down the hall with her high ponytail swinging across her shoulders. He waited with his heart in his throat, cursed by the unnerving image of her climbing out of her bedroom window to escape him. It was all he could do to remain still.

When she walked back into the kitchen, with an enormous purse in one hand and her keys in the other, he exhaled. Scarlet fidgeted with her keychain. "My car is in the garage. We can use the side entrance."

He nodded, following on her heels while she led him to the door on the side of the kitchen. "You know, I always wondered why you got a cabin with an attached garage and I didn't," he mused. "Is it because Pete Jackson is madly in love with you?"

She laughed while stepping into the garage, moving toward a sleek black four-door BMW. "Pete could never be in love with me, silly. He has his heart set on another woman at Blue."

"It's Betsy," Hunter stated, attempting to acclimate to the sight of Scarlet's car. He'd never imagined his freebird driving something like this. He assumed she would own a VW Bug with Dr. Seuss hats painted on the outside, or perhaps an orange van with pompom-fringed curtains and a peace symbol on the door. He hadn't expected a sensible sedan.

"You're right, Hunter. Pete does have his heart set on Betsy. Have you seen them together?"

"No, I haven't."

"Then how did you know?"

"They just fit," he explained, striding to the driver's door to open it for her. Scarlet glanced up at him before settling into her seat.

He shut the door behind her and rounded the hood, looking down at her license plate. Opening the passenger side, Hunter sat beside her on the smooth, tan leather. "Is, um, is this a rental car, Scarlet?"

"No, it's mine."

An outlandish grin spread his lips. He concentrated on buckling his seatbelt to prevent himself from bouncing up and down in sheer joy. Her license plate was issued in Virginia, which meant she lived within a few hours of Richmond, no matter where she called home.

She didn't travel here from Timbuktu. And he could get to her quite easily. If only she wanted him to.

Scarlet peered over at him. "Why do you think Pete and Betsy fit?"

Hunter forced himself to calm down. "Because he reminds me of a gnome and she reminds me of Mrs. Claus. They match. Just like us."

Scarlet's eyes widened. "Do I remind you of Mrs. Claus?"

"Of course not. You can't be Mrs. Claus. You're a bird."

"A bird?"

"Yes. Free and colorful and beautiful."

A smile tugged at her lips. "If I'm a bird, then what are you?"

"Well, when I first met you, I thought I was a statue. But now I'm pretty sure I'm a tree, with all of the cracks and crevices in the bark."

"Really? Do you like being a tree?"

"Yeah, I'm actually good with it." He stilled, focusing on her eyes. "Birds just love trees, you know."

Scarlet looked into him before turning toward the windshield. "Yeah, they do," she agreed, nibbling her lip while starting the engine.

Hunter grinned as she drove them to the main road. This day was going significantly better than expected. He'd accomplished so much already, even with Solemnly Sedate Scarlet beside him. Honestly, as much as he loved spending time with his forest fairy, this side of her captivated him. He wanted to know this woman. He wanted her to trust him, depend on him, and adore him. Just like the other woman did.

"Is it okay if we listen to music while I drive?" she asked.

Her voice pulled him from his thoughts. "What do you have?"

"Well, I can't get a radio signal up here, but my phone plugs into the console. It's in my purse, if you want to grab it."

"Sure." Hunter reached for her purse to rummage through the contents. The bag was insanely oversized, considering she only had her wallet and phone inside. He shook his head at the unsolvable mystery of women's purse needs as he grabbed the phone. Setting her bag back down, he began shuffling through her music lists. He made a selection quickly, turned up the volume on her radio, and listened as the smooth crooning filled the air.

"You didn't have to choose the Elvis collection just for me, Hunter."

"I didn't," he assured. "I like Elvis, too. Everybody likes Elvis. In fact, I think it's unconstitutional if you don't."

"Oh, wow. My mother would love to hear you say that."

"Well, I'll be sure to tell her, if I ever get the chance to meet her."

Scarlet's eyes darted to his before refocusing on the road. Her knuckles whitened against the wheel. Hunter reached out, smoothing his fingers across hers until she released her fearsome hold. Afterward, he dropped his hand down to rest on her thigh.

"I'm really looking forward to this ride with you, Scarlet."

She didn't respond to his loaded statement, and he honestly didn't expect her to. She was nervous right now, and doubtful, and confused, and he was okay with all of that. In truth, he needed it. He needed her to question every decision she'd made before this moment, and to realize there was more than one road this relationship could travel.

Scarlet stayed mostly quiet for the rest of the car ride, except for the few times she sang along with Elvis, which made Hunter smile as he listened. When they reached the bottom of the mountain, she turned onto another paved road. A town materialized in front of him, along with a vague memory of having driven by it two weeks earlier.

A beauty salon, a tailor, a hardware store, and a restaurant were among the miscellaneous offerings of Bottom-of-Blissful-Blue town. Scarlet pulled into a parking space between the hardware store and a women's clothing shop. She reached for her door handle, but he stopped her by squeezing onto her thigh. "Wait, please. I'll open it for you."

"Hunter, I am perfectly capable of opening my own..."

He jumped up out of his seat before she could finish her sentence. Rounding the hood, he made sure to get to her before she hopped out and scurried away. When he opened her driver's door, Scarlet grabbed her purse and stood, staring up at him with her brow furrowed.

Ignoring her apparent confusion, Hunter took her hand and threaded their fingers. He shut the door and pulled her toward the sidewalk. As they walked, he didn't bother to hide his ecstatic grin.

Scarlet exhaled. "Are you doing okay today?"

"Me? Yeah. I'm fantastic. I love taking a stroll through town with you. Because that's what we're doing now. We're strolling together."

"But we don't need to stroll. The store is right here."

"That's okay. It still counts as a stroll." Hunter leaned in for a quick kiss before shifting his attention to the storefront. "So, is this the underwear honor store?"

"I suppose it is."

"Hmm. It's odd they don't write that on a sign somewhere."

Scarlet laughed as he opened the door for her. She fastened their fingers together while leading him around the various racks and tables inside. Hunter felt more encouraged with every step.

When she eventually stopped at a table full of panties, he picked up a thong in hunter green. "This pair is nice. Is this your size?"

She looked to his hands. "Can I please pick my own?"

"Absolutely. I just think this color would look nice on you. It's my color, after all. And all of the underwear I tore off of you were black."

A woman cleared her throat brashly behind them. Scarlet's eyes grew three sizes as the shopper clucked her tongue and stepped away.

Hunter watched a delightful pink glow flush his little bird's cheeks. He bent down to whisper in her ear. "I guess I said that too loud."

"Just a bit," Scarlet agreed. But then she smiled, which made him smile. "Do you think I should get some different colors of underwear?"

"I do. I think you should get every color."

"But there are a ton of colors here, and you only tore five pair."

"It doesn't matter. I'll buy you every kind of underwear you want. I'll even buy you granny panties."

Scarlet burst out laughing, drawing the attention of two other shoppers. She clamped her hand over her mouth to muffle the sound.

He slipped his arm around her waist and pulled her flush against his side. "Don't hide your smile from me. Please."

She dropped her hand from her mouth to swat his shoulder. "Good Lord, Hunter! You can't say things like that to me in public! And how do you even know about granny panties?"

"I grew up with two women in my house. I know things. I'll be happy to buy some for you, if you want."

"No, no, no," Scarlet insisted. "You are not buying me granny panties. I don't wear those...very often. And I shouldn't need to buy any more until I am a granny. Although, I suppose I'll need to have kids before I can become a granny, and I'll probably want to wear granny panties when I'm pregnant, so I guess..."

"Pregnant?"

Scarlet's jaw dropped open. "Oh, well, I...I didn't mean anything by that. I swear I didn't. I promise you, I am on birth control."

Hunter reached his hand to her face, cupping her cheek. "God, you would look so beautiful pregnant."

She whimpered, her skin flushing hotter under his fingertips.

He wanted to kiss her. He wanted to kiss her so badly, and also do a bunch of other things that would be terribly indecent in public. But he stopped himself when he saw the look of utter fear written in her eyes.

Dropping his hand from her face, Hunter straightened. "I mean, I know you don't want to be pregnant now," he offered, working to act nonchalant. "You told me that the first time we went into the woods. You said you didn't want to be a single mother."

Scarlet touched her heated cheek. "I did say that."

"But you do want to be a mother someday? After you're married?"

She swallowed hard. "Yeah, sure. Someday."

"How many kids do you want?"

"Why...why are we talking about this?"

He shrugged. "I'm just curious. How many kids?"

"I haven't really thought much about it. Maybe two?"

"Two. That's a nice number. I like two."

Scarlet studied him, biting against her lip, before her gaze shifted back to the table. "I think I should finish shopping now."

Hunter watched her concentrate on making her selections. He probably shouldn't have pursued the topic of children just now, but he really was curious as to how many she wanted. He also wanted her to know he'd thought about having a baby with her, because he had. And it was a happy thought. Unexpected, but happy.

"I'd like to get these," she said, grasping several panties in hand.

He glanced down at her choices. "That's not one of every color."

"It's five. Thank you for offering to buy more, but this is all I need."

"At least you got the hunter green ones. I'm glad."

She gave him a tiny smile. "Let's go, okay?"

Hunter nodded, resting his hand on her low back while they moved to the cashier. He paid for their purchase, waiting for the woman behind the counter to wrap the underwear in frilly tissue paper and hand the decorative bag to Scarlet. He stayed close to her as they walked outside.

The chilled October air encased them, so he circled his arm around her shoulders. As soon as they stepped off the curb, Scarlet handed him her keychain. "Here, Hunter. You go ahead and get in the car. I need to use the restroom, and I believe the hardware store has one."

"But, I..."

"I'll just be a minute," she insisted, "then we'll head back to Blue."

"Oh." He barely got the single syllable out before she turned and bolted into the store beside the clothing shop. Hunter stared after her until she disappeared. Then he opened the passenger's side door.

He grumbled as he sat on the tan seat, irritated by her eagerness to get away from him. Not that he could blame her, after the pregnancy conversation. He honestly hadn't meant to upset her; he simply enjoyed talking about their future. He only wished she enjoyed it, too.

Hunter exhaled as he awaited her return. His eyes fell from the car's windshield onto the door of the glove box. He glared at the latch.

"Scarlet's vehicle registration is probably in there," he considered. "It should have her home address on it. All I have to do is reach inside."

His fingers fisted while he stared down temptation. Then he swore a stream of filthy curses, because he wasn't actually going to do it. He wanted nothing more than to know where she lived, but he needed her to tell him. If Scarlet didn't want to give him that information of her own free will, there was no point in having it.

With a growl of frustration, Hunter tore his gaze from her glove box. He surveyed the rest of the shopping center, until he zeroed in on a movie theater in the distance. His smile returned then, since he was still on a mission today. *Mission: First Date.* It was a romantic assignment, yet wrought with perils and uncertainties. And it had only just begun.

Scarlet emerged from the hardware store a moment later with her huge purse and frilly lingerie bag in hand. Hunter jumped out of his seat before she could take the necessary steps to the driver's door.

"Why did you get out of the car?" she asked when he joined her on the sidewalk. "We're driving back to Blue now."

"No, we're not."

"We're not?"

"Nope. We're going to see a movie."

"A movie? But that's not..."

He silenced her protest by wrapping both arms around her, pulling her onto his chest, and pressing his lips to hers. She resisted him for a few seconds, keeping her mouth sealed, until his tongue traced across the seam. Then she sighed and gave in, her body draping onto his.

"Mmm," he hummed against her lips after a proper, extensive kiss.

"Ugh," she groaned, prying open her eyelids. "That's really unfair."

"What's unfair?"

"The way you just grab me and kiss me whenever you want to change my mind about something. You are aware that you're using my attraction for you against me, right?"

"Wait a minute," Hunter demanded with a crooked grin. "Are you saying you're attracted to me? I did not know that."

"Wow. You think you're pretty cute, don't you?"

"Don't you think I'm cute?"

She rolled her eyes. "Lord, yes. Freakishly cute."

"Well, then. I think it's high time you sit next to your freakishly cute boyfriend in a movie theater. This is our first date, so we should do the things you enjoy. And I know how much you love movies."

Her fingers ran restlessly over his shirt. "Why do you think that?"

"Because you quote them *all* the time."

"I do not quote movies *all* the time."

"Yes, you do. You've quoted *Star Wars*, *Speed*, and *Spiderman* to me, all in the past few days."

"When did I quote *Spiderman*?"

"Last night, when we were in the bathtub together. You said your intelligence came with a lot of responsibility."

"That's not a quote."

"It basically is. 'With great power comes great responsibility.' Totally *Spiderman*."

She laughed as she fiddled with the buttons on his shirt. "Okay, maybe it sounded a tiny bit like that."

Hunter leaned into her. "I know you love movies, so let's go see one. Afterward, we'll have dinner. I mean, everyone has to eat, right?"

Scarlet huffed, but couldn't hide her smile. She arched up to peck him on the lips. "You're lucky you're so freakishly cute."

"God, don't I know it."

"Just let me put my bags in the car, then we can go to the theater."

Hunter struggled to maintain his composure. He thought it best that he didn't shout, "Hooray! Hooray!" and giggle like a schoolgirl.

~

SCARLET HADN'T GIVEN him her home address yet, or made him any promises for a future. But as Hunter sat beside her in the movie theater, he still felt a sense of accomplishment. This was a date, an actual *date*, which meant he'd basically won gold in the Romance Olympics.

He enjoyed winding his arm around her shoulder and feeling her rest her head against him in the darkened theater. He savored stealing a kiss whenever the mood struck him and loved how her eyes reflected the light onscreen as she gazed at him afterward. He adored it when she fed him popcorn and soaked in her giggles when he nipped at her fingers.

Hunter barely watched the movie – it was some romantic comedy about a stoic architect who figured out he was in love with his secretary after she took revenge on him for ignoring her for six years – since he spent nearly all his time watching Scarlet. After all, they were on a date.

Dinner proved equally amazing, seeing her seated across the white linen tablecloth of their cozy corner table. Solemnly Sedate Scarlet still sat with him, straight and pristine in her high-backed chair, with her napkin folded impeccably on her lap. But now, there was a glow of happiness to her. She made excited little noises while she read the menu, and then ordered enough food to feed a small horse, since she couldn't decide what she wanted and he told her to just get it all.

When the waiter walked away after removing their menus, she took hold of her water glass and downed several gulps with camel-like fervor.

Hunter grinned. "You're thirsty, I take it?"

"I am. That popcorn was so salty. I love movie theater popcorn, but I'm always parched afterward."

"You could get something else to drink, if you like. Maybe wine?"

"Thank you, but no. I have to drive us back to Blue after dinner."

"I could drive us back."

Her hand curled around the stem of her glass. "I'd rather drive, but I appreciate the offer. I appreciate everything you've done today. Truly."

"You mean, on our *date*."

A shaky laugh escaped her lips. "Yes, on our date. Although I still wish you'd seen Dr. Abbott earlier. You need your time with him."

Hunter set his hand out on the table, opening it palm-up to her. He'd been watching her fingers fiddle mercilessly with the stem of her glass and he just needed to hold them. She stared at his offering before resting her hand inside his.

He exhaled with her touch. "I promise I'll stay in therapy, Scarlet. You don't have to worry. I'm not afraid of it anymore."

"Does that mean you enjoy your sessions with Dr. Abbott?"

"I do. He helps put things in perspective, and gives good advice."

"Yeah? What kind of advice?"

"The other day, we talked about achieving a work/life balance."

"That sounds wonderful. Maybe Adrien could help me figure that out, too."

"Should I take that to mean you find your job stressful?"

"Well, I'm not the CEO of a giant corporation like you are, but yes, my work has stressors. It's okay, though. I can cope with it again now."

"Because your vacation at Blue helped you?"

"Because *you* helped me."

Hunter smiled. "Then I'm glad I could help," he assured, although he couldn't imagine he'd done anything as significant for her as she'd done for him. Running his thumb across her knuckles, he tried to soothe her restless fingers. "You know, I bet your mother would be proud of how you've ventured back into the woods these past weeks."

Scarlet returned his smile. "Yeah, I think she would be proud."

"Will you be able to see her when you go back home?"

"Unfortunately, I haven't seen my mother in nearly a year. After my father died, she moved to Vegas. She works as a waitress in a casino."

"A waitress? Really? Does she need the money?"

"Oh, no. Dad left her a fortune in life insurance. She works because she loves the excitement of the place. And because of Elvis. When I do visit her, we watch the impersonators sing. It makes us both so happy."

"Man, I'd love to see you in Vegas, singing and dancing with Elvis."

Scarlet laughed, but the bright sound died quickly in her throat.

Hunter shook his head. "I guess I'll never get to see that, will I?"

She glanced down to the table. "We both have lives to get back to."

"I suppose we do," he agreed, the wise words souring his stomach. "I have a company to run, and family and friends to spend time with. I also have a goddaughter to see, and hold, and spoil rotten."

Her gaze rose back to his with the mention of baby Evie. "I'm glad you have so many things waiting for you. They all sound wonderful."

"Yeah, they are pretty wonderful."

Except I won't have you, and you're what I want the most.

"So, what about you, Scarlet? What's waiting for you at home?"

"Oh, just work, mostly. And plants. I have a lot of plants."

Hunter chuckled, easily imagining her surrounded by a forest of greenery. "Anything else? Besides work and plants?"

"Like what?"

"Like people? You said you haven't had a boyfriend in a while, but maybe there's someone on the horizon?"

"There isn't. After what happened with my last boyfriend, I just…"

"What happened?" he asked, leaning forward. "Did he hurt you?"

"Oh, no. He was very kind. Actually, Richard asked me to marry him. And I said yes."

Hunter's heart stopped cold in his chest. "Y-you were engaged?"

"I was."

"But you didn't marry him?"

"No, I didn't. We were together for three years, and we planned to get married, but I broke it off before the wedding."

"Why did you break it off?"

"Because after my father died, it didn't feel right anymore. Richard was a cardiac surgeon, exactly like my father, and Dad died right on his desk. I questioned a lot of things when he passed, and after I broke up with Richard, I simply didn't find anyone else I wanted to be with."

"But didn't you tell me your father passed away two years ago?"

"He did."

"That's…that's a long time to be alone. I'm sorry."

"Thank you, Hunter. I'm sorry you've been alone, too."

He gave her a tender smile, appreciating her empathy. Although he couldn't get his mind off of the man he'd nearly lost her to, before he'd ever even met her. "So, you were with Richard for three years?"

"Yeah, I was."

"That's funny. I was with Clarissa for three years, too."

"Oh, right. She's the woman who asked you to marry her," Scarlet recalled, shifting in her seat. "Will you go back to her now?"

"Go *back* to her? Why on earth would I do that?"

"Well, you said Abbott gave you a new perspective. I just wonder if your new perspective includes being with Clarissa again."

"First of all, you were the one who gave me the new perspective. And as for getting back together with my ex, absolutely not."

"But maybe she can make you happy now."

Hunter shook his head. "No, she can't."

"You'll never know unless you try."

"Actually, I do know, because you helped me see it. Don't you remember that day in the woods, when I told you about Samantha?"

"Of course," Scarlet said, smoothing her palm over top of his. "I'll never forget that day."

"I won't, either. You told me so many things, and I couldn't even absorb everything then. But I do remember you saying I hadn't found the right woman because I'd been looking for the wrong kind of woman. That was the absolute truth. I didn't understand it when I was with Clarissa, but I do now. She could never be the right woman for me because she didn't challenge me at all. We didn't laugh together. We didn't play together. I didn't ache to touch her. I never dreamed of marrying her. And I couldn't imagine having children with her."

Hunter paused to thread Scarlet's fingers in his. "I didn't know who I was looking for before, but I do now. I know *exactly* who I want."

His little bird may have stopped breathing. She turned so still that he didn't think anything in her body moved at all. She obviously knew he was talking about her, and honestly, he felt perfectly happy about it.

"Hunter, I..." her voice trailed off as she held his fixed gaze.

He saw so many emotions pass through her eyes: longing, need, adoration, want, ache. Scarlet gripped hard to his hand, her bright, emerald green revealing everything he wanted to see. He definitely wasn't alone in struggling with these magnificent, overwhelming, amazing feelings. This woman sitting before him felt everything he did.

"I, uh, I just..." she tried to speak again, her words coming out breathy and more than a little frightened.

Hunter didn't want her to be scared. He held tight to her fingers, well aware of how terrifying all of this was. Two weeks. They'd met each other just two weeks ago. Yet now, he couldn't imagine enduring another day without her. As far as he was concerned, they'd lived a thousand lifetimes in the past few days. He'd come out on the other side with an entirely new outlook on life, and he owed all of that to her, which made his heart want to climb out of his ribcage and crawl across this table just to get to her.

"God, Scarlet, I hope I've said this already, but...thank you."

She blinked her eyes. "Wh-what?"

"Thank you," he repeated, still holding onto her as he smiled. "If I haven't said it properly before now, I should have. Thank you for everything you've done for me. Thank you for taking me along on your journey of self-discovery. Thank you for helping me understand my life. Thank you for showing me how to be happy."

Hunter's chest swelled as he spoke, filled to bursting with joy, excitement, and hope. He studied her, expecting to see all those things reflected back at him. He couldn't have been more wrong.

Scarlet's face fell. Her entire body deflated. Her lips pulled down, her shoulders sagged, and the light in her eyes dimmed.

He didn't understand. He could only watch her as she sat in silence.

After torturous seconds, she forced a smile and stiffened her spine. "You're welcome," she offered, her voice small yet determined. "I know you'll find a way to be happy once you return home. I want you to be happy. You certainly deserve it."

Hunter opened his mouth to speak, to tell her she was the one person in the world who made him the happiest. But their food arrived at that moment, and Scarlet pulled her hand away. He kept his own hand out on the table, in case she decided to hold onto him again. She didn't.

She made the effort to engage in small talk as they ate, but the air between them had changed. He couldn't comprehend it, since all he'd done was thank her. Yet now, she seemed a million miles away.

Scarlet remained distant through the rest of their meal. She didn't speak when they left the restaurant, or when they each slumped into the seats in her car. She stared straight ahead while she drove them back up the mountainside in the dark night. There wasn't much light in the car at all, but it was enough for Hunter to study the side of her face as she downshifted to scale the steep incline.

His forest fairy looked so sad, and he wanted nothing more than to soothe her weighted mind. Reaching out, he placed his hand on her shoulder. She tensed instantly, but he didn't let it deter him. He massaged her, pressing his fingers into her tight muscles.

She fought the soothing gesture at first, but eventually she moaned, melting beneath his touch. Hunter knew he was taking advantage of her body's response to his. He nearly felt guilty about it, until he recalled how often she'd used her therapeutic touch on him.

Kneading his fingers down her arm and onto her leg, he let the heat of his skin permeate the thin fabric of her pants. Scarlet whimpered while he stroked her. He shifted his fingers, skimming close to her inner thigh, making her squirm in her seat and catch her lower lip in her teeth.

Stark desire flooded his body as he stared at her mouth. So much of this day had been wonderful, but he still wanted more. They were almost back to her cabin now. It was almost time for her to fulfill her promise to spend the entire night in his arms.

Hunter squeezed onto her thigh in anticipation.

A needy groan escaped Scarlet's throat.

He remained so focused on the warmth of her body that he barely noticed the car slowing. When the sound of gravel crunching under tires reached his ears, he glanced up to see her cabin rapidly approaching. He grudgingly pulled his hand away as she fitted her car back in her garage.

The moment she parked, Scarlet grabbed her bags and leapt out. Hunter barely got one foot on the ground before she disappeared through the side door into her kitchen. With a derisive laugh, he exited his seat.

After crossing her garage and stepping inside her cabin, he shut the door firmly behind him. His eyes searched the dimly lit kitchen, noting that Scarlet had turned on the tiny light above the stove and tossed her bags on the countertop. He found her standing by the sink with her back to him, the faint ivory glow hugging her body.

Hunter's jaw clenched as he stared at her rigid spine. Despite the many joys they'd shared on their date, he knew he'd ultimately failed his mission. This steadfast woman wouldn't admit to the possibility of them having a relationship beyond this mountain. She wouldn't admit to anything except the prudent, sensible need for them to say goodbye.

He glared at her stiff spine and bunched shoulders – sure signs that she planned to put up a fight over the promise she'd made to spend the night with him. He'd clearly failed to convince her of their potential today. But he hadn't failed at everything, since he now knew for certain that Scarlet felt as strongly for him as he did for her. She wanted them to remain together, yet her logical brain wouldn't allow it. Her tenacious refusal to take a leap of faith frustrated him beyond belief, but he wouldn't let that deter him. He still clutched the end of his rope, determined to take one last shot at changing her stubborn-as-hell mind.

Closing the distance between them in a few long strides, Hunter came to stand behind her with his chest to her back. She exhaled shakily and gripped onto the counter. He eased his hands down her arms, covering her fingers with his, threading them together against the ledge.

Scarlet shifted inside the cocoon of his body. "So," she began, her voice barely a whisper, "we both know this is our last night together."

"Yes, we both know that. We also know you promised to spend an entire night in my arms before you left Blue."

"You're right, I did," she conceded, clutching tight to his fingers. "But I also promised to fulfill a fantasy of your choosing, and you never picked one. I think we should focus on that promise instead. I mean, there are so many different things we could try. You could tie me up, if you want. I still have the rope I borrowed from Pete."

Hunter stepped back, grabbed her by the hips, and spun her around to face him. He braced his arms beside hers on the countertop, caging her body. "No. I don't want that now. I want the *other* promise."

Her pleading eyes searched his. "But, Hunter..."

"*No.* You swore to me you'd spend an entire night in my arms, yet you've avoided it again and again. Tonight, I'm staying. In your bed."

"But we don't have to be in my bed. We can have sex anywhere – the counter, the refrigerator door, the couch, the floor. What about in the shower? We've never done that one before. It'd be fun, right?"

"The *bed*, Scarlet. We are going to make love in your bed, and in the morning, you'll wake in my arms. *Then* we can say goodbye."

She pinched her lips shut and shook her head.

Her silent refusal to fulfill her promise pissed him off even more. Reaching down, Hunter grabbed her ass with both hands and pulled her up onto him. "Wrap your legs around me," he commanded.

Scarlet gasped but still submitted. Her hands clung to his shoulders as he carried her through the kitchen. Her fingertips trembled against his shirt and her teeth gnawed on her lip, but he didn't stop.

Hunter strode into the hall, their path lit only by moonlight streaming through the cabin windows. He moved them toward her bedroom with utter resolve. But as he took his first step across the threshold to her elusive sanctuary, Scarlet reached up and grabbed hold of the doorframe above her head. Her knuckles whitened as she cemented them in place.

"Wait," she breathed. "What if we have sex here in the doorway? I'll hang on like this, and you can do whatever you want to me. I won't move my arms at all. I'll keep them above my head the whole time."

Hunter ignored her futile attempt to deter him. Securing her body to his chest with one hand, he reached his other hand to the underside of her arm and tickled her. Scarlet squealed and laughed, dropping her hands to grasp at his shoulders.

The moment she detached from the doorframe, he took the last few strides across her room and plunged them both onto her mattress. When they fell down together, he fell instantly in love with the sensation of her lying beneath him on a soft, welcoming bed.

Scarlet kept giggling for one more second. Then she focused on his eyes and stopped. She stopped laughing, or moving, or even breathing. She stopped everything to gaze up at him in utter desperation.

She obviously didn't want to be here. But Hunter wanted to be here. Her suitcase had been lying on this bed mere hours ago, and he'd been forced to watch as she painstakingly packed everything away, and it killed him to think she would leave here and not look back.

Taking her face in both his hands, he stared into her in the moonlit room, trying to read her thoughts in her eyes. He knew she planned to return to the real world tomorrow, the world of Solemnly Sedate Scarlet. Over the past two weeks, she'd struggled to keep that side of herself away from him, to only be the freebird who came to live for these few days at Blue. Now, he could see how torn she felt, torn between what she wanted to do and what she needed to do. God, she looked so scared.

Hunter watched the fear move through her as she lay here beneath him. The sight made his heart pound and his stomach twist. He never, ever wanted her to be frightened. Certainly not by him.

Forcing himself to exhale, he slipped his fingers gently into her hair and gave her a tender smile. "It's okay," he assured. "I already know."

"What do you know?"

"I know why you don't want to be in this bed with me."

Her head tilted. "Why don't I?"

"Because it's too intimate. It's too close to reality. To be perfectly honest, I think you've done an amazing job of keeping reality away from us while we've been on this mountain. But I'm not afraid of it anymore, which is entirely because of you. So, tonight, I don't want the fantasies. I don't want to tie you up on the couch or fuck you on a countertop. I just want to be here in bed with you. I want us to make love, like two people who are together in a real world."

Scarlet whimpered.

Hunter sighed. "It took me a while to figure it out, but I understand now why you never let me stay the night. You've been trying so hard to protect us from the pain we're going to feel when we say goodbye tomorrow. And yet, despite all your efforts, the fact remains that we're both in this thing too deep. Tomorrow is going to hurt like hell and there's nothing you can do to save us from it."

"I'm sorry," she whispered, holding his eyes with hers. "I'm so, so sorry. I never meant for either of us to experience that kind of pain."

"I know you didn't, and I appreciate you wanting to protect me. But it's still going to happen. It's going to happen no matter what we do at this moment, and I just really want to have you in my arms right now. I want you in my arms all night long. But I can't make you want the same thing. I can't force you to be here with me, and I won't try."

"What do you mean?"

"I mean I release you from your promise."

"You *what*?"

"I release you from your promise. You don't have to spend the night in this bed with me. We can leave here and go have sex anywhere you want. We can get in the shower right now, if you like. I promise I will be very involved in the act of shower sex, and I promise I will make you come. Multiple times, if that's what you want."

She shook her head. "No, I don't want that. Well, I mean, I want you to make me come, of course. Who wouldn't want that? I'd truly be mentally unstable if I said I didn't want that, and you're so good at it, by the way, although I know you know that by now, especially after the bathtub incident last night, and I just..."

"Scarlet. Take a breath. Please."

"Oh. Right. Sorry. I'm just...I'm nervous."

Hunter traced the side of her face. "I'm nervous, too."

She leaned into his touch. "I do want to be in this bed with you. I swear I do. I want us to make love."

"But?"

"But it's not going to change what happens tomorrow."

He blew out a breath. "I know that. Damn it, I know. I just don't want to think about tomorrow right now. I want to be here, with you, tonight. Can you give me that? Can you be here with me?"

Scarlet considered her answer forever. When she finally nodded, the harrowing ache in his chest eased the tiniest bit. "I can be here with you, Hunter. I want this so much. You have no idea."

"Well, I...I think I may have some idea."

She smiled at his massive understatement. He watched her smile for a long minute before sinking his forehead onto hers. Hunter closed his eyes and stilled, taking his time to breathe her in.

This feeling pulsing through his body now was incredible. Knowing she was present and willing. Knowing she wasn't going to run from the bedroom, or usher him out of the door at the end of the night. Knowing she wanted to be with him as much as he wanted to be with her.

He kept his eyes shut, concentrating on the sound of her steady exhales. Scarlet slid her fingers up into his hair, threading through the thick strands to hold him to her. He wrapped his arms around her back, sinking them both down farther into the mattress.

She smiled again, this time against his lips. The joy of it filled his heart to bursting, so he pressed his mouth to hers for just a moment. At least, he told himself it would only be for a moment. Hunter didn't want to get too carried away, for fear this night would pass too quickly. He was determined to savor every second, and yet the instant he felt her lips on his, he lost himself to that bliss.

Her mouth was perfect. She was perfect. He had to taste her, so he eased his tongue past her lips, relishing the smooth wetness waiting for him. Scarlet responded immediately, eager and desperate for his kiss. Her fingers fisted against his scalp while he banded her more securely in his arms. His muscles shook with the effort of holding her under him without crushing her.

She gasped when he pulled back for air, her entire body vibrating with need. Hunter had to shift his hips, struggling to ignore the straining of his erection against his zipper. All he'd done was kiss her for a few blissful minutes, yet he could barely fight the urge to bury himself in her warmth this instant. Finally having her beneath him in bed was just too damn overwhelming, so he pressed his lips to hers again, tightening his hold on her body in order to roll them both over on the mattress.

The moment Scarlet lay on top of him, she eased her knees down onto the bedspread. Tucking her thighs close to his hips, she adjusted herself over the ridge of his erection. He'd hoped this new position would somehow lessen his immediate, clawing desire for her. But she just kept kissing him, winding their tongues together as she pressed her body harder onto his, and it only made him want her more.

Scarlet pushed her breasts into his chest and shifted her hips to rub herself over his stiff length. Their breaths mingled, hot and gasping. Hunter clung to her, his arms spanning the width of her body twice over. He clung to his bounding bird, his frolicking forest fairy, with urgent need. Yet he also clung to the sober, practical woman who'd spent this last day with him. He clung to *his* Scarlet, who was both women in one.

She didn't stop touching him, not for an instant. Her hands roamed across his shoulders, up his neck, and into his hair. She cradled his head with her fingers while kissing him a dozen different ways – sometimes frantic and sometimes gentle, sometimes fierce and sometimes loving.

Hunter happily drowned in each sensation, barely noticing when she started pulling away. But then he felt the retreat of her body. His eyes shot open as Scarlet backed off the mattress to stand at the bedside.

Panic sliced through his chest. He bolted upright, perching himself at the edge of the mattress, grabbing onto her hips to prevent her escape. Thankfully, she didn't attempt to leave. She merely smiled at him as she reached up to pull the tie from her ponytail.

Hunter remained seated on the bed while looking up to her face. The pale light streaming through the window haloed her body in a dark blue glow. He watched in hunger as her ebony curls fell in loose waves to her shoulders, only wishing he'd been the one to set them free.

Gripping onto her hipbones, he pulled her closer to cradle her knees between his thighs. Scarlet dropped her hair tie to the floor and reached for the hem of her blouse. He covered her fingers as she gathered the material so they could both raise her shirt together, until he couldn't reach any further and she finished for them. After allowing her shirt to fall to the ground, she brought her hands back to rest on his shoulders.

Hunter sighed with the gentleness of her touch. Her stomach lay bare before him, so he banded both arms around her back, securing her in place as he pressed his forehead into her soft skin. Scarlet ran her hands from his shoulders to his neck and back again while he filled his lungs with her fresh soap and tiny flowers. Her bellybutton sat beneath his mouth, so he slid his lips over that little circle, listening for her easy giggles to float into the cool, dark air.

When she withdrew her hands, Hunter's eyes darted up to watch her reach around her back. She unclasped her bra, drawing the black lace over her arms before letting it join her other clothes on the floor. She stood before him, half-naked and encased within his thighs, and smiled.

He stared at her for a long while, drinking in the sight of her curved pink lips, the black curls resting over her shoulders, and the rose peaks of her breasts tightening beneath his hungered gaze. As he stared, he ran his palms over her bare spine again and again, until his hands came to rest at her hips. Then he traced the waist of her pants to the front, popped open the button, and curled his fingers into the fabric.

His eyes fell to watch as he pulled down, easing the soft material over her softer skin, trying to memorize every inch he revealed. Hunter pulled her panties down at the same time, leaning in to press his mouth to her bared hipbone. He kissed across that flesh-covered line, tracing it with his lips and his tongue.

Scarlet wriggled and squirmed with the ticklish feel of his mouth, until she finally burst out laughing and took a step back. He glanced up to her, mesmerized by the look on her face as she beamed down at him. Resting one hand against his shoulder, she steadied herself while kicking her shoes in the corner and stripping off her pants. When she finished ridding them of the last of her clothing, she straightened before him.

His little bird stood only a few inches away, completely bare and so goddamn gorgeous, and there was way too much distance between them. Hunter stood from the bed, keeping his eyes pinned to hers, watching her chin tilt up as she followed his heated stare. The moment he stood at his full height, he stepped into her, took her face in both hands, lowered his mouth to hers, and kissed her for all he was worth.

Scarlet grabbed onto his forearms to keep herself upright. When her legs swayed, he pulled back just enough to listen to the tiny, panting gasps escaping her lips. Her hands dropped from his arms to his waist, gathering the hem of his shirt with a firm grasp. Hunter watched the desire and determination in her eyes while she drew the fabric up his chest. He helped her when she needed it, pulling the unwanted clothing over his head as quickly as possible, impatient to see her reaction.

Her eager eyes fell to his bare chest along with her fingers. She looked positively entranced by his body, tracing each line of muscle across his abdomen, apparently awed by her ability to touch him. Hunter dropped his shirt and pulled her closer, grounding her in place despite his certainty that she wasn't going anywhere tonight. Slipping his hands from her hips to her bottom, he stroked her rounded flesh, equally awed by his ability to touch her. She was the soft to his hard, the curves to his lines, and they fit perfectly together. He knew that like he knew his own name.

Scarlet whimpered while watching herself touch his chest. Her desire for him pulsed through her fingertips and Hunter expected her to reach down now, to undo the button on his pants and continue what they'd started. She didn't. One of her hands slipped upward instead, roaming and seeking until finding a home over his heart. She looked to his face when her palm flattened onto his heated skin.

Hunter stared down at her shadowed face, seeing the most beautiful smile spread across her lips, even as tears welled in her glassy eyes. Her fingers curled into his chest, trying their damnedest to reach inside. He froze in place while her hand shifted slowly and deliberately over his pained, pounding heart.

Good God, Scarlet, just take it. It's already yours. You may as well physically remove it and carry it home with you in your gigantic purse.

He dropped his arms to his sides, currently unable to reconcile his forceful need for her with the understanding that he must watch her walk away in the morning. For the first time tonight, Hunter wanted to run from the inevitability of that pain. But she didn't let him. She wrapped her fingers around his wrist and pulled his hand up to her chest instead, laying his palm over her heart and pressing it against her with quivering fingers. He swallowed hard at the sight.

Scarlet gave him another watery smile before resting her forehead on his shoulder. Her fingers covered his, securing his hand to her chest. He wanted to reach inside her now, to capture her heart and take it home with him, just as she would surely take his. But he knew he couldn't, so he closed his eyes and dropped his face into her hair, concentrating on the fluttered pulsations of her heartbeat beneath his palm.

Hunter didn't know how long they stood like that. Her pulse raced for the longest time while she held him to her, matching each of his own threaded beats. Eventually, she calmed beneath his touch. She took several deep breaths in and out, and when she finally raised her eyes back to his, they no longer brimmed with tears.

Releasing her hold on his hand, Scarlet arched up on her tiptoes. She pressed her mouth to his, smooth yet insistent. Hunter followed her lead, kissing her with intention, hungry for her taste. Her hands slid over his hips and onto the waist of his pants. He kissed her harder as she popped open the button, pulled down the zipper, and reached for him.

Her fingers encircled his erection, warm and firm. He sucked in air, his lips stilling against hers so he could steady himself. Scarlet stroked his rigid shaft up and down, over and over, causing his thick length to twitch into her bare belly. Her feet shifted against the floor in time with the motion of her hand, pressing her body rhythmically onto his while he throbbed beneath her fingers.

Holy fucking hell, he wanted her. Honestly, *want* didn't begin to describe his level of desire. This was a bone-deep need, one he could barely comprehend. He needed her surrounding him, accepting him, holding him together. He needed her *now*, and he was mere seconds away from pushing her against the wall and burying himself inside her.

But that just wouldn't do. Not tonight.

Hunter reached for her arm and squeezed. Scarlet glanced up to him in question when he halted her actions. He answered her with a soft smile before removing her hand from his overly eager flesh. Bringing her fingers up to his mouth, he kissed each one of them before pressing another kiss to her forehead.

He didn't want to leave her. Not for a second. But he definitely wanted to have her in bed, and they weren't going to get there this way.

Stepping over to the mattress, he reached down to pull back the covers. The sheets were red, just as he always imagined they'd be. They were Scarlet's red, and he couldn't imagine anything better than having her inside them now.

Hunter pivoted back to her, sighing in relief when he saw she hadn't moved. He returned to his freebird, banded her in his arms, reached down to grasp her bottom with both hands, and lifted her onto his chest. He didn't have to tell her what to do next. She instantly wrapped her legs around his waist, pinning his stiff length between their stomachs.

As he carried her to the bed, the wet entrance to her sex pressed against his skin. He groaned while placing her on the mattress, bracing himself on one knee so he could control her descent. He made sure her head eased onto a pillow, and her entire body rested comfortably in the soft bedding, before withdrawing his arms. Then he stood back up to toe off his shoes and fully remove his pants.

Scarlet waited patiently for him, even though her fingers balled and her feet shifted restlessly against the sheets. Hunter undressed quickly, although not too quickly, since he liked seeing her here. He liked seeing her muscles clench and her body shiver in anticipation of his touch.

Once he stood entirely naked, he stepped back to the bed and stared down at her. She lay against the mattress, gazing up at him under heavy eyelids, with her halo of hair spread across the pillow and a serene glow lighting her face. Damn, she was an actual angel. A pure, untarnished angel sent here just for him, if only for these few days. And if this brief amount of time together was truly all they were meant to have, then it would have to be enough. He'd been blessed to even have this much.

Scarlet reached her arms out to him, silently begging him to join her. Hunter couldn't stay away any longer. He eased onto the bed, fitted his knees between her parted legs, and lowered his body over hers. But he didn't enter her. Not yet. First, he needed to experience her warmth. He needed to accustom himself to the feel of her bare flesh beneath his own, since he knew the sensation would take his breath away.

He struggled to fill his lungs when he rested fully down on her, positioning his hips to the side so his rigid length lay against her thigh. He placed his forearms on the mattress to support some of his weight, since he didn't want to crush her – he wanted her comfortable, happy, and at peace.

Scarlet sighed as his body covered hers. She reached up, tracing the outline of his lips. "This is wonderful, Hunter."

Unsure if he could manage to voice his agreement right now, he simply nodded while dipping his mouth down to hers. She met him eagerly, sealing their lips together, moaning and humming in response to his kiss. He paid rapt attention to her needy noises as he slipped his mouth across her cheek and down her neck, tasting the skin over her collarbone and feeling the pulse point of her throat beneath his tongue.

Scarlet clung to him, her fingers clutching his shoulders, even as her legs spread wider. She arched her hips up to press into the ridge of his erection, making his cock throb against her inner thigh. Hunter buried his face into her neck, knowing full well where this led and unable to bear the thought of it being over too soon. He never wanted this to end, and yet he needed to be inside her like he needed air to breathe.

Looking back to her face, he witnessed the stark desire in her eyes. Scarlet smiled up at him, like she did when they were in the forest together, when she saw the sun shining through the leaves in sparkling silver and gold. It was the smile of his freebird, the fairy who'd flitted her way into his soul and brought all her light with him. Hunter needed nothing more than to be surrounded by that light now.

He held her heated gaze as he aligned their hips, running his aching length through the outer folds of her sex. She was so warm, and so wet, and he found the opening to her body instantly. When he pressed the head of his cock inside her, she grabbed hold of his forearms and held tight, biting her lip and whimpering.

His pulse sputtered while he watched her. It took every ounce of control he possessed to not plunge deep inside her this instant. But he simply couldn't do that. He needed to take his time. He needed to love her so fully and thoroughly that she would never be able to forget him.

Lord knows, he could never forget her.

Hunter forced himself to still, with his body barely inside hers, even as his shaft twitched and begged for more. Scarlet watched as he warred with his desires. She rocked her hips up, coaxing him farther inside, coating him in her warmth and wetness. Then she smiled again, the pure, undiluted emotion in her eyes shining like a beacon. He could tell his little bird wasn't holding anything back right now. She focused every bit of her heart, body, and soul on him, and he wanted all of that, so he finally allowed himself to sink fully inside.

Her eyes widened as they joined. Hunter groaned out loud, having trouble reconciling the pleasure with the pain. He'd entered her so many times before, but never quite like this. So warm and welcoming, like home. Like a home he never thought he deserved.

Scarlet held tight to his shoulders, pulling him closer, inviting him deeper. She gazed up at him with raw need and undiluted longing and he wanted to stare back at her forever. He wanted to bask in this perfect world they'd found in each other...except that it wasn't perfect at all. Nothing about this was even remotely perfect, because as much as she felt like home, he knew this was actually her way of saying goodbye.

Hunter couldn't bear that thought right now. He couldn't reconcile any of it, so he dropped his forehead onto hers and concentrated on breathing. She merely held him closer, circling her arms across his neck, wrapping her legs around his back, and linking her feet over his spine. She held him to her with every part of her body, and with all of her heart, clinging without any semblance of restraint.

Dear Lord, why does this ever have to end? I want her with me. I want her with me for every single day of the rest of my life.

Hunter raised his eyes to hers, reaching out to cradle his little bird's face in his hands. "I'm going to miss you," he confessed, his voice broken and shaking. "I'm going to miss you so damn much."

Her tears returned with a vengeance. They sprung up quick and clear, brimming in the dim light. She didn't say anything, even though a sob choked its way from her throat. Scarlet only nodded, over and over.

Hunter squeezed his eyes shut, since it hurt like hell to see her on the verge of crying. He ran his fingers over her cheeks as her fists balled against his spine. She released a shuddered exhale just before her tears spilled out onto his fingertips. He didn't want her to cry, but he couldn't stop her. Honestly, he could barely stop himself. He did the only other thing he could, pressing his lips to her wet skin, tasting the salty sting against his tongue while kissing her over and over again.

Scarlet tried to compose herself. She took deep inhales, and sniffled, and pressed her body closer to his, but he still felt her quake beneath him. He understood now that he needed to finish this. It was too painful for her. It was too painful for him. He couldn't stay here inside her forever. That wasn't possible, and to try would only torment them both.

Hunter began moving, pulling out and pushing back in, as he pressed fevered kisses to her lips and face. Scarlet gasped and rocked against him while he drove himself inside her again and again. Her tight, slick sheath encased him fully, a sensation more heavenly than anything on earth, and yet as painful as the worst torture he could imagine. He grit his teeth together and kept going, determined to put an end to this.

Lunging into her with purpose and precision, he made every thrust count. But then her tiny voice breached the cool, still air. "Hunter?"

He stopped all his actions immediately and looked to her eyes. "Yes?"

"Will you hold my hands? Please?"

Memory after memory accosted him – of all the times she'd asked him to hold her hands – of all the times she'd begged him to touch her, with and without words. He grabbed hold of both her hands now, one in each of his, and brought them to rest against the pillow beside her tousled hair. The movement shifted his body down fully onto hers, and Scarlet moaned as she laced their fingers.

She smiled up at him through her tears. It was a beautiful smile, a perfect smile, and he wanted to see it. He kept his eyes latched to hers when he started to move again.

Hunter rocked into her, slow and steady, studying every emotion that crossed over her face, witnessing her desire and her need as they built and swelled and burned. Eventually, she began to whimper in time with his thrusts, her inner muscles tightening perfectly around his shaft. He refused to look away from her and she never looked away from him. Her fingers wound inseparably with his as their bodies glided together, soft and hard, hot and wet, deep and penetrating and complete.

When she came, her lips parted and her breath hitched, yet her eyes stayed pinned to his. Her body shuddered, still clinging to his as she tried to focus. Hunter wanted to watch her forever, to bask in her beauty for the rest of his life, but his physical needs overruled his wishes.

He let himself go, drowning in the pleasure of her body as he had so many times before – although never quite like this, with the definitive knowledge that this was the last time. Even as he surrendered to the ecstasy, even as he rocked and throbbed and poured inside her, the agony in his heart grew too powerful to be ignored. He couldn't fight the tears that fell from his eyes to join those streaming down her cheeks.

She blinked as she looked up at him, arching up from the pillow to press her forehead onto his. "Hunter. Hunter."

"Scarlet," he moaned, gripping her fingers inside his own. He kissed her again, joining their mouths and tongues while their bodies pulsed in time together. They lived out each final second with their limbs intricately entwined, falling slowly back down to earth. She stayed with him the entire time, her lips never leaving his. He held onto her for what felt like forever, although he knew it wasn't, and couldn't be.

Eventually, he rested his forehead onto her shoulder, released his grip on her hands, and waited as she extracted her fingers from his in order to ease them onto his back. His tears finally dried, and he knew hers had as well, since he could no longer feel that wetness against his skin. Hunter was happy for it, grateful she no longer cried because of him, and dreading the thought of seeing those tears again in the morning.

He stilled, hesitant to even twitch a muscle. Scarlet didn't attempt to leave. She just drew her hands up and down his spine, lazily tracing her fingers over his skin. As she petted him, she hummed beside his ear. He couldn't quite discern the tune, but it sounded like an old Elvis ballad.

The song was soft and sweet and wonderful, and Hunter lifted his head to see her again. "What are you humming, honey?"

"Was I humming? Oh, I guess I was. I didn't realize."

"I like it when you hum. I always love hearing your voice."

She smiled in response, which lit a spark in her sad eyes. "Should we get under the covers now? I don't want you to get cold."

"I'm not cold. But I suppose we should get under the covers."

Hunter left her body with great reluctance. Sitting up to gather the edges of the sheets and quilt in his hand, he pulled the warm, cozy fabric around them both as he lay back down beside her. Scarlet burrowed immediately into his chest, so he threw one of his legs over both of hers and wrapped his arm around her back.

He drew her closer, grateful for her warm breath against his neck, her dainty fingers resting on his chest, and her soft breasts pushed into his skin. Pressing his face into her hair, he filled his senses with the feel and sound and smell of her. He ran his hands over her body, trying to live in this moment alone, and not consider what tomorrow would bring.

Scarlet's fingers spread out over his heart. "Hunter?"

"Hmm?"

"Will you be okay? I mean, I probably don't have the right to ask, but I really need to know. You will be okay after I leave, won't you?"

For a brief moment, he considered telling her he wouldn't be okay, just to see if that would make her stay. But he couldn't put that burden on her shoulders. Not when she was trying so hard to do the sensible thing for them both – the goddamn sensible, rational, logical thing that obviously devastated her as much as it did him.

Hunter sighed. "I'll survive, Scarlet. What about you?"

She nodded against his shoulder. "I'll survive, too."

He slipped his hand over her hair, trying to wrap his mind around her answer. He couldn't imagine his frolicking freebird merely surviving. The woman he'd known for the past two weeks danced and sang and bounced. That's what he wanted for her. He didn't want her to lose that joy from her life. He didn't want her to lose the hope in her eyes.

Scarlet pressed her lips to his neck, sending goose bumps down his arms. "You know, you never used the fantasy I promised you. We do still have a little more time together tonight, if you want me to fulfill it."

Hunter shook his head. "No, thank you. I appreciate the offer, but I prefer to remember us just like this."

"You're not going to use your fantasy?"

"No, I'm not. Knowing there's a gorgeous woman somewhere in the world who owes me a fantasy will put a sparkle in my eye every day. People will always wonder what I'm thinking. It'll be worth it."

Scarlet laughed, which shifted her bare skin against his, which made his arms tighten around her. "So...do you really think it was worth it?"

Hunter understood the weight of her question. He also knew his answer without hesitation. "Yes. It was worth it."

"Are you sure? The first night we were together, you said you didn't have any regrets. But I'll understand if you've changed your mind."

"I haven't changed my mind," he assured.

The only thing I will ever regret is letting you go.

Hunter wanted to tell her that now. He wanted to tell her the thought of losing her was unfathomable, and he knew she hated the thought of losing him just as much, and they could find a way to be together if they just tried hard enough. He wanted to convince her of all of this, using elegant, intelligent words – words he wasn't capable of at the moment.

As his forest fairy settled further against his chest, and ran her fingers over his heart, and sighed into his skin, Hunter decided not to say anything. She felt so warm and tranquil and flawless in his arms, and he didn't want to risk disturbing this perfect peace. He chose to save his speech for tomorrow, for when she woke, soft and snuggly in his arms. In the morning, he would look down into her sleepy eyes and assure her that life could always be like this for them. He would try like hell, one more time, to convince her to give them a chance beyond this mountain.

"I'm glad you haven't changed your mind," she whispered, her voice already thick with exhaustion.

"I'll never regret a moment we spent together, Scarlet."

"Me, neither. I'll never regret a moment of us. Never, ever."

Hunter tried to pull her even closer. She didn't complain at all when he practically smothered her in a full-body embrace. She only snuggled further inside his arms and nuzzled her face into his neck.

After several minutes, her breathing evened out. He wondered if he would finally get to feel her asleep in bed with him. It took a few more seconds, but then he heard her tiny snores. Her fingers still lay over his heart, even in her sleep.

He placed a kiss on the top of her head. "Goodnight, my little bird," he spoke into her curls. Then he finally closed his eyes.

~

HUNTER WOKE to the warmth of sunshine splaying across his face. He basked in the realization that he was not in his bed. He was in Scarlet's.

With a smile consuming his face, he reached for her. His hand eased to his side, searching for her body, needing to pull her back to him. But all he felt were pillows and sheets.

He ceased all his movements, straining to hear any noises coming from the other rooms in the cabin. But everything was silent. A deep hollowness settled inside his chest.

He didn't have to open his eyes to prove what he already knew.

His Scarlet was gone.

1 2

DISCOVERIES

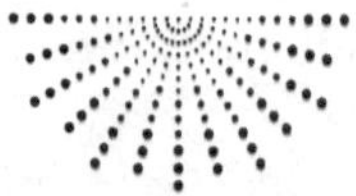

Hunter lay in Scarlet's bed, staring up at the ceiling. He could still smell her scent everywhere – in the sheets, in the air, on his skin. The bed was warm, but not as warm as it would be with her beside him.

He held his breath, hoping to hear sounds from other rooms of her cabin. He only heard the inexplicably cheerful chirping of birds outside her window. His heart sunk, heavy and painful, inside his chest.

She's gone.

He'd known he would have to accept that truth eventually. Just not yet. He honestly believed he'd wake with her in his arms. He thought he'd have one last opportunity to convince her to give this relationship a chance in the real world. Instead, she'd left without saying goodbye.

Hunter pressed his fingers into his eyelids, knowing she'd actually said her goodbyes last night, even if not entirely in words. To be honest, he understood why she left before he woke today. Saying goodbye this morning would have been too damn hard on both of them.

Images of the two of them together in this bed – wrapped up in each other, clinging to each other, loving each other – accosted his mind in the most gorgeous and painful way. He could still feel her skin against his, taste her salty tears, and hear her voice as she chanted his name. Shaking his head, he sat up at the edge of the mattress. These memories were too damn raw. He couldn't stay here in her cabin, yet he also couldn't imagine being anywhere on this mountain without her. Staring at his strewn clothes on the floor, he reluctantly reached for his shirt. Then he caught sight of her nightstand and froze.

A letter lay there, beside him. A letter in a woman's scrolled handwriting. His eyes scanned to the words at the bottom of the page: *Yours, Scarlet.*

Hunter's pulse raced while he stared at the paper.

He reached for it, grasping it hard in both hands, and read:

My Dearest Hunter,

First and foremost, I must ask you to forgive me. I promised to stay the entire night with you and I didn't. I'm sorry. You once told me you couldn't imagine having to watch me walk away from you, and honestly, I couldn't bear the thought of doing it. I know it was cowardice on my part, but I hope you'll forgive me for wanting to spare us both that pain. I also hope our last memories of each other will be happier this way.

I must also apologize for writing you a letter. I hesitated to do it, since the letter you received back in your high school locker room hurt you deeply, and the last thing I ever want to do is hurt you. But I still have things to say, and not enough time to say them, so I decided to write my thoughts down. I hope you'll indulge me by reading, and I hope you'll find a way to see this letter as something positive.

I never spoke with you again about what happened between you and Samantha all those years ago, since I promised I wouldn't say anything else while we were at Blue. Now that I'm leaving, I need to get a few things off my chest, and I pray you'll allow it. The most important thing I have to tell you is that what Samantha did was not your fault. I know I said those words before, and I know you heard me. Still, I want you to see them in writing. I want you to understand them without any doubt.

You were so young when all of that happened. So young, and not yet capable of understanding the effect it had on your mind and your soul. I understand how your need for control grew from your grief. In truth, I'm amazed by the positive choices you made because of it. You became a strong, steadfast leader, and I couldn't be more proud of you. But now, I hope you'll see the control you hold over your life, and everyone else's, isn't doing you any favors. The guilt you've carried with you since high school has prevented you from experiencing the miracles this world has to offer. You deserve so much more. You deserve everything. Please know that. Please know you deserve all the love in the world.

You shared yourself so deeply with me that day in the woods, and I will never forget the trust you placed in me. You also asked for my forgiveness, and I willingly and absolutely gave it. Now, my greatest wish is for you is to allow yourself forgiveness for the events that were not, in any way, within your control. You are an amazing man, with such capacity for laughter, joy, and love. You let me see the beauty and the light inside you, and I'm so grateful to you for allowing me to see.

In truth, I am grateful to you for so many things. I want to thank you for being here on this mountain with me. I needed you, Hunter. I had no idea, when I found you by the side of the road, how much I needed you. I can't possibly tell you all the ways you've helped me. Please just know that our time together was one of the best experiences of my life. I have never allowed myself the freedom of a relationship like ours before, and every moment we shared was wondrous and magical and perfect.

All I have left to give you now, after my apologies and my gratitude, is hope. My hope is for you to let other people see this man I've seen. I hope you'll let them see your fun, playful, adventurous spirit – the one that lit up my world for these two precious weeks. If you allow that man to live and breathe, I know you'll find the life you're searching for.

Thank you, again and again, for everything. And until the day you put me from your thoughts, hopefully with a smile, please know you will never be far from my heart.

Yours, Scarlet

Hunter sat, stiff and silent, holding the letter in his hands. His eyes returned to the top of the page, his pulse surging as he read the letter over. And over. And over. He read until he'd memorized every word. Then he set the paper down carefully on the mattress beside him.

He stared at the floor, unseeing, trying to wrap his mind around her words. He fisted his fingers into her sheets, painfully aware he'd had her here with him, in every way, mere hours ago. Last night, he believed he understood how deeply Scarlet cared for him. Now, he knew the woman who wrote him that letter cared more about his happiness than her own.

The weight on his chest grew heavier with each passing second. He stood, needing to get the hell out of this cabin if he wanted even a remote chance of breathing normally. Hunter pressed his eyes shut as he pulled his clothes on, since it hurt too fucking much to see her mussed sheets and indented mattress. He'd worked too hard to have her here, only to have this be the place where she said her goodbyes.

The instant he finished dressing, he grabbed the letter and shoved it in the pocket of his pants. He strode from her bedroom and rushed down the hall, pushing one foot in front of the other, determined to escape as quickly as he could. Yet when he arrived at her front door, his footing faltered. He came to a stuttered halt, horribly aware that walking out of this door meant leaving everything behind.

Hunter dragged in a deep breath and blew it out. His eyes drew to the kitchen, seeing Scarlet sitting naked on the counter. He shifted his focus to the living room floor, where her body wrapped around his on the Twister mat. He looked to the couch, feeling her asleep on his lap.

He drank in every memory he could, until his gaze finally turned to the far wall, seeking out the picture of her fantini bird. Hunter knew how much the blurry photo meant to her, and he wanted to see it again. But to his surprise and dismay, it wasn't there anymore. The log wall sat empty, just as it had the first night he'd stepped foot in this room.

His body drew toward the empty wall. Coming to a standstill in front of the blank surface, he stared at the knotted pine. He wished the photo she'd nailed here had been an actual image of her imaginary bird. Maybe then, she would believe in magic again. Maybe then, she would believe their relationship could exist in the real world, too.

Hunter sighed as he looked over the gnarled log wall, searching out the hole she'd hammered into the wood. He remembered how angry he'd been with his forest fairy when he realized she'd nailed a picture to a wall that wasn't hers. He remembered chastising her for it.

Amazingly, it wasn't difficult to locate one hole in the wildly uneven surface. It wasn't hard at all, because the residual mark it left was wet. His brow furrowed as he reached out to run his forefinger over the sticky substance. Apparently, Scarlet had taken the time this morning to fill the tiny divot with wood spackle.

Hunter ogled the brown paste now drying on his skin. "Where in the hell did she get wood spackle?" he wondered aloud, pondering the question for only a second before recalling her trip to the hardware store in town last night. She'd said she had to use the restroom, then emerged from the store carrying her absurdly oversized purse and eager to return to Blue. "Wow, Scarlet. You certainly went through a lot of trouble to hide your spackle purchase from me."

He honestly didn't know why she'd gone so far to conceal it, except that

Frolicking Freebird Scarlet had told him she wouldn't buy spackle to fill this hole. Evidently, Solemnly Sedate Scarlet had changed her mind. Rubbing the brown paste from his fingers, he huffed out a laugh. "Damn, you really wrapped things up, didn't you?"

Solemnly Sedate Scarlet had worked diligently to set everything straight before she left: she'd tried to fulfill all her promises to him; she'd told him goodbye, both with her body and her letter; she'd said her piece about his past; and she'd spackled this wall. She'd filled in all the gaps, literally and figuratively, so she could return to her life without remorse. But no matter how hard she'd tried to do right by him in her final hours at Blue, none of those things made her leaving hurt any less.

Hunter spun away from the wall, forcing himself toward the front door, his blood rushing fiercely through his veins. The only thing he wanted in the whole world was to see her, but he couldn't, which made him desperate for some semblance of human contact. He needed to talk to another person right now, someone who would understand his pain.

He knew the person he *should* talk to about all this. After all, he was a patient at a psychiatric retreat, and the appropriate thing would be to seek out his therapist. Yet he couldn't imagine doing that, since he'd never before discussed Scarlet with Abbott. Hunter felt fairly certain his by-the-books doctor, who also happened to be Blissful Blue's Medical Director, wouldn't approve of two patients having a heated sexual relationship while undergoing therapy.

Hunter huffed, unable to bear the thought of listening to the stern, fatherly lecture his doctor would give him right now. He needed to talk to someone who actually understood his dilemma. He needed Tyler Hensen, who'd looked like a kicked puppy the day Jocelyn left Blue.

Forcing himself to grasp the door handle, Hunter took one last look around her cabin. A million memories barraged his brain, accompanied by more pain than he could currently manage. He yanked on the handle, working to breathe as he pushed his way out into the cold morning air.

After slamming the door shut behind him, he strode off the porch, up the gravel path, and onto the main road, turning right toward Tyler's. While Hunter marched down his friend's driveway, he acknowledged the fact that he was right in the middle of the moment he'd been dreading all week. Scarlet had left him, and she'd torn a fucking hole in his heart, just as he knew she would.

The pain of her absence pulsed through his veins like wildfire. Yet, oddly enough, it wasn't the worst thing he could imagine. He hadn't hurt like this in as long as he could remember, which made him realize the worst thing in his life was what he'd been doing *before* coming here.

Before coming to Blue, he'd felt nothing. He'd felt nothing at all. And that truth hurt worse than anything else ever could.

Hunter stepped faster when Cabin 11 came into view. He struggled to keep his heart inside his chest as he bounded up the steps and knocked on the door. Rustling sounds came immediately from behind the logs.

"Hey there, buddy," Tyler greeted when he opened the door. "I wasn't expecting you. When you didn't meet me earlier at the gym, I figured I wouldn't get to see you at all today."

"I'm sorry. I know I haven't been around. Some things happened in the past few days, and I hoped we could talk. If you have the time."

"Sure. There's nothing but time up here. You want to come in?"

"That would be great."

Tyler waved him inside. "Sorry the place is a bit messy."

"That's no problem," Hunter assured as he stepped into the living room. The next instant, he had to school his reaction. Tyler's cabin wasn't just messy. It was a veritable pigsty, with clothes and dishes strewn over the furniture and floor. Hunter hesitated to move at all.

"Here, let me clear a place for you," Tyler offered, yanking a few shirts up from the couch. "Have a seat."

Hunter eased tentatively onto a cushion as he watched his friend clear another spot on the facing chair. He zeroed in on the dark circles under the man's eyes. "I hope you don't mind me saying this, Tyler, but you look like hell today."

"Wow. Well, right back at you."

"What's going on? I haven't seen you this upset since Jocelyn left."

Tyler shook his head. "That's the funny thing, though. I'm actually not upset. Not at all."

"Then why do you look like you went ten rounds in a boxing ring?"

"It's funny you put it that way, since I do feel like I've been hit in the chest. But that's not a bad thing, I swear. I just think...I think I'm finally in love."

"In love?" Hunter echoed. "With who? Mitzi Fisher?"

"*Mitzi*? Hell, no. That woman is a serious ice queen. And I've met my share of ice queens up here, let me tell you. But that woman deserves her own ice castle."

"Well, if not Mitzi, then who?"

"Her name is Natalie Abbott. She's Dr. Abbott's daughter."

"Abbott's daughter? When did you meet her?"

"Yesterday. She's up here visiting her dad."

Hunter shifted in his seat. "Wait a minute. You met this woman *yesterday*, and you already think you're in love with her?"

Tyler's shoulders bunched. "Look, I know how it sounds, and I know it's the real reason I'm here. But I think this could be different. I think I could actually change. Don't you think I could change?"

"I don't understand. What sort of change do you need?"

"You know what? It doesn't matter. You came here for my help, and all we've done is talk about me. Tell me what's on your mind."

"Right now, you are what's on my mind. Please tell me the real reason you're here. I truly want to know."

Tyler looked him in the eye for a long minute before his shoulders finally fell. "It's because I'm...I'm a sex addict."

"Oh. I see." Hunter stilled. "Since when?"

"Since forever, I guess. At least, since I knew what sex was. All my therapists say it's an unhealthy coping mechanism I developed because I suffered childhood trauma. You see, my mom died when I was little. A mugger robbed and shot her, then left her to die in an alleyway."

"My God, I'm so sorry."

"Thanks. It might not have been the worst thing ever, except my father never got over what happened. Apparently, I didn't, either. The doctors say I never had the ability to form healthy relationships with women as a child, and I've always missed my mother's love, so now I seek it out in other women. Lots and lots of other women. I don't know if I believe all of that, but it makes sense, I suppose."

"So, that's why you stay in therapy? And why you come to Blue?"

"Yup. That's why."

"I guess it's good you're aware of what's happening in your life."

"Oh, you know how it goes," Tyler said with a shrug. "Once upon a time, I would've been labeled a womanizer or even a chronic bachelor. Nowadays, they diagnose you with a disease and give you therapy. And I really do enjoy therapy. I mean, in my younger years, I went from woman to woman with no remorse at all. But since I started counseling, I feel a bit guilty. They tell me that's progress."

Hunter stared at him. "I'm...I'm glad you're making progress?"

"Thanks, buddy. I believe I am. Especially since I fell in love with Natalie. I think she might be the one woman I can finally commit to."

"Natalie, the woman you met yesterday."

"Yeah, that's the one. I can tell you don't agree with me, though. I guess you don't believe in love at first sight?"

"I, um..." Hunter mumbled, certain he should impart his friend with a lengthy sermon on the impracticality of such a thought. Two weeks ago, he would have told Tyler he was nuts for even considering such a thing. Now, he wasn't sure what to say. "I guess I just...I don't know."

"You don't know? Do you really not know if you believe in love at first sight?" Tyler studied him before cocking his head. "Oh. I see what's going on."

"What do you see?"

"I see why you needed to talk to me today. She left this morning, didn't she? That woman you've been with since you came to Blue – the one you never wanted to kiss-and-tell me about?"

Hunter scrubbed his hand across the back of his neck.

"So?" Tyler prodded. "Was it love at first sight between you two?"

The memory of Scarlet stepping out of the forest for the first time – with her rugged hiking boots and huge camera and enchanting smile – entered Hunter's mind and refused to leave. "No, it's..." he hesitated, fisting his fingers. "It's not possible to fall in love at first sight."

"Hmm. We're just going to have to agree to disagree on that, since it's pretty damn obvious you fell in love with her. Perhaps not instantly, but sometime over the last two weeks."

"No, no. I didn't fall in love with her. Definitely not."

"Definitely not?"

"Definitely not." Acid pushed into Hunter's throat. He swallowed hard. "Except that *definitely* is such a strong word. It's a really strong word, and I don't know if I should use it. Because...I guess...maybe."

Tyler grinned. "Maybe?"

"Maybe."

"You maybe fell in love with her?"

"Yeah, well, I mean...I could go as far as to say probably."

"You probably fell in love with her?"

"Probably," Hunter reiterated, watching an easy smile settle on his friend's lips. He pinched the bridge of his nose. "Goddamnit, Tyler! *Yes*, okay? I fell in love with her. I am completely, madly in love with this woman. You have no idea. I can barely comprehend it myself."

Tyler chuckled as he settled back into his seat.

Hunter huffed. "I'm glad this amuses you."

"Oh, it does, but only because I understand it so well. You don't have to earn approval in this cabin, you know. You can talk to me about anything."

"I do know. And I must admit, that's exactly why I came to you. But now, I don't even know what to say."

"Then why don't you just answer a question for me?"

"Okay."

"What are you still doing here?" Tyler asked, staring intently across the span of the cluttered room.

"What do you mean?"

"I mean, if you love this woman and she left, why in the hell are you still sitting here, talking to me? Why aren't you packing your bags right this minute and going to find her?"

Hunter's body deflated. "Because she doesn't want to be found."

"Are you sure about that?"

"Yeah, I'm pretty sure."

Tyler leaned forward in his chair. "No, buddy. I'm not asking if you're *pretty* sure. I'm asking if you're absolutely, positively, there's-no-way-in-hell-I-could-possibly-be-wrong, completely fucking *sure*."

Hunter's mind reached to the restaurant last evening, where he'd witnessed such fevered emotions in her eyes. His muscles clenched with the memory of her body clinging to his in her bed. His thoughts reeled with every word of the letter now burning a hole in his pocket.

"No," he admitted aloud. "I'm not that sure."

"Then I'll ask again. What are you still doing here?"

"You just...you don't understand, Tyler. I tried. I really tried. She and I went out on a date yesterday, and I did everything I knew to do. It was fun and romantic and perfect, and if she wanted to be with me in the real world, she would have said something last night."

"So, I assume you told her."

"Told her what?"

"How you feel. Yesterday on your date, did you or did you not tell this woman how much you love her?"

"Well, I didn't use those exact words. But I'm pretty sure she knows. I mean, I told her she's the only woman I want. And that I could imagine marrying her. And that I'd love to see her pregnant. And then I asked how many kids she'd like to have..."

Hunter's voice trailed as his eyes widened. "Holy shit!" he hollered. "I can't believe I actually said all of that! I probably terrified the poor woman! Good Lord! We've only known each other two *weeks*, yet there I was, telling her how I want the rest of our *lives* to be. It's no wonder she ran away from me. I must have sounded like a *lunatic*."

"Maybe you did. Or maybe you sounded like a man who finally knows what he wants out of life. Either way, she deserves to hear how much you love her. I think you should go find her and tell her."

"Why? So I can scare her more? Or have her tell me we haven't known each other long enough to feel this way? She'd be right, you know. I don't have any business talking about being in love so soon."

Tyler offered an empathetic nod. "I get it, man, believe me. It's scary as hell to put yourself out there like that. It feels like you're walking on a high wire with no safety net. But if she's the person you truly want to be with, then isn't she worth the risk?"

"But what if I'm wrong?" Hunter countered. "People don't fall madly in love in two weeks, yet I still babbled about us getting married and making babies. She must have thought I'd lost my grip on reality. She warned me the emotions at Blue are weird and overpowering and don't translate into real life. I understood it at first, but then I stopped caring about normalcy, because I just wanted to be with her. She was right, though. People don't fall madly in love in two weeks."

"You already said that part."

"Which part?"

"People don't fall madly in love in two weeks. You said that twice."

"So?"

"So, I think you're trying to talk yourself into it. Because you actually did fall madly in love in two weeks."

Hunter stared at the ground, knowing full well that his friend spoke the truth. "God, Tyler, do you want to know what the worst part is?"

"What's the worst part?"

"It didn't even take the whole two weeks. I don't know if I believe in love at first sight, but I know it didn't take the whole two weeks."

"Well, then. Congratulations, buddy. You're in love."

"Yeah, thanks. Even though nothing about this makes any sense."

Tyler laughed. "Hell, does it have to? Who ever said love makes sense? I never saw that written anywhere. No therapist ever looked me in the eye and told me I would know when I was really in love because it would make perfect sense. Maybe it works that way for some people, but I don't think love is supposed to make sense. It just is."

Hunter nodded with those words. On one level, he understood them. After all, he was in love with Scarlet beyond sense or reason. To be honest, he'd known it for a while. But he also knew love wasn't always the answer to everything. Chasing her down to confess his emotions could do a hell of a lot more harm than good.

As his mind waged war with his heart, he met Tyler's inquisitive stare. "I really appreciate you talking to me, but I should go now."

"Are you going to be okay, Hunter?"

"Yeah, I am. Thank you for listening, and for the advice."

"I'll feel better if you think about actually taking my advice."

"I imagine I'll think about little else," he admitted while standing.

"Well, good." Tyler followed him to the front door. "Will I see you tomorrow? Or will you be off to find your woman? As much as I enjoy our basketball games, I won't be upset at all if you don't show."

Hunter stepped onto the porch. "I wish I could give you an answer."

"Oh, you don't have to answer me now. Just know I plan to be here in my cabin all morning. If you show up on my doorstep, we'll go play some hoops. If you don't, I'll wish you and your lady the best of luck."

"Thanks, Tyler."

"Anytime."

Hunter nodded before trudging down the porch stairs. He heard the cabin door latch shut behind him, the hollow sound echoing off the trees. He cringed as he walked forward alone.

Should I go find Scarlet? Should I try to change her mind about us again? Should I tell her I'm madly in love with her and want to marry her as soon as humanly possible? Will she scream in horror if I do?

Hunter wondered if he had, in fact, terrified her yesterday. He'd smothered her in romance during their date, as intended, yet now he questioned if it had all been too much. Perhaps it was.

Or perhaps it wasn't. His little bird had told him the attraction they shared only freaked her out at first. Once they were fully together, she decided to embrace it. She embraced every emotion they experienced with each other, because when she was with him, she felt truly alive.

Hunter understood that now. Love, joy, pain, sorrow, desire, hope – they all gave him life. Two weeks ago, he'd had one foot in the grave.

"Damn it, Scarlet," he grumbled as he shuffled across the main road and onto his driveway. "Why did you leave?"

That was the big question. He had a million questions, but that was the one that truly mattered. She had to know how he felt about her. He hadn't been coy about it, not at dinner last night, or in bed after. But apparently, his love wasn't enough to keep her here.

"Why did you leave?" he asked again, his footsteps slowing when his cabin appeared in the distance. His fists clenched at the thought of being alone inside those log walls. He honestly couldn't bear the thought of being trapped in there all by himself.

By the grace of God, Hunter saw a friend waiting for him. Colin sat on the porch steps, huddled up against the cold in his red hoodie, with his food truck parked a few yards away.

"Hey there!" Hunter shouted as he ran the rest of the way.

"Hey yourself," Colin replied, scooting over to offer room on the stair beside him. "I hope you don't mind me waiting here for you."

Hunter dropped down to sit shoulder to shoulder with the boy. "Hell, no, I don't mind. Actually, I'm extremely grateful to see you."

"Yeah, I thought you might say something like that. I know how hard it is to still be up here after she leaves."

Hunter glanced at the young man's dejected expression while he stared out into the evergreens. "You're missing Scarlet, too, I take it?"

"I am. I always miss her after she's gone. When she's here, I feel like I have stability. When she's here, I feel like I have a home."

"Home," Hunter agreed, silently repeating the word over again as he listened to the wind rustle the leaves. "I know exactly what you mean."

They sat in silence for a while. It was the most peaceful he'd felt all day. He wished his friend didn't have to hurt like this, but he took solace knowing the person beside him understood some of his pain.

"I didn't know where to bring your lunch tray," Colin finally said. "I knew she'd gone, so I thought you'd be here. When you weren't, I decided to wait for you. I wanted to make sure you had some food."

"Thanks for always looking out for me."

"Sure."

Hunter watched the boy rub his hands together. "Is there something else on your mind, Colin?"

"Yeah, actually, there is. But it's definitely on the personal side, and I know you're an official guest here, and I'm just a truck driver."

"Hell, you're not *just* anything, man. You're my friend."

Colin grinned before glancing to the ground. "Thanks."

"It's only the truth. Please tell me what's on your mind."

"Well, it's about Scarlet. I don't know what happened between you two up here, and I'm not asking you to tell me. In fact, I'm trying really hard not to imagine it. But she's been my friend for years..."

"For years?"

"Yeah. She was here the day I arrived. She was the first person at Blue to throw her arms around me and ask how I was after my parents died. She always looks out for me, always talks to me, always listens."

"That does sound exactly like her. She's wonderful, isn't she?"

"She is," Colin confirmed. "She's the most wonderful person I know, and having known her as long as I have, I can honestly tell you she's looked happier in the past two weeks than ever before. And since the only difference I can see in her life is you, I want you to know how much I appreciate it. Whatever you did to change things for her, I'm grateful you could put a smile on her face. Even if it was only for a handful of days."

Hunter blinked against the moisture in his eyes. He didn't reply, since he was at a loss for words. All he could do was watch while the young man smiled softly to himself before standing.

"Well, that's really all I had to say, so I'd best be going. I set your lunch tray on the kitchen counter inside. I hope you don't mind me letting myself into your cabin, but I wasn't sure if I'd get to see you and I didn't want to leave the food on the porch for too long."

"Thank you," Hunter replied when he found his voice. "Not just for lunch, but for everything."

"Sure." Colin stepped off the porch and onto the gravel, moving toward his truck. When he reached for the door handle, he turned back. "You know, you asked me once if romantic relationships ever worked out beyond these mountains."

"Yeah, I remember it well."

"And I remember telling you they didn't."

"That is what you said."

"Well...maybe I was wrong. I mean, I wouldn't be at all upset if you proved me wrong."

As Colin jumped into the driver's seat and drove away, Hunter stared after him. He sat on his porch steps for what felt like hours. He may never have entered his desolate cabin again, if it weren't for the grumblings of his stomach.

Forcing himself into his living room, Hunter slumped onto the couch with his tray. The letter in his pocket crinkled as he sat, so he took it out and unfolded it while shoving food in his mouth. He didn't really taste anything. He just concentrated on the words she'd left him.

He read his favorite sentences over and over, studying the strokes of his little bird's handwriting. He imagined the soft contours of her face as she'd put her thoughts on paper. He imagined the tears in her eyes as she'd poured her heart out to him. In truth, after what Colin had just told him, reading her letter again now made one thing perfectly clear.

Scarlet is in love with me.

Hunter smiled with that perfect knowledge. But his smile fell before he even had the chance to enjoy it. Scarlet loved him, yet she'd still left Blue without him. Which meant she didn't know she loved him. Or she did know, but it didn't overcome her reasons for leaving.

Honestly, neither possibility was great.

The first one, he hoped he could fix. He just needed to find her, so they could spend time together in the real world. Maybe then, when she saw how good things could be, she would acknowledge how she felt.

As for the second possibility, he didn't really know how to fix that. If she knew she loved him, he couldn't understand why she still felt the need to run away. Which brought him back to the same damn question.

Why did you leave, Scarlet?

His gourmet meal sat like a rock in his stomach. Hunter dragged himself off the couch, folded up her letter, and shoved it back in his pocket. He walked his tray to the porch, setting it down before straightening to look into the evergreens.

A firm breeze swirled through the trees, drawing cool air across his skin. The scents of pine and earth filled his nostrils. Leaves spun at his feet, their tiny red-and-green bodies twirling over his shoes.

The smile returned to his face as he watched and listened. The woods called to him so clearly, as if they'd sung his name out loud. *Her* woods called to him, and that was exactly where he needed to be.

Hunter stepped forward, wanting to run into the forest this instant. But he couldn't, because he had a therapy appointment. Pivoting on his heels, he strode back into his cabin, picked up the phone, and dialed.

"Blissful Blue, this is Betsy. How may I help you?"

"Hello, Betsy," he greeted the woman who answered. "It's Hunter."

"Oh, hello, dear! How are you doing this fine afternoon?"

"I'm...I'm here. But I won't be there. Today, I mean. I need to cancel my appointment with Dr. Abbott."

Betsy exhaled. "But you're supposed to be here in a few minutes. This is the third day in a row you've cancelled therapy, and I'm starting to worry. Do you need help? I can send Pete over to your cabin."

"No, that isn't necessary. I'm okay. I just need some time to think."

"Well, I do understand that. But I also want to make sure you're getting all the help you need. That's what we're here for, you know. That's the whole purpose of Blissful Blue."

"I know. I will get more therapy, I promise. Just not today."

"How about tomorrow?"

Her persistence made him chuckle. "Okay, yes. Tomorrow."

"You'll come to see Dr. Abbott tomorrow? You promise?"

"I promise. I'll be there tomorrow."

"I'm putting you down for an 8 a.m. Bright and early."

"I'll be there. Scout's honor."

"Were you ever a Scout, Hunter?"

"Not technically. But I'd like to think I have an honorary title."

"Okay, then. I'll take you on your Scout's honor."

The obvious pride in the woman's kind voice made him smile. He hoped he might still get a Christmas gift this year, if Mrs. Claus had anything to do with it. "See you tomorrow, Betsy."

"Until then."

Hunter hung up the phone and rushed back outside. He barely got the door shut before vaulting off the stairs toward the woods behind his cabin. The fresh breeze petted his skin as the evergreens drew him in.

He wandered through the forest for hours. Not because he was lost. On the contrary, he knew exactly where he was.

Hunter thought a lot on his journey. He thought about Tyler, who didn't have a mother growing up, and sought refuge in the arms of woman after woman. He thought about Colin, who'd lost his parents to a car accident, yet chose to drive a truck as his occupation. He thought about his own parents, who'd given him unlimited, undeniable, unfaltering love from the moment he'd been born. That was the kind of love Hunter was used to. It was the kind of love he wanted to give.

He'd never been able to give love the way he wanted to before. He'd never been able to understand why his relationships didn't work out the way he planned. But after these weeks at Blue – after acknowledging the guilt he carried over Samantha and how that guilt drove him to try to control every-thing and everyone around him – he realized *he* was the person preventing his happiness.

Scarlet had forced him to see that truth. She'd shown him what he needed to change in his life in order to be happy, and assured him that he deserved all the love in the world. All Hunter desired now was to give his unlimited, unde-niable, unfaltering love to her.

The depth of that desire terrified him, even though the emotions them-selves weren't frightening. Knowing how much he loved his forest fairy actu-ally soothed him in a way he hadn't thought possible. But to chase her down – to find her against her will and shout out his love at the top of his lungs – sounded insane. It meant taking the ultimate leap of faith. It meant throwing away every logical thought, giving up any semblance of control, and putting his life entirely in her hands.

As he walked through her woods, he acknowledged what he wanted to do. He wanted to step onto that high wire, trusting she would catch him. He only wished he knew why she'd chosen to leave him behind.

Scarlet's red maple appeared before him then. Hunter froze when he saw it, staring at the dark crimson leaves the way she had just days ago. He remembered holding her here as her body trembled, and hated that he'd never discovered what took the color red away from her.

Forcing himself away from her favorite tree, he moved farther into the woods. He wished she had asked for his help while she was here. He wished she'd relied on him the way he'd relied on her.

Unfortunately, Hunter knew she would never have asked for what she needed. She'd spent all her time at Blue wandering through the woods and encouraging him to go to therapy, yet he didn't think she'd attended any therapy herself. He wondered if Solemnly Sedate Scarlet ever asked anyone for help. She probably didn't. She was resourceful and brilliant, and she would figure out a way to exist, in spite of her own needs. She was tougher than she looked, and she would survive.

Hunter's steps ground to a halt. He stopped because he'd reached his destination: Scarlet's oak tree. He recognized it easily, with all its cracks and crevices. Even the dirt floor at his feet looked familiar.

He sat in that dirt now, where he'd lain with her time and time again. Easing down onto his back in front of the oak's thick trunk, he looked up into the towering branches. Hunter hoped to catch sight of her yellow-crowned purple fantini. He wanted to be able to run to her and tell her the bird wasn't only in her imagination. Then, in his very next breath, he would tell her she didn't have to survive on her own. He would tell her she could live – truly live – with him.

Staring up at the branches of her tree, Hunter watched the sunlight play off of the colorful leaves. He watched the gold and silver sparkle from the bright sky all the way down to where he sat. It was enormous, this world. As enormous as ever. But it didn't scare him anymore.

He settled fully onto the earth while looking up to the blue. A smile tugged at his lips. "Samantha?" he whispered. "Can you hear me?"

The guilt he'd carried for so long released the moment he said her name, lifting a steel weight off of his chest.

"I hope you can hear me," he continued, his voice raw but clear. "I know I've never spoken to you before, but I hope you'll still listen, because I've wanted to talk to you for so long."

Hunter's smile fell. "I'm sorry," he said, focusing on the leaves above. "I'm sorry I failed you. If I'd truly known you, I'd like to think I could have changed something for you. I'd like to think I could have shown you all the happiness life has to offer. I'd like to think I could have helped you see that there was an entire world waiting for you."

He sucked in a deep breath. "I don't know if you've been watching me. If you have, you already know I tried to make my life perfect. I tried to control everything, since I thought it would honor your memory. But I failed you. I failed us both, because perfection should never have been my goal. My goal should have been to enjoy my life, to enjoy a *good* life. I should have embraced every bit of it. The laughter and the joy. The beauty and the magic. Even the pain."

His eyes closed as he listened to the whispered breeze flow through the trees. "I've made so many mistakes, but I'm going to fix them now. I'm going to honor your memory by feeling all that I can. It won't always be easy for me – and I know I can't change overnight – but at least I understand what I need to do. I want you to know I'll never forget you, Samantha. I'll never forget the responsibility you gave me to keep your spirit alive. Only now, I'm going to take on that responsibility in an entirely new way. I'm going to allow myself the happiness I believe you'd want for me. I will climb mountains, and play in the forest, and love with all my heart. And if you can hear this, I hope you're smiling. I truly hope you are."

Hunter exhaled slowly. He opened his eyes to see the beauty of each leaf above his head. When the cool air brushed over his skin, softly and gently, he knew she'd heard him.

～

He ran faster than he ever had in his life. Through bramble and underbrush, around rocks and branches, Hunter focused solely on getting out of the woods. He leapt over a fallen log or two, laughing when he landed unharmed on the other side.

By the time he emerged at the back of his cabin, night had fallen. He wanted nothing more than to jump in his car this instant, to speed down this mountain toward his little bird, but he couldn't leave tonight. He still had to pack, say goodbye to his friends, and attend therapy in the morning, since he'd promised Betsy he would.

Taking his porch steps two at a time, Hunter entered his cabin with renewed determination. His dinner tray waited for him on the kitchen counter, which reminded him of another thing he had to do before he left tomorrow. Walking down the hall to his bedroom, he opened the safe in his closet and pulled out his checkbook, remembering how he'd brought it here in case this weird retreat didn't take credit cards.

Grabbing the souvenir Blissful Blue pen off his nightstand, he wrote out one check. He didn't fill in the name, because he didn't know it entirely, but in the *memo* section he jotted down the address for Gregory Global. Then he set the check on his dresser.

He reached for his suitcase next, hastily tossing his clothes inside. He tidied up the rest of the cabin before sitting down to eat. Colin had brought him steak tonight, which was tasty, but certainly not as delicious as it was the night Hunter used Scarlet's backside for a plate.

His pulse raced with the thought of seeing her again, even though he knew she was going to be pissed as hell when he showed up on her doorstep. She'd be angry that he'd left Blue early, and hadn't finished therapy, and had tracked her down. In truth, the thought of her wrath appealed to him. Hunter wanted to see the blaze in her emerald eyes, to hear her loud voice as they argued, to watch her stomp her foot at him. He wanted to witness all her emotions on full display, to verify how much she still affected him, and to prove how much he still affected her. Even in the real world.

He smiled when he finally finished his meal and set it back on the porch. It wasn't terribly late, but he decided to go to bed anyway. He wanted a good night's sleep before his adventure tomorrow.

Hunter slept straight through until morning, having nothing to weigh him down. He knew what he wanted out of life, and who he wanted beside him. He didn't have any doubts, which freed him entirely.

He woke before the birds even had a chance to start chirping at him. He showered, dressed, and packed the last of his things. He took his briefcase and luggage out to his Porsche and tossed them in the trunk.

The food truck crunched down the driveway just as he started to turn back toward his cabin. He brightened further when Colin approached.

"Good morning, Hunter," the boy offered, jumping out of his seat to make his way around the back of the truck.

"Good morning, Colin."

"You're up early."

Hunter took his tray from the young man's outstretched arms. "I am up early. I'm leaving today."

"Leaving? Don't you have until the end of the week here?"

"I do, but I've decided to head out early. Actually, I'd like to give you something before I go. Can you wait here a minute?"

"Yeah, sure."

Hunter walked into his cabin, set the tray down, and grabbed the check he'd written the night before. He bounded back outside. "I need you to take this," he stated, placing the slip of paper in Colin's hand.

"Why are you giving me a check?" Colin questioned before glancing down. "Holy fuck, Hunter! Why are you giving me a check for *fifty thousand dollars*?"

"Because you need to finish school and you can't do it up on this mountain. I know Blue has been a refuge for you. I know you needed to be here for a time, and I respect that you sought help. But I think you're okay now. I know it's not up to me to make that decision, but I want you to know I believe you're okay. I believe you can leave here and go back to the real world and live your life again."

Colin shook his head as he gripped onto the check.

Hunter's eyes shifted to the young man's trembling fingers before looking back to his face. "I want you to know this isn't charity, Colin. It's an investment. When you're done with school, I want you to consider taking a position at my company. Gregory Global's address is on the check. I know good workers when I see them, and I wouldn't be a very intelligent businessman if I didn't try to get them to come work for me. So, will you take the money?"

"I...I don't know what to say."

"Say you'll let me invest in you. Write your name on that check and cash it. Then go back to school, and come see me when you're done."

Colin didn't speak for a long minute. A tear fell from his eye when he finally nodded. "I will. Thank you."

"You're welcome. Promise you'll consider working for me?"

"Yes, Sir."

"Hunter," he corrected. "I'll always be Hunter to you."

Colin grinned, swiped the wetness from his cheek, and turned back toward the truck. He hopped into the driver's seat, started the engine, and sat. He didn't move at all for lengthy seconds, until he finally rolled down the window and stuck his head out.

"Hey, Hunter?"

"Yeah?"

"You are going after Scarlet now, right?"

He met the young man's stare. "I am. I will find her, come hell or high water."

Colin nodded in satisfaction. "Good."

Hunter smiled while watching his future employee drive away. Stepping back inside his cabin, he spent his last few moments eating breakfast. When he finished, he returned to the porch and locked the door behind him. He stared out into the evergreens, took one more breath of mountain air, and headed to his car.

The Porsche performed fairly well as he drove toward Cabin 13. He hoped the hobbled vehicle would take him all the way home, since he needed to get to Gregory Global as soon as possible. This was Monday, which meant his friend Clay would be working in IT, which meant the computer guru could track down Scarlet's address in the blink of an eye.

Hunter wasn't exactly sure what he would tell Clay in order to avert the suspicion that he was stalking some poor woman. Then again, he actually would be stalking Scarlet – in what he thought of as a pleasant and loving way. Which was probably what most stalkers thought.

"Shit, this is going to be a rough day," Hunter mumbled while pulling into the parking lot of Cabin 13.

"There you are!" a woman called when he stepped out of his car.

Glancing to the front door, he smiled up at Mrs. Claus. "Hi, Betsy."

"You kept your promise," she said, holding her arm out to him.

"I'd never want to let you down," he assured, taking her hand as she tugged him into the building toward Abbott's office. "I truly appreciate your support."

"We always try to be supportive here. You can come anytime."

"I know that, but I won't be back. At least, not on this visit."

Betsy's footsteps halted in front of Abbott's door. "What do you mean?"

Hunter met her eyes. "I'm leaving Blue after my session today."

"But...that's not..."

He rested his hand over hers. "Betsy, I'm okay. Really. I'm not running away from anything. I'm running *toward* something. It's something I've been searching for my entire life, and I'm going to be fine. I'm going to be better than fine. I want you to know that. And I want you to know how grateful I am for all your help."

It took a few seconds, but she finally smiled. "Well, I'm sad to watch you leave so soon. But I can see how certain you are, so I'm also happy for you. I wish you the best of luck."

"Thank you."

Betsy squeezed his hand before turning away. Hunter watched her long red skirt shuffle around her black boots before he knocked on the door in front of him. He waited for the deep voice to say, "Come in."

Adrien Abbott sat behind his stately desk. "It's good to see you, Hunter. After you cancelled your last three appointments, I'd started to worry I wouldn't have the pleasure of speaking with you again."

"I'm sorry about cancelling."

"I'm just glad you're back. Would you like to have a seat?"

"Sure," he agreed, settling into the opposite chair. "I must tell you, I'm not here for a full session. I need to leave as soon as possible."

"Leave? To go where?"

"Back home."

Abbott stared at him. "You're going home today?"

"Yes. I only came to say goodbye and to thank you for your help."

"You're welcome, but you still have almost a week left at Blue. I think it would be worthwhile for you to stay, to continue therapy."

"I understand, but I have issues to attend to back home. They're things that can't wait any longer, as far as I'm concerned."

The doctor observed him from across the desk. "Honestly, I'm sorry to hear that. I think you've come a long way, but I don't think you're done."

Hunter nodded, knowing Scarlet would tell him the same thing. "You're right. I need to keep improving, and I fully intend to continue therapy when I get back to Richmond. My friend Will can help me."

Abbott frowned. "You mean Dr. William Rand."

"Yes, he's my best friend. I've told you about him before."

"I know you have, and I know William is an excellent physician. He's one of the traveling doctors who comes to Blue from time to time."

"He's the person who convinced me to come here in the first place."

"And that's wonderful, Hunter. However, I don't believe it's a good idea to continue therapy with someone you're so close to."

"Oh. That makes sense. I'll have to find another therapist when I get home."

"I could give you a recommendation," Abbott offered. "It just so happens that one of our other traveling psychiatrists at Blue lives in Richmond, too. She's an excellent therapist."

"That sounds perfect," Hunter agreed. "What's her name?"

"Dr. Tracey."

"I'm...I'm sorry. What did you say?"

"Her name is Scarlet Tracey. Dr. Scarlet Tracey."

HUNTER

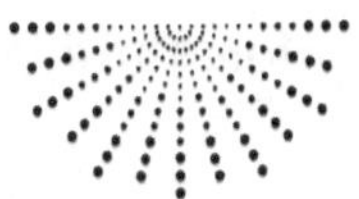

Hunter sat stiffly in Abbott's office, gawking at the man across the desk. The words still hung in the air, attached to the doctor's lips in a little cartoon balloon: *Her name is Scarlet Tracey. Dr. Scarlet Tracey.*

"Did you...did you just say...could you repeat that?"

Abbott's brow quirked. "Her name is Scarlet Tracey. She's one of the visiting physicians who travel up here to Blue to treat patients. She's actually a colleague of your friend, William. They both have offices in Richmond, although not in the same practice."

Hunter couldn't feel his arms. "Scarlet is Will's colleague."

"Yes. Occasionally, they both work here at the same time."

"Scarlet and Will work together."

"That's right."

"And she's a *doctor*."

"She is," Abbott verified, leaning forward in his chair. "Have you already met Dr. Tracey?"

As the older man's eyes pierced his, Hunter braced his spine against the back of his chair. He remembered that stern, scrutinizing glare. It was the same one his high school football coach used to give him when he showed up to morning practice bleary-eyed after a night of partying. Despite his current level of shock and confusion, he knew that look wasn't a good one.

Forcing his body to relax, Hunter met the doctor's severe gaze head on. "Yes, I've met Scarlet. She lives in Richmond."

"You met her in Richmond?"

"I've met her," he acknowledged, trying to stick to the truth.

Abbott examined him from across the desktop. Hunter kept his face as expressionless as possible until the doctor settled back in his chair.

"Well, since you already know Dr. Tracey, I suppose you shouldn't continue your therapy at home with her, either. We'll have to find another physician for you to see."

"Yes, I'll do that," Hunter agreed, jumping up from his seat. "I'll talk to Will when I get home. But right now, I really need to leave."

"I'm sorry to see you go."

He shook the man's hand before turning toward the door. "Thank you again for all your help, Dr. Abbott."

"Of course."

Hunter couldn't get out fast enough. He didn't look around him as he hurried down the hallway and out of Cabin 13's front door. He just needed to get outside. He needed fresh air, and lots of it.

The cool breeze struck him in the face the instant he stepped onto the porch. Hunter struggled to draw it into his lungs. He moved in a haze toward his Porsche, the crunching gravel rocks under his shoes barely audible over the voracious pounding of his heart.

My God, she's a doctor. Scarlet is a doctor here.

He paced in front of his car door, replaying every moment they'd spent together. It was all so obvious now: the way she spoke to him, the way she looked inside him, the way she opened him. She was a doctor here and he was a patient.

Except that Scarlet told him she was on vacation. He didn't know if that was true, but it felt true, since she'd been vulnerable with him. So vulnerable. Also, he didn't think a doctor would treat a patient the way she'd treated him.

Unless she's a sex therapist. Good Lord, is she a sex therapist?

"No," Hunter answered himself. The woman he'd been with these past weeks was a sexual innocent. She'd been exploring her own needs and desires with him. She was not a sex professional, by any means.

But if she's not a sex therapist, what the hell happened between us?

"Damn it, damn it, damn it," he grumbled, feeling like a fool for not figuring out the truth. He should have seen it. He should have known. Yet it never crossed his mind that his forest fairy could be a doctor here.

Hunter raked his hands through his hair, his brain firing thoughts as rapidly as a machine gun. Apparently, everyone on this mountain knew the truth about Scarlet. Everyone but him. He couldn't comprehend how she'd managed to keep it a secret the entire time. She'd lied to him from the moment she met him. From the very first moment to the very last.

The ache in his heart transformed swiftly to stone, stiffening his muscles and leveling his thoughts. He'd been too stunned to be angry before, but now he felt it: the surge of heat in his veins, the raw sting of betrayal behind his eyes. Scarlet never told him the truth. She'd had so many opportunities, but she'd never told him.

Then she just *left*.

Hunter needed the truth now, more than ever. Yanking open his car door, he jumped into his seat and peeled out of Cabin 13's driveway. The trip to Cabin 11 happened in the blink of an eye. Hunter leapt out of his car and onto Tyler Hensen's porch steps in an instant, prepared to slam his fist into the door over and over until the man appeared.

Hunter managed to stop himself. He froze in front of the door with his balled hand trembling. Something was wrong about all of this. He knew it the moment Abbott stared him down across his desk.

Struggling to organize his thoughts, Hunter considered the day he'd seen Tyler walking away from Scarlet's cabin. He'd been outraged to witness another man leaving her driveway, but she'd said that Tyler only needed a friendly ear. She also said he wasn't supposed to be there.

But if she's a doctor at Blue, why wasn't Tyler supposed to see her? Isn't she obligated to see patients? Isn't that what doctors do?

Hunter stared blankly at the logs before him, trying to reconcile even one of the million questions addling his brain. He didn't know much of anything at the moment, but he did know one thing: he didn't want to hurt her. Scarlet had helped him. No matter how it happened, or how many lies she'd told, she'd helped him. He didn't want to repay her by creating more problems in her life, even despite the betrayal he felt now.

Standing with wobbly legs on Tyler's porch, Hunter took huge gulps of air. He remained in place for several minutes, until he believed he could have a rational conversation with another human being without turning into the Hulk. Then he raised his hand to knock once. Or twice.

Fumbling sounds came from behind the door before it cracked open. Tyler blinked against the morning sun. "Hunter? You here already?"

"Oh, hell. I'm sorry. Did I wake you?"

Tyler yawned while straightening his shirt. "Maybe a little."

"I'm so sorry, man. I know it's early. I just really need to talk."

"Yeah, sure. Come on in."

Hunter stepped over the threshold as soon as his friend stepped back. He worked to not trample on any of the debris littered about the floor. Settling himself purposefully into a small cleared spot on the couch, he waited for Tyler to slump into the chair across from him.

"Not that I'm not happy to see you," Tyler began, swiping his hands across his eyelids, "but I have to admit, part of me hoped you wouldn't show up this morning. I hoped you'd take my advice to chase after your lady."

"I listened to your advice. I swear I did. I just..." Hunter's words trailed as he shook his head. "I actually came here today because I need to ask you a few things about one of the doctors who works up here."

"Yeah? Which one?"

"Dr. Scarlet Tracey."

"Dr. Tracey? How do you know about her?"

"I had a therapy session with Dr. Abbott this morning. I told him I plan to head back to Richmond today and he recommended Dr. Tracey as a physician I could continue my therapy with at home."

A giddy grin spread Tyler's lips. "Then you *are* leaving today?"

"That...that was the plan."

"You mean it's not the plan anymore?"

"I don't know. Maybe. But Abbott thinks I should continue therapy when I get back, so I need some information on Dr. Tracey before I go."

Tyler nodded. "Yeah, keeping up with therapy is always a good idea. And Dr. Tracey is the best. A real professional."

"I take it you've been treated by her before?"

"Oh, sure. Whenever I get the chance," Tyler confirmed, sagging further into his chair cushion. "Unfortunately, I live in New York and she lives in Richmond, so I can only see her when I come to Blue. I remember when she first started working here, straight out of her doctor-residency-thing. She was a live-in physician at Blue for almost a year before she moved away to do private practice. It didn't take her long to build up a following, even as young as she was. She has this uncanny ability to see people for who they really are. It's like she was born with Superman laser eyes that let her see straight through bullshit."

Hunter would have laughed out loud, if he were capable right now.

"I actually schedule my visits here to coincide with hers whenever possible," Tyler continued. "Although I do like to stay a bit longer than the standard three weeks, for extra relaxation time. And, you know, extra time with the ladies."

Hunter ignored his friend's suggestive eyebrow waggling. "Why do you schedule your visits to coincide with Dr. Tracey's?"

"Because she specializes in addictive personalities. I'm sure she can handle anything, but addiction is her focus. I fit right into her wheelhouse, so to speak."

"Then I suppose you had sessions with her while she was here this time? As I understand it, she's been at Blue for the past three weeks."

Tyler's mouth pulled down at the edges. "No, I didn't get to see her. I mean, I did the first week, but everything changed after the lecture."

Hunter perched at the edge of his seat. "What lecture?"

"Do you remember the first time I saw you at the gym? You asked me what I'd found missing from my life, and I told you I found appreciation?"

"Yeah, I remember."

"Well, that came from Dr. Tracey's lecture. All the patients had gathered to hear her speak at the end of her first week. She gave an amazing talk about appreciating the beauty of life – about appreciating all the little things around us. It was a wonderful, inspiring speech, and we were all so excited by it. But at the end of the lecture, she announced she wasn't going to see any more patients during her visit this time."

Hunter's heart stopped. "Why not?"

"Because she was taking a vacation."

"Really? She's been on vacation for the past two weeks?"

"She has. Honestly, it's the strangest thing. I've never known a doctor to take a vacation here among the patients. But she let us know, as soon as she finished her talk, that she wouldn't be seeing any of us until the next time she came back to Blue. Dr. Abbott was at her lecture, too, and he confirmed that no one would be able to have any sessions with her for the remainder of the time she was here."

Hunter's heart surged back to life. "So, she really wasn't treating any patients for the last two weeks?"

Tyler shrugged. "Not as far as I know. And it really pissed me off, too. When you travel all this way to see a specific doctor, you should be able to see them."

"Yeah, I guess that's...yeah."

"But I can see her point of view, I suppose. Everyone needs a vacation, right? Although I never really thought of her as needing one."

"Why wouldn't you think she needs one?"

"Because she's so straight-laced and organized. She's one of those people who obviously has her life in perfect order. I guess that's why patients like me flock to her. We all have these messy, addictive personalities, and she's a pillar of order and professionalism. In truth, I've always aspired to be just like her."

Hunter stared the words out of his friend's mouth. None of it could be true. Those words didn't describe his freebird. Not at all.

"I was genuinely surprised to hear her give a lecture on appreciating life," Tyler added. "That speech wasn't what I've come to expect from her. She's always been a positive person, but normally so reserved. I'd even go so far as to call her anal-retentive. I mean, you should have seen her cutting up her steak."

"Her steak? What do you mean?"

"Oh, it was really something. I went to see her about a week ago, even though I wasn't supposed to. Do you remember how messed up I was the morning after Jocelyn left?"

"I do. You looked like a kicked puppy when I saw you at the gym."

"Yeah, well, I really needed someone to talk to. I mean, don't get me wrong, it was nice talking to you. But I needed professional advice, so I went to Dr. Tracey's cabin that afternoon. I'd figured out which one was hers, by process of elimination. It felt kind of naughty, going to see her when I knew I wasn't supposed to. I liked it. A lot."

Hunter stiffened with his friend's inglorious smile. "What happened when you arrived at her cabin?"

"She said I wasn't supposed to be there. She said it'd be unethical for her to treat me while she was on vacation. But I begged her to listen, so she did. She gave me a few minutes of her time, to get the load off of my back. And the entire time I spoke, she was busy cutting up a filet mignon into teeny, tiny pieces. That steak looked so delicious, I wanted to just dig in. But she meticulously dissected it, arranging only the best bites onto a proper china plate. So damn weird."

Hunter's fingers twitched with memories he couldn't afford to dwell on right at this moment. "So, Dr. Tracey listened to you when you asked her? She helped you even though she wasn't supposed to?"

"Sure. I knew she would. She has that need to help people. It's a marvelous thing, how some doctors have that urge, no matter what. She listened to me and she gave me sound advice. Of course, I don't ever take that advice. Maybe if I saw her all the time, I'd learn to fix myself. But my therapist back home isn't very good. Great legs, though."

"Wait...who?"

"Who what?"

"Who has great legs?"

"Oh. My therapist back home," Tyler clarified. "She's hot. Don't get me wrong, Dr. Tracey has awesome legs herself. It's just too bad they're connected to such a frigid body, if you know what I mean."

Hunter fisted his hands against his thighs. "Frigid body?"

"Yeah, man. Believe me, I've tried to unfreeze that ice. But it's like she never even notices me flirting with her."

"You *flirt* with her?" he growled, ignoring the pain of his own fingernails digging into his palms.

"Well, sure. I've tried to come on to her plenty of times."

Hunter's entire body bristled. He couldn't stand the thought of Tyler touching her. He couldn't fathom any other man ever touching her.

"I used to tell her all about my sexual encounters," Tyler continued, oblivious to the rage swelling inside the man on his couch. "I would go into a *lot* of detail, to see if I could get a reaction. I wanted to see her eyes widen, or a blush on her cheeks – anything. But she never changed her expression while I confessed my sins. Not once. I know she treats a lot of sex addicts, so she hears that crap all the time, but I thought my blatant descriptions would be enough to rattle her."

Hunter nearly bit through his tongue.

Tyler sighed. "But she gave me nothing. No reaction whatsoever. Hell, you think Mitzi is an ice queen? She's got nothing on that cold-ass doctor. I honestly don't know if Scarlet Tracey has ever spread her legs. What she needs is some good, old-fashioned, in-and-out fuck..."

"Damn it, Tyler! Stop! Stop talking about her like that! Or I swear to God I will beat the living shit out of you!"

Tyler's mouth fell open. "Oh. Wow. Sorry, man. I'll stop."

Hunter attempted to reign himself in. "No, I – I shouldn't have threatened you. I just...I can't even..."

The silence stretched between them. Tyler's eyes grew wider by the second. A choking sound escaped his throat before he spoke. "My God. It's *her*, isn't it? The woman you're in love with? It's Dr. Tracey."

Hunter squeezed his hands together. "Yeah, it's her. It's Scarlet."

"She's the woman you've been with for the past two weeks?"

"Yes."

"Oh," Tyler croaked. He sat very still, staring at him across the living room. A moment later, his head shook. Almost imperceptibly at first. But then harder and harder. "Fuck, Hunter. Fuck, fuck, fuck. This isn't good. This is actually really, really bad. Shit. *Shit*. Please tell me you didn't say anything to him."

"Who?"

"Abbott!" Tyler leapt from his chair to pace the cluttered floor. "Holy hell! Tell me you didn't say anything to Abbott about the two of you! I can't lose her! None of us can!"

"What are you saying? Would Abbott fire her if he found out?"

Tyler stopped dead in his tracks, panic running over his face. "You don't understand. He wouldn't just fire her. He would bring her up on malpractice charges and make sure she never worked as a doctor again anywhere. And I can't even begin to tell you how many people that would hurt. We rely on her, man. We *all* rely on her."

Hunter's stomach sank to his feet. "I didn't say anything to Abbott. Not a word, I swear. I don't want to hurt anyone."

"Thank God," Tyler breathed, collapsing back into his chair. "I still don't get how it happened, though. I know you haven't been in therapy before, but sexual relationships between doctors and patients are so forbidden, it's beyond words. It's what always made it fun for me to flirt with her, since I knew she'd never accept my advances. But now, knowing what she did with you, I'm just so fucking stunned. I can't comprehend what made her cross that line. The Dr. Tracey I know would never break the rules like that. She'd never do anything to jeopardize a patient."

"I was not her patient, goddamnit!" Hunter hollered again, unable to control the volume of his voice. "She wasn't working as a doctor the past two weeks! She was on vacation! And Abbott knew it!"

Tyler held his hands up in surrender. "Okay, buddy. It's okay. I see where you're coming from."

"Do you really?"

"Yeah, I really do. But as much as I hate to tell you this, it won't matter to Abbott. He's strictly by-the-book. And Scarlet is normally so perfect. So straight and narrow. I'm just...I'm completely confused. Why in the hell would she do something this reckless?"

Hunter stared at his friend, already knowing the answer.

She did it because I needed her. And because she needed me.

Hunter's pulse raced beyond control. The room spun around him, making his stomach lurch. All he wanted was to see her, to touch her, to hold her. He needed to look into his freebird's adoring eyes, and watch her lips pull up in a loving smile, and feel the soothing softness of her skin. That would calm him. That would set his world right again.

He shifted restlessly against the couch, despising the fact that he was still stuck on this godforsaken mountain. "I can't stay here anymore, Tyler. I have to find her. Now. Do you have the address to her office?"

"Yeah, yeah, I have it," he answered, rising from his chair to grab his wallet off the kitchen counter. He shuffled through several business cards before grasping one and turning back.

Hunter stood and reached out his hand.

Tyler started to give him the card, but pulled back. "Wait a minute."

"Wait? For what?"

"It's just...you're so angry today, Hunter. I've never seen you like this, not even when you first came to Blue. I want to know why."

His breath hissed through clenched teeth. "I'm trying very hard to be polite right now, Tyler. Please just give me the *goddamn* card."

"Not until you tell me why you're so *goddamn* angry."

Hunter fisted his hands at his sides, his entire body vibrating, until the words finally exploded from his throat. "It's because she never told me! Two weeks we were together! In every way! But Scarlet never told me she was a fucking doctor! And I think I had the right to know!"

Tyler's jaw dropped. "Oh. Well, shit. That…that is bad."

"Yeah," Hunter huffed. "It is."

"You know, maybe I shouldn't give you her address. Seeing her now may not be the best thing for either of you. You should take some time to calm down first."

"I don't need time. If you don't give it to me, I'll find her myself."

"Hunter, why don't you…"

"Just give me the card," he growled.

Tyler puffed out his chest and looked him squarely in the eye. "I'm not giving you this until you swear to me that you won't hurt her."

"What?"

"I want you to say the words! Swear you won't hurt her!"

Hunter observed his friend's brave front. He knew this man – who'd said such crass things about a cold-ass doctor just moments ago – would fight like hell to defend her honor. He stared at his rigid stance for one more moment before heaving a sigh.

"God, Tyler, I would *never* hurt her. I *love* her. I am madly, wildly in love with her and you know that. And yes, I'm pissed as hell right now, but that doesn't change how I feel about her. I swear to you, I will never hurt Scarlet in any way, shape, or form. I just need to see her again. I just need her. Please help me. *Please*."

"Well, damn, man. You really are in love with her, aren't you?"

"Yes. I really am."

"Okay, then." Tyler handed over the card with a firm nod. "I want you to know, as far as I'm concerned, this conversation never happened. I won't mention a word of it to anyone. Ever. If that woman loves you as much as you love her, and you find a way to make things work, rest assured I won't tell anyone what happened between you up here. Your secret will go with me to my grave."

"Thank you," Hunter said, taking the business card in one hand and shaking his friend's hand with the other. "Seriously. Thank you."

"Of course."

"I'm sorry I yelled at you."

"Eh, no worries. I probably deserved it. I just want you to be happy. And I'd love to see Scarlet happy, too."

Hunter smiled for the first time. "That's all I want," he assured, glancing down at the business card he now held. He read the first line: *Dr. Scarlet Tracey, Richmond Psychiatric Partners*. Next, he read her address. Then he read it again. And again.

"Good Lord, Tyler. Is this her...her office?"

"Yeah. I mean, I've never been there, but that's the address."

"No, but...you don't understand. This building is across the street from Gregory Global. I can see this building from *my* office."

"Well, that's good, right? It means you won't have far to go."

Hunter looked back to his friend, painfully aware that those words weren't remotely true. Scarlet knew he was the CEO of Gregory Global, which meant she also knew they'd be right across the street from each other when they returned to the real world, and yet she'd still left without telling him the truth. Which meant he actually had a long, long way to go if he was ever going to change her mind.

Hunter spun toward the door. "Thanks again, Tyler. I won't forget this. You've been a real friend to me."

"You've done the same for me. Maybe I can give you a call if Hensen Incorporated decides to open that Richmond branch?"

"Yes. Please do."

"Great. And I promise I won't ever flirt with your woman again."

Hunter stiffened when he arrived on the porch. "I think that's best."

"I do, too," Tyler agreed with a chuckle.

Stepping to his Porsche, Hunter smiled and waved goodbye to his friend. Once the cabin door shut, he dropped down into the driver's seat of his car. He sat, alone and still, and stared at Scarlet's business card.

Dr. Scarlet Tracey. The woman who'd opened him up and turned his whole world upside down. The woman who'd risked losing her entire livelihood in order to help him. The woman who might actually think of him as her patient.

Hunter shuddered. Reaching into his glove box, he grabbed his dead cell phone and plugged it into his car charger. He set Scarlet's business card in the seat beside him, started the engine, and pulled back out onto the main road, headed straight toward her office.

He honestly didn't know what he intended to say when he saw her. And he didn't have a clue how she'd reply. He only knew he needed to look her in the eyes when she finally told him the truth.

Hunter passed the entrance to Scarlet's Cabin 10, and his own Cabin 9, as he made his way off the mountain. When the information cabin eventually showed up on his right, he grudgingly pulled the car over for one final stop on his way out. He glared at the worn wooden entry marker – *Welcome to Blissful Blue Retreat* – before killing the engine.

After jumping out of his seat and plodding up the gravel, he yanked open the front door. The pine and cinnamon scents still accosted his nose when he stepped inside. The fireplace still glowed. And the little gnome still sat behind the desk.

"Well, hello there, Hunter. Good to see you."

"Pete," Hunter acknowledged, barely containing his sense of betrayal as he moved toward Blue's kindly old caretaker.

"What brings you to my neck of the woods?"

"I'm leaving today. I'm here to check out."

Pete raised one bushy gray eyebrow. "You're checking out? That's surprising. Don't you have another week with us?"

Hunter stared the gnome down. "Yes, I do. And don't pretend you don't know I'm checking out, since I'm sure Betsy already told you."

Pete observed him with a keen eye before resting his hands on the desktop. "Betsy did call to let me know. She's concerned about you."

"Well, I wish everyone around here would stop *lying* to me in the name of *concern*," Hunter huffed, shuffling his feet against the log floor.

"Hmm," Pete considered, tapping his finger to his chin. "Seems to me you've got a lot on your mind. Maybe leaving isn't the best thing."

"No, it definitely is. I have to get out of here. I have to head back home. I have to see her, and..."

"Who do you have to see?"

Hunter clamped his lips shut, staring down at the ground before meeting the man's eyes once again. "God, you're right. I have a hell of a lot on my mind."

"You want to talk about it?"

"I do. I want to ask you so many things, if you'll let me. But first, I need to know you'll keep our conversation in strictest confidence. You have to do that anyway, don't you? Because I'm a guest here?"

"Yes, Hunter. But I would keep our conversation in confidence even if you weren't a guest. I can promise you that."

"Then I'd like for you to tell me about Dr. Tracey."

"Scarlet?" Pete asked, his languorous voice hanging on her name. "She's wonderful. One of the best physicians who ever comes up here."

"And how would you describe her? Her personality, I mean."

"Well...I guess I would say she's soft. Soft and lovely and kind."

"Soft and kind? Not uptight and straight-laced and cold?"

"Cold? Goodness, no. Scarlet is a sweetheart. She's like a daughter to me, to tell you the truth. To me and Betsy both. We just love her. She's very easy to love."

Hunter closed his eyes, needing a moment to catch his breath before refocusing on the older man. "Can I ask you another question, Pete?"

"Sure thing."

"Several days ago, did Scarlet ask you for a rope?"

"Seeing as you already seem to know the answer, I'll admit she did."

"Did you ask why she needed it?"

"She said it was for a trust-building exercise."

"With a patient?"

"I assumed so."

Hunter's gut lurched. "No. She wasn't seeing any patients for the past two weeks. She was on vacation."

"Yeah, she was on vacation. But it didn't surprise me that she was still trying to help someone, even if she wasn't getting paid for it."

"So, you just gave her a rope? Up on a mountain full of psychiatric patients, you gave her a rope simply because she asked?"

"I did."

"Did you give her a hammer and nail to hang a picture in her cabin?"

"I sure did."

"And if she'd asked you for a shotgun and a chainsaw, would you have given her those, too?"

Pete chuckled. "I believe I would have. I trust that woman. I trust her with my life. Honestly, I'd trust Scarlet Tracey with anyone's life."

Hunter held his breath, waiting for the man to say something else about all of this. But the little gnome simply sat in silence. "Aren't you going to ask me how I know so much about Scarlet, Pete?"

"Nope. I'm not."

"Why not?"

"Because you said you wanted to talk in confidence, and I figure the less I know, the more confidential this can be. I don't intend to utter a word about this conversation ever again. Not to anyone."

Hunter studied the caretaker for another minute, working to grasp all the scraps of information slamming into his brain from moment to moment. As he stood, he absorbed the even, easy temperament of the man before him. "I'm sorry if it seems like I'm grilling you. I don't mean to be rude. I really do appreciate everything you've done for me."

"I know you do. I hope you found what you were looking for here."

Hunter sealed his lips, unaware of how to reply at the moment.

"I remember, you know," Pete assured in his silence. "I remember how strange everything felt the first time I came to Blue as a patient."

"You...you were a patient here?"

"I sure was. I used to have a big job in a big city, just like you. I was the CFO of a huge financial institution. I spent too much time at the office, and not enough time with the people who matter, and eventually I lost my marriage because of it. Then my daughter got sick. She got really sick with cancer, and she died at the age of thirty-two. When I lost her, I lost myself. That's when I came here for the first time. Then I came back again, and again, until I decided to stay."

Hunter gripped the edge of Pete's desk as he listened. "God, I'm sorry. I'm so sorry about your daughter."

"Thank you. It's been several years, and I still miss her every day, but everything heals with time."

Everything heals with time. Hunter knew those words. Scarlet had assured him of that. She'd said so many things to him – so many beautiful, wonderful things – and he wanted to hear them again. He wanted to hear the luster of her voice, and the ringing of her laughter, and the sweetness of her whispers and moans.

"I'm glad you found what you were looking for here," Hunter told the caretaker. "I did, too. I found what I was looking for."

"I'm glad. Now hold onto it with both hands and don't let go."

"I promise. Goodbye, Pete. I'll see you again someday."

"That sounds like a plan to me. Be sure to take care of yourself, Hunter. And always take care of the people you love."

He gave the kind old man one last smile before leaving the warmth of the welcome cabin. As he walked away, Pete's words roiled in his brain. Hunter wanted to take care of Scarlet. But would she let him? Would she let him take care of her now, after she'd taken care of him since the moment they met?

He shivered as he stepped outside, fearing the truth of how Dr. Tracey saw him. He didn't want to believe she'd ever thought of him as her patient. Not that he wasn't a patient here – he most certainly was – but not *her* patient. He believed they'd *both* come here for help.

"Damn it," Hunter cursed for the thousandth time today.

Gravel crunching beneath tires caught his ears. His eyes darted up to see the Blissful Blue food truck park beside his Porsche. Colin dropped out of the driver's seat, starting up the path toward the welcome cabin.

"Hey there," he greeted as he strode forward.

Hunter pinned his eyes on the boy in the red hoodie.

Colin fiddled with the folded piece of paper he carried in his hand. "Are you heading back to Richmond now?"

Hunter didn't answer the question. He just glared.

The boy stopped in his tracks. "What's wrong, Hunter?"

"I think you know what's wrong," he answered, giving the boy the same stern look Abbott had given him earlier today.

"Oh," Colin said, his face falling. "I guess this is about Scarlet?"

"Damn straight it is. You do know she's a doctor, right?"

"Yeah, I know."

"And you know she kept that fact a secret from me?"

"I do. She...she told me she didn't want you to know."

Hunter shook his head, hating to hear those words, even though he felt grateful for the truth. "Did you at least her ask why?"

"No, I didn't."

"Why not? Why wouldn't you question her reasons?"

Colin squared his shoulders. "Because I trust her. That woman has a gift. There are a lot of doctors in this world, but only a few have a way with people that defies explanation. Scarlet is one of them. She helped me from the moment we met. I never paid her. I could never afford her. But she helped me anyway, because that's just who she is. And I'm positive – absolutely positive – that whatever her reasons were for not telling you, they must have been pretty damn good."

Hunter huffed out a laugh, unable to remain upset with the earnest young man standing before him. Instead, he glanced down to the paper in his hand. "What is that you're carrying, Colin?"

"It's my letter of resignation. I came here to give it to Pete. But maybe I shouldn't, in case you want your check back."

"Why would I want my check back?"

"Because I didn't tell you the truth about her."

"God, no," Hunter sighed. "I'm certainly not going to hold a grudge against you, especially when all you've ever done is try to help me. Only an asshole would do that. And I'm not an asshole."

Colin grinned. "I know you're not."

"Go turn in your resignation," Hunter instructed. "And cash the check. I'm headed out, but I hope to see you when you finish school."

"You will. I promise."

"Good," he said, patting Colin's shoulder before moving to his car.

"So, does knowing the truth change anything?"

Hunter halted in place, turning to meet the boy's steadfast gaze. "What do you mean?"

"Are you still going after Scarlet? Now that you know the truth?"

Hunter fisted his keys. "Yes, I'm still going after her."

"I'm glad," Colin said, although the look of concern on his face hadn't diminished at all. "I know I probably don't have the right to ask, but could you promise me something, Hunter?"

"What's that?"

"Will you listen to her? Will you take the time to really listen to whatever she has to say about all this?"

"Of course, Colin. I fully intend to listen to her."

"That's wonderful. Really wonderful. But..."

"But what?"

"I'm afraid it'll be an uphill battle to change her mind. Scarlet has one hell of a mind."

"Believe me, I know," Hunter agreed, shoving one hand roughly through his hair. "I'm fully aware that it will be an uphill battle. It's just going to be a steeper incline than I originally thought."

"Well, I'm definitely rooting for you. I don't have pom-poms with me or anything, but if I did, I would shake them."

Hunter chuckled. "I appreciate the thought. Now stop talking to me and go talk to Pete. You have things of your own to accomplish."

"I'm going right now. Good luck."

"Good luck to you, too," Hunter replied, settling into his Porsche for the long ride home.

～

THE JOURNEY down the mountain was bumpy, both from the spare tire and his turbulent thoughts. Hunter could hardly reconcile everything he'd learned about Scarlet today. The strangest part wasn't even her being a doctor – it was learning how Tyler, Pete, and Colin saw her.

She was a different person to each of these men. To Colin she was a home, representing the stability he'd lost. To Pete she was a daughter, fulfilling a missing piece of his heart. To Tyler she was order and perfection, a goal to strive toward in his unorganized, unbalanced life.

Apparently, Dr. Tracey became whoever her patients needed her to be in order to heal themselves. Which left Hunter to wonder if she'd become the person he'd needed for the time he'd needed her. If that were true, then she'd only ever been an actress playing a role for him. If that were true, then he never knew the real Scarlet at all.

He shook his head, barely noticing the evergreens flying past his car as he sped toward her. Hunter refused to believe that Scarlet had only been acting with him. He'd seen her. He'd seen the real her. He'd watched her struggle with the two sides of herself, the frolicking freebird versus the solemn doctor. He'd been front and center – the only audience member to witness that epic battle.

Maybe Scarlet had started their relationship with the intention of being his doctor, whether he wanted it or not. Maybe she'd started as an actress in a role, playing mind games and telling far-fetched lies, in order to open him. But from the night she'd promised not to lie to him anymore, she became herself. She let him see her struggles. She allowed herself to be truly vulnerable. And she let herself feel for him.

His little bird fell in love with him, just like he fell for her. They'd seen and embraced the most real versions of each other, and that wasn't something Hunter felt the need to be ashamed of. On the contrary, he believed a truth like that should be celebrated every second of every day.

He smiled despite the uncertainties that lay before him. He knew this war with Dr. Tracey was going to be an uphill battle, but he was perfectly willing to fight it. And he *would* win.

When Bottom-of-Blissful-Blue town appeared on the horizon, Hunter wanted to ignore it. He wanted to drive straight back to Richmond, go directly to Scarlet's office, barge his way in, tell her he knew she was a doctor and didn't care that she'd lied about it, and assure her they could live happily ever after from this day forward.

Unfortunately, he wasn't going to get what he wanted. First, because his wobbly spare tire barely made it down the mountain and into the parking lot of the mechanic. Second, because he *did* care that she'd lied about being a doctor. He needed to hear her explanations, and understand her reasoning, so they could truly live happily ever after.

The moment he parked in front of the auto shop, he went inside to speak to the mechanic in charge. Hunter offered a ridiculous amount of money to have his car fixed immediately, and the grizzled man was more than happy to oblige. He grabbed his cell and stepped around the side of the building while Earl pulled his Porsche into the repair bay.

Hunter paced back and forth beside the store's white-painted bricks, holding onto Scarlet's business card and staring at the phone number he already knew by heart. Eventually, he forced himself to stand still in the deserted alley. Then he dialed the number to her office.

After several rings, a woman's stern voice came across the line. "Richmond Psychiatric Partners, how may I direct your call?"

Hunter cleared his throat. "I need to make an appointment."

"Certainly, Sir. Do you know which doctor you'd like to see?"

"Dr. Scarlet Tracey."

"Of course. I'll direct you to her assistant. One moment please."

He heard a few seconds of music – an instrumental version of an old Rolling Stones song – before a different female voice addressed him. "Hello, this is Marie. How may I help you today?"

This woman sounded older, and soft and pleasant, and he smiled. "Hello, Marie. I need to make an appointment to see Dr. Tracey."

"I can certainly help you with that. Can I have your name, please?"

"Yeah, sure, it's um..." Hunter looked up to the trees in the distance. "Forest. Mick Forest."

"Okay, Mr. Forest. I assume you're new to Dr. Tracey's practice?"

"I am. Is that a problem?"

"No, that will be fine," Marie replied as Hunter listened to the clack of computer keys in the background. "Very good, then, Mr. Forest. Dr. Tracey's next appointment is in nine weeks."

"*Nine weeks?*"

"Yes. She recently returned from vacation and her schedule is heavy."

He shook his head. "I need to see her sooner than nine weeks."

"Well, if you're flexible with your choice, I could redirect you to Dr. Asa."

"Who?"

"Dr. Asa. He's one of Dr. Tracey's partners. I assure you he's very good, and should have an opening sooner."

"No, that won't do. I need to see Dr. Tracey as soon as possible."

"Well, I wish I could assist you, but..."

Panic rose in his chest. "You don't understand. I *have* to see her."

"I'm sorry, but that just isn't feasible right now."

Hunter closed his eyes. *Please forgive me for what I'm about to do.*

"I really need your help here, Marie. If I don't see Dr. Tracey today, I think something bad will happen to me."

The woman inhaled sharply. "Mr. Forest, if you're having thoughts of harming yourself, I implore you to go to the nearest hospital."

Fisting Scarlet's business card, he sighed. "I have no plans to hurt myself. I just have to see her today. Please. *Please.*"

"Can you...can you hold on? I want to see what I can do for you."

"Yes, I'll wait. Thank you."

The elevator music returned to his ear. Hunter resumed pacing beside the white bricks, trying to keep his mind blank. When the woman returned to the line after several minutes, he held his breath.

"Okay, Mr. Forest. Dr. Tracey says she'll be able to work you in at the end of her sessions today. Can you be here at 5:30 this evening?"

"Yes, absolutely. Thank you, Marie."

"Will you be safe until then?"

"I will. Thank you again."

"Of course. We'll see you at 5:30, Mr. Forest."

Marie hung up. Hunter stood entirely still, listening to the silence on the other end. He couldn't believe what he'd just said in order to see Scarlet. Then again, desperate times called for desperate measures.

Pressing his eyes shut, he leaned back against the cool bricks. He wondered what Dr. William Rand would think of all this. He feared what his best friend would say if he knew how low Hunter had stooped to get what he needed.

"Will, buddy, I miss you," he thought aloud, picturing the man he loved like a brother. Hunter couldn't wait to see his friend again. He also couldn't wait to see his goddaughter, Evie. And he truly couldn't wait until he and Scarlet could have their first dinner with Will and Maggie. Anticipation built as Hunter imagined introducing his girlfriend to his best friend. He imagined watching the happiness on Will's face when he realized he already knew the woman Hunter loved.

"Good God, Will already knows Scarlet," Hunter reiterated out loud, his spine stiffening against the brick wall as he considered that truth. "He's know her for years, according to Abbott. Hell, did Will know Scarlet would be at Blue with me? Did he intend for the two of us to meet? Was this all some sort of elaborate matchmaking scheme?"

Hunter grasped hard to his phone. "No. That's a ridiculous thought. Will wouldn't do that. He's strictly by-the-book, just like Abbott. He wouldn't encourage a relationship between a doctor and a patient. Or...or would he?"

Hunter's fingers began dialing his friend's number before he had the chance to think it through. Will's phone rang only once.

"Hunter? Is that you?"

"Yeah, it's me. Man, it's great to hear your voice. Is this a good time? I didn't interrupt your work, did I?"

"I'm between patients right now," Will assured. "It's great to hear you, too, although I didn't think you'd call for another week. I know cell phones don't work at Blissful Blue."

"Yeah, I'm...I'm not at Blue anymore."

"What do you mean you're not at Blue?"

"I left today. I'm coming home early."

Will's deep laugh emanated over the phone. "Well, damn. You couldn't do it, could you? You couldn't let go, even for three weeks."

"That's not true. I let go, Will. You have no idea how much. I met someone up at Blue – someone who changed my whole life – and I'm coming home now because I'm finally ready to live that life."

"Wow, man. That sounds pretty wonderful. I mean, it sounds really fast, but still wonderful. Can I ask who changed your life?"

Hunter smiled at the tree line in the distance. "Her name is Scarlet."

"Scarlet? Do you mean Dr. Tracey? Was she up there with you?"

"Yeah, she was. I take it you didn't know she was up here?"

"No, I didn't."

"Really? You *swear* you didn't know?"

"What's that supposed to mean?"

"It's...it's nothing. She just told me you two know each other."

"Yeah, we do. She and I work at Blue together from time to time. Occasionally, we see each other here in Richmond, too."

"But you didn't know she'd be up here with me?"

"No, Hunter, I don't keep track of her schedule. However, I am glad she was there to help you. Did you attend some of her lectures?"

"Um, yeah. You could say that. Listen, Will, do you think I could see you sometime soon? I'd really love to talk to you in person."

"Sure, anytime. You know where I live."

"I do. Thank you. For everything. I'll let you get back to work."

"Okay, then. Take care of yourself."

"You, too."

Hunter exhaled as he ended the call, still staring out at the line of trees leading to Blissful Blue. He struggled to comprehend how Scarlet could work across the street from him, and be colleagues with his best friend, yet remain a stranger until the day his car blew a tire on the side of a mountain. He'd never believed in Fate, but he had to wonder if these trees had been trying to tell him something when they sent a squirrel out of the underbrush to leap in front of his car.

"Mr. Gregory?" a gruff voice called from around the corner.

Hunter stepped away from the side of the building. "Yes, Earl?"

The mechanic gave him a lazy smile. "I think everything is good for travel down the mountain now. You're all set to go back home."

"Thank you. I'm sure you're right."

～

THE TRIP back to Richmond took several hours. Hunter stopped only once to grab a bite to eat, lamenting the fact that it wasn't gourmet, nor delivered to his door. Otherwise, he passed the lengthy drive listening to music. As soon as he could get a satellite radio signal, he tuned into the all-Elvis channel and sang along to the songs he knew by heart.

When he finally arrived on the street where he'd worked nearly every day for the past dozen years, his instinct was to turn into the parking lot of Gregory Global. But he didn't. He made a left instead, pulling into the parking garage beneath Scarlet's office building.

Hunter had arrived a few minutes early for his appointment, but he couldn't stay in his car any longer. As he walked through the parking area to the first floor, he drank in his surroundings. Security guards waited just past the front entry doors, instructing him to remove his keys and watch in order to pass through the metal detectors. The burly guards observed him with keen eyes while he cleared the detectors, but Hunter merely nodded at them, reassured by the safety of Scarlet's workplace.

After retrieving his personal effects, he found a restroom near the elevator. He spent a moment checking his appearance in the mirror, recognizing the same face he'd seen the day he arrived at Blue, with the same crinkles at the corners of his eyes. But this face didn't look worn and weary anymore. And the crinkles looked more like laugh lines.

He smiled at his reflection before exiting the washroom. With Scarlet's business card in hand, he verified her office suite number while stepping onto the elevator. His stomach flipped as he pushed the button for the 17th floor and stood in place, waiting as patiently as possible.

When the *ding* announced his arrival, Hunter clenched his fingers and stepped out into a long hallway. He turned to the right and walked to the end of the hall, finding an opaque glass door that read: *Dr. Scarlet Tracey, Richmond Psychiatric Partners*. Sucking in a deep, fortifying breath, he reached for the handle and stepped inside.

The waiting area was bright and homey, with floor-to-ceiling windows that showcased the city skyline in the glowing evening sunset. Two couches lay at angles before the windows, and a reception desk sat to his right. The thin, middle-aged woman behind the desk jumped up.

"Mr. Forest? Is that you?"

"Yes, hello," Hunter offered, trying to soothe her obviously frazzled nerves with a warm smile. "Are you Marie?"

"I am," she acknowledged, walking over to shake his hand. "I'm so glad you got here safely."

He gave her small hand a gentle squeeze before releasing it. "I did. I'm sorry I'm a bit early."

"Oh, no, that's okay. Dr. Tracey still has a patient with her now, but it should just be few moments until she's available. You can fill out some paper-work for me while you're waiting."

"Paperwork?" he questioned, as if he'd never been to a doctor's office before. *Of course there's paperwork, Hunter.*

"Yes, let me just grab that." Marie pushed her short brown hair behind her ears as she turned back to her desk.

He observed the woman while she bustled around, gathering a pen and clipboard along with several forms. Hunter felt increasingly guilty about the lies he'd told her, since he would be seeing this woman quite a lot in the future. Sooner or later, she would have to know the truth.

"Here you are, Mick," Marie said when she stepped back to him and handed over the paperwork. "Is it okay if I call you Mick?"

"Um, sure."

"Wonderful. Please fill in the first two forms completely, and initial the third form here, here, and here, then answer the questions on the fourth page. If you have your insurance card with you, I can take that."

"You need my insurance card?"

"Yes, if you have it with you."

"I – I don't," Hunter lied again.

"Oh, well, do you want to bring me that information later?"

"I guess so."

Marie's face softened. "Do you need financial assistance, Mick? I assure you, it won't be a problem if you do. Dr. Tracey has programs in place for patients who are unable to pay. She also runs a free clinic downtown, for both individual and group therapy sessions."

"She runs a free clinic, too?"

"Yes. Do you need information on that?"

"No, it's...I'll just pay cash. Is cash okay?"

"Of course," Marie said, gesturing to the couch. "Why don't you have a seat? You can make yourself comfortable while you wait."

Hunter eased down into the couch cushions, staring at the clipboard in his hand. He wrote his fake name at the top of the first form, but tried to answer everything else truthfully. After all, he was perfectly fine with Scarlet having his real address and phone number. He actually wanted her to become very familiar with that information, the sooner the better.

When he came to the fourth piece of paper, he realized it was some sort of basic psychological assessment. He read the first question at the top of the page: *How are you feeling today?*

Hunter stared at those words long and hard, trying to decide the most truthful answer. Honestly, he felt a hundred different things right now. He was angry still, at least a little, that Scarlet lied to him about being a doctor. He was also excited, eager to see her now with that truth exposed in stark light. He was curious, too, wondering how she would respond when she realized he'd come for her. And he was nervous, not knowing just how hard she would fight him.

Yet, as Hunter waited impatiently to walk back into her life, what he felt most was the pull – the undeniable draw he always felt toward her, from the first moment they met. His Scarlet sat on the other side of the wall before him, and he just wanted to see her, plain and simple.

Putting his pen to paper, Hunter jotted a few things down. He wasn't entirely sure of everything he wrote, but he did get through to the end of the questionnaire. Then he walked the clipboard back to Marie.

She smiled at him from behind her desk. "Thank you, Mick. Here's your bill."

He read over the paper she handed him. His eyes bulged a bit, since he couldn't believe how expensive it was to have an appointment with Dr. Tracey. *No wonder Colin can't afford her.*

Reaching into his wallet, Hunter pulled out several hundred-dollar bills and handed them to Marie. He honestly didn't care how much this cost. He would throw a million dollars on the desk right now if it meant he could finally see his little bird in the real world.

After Marie took his money and handed him a receipt, Hunter went back to sit on the couch. He tapped his fingers together as he watched Marie enter information in her computer. His leg bounced up and down.

He felt too much like a patient right now. Sitting in this waiting room, with a receptionist and paperwork and all manner of formalities, was how it felt to be Scarlet's patient. But this wasn't what existed between them up on that mountain. He wasn't her patient at Blue, damn it. No matter what anyone else thought.

A moment later, the large mahogany door to the right of Marie's desk swung open. Another woman emerged, this one far younger than him, with eyelids swollen as if she'd been crying. She barely glanced in his direction before turning toward the reception desk.

"Can I make my next appointment, Marie?"

"Certainly, Cindy. Give me just a moment."

Marie lifted her head back to Hunter, motioning her hand toward the door. "You may go in for your session now, Mick."

Hunter nodded and stood. His palms dampened as he stepped toward the inner office. His pulse tripped when he pulled open the door.

The last time he'd seen his Scarlet, she'd been naked and curled up against his chest. She'd made love to him, with all of her heart and body and soul, and fell asleep in his arms. Warm, soft, and peaceful.

Hunter stepped quietly into the back of her huge, elongated office, easing the door shut behind him without making a sound. The first thing he noted was that her office reminded him of Blue. It was vast and spacious, with the walls paneled in the same dark mahogany as the door, and there were plants – so many, many plants – from floor to ceiling. A pristine leather couch lay some yards before him, then several chairs, then an oversized desk with a laptop on it.

Scarlet sat behind the laptop with her eyes focused on the screen.

Hunter remained standing in the back of the room, wholly unnoticed, and watched her. Less than two days had passed since he'd laid eyes on his forest fairy, but it felt like forever. The last time he'd gone this long without seeing her, he'd only made it thirty-six hours before desperation kicked in. This time, he'd made it just slightly longer.

Scarlet's fingers flew across the computer keyboard while she typed. She remained oblivious to the fact that he'd entered the room, so he listened to the click of the keys while observing her. His freebird looked just as he remembered, mostly. Her skin was still a perfect cream, her lips still a gorgeous pink, her eyes still bright as jewels. She wore her hair up in a ponytail today, like she had the last day they were together at Blue. But now, she also wore glasses.

Hunter cleared his throat. "I didn't know you wore glasses."

Scarlet stopped typing.

He watched her chest rise on a sharp inhale. He watched her fingers tremble as she closed the lid of her laptop. He watched her bite into her lip before focusing on him across the expanse of the room.

"I only wear them when I read."

"Well, that explains it. After all, we didn't do much reading while we were together. Did we?"

Hunter took a few steps closer, staring her down.

Scarlet shifted in her thick leather chair. "So...you're Mr. Forest?"

"I am."

"I really should have figured that out. I just wasn't expecting you."

"Did you honestly think I wouldn't find you, Scarlet?"

She swallowed hard. "Yes. No. I don't know. I guess I didn't think you'd find me this soon. You're supposed to still be at Blue."

He ignored that statement entirely, turning instead toward the wall of greenery beside him. "You have a lot of plants. I remember you telling me you had a lot of plants, but damn, this is a lot of plants." He touched the one closest to him, his fingertips grazing the feathery leaves.

"That's a fern," she explained. "They grow well, even in low light."

Hunter glanced back to her. "An ideal for patients to strive toward?"

She blinked behind her glasses. "Something like that."

He nodded and turned away again, moving around the perimeter of the room, soaking everything in. He kept walking until he stood a few feet from her desk. His eyes skimmed the diplomas hanging on the wall.

"I see you've received a lot of degrees and honors, Dr. Tracey. I suppose I should be happy to know I was in such good hands at Blue," he said, well aware it was a low blow, but unable to stop himself.

She gave him only a tiny whimper in reply.

Hunter read each of her hard-earned accolades. When he finished, he stepped toward the corner of the room to look out over the city. He stood encased by the tall glass windows, staring out at the building across the street. "That's my office, you know. Gregory Global. You can see the 'GG' on the side of the building."

"Yes. I'm well aware of that."

"Since when?" he questioned, turning his head toward her. "When exactly did you know we worked across the street from each other?"

Scarlet straightened in her seat, squaring her shoulders against the high backrest. "Since the moment you told me your last name."

"You mean the first night we played Twister on your cabin floor?"

"Yes, then."

He smiled, remembering how adorable she'd looked with tiny hairs sticking out of her messy bun after they'd wrestled for hours on a plastic mat. That wasn't how she looked now, though. This Solemnly Sedate Scarlet was entirely different, all tightness and determination.

"That night feels like a lifetime ago. Like a fantasy," he admitted.

"That's because it was a fantasy, Hunter. Blissful Blue wasn't real life. We both know that."

He couldn't help but cringe with her predictable reply. He hid his reaction as best he could, refusing to acknowledge her response. Instead, he stared out of the windows and gathered his thoughts.

When he finally turned back, Hunter watched her chin rise with his approach. He stopped a few feet away from her chair, not wanting to appear too confrontational. At least, not any more than he had to be.

He observed Dr. Tracey for a long minute: the rigidness of her spine; the clear, focused green of her eyes; the shallowness of the breaths she held steady inside her chest. He wished he could see his forest fairy now, all bubbly and bright and voracious for life.

As Hunter longed for even the slightest indication of his freebird's existence in this office, Scarlet's gaze darted toward her desktop. He followed her line of sight to the two little leaves resting on the flat wood surface – green with red and red with green. The leaves that had once clung to her hair in the forest at Blue were here now, on her desk.

He smiled wildly at the two tiny freeloaders. When he looked back to Scarlet, she shifted her hands to the arms of her chair. Her fingers squeezed tight to the padded leather.

"So, Hunter. I imagine you have a lot of questions for me."

He chuckled softly at her therapist's tone. He knew it well, since it was the same one Will and Abbott often used. Hunter stared at her fingers, watching her knuckles whiten against the armrests.

"Actually, Scarlet, I only have one question for you."

"Just one?"

"Yes."

"What is it?"

He fastened his eyes to hers. "Why did you leave?"

"Why did I leave? Are you really asking me that?"

"I am. And I don't want to hear that it's because I never knew you were a doctor. Or that you thought of me as a patient, which would have made our relationship unethical. Or that Abbott might have found out about us, which could have destroyed your medical career."

Her eyebrows shot up above the rim of her glasses. "Are you saying those aren't good enough reasons for me to leave?"

"No, actually, those are all perfectly fine reasons for you to leave. But I don't think any of them are the real reason you left, because if they were, you would never have allowed yourself to be with me in the first place. So, what I want now is the *real* reason. And please don't repeat that damn movie quote about the fate of relationships based on intense experiences, because we're not on a speeding bus anymore. We're in the real world, dealing with reality, so that quote no longer applies."

"Well, it kind of still does," Scarlet corrected.

"No, it doesn't. Besides, you do know those two characters from *Speed* end up as a couple, right? There's a sequel and everything."

"Yeah, but the sequel was awful."

"That's only because Keanu Reeves wasn't in it," Hunter insisted, pausing to watch her lips curve up. Her smile made his pulse bound. "I promise we can talk about movies later, honey. We can curl up together on my couch with a big bowl of popcorn and talk about movies all night long, if you want. But first, I need an answer. Why did you leave?"

"Hunter, I..."

He took one step forward. "I know you didn't want to leave me. I *know* you didn't. That last night, when we made love, you clung to me like your life depended on mine. And the letter you wrote me? Dear God, your letter – I've read it a hundred times. The woman who wrote that letter cares so deeply for me. I know this isn't what you want. I know you don't want us to be apart. So why, in the name of all that's holy, did you leave? Why didn't you just stay and tell me the truth?"

Scarlet watched him the entire time he spoke. Her lips quivered and her eyes watered. Still, she managed to hold him with a steadfast stare.

"When I first met you," she began, her voice as poignant as her gaze, "you were so closed. So angry. You weren't ready for therapy. And I knew, from the moment I saw you crouched and grumbling by your blown tire, that if I told you I was a doctor – even one on vacation – you'd run screaming in the opposite direction. So, I made the decision to not tell you. I decided to wait until you got used to the idea of being at Blue, and until I figured out how to help you."

"But why would you need to help me? You were on vacation."

"Yes, I was, but..."

"No, Scarlet. You were on vacation, the same as I was, and you shouldn't have felt the need to play doctor with me."

She collapsed back against her chair. "You're right. I shouldn't have. But I just needed to do it. As much as I'd promised myself I would take a step back for those two weeks, when I saw you, I couldn't turn that part of me off. I needed to help you, because that's who I am. I'd been doubting that fact before I went up there. I'd been questioning everything in my life, if I'm being brutally honest."

"I like brutal honesty," he interjected. "Give me all of it."

She sighed. "I tried to give you honesty at Blue. I swear I did. I told you the reason I went there was to reconnect with my roots and find my joy, and that was the truth. I needed to take that journey because I'd been struggling here in the real world. I'd been questioning every decision I'd ever made, questioning my very identity. You basically caught me in the middle of a mid-life crisis."

"A mid-life crisis?"

"Yes, for lack of a better term. Although that may be a rather bad choice of words, since I'd really like to live past the age of 64."

Hunter couldn't help smiling.

Scarlet returned the gesture briefly before her eyes fell to study her fingers. "I tried to not struggle while I was at Blue," she admitted. "I tried to be happy and carefree for once in my adult life, and I did a lot of things I normally wouldn't have – a lot of things I *shouldn't* have."

"Are you talking about us becoming lovers?"

"Yes," she whispered, her entreating gaze drawing back to his face. "I hope you can forgive me for entering into that kind of relationship with you. I never should have done it."

"There's nothing to forgive," he assured, wishing he could simply take her in his arms and soothe her troubled mind. But there was still too much left unsaid. "You were on vacation, Scarlet. And you told me we shouldn't get involved that way, but I didn't listen. I basically seduced you, especially the first night we were together."

"No. You're not to blame here. I should have fought harder against it. I knew it was wrong, but I just kept telling myself it was okay, because we're both adults and our relationship was consensual."

"It was consensual. I don't feel violated, if you're worried about that. And I still don't regret anything. You said you didn't, either. That last night in bed, you said you'd never regret a moment of us."

"And I don't," she vowed. "Even if I lose everything because of it, I'll never regret a moment I spent with you."

Hunter shook his head. "Lose everything? My God, you don't have to lose *anything*. I have no desire to hurt you. You must know that."

"I do know, but I also understand if you feel betrayed. Honestly, I'm still amazed you never found out I was a doctor while we were at Blue. I figured Colin would accidentally mention it, or you would hear it from Tyler, or Abbott. In the back of my mind, it was always a concern."

"Because you thought Abbott would be angry and you might lose your medical practice?"

"No, Hunter. Because I knew it would hurt you to find out that way, and hurting you was the last thing I wanted to do."

His brow rose. "Didn't you care that you might lose your practice?"

"Yes, I cared. At first, I cared a lot. But then, when you opened up to me, and I could see you starting to truly *live* again, I decided any consequence I might face for my actions would be worth it."

"I don't understand. What about the nine-week backlog of patients waiting to see you here? What about the free clinic you run? What about Tyler and Colin and Pete and everyone else at Blue who relies on you? Are you saying that losing everything you've worked to build all these years would have been worth it, just to help me?"

Scarlet stared straight into him. "Absolutely."

Hunter shifted his stance, his chest tightening to the point of pain. "Well, I don't think that'll be an issue. The few people who knew about us at Blue are all ridiculously loyal to you. Tyler promised me he would take his knowledge of us to his grave. And Pete didn't know much, but swore himself to secrecy anyway. And I think Colin would lay himself down on train tracks before he'd ever hurt you."

"They're...they're all such wonderful people."

"They all adore you. But not as much as I do."

Her breath hitched with his words. He could practically see her heart pounding beneath her blouse. "Please tell me," he begged, his fingers twitching from the crushing desire to touch. "God, just tell me. Why did you leave?"

Hunter watched her forever, hoping for some simple explanation to gush from her perfect lips – a basic protest he could overcome with a few artful words – so he could reach for her and end their suffering.

When she didn't answer, he sighed. "Is it really because I didn't know about you being a doctor? I wish you'd just told me. I mean, I get why you didn't tell me at first. You thought I'd run away screaming, and you were right, I would have. But things between us became a lot different after that, so why didn't you tell me once we were together?"

Scarlet smiled wistfully. "I wanted to tell you, believe me. I thought about it all the time, but I knew it would change everything. Even if you didn't run away screaming, you'd still see me as Dr. Tracey, and I didn't want to be her. Not with you. I wanted to be the free, adventurous, happy Scarlet, the one I hadn't been in as long as I can remember. And I know it was a terribly selfish thought, but I told myself it was okay, since you and I only had a few days together."

"So, you were just never going to tell me?"

"Actually, there was a moment when I almost told you everything."

Hunter took a step toward her. "When? When was that?"

"That last night at the restaurant. You sat with me and held my hand and told me about the woman you wanted to spend your life with. I wanted that woman to be me. I wanted it so badly. But there was this lie – this huge lie between us – and I knew I had to tell you the truth."

"Then why didn't you tell me right there?"

"Because you thanked me."

"*What*?"

"You thanked me for helping you at Blue. For helping you understand your life, and for helping you learn how to be happy. Don't you remember?"

"Yes, I remember. And I meant every word. But what the hell does that have to do with anything?"

"It confirmed what I already knew: you were a patient at Blue, a patient who needed help, and I helped you. And yes, I was on vacation. But that doesn't change the fact that our relationship was therapeutic, and all therapy is based on trust. If I'd sat in that restaurant with you, and told you I was really a doctor at Blue, it would have destroyed your trust in me. Which could have destroyed all the progress you'd made."

Scarlet sucked in a shaky breath. "You told me I helped you to be happy, Hunter, and that's all I want for you. How could I have told you the truth then, and risked destroying your trust and happiness, just to fulfill my own desire to be with you? I'd already been so selfish, yet that would have been the most selfish thing I could possibly do. Ever."

Hunter stared at her in disbelief, coming to the realization that she'd done all this for *his* benefit. "Scarlet, you literally just said you want to be with me. You do realize that, right?"

"Is...is that all you took from my speech?"

"Yup. That's all I took from it."

She huffed out a laugh. "Well, as sorry as I am to admit it, none of that matters. What I want in this situation doesn't matter."

"How can you even say that?"

"Because I have to do what's right here. My wishes don't matter."

"They matter to me."

A whimper escaped her throat. Scarlet leaned forward in her chair, pinning him in place with a solemn stare. "I liked who I was up on that mountain, you know. I loved being that person with you. But please understand, that's not who I really am. I'm not the free-spirited woman you met at Blissful Blue. *This*," she said, motioning to the room, "is me. Dr. Scarlet Tracey. This is who I am."

Hunter finally saw the forest through the trees. "Good Lord, is that it?" he questioned, wondering if it could truly be this simple. "Is that what this is all about? Do you actually think I don't know you? Is that why you didn't tell me you bought wood spackle at the hardware store?"

"I...I did use the restroom in the hardware store. Honest."

"I don't doubt that, but you also bought wood spackle and didn't tell me. I'm just now realizing it's because you think I wouldn't have understood. You think I only saw the person you allowed yourself to be for those few days: the reinvigorated Girl Scout running around in the forest. But you couldn't be more wrong."

Scarlet's brow furrowed in confusion.

Hunter stepped forward, closing the gap between them to mere inches. "I can't believe you honestly think you hid yourself from me. You didn't. I saw those moments when your façade cracked, when you mourned being on vacation, and when you regretted lying to me. God, that last day we were together in the forest, you practically came unglued, begging forgiveness for pushing me to take such a hard look at my life. I didn't know why you felt so guilty about it at the time, but I did know the woman who shook and sobbed in my arms was neither carefree nor untroubled.

"And those aren't the only things I saw, either. There were so many little things, too. Like how you lined up your toiletries precisely in the bathroom, and how you packed your luggage like a schoolmarm, and how you went out of your way to buy wood spackle to fill in the holes you'd made. I saw you, Scarlet. Or, I should say, I saw *both* of you."

Her eyes widened behind her glasses. "Both of me?"

"Yes. I'm very much aware of the two sides of you. Hell, I even named them."

"You *named* them?"

"I did. The carefree forest fairy – the one you called 'Scarletson' the night we played Twister – I call her Frolicking Freebird Scarlet."

She giggled, a sound as bright as any he'd ever heard. "Freebird?"

"My freebird. She was the person I was with most on that mountain. But I also saw this person, the one sitting in front of me now. I named her Solemnly Sedate Scarlet. And no, I didn't know she was a doctor, but I knew she existed. Because I watched you, honey. I was right there beside you, and I watched you struggle, trying to decide which woman you really were. Which woman you *are*."

"The answer is this woman," she spoke without hesitation. "I can't be that freebird. Too many people depend on the person I am right now – sometimes with their very lives – and I've realized this is who I was always meant to be."

Hunter moved even closer, until she had to tilt her chin up to match his intent gaze. "Okay, fine. You've decided to leave the freebird behind and be this person again. Now you're back here helping others, and even though I may not agree completely with your logic, I do understand it. But I honestly don't see what any of this has to do with us. I don't see why you can't help people and still be with me."

Scarlet shook her head. "It's because I'm not the person you were with on that mountain. I'm not the freebird. I'm Dr. Tracey, a physician at Blissful Blue. And you were a patient, Hunter. A *patient*."

"No. You were on vacation. We were *both* patients."

"It doesn't matter. What I did was wrong."

He threw his hands up in the air. "Then I forgive you! Damn it, Scarlet, I forgive you! Now we can just move on!"

She grimaced with his outburst, her eyelids blinking rapidly behind her dark frames. He reigned in his temper as quickly as he could, but it was too late. The damage was already done, and the woman he thought he'd been reaching had closed herself off to him again.

Hunter watched her entire body clench inside the confines of her chair. He wanted to touch her so badly, to feel the connection of his skin to hers. The severity of that desire stole the air from his lungs.

Scarlet held still as stone while she observed him, waiting patiently until his shoulders eased from his ears and he possessed the control to match her somber gaze. "You've asked me for the real reason I left, Hunter, and I'm going to answer your question now. I simply request that you listen to everything I have to say."

He nodded slowly, although he didn't back away from her at all.

"I go to Blue several times a year to see patients," she began, her voice calm and steady. "I actually started my practice at Blue, and I've always enjoyed my time there as a physician. But on this visit, for the first time ever, I asked Dr. Abbott if I could spend two of my three weeks in personal reflection. At first, he refused. He didn't think it was a good idea for me to be there and not treat patients, since it would confuse those who came specifically to see me. I understood his point, but I wanted so desperately to have my journey in those woods, that I begged him until he relented. It wasn't easy. I had to promise not to communicate with any guests after that first week. I had to promise I wouldn't attend any common functions, or be seen around the grounds. I basically had to promise Abbott my firstborn child, just to be there by myself for those two weeks. But I knew it would be worth it, because I needed that time.

"I told you a few days ago that I felt weak and beaten when I got to Blue. It was the absolute truth. I needed my vacation there, so I could recharge myself and come back to the real world as Dr. Tracey. I know I never should have involved you, but I did, and I still don't regret it. I'll never regret a moment of it, because when I saw everything you'd been struggling with for so many years, I realized my journey at Blue was always supposed to be bound to yours."

She paused to give Hunter a tender smile. "Do you know I actually got lost in the woods, the day I met you? I've never gotten lost in those woods before, but the day you arrived, I got a bit turned around and came out of the forest farther down the road than normal. I recognized where I was immediately, once I stepped out of the tree line. Then I saw you crouched down by that tire, held up by the flitting of a squirrel. It felt so random, so arbitrary. Days later, when you told me your last name, I marveled at how many times we'd probably passed each other here on the street and never met. Yet that day at Blue, I got lost in the woods, and you got waylaid by a squirrel, and our paths collided.

"I'm honestly amazed by how the stars aligned for us on that mountain. The more time we spent together, the more I understood I was supposed to be there for your journey. I believe I was always meant to guide you, from that very first moment. Realizing that truly helped me. It helped me remember why I chose to become a doctor in the first place. Knowing I could pull you out of that deep, dark forest you'd created for yourself meant I could do the same for others, and I'm grateful I had the opportunity to be with you for those two weeks.

"Looking back on our time together now, I hope you understand why I didn't tell you the truth about me. I hope you understand that I never wanted to harm you by breaking your trust. Instead, I chose to return to reality, to the life I was always meant to lead. I chose to leave so you could finish healing, because healing takes time and you haven't had enough of it yet. And I knew, when I arrived back home, I would have to look out of my office window and see your building across the street. I knew I would have to sit here, with you practically in reach of my fingertips, and not say a word. But I made that decision, and I stand by it. Blissful Blue gave us both what we needed in order to move on with our lives, and now it's time for us to do that."

Scarlet clenched the arms of her chair. "I can't be your frolicking freebird here in the real world, Hunter. And you need to let me go, so you can move on. So we can *both* move on."

He stood in place, fully stunned and entirely mystified.

Let her go? A minute ago, she admitted she wants to be with me, and now she thinks we should move on? What the hell?

Hunter took another step toward her, erasing the space between them completely. "You know, Scarlet, if you wanted me to believe there was no hope for us, you never should have written me that letter."

She blinked several times. "I'm...I'm sorry."

His jaw clenched with her words. He didn't need any more apologies. He just needed her. He just needed them.

Hunter held her steadfast gaze for the longest time. Dr. Tracey sat rigidly before him, full of determination and resolve. He knew he couldn't get through to her right now. Her walls were too thick and high and his mind was too tossed and tortured. This argument was just going in circles, and he couldn't figure out how to change the direction.

Exhaling harshly, Hunter resigned himself to the only course of action he currently possessed. "I'm going to leave now, Scarlet."

"Yes...good. I think that's for the best."

Goddamnit! No, it's not! Why can't you see that? Why can't you just admit we're better off together?

He kept his eyes fixed on hers, studying the emerald green behind her glasses, searching for the woman he'd known on the mountain. The woman who'd bounced and bubbled and giggled. The woman he'd kissed senseless for hours on end. The woman who'd come so hard for him that she forgot where she was and banged her head into furniture. The woman he'd made love to just two nights ago, who'd achingly whispered his name as tears ran down her face.

Hunter wanted nothing more than to see that woman right now. He wanted nothing more than to touch that woman. His eyes trailed down her body, drinking her in. He soaked in the slope of her shoulders under her tailored blouse, the curve of her hips beneath her pencil skirt, and the perfection of her tiny feet inside her heels.

Damn, she had high heels on. Red ones. He wanted to fuck her in them. He wanted to fuck her right out of them. Then he wanted to take her back to his house and make her dinner. Then snuggle up with her on his couch and talk to her for hours. Then lay her down in his bed and make love to her over and over again.

By the time he finally managed to peel his eyes away from the sight of her heels, and drag his gaze slowly back up to her face, Scarlet barely breathed. He wasn't sure what she saw in him right now, but whatever it was, it obviously set her body on fire. She shifted nervously in her seat, unable to sit still beneath his shameless exploration. When her tongue darted out to wet her lips, Hunter couldn't stand the wait any longer.

He dropped forward, clamping his hands onto her chair's armrests, with the tips of his fingers overlapping her own. The air lodged in his throat as he pressed his forehead onto hers. Inhaling steeply, he filled his lungs with her fresh soap and tiny flowers.

"God, I missed you," he breathed against her lips. "It's only been two days since I felt your skin on mine, but I swear it's been a lifetime."

"H-Hunter," she whimpered, her fingertips shifting beneath his.

Their mouths hovered close together, sharing the heat of the air between them. Scarlet sat up in her chair, her entire body straining toward his. His freebird wanted his touch. She wanted his kiss.

He knew he could simply take a kiss from her now. He could take a hundred kisses. Hell, he could take all of her, for this one moment. He could snatch her up out of this chair and set her down on her desktop and do whatever he desired. She would let him. She wouldn't be able to resist this unearthly pull between them.

But he couldn't. He wanted so much more than just this one moment. He wanted everything.

Hunter held himself suspended above her, enjoying the feel of her shallow, puffed breaths on his skin. Eventually, he pulled away from the ungodly temptation of her mouth. He pressed a kiss to her forehead, relishing her smooth skin beneath his lips, savoring the soft sighs escaping her throat. When he eased back to look on her face, her eyes were closed, her dark lashes resting heavily against flushed cheeks.

Leaning down once more, he whispered beside her ear. "I'm leaving now, Scarlet. But rest assured, I will be back. This isn't over between us. Not by any stretch of the imagination."

Hunter walked away before she had the chance to reply. He couldn't bear to hear any more of her logical protests today. He just wanted to get out of this office. He wanted time to think this through, to figure out what weapons he needed in order to fight this battle on different terms.

The moment he exited through the thick mahogany door and stepped into the reception area, Marie jumped up from her seat. "Did everything go well during your session, Mr. Forest?"

He stopped dead in his tracks. "That's not my real name, Marie. My name is Hunter Gregory."

"Good heavens! Do you mean *the* Hunter Gregory?"

"I do. And I think you and I should get used to seeing one another, since I'm going to be coming back here. A lot. But not as a patient."

Hunter gave her a brief nod before pivoting on his heels. He didn't stop moving after that. He marched down the hall, into the elevator, through the lobby, and out to the parking garage. He didn't stop moving until he sunk into the driver's seat of his Porsche and gripped the wheel. Then he stared blankly ahead as he worked to calm his body.

That meeting with Scarlet didn't go the way he'd wanted. He'd wanted her to abandon all her stubborn logic and reason. He'd wanted her to embrace the joy they'd found up on that mountain and give them a chance to hold onto it here, in the real world.

Her continued resistance, now that he finally knew the truth about her being a doctor, just didn't make any damn sense. Despite portraying the serious, stoic physician today, she still looked at him like he was an oasis in the middle of the desert. Scarlet loved him. He felt more certain of that now than ever.

"Why won't you admit how you feel about me?" he questioned her as he sat alone in the dark, cool cavern of his car. "Is it because you truly think I don't know you? Or do you actually believe you can't be my forest fairy and still help your patients?"

Hunter shook his head, unable to accept the thought of her burying her frolicking side forever. He couldn't fathom her merely surviving. Not his freebird. She had to break free of the cage she'd created, and he had to help. He would not abandon her, even though he had no clue how to change her mind. He just needed someone to help him figure this out. He needed the one person who would tell him the absolute truth, without pulling any punches: Dr. William Rand.

Starting the car engine, Hunter drove out of the parking garage and onto the main road, headed straight to his best friend's house. He knew Will would listen to everything he said, and come back at him with sound, reasonable arguments. If Hunter could find a way to counteract those arguments, and convince Will of the rightness of this relationship with Scarlet, then he believed he could convince anyone. Including her.

Hunter didn't remember half of the trip to the Rands' home, since he'd traveled these roads a million times. His body finally calmed when he arrived in front of Will and Maggie's two-story house, the one with the blue siding and white shutters and the red rosebushes surrounding the porch. This was a true home, with people who loved and supported each other inside, and Hunter always felt grateful to spend time here. After exiting his car, he strode up the sidewalk and knocked at the front door. A moment later, his friend answered.

"Hey, man, good to see you," Will said, stepping back to let him in.

Hunter looked to the large, hulking doctor as he shut the door behind him. He closed the gap between them, throwing his arms around Will's shoulders. The hug stunned Will for a second before he returned it.

Hunter eased back to meet his friend's eyes. "Good to see you, too."

"Apparently. What was the hug for?"

"Oh, nothing much. I just found out while I was at Blue that you once gave a lecture there on the benefits of therapeutic touch."

Will chuckled. "You're right. I did."

"Yeah, but you and I don't have any therapeutic touch between us. Unless you count punching each other in the boxing ring, which I don't want to count. So, I thought I'd change things up a bit."

Will grinned, nodding his acceptance of this new status of their friendship. Hunter returned the gesture before catching movement out of the corner of his eye. He looked over to find baby Evie sitting on the living room floor, gnawing on a brightly colored plastic toy. She turned her wide, dark eyes up to his and smiled and hiccupped simultaneously.

"Well, look at that. I think Evie remembers me."

"Of course she remembers, Hunter. You've only been gone two weeks."

He looked back to Will. "May I pick her up?"

"Sure. Anytime."

Hunter's pulse skittered while he approached the tiny person. He wasn't sure why he felt so nervous to hold her, except for the fact that he'd never done it before. When he bent down to reach for the bubbly girl, she bounced on her diapered butt and squealed.

She was heavier than he'd imagined, and softer and warmer than he could have imagined. As he pulled her onto his chest, Evie dropped her toy to the floor and grabbed hold of his shirt, beaming up at him. "Hi, Evie," he said, softening his voice while taking one of her chubby little hands in his fingers. "You remember me, don't you? You know your godfather. Can you say *godfather*?"

She giggled, a chunk of drool falling from her lips onto her shirt.

"That is hard to say, isn't it? Maybe you can call me your uncle instead. Uncle Hunter. I like the sound of that. Do you like the sound of that, Will?" he asked, turning back to his friend.

Will's eyebrows shot up to his hairline. "Damn, Hunter. When you said on the phone that your whole life changed up at Blue, I thought you were exaggerating. But now, I don't think you were."

Hunter looked back to the little girl, holding her tiny body securely to his. "Thank you for sending me up there, Will."

"You're welcome. I'm just happy Blue helped you. I'm also happy Scarlet was there to guide you. She's an amazing woman."

"She's the absolute best," Hunter agreed, sighing as he stared into Evie's bright eyes. It felt so good to be able to hold this little person – to watch over her, protect her, and love her. He wanted to do this for his own daughter someday, the baby girl he'd imagined in Scarlet's arms.

Glancing back to his friend, he saw Will's gaze narrow at him just before Maggie walked into the room.

"Hunter!" she exclaimed. "Look at you! You're a natural with her!"

"Oh, she's just easy to be with, I think."

Maggie gave him a warm smile. "Well, as excited as Evie obviously is about being held by her godfather, it's actually time for her bath. Why don't I take her, so you and Will can visit?"

Hunter nodded, even though he didn't want to let the warm bundle out of his arms. As he passed the tiny girl off to her mother, he said, "Thank you, Maggie."

Her brow crinkled. "For what?"

"For everything you do. For allowing me to be a godfather to such an amazing little girl. And for making my best friend so happy."

Maggie blinked, her eyes darting to Will's before returning to his. "You're welcome," she replied, squeezing his arm before stepping away.

Hunter watched the two ladies travel down the hallway. When they disappeared from his sight, he turned to his friend.

Will stared at him. Hard. "What's going on with you, man?"

Hunter huffed out a laugh, since Will could always see through him. "I just really need to talk to you."

"What about?"

"About Scarlet."

Will crossed his arms over his chest. "You know, I call her Scarlet because she's my friend. But I think you should call her Dr. Tracey."

"No, Will. She wasn't Dr. Tracey up on that mountain. Not to me. She was on vacation, just like I was."

"On vacation? Are you sure? The physicians who work at Blue don't take vacations there."

"Not normally, no. But she did, and that's how we met."

"On vacation," Will echoed, his eyes shifting to the floor before meeting Hunter's again. "Was she okay?"

"What do you mean?"

"I'm asking how Scarlet was when you saw her. Was she okay?"

Hunter stood at attention. "Why wouldn't she be okay?"

"It's nothing, I just..."

"No. It's definitely not nothing. You know something about her, don't you? I need you to tell me. I need you to tell me *now*."

"Hunter..."

"Dear God! Is Scarlet really a patient of yours?"

The muscle in Will's jaw twitched over his clenched teeth.

Hunter stepped closer to his imposing friend. "Tell me something about her. Anything. Please."

"I think you know I can't give you any personal information. It would go against the ethics of doctor-patient confidentiality."

"Then she *is* a patient of yours?"

Will gave him a stern glower. Hunter eased back, trying to appear less confrontational. He knew Dr. Rand wouldn't hesitate to shut this conversation down if pushed too hard.

"I'm...I'm sorry, Will. I just really need some information on her."

"And I'm sorry, too, because I can't answer you. All I can say is *no*, Scarlet is not my patient. But she is a colleague, and we have spoken personally from time to time, so I don't feel comfortable sharing the things she told me in confidence."

"She needed your help with something, then? What was it?"

Will exhaled heavily. "Everyone has their demons, Hunter."

Salted tears stung his eyes. He knew his little bird had been struggling with problems at Blue, but to hear it confirmed was too much. He didn't want her to have any demons. He didn't want anything in this entire world to clip her wings.

Swiping his hands across his face, he worked to steady himself. Will observed him for a moment before tilting his head toward the hall. "Why don't we go sit in the kitchen and talk? Maggie made fresh lemonade today. I can pour you a glass."

Hunter's besieged mind latched to one word. "Lemonade?"

"Yeah. Come have some."

He trailed behind his friend down the hall, taking a seat on one of the bar stools around the kitchen island, while Will set a glass in front of him. Hunter watched the sunny yellow liquid pour into the ice-filled cup, accepting it the moment he could. He took a huge, eager gulp before setting the glass back down. Then he frowned.

"Don't you like it, Hunter? You usually love Maggie's lemonade."

"I know I do. It's just...it has a lot of sugar in it."

"It's the same amount she normally uses."

"Oh, there's nothing wrong with it. I appreciate you giving it to me." Hunter pushed the glass away. "It's just not what I want."

"Okay, well, would you rather have a beer?"

"No, thanks. I want to keep my head on straight."

Will leaned against the counter, regarding him. "Damn, man. You're pretty deep in thought right now, aren't you?"

"Yeah, you could say that."

"What are you thinking?"

Hunter didn't blink. "I'm thinking I'm in love."

Will's eyes bulged. "*Excuse me?*"

"I'm in love with Scarlet," Hunter declared, relieved to finally admit the truth to his best friend. "Completely, head-over-heels, in love."

Will stared him down for painful seconds before the expected lecture began. "Come on, man. Seriously. I want you to think about what you just said to me. Do you honestly believe you're in love with a woman you met *two weeks* ago?"

"Yes, I do, because it's true. And that's not the problem. The problem is she refuses to be with me now that we've left Blue, and I don't know why."

"You truly don't know why?" Will echoed, his obvious concern apparent in his voice. When Hunter shook his head, Will exhaled. "Okay, then. Can I ask you a personal question? I mean, I'm pretty sure I know the answer. But I think it's an important point to cover, if you and I are really going to talk about this."

"Go ahead and ask."

"Were you and Scarlet physically intimate while you were at Blue?"

"I...I don't know exactly how to answer that," Hunter hemmed. "Are you asking me only as a friend?"

"What do you mean?"

"I mean I don't want her hurt by this in any way. So, if you're going to feel the need to report some sort of medical malpractice, then I will have to inform you that she was on vacation, just like I was, and..."

"*Hey,*" Will stopped him. "I'm asking as a friend. Only as a friend."

Hunter wound his fingers together on the countertop. "Then, yes. We were physically intimate. We were...quite involved, actually."

"Yeah, that's what I figured."

"Why would you figure that?"

"Well, aside from you thinking you're in love with a woman you just met, I can tell by the look on your face – not to mention how differently you're acting around Evie and Maggie and me – that something pretty significant happened between you and Scarlet up there. The two of you being together physically explains a lot, from a psychiatric perspective."

"What does it explain?"

Will sighed. "You won't want to hear this, but there's a phenomenon that can occur sometimes between patients and therapists. It's called erotic transference."

"Erotic transference? What on earth is that?"

"It's when a patient assumes an emotional connection to their physician, secondary to the profound interactions that come from therapy. The patient feels a sexual attachment because that caregiver has fulfilled a significant need in their life. It can be an intense problem under normal circumstances, so I imagine it would be compounded exponentially in the face of an actual physical relationship."

Hunter's jaw unhinged. "What the fuck, man? Are you actually suggesting I developed some sort of schoolboy crush on my teacher?"

"It's just a thought, Hunter."

"Well, it's a horrible thought! I'm a grown man and I'm well aware of what love is! And Scarlet was never my doctor! Just because we were lovers doesn't mean I've got this goddamn erotic transference!"

"Maybe not. I'm only telling you the phenomenon exists. Any psychiatrist worth their salt knows it's a potential problem, and whether Scarlet was on vacation or not, she *is* a psychiatrist. Even if she wasn't your actual doctor on that mountain, I can guarantee she still held herself accountable for your wellbeing."

Hunter's mind latched to the image of Dr. Tracey – sitting behind her stately desk – glaring at him behind her glasses. "Holy hell, Will. That's it, isn't it? Scarlet thinks she acted as my physician at Blue, and therefore my emotions came from a therapeutic relationship. That's why she refuses to be with me now. She thinks I'm suffering from a psychological syndrome, so what I feel for her isn't real."

Will pressed his lips shut in silent confirmation.

"That's bullshit," Hunter retaliated. "I was never her patient. We were just two people helping each other out for a few days, and during that time, I fell in love with her. And you know what? She fell in love with me, too. Scarlet is in love with me."

The doctor exhaled heavily, his huge shoulders falling.

"God, Will, please stop looking at me like that."

"Like what?"

"Like you're going deeper into psychiatrist-mode. I've had plenty of therapy – with my *actual* physician, Adrien Abbott – and I'm more aware of what's happening around me now than I've ever been in my life. I'm telling you, Scarlet is in love with me."

"I'm not telling you she isn't. I just need you to see that you've been through a life-changing event these past two weeks, and it puts you in a place of emotional vulnerability. What you're feeling now may not be the way you'll feel after you've had a chance to step back and see this without your rose-colored glasses."

"I'm not fucking wearing rose-colored glasses!" Hunter hollered.

Will arched an eyebrow and flexed his giant arms.

Hunter raised his hands in front of him, surrendering instantly. "Okay, okay, I realize that was an emotional outburst. I'll admit my feelings are pretty raw at the moment. But I *want* to feel this. I haven't felt much of anything in forever, and I think you know that, which is why you told me to go to Blue in the first place. God, I haven't been happy in as long as I can remember – not until two weeks ago, when Scarlet walked into my life. And I know I'm vulnerable, and I know this experience hit me like a ton of bricks, but that doesn't mean what I feel isn't real. It doesn't mean this isn't the right thing for me, or for her."

Hunter froze the moment he finished his confession. *Damn, that's the answer. I need to make Scarlet see that what we have between us is real. I need to prove to her that the magic we knew at Blue can still exist in this world. Maybe then she'll let herself be happy. Maybe then she'll let herself be the freebird I know.*

He looked back to his quiet, commanding friend. "Do you remember what you said to me a few years ago, Will? When you told me that love was about finding someone who is the right fit?"

"Yeah, I remember."

"Well, I found her. No matter what it sounds like, or how quickly it happened, or how strange it seems, I know I found her."

Will didn't move or speak. He just stood there, staring.

"Please understand," Hunter implored. "For the first time in my life, I know exactly what I want and what I need, and I'm not going to let anyone tell me that I have some sort of syndrome, or that my feelings aren't based in reality. I love Scarlet. I love her with all my heart."

The doctor's dark eyes evaluated him, seeing straight inside.

Hunter remained firm beneath the harrowing scrutiny.

Eventually, Will responded. "Look, man, I know you. I know how strong you are. Maybe you're not experiencing erotic transference at all. Maybe you genuinely feel for Scarlet, and it doesn't have anything to do with being in therapy. But I'm telling you, if you want to convince her of that, you'd better know without a doubt that it's the absolute truth. Because she's one hell of an intelligent woman, and she's going to be highly aware of every possible pitfall in your relationship."

"I love her, Will."

"I know you believe that, but I'm not the one you have to convince."

Hunter straightened in his seat. "Then I'll convince her. She's the person I've been searching for my entire life. I have no doubts. None."

Will stared at him for another long minute. It actually felt like an eternity. Finally, he nodded and smiled.

"Then go be with her, Hunter."

14

SCARLET

Dr. Scarlet Tracey sat behind the desk in her office, staring at her computer screen. Mrs. Sanderson had just left, leaving Scarlet alone to enter a progress note into her patient's chart. Mrs. Sanderson had been in sessions for almost a year now, after the car accident that left her addicted to prescription medication for her back pain. That pain and addiction had manifested itself in every aspect her life, and she now had trouble seeing the forest for the trees.

Scarlet tried to help her see, to show her that happiness could still be found. Whenever Mrs. Sanderson came for therapy, Scarlet plastered a smile on her face. She spoke openly and warmly, encouraging her patient to look for beauty in the everyday. Mrs. Sanderson responded well to treatment, but still returned for her regularly scheduled appointments like clockwork. She was healing, and healing took time.

The computer screen stared back as Scarlet attempted to compose her thoughts. If she could just write this one last progress note, she could finally leave her office for the day. Unfortunately, she couldn't get her thoughts together in quite the right way. She hadn't been able to find clarity in much of anything...not since Hunter left this office on Monday evening, swearing he would return.

It was Wednesday now. Two whole days had passed since she'd last seen him. Two days had passed since he'd looked on her for the first time in the real world and insisted he knew exactly who she was.

Scarlet closed her laptop. She slid the computer into its case on the floor, unable to refine her thoughts enough now to make an intelligent annotation. God, she really needed to pull herself together. She had clinic hours to run later tonight, and those patients needed her focus.

Nearly the entire day had felt as blurry as it did now. Only her morning had transpired in the usual fashion. She'd woken up before dawn, showered, and dressed in a peach silk blouse and black skirt. She'd brushed out her curls and secured them up on her head in a tight ponytail before slipping on her glasses. Then she'd made her way into the kitchen of her apartment and downed nearly a gallon of coffee to revive her mind. That, apparently, was where she'd gone wrong. The moment her mind woke, it clung to Hunter Gregory and refused to think of anything else.

Turning toward the corner of her office, Scarlet stepped to the floor-to-ceiling windows, soaking in the impressive sight of the Gregory Global building across the street. *Is Hunter there today? Did he forgo his last week of vacation to return to work? Is he staring out of his window, right back at me?*

Her gaze fell all the way down his building to the common area beside the entrance – the marble square with the scenic water fountain and stone seats – where she often sat to eat her lunch. She wondered how many times she'd passed Hunter while walking through that little square. She wondered how many times they'd been within reach but never met.

Pressing her glasses up higher on her nose, Scarlet noted the dark gray clouds rolling in over the city. She hugged her arms, since her thin blouse did little to keep her warm today. In truth, she hadn't felt warm since she'd had Hunter's arms around her in her bed at Blue.

She knew what she'd been doing that last night, when she'd left him to sleep alone in her cabin. What happened between them was too fast. They'd each been in the middle of an emotional tornado while they were on that mountain, complicated outrageously by the physical relationship they'd chosen to engage in, and they both needed time to stop spinning.

The feelings they'd shared at Blue were impulsive, rooted in desire and temptation. In truth, she hadn't had much personal experience with either of those emotions prior to him. The way Hunter could make her feel with merely a look, with the simplest of touches, went far beyond anything she'd ever known. Her craving for him overcame her sensibilities in a few short days, leading her into a relationship she never intended to pursue.

Scarlet remembered how guilty she'd felt the first night she crossed the line she couldn't uncross. She remembered sitting naked on her kitchen countertop while Hunter escaped to her restroom. She'd pulled her robe back on, thrown her torn underwear in the trash, and stood on her cold wood floor, worrying herself to death over the possibility of having harmed him. Her mind only eased when he returned, assuring her he would never regret what they'd done.

She traveled full circle in those weeks at Blue, from feeling guilty about the weakness of her desires to feeling grateful for every moment she had with him. She relished the chance she'd been given to leave the sedate physician behind and embrace every emotion Hunter created inside her. She knew it couldn't last, of course. Everything at Blue was a fantasy and not something they could bring home to the real world. But as much as her mind understood that fact, her body refused to agree.

Looking down now at the quaint marble square in front of his building, Scarlet ran her fingers across her lips, recalling a thousand kisses he'd placed on them in a matter of days. She couldn't blame her flesh for its innate chemical response to him. But she could definitely blame her heart for wishing he would keep his promise to return to her.

Dear Lord, she wanted him back. She wanted his arms around her, his voice in her ear, his heat soaking through her skin. It had only been four days since he'd made love to her, and only two days since she'd last seen him, but she could already feel the loneliness creeping back in. She'd thought it was difficult to leave him alone in her bed after they'd made love, but it was nothing compared to the torture of looking him in the eyes, here in her office, and telling him to let her go.

A knock came at her door, making Scarlet jump in her black leather heels. Her eyes darted to the back of the room, staring at the knob while it turned. She watched in shameful anticipation for the person on the other side to enter. When they did, her heart sank dejectedly to her feet.

"Oh, Marie. It's you."

"Yes, it's me. I'm sorry to just walk in, but I knocked several times. You must not have heard me."

Scarlet smiled at the sweet older woman, who was more friend than employee. Although, in the past six months, she'd become more mother than friend. "I'm sorry I didn't answer. I was just thinking."

"Well, I'll leave you to your work, then. I only came to tell you I'm going home in a bit, after I finish up some filing." Marie stepped farther into the room, holding a wrapped brown paper package in one hand. "I also came to bring you this. It arrived by courier a few minutes ago. The return address says it's from Hunter Gregory."

"It's from Hunter?"

"Yes," Marie verified, tilting her head while she approached. "Are you okay with this, Scarlet? Is this Hunter-person bothering you? I could take the package down to security, to have them open it."

"No, that's not necessary," she replied, moving to the other side of her desk to reach out her hand. "It'll be fine."

"Are you sure? You know how I worry about you."

"I appreciate that, as always, but it's honestly fine."

"Hmm. If you're certain."

"I am," Scarlet assured as she accepted the package.

"Okay, then. I'll let you know when I leave for the night."

She gave her assistant a warm smile. "Thank you."

Marie nodded before exiting the room. The moment the door closed, Scarlet returned to her desk chair and sank down in the soft leather seat. She sat very still, staring at the innocent-looking parcel in her hand. Her heart thudded at the sight of her name in Hunter's bold handwriting.

She ran her fingers over the brown paper surface before easing one edge open and pulling the contents out. Apparently, Hunter had chosen to send her a book: *A Field Guide to North American Birds*.

Her brow crinkled, even though she knew this book well. She had an old, well-read copy at home. This was the newest edition, however, and she stared at the colorful cover for a long while. Eventually, she opened the book to find an inscription inside:

For Scarlet, my favorite birdwatcher
Reality is what we make it
Yours, Hunter

She read the words again and again, turning them over in her mind, before noticing a bookmark inside the back of the thick volume. Opening to the designated page, she pulled out the placeholder. The bookmark itself was a photograph of the morning sky – with gorgeous, fiery reds radiating out from the brimming sun – and she smiled at the sight before turning her eyes back to the book.

Nestled there in the pages, under the letter *Y*, was a picture of a purple bird with a yellow crest on its head. Scarlet stared at the photo, amazed by the realistic look of what must be a computer-edited image. The page had been placed expertly inside the book binding, blending in seamlessly with all the other pages. Her eyes drifted from the picture to the caption beneath it. *The Yellow-Crowned Purple Fantini*. The air caught in her chest as she read the description that followed:

The yellow-crowned purple fantini is a rare species discovered by noted avian enthusiast Dr. Scarlet Tracey of Richmond, Virginia. After years of searching,

Dr. Tracey finally found her bird in the Blue Ridge Mountains. The fantini has a deep purple body and a large, bright yellow cap of feathers that rise above its head when angry. At first glance, the fantini can appear quite crazy, especially when performing dance moves that make it look rather chicken-like. But upon deeper inspection, this bird is actually soft, tender, loyal, loving, and brave.

The fantini is one of the rarest creatures in the world, and the most beautiful, inside and out. It can often be found deep in the woods, among the tallest oaks and the littlest pines. The fantini's favorite activity is to hop through tree branches, perching among the leaves and pecking its way into all the little cracks and crevices in the bark.

If you're fortunate enough to catch sight of this amazing bird, please don't attempt to lock it in a cage. The yellow-crowned purple fantini won't survive behind bars. This bird needs to be free to live and explore and dream. This bird needs to fly.

The book shifted as Scarlet held it with trembling fingers. Blinking away the moisture behind her glasses, her eyes returned to the top of the page to read it all again. When she finished, she looked to the two tiny leaves sitting on the corner of her desk. She reached for both, taking the stems in hand to twirl them together. Green with red and red with green.

My freebird – that's what Hunter had called her when he stood in this room two days ago. *She was the person I was with the most up on that mountain,* he'd said. Scarlet knew he was right. She'd felt entirely free when she was with him.

Hunter elicited a response in her that defied explanation. Everything about him called to her on a primal level, erasing years of loneliness with just the touch of his fingers. She wanted to cling to those wondrous sensations, to remain by his side for every second of the rest of her life.

But that was the selfish part of her talking. The selfish, wanton woman who'd nearly risked all of his emotional and psychological progress by confessing her sins that night at the restaurant. She'd nearly told him that she was a doctor, and that she'd lied to him about it from the moment she met him, and that she wanted them to be together despite the million obstacles preventing it. The fact that she'd come so close to crushing his trust in her was downright shameful.

Scarlet knew Hunter's freebird wanted nothing more than to be with him. She also knew the sensible, logical physician inside her had made the decision to leave him up on that mountain. Unfortunately, she couldn't be sure which woman broke down on the way home from Blissful Blue. She didn't know if it was the freebird or the physician who'd started crying the moment she snuck out from under his warm, heavy arm as it lay across her bare hip. She wasn't sure who'd sobbed through every second of writing him that letter, or who'd barely been able to see the dark, pre-dawn road as she drove down the mountain.

She only knew it was the doctor who pulled everything together once she'd arrived back in Richmond. It was Dr. Tracey who'd made her gather her wits, and unpack her bags, and attempt to sleep, and wake on Monday morning to dress and come to work. It was Dr. Tracey who'd smiled at Marie, and who'd replied that her vacation was restful when asked, and who'd forced herself back into her office chair, assuming the proper demeanor in order to see patients again.

And it was definitely Dr. Tracey who'd told Hunter, right here in her office, that they were better off apart and that he needed to let her go. Scarlet knew it was the doctor who'd said those words, because his freebird had screamed and clawed at her the entire time – begging to stay with him, to wrap her body around his and never let go.

The doctor inside her won two days ago. She won because it was the right thing to do. Hunter had been through so much on that mountain, and now he was open and exposed and raw. He needed time, more than he needed anything else at this moment. Time to himself. Time to heal.

Scarlet looked back to the book, placing the two forest leaves onto the page alongside her fantini bird. She pressed the book deliberately shut, trapping everything inside. As much as she wanted to live there, among those beautiful thoughts and picturesque words, she knew they belonged in a fantasy world that didn't exist here in this office.

"I already told you *no!*" Marie shouted, her distressed voice emanating from the other side of the wall.

Scarlet stood from her chair. "Marie?"

"Do not go in there, Mr. Gregory!"

"I promise it's okay, Marie," Hunter assured as he forced open the door, still looking into the older woman's eyes.

"No, it is *not*," she told him, following on his heels. "Dr. Tracey has no further appointments today, and you are just..."

"Marie! Hunter!" Scarlet barked.

Both of them stopped cold in their tracks. They stood in the middle of Scarlet's office floor and looked to her. Hunter's eyes caught hers that instant, staring straight inside.

Scarlet forgot to breathe. She simply forgot, because he'd come back to her, as powerful, tempting, and intense as ever. She gripped his book in her hand, needing the support when her knees buckled.

Marie folded her slender arms across her chest. "I tried to stop him, Dr. Tracey, but he wouldn't take *no* for an answer. Please say the word, and I will call security to have him *removed* from this office."

Hunter's potent gaze gripped Scarlet in a vice from across the room. She could feel her body pulling toward his and had trouble producing words. "It's – it's okay, Marie. I'll see what Mr. Gregory has to say."

"But he has a briefcase with him, and he refused to let me examine the contents before he came *barging* in here."

Scarlet glanced down, seeing Hunter's knuckles whiten against the handle of the case he carried. When her eyes rose back to his, he shook his head. "She doesn't need to see what's inside the briefcase, Scarlet."

Marie snorted. "Should I call security now, Dr. Tracey?"

Scarlet observed him for another moment, the calm determination written across his face simultaneously soothing and intriguing her. "You don't need to do that, Marie. Everything will be fine here."

"Are you sure?"

"Yes. I promise I'm okay. You can leave us now."

Marie didn't move for several more seconds. She just stood there, side-eyeing Hunter. Finally, she pivoted on her heels. "I will be waiting *right outside this door,*" she emphasized with another glare at his back before shutting the thick mahogany wood behind her.

Marie managed to make the door slam, which Scarlet had never heard before. The sound echoed through the room, reminding her she was now alone with the man she'd grown to need in ways that bordered on unnatural. She straightened her spine as she met his brazen stare. "What are you doing here, Hunter?"

He shrugged beneath his tailored black sport coat, shifting the white button-down beneath. His shirt was undone at the collar, revealing the hollow at the base of his neck – the one she'd kissed more times than she could count. "I told you I'd be back. So, here I am."

Scarlet's eyes fell to his briefcase. It wasn't a typical business case with metal locks. This one was made entirely of leather, with a thick, detailed strap holding it shut. "That's a very handsome briefcase."

"Do you like it? I bought it yesterday."

Her gaze darted back to his. "Just yesterday?"

"Yes."

"Care to tell me what's in it?"

"Not really."

"Why not?"

"Because we'll get to that later...if we need to." Hunter pointed to the space the other woman had just vacated. "I swear to you, I will find a way to get Marie to like me. I realize she doesn't now, and I can't blame her, since we got off to a rough start. But I will win her over."

Scarlet smiled despite herself. "I don't doubt that you can."

He returned her smile with that dangerous-yet-delightful curve of his lips that made her toes curl inside her heels. She set the book down on her desktop so she could grasp the wood edge in both hands. Damn, he was intimidating. He always had been, from the first moment she'd laid eyes on him, when she'd felt the freebird inside her clawing toward him.

Hunter watched her watching him. Eventually, he loosened the fierce grip he had on his briefcase handle and glanced down to the book on her desk. "I see you got the gift I sent."

"Yes, I did. It's lovely. Thank you."

"I'm glad you like it. I really hoped you would, even though I can't take all the credit. My head IT guy, Clay Saunders, helped me. Turns out, he's quite the romantic. When I told him I needed to make a gift for my girlfriend, he jumped all over it."

Scarlet's mouth fell open, since she couldn't believe Hunter told someone she'd never met that she was his girlfriend. She didn't know how she was supposed to feel about that. She only knew she should probably feel more upset by it than she did.

He started toward her, spanning the floor in purposeful, determined strides. As he approached her desk, Scarlet stepped backwards. She didn't have a choice in the matter. Retreat came instinctually, since the closer she stood to him, the less chance she had at logical thought.

By the time he made his way around her desk – to occupy the same spot she had a moment ago – she'd backed herself into the corner by her office restroom. "Hunter, the gift was very sweet of you, but..."

"Clay did the picture. He also figured out how to attach the page inside the book, since I didn't know how to make it look that good. But I promise you, all the words were all mine."

"They...they were beautiful words."

"Well, you once told me I'm a poet. And I am. But only with you."

Scarlet's lower lip quivered. She bit into it to stop the unwanted movement. Hunter's gaze drew to her mouth, lingering for a harrowing minute, before he pivoted toward her desktop. Pushing the book off to the corner, he set his briefcase down in the center of the wood surface.

"So, tell me, Scarlet. How have you been?"

Her brow rose. "How have I been?"

"I mean, since I saw you on Monday," Hunter clarified, turning back to her. "Damn, was it just Monday when I was last here in your office? It feels much longer than that to me. Does it feel like it's been a lot longer than two days since we were together?"

She sealed her lips shut.

"Honestly, it feels like forever," he continued in her silence. "I remember that one time at Blue, when I was away from you for thirty-six hours, and it felt like an eternity. I guess I haven't learned how to be without you for more than two days at a time yet. I suppose I'll have to work on that. Maybe I'll even figure out a way to go for a whole week without you, once we've been married for thirty or forty years."

An involuntary gasp left her throat. She reached up to her glasses, pushing them hard against her face. Her fingers clenched when they fell back to her sides.

Hunter's eyes narrowed on hers, his next words even and precise. "I think you know I want to be with you. I believe I've made that abundantly clear. However, in case you have any doubts, let me erase them now. I want to be with you, wholly and without question. I want you in every possible way. From this moment forward. Period."

She opened her mouth to respond, but nothing would come out.

"You do understand that, don't you?" he questioned.

Scarlet did understand. She knew he wanted them together. Yet his certainty, in such an uncertain situation, caused her even more alarm.

She tried like hell to compose herself beneath the scrutiny of his stare and the hellish beauty of his words. Brushing at the invisible creases in her skirt, she shifted inside her heels. "Hunter, I...I do understand your wishes. I just don't think they're realistic."

He stood beside her desk, examining her, absorbing every uncertain movement she made. Eventually, he shoved his hands into his pockets and sighed. "I know you intend to argue with me. I know you have reservations about us being together, and I've thought long and hard on all your possible protests. After due consideration, I've come to the conclusion that there are two major obstacles to our relationship."

Hunter turned away from her to step toward the window in the corner. Scarlet felt grateful for the extra space he put between them.

"Only two obstacles?" she countered.

Looking out of the glass, he absorbed the view of his building across the street. He sucked in a breath, shifting his broad shoulders beneath his coat. The simple action pulled a whimper from her throat.

"I said two *major* obstacles," he clarified. "I know there are more, but if we can overcome these, the rest of your protests should fall away."

Hunter glanced back to her. The light from the window highlighted the strong contours of his face, even with the grayness of the sky. "I want to tell you what these two things are, Scarlet. Will you let me?"

She knew she should stop this, here and now. The longer she allowed him to speak, the less chance she had of resisting. She already fought her desire to go to him, to throw her arms around his neck and simply give in to everything he wanted them to be, so she should definitely shut him down before he even had the chance to begin. But as he looked to her with his tender, pleading gaze, she couldn't find the strength.

"Yes," she whispered. "I'll let you."

He closed his eyes for a moment, smiling softly to himself before refocusing on her again. "The first obstacle is that you think I don't know you. You think, because I didn't realize you were a doctor when we were at Blue, it means I don't know who you truly are."

Her chest constricted with that painful truth. "What's the second obstacle?"

"You don't believe my feelings for you are real. You believe I'm suffering from a psychological syndrome called erotic transference."

Her eyes widened. "Where did you hear that term?"

"From Will Rand."

"You spoke to Will about me?"

"Yes, I asked him about you. I asked him to tell me everything he could about you. He wouldn't do it, of course. He'd never break your confidence. But I did speak with him, after you and I met here Monday, because he's my best friend and I needed his advice."

She couldn't help smiling. "I'm glad you have a friend like Will."

"I'm glad, too. And I'm happier than ever that he's a psychiatrist, because he mentioned this erotic transference issue to me, and that gave me the opportunity to research it."

"You actually researched it?"

"I did. I'm a businessman, Scarlet. I do research so I'll have all the facts, so I can arm myself with the proper tools for battle. After Will and I spoke, I knew you were going to come at me with this particular protest and I needed to know what I'd be up against. I'll admit now that I can see how this particular syndrome could be a concern of yours."

She leaned toward him. "Can you really see that?"

"Well, I can see how you've convinced yourself that I suffer from it. You believe our time at Blue was therapeutic in nature, because you are occasionally a physician there, and because you felt responsible for my wellbeing. So now, you're afraid my feelings are based on a reaction to therapy, and are therefore not based in reality. That's all true, isn't it?"

"Yes," she admitted. "That's all true."

Hunter nodded. "Good. I mean, it's good you admit it's a concern of yours, because I'm here to tell you it shouldn't be. I understand how you arrived at that conclusion, but there is one flaw in your theory. One beautiful, magnificent flaw."

"What flaw is that?"

"I never saw you as a doctor. Erotic transference evolves out of a patient-physician relationship, and I can't have that syndrome if I never saw you as my doctor. And I swear to you, on my life, it never once crossed my mind. You were my friend on that mountain, and you were my lover." He hung on that last word, running a harsh hand through his hair. "God knows, you were definitely my lover. But you were never my doctor. Not the way I saw it. Not the way I *see* it."

Scarlet struggled to take in air. A huge part of her wanted to say he was right, and everything between them was perfect, and it would all work out the way they both desired. But reality wasn't that kind.

"Okay, Hunter. I'll admit erotic transference occurs between a patient and physician in a therapeutic setting, and you never knew I was a physician. But I think you can still see that things moved pretty quickly between us up on the mountain. You do see that, right?"

He gave her a begrudging nod.

She sighed. "Then don't you think your feelings for me could be a reaction to finally being in tune with the emotions you've repressed since high school? And the therapy you received at Blue, whether it was from me or from Abbott, is the reason you feel that way?"

Hunter huffed out a laugh. "I know what you're getting at. You want me to admit that I was basically your patient at Blue, which means my feelings for you are a side effect of therapy. And you know what? I'll agree with part of your argument. I'll admit you opened a floodgate of emotion in me. But just because I feel things more deeply now than ever before doesn't mean my feelings are baseless or wrong; it only means that I finally understand them. And I think understanding myself is a good thing. Don't you?"

Scarlet didn't answer. She couldn't answer, not in the way she should. Instead, she stood mutely and studied him.

Hunter held her unwavering stare for a long while before turning back to the window. He looked down to the street below them. "Have you ever been down to the outdoor square in front of my building? Have you ever gone outside to sit by the marble fountain?"

"Yes," she answered. "Sometimes, I go there to eat my lunch."

"I do, too. When I was here Monday, you told me you were amazed by how the stars aligned for us to meet up on that mountain. The more I thought about it, the more it amazed me, too. How many times have we passed each other here on the street? How many times have we eaten lunch together, sitting by that fountain? How many times have we stood side by side, completely unaware of everything we could be?"

He didn't wait for her reply. He just shook his head and continued. "It frustrated me like hell over the past couple days, to think about all those missed opportunities. I asked myself why it took a squirrel darting in front of my car on a desolate mountain road for me to find you. I thought a lot about that question, and I believe I know the answer."

"Yeah? What's the answer?"

Hunter looked back to her. "It's because that was the moment I needed to find you. And that was the moment you needed to be found."

Her pulse leapt with his words, bounding through her entire body.

"I've done a lot of things in the past two days, Scarlet. But mostly, I've thought. I've thought about every word you ever said to me, and all the things I've watched you do, and everything I've learned from the people in your life. I've thought about you every single moment since I walked out of this office on Monday, and I've come to the conclusion, absolutely and without doubt, that I found you on that mountain. I found the real you. I *know* you, up and down, inside and out. And because I know you, I already know what you're thinking about all of this."

She couldn't tear her eyes away from him. "What am I thinking?"

"You're thinking I couldn't possibly understand who you are after only being with you for two weeks. And I couldn't have known the real you up on that mountain, since I never knew you were a doctor."

Scarlet gave him a soft smile. "That's true," she admitted.

He mirrored her tender gesture. "I know it is, but I'm going to prove you wrong. Because right now, I'm going to tell you all about yourself."

"You mean you're going to tell me about me?"

"I am, and I want you to stand there and really listen to what I have to say. When I'm done, if you can honestly tell me I don't know you – that I don't know who you are deep down in your soul – then I promise I will walk out of that door and never come back." Hunter paused to take a shuddered breath. "I promise I'll never try to see you again. Or call you. Or contact you by any means. If I pass you on the street, I will turn my head and look the other way. I'll pretend I never knew you at all. I swear I will."

Blinding tears consumed her vision. Scarlet blinked back the bitter sting and swallowed hard. She couldn't respond, since the thought of him treating her like a stranger left the darkest ache in her heart.

Hunter balled his hands. "So, will you let me tell you who you are?"

All she could do was nod.

He offered a grateful smile before turning his gaze to the window. "I'll start from your childhood, when you were a really happy little girl," he began, looking to the gray clouds hovering over the city. "You had parents who loved you dearly, each in their own way. A free-spirited mother, who took you into the woods for adventures and taught you to appreciate all the little things life has to offer. And a stern, intellectual father, who pushed you to strive for all your mind could achieve and taught you that a life lived in the service of medicine and humanity was the noblest profession. You had two loving parents, who showed you two paths for your life. But they were a bit too different from each other, and they weren't able to teach you how to wind those paths together."

Her tears returned, fresher and hotter. Scarlet fought them back so she could focus. She glued her brimming gaze to Hunter's profile.

"But you did grow up happy, at least," he spoke to the clouds. "You remained quite innocent, even as you got older, since you spent so much time wandering in the forest with Girl Scouts, and giggling with your best friend, and talking to plants. You stayed innocent right into college, enough that you managed to eat a pot brownie without your knowledge, because you thought brownies served at college drinking parties were made with Betty Crocker recipes."

Scarlet laughed, the sound drawing his eyes. Hunter smiled at her again – an adoring smile she felt across every surface of her skin – and she took a moment to appreciate its beauty. Then she pressed her lips together, knowing she was supposed to be quiet while he spoke. He turned back to the window with that same sweet grin still on his face.

"You were a happy, innocent college student, and you rambled when you were nervous," he told her. "Your overpowered brain simply thought too much at once, and the words tumbled out whenever you felt stressed or excited. Which was a lot, I imagine, since college is challenging for normal people, but even more so for someone who felt the need to achieve all of the degrees and honors now hanging on your wall. So, you thought it best to seek out therapy to fix your nervous-talking, which your mother most likely thought was adorable, but your father probably saw as a hindrance to your success. I imagine the idea for therapy came to you after a particularly riveting Psych 101 class in your freshman year."

"Professor Price," Scarlet supplied.

Hunter winced with her disruption. He looked back to her and stilled. Then he stood, silent and stern, just staring into her eyes.

Her fingers wound together. "Sorry," she offered. "I know I'm only supposed to listen right now, but Professor Price's face just popped into my head. Price Psych – that's what we called his class. He looked like Julius Caesar, minus the leaf headband over his ears. But I know that's not important right now, and I'm going to be quiet again."

Hunter's head tilted, although his gaze remained firm. "You can talk during this if you want to. Just as long as you don't argue with me."

Her brow rose at the veiled command, but she felt too captivated by his story to stop it now. Settling back into her heels, she nodded again.

With her acquiescence, he diverted his eyes back to the sky. "As I was saying, you entered into therapy in an attempt to control your magnificently wandering mind. During your sessions, you began to see what the doctors could do and what it meant to devote yourself to helping people. You started to understand why your father spent his life the way he did, and you began to think your mother didn't know what she was talking about when she told you to be wild and carefree. You were also terribly aware of your level of intelligence, because how could you not be? So, you took an acute look at your life and decided to grow up. You decided to devote yourself to the service of others, and you went from college to medical school, where you grew up fast and hard."

When Hunter stopped to look at her, Scarlet's pulse ran a mile a minute. "I imagine you discovered your latex allergy sometime during medical school."

"Oh, yes," she agreed. "It was awful. There were rubbers everywhere."

A deep chuckle erupted from his chest.

Scarlet replayed the words until her face grew hot. "Just so we're clear, I meant rubbers as in gloves. And by that, I mean gloves for your hands. There were a lot of hand-gloves. Not other-body-part gloves. There weren't many of those. And I'm allergic to them all, so..." Her words trailed as Hunter held her with an impassioned stare.

"That brings me to the next chapter of your life – the boyfriends," he said, pivoting fully toward her. "You had a few over the years, but only assholes who never gave you more than one orgasm. Then you met Richard, who was a cardiac surgeon, just like your father. You probably found him after you graduated medical school, and I imagine Dr. Richard What's-His-Name seemed like a perfect match for Dr. Scarlet Tracey. I imagine that relationship made sense at the time, and you might have even convinced yourself you were happy. Happy enough to agree to marry him when he asked you.

"In your mind, life was as it should be then. You were engaged to a proper doctor. You were helping people, like your father wanted, and your mother certainly wasn't ashamed of you. How could she be, when you were doing such good? But then something happened, and it shook your entire world. Something happened that forced you to take a severe look at your supremely structured life."

Scarlet stood perched on the edge, anxiously awaiting his next words, even though she'd lived every moment. "What happened?"

"Your father died," he answered, his face falling. "He died right on his desk at work, and no one found him until the next morning." Hunter's eyes drifted to her desktop. "I imagine you've slept on this desk before. I imagine even Marie couldn't get you to leave here some nights, when the workload was too heavy."

Scarlet gulped, forcing down the truth.

His eyes returned to hers. "This is where your life started to unravel. This is where your identity crisis began, because somewhere on the path of dealing with the emotions surrounding your father's death, you began to examine your own life as a doctor. You knew you were good at being a psychiatrist, since you had a gift – you had the ability to become whatever your patients needed you to be, in order to earn their trust. For Pete, you became a missing daughter. For Tyler, you became a pillar of normalcy. For Colin, you became a stable home. You did it because you could look into them all so easily, and you knew if you met their needs, they would let you delve into their darkest fears.

"You were terribly good at opening people up, probably from the instant you set your mind to practicing psychiatry. But then you lost your father, and there you were, seeing how he lived and died for his work. You were engaged to a man just like him, a man who bored you to tears. Richard bored you because he didn't know the real you. How could he? You never let him see that bright, boundless girl you'd once been. And you filled so many roles for so many people – including him – that he couldn't possibly know the real you. Honestly, no one could. When you realized that truth, you broke off your engagement.

"That decision, while wise, left you with no fiancée, no father, and a somewhat-estranged mother who picked up the pieces of her life and moved to Las Vegas. After that, you were alone. Entirely alone, and neck-deep in a job where you felt like you had to lose your identity, day after day. But you told yourself it was okay, because you were helping people and that made all the sacrifices worth it. You told yourself it was fine to go home alone every night, and bury your head in distractions like movies, which offered an easy escape from reality."

Hunter stopped to catch a breath, but Scarlet couldn't. His words ran hot as wildfire beneath her skin, and she wanted nothing more than to crawl out of it. When his voice returned, as powerful and passionate as ever, she forced herself to remain motionless.

"But there was still that part of you, Scarlet – the frolicking bird – begging to be free. It was that woman who listened as some of her female patients talked about how they'd never been able to have an orgasm, and you felt relieved you could. Except you also had to listen to your sex-addicted patients confess their exploits in great detail, and you had to keep a straight face through those sessions, for their sakes. You could never reveal how their words bothered you, or how curious you were for experiences of your own. You tried not to think about how empowering it would feel to blindfold a man, and tie him up, and do anything you wanted to do. You tried not to imagine being tied up yourself, since you would never act on your fantasies. The sedate doctor you'd become simply wouldn't allow such hedonistic explorations.

"Instead, you repressed your desires. You buried everything down deep, and concentrated on being the person you had to be, to support everyone else. You went to work, and volunteered at your clinic, and helped your community. Then you went home alone every night, assuring yourself that your life was rich in many ways. Which is true, of course. I've seen firsthand some of the people you've helped, and I know how they rely on you. I'm sure that's an incredible feeling, to know you can give someone what they need to live a better life."

Hunter paused his speech, his shoulders bunching beneath his coat. "But then, something else happened," he said, the words barely above a whisper. "Something that shook you all the way down to your soul, and it...it took the color red away from you."

Tears welled in his eyes. "I know this thing hurt you so deeply, honey. It was angry and violent and bloody, and it hurt you in the worst way. And I don't know what it was. I admit I don't know. But only because you haven't told me. Yet."

Scarlet's chest squeezed to the point of suffocation. She fought back tears of her own, but they still won, spilling down her cheeks behind the frames of her glasses. She turned toward the multitudinous plants running the length of her office wall, absorbing the peaceful sight as she struggled to control the pain. When she finally found the courage to look back to Hunter, he matched her solemn stare.

"I hope someday you will, Scarlet. I hope you'll share this thing with me, since I know it affected you profoundly, and I want you to tell me about it. Maybe I won't be able to help you. Maybe I won't have any good words of advice. But there is one thing I know I can do for you."

She sniffled. "What's that?"

"I can listen. If nothing else, I can listen to you, and be here for you. I want that. I want to be here for you. I want it so badly."

God, his words were beautiful. They were absolutely gorgeous, and she wanted to band them tight to her chest and never let go. It was all she could do to stand so far away from him as they both trembled. It took every ounce of strength she owned to not leap across the floor and hurl herself into his arms.

"Whatever this thing was," he continued, "I believe it's the reason you felt weak and beaten when you went to Blue. I believe it's the reason you felt desperate enough to beg Abbott for a vacation."

Scarlet nodded. She didn't even realize she was doing it. Not until she saw Hunter study the movement, absorbing her silent confirmation.

The muscle in his jaw twitched before he spoke again. "I've got to be honest; I'm pretty pissed off at Abbott for making you beg to stay there. You shouldn't have had to do that. He should have let you be at Blue on your own terms, and attend any of the functions, and receive all the therapy you needed. Instead, you didn't get anything of the sort. You spent your days wandering in the woods, and your nights with me, and despite your immeasurable level of self-reliance, I think you would have benefited from actual sessions with another doctor."

Hunter leaned toward her. "You know, Will is worried about you. When I told him you were on vacation at Blue, I could see the concern in his eyes. And even though he wouldn't tell me what you'd spoken with him about, I realized something. While you mostly treat people with addictions – sex addicts like Tyler and work addicts like me – Will treats a lot of soldiers and police officers. He specializes in helping people with posttraumatic stress, so I think you went to him because of the trauma you suffered from whatever took the color red away from you."

Scarlet brushed the tears from her cheeks. "Will is a good listener."

"Yes, he is. So are you. You spend every day listening to people talk, and I can't even imagine all the things they say. I can't imagine all the burdens they unload onto your shoulders. I know why you chose to go to Blue, and why you needed to recharge yourself, since the problems facing you here had become too much to bear. I also know you spent your first week there seeing patients, because you'd promised Abbott you would, and you spent your evenings wandering in the woods, trying to reconnect with your inner Girl Scout.

"Then, right before you started your vacation, you gave a lecture to all the patients. You spoke to them about appreciation – about searching out and loving all the little things life has to offer – because that's what you were trying to remember how to do. The very next day, you went for a walk in the woods, and you got a little lost, and you came out farther down the road than normal. That's when you saw me, crouched down and grumbling by my tire."

Hunter's brow furrowed. "To be perfectly honest, I'd like to think that when you first laid eyes on me, a part of you – even a tiny one – thought about leaving me there and walking back into the trees. I'd like to think a part of you has some sense of self-preservation, enough to keep you from poking a big, growly grizzly bear with a stick. But I know that's not the case. I know you didn't think twice. You just came to help."

He looked straight into her, grounding her in place. "You know, Scarlet, the last time I stood here in your office, you told me that entering into a relationship with me was a selfish decision. But I assure you, that's far from true."

Her jaw unhinged. "My God, how can you even say that? Being with you at Blue is the most selfish thing I've ever done."

"No. It wasn't selfish at all."

She started to protest, until Hunter took a step toward her.

"The selfish thing would have been for you to leave me there," he insisted. "The selfish thing would have been for you to take one look at me, spin on your heels, and run. The selfish thing would have been to turn your back on someone who desperately needed your help. But you would never do that, because that's not who you are. You're kind and loving and generous, and you'd never turn away from a person in need. Instead, you walked over, smiled your beautiful smile, and looked inside me. You saw how I suffered and you made the decision to change my life for the better. And you did. You opened me up entirely, and I'm so grateful for that. But I'm even more grateful that you opened yourself up to me. I hope you realize you did that, too. I hope you know how much you opened up to me while we were on that mountain."

He paused for her acknowledgement, but it wasn't necessary. She couldn't deny the truth, even if she wanted to. "Yes, Hunter. I know."

A smile tugged at his lips, although he didn't relax his rigid stance. "I'm glad you know. I love how you let me see the imaginary bird flying through your mind, and the innocent girl who wanted to explore her sexuality, and the somber woman who struggled to keep her head above water. You let me see *all* of you, and I think I might be the only person who ever has. I think I'm the only person in the whole world who knows every single part of you."

Hunter took two steps forward, closing some of the gap between them. "Now tell me, please – am I right? Am I right to think I know you? Or do I need to keep the promise I made earlier, and walk out of that door, and never lay my eyes on you again?"

Scarlet's heart stopped cold in her chest. The repulsive thought of him walking away forever sent icy shivers raking across her skin, and she knew there was no way in hell she could make herself tell the lie that would force him to leave. Sucking a deep breath into her lungs, she faced him head-on. "You're right about everything, Hunter."

"Really? You actually admit I know you?"

"Yes. I admit you know me."

With her affirmation, his shoulders finally fell. "Thank goodness for that. Can I assume now that you have no further protests against our relationship? Can we simply agree to move on with our lives together?"

Her heart sunk into her stomach. "No, I can't simply agree."

"Why not?"

"Because things between us are still complicated."

"What things? What's left that makes this complicated?"

She shifted in her heels, struggling to remember all the protests that made perfect sense to her before he entered this room today. "Well, for one, there's the matter of Abbott finding out about us."

"You were on vacation."

"I know I was, but that won't make a difference to him."

Hunter shrugged. "Then Abbott never needs to know our paths crossed at Blue. We can make up a story about how we met. Honestly, my family thinks I've been in Cozumel for the last two weeks with friends from work, and my work thinks I've been mountain climbing with my parents, so I'll need something to tell everyone. The only thing I said to Clay when he helped me with your book yesterday was that my trip was cancelled. I think we should tell people that we met each other while eating by the fountain in the marble square, and I was so enamored when I saw you, I cancelled my vacation to get to know you better."

Scarlet enjoyed imagining their quaint, meet-cute scenario, complete with shared sandwiches and bashful smiles. "That would be a lovely story, if it were true. But I don't want to keep secrets about how we met. Believe it or not, I don't want to start a relationship by telling lies."

"Well, I prefer not to do it this way, either. But I don't ever want our relationship to hurt your career, so I can't risk Abbott discovering the truth. Besides, I think it's okay to keep secrets *with* each other. As long as we don't keep secrets *from* each other."

She absorbed the easy certainty in Hunter's eyes. "Wow. This is all just... it's all so simple for you, isn't it?"

"What do you mean?"

"This – us – everything. You don't see the complications."

"No, I don't. I know you see a ton of obstacles, but I don't see any. My feelings for you are crystal clear, and I have no doubts about them. This is simple for me. I want it to be simple for you, too."

Scarlet twisted her fingers together. "But I don't know if I can be the person you want me to be. I don't know if I can be your frolicking freebird in the real world. Here, I'm a doctor. I'd questioned that fact when I went to Blue, but you helped me realize I will never truly be happy unless I'm taking care of my patients. This is just who I am."

"Okay," he agreed. "You can be whoever you want. I'm not asking you to leave your patients. I'm only asking you to be with me, too."

"But Hunter..."

"No. Don't 'but Hunter' me. You keep trying to tell me you're not the same person I knew on that mountain, but that's not true. You're as much the frolicking freebird as you are the solemnly sedate physician. You've just never tried to be both women at the same time."

"You're right. I haven't tried it, because it won't work. I have to be this person, so I can put my heart and soul into my job. The people here count on me with their lives. I can't let them down."

"Then don't. Be a doctor, Scarlet. Be a straight-laced, hard-ass doctor while you're in this office, if you think that works best. But then leave here at the end of the day and come home to me. Come home and be my freebird. Because I need her. I need her so damn much."

She blinked against the next round of tears in her eyes.

Hunter took another step closer. "But I swear, I'm really not trying to make you choose. If you decide to stay the hard-ass doctor all the time, I'll be perfectly happy. She challenges me, and I love that. I want you to be whichever woman you want to be. Or you can try something entirely different – you can try being both at the same time. After all, you helped me as the frolicking free-bird, so I think you can be her and still be a doctor. All I want is you, no matter who you decide to be."

Scarlet whimpered, banding her arms around her stomach to hold herself together. This gnawing hunger inside her grew even more potent, while the logic she clung to frayed at the edges.

Hunter stared down at her clenched arms before looking back to her eyes. "You know, I've come to realize I owe you an apology."

Her brow rose. "What on earth for?"

"For that day in the woods, when I told you about Samantha. After I told you what happened with her, you said so many things to me. You tried to get me to understand the impact that experience had on my life, especially with the decisions I'd made at work. Honestly, I couldn't process much of anything at that point in time, except anger. I was so angry with you, thinking there was no way in hell a frolicking freebird could possibly understand what it means to hold the lives of so many people in their hands, like I do. But I was wrong. I was terribly wrong, because you truly hold lives in your hands, and I understand that now.

"You said a lot of things to me that day, Scarlet. You said I was putting all of myself into my work. You said I was giving my whole life to my employees. You said I was giving them everything, and leaving nothing for myself, and it was killing me. And you were right. I was doing all of those things. But what I can see now, so starkly, is that you weren't just talking to me. You were also talking to yourself, because you're doing the exact same thing. You're giving all of yourself to your work – you're giving all of yourself to your patients – and you're not going to be able to breathe like that for much longer."

Hunter's fists clenched at his sides. "You've never allowed yourself a full life of happiness as an adult, and it just...it kills me. It kills me to see you here in your office, caged and alone. This life is suffocating you, and I'm so goddamn scared you won't be able to get through it."

She shook her head violently. "No. I can get through it. I *can*."

"Well, if you're that determined, then I believe you. I know you're not easily broken, honey. But is this what you really want? Are you going to be happy just getting through life? Are you going to be happy merely surviving? Because you deserve to be happy."

Tears streamed down Scarlet's face again. It took several gulped breaths to steady herself. When she finally reigned in her emotions, she met his raw stare. Hunter's body vibrated with energy, obviously struggling to keep his distance while she cried.

After smoothing her fingers over her damp cheeks, she settled her arms to her sides. She stood tall and forced a smile onto her lips, focusing on his deep blue eyes from across the room. "I appreciate everything you've said to me today," she began, keeping her voice calm and clear. "All of your words are beautiful. Unfortunately, I'm not sure if I can be both the doctor and the freebird. And even if I could try to be both, I don't think now is the best time. You and I went through so much up on that mountain. We're each emotionally raw. Please tell me you can see that."

Hunter glared at her, even as he nodded. "Yes, I can see that."

"Then please understand I'm not contradicting you because I want to. I don't want to fight this thing between us. But I have to, since now is not the time for either of us to enter into a long-term relationship." Scarlet stopped speaking when her stomach ground against itself.

"Maybe it won't be this way forever," she offered in consolation. "Maybe someday, after we've had the necessary time to heal, we can find our way back to each other. I'll even admit I'd really like for us to be able to do that, at some point in the future. But I don't think it's here and now."

Hunter stood at attention, listening to everything she had to say. She knew he listened, because the muscle in his jaw worked overtime with the words he obviously didn't want to hear. When he finished listening, he huffed. "Well, frankly, I don't agree with any of that. I don't want to put our lives on hold, just hoping we might find our way back to each other someday. We've spent years passing each other on the street, never knowing what could be. But now that I'm certain of what can be, I refuse to let it slip through my fingers."

"Please understand," she implored. "I'm honestly trying to do the right thing here. This isn't about what we want. This is about what we need. We need time to heal – we *both* need time to heal."

His eyes locked onto hers. "Why can't we heal together?"

"Because it...it doesn't work that way."

"Who says it doesn't? Some professor? Some psychology book? Or you? I know you've been on your own for a long time, and you've felt alone for even longer. But that doesn't mean you have to handle all of this by yourself anymore. I'm here now. I'm right here with you."

Scarlet ran his words over in her mind, holding on to them for as long as she could. When he took several more steps forward, she struggled for air. He stood beside her desk again now, so much closer.

"I can tell you with absolute certainty," Hunter vowed, "thatI will heal better with you by my side. And I truly believe you'll heal better with me by your side."

"No, but that's not..."

"God, stop!" he yelled, throwing his hands up in the air. "Just stop! I don't want to hear the end of that sentence."

He started pacing back and forth in front of her desk. The air lodged in Scarlet's lungs as she watched. He looked like a captive beast, with hunger and frustration roiling off his skin.

She remembered now why she'd given him the color hunter green. Despite the shackles she'd placed on him today, the man before her was a hunter – skillful, intelligent and predatory. He was primal and powerful, and she'd known patients just like him. She'd treated so many of them, both men and women, and had years of schooling and experience to manage turbulent situations with such challenging individuals.

Scarlet tried like hell to recall her training. As a physician, she knew what she should do: set defined limits and insist there were no arguments to be made. There was only one answer to be had, which was to step away from each other. But even though she understood the necessary boundaries, she still struggled to set them. As powerful as the man before her was, he now looked trapped and scared. His emotions were scattered in pieces, their edges ragged and sharp, which she knew was her fault. All of this was her fault.

"I'm – I'm sorry," she breathed, her heart reaching for his as he paced relentlessly across the floor.

"No," Hunter snapped. "No more apologies." He stopped moving to stand beside her desk again, staring her down. "Good Lord, you're stubborn. I already knew that, but hell. You're so *goddamn* stubborn."

"This isn't about being stubborn. It's about doing what's right."

He didn't move a single tensed muscle, yet she could still feel his boiling energy pulsing at her in waves across the meager space separating them. Every nerve in her body heightened while she watched him take several deep breaths. "I know you're trying to do the right thing here," he finally admitted, his voice steady again, even if he was unable to fully mask his frustration. "I get that you want to do what's best for me. I really do. But I know *you* are what's best for me. And I know *I* am what's best for you. So, you'll have to forgive me for refusing to believe that walking away from you is the right thing to do. For either of us."

Scarlet worked to maintain a brave front. She straightened her spine, pressed her shoulders back, and lifted her chin. Still, her gelatinous legs barely supported her. "Well, I hope you'll reconsider that thought."

Hunter stared the words out of her mouth. She hoped she'd done enough to convince him of her point. This pull they had to each other – this insane level of emotion they shared – was entirely out of control. These feelings simply weren't realistic for two people who'd only known each other for a handful of days.

He examined her from head to toe. Hours passed as she held herself firm beneath his inspection. Eventually, his expression changed. His gaze fell to the ground, his hands unclenched, and his body calmed. He finally looked...resolved.

Scarlet's eyes widened with the realization that he wasn't going to challenge her anymore today. When Hunter raised his head back up, she could tell by the look on his face just how resolved he was. She held her breath when he opened his mouth, preparing herself to hear one statement: *I'm going to leave now, Scarlet.* She was ready to hear it. She really was, no matter how much it would hurt. However, that wasn't what came out of his mouth at all.

Instead, he looked straight into her and said, "I really tried to give you a choice in this matter. I hope you can see that."

Her brow knitted. "What does that mean?"

Hunter shook his head as he turned, reaching for the briefcase he'd set on her desk. "It means I gave you ample opportunity to make the right decision. I honestly thought, once you heard everything I had to say today, you would allow us to be together. But you still refuse to give us what we deserve, so I'm going to have to do this the hard way."

Scarlet's entire body stiffened. "What exactly is the *hard* way?"

He grasped his briefcase and unfastened the leather strap. "You know, I really hoped when I arrived today that I wouldn't have to open this case. But I have no choice at this point, because I came here for a very specific goal, which I have yet to achieve. I want something from you, Scarlet. I want one simple little thing from you, and I've tried using both romance and logic to get it, yet neither of those has worked. So now, I'm left with only one other option."

"Wait a minute. What do you mean you tried romance and logic? And what's the other option?"

"I tried romance on our first date, in the town at the bottom of Blue," he explained while flipping the strap open. "I tried to show you how good we could be together, and at the end of our date, we made love and you fell asleep in my arms. I thought it was a pretty damn perfect day, and yet you still weren't with me when I woke up the next morning, so I know romance isn't going to get me this thing I want from you today. I've also tried to reason with you – the last time I was here in this office, as well as just now – but that hasn't worked for me, either."

Hunter pulled open the briefcase. "Don't worry," he assured, looking down at the contents she couldn't see from this angle. "I promise I'll be more reasonable in other situations. I also promise there will be plenty of romance in the future. Just not right now."

Scarlet cringed with his declaration. This man was resolved, but it definitely wasn't the kind of resolution she'd expected. There was an entirely different sort of certainty emanating from his skin, one she could feel across the scant distance between them.

She had to lick her dry lips in order to speak. "If...if you want something from me, then tell me what it is, and we'll discuss it."

"No. I'm done trying to talk this out rationally."

"Does that mean you intend to be *irrational*?"

He chuckled, the sound dark yet lulling. "I wouldn't say I'm going to be irrational. I'm just using another approach to get what I want."

She worried her lip with her teeth when Hunter began pulling items from his mysterious briefcase. Arching on her tiptoes, she attempted to peek at what lay inside. But he was too damn tall, and his shoulders were too infuriatingly broad, and she couldn't see anything at all. Her pulse bounded as he set three items down on the edge of her desk.

"Are those scarves?" she asked, settling into her heels when he turned to her.

"They are. I bought red, green, and blue ones. The colors seemed fitting, given our history. I think they're pretty, especially the red one with the little roses on it, although I don't know how good my taste is. I wish Maxine was home from Paris already, so I could have taken her shopping with me, but I had to do it myself. I do hope you like them."

"They're lovely. But why did you bring them here?"

He didn't answer. He just pinned her with his eyes while a devilish smile curved his lips. Scarlet's face blanched in his silence, since the only time they'd done anything with a scarf before was when she'd blindfolded him that night in her cabin. But Hunter had *three* scarves now, and she wasn't sure what he intended to do with all of them.

He stepped away from his briefcase then, grabbed hold of her chair, and pushed it to the far wall. His sweltering, feral gaze raked over her body as he moved back to the desk. Scarlet inched backwards on instinct, crowding her spine onto her washroom door.

When Hunter reached her desktop again, he took the green scarf in one of his hands. As she watched him run the fabric between his fingers, she forced herself to accept the truth of his unspoken intentions. *Sweet heaven, he plans to tie me up and blindfold me. Holy hell.*

She pressed her lips shut, unable to do anything but watch while he reached into the briefcase again. He pulled out another object and set it down beside the scarves. This item was a red plastic egg.

Scarlet's head tilted. "What is that egg? Is it what I think it is?"

"Depends on what you think it is."

"It looks like silly putty."

"You're right. It's silly putty."

"Dear Lord, what are you planning to do to me with silly putty?"

Hunter grinned. "Not a damn thing. I just stopped by a toy store yesterday to pick up some gifts for Evie and I saw this. I remembered you saying it was one of the handiest things on earth, so I thought you might like to have some."

"Oh. Well, thank you. It's sweet that you remember."

"I remember everything you ever said to me," he stated. "But do you remember what I said *my* handiest thing on earth is?"

Her knees buckled. "Y-you said duct tape."

"That's right. Duct tape."

Hunter didn't take his eyes off of her as he reached back into the briefcase and grabbed hold of a thick roll of gray tape. He held it in both hands, his fingers playing with the starting edge.

Scarlet whimpered. "What are you going to do with that?"

"What do you think I'm going to do with it?"

"I don't know...tape my mouth shut?"

He laughed, his shoulders shaking beneath his expertly tailored coat. "I would never do that. I love your voice too much. Honestly, I love your mouth in general, so I definitely want to maintain access to it."

Turning back to her desk, he held the tape roll in one hand as he opened and shut her desk drawers with his other hand.

"What are you searching for, Hunter?"

"Scissors. You do have scissors in here, don't you? I knew I'd never be able to get them through the metal detectors downstairs, and I couldn't risk those beefy guards opening my briefcase. After all, I bought a case with a leather closure just so it wouldn't set off any alarms. And you can rip duct tape with your teeth if you have to, but the taste is quite unpleasant. Although not as bad as pure lemon juice, of course. You must have scissors in here somewhere... ah, here we are."

He pulled his find from the bottom drawer on the left, where she kept her scissors lined up perfectly beside her stapler, hole punch, and paper clips. "Wow. This is a highly organized drawer, Dr. Tracey."

Hunter gave her a knowing look as he stood, setting the scissors and tape down beside each other before walking to the other side of her desk. Scarlet's body leaned toward his as he moved farther away. "What are you doing now?"

He didn't answer immediately. First, he reached for his jacket, eased the crisp material off his shoulders, folded it up, and laid it on the side of her couch. Next, he undid the buttons on his shirt cuffs and rolled each sleeve up to his elbow. She tried with all her might to not moan at the sight of his muscles moving beneath his forearms as he worked.

"I'm doing what needs to be done," he finally replied, the words making the tiny hairs on the back of her neck rise beneath her ponytail.

Scarlet kept perfectly still when he began his next task, which was to rearrange the furniture in her office. He grasped two of the wood-slatted chairs sitting in front of her desk, one in each hand. He lifted them easily, even though they weighed a good bit, his biceps tensing as he carried them around the desk. Hunter set the two wood chairs down in the space her leather chair normally occupied, with their backs up against her desktop, spaced body-width apart with one to either side of his hips.

She frowned as she watched, trying to determine his purpose. Did he want her to sit on one of the chairs? Was he going to sit on the other one? That didn't make any sense. Not if he intended to tie her up. Unless he intended for her to sit on the desktop, and spread her legs open, with one foot bound into each chair...

Scarlet's heart tripped. "Hey, why don't, um, instead of, uh..."

Her pitiful protest was silenced by the screeching sound of tape being stripped away from the roll. She stood in disbelief as he used her scissors to cut one extremely long section of the sticky gray material.

"Good Lord, Hunter. Do you really intend to use that tape on me?"

He peeled off a second strip of equal length before turning toward her. "I do, actually. I'm about to be very demanding with you, Scarlet."

The domineering look in his eyes sent shivers flitting down her spine. Not shivers of distress, or resentment, or fear. God help her, these were shivers of anticipation. "What exactly do you mean by *demanding*?"

"I mean that I'm going to use your body's response to mine against you, in order to get what I want. Because we both know that I can."

Her jaw dropped. "That's – that's not fair."

"You're right. But I don't intend to play fair anymore today."

When he returned his attention to the long strips of tape, Scarlet groaned. "The duct tape looks like it's going to be extremely painful."

"It doesn't have to be," he assured, pressing both pieces of tape together, so the adhesive sides clung to each other. "See that? Now it's not even sticky. It's just a really good form of binding."

"Binding?"

"Yes," he confirmed before cutting another lengthy strip. "I worried yesterday, when I devised this holy-hell-Scarlet-is-even-more-stubborn-than-I-thought back-up plan, that you might have a reaction to the duct tape because of your allergy. So, I did my research. Did you know there's an American Latex Allergy Association? They have an informative website, with lists of everything containing latex. I'm fairly certain you shouldn't have a reaction to the outside of the tape, but I bought the scarves to protect your skin, just to be safe."

Scarlet watched him tear off a fourth piece of tape and stick it to the third one, once again concealing the adhesive inside. Her heart banged against her ribcage. "Please," she entreated. "We don't need to do all of this. Just tell me what it is you want from me."

He lifted the two strips of binding, tugging on them to test their strength, before setting them back on the desktop. "Oh, I don't want much. It's honestly a simple little thing I'm going to ask you for. But I want it more than life itself, and I'm definitely going to get it."

"Can't you just tell me what it is?"

"Nope. Not yet." Hunter placed the tape roll back into his briefcase, closed the leather strap, and set the case onto the floor. He moved the scissors and silly putty egg off to the corner, to sit beside her book. The moment he'd cleared the desktop, he refocused all of his energy on her.

"I'm ready for you now," he stated. "Will you please come here?"

Her mouth ran dry when she witnessed the determined look in his eyes. She shook her head without her even realizing it.

He smiled in response to her muted denial. "You must know I'm not really asking. I'm just trying to offer a pretense of politeness, for your sake. If you don't come over here, I will come get you."

"H-Hunter..."

"Scarlet, you're going to come here and stand by this desk. You're going to let me blindfold you and tie you up, because you're curious about it, and because deep down you actually want me to do it. You know your body wants to be close to mine. You want me to touch you, and I will, and I promise there will be nothing physically painful about it when I do. In fact, I assure you it will feel very, very good."

She struggled to remain upright. "I – I know perfectly well what you're doing right now."

"What is that?"

"You're telling me what's going to happen, and how I'm going to feel about it, so I'm more likely to submit passively to your demands."

His eyebrow quirked. "Is it working?"

"That's...that's beside the point, and I think..."

"Scarlet?"

"Yes?"

"Will you please stop thinking for one second and just come here?"

She planted her heels firmly on the ground. "No. I will not."

He didn't budge an inch. "Come here. *Now.*"

Her brow arched above her glasses as she held him in place with an indomitable glare. That glare finally made the smile fall from his lips.

Hunter exhaled before addressing her in a surprisingly rational tone. "Look, I know you have a strong will. You know I do, too. I'm fully aware that your will and my will are going to have issues for the rest of our lives. To be perfectly honest, I'm looking forward to all the times they're going to clash.

But today, I am going to win this battle of wills, no matter what. I will get what I want by any means necessary."

"Even if I refuse to cooperate?"

"Well, the way I see it, you have two options at the moment. You can either come over here as I've asked, or you can yell for Marie to call security. Because the only way I'm leaving here – without getting what I want – is if those gigantic guards charge up seventeen stories, barge into this room, and drag me away, kicking and screaming. And I do mean literally kicking and screaming. I'll resist them so hard, they'll have no choice but to haul my belligerent ass off to jail."

Hunter matched her resolute stare across the space separating them. "I can just see the news headlines now, Scarlet: Millionaire CEO Hunter Gregory behind bars after being dragged from local psychiatrist's office. Damn, all of that horrible publicity, when I've spent my entire adult life trying to stay out of the tabloids for the wellbeing of my employees. Gregory Global stocks will take a significant hit when that story breaks tonight, which will affect every person in the building you see from your window each day. I think it would be a real shame to put the livelihood of all those families in jeopardy. Don't you?"

His question hung in the air for a solid minute. He stood tall and straight, without flinching in the least. Meanwhile, Scarlet's mind spun, wondering if there was any chance in hell that he was bluffing.

"You know I'm serious," he said, making her question whether he'd read her thoughts or she'd spoken out loud. Although she was fairly certain she hadn't said a word, since her throat felt entirely constricted.

After forever, she managed to huff. "This is truly unfair."

"I already told you – I'm not playing fair today."

"But this is blackmail, Hunter. It's *emotional* blackmail. Your need to control this situation has made you stoop to a level far beneath you. Your actions are borne entirely out of desperation."

"Hell, don't you think I know that? I am fully aware of how far down I'm stooping. And of how insanely desperate I feel."

"Then can't you see what it all means? The desperation we feel comes from powerful, wrenching emotions. You need time to deal with those emotions before you even *think* about moving forward with a relationship. *Please* tell me you see that."

When she finished speaking, Scarlet held her breath. She focused on him with her entire body, hoping beyond hope that he would finally accept the reality of their situation.

After an unreasonably long minute, the fire in his eyes softened. "Do you realize what you just said, Scarlet? You said we."

"What?"

"The desperation *we* feel. That's what you said."

"Well, I...I..."

"You're as desperate for me as I am for you," he concluded, pushing the sleeves of his shirt higher and crossing his arms in front of his chest, defining his forearms in a way she shouldn't have noticed.

She quieted, unable to deny his statement.

In her silence, Hunter offered an empathetic smile. "You know, a few moments ago, you asked me to understand that you're trying to do the right thing here. Now I'm just asking for the same understanding, because I believe I'm doing the right thing, too. I truly, honestly believe I'm doing what's right for us. I'm fighting for our *lives* here today – for *both* our lives. You didn't abandon me to suffer alone up on that mountain, and I'll be damned to hell before I abandon you to suffer alone in this office."

Scarlet stood, utterly immobile. His words rang in her ears, barely audible over the hammering of her heart. She felt her walls crumbling around her, both personally and professionally.

Hunter tilted his chin down and narrowed his gaze. "I'd appreciate it if you let me know how this is going to happen. Are you going to come over here of your own free will? Or do I have to come get you?"

She somehow managed to shake her head, since giving in to this controlling behavior of his went against every shred of sense she owned. But even more than that, as she stood beneath the scrutiny of his deep blue eyes, she couldn't be sure her legs would actually carry her that far.

He gave her another few seconds to comply, despite her silent refusal. When she didn't move at all, he started toward her. He barely placed one foot in front of the other before Scarlet whimpered.

"Wait," she said, raising both hands in front of her. "I'm coming."

"You are?"

"Yes. Just...just give me a minute."

Hunter smiled as he resettled beside her desk.

She dropped her hands back to her sides. Her feet wobbled in her heels when she took the first step toward him. Working to keep her head held high, she balled her fists to hide her shaking fingers. When she arrived at the edge of her desk, she stopped.

He stood mere inches away. Her stomach lodged in her throat while she looked up to him. He stepped to the side, sweeping his arm out in an open invitation. "Come stand between the chairs. Facing me. Please."

Scarlet did as instructed, backing up between the two chairs until she felt the desktop edge against her skirt-clad bottom. Grasping onto the wood frame for a faint semblance of stability, she pressed her shoulders back and attempted a veil of defiance. "I don't know why you're bothering to say please at this point."

Hunter chuckled when he faced her. "Well, I was trying to maintain a sense of decorum. But I'll be happy to stop, if that's what you want." He took two steps closer, erasing nearly all the space between them, immediately drowning her in the heat of his body.

He didn't touch her at all. He just stood there, smiling down into her eyes. "How are you feeling right now, Scarlet?"

"Feeling? Are you actually asking me how I'm *feeling*?"

"I imagine you're feeling all kinds of things. Emotions are messy."

"You're right. Emotions are messy. And acting on them isn't necessarily a good thi..."

He cut off her words with a simple action. It wasn't even a kiss, like he'd used to silence her in the past. This time, all he had to do was lean forward. He closed his eyes, pressed their foreheads together, and breathed in deep. Scarlet lost her words entirely.

"God, you smell good," he whispered over her lips. "I'm so used to your scent. And the warmth of your body. It's only been a few days since I had you beneath me in bed, but I've barely been able to sleep since. I miss your warmth. I miss your scent. I miss all of you."

He put his hands on the desk, in the space between her hips and her clenched fingers, and she inhaled sharply. She wanted to say something, but then he grazed his mouth across hers.

"Have you missed me, Scarlet? Has your body ached for mine?"

She groaned, biting her lip, trying like hell not to give in.

Hunter lifted his head to pin her eyes. "Answer me. Please."

Scarlet couldn't think straight. Not with him looking at her like he could devour her whole. Her hands shifted closer to his against the desktop. "I, um... perhaps...a little."

"Hmm. I didn't really catch that. Could you repeat it?"

She huffed. "Damn it, *yes*. I've missed you. Are you happy now?"

"Oh, I am," he answered with a wicked grin. "I'm actually ecstatic. But is there anything else you want to tell me?"

"What do you want to know?"

He lifted one hand, reaching behind her head to grasp her ponytail. "Have you ached for me? Did you lay in bed last night and wish you had me beside you, touching you and kissing you and making love to you? Is that what happened in those dark hours?" He curled his fingers over her hair tie and tugged. "Or maybe you didn't imagine me making love to you. Maybe you imagined me fucking you. Maybe you wanted to fulfill more of your repressed fantasies. Maybe you imagined me fucking you in the shower, like we never got to do at Blue. And maybe you had to touch yourself right then, just to give your body some relief, since you didn't have me to help release all of that pent-up energy. Because you knew, if I was there, I would touch you everywhere and taste every inch of you. You knew, if I was there, I would…"

"Please," she panted. "Please stop."

He slipped the tie from her hair, slowly but surely, until it dropped onto the desk. Her loose black curls fell to her shoulders. Hunter hummed his approval at the sight. "Mmm. Stop what?"

"Everything. It's not fair to use my attraction for you against me."

"You're right. It isn't. But then again, I've heard all is fair in love and war." He inched closer, his warm breath brushing against her skin. "I need you to do something for me right now."

"Wh-what?"

"I need you to lift your skirt."

"No, that's not…"

"Lift your skirt, please."

"I need you to be reasonable right now, Hunter. This is my office. *My office*. Marie is right outside that door, and there's no lock on it."

"Lift. Your. Skirt. Now."

Scarlet's nipples tightened. "You know I can't give in to this. You're supposed to be working on your control issues."

"Sometimes you like my control issues," he reminded her, rubbing the tips of their noses together. "I distinctly remember you saying you want me to be my controlling, demanding self when we're together."

"I told you that up at Blue. Not here."

"And yet here we are, back in the real world, and you still want me. I can see that so clearly. Your pupils are blown, your body is trembling, and your breaths are coming fast and shallow to your chest. You're just aching to feel me inside you, aren't you?"

She closed her eyes and shuddered. "That's not a fair question. You already know how much I want you."

Hunter smiled against her lips. "I do know, and I'm so damn glad. I'll admit that a lot of things are different here in the real world, but I'm going to prove to you that nothing has changed between us. I still want you, you still want me, and I'm still going to fuck the hell out of you. The only difference is that today, it'll be on the desk in your office."

He skimmed his mouth across hers, light and feathery, and she nearly toppled over straining for more pressure. He chuckled when she caught herself before falling. Scarlet straightened in front of him, frowning at the smug look on his face.

"I can see you're frustrated that I haven't kissed you yet."

"Maybe," she conceded. "Why haven't you kissed me?"

"Because I'm not going to kiss you until you ask me. Kissing is very intimate. It carries a lot of emotion. So, I'm not going to just *take* a kiss from you. If you want that kind of intimacy, you're going to have to let me know." He leaned down again, running his stubbly cheek across her soft one. "I won't kiss you on the lips until you ask me. Or until you *tell* me. I must admit, I won't mind at all if you demand that I kiss you. And if you do, I promise I'll follow your orders exactly. But until then, I'll content myself with kissing you in other places."

He pressed his face into her neck, his forehead burrowing into her hair. His lips slid over her skin, the prickles on his chin scraping across her shoulder and sending chills down her spine. "Please," she breathed, "just tell me what it is you want from me."

"Mmm," he hummed into her throat. "I want you to lift your skirt."

"Is that really the thing you want from me?"

His eyes returned to hers. "Oh, no, that's not the actual thing I came here to get today. That's just the thing I want right this minute. I want you to lift your skirt for me."

"You know I can't. I absolutely *cannot* do that here."

He exhaled in frustration. "Damn it, Scarlet. You're not actually going to make me use my fantasy on this, are you?"

"Your fantasy?"

"The one you gave me at Blue, when you promised to fulfill any sexual fantasy of my choosing. You never did fulfill it. I brought it home with me, and I still have it."

"No, Hunter. That fantasy was only meant to be between us on that mountain. It was never supposed to follow us home."

"But it did follow us home. Maybe it shouldn't have, but it did. And I know you'll honor it, because Dr. Tracey would never break a promise."

She nibbled her lip, which drew his attention to her mouth, which pulled a moan from the back of his throat.

"God, honey, please don't make me use my fantasy on this. I want to hold onto that promise, because I love knowing you gave it to me. I want you to lift your skirt now simply because I've asked. I want you to do it because you actually *want* to do it. Because you want me to touch you. Because you want to feel me as much as I want to feel you."

Her entire body throbbed. She stared hard into his darkened eyes, witnessing so many emotions inside him. Desire. Determination. Lust. But those weren't the emotions that made her heart stutter in her chest. The longing, the ache, the need she saw – those were the things that stole her air. She knew everything Hunter felt was mirrored inside her eyes. He saw it all, so there was no point in trying to hide.

Her hands unclenched from the desk to reach for the hem of her skirt. She drew the fabric slowly up her thighs. When the soft material bunched at her stomach, she watched his throat shift on a hard swallow.

For a long moment, he didn't look down. He just looked straight into her, until Scarlet shifted impatiently inside her heels. Then his eyes drifted slowly to her waist.

Hunter's gaze roamed over her tensed fingers before easing farther down, to the juncture of her thighs. A low growl escaped his chest. "You're wearing the hunter green thong I bought you," he noted, his voice rough as sandpaper. "Did you think about me when you put them on this morning? Did you think about how you'd be wearing my color?"

"I – I did."

Her confession pulled his eyes back to hers. "I suggest you take them off. Now. Since I would hate for them to get torn."

She obeyed, because she didn't want them torn, either. And because she was really fucking tired of fighting her need for this man. Slipping her fingers inside the straps at her waist, she eased the silky material down to her thighs before allowing it to fall to the floor. She kicked the panties off to the side before straightening in front of him again.

"Very good," he praised. "Now sit up on the desk, please."

Scarlet didn't argue this time. She propped herself on the desktop, the bare cheeks of her bottom cooling instantly with the temperature of the smooth wood. Her fingers returned to the ledge, gripping tight.

Hunter leaned in closer, his chest coming flush with hers. He dipped his head down to kiss up her jaw and whisper in her ear. "I'd like you to spread your legs for me now. Place one of your feet into each chair."

She did as he told her, again, setting one black heel onto each chair so her calves rested against the slatted wood backs. The cool office air shifted over her heated inner thighs, making her shiver. With her skirt bunched at her waist, she realized she now sat entirely open to him. That fact didn't bother her nearly as much as it should.

Grabbing the red and green scarves, along with both strips of tape, he knelt onto the floor. Scarlet heard the air catch in his lungs when he settled before her. "Damn, you're wearing high heels today. You never wore heels at Blue."

She smiled down at the top of his head while his fingers ran across the black leather straps of her shoes. "I always wear heels to work."

Hunter's eyes darted back to hers. "I may have to visit you at work quite often, then."

The promise inherent in his words didn't make her heart jump in her chest, or cause wet heat to pool between her thighs. Of course it didn't, because that would be wrong. So very, very wrong.

Scarlet watched in shameless anticipation as he returned his attentions to her feet, slipping the green scarf around her left ankle and the red around her right. "I need to use the scarves to protect your skin," he explained while wrapping the strips of duct tape over the fabric. "And I realize I could have simply used the scarves to tie your legs to the chairs, but it felt more poetic this way."

She didn't respond, since the idea of him putting so much thought into tying her up rendered her speechless. She held perfectly still as he finished securing her ankles to the chairs with the long strips of gray binding. When he was done, his gaze drifted slowly across her calves and up her thighs, until settling decisively on the juncture of her legs.

Hunter inhaled sharply as he stared at her sex. The next instant, he stood fully upright, pushing his hips between her thighs to align their bodies. "Sweet hell, honey. You're already wet for me. I can actually see how wet you are."

Scarlet groaned out loud with the raw hunger of his voice.

"You know you're already wet for me, don't you?"

"Yes," she admitted, unable to tear her eyes away from his.

"Good God, I want you so much right now. I want to be inside of you so badly, it fucking hurts like hell."

"Damn it, Hunter. Just put us both out of our misery. Please."

"No, Scarlet. I'm sorry, but not yet."

She held tighter to the desk. "Then tell me what you want from me."

"Oh, I promise I will...in a little while. You know, I must say I'm already used to seeing you with your glasses on. They make your eyes look even more beautiful than usual, so it's truly unfortunate that I have to take them off now."

Hunter grasped the frame in both hands and slipped it off of her nose. After setting her glasses on the desk, he reached for the blue scarf and swept the fabric across her face. Scarlet's eyelids drifted closed.

His fingers knotted the fabric against the back of her hair before she felt his hands return to rest beside her hips. "How is it? Not too tight?"

Scarlet shook her head beneath the blindfold. "It's not too tight."

"Good. Can you see me?"

"No," she whimpered. "I can't see you at all."

He leaned in, pressing his lips beside her ear. "I know how much you want to see me right now. I remember the feeling all too well. The night you blindfolded me, I was desperate to see you. But I'm going to say the same thing now that you said then. Just feel. I want you to *feel*."

She pressed her eyes shut behind the silky scarf.

He kissed the tip of her nose. "Stay very still, just for a second."

Scarlet's ears pricked up with the sound of his fading footsteps. "Why? Where are you going?" she questioned, unable to hide her panic.

"I'm just going to use the sink in your restroom to wash my hands. I promise I'll be right back," he called from across the room.

Her brow crinkled behind the scarf when she heard the water running in the distant sink. A minute later, it stopped. "Why did you need to wash your hands?"

Hunter came back to her then. She knew he'd come back because she could feel the warmth of his body next to hers. She sighed in blissful peace, even despite being blindfolded and having her legs tied to chairs.

"I had to wash off any residue from the duct tape," he told her. "I can't risk you having a reaction. I really need to be able to touch you."

Scarlet blushed beneath the blindfold, just now realizing he hadn't touched her skin once since he'd pulled the tape from his case. He'd touched her hair, glasses, and shoes, but never her skin. "Thank you for being so cautious, but I don't think a little duct tape will hurt me."

"Well, I don't want to take any chances. I never want to hurt you, honey. Never, ever."

Hunter's cool, freshly washed fingers eased up one side of her face, carrying the scent of lemon from the soap on her bathroom sink. She liked the fresh smell, but she preferred the way he smelled. She couldn't really describe his scent in words. She only knew it was warm, and woodsy, and reminded her of being in the forest she loved so much.

He took a step closer and she leaned forward to breathe him in. His mouth returned to her neck, kissing leisurely down to the crook of her shoulder. His other hand found its way to her hip, curling into her bare skin. Scarlet moaned with the feel of his cool fingers on her fiery flesh.

She desperately wanted to touch him now. She wanted to peel her hands away from the edge of the desk and grab hold of him. Which truly confused her – not because she couldn't, but because she could.

"Um, Hunter?"

"Mmm?"

"Aren't you going to tie my hands together now, like I tied yours together the night I blindfolded you in my cabin?"

He eased back, until she couldn't feel his warm breath on her skin anymore. "Hell, you don't have to remind me of how you tied my hands that night. I'll never forget the pain of not being able to touch you."

"So, you're *not* going to tie my hands right now?"

"No, I'm not. I want you to be able to touch me, if you want to."

"You know I want to touch you."

"Then go ahead. Touch me as much as you like."

Scarlet reached up that instant, grabbed his shirt collar in both hands, and yanked him toward her. Hunter's breath caught when his chest slammed into hers, nearly toppling her backwards onto the desktop. He flattened his palms beside her hips, catching them both before they fell.

"Wow. You have a seriously ferocious grip on me, Dr. Tracey."

She eased her fists open a tiny bit.

He pressed a kiss to the shell of her ear. "That wasn't a complaint. I've wanted you to touch me every single second since I woke up without you in the bed in your cabin. Not having you there was torture. It's been torture every moment since. I just miss you all the time."

Tears stung the backs of her eyelids. "It's been torture for me, too," she whispered, immediately guilt-ridden by the admission. She honestly believed she should set her own needs aside, but Hunter was clearly absolute in the conviction of his emotions, and that resolve lulled her and soothed her and pulled her even closer.

His lips hovered over hers. "I'm sorry it's been torture for you, too. But I have to admit, I'm so fucking glad you feel the same way I do."

Scarlet couldn't help the laughter bubbling up from her throat.

He nudged her nose with his. "God, I love hearing you laugh."

She squeezed tighter to Hunter's collar, wishing he would just kiss her already. He'd told her he wouldn't until she asked, and she knew he wouldn't budge on that point. She also knew he was right about kissing being intimate. She'd resisted kissing him at Blue as long as she could, for just that reason. But she definitely didn't feel like resisting anymore.

Reaching for the top button on his shirt, Scarlet worked it open with unsteady fingers. She managed to pop all the buttons, despite her blindness and incoordination. The moment she'd fully bared his chest, she settled her hand over his heart.

"Damn, that feels amazing," he sighed, pressing kisses up her jawline. "I missed feeling your hand on my heart."

It's my heart, she corrected, silently chastising herself for the greedy thought. It was far too possessive and unruly. And yet she'd felt that way much longer than she wanted to admit.

"Touch more of me, Scarlet. Please."

The pain in his voice as he begged for her touch made her thighs clench around his waist. Slipping both hands under his shirt, she ran her fingers across his shoulders and up to his neck. Hunter cursed while wrapping his arms around her back and grabbing two handfuls of her ass. He palmed her cheeks, his fingertips inching closer and closer to her center seam.

Scarlet's flesh sweltered, from both the pleasure of what he already gave and the demand for more. Her breaths came in staccato pants when he dragged his mouth down her neck, leaving a trail of wet, needy kisses in his wake. Then Marie's voice came from the other side of the door.

"Dr. Tracey, is everything okay?"

Scarlet stiffened instantly, her fingers digging into Hunter's shoulders. She pulled at the ties on her ankles as his rough beard scraped her throat. Her door was not locked. Her assistant could walk in right now and see her bound, blindfolded, and bare-assed on her desk.

Panic nearly overtook her entirely before she heard his voice.

"Tell her you're good," Hunter spoke against her neck, his command quiet yet firm. "Tell her she can go home now."

Scarlet cleared her throat. "Y-you...you can go home now, Marie," she managed to announce on her second try. "Everything is good here. I'm perfectly good now."

"Are you sure you're okay, Scarlet?"

Hunter pressed his lips to her shoulder, nipping at her skin.

She didn't think twice about her response. "Yes. I am. I promise."

"Okay, well...goodnight then."

"Goodnight. See you tomorrow."

She heard her assistant's footsteps padding into the distance while Hunter's mouth moved down to nibble on the edge of her collarbone. His tongue darted out to wet her skin. Grabbing his face in both hands, Scarlet pulled his face back to hers. "That was too damn close."

"Mmm," he hummed, his panted breaths mixing with her own. "I'm glad she's gone, because now we have this whole office to ourselves. I can do anything I want to do to you. I can do anything *you* want me to do to you. What do you want? I'll do anything you desire. Anything at all."

"Dear God! Just kiss me already!"

His mouth landed on hers that instant, stealing the air from her lungs. Hunter kissed her ravenously, insatiably, every movement full of heat and need and possession. He pushed one hand into her hair, his fingers threading her loose curls before fisting tight against her scalp, allowing him to hold her steady as he explored her with his tongue.

When he finally pulled away, after several long, flawless minutes, they both gasped for air. "Your mouth is so fucking perfect," he groaned. "All of you is perfect. Your soft skin, your gorgeous smile, your beautiful voice. You're like a drug to me, and I can't get enough of you, no matter how hard I try."

She dropped her forehead onto his and heaved a sigh.

Hunter chuckled. "And before you start getting all doctor-y on me, just know that I'm perfectly happy with my addiction to you. It's not something you need to cure me of, because it doesn't do me any harm. Quite the opposite, actually. Wanting you makes me feel alive, and I've needed to feel that for as long as I can remember."

"*Alive*," she repeated, the word a prayer on her lips.

"Yes, honey. I've only been surviving for so long, and I know you have, too. We make each other feel alive. We have since the moment we met, and I don't want to run from it. It's a gift to feel this way. It's an amazing, incredible gift, and I don't ever want to let it go."

He smiled against her mouth before kissing her again, sweeping his tongue past her lips to tangle with hers. This kiss was strong and insistent, drawing her fully into him. Scarlet slid her hands up his jaw, holding him in place as his mouth slanted over hers.

Hunter dragged his hands away from her backside to run down her legs. He smoothed his palms across her thighs once, twice, three times. Then his fingers drifted inward, toward her throbbing sex.

She whimpered into his mouth as he slipped one hand down between her legs. He teased the edges of her slick folds, but didn't enter her at all. "Now, about this thing I want from you," he said, his husky voice hanging on the words. "I want you to promise you're going to give it to me, no matter what it is, no questions asked."

"Are you serious? Do you really mean no questions *ah...*"

He drove one finger deep inside her, silencing her instantly. Drawing that finger slowly back out, he dragged the wetness from her sex all the way up to the tender bundle of nerves at the top of her folds. An electric pulse skittered across her skin, originating from the pressure of his fingertip and moving outward over every surface of her body.

"Mmm...that's...damn," she stuttered.

"Does this feel good?"

She grasped onto his shirt for support. "God, yes."

"It feels good to me, too," Hunter growled, slipping his finger down to her sex again, freshly lubricating his path with her wetness, before dragging it back up to where he started.

Scarlet shivered. *Sweet hell, how awful is this thing going to be? What does he want so badly that I can't even know what it is first?*

He circled her tender nerve bud as he pressed the hard ridge of his still-clothed erection into her thigh. "Please," she begged, her eyes rolling back behind the blindfold with the feel of his stiff length rubbing against her. "I want you inside me."

Hunter plunged his finger back into her soft sheath, making her hips buck against the desk. "I want that, too. You have no idea how much. I want to feel you surrounding me, soft and wet and warm. I want you with everything I am. But I need this thing from you first."

"Good Lord, what is it? Just tell me."

"Will you give it to me? No matter what it is?"

Scarlet bit into her lip so hard, she nearly drew blood. Hunter's hand – the one not buried inside her – moved to her face. She felt his thumb trace the outline of her chin before pulling her lip from her teeth.

He pressed his mouth to hers, smoothing his warm, wet tongue over her tender skin. "Tell me you'll give me what I want, Scarlet. It's not a big thing. I swear it's not. It's a small thing, a simple thing. It'll be easy to give it to me. Just say you will."

"But...but I..."

Hunter peppered tiny kisses across her cheek. "Say yes."

She pressed her eyes shut tight behind the scarf as his hot breath ignited her skin. Damn, he was so close. So close, so warm, so strong. He filled her senses, and she wanted to wrap herself around him and never let go. She wanted all of him, too desperately to deny.

"Yes, Hunter. Yes. Tell me what you want and I'll give it to you."

His entire body stilled. Scarlet actually felt him tremble against her, just for a moment, before he pulled his finger out of body. She groaned at the lack of contact, until he returned both hands to her thighs and tightened his fingers into her skin.

"You promise you'll give me whatever I want?"

"I promise," she vowed.

He smiled against her lips, his hands now slipping across her legs in a gentle rhythm. "Okay. What I want from you is...a second date."

Her brow lifted behind the scarf. "A second date? That's it?"

"That's it. We already had our first date, and now I want a second one. See? That wasn't so bad, was it?"

"No, it wasn't."

"I told you it was a simple thing."

Scarlet shook her head, since nothing about this felt simple at all. "I'm sorry, but I can't go on a date with you tonight, because..."

"Because you work at your free clinic on Wednesdays. I know."

"How do you know?"

"I told you; I did my research. I know you volunteer Wednesday nights, and you have other doctors man the clinic the rest of the week. Which means you'll be able to spend the evening with me tomorrow."

"Well, yes, I suppose tomorrow is good."

Hunter leaned in closer. "Tomorrow *is* good. Besides, I can't have a date with you tonight, because I already have another date."

"You have *another* date?"

"I do. Her name is Evie and she's absolutely adorable. Although she does drool quite a bit. Not as much as you do when you fall asleep on my chest, but there is drool."

Scarlet worried that her swelling heart might actually burst. "Are you really going to spend tonight with your goddaughter?"

"I am. I told Will and Maggie to go out and enjoy some alone time together, so I could have my time with her. I bought Evie all kinds of toys, too. I mean, I'm sure she'll grow to love me for my charming personality. But I figure showering her with gifts can't hurt, either."

Scarlet wrapped her arms around his neck. "She will love you for your charming personality. She'll also love you for treating her so well, and for always being there when she needs you. She'll love you forever, even when she's a little mad at you for not agreeing with her decisions."

"I see. Well, I'm glad she'll still love me even when we don't agree. However, I would like to make it perfectly clear right now that you and I are in utter agreement about our second date."

Scarlet exhaled. "Yes, we're in agreement."

"Wonderful. But I would still like to hear you say the words."

"What words?"

"I want you to say, 'I promise to come to your place tomorrow night at seven, for our second date.' Can you do that, please?"

She smiled despite herself. "I promise to come to your place."

"Tomorrow night at seven."

"Tomorrow night at seven."

"For?"

"For our second date."

"That's good, Scarlet. So good."

Hunter slid two fingers back inside her while pressing his thumb deliberately against her tiny bundle of nerves. She squealed, wrenching her hands into his hair as her legs pulled futilely against the restraints. While he eased his fingers out and back in again, an involuntary shudder ran the length of her body. "Don't worry," he whispered beside her ear, "I'm going to take care of all of this pent-up energy of yours. But first, I need to let you know something."

"What is it?"

"Do you remember that day in the forest, when you released me from my promise to tell you what happened back in my high school?"

"I – I do."

He shifted his fingers inside her body, pulling a moan from deep in her chest. "And do you remember that last night at the cabin, when I released you from your promise to spend the night in bed with me?"

"Yes, yes, I remember."

"Well, the thing is, I know this promise you just made was ill-gotten. I'm well aware that I coerced you into making it, but I don't feel guilty about it, and I'm not going to release you from it. I *do not* and *will not* release you from this promise. Do you understand?"

Scarlet huffed. "You do realize you're being kind of despicable, don't you?"

He chuckled, the warm sound echoing through his chest into hers. "Despicable? No, I don't like that word. Let's go with *scoundrel*. I'm being a scoundrel right now. But that's okay, because my Scarlet thinks scoundrels are sexy."

When she matched his laughter, he pressed his mouth to hers and swallowed the sound. Hunter shifted his wrist to push his fingers deeper inside her, palming the folds of her sex. Scarlet wriggled against his hand, eager and desperate for the full release she'd only known with him. Her tongue swept across his as she ran her hands down his bare chest, her fingers digging into his warm skin.

"Damn, I love it when you touch me," he breathed, nipping at her lips. "I feel so fucking possessive of you. I probably shouldn't feel that way, should I? I know it's a caveman-like thought. Part of the reason I wanted to tie you up today was because I wanted to have you at my mercy. But that's only because the night you tied me up, I was at your mercy. I've been at your mercy ever since. Tell me you know that."

She cringed behind the blindfold. "I do know, and I should apologize for it."

He pushed his fingers up to the top wall of her sex, making her writhe against the desk. "No. Don't ever apologize for that. I'm grateful I get to feel this way."

Raw, perfect emotion bathed her mind and swelled her heart. Scarlet reached for the button on waist of his pants, wanting him joined with her in every possible way. Hunter moaned with her greedy actions.

"Honey, I...I don't want you to feel like we have to have sex today. We don't. I can make you come right now with just my fingers."

"No, I don't want that," she insisted, easing his zipper down over his rigid shaft. "I want *you*." Scarlet took his cock in both hands, encircling his fearsomely stiff flesh. He felt hot and pulsing and alive against her palms, and she squeezed onto him, licking her lips in anticipation.

"Fuck," he panted. "That is just...amazing."

"Please take your fingers out of me now."

Hunter did as she asked, returning his hands to her ass, gripping one cheek tightly in each hand. She drew him closer, rubbing his taut erection against her slick folds, coating him in her wetness. Slipping her bottom forward on the desk, she aligned their hips to place the head of his cock at the entrance to her sex. When she released her grip on his shaft, she grabbed onto his shirt and twisted her fingers into the fabric. She waited forever for him to enter her. But he didn't.

He held entirely still, his mouth hovering maddeningly over hers.

"Holy hell," she cursed. "Please."

Hunter smiled against her lips. "Please what?"

"Will you please?"

"Will I please what? I want to hear you say the words. Tell me what you want me to do to you."

"I want you to fuck me. Will you fuck me? Please?"

"Hmm. Are you saying that Dr. Tracey, renowned psychiatrist of Richmond, wants me to fuck her right here, on the desk in her office?"

"Oh my God, yes. It's me. Dr. Tracey. I'm asking you to fuck me on my desk. No, I'm *telling* you to fuck me on my desk. *Now*."

He drove inside her.

They both sucked in air, deep and harsh.

Hunter's hands fell from her ass onto the desktop, the banging sound echoing off the walls. His chest jutted into hers, pinning her fingers flat between them. "How is this even possible?" he breathed beside her ear. "I swear you feel better and better every time I sink inside you."

Scarlet nipped at his jaw. "Has it only been four days since you were inside me? It feels like it's been forever."

"It has been. It's been forever," he agreed, running his lips across the shell of her ear. His tongue darted out, wetting the skin just below her earlobe. He exhaled against it, sending chills up her spine.

She bucked, straining her ankle ties to coax him farther inside. His cock throbbed against her inner walls, hot and thick and filling. Snaking her hands up his chest, she dug her fingers into his skin.

"I need you to stop moving for a minute, Scarlet. I need some time to get myself under control."

"I don't want you to get yourself under control. Not right now."

"Please, honey. I need to do this."

With a harsh sigh, she dropped her forehead onto his shoulder. She stilled her entire body, even though the inaction went against all her current desires. She just wanted him to come inside her. She wanted to feel that pulsing sensation again, to feel him empty himself deep in her sex as she clamped her walls around him and thrashed in ecstasy.

She listened intently while Hunter inhaled and exhaled several times. Eventually, his fingers returned to grip the cheeks of her ass. He pulled his cock entirely out of her body, just a second before plunging all the way back in. When their hips met fully, pressing his flesh into her taut circle of nerves, she cursed and begged simultaneously.

"Mmm," he murmured beside her ear. "Now isn't this better? Isn't it better when I'm in control?"

Scarlet wound her fingers into his hair. "You're not actually trying to get me to say that I like it when you're in control of me, are you?"

He chuckled, making his thick erection twitch deliciously inside her. "You don't have to say it. But I won't fault you if you do."

She bit her lip to keep the words from tumbling out of her mouth.

"Perhaps you'll admit that to me one day," he suggested, inching his fingers closer to the soft seam of her bottom. "Fuck, I love your ass."

Her hands fisted against his scalp. "You've mentioned that before."

"And I'll mention it again." He pressed a kiss to her chin. "And again." Another kiss to her jaw. "And again." Another to her cheek.

Hunter gripped tight to her flesh, edging out of her just far enough to drive back in again, pushing hard against her body. Scarlet whined and moaned, yanking at her bindings, desperate to clamp her legs around him. "For the love of all that's good, will you please untie me now?"

"Why?" he questioned, his warm breath tickling her face. "Is it because you're aching to wrap your legs around me?"

A strangled laugh escaped her throat. "The way you read my mind is scary."

"I can read your mind because I know you inside and out. I know you want to wrap your legs around me because you always held onto me so tight when we were up on the mountain. You clung to me with your whole body, every time I was inside you, like you never wanted me to leave. I never wanted to leave you, either. I always want to be inside you, and not just physically." He withdrew his full length before gliding back inside. "Although I must admit, this is perfection."

Hunter repeated the motion again and again, pulling out and sinking back in, sending frissons of lightning coursing over her skin. "I'm sorry I can't untie you, Scarlet, but I need this. I need you to feel desperate to wrap your legs around me. I need you so desperate to hold onto me that you won't be able to stay away, even after I leave here today. And I know that's wrong of me, but you already know how desperate I am to have you with me, and I need you to be just as desperate."

Tears sprang up behind her blindfold. "I – I am, Hunter. You must know that. I'm just as desperate for us as you are."

He stopped breathing. He stopped moving altogether, held captive in silence for a long minute. Then he reached for her face, steadying her in both hands. "Damn, that's the best thing I've ever heard in my life."

His mouth landed on hers, fiery and demanding. Their tongues tangled as he thrust his cock inside her, over and over, pressing her back on the desktop with each determined pulse of his hips. Scarlet pulled harder against the binds at her ankles, straining her thighs to keep his body close to hers. Hunter aided her with her struggles, grabbing her ass in both hands and yanking her toward him. He pulled her to the very edge of the desk and buried himself to the hilt inside her swollen walls. She cried out, her entire body quaking with sweet, hellish desire.

"Come for me," he panted against her mouth. "I need to feel you come apart around me."

Scarlet complied instantly. She didn't have a choice in the matter. He'd strung her flesh so tight, her nerves so raw, that just the sound of his voice sent her careening over the edge, drowning before she realized how far under she'd gone.

She gripped his shoulders, clinging to him as her world exploded. Hunter held her back just as tightly, his thick arms banded around her back while his hips pumped mercilessly into hers. His perfectly sinful movements slowed over time, yet he still milked every sensation, eliciting deeper moans from her throat with each deliberate thrust.

Scarlet shivered with the final firings of her nerve endings, with every last throb of the orgasm he'd drawn so deliciously from her body. As reality returned slowly to her mind, her brow furrowed. In the haze of her ongoing delirium, she hadn't noticed his restraint. Yet now, she could think of little else except the fact that he remained rigid and swollen inside her. She hummed while his thick length continued to stretch the walls of her sex to its limits, blissfully aware that he hadn't allowed his own release, which meant they could have even more of this.

Hunter pressed a kiss to her forehead, making her sigh with the tender sensation. Then he untangled himself from her clinging grasp and pulled out of her body completely. He left her panting and shifting on her desktop, wondering what would happen next.

Will he untie me now? Will I finally get the chance to wrap my legs around him? Or will he spin me around and bend me over my desk, so I can feel his chest against my back while he takes me from behind?

Anticipation spurred her racing heart. Scarlet waited impatiently behind her blindfold as his warm, strong hands eased down her legs. He untied the tape from her left ankle, unwrapped the scarf, and smoothed over the skin beneath it. He released her right ankle in the same manner.

She didn't remove her feet from the chairs, even after he'd freed her. She didn't know what his next plans were, but she sat prepared for anything. Confusion muddled her brain when she heard his zipper close. Yanking the scarf from her face, she blinked her eyes into focus.

Hunter stood a few feet away, with his erection stuffed back inside his pants. Currently, he was refastening the shirt buttons she'd undone. "Why are you dressing?" she questioned. "Aren't you going to finish?"

He closed his last button before meeting her eyes. "No, I'm not."

"Why on earth not?"

"Because this wasn't about me, Scarlet. This was about you."

"But what about..." She motioned to his wildly tented pants.

Hunter shrugged. "Yeah, that's going to be really annoying for a few more minutes. Then it will calm down."

"It doesn't have to, you know. I'm perfectly willing to..."

He stepped between her legs before she could finish her protest, kissing the hell out of her, until her toes curled inside her high heels. Once he'd silenced her properly, he groaned against her lips. "Don't think for a second that I don't want to finish. I'm making a point, here."

She looked to his eyes, taking a moment to absorb the bright blue she hadn't been able to see behind her blindfold. "Your point is noted and appreciated, but that doesn't mean you have to suffer. I'd be happy to finish things for you. Maybe with my mouth?"

Reaching to her face, Hunter tilted her chin up and gave her a crooked smile. "Let me make sure I'm hearing this correctly. Is Dr. Tracey saying she wants to give her boyfriend a blowjob right here, in the middle of her office?"

Scarlet tried not to smile. But when she looked into his adoring, playful eyes, her lips curved up of their own accord. "Yes, that's exactly what I'm saying."

"Then will you please say it?"

"What do you want me to say?"

"I want you to say, 'I, Dr. Tracey, want to give my boyfriend a blowjob in my office.'"

She cocked an eyebrow. "Are you really going to make me admit how much I want you? Again?"

"Scoundrel. Remember?"

Scarlet's heart flipped in her chest with the gleam of delight in his eyes. "Okay, yes. I want to give my boyfriend a blowjob in my office."

Hunter's teasing grin fell. He grabbed her face in both hands, leaned down, and bit into her lower lip. He tugged it into his mouth before soothing it with a kiss. "You forgot to say the 'Dr. Tracey' part."

She moaned before she could reply. "I, Dr. Tracey, want to give my boyfriend a blowjob in my office."

His arms snaked around her waist to pull her harder against him. His thick erection pulsed between her bare thighs as he stared into her. "You have no idea how much I want that. You have no idea how much I want to see your lips wrapped around me. You have no goddamn clue how much I want to fuck your gorgeous mouth."

Scarlet whimpered, struggling to hold herself upright.

Hunter ran the side of his nose against hers. "Will you let me come in your mouth, honey? Can I come right on your tongue?"

Her hips jumped. "Yes. *Yes.*"

He thrust his stiff length against her sex, with only the thin material of his pants separating them. "Are you just aching to taste me?"

Some sort of bizarre noise bubbled up from her throat. It was a sound she'd never made before, ever. "God, yes, I want to taste you."

"Mmm," he murmured against her mouth, his tongue darting out to trace the seam. "That's how I feel about you, too. I could taste you all day. I could bury my face between your legs and lick you for hours on end, making you come on my tongue over and over, until you beg me to stop because the pleasure is just too fucking intense to bear."

"Holy damn it, Hunter! Take your pants off!"

Her fingers dove for his zipper, but he grasped her wrists before she accomplished her goal. Drawing her hands up to his mouth, he pressed a soft kiss into each palm. "As good as that sounds, I need to leave before I can't. If I stay here, I'm either going to come in my pants, or break down and fuck your mouth. And I didn't intend for either of those things to happen when I showed up here today."

He released her hands, placing them down onto her thighs. He made sure she could hold herself straight on the desktop before he backed away. Scarlet dropped her feet to the floor, her heels catching her when she stood. She pushed her skirt back down her legs while watching him bend over to grab her underwear off the ground.

Hunter grinned as he handed them to her. "I will, however, take a rain check on the blowjob, if that's okay with you."

"A rain check?" she echoed, tossing her panties onto the desk.

"Well, it is raining."

She glanced outside, to the gray clouds now pouring sheets of water over her office windows. The raindrops pummeled the glass panels, yet she hadn't even noticed the melancholy sound. Scarlet turned her eyes back to his. "Okay, you can have a rain check."

"Come to think of it, you promised me a blowjob the night you tied me up in your cabin. With whipped cream, if I recall correctly. So, that's actually two you owe me. Not that I'm counting, or anything."

She laughed. "Well, then, you now have *two* blowjob rain checks."

"I like the sound of that," he said, reaching around her to grab the two chairs. He walked them back to the front of her desk and set them in their place. Then he rolled down his sleeves and grabbed his jacket.

Once fully dressed, Hunter returned to stand before her. Reaching into his pocket, he pulled out a piece of paper and set it on her desk. "I wrote my home address down for you. I'll see you there tomorrow night at seven. Okay?"

"Okay."

"Promise you'll be there?"

"I promise."

He leaned in, peppering several more kisses over her lips before picking his briefcase up off the floor. When he straightened, he glanced down at the conspicuous bulge still tenting his pants. "Man, I'm glad Marie already left. It's going to be difficult enough to win her over without her seeing me walk out of your office in this condition."

Scarlet giggled, the sound drawing his full attention.

Hunter's eyes roamed across her face. "I'm so glad I met you two weeks ago, down in the marble square beside the fountain."

She absorbed the hope written in his deep blue. "I'm glad you came over to talk to me while I was eating my lunch."

"Well, once I saw you, I had to talk to you. I had to know you."

"You do know me, Hunter."

"And you know me. I'll see you tomorrow."

Scarlet stood and watched, intent on every movement of his body, as he strode across the floor. He turned back only once, giving her a playful wink, before exiting the room. When the door closed behind him, she stepped over to her leather chair. Pushing it back in front of her desk, she slumped down into the seat. She stared at her desktop for a long minute before reaching for the red plastic egg and popping open the lid. Gathering the soft putty from inside, she squished it between her fingers and smiled.

15

REALITY

Scarlet sat behind her office desk with her chair turned to the window, staring out at Hunter's building across the street. She'd had her eyes glued to Gregory Global for a while now, enjoying the fact that his work was so close to hers. Also, looking out of the window meant she didn't have to look at her desk, where they'd had sex just yesterday.

Her face grew hot with the memory. She'd brought in bleach wipes to clean off the surface this morning, since that seemed like a good thing to do. Although she wasn't sure, having never had sex in her office before. But she figured bleach couldn't hurt.

It had been a long night working at her clinic last night, and a long day of seeing patients today, with her mind churning. Scarlet couldn't not think about what happened with her and Hunter yesterday. Everything they'd said and done left her excited, nervous, hopeful, and frightened – frightened of taking this step into new territory, of trying to be with someone who swore he wanted all of her.

Honestly, even after having a whole day to think about it, she wasn't exactly sure what had occurred here between them last evening. She only knew she'd made Hunter a promise and she intended to keep it. In just a few moments, she would drive to his house for their second date.

A second date – that was all he said he wanted from her. A second date was a simple thing, just as he said it would be. She could do this.

But only if they took things *slow*.

Scarlet knew beyond a doubt that if they were going to make this relationship work in the real world, then caution would be the key. They needed to take everything one step at a time, over a span of time. That was a scenario she could work with: a slow, methodical transition from the fantasy that was Blue to the reality now stretching out before them.

She was prepared to begin that journey with Hunter tonight, perhaps over a lovely meal at his dinner table.

Are we going to have dinner? We never actually discussed it.

After their meal, they would sit on his couch and talk.

But just talk. That's all.

When they finished talking, she would give him a kiss goodnight.

Or maybe two, or three. But definitely no more than three.

Then she would go home.

Alone.

It would be a lovely date. They would probably even agree to have a third date soon, perhaps sometime next week. Next week would be good timing. Nice and slow. Slow was the key. Slow, slow, slow.

I guess I haven't learned how to be without you for more than two days at a time yet. I suppose I'll have to work on that. Maybe I'll even figure out a way to go for a whole week without you, once we've been married for thirty or forty years.

Scarlet winced at the sound of Hunter's voice into her head. As certain as she was about embarking cautiously on a relationship, she knew he didn't want to wait for anything. He wanted them together right now, which meant Dr. Tracey would have to reign in his extreme thoughts.

The physician inside her understood how important it was that they take baby steps moving forward. They could try dating in the real world, and use terms like boyfriend and girlfriend, and see if they still enjoyed spending time together with their feet planted firmly in reality. If they were truly meant to be together in the long run, then the rampant, fantastical emotions that sprang up so quickly between them at Blue would eventually grow into something sturdy and stable.

Scarlet hoped that would happen. She wanted to believe they were meant to be. But only time would tell. Only time.

She nodded to herself, silently confirming the rationality and validity of her plan. It was a good, solid plan for their future. She just hoped Hunter would be reasonable enough to agree with it.

Standing from her chair, Scarlet grabbed her purse and keys. She spent a moment gazing at the wall of plants in her office, drawing strength from their peaceful beauty, before walking to her door. The instant she pulled on the handle, an overwhelming smell hit her squarely in the face.

She gasped as she stepped into the office reception area, struggling to wrap

her mind around the sight before her. Dozens and dozens of flower vases –
filled to brimming with vibrant, fragrant blooms – decorated every flat surface.
"Um, Marie? What's all this?"

"Goodness, I have no idea," Marie replied, wringing her hands.

"It looks like a florist's shop threw up in here."

"I know! They all arrived just a few minutes ago. I thought they must be
for you, but they're actually for me."

"Really? Did Manny just decide to tell you in the most adamant way that
he loves you even more today than he did twenty-three years ago?"

"No, no. It wasn't my husband who sent them."

"Oh. Then is there a secret admirer I should know about?"

A blush lit the woman's cheeks. "I have no idea. The card just says, 'Marie,
Thanks for all you do – H.' I don't know who that could be."

Scarlet burst out laughing. "Oh my God, they're from Hunter."

"Hunter? Do you mean Hunter *Gregory*? Why on earth would he send me
a greenhouse-full of flowers?"

"Because he wants you to like him."

"I don't understand. Why would he care so much?"

Scarlet inhaled steeply. "It's because he's...he's my boyfriend. He wants to
be friends with you, since he knows you're a part of my life."

Marie's eyes bulged. "Hunter Gregory is your *boyfriend*?"

"Yes," Scarlet admitted for the first time to anyone but him.

"I – I didn't even know you were seeing anyone."

"It all happened very recently. I'm sorry I didn't tell you sooner. I know it
would have made things easier between the two of you."

"Well, I appreciate your apology, but..."

She absorbed the look of concern on Marie's face. "But what?"

"But I can't help feeling protective of you. I know Hunter Gregory is
wealthy, but that doesn't necessarily mean he's a good person."

Scarlet smiled. "He *is* a good person. Also, he makes me incredibly happy.
Happier than I've been in as long as I can remember."

Marie studied her for a moment before matching her contented smile.
"That's what I care about the most. You deserve to be happy."

"You know, Hunter assured me of that just yesterday."

"Well, if that's the case, then I'll give him a chance."

"Good. I'm glad."

"Are you going to see him tonight?"

"I am. Right now, in fact."

"That explains why you wore your hair down today. I was surprised, since
I haven't seen it down in over six months."

Scarlet's stomach lurched. "Yes, it's...it's been a while. I should go now. I'll see you in the morning, okay?"

Marie nodded. "Bright and early."

Stepping toward the outer door, Scarlet clamped her fingers around her car keys, holding tight to that small sense of stability. She made it down the elevator, past security, and to the parking garage, with only mild panic symptoms. But once she sat in her driver's seat, pulled Hunter's address from her purse, and stared at his bold handwriting, she developed a lot more difficulty breathing.

Sitting here in her car, preparing to head to his place for their second date, felt really real. She wanted their relationship to be grounded in reality – she truly did – but facing that reality still scared the hell out of her. There were things in her life Hunter knew nothing about, things she'd never intended to tell him during their brief time at Blue, and she just wasn't sure if she could relive those events anytime soon.

Calm down, Scarlet. Tonight is only a slow beginning for you both.

She inhaled steeply, working to settle her fears, yet her hands still shook when she started the engine. Her eyes darted to the clock on her dashboard: 6:15. It was too unfashionably early to arrive at his place now, even though she prided herself on being early. When her empty stomach growled at her, she decided to stop by a grocery store on the way.

Taking a tiny pit stop shouldn't have been a problem, except once Scarlet got to the store, she couldn't decide what to get. She honestly didn't know if Hunter had plans for dinner, and couldn't call to ask, because they'd never exchanged phone numbers. She wandered the aisles before finally deciding on some fancy cheddar cheese and a bottle of wine, figuring she could survive on the cheese as a food source if she had to, and the wine would help settle her nerves. Hopefully.

By the time she returned to her car, it was 6:50. His place was fairly close according to the map on her phone, so she could still get there by 7:00 if she didn't dawdle. Unfortunately, she got turned around on the interstate between the store and his building. When she finally pulled off on a random exit to make a U-turn, she was already officially late.

Sometime later, Hunter's building came into view through her windshield. A sense of relief flooded her veins, until she realized the building was huge, and immaculately structured and detailed, and reeked of wealth. Scarlet gripped the steering wheel as she drove beneath the high rise into the underground parking garage, pulling her sedan in an unmarked space in the visitor's section.

Her eyes drew to the clock. 7:21. *Damn it.* She hated being late.

Tossing the block of cheese into her purse, she grabbed the wine bottle by the neck and stepped outside, balancing on her silver heels for a moment before shutting her door. She pulled her purse over her shoulder and smoothed out the wrinkles on her bright blue blouse and ivory skirt. Then she focused on walking with a minimum of trembling as she made her way into the lobby of the imposing building.

Once inside, Scarlet approached the security desk with her head up. She glanced at the handsome man standing behind the large, ornate desktop. He wore a guard's uniform and busily studied a feed on a video monitor...right up until he heard her approach.

His eyes sparked the instant he saw her. "Thank God you're here."

She glanced to his badge: *Seth Mills*. "I'm sorry; do I know you?"

"No, but I know you. That is, if you are Dr. Scarlet Tracey, Hunter Gregory's girlfriend."

"He...he told you I'm his girlfriend?" *Is he telling the whole city?*

"That's not all he told me," Seth added with a mischievous grin. "He said you were more beautiful than I could imagine, with ebony hair, emerald eyes, and lips as pink as flower petals – I'm fairly certain those were his exact words. And he wasn't wrong, although I probably shouldn't say so, since he informed me that if I tried to charm you in any way, he would have some truly horrible things to say to me."

Scarlet had to clear her throat to utter a single word. "Oh."

Seth chuckled. "It's okay; Hunter's been my friend for years. We speak fairly candidly with one another, although I've never seen him act like he has tonight. I'm grateful you finally made it here, since he's been calling me every five goddamn minutes for nearly an hour, asking if you've arrived yet. Maybe now I can stop talking on the phone and get some actual work done."

"I'm so sorry, Seth. May I call you Seth? I didn't intend to be late. I just got a little turned around on the highway getting here, and..."

His phone rang. "Hold onto that thought," he told her, lifting the cell to his ear. "Yes, Mr. Gregory...Yes, she's here now...Yes, it is wonderful...No, I promise you she's fine; she just got a little turned around on the highway...No, I haven't kept her down here, talking to me *forever*...Yes, I'll send her up right away...You're welcome."

Seth shook his head while meeting her eyes. "Yes, please do call me Seth. And as much as I enjoy your company, I should probably send you up to see Hunter now. If I don't, I'm afraid I'll never hear the end of it."

Scarlet forced a smile as her heart thumped a thousand times a minute. "I don't know exactly which apartment is his. What floor do I go to?"

"The top floor."

"Thank you, Seth. It was very nice meeting you."

"It was nice meeting you, too, Dr. Tracey."

"Please, call me Scarlet," she encouraged while stepping past the desk. After pressing the "up" button on the elevator panel, she looked back to the guard. "Um, which way do I go once I get to the top floor?"

"Straight ahead."

"Great. And which door will it be?"

"There's just the one door, Scarlet."

Her brow rose. "You mean he owns the whole top floor?"

Seth's head tilted. "You do know his family is filthy rich, right?"

"Um, well, they're the Gregory family, so..." The ding of the elevator rescued her. She waved before stepping inside and hitting the top button. Seth grinned at her while the door closed. The moment she stood alone, Scarlet gulped. Her fingers clenched the neck of the wine bottle as she stared at the shiny silver insides of the ornate elevator.

She'd never stopped to consider the truth of Hunter's family before. She'd never needed to, since it had always just been the two of them – Hunter and Scarlet – alone. Other than a few brief moments with Colin and Marie, no one else in the world had ever even seen them together.

But it wasn't going to stay that way forever, not if they planned to make this relationship work long-term. Eventually, they would share time with family and friends, and tell the lie about how they'd met in the square by the fountain outside of Gregory Global. Scarlet definitely wasn't ready to do any of that, even though the Gregory wealth itself didn't alarm her. What truly bothered her was how the people in his life might react to them being together so quickly. Also, she wondered if Hunter's family – his mountain-climbing parents and world-traveling sister – would all be as intimidating as he was. She could barely manage *his* control issues. She didn't know if she could ever have enough training to handle an *entire family* of them.

"God, don't think about that right now," she chastised herself when the elevator neared the top floor. "Tonight, you only need to concentrate on the beginning of your relationship, and on taking things slow."

Those words made sense, and when the elevator bell rang at the top floor, Scarlet felt better about their impending snail-paced relationship. That tiny sense of calm lasted exactly two seconds. The instant the door opened, Hunter stood there in the hallway – in all of his mesmerizing, nerve-wracking glory – glaring at her with steely, piercing eyes.

"You're late," he growled, his body consuming her field of vision.

"I'm...I'm so sorry...I just got..."

He grabbed her around the waist, lifted her out of the elevator, and set her down in the empty hallway. Then he pressed her up against the wall and kissed her. Except it wasn't just a kiss. It was a declaration.

Scarlet's arms dangled limply at her sides, her fingers barely able to keep a hold on the wine bottle, as he invaded all her senses. She didn't protest the brazen intensity of his demanding mouth and enveloping body, although she probably should have. She'd simply missed him as much as he'd obviously missed her, and decided to let the moment be.

When Hunter finally dragged his lips away and dropped his forehead onto hers, neither of them could catch their breath to speak. He curled one hand around her waist while edging the other up into her hair. As his taut muscles eased, he smiled against her lips. "You're here."

"I'm here," she assured, gripping onto his forearm with her free hand.

"I was worried sick, you know. I expected you to be early."

Laughter bubbled up from Scarlet's chest. "Actually, I'm almost always early to everything. I just got a bit turned around on the highway."

He eased back to see her face. "Can I have your cell phone, please?"

"Oh, um, sure." She dug in her purse until she found it.

He grabbed the device and started pushing buttons.

"What are you doing, Hunter?"

"Programming my cell number in here. And my home number. And my work number. Now, I'm going to call my phone from yours...and there we go. I have your number, too." He pinned her eyes when he handed her phone back. "Please, please call me if you're ever going to be late again. Just so I don't have a heart attack. Okay?"

"Okay. I'm sorry I'm late."

"At least you're here now," he said, settling both hands on her waist. "Honestly, I was afraid you might not show. I know the promise you made me yesterday was done under duress, and I wouldn't have blamed you if you didn't come tonight. But I'm so damn grateful you did."

Memories of being half-naked on her desk, begging him to fuck her, rushed into Scarlet's mind. Fire ran beneath her skin, making Hunter's eyes grow dark as he watched her blush. She dreaded them being alone for much longer in this hallway, where he could easily fuck her against this wall. Not because she thought he would do it, but because if he didn't, she might beg him mercilessly until he did. And that would go directly against her very rational plans to take things slow.

In order to divert that impending disaster, she said, "I brought wine." Scarlet held the bottle up as proof, ultimately proud that she hadn't dropped it when he'd kissed the hell out of her straight off the elevator. "I also have a block of cheese in my purse, since we didn't talk about whether or not we're going to have dinner. I just thought I'd bring a little something along. For a snack. Or an appetizer. Or whatever."

Hunter chuckled. "I promise I'm going to feed you. I know you've been at work all day and must be starving. I made us dinner."

"Really? You cook?"

"I do. I actually like to cook, when I find the time. I can't say it will be as good as the food at Blue, but it's definitely passable."

"I'm sure it's more than passable, and certainly better than anything I could do. I can't cook at all. I'm absolutely horrible at it."

He slipped his hand up her jaw. "Well, I guess you can't be perfect at everything."

"I – I'm not perfect," she insisted, nibbling against her lower lip.

Hunter pulled her lip from her teeth with his thumb. He pressed a soft kiss to her mouth. "You're perfect to me."

She whimpered with the sincerity in his voice.

"So, I'll be the cook," he announced as he straightened. "See? That worked out incredibly easy. Our first relationship question of the night, and we tackled it head-on. We're simply amazing together."

The gleam in his eyes made her smile. "You cook and I'll do dishes?"

"Wow, this just keeps getting better and better." Hunter gathered her free hand in his, pulling her down the wide hallway toward the single-entry door straight ahead. "But no dishes for you tonight. And in the future, I'll never mind helping with them."

Scarlet trotted along behind him, mentally preparing herself to step inside his full-floor home, until he stopped abruptly a few feet from the door. He turned to her, his body only inches away, and pinned her eyes.

"I, um...I think I owe you an apology, Scarlet."

Her head tilted. "An apology? For what?"

"For Maxine."

"Your sister, Maxine?"

"Yes. She's here. She flew in from Paris yesterday evening for a surprise visit. Honest to God, I had no idea."

"You mean Maxine is here right now, in your apartment?"

"She is. And my mom and dad, too."

"Your *what*?"

"My mom and dad."

"Hunter, are you telling me your *entire family* is in there?"

His brow furrowed. "Yes."

Scarlet feared that her eyes might actually pop out of their sockets. "Well,

I'll...I'll just come back another night, then. Obviously, you weren't expecting them to be here, so we'll have to reschedule."

"Oh, no, I expected them to be here," he said, squeezing her hand. "I mean, I wasn't expecting Maxine, but I invited my mom and dad."

"Wh-why did you invite your mom and dad to our *date*?"

He grinned ear to ear, the kind of grin that normally melted her heart down into her shoes. But she couldn't melt right now, since her entire body had frozen solid. He took a step closer, forcing her to crane her stiff neck to match his gaze.

"Because I want you to meet them. And I want them to meet you."

"Hunter, I...I can't..."

"Here we go," he announced, wrapping his arm around her waist while pushing the door open. He pulled her forward into the ginormous front hall of his top-floor home. The moment they entered, three impeccably dressed people sauntered up to them.

"Well, here she is," Maxine said, pushing her short brown hair behind her ears while looking to Scarlet with the same sparkling blue eyes as her brother. "I guess I owe you twenty bucks, Dad."

"You sure do," the older, distinguished-looking gentleman agreed with a smile. "I told you he didn't make her up."

"Oh, you two," the other woman admonished. "Behave yourselves or she'll run away. It's a pleasure to meet you, Scarlet."

Hunter's beautifully poised mother offered her hand to shake. Scarlet lifted her hand, too. Except she forgot about the bottle of wine she still held – and she just let go of it.

Hunter dove down, catching the bottle with lightning-fast reflexes, just before it hit the ceramic tile floor. "Whoops," he said. "Got it."

Scarlet gnashed her lower lip in her teeth as she looked to his face.

"Crisis averted," he assured, setting the bottle down on the hall table.

She blinked a few times before refocusing on his mother, finally managing to shake her hand. "I'm so sorry, Mrs. Gregory. I can't believe I just dropped that. I'm just...it's a pleasure to meet you, too."

"Call me Olivia, please," she encouraged, the tone of her voice more regal than any Scarlet had ever heard in real life. "This is my husband, Hugh, and my daughter, Maxine. I figure introductions are in order, in case you haven't heard as much about us as we have about you."

Scarlet's brow skyrocketed. "You've heard about me?"

"Goodness, Hunter hasn't stopped talking about you for days. We've been looking forward to this evening ever since he invited us."

"When did he invite you, exactly?"

"Hmm. I believe it was Tuesday night."

Scarlet stared in bewilderment. "Tuesday?" *Before I even agreed to a second date, Tuesday?* "Oh, well, that's, um…"

"Oh my God, Hunter!" Maxine piped in, crossing her slender arms across her chest. "You didn't tell her we were going to be here, did you? You actually sprang your entire family on your new girlfriend without even telling her? What in the hell were you thinking?"

"Well, Maxine, it wouldn't have been my entire family if you hadn't barged in here unannounced."

"But still, big brother! What were you trying to do to the poor woman? Give her a stroke?"

Hunter glowered at the tiny, fiery brunette. "Will you all excuse us for a minute?" he asked, grasping Scarlet's hand to coax her away.

Maxine snorted. "Sometimes you are amazingly dense, you know."

"Have some of the appetizers I set out, please," he called over his shoulder while guiding Scarlet through the main room.

She stumbled along beside him, her footsteps barely functional. A large dining table sat to her left, with five elegant place settings in china and crystal. A vast living room sat to her right, full of designer furniture and gorgeous artwork. Hunter's home was absolutely delightful, but she couldn't appreciate any of it, given her current situation.

He pushed them both through a swinging door into his kitchen, which was gigantic and pristine. As the door swung closed behind them, Scarlet stared at the gourmet cooking pots hanging from the racks above her head and the thick granite countertops at her waist. Hunter pulled her farther inside, up to the massive kitchen island, before finally letting go of her hand. Then he stepped back, looked to her face, and stilled.

She stood, barely conscious and forcibly mute. She opened her mouth, desperate to speak, but nothing came out. Nothing at all.

Hunter exhaled slowly as he studied her. "I suppose you have a lot of questions for me," he began, keeping his tone soft and calm.

She managed to squeak out noises, although not actual language.

He gave her a tender smile. "Well, while you're thinking, I'm just going to take dinner out of the oven."

Scarlet watched him turn toward the double stove. He grabbed a potholder, opened one door, and pulled out a pan of food. The smell was delectable, and her empty stomach growled its approval. Hunter set the pan down, picked up a pair of tongs, and began transferring the food to an ornate china platter. "I made chicken cordon bleu," he informed her while he worked. "I hope you'll like it. It's my mother's favorite, so I thought it would make her happy. Also, it'll have the side benefit of keeping her mouth full. I know she can be a little bit intimidating at times. Honestly, my whole family can be a little bit intimidating."

Just a little bit? Really? Good God, Hunter!

Once he'd arranged the chicken artfully onto the platter, he moved to the sink, washed his hands, and dried them on a towel. He merely went about his business, preparing their dinner, as if this entire situation were perfectly normal. His nonchalant attitude freaked her out beyond words.

Breathe, Scarlet. Breathe.

She did as she instructed, working on life-sustaining measures. After forever, she managed to utter one single word. "Simple."

Hunter turned back, focusing his entire body on hers. "Simple?"

She narrowed her eyes. "Yes, simple – that's what you said you wanted from me yesterday – you said you wanted a *simple* thing."

"You're right; I did. I wanted you to meet my family, and now you're meeting them. I'd say that's pretty simple."

"You actually think introducing me to your entire family on our second date is *simple*?"

"Yes, I do. If we're going to spend the rest of our lives together, I think we should get to know each other's families as soon as possible. I'm just making sure that happens." Hunter shrugged. "Simple."

Scarlet fell mute again. She shook her head, over and over, looking around the enormous room for something easy and functional she could do to orient herself to time and place. Pulling her purse off her shoulder, she set it on the counter and reached inside, searching for the one task she knew she could perform right now. "I need a knife," she told him.

"A knife?"

She pulled the block of cheddar from her bag, set it on the granite countertop, and looked back to him. "Yes. I need to cut the cheese."

Hunter's lips twitched, working to repress a smile.

Scarlet replayed the words in her head. "Oh my God! I can't believe I just said that! And it's still as mortifying now as it was when I was ten."

He turned away to find her a knife. She watched his shoulders shake beneath his shirt. "You'd better not be laughing at me right now, Hunter."

"I would never laugh at you," he insisted, placing a cutting board and knife in front of her before taking two steps back.

Scarlet grabbed the knife, her knuckles whitening against the handle. "Just so you know, I'm probably going to say something ridiculous like that in front of your family, because no matter how much I want them to like me, I'm so flustered right now, I can't even think straight."

Hunter observed her with puppy-dog earnestness.

She couldn't accept the look of pure adoration in his eyes at this moment. "You know you fluster me even under normal circumstances," she told him as she looked down, hacking into the block of cheddar. "I worked very hard to get my nervous speech under control when I was younger. I went to therapy for years to fix it, and I did. I conquered it. I hadn't rambled at all, not once since I was twenty-two years old, until I met you. Then there I was, lying on the ground with you in that forest at Blue. I felt your hands on me, and the next thing I knew, I started rambling about latex allergies and condoms and getting pregnant. I even think I said something about sperm banks. Sweet Lord, did I really talk about sperm banks? I think I did, but I can't be sure. But that's the thing – that's what you do to me. You change everything, every second I'm with you. You make me feel so damn much all the damn time. You make it so I can't think straight at all. And now here we are, with your entire family outside those doors, and I'm terrified something preposterous is going to come flying out of my mouth and then..."

"I love you, Scarlet."

"...they won't know what kind of woman you've brought home..." Her words collapsed in her throat. She gripped the knife handle for dear life as her eyes rose slowly to meet his. "What did you say?"

He stepped forward, erasing the space between them. "I love you, Scarlet. I love you. I know I probably picked a really bad moment to say that for the first time, but I just needed you to hear it."

Her entire body trembled.

Hunter eased his hand to her face, holding her steady. "And I swear to you that I am positive about how I feel. I'm not suffering from erotic transference, because that syndrome is about a person searching for the love they missed during childhood, and I don't have that problem. I've always been loved. My mother, father, and sister love me without bounds. It's a gift I've always been aware of, a gift I've treasured. I know what love is. I even know *how* to love. I've just never found the right woman to give my love to. Not until now."

His fingers shifted across her cheek. "I love you, Scarlet. I love you with everything I am. And those people out there – who've known me and loved me for my entire life – are going to see exactly how I feel about you. I can't hide it from them, and I don't want to. They're going to see it, and they're going to love you, too. Now please put down the knife, and come have dinner with my family."

Hunter pressed his lips to hers. The kiss was warm and soft and soothing, and she breathed in his woodsy scent while he dwelled against her skin. When he straightened, he reached for the knife she held.

Extracting the blade from her fingers, he set it down beside the partially carved block of cheddar. He lifted the cutting board and held it out to her. "Do you think you can carry this out to the dining room? I need to carry the chicken platter."

Scarlet nodded, accepting the board from his outstretched hands.

"Everything is going to be okay," he reassured as he gathered the platter from the stovetop. "You know I'll be right here beside you."

Hunter smiled when they walked away from the island together. He pushed on the kitchen door with his elbow, holding it open for her. Scarlet followed him out to where his family sat around the table.

"Oh my goodness, is that what I think it is?" Olivia cooed.

"Chicken cordon bleu," Hunter announced, setting the platter down between his mother and sister. He moved around the table, pulling out a chair for Scarlet to the left of his own.

She plastered a smile on her face while she sat between Hunter and his father, across from his sister. "I brought the cheese," she said.

Olivia nodded. "Well, that's lovely," she praised before turning to her husband. "Remember when we took that trip to Holland, Hugh?"

"Yes, I sure do. Beautiful country. And the cheese was incredible. Did you know people actually wear wooden shoes there? It's probably just to delight the tourists, but still."

"Ugh. Wooden shoes," Maxine groaned, grasping one of the goblets of wine sitting on the table. "Fashion nightmare."

"It was perfect, Maxine," Olivia defended, helping herself to the chicken. "And so is this meal. We haven't had a real family dinner in ages, and I haven't had Hunter's cordon bleu in as long as I can recall."

He smiled. "I knew you'd like it, Mom."

"Yeah, Hunter made your favorite dish," Maxine added while taking her own serving. "It's like he's buttering you up to hear some shocking news. But I can't imagine what, since Scarlet is so adorable. There's no reason to butter you up because of her. Unless...unless she's pregnant."

"Maxine!" a chorus of voices rang out – every voice except for Scarlet's. Even Maxine shouted her own name.

"Geez, it's so easy to rattle you guys," the young woman noted with a giggle of satisfaction, taking a sip of her wine before setting it back by her plate. "Besides, I don't see what the big deal is anyway, since Mom would probably love it if Scarlet was pregnant. I know she wants a little Gregory heir running around in diapers, and I'm certainly not there yet."

Scarlet shook her head. "I'm...I'm not pregnant," she squeaked.

"Of course you're not, dear," Olivia reassured. "And even if you were, it would be *none of our business*," she emphasized her words while shifting her intent stare to her daughter.

Maxine sighed dramatically, settling heavier into her chair. Scarlet observed Hunter's sister for a moment, wondering what would pop out of her mouth next. Then Maxine looked to her across the table, gave her a big, gorgeous, heartwarming smile, and winked.

Scarlet could have kissed the girl right now. She wanted to reach across this table, grab Hunter's sister by her ears, and plant a big one right on her mouth. Maxine had jumped into this tenuous situation with both feet, crushed the barriers of formality into little pieces, and made Scarlet feel more at home than she could have possibly imagined.

She smiled to herself as she looked down to the chicken Hunter set on her plate. Hugh nudged her elbow, handing her a bowl of mashed potatoes, which was one of several side dishes that waited on the table. The fluffy, buttery concoction was still warm, and Scarlet heaped a serving onto her plate while the other sides were passed around.

"Why don't you tell us about Paris, Maxine," Olivia suggested.

Maxine nodded vehemently, and barely stopped to catch a breath for a very long time. As everyone dug into their meals, she regaled them with stories of the Parisian people and culture, of parties and shopping and forever friendships. Scarlet listened intently, nodding, laughing, and exchanging comments with the vivacious young woman across the table.

The joy of Maxine's impassioned personality was infectious, helping to slow Scarlet's rapid pulse. She still looked to Hunter from time to time, just to assure herself that he remained beside her. She always found his deep blue eyes fixed intently on her face, vigilant as ever.

By the time they finished their meals, the atmosphere had lightened considerably. Scarlet found herself relaxing, up until Hunter said, "Let me just take these plates to the kitchen and I'll bring out dessert."

She jumped in her seat. "I'll help you."

"Nonsense," Maxine huffed. "You're the guest here. I'll help."

Hunter smiled while he and Maxine stood from the table. They cleared everyone's plates and moved to the kitchen together. Then Scarlet found herself alone with Mr. and Mrs. Gregory.

Lifting her chin, she focused on the flawless woman across the table. "So, Hunter tells me you both went mountain-climbing for your birthdays. Which, if I remember correctly, are just two days apart."

Olivia nodded as she dabbed her mouth with her napkin. "You're right, they are. And the trip was simply amazing. Wasn't it, Hugh?"

He nodded. "Amazing, indeed. I'm glad we took on the challenge."

"Where did you go?"

"Mount Rainier in Washington," he answered, turning his pale blue eyes to hers. "We went with a group and had a guide, so it wasn't exactly as adventurous as it sounds."

Scarlet grinned. "I don't know about that. I think it's still pretty spectacular to get out there and explore. I love the mountains, too."

"You do?" Olivia questioned, drawing her gaze.

"Yes, I really do."

"You would have loved the view from the top, then. It was simply exquisite – lush valleys and volcanoes. Astounding."

"It sounds incredible," Scarlet sighed. "I'd love to climb Rainier one day. Did you happen to see any birds? Washington's state bird is the American goldfinch. It's quite beautiful, with a yellow body and black wings, and just a bit of black on the top of its head."

"You like birds, I take it?"

"Oh, yes. I did a lot of hiking and bird-watching as a child."

Olivia paused her next question when the kitchen door swung open and her children returned. She looked up at her son. "Hunter, Scarlet was just telling us how much she would like to go mountain climbing."

He nodded as he carried a rectangular plate over from the kitchen. "Yes, Scarlet loves nature. She always has, ever since she was little."

Hunter set the plate down in the center of the table. When Scarlet saw what was on it, a giggle burst from her throat. She looked up to him, watching in wonder as he grinned like a schoolboy.

"Dessert is served," Hunter said, reseating himself beside her.

"Um…" Olivia hemmed. "What are those, dear?"

"They're Twinkies, Mom. They're Scarlet's favorite food."

The woman's brow rose. "This is your favorite food?"

"It is," Scarlet admitted. "Thank you so much, Hunter."

"Anything for you," he answered, offering her first pick of the spongy treats before them. "I love them, too," he added, grabbing his own and shoving a bite in his mouth. "I mean, it has something in the middle that you didn't even know was there. It's a complete surprise."

Maxine took a Twinkie next. "This is a surprise, alright."

"Well, I think it's a great idea," Hugh concurred, lifting the tray to his wife. Olivia accepted the dessert with her forehead crinkled. She sniffed it, pressed it to her lips, and nibbled the edge.

"God, Mom, just bite into it already," Maxine encouraged. "There's frosting in the middle – that's the part you want to get to."

"I'm getting there, *dear*," she retorted with an arched eyebrow.

Hunter chuckled as he watched his mother struggle with her dessert.

Olivia took another bite and a dollop of cream mushed onto her chin.

"You've got a little something right there," Maxine informed with a twinkle in her eye.

Olivia reached for her napkin, wiping her mouth. "Did I get it?"

"Yup. It's all good now."

"Wonderful," she said, refocusing on her son. "Now, back to what I was saying, Hunter. Scarlet says she loves nature and would enjoy climbing with us."

He nodded. "I'm sure she would. She is a Girl Scout, after all."

Scarlet shook her head. "I *was* a Girl Scout."

"You still are, honey."

Maxine laughed hysterically, until tears clouded her eyes. "Well, get a load of that! Hunter Gregory is dating a Girl Scout! Now *there's* a sentence I never thought I'd utter."

Hunter glared at his little sister. She mouthed the word, "What?"

"I'd love to have a Girl Scout with us next time," Olivia interjected. "I'm sure you'd be a better guide than the one we had up on Rainier."

"Oh, I don't know about that," Scarlet replied. "But I might be able to point out some interesting birds, at least."

"Yes, I bet you could. You must come with Hugh and I, the next time we go. Although it would just be the three of us, I'm afraid, since my son won't climb. He doesn't care for the outdoors."

"I'll come," Hunter said.

All eyes at the table turned to him. His mother's widened the most. "You'll...you'll come mountain climbing with us?"

"Sure. If Scarlet wants to go with you, then I'll go, too."

Olivia's mouth opened, but nothing came out.

Maxine's mouth was another story. "What the *hell*, Hunter? Are you kidding me right now? You *hate* nature. I could barely even get you to take me to the *park* when I was little, and all I wanted was a push on the swings. Yet now, you're all set to go mountain climbing?"

He shrugged. "I changed my mind about nature, Maxine. I wasn't looking at it the right way before. I didn't appreciate all the beauty."

"Good God, this just gets more and more interesting," she mused, shifting her focus to Scarlet. "Tell me, please – how did you two meet?"

Scarlet stiffened immediately, not wanting to lie to anyone, let alone Hunter's whole family. She turned to him, meeting his eyes that instant. He set his hand out on the table for her to take. She didn't hesitate.

Hunter smoothed his palm across hers, his fingers easing over her wrist, calming her instantly. "Scarlet works in the building across the street from Gregory Global," he answered, his eyes still latched to hers. "I can see her office from mine, yet I never knew she existed. I'm just fortunate she sometimes eats her lunch outside in the marble square."

"I do," she agreed. "I sit outside when the weather's nice, watching the birds hop by and listening to the water splash in the fountain."

"And you were there that day, eating your lunch," he continued, his voice softened for her ears only. "You were sitting on one of the stone benches and I saw you from across the square. You didn't see me at first, since you were busy. But I saw you, and I nearly tripped over my own two feet when I did."

"Well, you did almost trip when you walked over to me."

"That's only because you were feeding your sandwich to a squirrel, and the damn thing dove in front of me to catch a piece of bread."

"It didn't *dive* in front of you," she corrected, her fingers tracing over his palm. "It was just living its life, and you happened to be there."

"Oh, it absolutely dove in front of me. And I nearly fell on my face. But that just made you reach out to catch me, so I forgive the squirrel."

Her fingers stopped moving. "You forgive him?"

"I do. I might even *like* him. But if you tell anyone, I'll deny it."

Scarlet smiled with her whole body. Hunter chuckled.

"Umm," Maxine hemmed. "In case you forgot, dearest brother, there are actually other people here and we heard all of that."

He looked grudgingly back to his sister. "What?"

"We heard the part about you liking the squirrel, so you can't deny...oh, never mind. When exactly was it that you tripped over a rodent and landed in Scarlet's lap?"

"Uh, well, it was very recently."

"Recently?" Olivia questioned her son.

"Yes."

"Weren't you in Cozumel with your friends for the last few weeks?"

"No, I didn't go to Cozumel. I stayed with Scarlet."

Maxine sat up straighter. "You mean you cancelled your vacation to Mexico to spend time with a woman you *just met*?"

"Yeah, I did."

"Then are we talking about a love-at-first-sight scenario here?"

Hunter squeezed Scarlet's hand. "Pretty much."

Maxine turned to Scarlet, staring the same question into her eyes. *Was it love at first sight?* She didn't know how to answer the unspoken query, since this certainly wasn't the time or place to make emotional confessions to her boyfriend. Her fingers clamped onto his.

The awkward silence became deafening until Olivia crooned, "My goodness, these really grow on you." She bit down into her Twinkie and gave a tight-lipped smile as she chewed. "Mmm. Quite good."

Scarlet refocused on Hunter's mother. "I'm glad you like it."

"Oh, I do," Olivia agreed once she'd swallowed the spongy mush and washed it down with a gulp of wine. "Now, why don't we talk more about you? My son tells me you're a doctor."

"Yes, I am."

"You must be brilliant, then."

"Well, I wouldn't..."

"You don't have to be modest," Hugh assured with a gentle smile. "Have you discovered the cure for cancer yet?"

Scarlet returned the soft-spoken man's smile. "No, I'm afraid not."

"There's always tomorrow."

"I bet she can do it," Maxine declared. "She's obviously some sort of miracle worker. What kind of medicine do you practice, Scarlet?"

"It's, um...it's psychiatry."

Maxine's eyeballs nearly fell on the table. "*Psychiatry*? Oh, crap! Did you put Hunter on medication? Is that what's happening here?"

"Goddamnit, Maxine," he growled. "Give it a rest."

She matched his feral glare. "I'm just saying, you being on drugs would go a long way in explaining all of this."

Hunter's brow rose. "Do I need to pin you down on the floor and tickle-torture you like I did when we were kids?"

"Holy hell! Don't you even *think* about..."

"Hunter! Maxine!" Olivia shouted, her eyes blazing before she calmed her tone. "The two of you do know how to behave properly in front of a guest, don't you? Because that fact is in question right now."

Olivia focused on Scarlet the moment her composure returned. "I apologize for my children. They get a bit unruly around each other."

"Yeah, we do," Maxine agreed, also looking to Scarlet. "Seriously, though, please tell me the truth. Did you put Hunter on meds?"

Scarlet cringed with the question. She realized something just now, something she hadn't considered before. As much as Maxine loved her brother, and as much as Olivia and Hugh loved their son, Hunter had opened himself up to their scrutiny tonight. He'd opened himself up to a veritable firing squad, simply by putting his love for her on the table – almost literally – in front of his entire family.

Scarlet hadn't considered the magnitude of his actions before now. She'd been too caught up in how this night affected her. Yet it was Hunter who was actually affected most, by exposing his heart to the people who knew him longest and best – the people who had the highest expectations, and were therefore the hardest to be vulnerable with.

Looking back to the man by her side, she matched his vigilant, protective stare. "No, Maxine, that's not what's happening here," Scarlet reassured as she eased her hand across his.

Hunter captured her fingers, holding her steady. He focused entirely on her face, watching with tenderness, love, and hope. She gripped him back just as tightly. "What's actually happening here is that your brother is being so strong. He's being so brave. He's courageous. He's determined. He's fearless. He's..."

"Happy," Hunter supplied.

"Happy," Scarlet echoed.

He smiled into her eyes, warm and boundless.

For several perfect minutes, she let everything else in the world leave her mind. She allowed herself the solace of this moment, simply holding onto him, content to stay in their blissful cocoon forever. Until she realized the room was entirely silent, and had been for some time.

When she finally pulled her gaze away from Hunter's, she looked first to Maxine. The girl's lower lip quivered as she attempted to reign in her emotions. Scarlet offered his sister a smile, which was returned in spades. Then she looked to the other woman at the table.

Olivia gazed on her son with tears in her eyes. Her fingers trembled against the tablecloth. She swiped at the moisture in her eyes with her napkin, inhaling steeply as she shifted in her chair.

After another brief moment of silence, Hunter's mother cleared her throat. "Well, it's been wonderful meeting you this evening, Scarlet. So very, very wonderful. This has been an enlightening experience for all of us, I think. And I would just like to say..." Olivia paused to stiffen her spine and lift her chin, "...that if you aren't pregnant yet, I hope you will be soon. Perhaps tonight."

"Mom!" Hunter and Maxine shouted in tandem.

"Well, I think that's our cue to exit," Hugh announced. "Come on, dear. Let's leave these two alone for...whatever they need to do."

"Oh my God," Maxine grumbled. "I think I'm gonna die."

Scarlet understood that sentiment. If it weren't for the wild banging of her heart in her ears and the fiery heat of Hunter's fingers clenching hers, she wouldn't be sure whether her body sustained life at all.

Hugh stood and walked around the table to pull Olivia's chair out for her. Hunter mimicked the action for Scarlet. When she stood, he wound his arm around her back and gripped onto her hipbone, keeping her body close to his while they followed his parents to the door. Scarlet clung to the back of his shirt, needing the support, even though it probably seemed as if they couldn't keep their hands off of each other.

Hugh opened the door for his wife as Olivia turned her eyes back to them. "Thank you for a wonderful evening, Hunter and Scarlet."

"You're welcome," they answered together.

Olivia smiled. "You coming, Maxine?"

The young woman stepped up beside Scarlet and shook her head. "In a minute. I drove myself here, so I can drive myself home."

"Very well, but don't overstay your welcome, please."

"Yeah, Mom, I know. Lots of baby-making for these two to get to."

Olivia raised her brow and Hugh shook his head before they exited.

"Bye, Mom and Dad," Hunter called after them as he closed the door. He didn't take his arm from Scarlet's waist, which she very much appreciated, given the twinkle in his sister's eyes.

Maxine observed her for a solid minute, until a wild grin consumed her face. "Man, Scarlet, you are such a breath of fresh air."

"I am?"

"Oh, yes. You're different and lovely and wonderful. I'm sorry if I seemed a bit harsh on my brother tonight. I hope I didn't upset you."

"Not at all. I may be an only child, but I understand sibling rivalry."

"Rivalry? Geez, I wish that's all this was. In truth, it's a dictatorship. This man standing here with you now, all adoring-and-clingy, made my entire teenage life a living hell. If he'd had his way, I would have been dressed in Amish clothing and sitting behind a spinning wheel all day."

He sighed. "I wasn't that bad, Maxine."

"I know you did it because you love me, Hunter. But you were a tyrant. You have to realize that."

"Okay, okay. Maybe I was a bit of a tyrant. Just a bit."

"Well, that's more than you've ever admitted to before, so I'll take it." Maxine turned back to Scarlet. "I really do think you're a miracle worker. Would you like to go out for lunch with me sometime?"

"Goodness, yes. I would love that."

Hunter's head cocked. "How long are you going to be in town, sis?"

"Oh, I guess I forgot to tell you. I'm moving back here next month."

"What? You're moving back? Why didn't you tell me sooner?"

"I wanted it to be a surprise. I was going to tell you over dinner, but then *this*," Maxine paused to motion between Scarlet and him, "happened, and I became the surprised one. But I'm not moving back so you can rule over me with an iron fist again. Just so we're both clear on that."

His arm tightened around Scarlet. "I won't. I'm really happy you're going to be here again, and I promise to put my iron fist away. I do realize you need to be free to lead your own life."

Maxine's jaw unhinged. "Holy hell! I think you just quoted the crab from *The Little Mermaid*."

"Oh my God, he did," Scarlet agreed, giggling as she tilted her face up to his. "But then again, he does quote movies *all* the time."

Hunter smiled down at her. "I do not quote movies *all* the time."

"Well, you do quote a lot of movies. I'm just saying."

He growled, the sound both teasing and tempting. Scarlet had difficulty catching her breath when his eyes darted to her mouth. She fisted his shirt as his fingers twitched against her hipbone.

"I do believe that's my cue to exit," Maxine huffed. "Seriously, I've felt like a fifth wheel all night long, watching the lovey-dovey couples. I mean, Mom and Dad have been always bad enough, but now I have to deal with you two on top of all that?"

Hunter stared her down. "Get used to it, Maxine."

"Ugh," she grunted. "Please tell me there are some eligible bachelors at the Richmond branch of Gregory Global. I'm not asking for much, I swear. I only want someone young, sweet, smart, and handsome. Also, it wouldn't hurt if he had a haunted past. But not *too* haunted, if you know what I mean. Maybe just mild-to-moderately haunted."

"I'll keep my eyes open," Hunter grumbled.

Maxine grinned. "It really was nice to meet you, Scarlet. Honestly, I can't tell you how happy I am that you're here."

"Thank you. I can't tell you how happy I am to be here."

The bubbly young woman grinned before shifting her attentions back to her brother. "Walk me to the elevator, Hunter?"

"Yeah, sure," he agreed, pressing a kiss to Scarlet's cheek.

She smiled while the siblings walked into the hallway. Maxine waved and she returned the gesture. "Be right back," Hunter told her.

The moment the door closed, all the air rushed from Scarlet's lungs.

Her mind ran a mile a minute, but didn't have any clue where to go. This night had been so bizarre. And fun. And scary. And wonderful.

Her pulse bounded as she stepped into his living room and stared blankly at the wall. She still had a few bones to pick with Hunter. She definitely had some grievances to air, and some points to drive home. Yet they all felt muddled and silly, given the words he'd spoken earlier.

I love you, Scarlet. He'd said it with such openness, such certainty.

I love you, Scarlet. God help her, she didn't doubt him.

She probably should have made some sort of rational argument against a declaration that strong – hell, Hunter had even countered an argument she should have made, but didn't – yet she still didn't think to fight him. She simply accepted his declaration of love, because she could see the truth of it in his brilliant blue eyes.

Scarlet laughed, a bright, bubbly sound that filled her body with joy. She barely heard the click of the closing door as Hunter came back inside. He stood across the room, frozen in place, while he studied her with those brilliant eyes of his. She remained entirely still, waiting in breathless anticipation. Eventually, he gave her a soft smile. She returned it without hesitation. That simple acknowledgement was apparently all he needed.

Hunter closed the gap between them that instant, striding purposefully across the floor until he could take her in his arms. He pulled her onto his chest, flattened both his hands on her back, pressed his forehead to hers, and exhaled. "God, it feels so good to have you here with me."

"It feels good to me, too," Scarlet admitted, resting her palm over his heart. "Can I ask what your sister said to you in the hallway?"

He chuckled as he raised his head to meet her eyes. "Oh, Maxine had quite a lot to say. Mostly, she thinks you're wonderful."

"Mmm. I think she's wonderful, too."

"She also said you're sweet, fun, and lovely, and she wants to spend oodles and oodles of time with you – those were her exact words."

"Wow. She did have a lot to say."

Hunter grinned. "That wasn't even all of it."

"No? What else was there?"

"She said she's never seen me happier or more in love in my entire life, and she hopes I don't fuck this up."

Scarlet's brow rose. "Oh."

"You look surprised."

"I am surprised."

"Well, I'm not. If you didn't notice, my sister is very outspoken, especially with me." He leaned in to press a soft, tender kiss to her lips, humming in contentment. "Besides, I already know I love you more than I've ever loved anyone. I also know I'm happier than I've ever been. And I totally agree with the not-fucking-it-up part, too."

Scarlet gulped in a breath.

Hunter ran his fingers up her jaw, watching the movement intently. "Are you doing okay now? I know tonight was a lot all at once."

"It was quite the surprise."

"I'm sorry. Well, I'm not sorry about having all of you in the same room, but I am sorry I sprang it on you. I know I shouldn't have."

Her fingers curled into his shirt. "Then why did you?"

"I just didn't think you'd come if I said my family would be here."

"You're right; I wouldn't have. I mean, don't you think meeting your whole family on our second date is moving a little fast?" Even as the words left her lips, Scarlet already shook her head. "Wait, don't bother answering that. Everything between us happens at the speed of light, so I should really be used to it by now."

He chuckled, the warm sound rumbling through his skin and into hers. "Everything does move quickly between us, and I know it can feel like a fantasy. You've always said our time at Blue was a fantasy, and in a lot of ways that's true. But we're back to reality now, and I want everything between us here to be grounded in reality. I need you to believe that what we have together is real, and I honestly couldn't think of anything more real than having you meet my family."

Scarlet worked to absorb his words. "Well, I guess I can see why you did it, although I'd like your promise that you won't surprise me with any more family dinners in the future. I mean, I would actually enjoy more family dinners. I'd just like to know they're coming."

"I promise," he said, smoothing his hand up and down her spine. "Was it really that bad when you found out they were all here?"

"Yes, Hunter, it was that bad. It freaked me out completely."

The wounded look on his face made her chest tighten. "Actually," she offered, "the worst part is I was too stunned to fully appreciate how beautiful your home is. Did you decorate it yourself?"

"No, I've never had time for that kind of thing. I hired a designer."

"Oh," she said, glancing around again. As opulently adorned as the room was, there was nothing to personalize it. No picture frames. No half-burned candles. No tiny trinkets with memories attached to them.

"Hmm," Scarlet considered, "now that I think about it, this place could really use a few plants."

"You can bring as many plants in here as you like."

She looked up to Hunter as his eyes roamed across her face. His home stretched over this building's entire top floor, yet they were pressed so closely together that they barely occupied a square foot. No boundaries of personal space existed between them anymore, if they ever truly had.

Scarlet knew she should step away, since her goal tonight was to take this slow. Instead, she melted into him, happily drowning in his eyes, while he encouraged her to bring her things into his home. It felt both wrong and right at the same time, and she hung her head, ashamed of her own indecisiveness. Playing with the buttons on his shirt, she decided to change the subject. "So, how did your date with Evie go last night?"

"Oh, it went fine. Better than fine. I know Maggie was nervous to leave us alone for so many hours, but I came through. I had Evie fed, bathed, and in bed before they got home. Although I'm not sure about the diaper-changing thing."

Scarlet raised her eyes back to his. "Was it difficult for you?"

"You could say that. I'd never done it before, and even though I knew what to expect, it was still something. I may have dry-heaved once or twice. But Evie thought that was hysterical, so it worked out well."

Scarlet giggled and Hunter gave her a crooked grin.

He ran his fingers across her cheek. "Will and Maggie were really happy with how well I did, so I offered to babysit again in a few weeks. I thought maybe you'd like to join me the next time."

"Yeah, I think I could do that. I'd love to meet your goddaughter."

Hunter smiled even wider, just before pressing a kiss to her mouth. It was soft, tender, and sweet...right up until he smoothed his tongue across her lips and groaned. "Come with me, Scarlet. It's time for bed."

Her brow shot up. "Bed?"

"Yes, it's late. We should head to bed now."

She shook her head immediately, struggling to clear her jumbled brain. "I don't think that's a good idea."

"You're right. It's not a good idea. It's a *fantastic* idea."

Hunter slipped his hands down her arms before taking a step away.

Scarlet worked to hold herself upright. "I – I really can't stay."

"Sure you can." He turned, striding through his living room toward the back of his home, effectively preventing her from having a face-to-face conversation with him.

"*Hunter*," she protested to his confidently retreating form.

"*Scarlet*," he growled in response.

She ground her feet into the floor. "You know, I would really like for you to listen to me right now. I am telling you that I cannot..."

"You're staying the night!" he announced in a deep bellow, not even bothering to look over his shoulder as he disappeared around the corner.

She stood right where she was.

He gave me a command! A goddamn command! What the hell?

Scarlet clenched her teeth while glaring at the empty space he'd just occupied. Hunter could not tell her what to do. He couldn't demand she stay the night and then expect her to stay. If they actually intended to have a real relationship, she couldn't give in to his controlling behavior all the time. That wouldn't do him, or her, any good.

Hunter needed to understand these things. She needed to set him straight this very minute. Unfortunately, in order to make her points of contention clear, she had no choice but to follow him into his bedroom.

Pulling a deep, filling breath into her lungs, Scarlet gave herself a pep talk. "You can do this. Yes, Hunter is intimidating, but you are a doctor with years and years of experience. You can handle this, damn it."

Taking one slow step at a time, she moved purposefully though his living room into the back hallway. She approached the first of several doors, which turned out to be the entrance to a giant master bedroom. Stopping just inside the doorframe, Scarlet stiffened her spine. She tried not to dwell on how gorgeous his room was – with its massive king bed, dark cherry headboard, and brilliant blue bedding to match his eyes – but it was hard to not notice her decadent surroundings.

Hunter observed her closely. He stood several feet away, beside a cushioned, ornately carved chair. He'd kicked his shoes off under the chair seat, and now stood in bare feet on the lush tan carpet. He didn't say anything as he watched her. He just started unbuttoning his shirt.

Scarlet focused on his eyes, refusing to let her gaze drift down to the wall of his bared chest. She pressed her shoulders back with great effort. "Hunter, what you just said to me out there wasn't appropriate."

He held her eyes as he undid the last button. "I am aware of that."

"Did you hear me correctly? I said it *wasn't* appropriate."

"Yes, I heard you. And I freely admit that it wasn't appropriate."

"I'm...I'm being serious here. You can't simply *demand* that I do whatever you want me to do, whenever you want it done."

He shrugged his shirt off and laid it across the chair, leaving him in nothing but terribly well-fitting dark pants. "You're absolutely right."

"That type of communication is not going to work between us," she continued, maintaining his unwavering gaze from across the room. "Not if we plan to have a real relationship."

"I completely understand," he said, his bare feet now padding across the carpet toward her.

She shifted in her heels. "No, I mean it. You have to listen to me *all* the time. You have to really *hear* me, and give me a say in *everything*."

He stopped walking when he stood inches away. "I totally agree."

"Good Lord! Are you just agreeing with everything I'm saying in order to get me to stop talking? Because that's what it feels like."

"No, not at all. I'm agreeing with everything you're saying because I actually agree with everything you're saying."

Hunter slid his hand into her hair. "I've been acting like a scoundrel over the past two days, Scarlet. I know I have. My bad behavior comes from desperation, but that doesn't excuse it. Honestly, the only reason I demanded you stay the night just now was because I knew it would piss you off. I knew you'd come in here to give me a piece of your mind, and it worked." His fingers wound into her curls. "But you're here now, and that's all I wanted. Mission accomplished, so I'm going to behave myself from this point forward. I promise."

Her reply failed when his other hand trailed across the waist of her skirt.

"I want you here with me," he told her. "But, of course, you have the right to leave. You always have the right to leave, and I understand that. I'm just hoping you won't, because I need you here. I *need* you, so I'm asking you to stay with me. Will you please stay?"

Scarlet's heart swelled as she stared into his deep, loving, hopeful blue. "I love that you want me here," she confessed. "But even though you're still on vacation, I'm not. Tomorrow is Friday, and I have to go to work. I actually have to wake up really early, and besides, I didn't bring any of my personal items with me to stay the night."

"I'm fully aware that you have to work tomorrow," he insisted. "I intend to have you awake and alert first thing in the morning. I have croissants and orange juice in the kitchen, along with tons of coffee. And as for your personal items, I'm pretty sure I've got that covered, too."

"What do you mean you've got it covered?"

"Well, let me just double check the bathroom situation." He stepped away from her to walk through the doorway beside the chair. She stared after him for the few seconds it took him to return. "Yes, I do believe everything you need is there. I have all of your personal items, including a nightgown."

Scarlet's tangled brain only heard one word. "Nightgown?"

"Yes."

"Did you really buy me a nightgown? And does that mean you don't want me naked in bed with you?"

Hunter chuckled. "Normally, I'd definitely want you naked in bed. But I need you fully clothed tonight, because I don't want us to have sex."

"You don't?"

"No, I don't. Not that I don't want to have you – Lord knows I'd be struck by lightning if I said I didn't want to have you in every possible way – but I don't want us to do any of that now."

"Really? Is this because of all the pregnancy talk that went on with your family at the dinner table?"

He grinned. "No, that's not why I don't want to have sex tonight."

"Then why don't you want to?" she asked, unsure as to how she went from refusing his advances to being upset that he didn't want to have sex.

"Because this is reality," he answered, "and real-life couples don't have sex every day. At least, that's what it said when I researched it. The statistic for the average married couple to have sex is only twice per week, which seems pitifully low to me, since I'm going to want you more than that. Honestly, if you're willing to go against the norm and try for sex every day, I'm certainly not going to protest. I have great faith we could prove that statistic wrong if we wanted to, and we can start working on proving it wrong any time you'd like, well, except for right now, because, as I already mentioned, I don't think we should have sex tonight, and..."

"Hunter?"

"Hmm?"

"You're rambling a little."

"Am I? Well, damn. Sorry."

"You don't need to apologize to me for that. Ever."

He leaned down to press a kiss to her forehead. Scarlet felt his shallow breaths moving through his chest while his lips dwelled on her skin, and she knew he was just as nervous about embarking on this journey into reality as she was. Slipping her hands up his bare chest, she rested her fingers over his heart.

Hunter sighed. "Will you stay here with me, Scarlet? Will you please stay the night in my bed, and let me hold you until morning?"

A smile spread her lips, one she couldn't have stopped if she tried. "Hmm. I guess I should go try on my new nightgown."

He nodded wildly. "Yes, that...that would be perfect."

When she pulled away, Hunter held her hand as long as he could. Once their fingertips finally parted, Scarlet stepped into his master bathroom. She shut the door, slumped back against it, and exhaled.

Her unsteady fingers moved to her blouse, unbuttoning the front while she absorbed her surroundings. His bathroom held an enormous soaking tub, a large rain shower, and a sink with two basins, all of which were worthy of her attention. But she couldn't focus on anything but what she saw on the countertop. Sitting there, lined up perfectly, were all of her personal items. It was every brand she used, in precisely the order she used them, arranged exactly as they'd been at Blue. Hunter had even bought her brand of shampoo and conditioner and set them on the edge of the bathtub, along with vanilla bubble bath and candles.

Scarlet's mouth gaped as she finished unbuttoning her shirt. She tried like hell to not overanalyze everything she saw, although she knew she'd have to later. Instead, she focused on the open shelves beside the sink, where he'd lined up multiple pairs of thong panties in every color of the rainbow. Lying beside them was a very unusual nightgown.

Her eyes remained glued to the gown as she stepped toward it. She'd expected something in silk or satin, something soft and skimpy to slip deliciously over her skin. When she picked up the curious garment by the shoulders, the lengthy hem unfolded and fell all the way to the floor. She stared at the red-and-green checkered flannel material, highlighted by white eyelet lace at the gathered collar and cuffs.

"Those would be the cuffs on the oddly long sleeves," she mused.

Scarlet wasn't entirely sure why Hunter wanted her to wear something this homely. Shaking her head, she set the nightgown on the countertop. She removed her shirt, bra, heels, and skirt before slipping off her underwear. Looking to the line of rainbow panties, she tried to decide which color to wear.

Her mind reeled as she absorbed everything before her. In truth, if she thought too hard about all the things he'd bought, she'd begin to feel like a kept woman. She might even think he was still trying to control her, which she knew wasn't true. She knew he didn't want to cage her. On the contrary, Hunter wanted to set her free.

Her eyes shifted to the mirror over the sink, drinking in her naked reflection. Her eyes were bright. Her cheeks were flushed. The skin over her chest was a smooth cream. It wasn't bruised anymore, not like it had been after that day of reckoning in the woods.

Scarlet brought her hand up to rest over her heart, feeling her smooth skin and strong pulse. Her flesh had healed fully since that fateful day. She wanted to heal, too. God, she wanted to heal so badly.

Picking up the unsightly nightgown, she pulled it over her head and pushed her hands all the way to the ends of the sleeves. She shimmied her hips until the thick material sank to her ankles. When Scarlet glanced back to the mirror, she giggled at the ridiculous picture she painted.

Grasping the hairbrush he'd left for her on the counter, she swept it through her loose curls. She took another minute to brush her teeth before looking back to the rainbow of panties. She tried again to decide which color to wear...and then decided to not wear any at all.

Her pulse skipped as she turned to pull open the door. She switched off the bathroom light while taking a step into the bedroom. He'd turned off the overhead light in here, too, the only glow now coming from a small lamp on his nightstand.

Hunter lay on the mattress, his body bathed in the pale yellow halo. He'd changed out of his slacks into a pair of black sweatpants that hung low on his hips. His chest was still bare, as were his feet, and his lips pulled into a soft smile when his eyes met hers. She dislodged her tongue from the suddenly dry roof of her mouth while striding forward.

"So, how did I do?" he asked, sitting up at the edge of the bed and planting his feet onto the carpet. "Did I get everything you need?"

"Yes, you did. I have to say, that was pretty impressive in there."

He reached for her hips the moment she came close, pulling her body firmly between his thighs. "I hope it's okay that I bought you a few things to keep here."

"Yeah, it's okay," she said, resting her hands on his shoulders, feeling his muscles relax beneath her touch. "Although, I must admit, this is not the kind of nightgown I expected you to get me."

Hunter chuckled as he looked up to her face. "It isn't?"

"Not at all. I thought you'd opt for something silkier. And shorter."

"Oh, I wanted to pick something like that, believe me. But when I looked at all those skimpy slips in the store, I could imagine fucking you in every single one of them. And since that wasn't my goal for tonight, I had to pick something entirely different."

"Then you don't want to fuck me in this nightgown, I assume?"

Hunter's gaze drifted down slowly and hungrily, over the frumpy lace collar and fully buttoned plaid front, onto the tiny swell of her belly. He exhaled heavily. "Actually, you look incredibly sexy right now. I definitely want to fuck you in this, too."

"Good Lord! Are you being serious? How can you possibly think I look sexy? You basically dressed me like a garden gnome."

His hands tightened around her hips. "Sweet hell, you're right," he whispered, staring at her flannel-covered stomach for another minute before dragging his gaze back up to her face. "Um, Scarlet?"

"Yes?"

"I'm going to need more therapy. Apparently, I've developed a gnome fetish."

She burst out laughing. "Well, that is definitely a problem. But don't worry, I'll help you get through it."

"Thank God," he breathed, smiling up into her eyes.

Easing her fingers over his face, she explored the curves of his ears and the stubble on his jaw. Hunter sighed with her caresses, his hands sliding from her hips to her back, hanging low on her spine. His thighs tightened around hers, locking her in place.

"Can I just...can I ask which color of underwear you picked?"

Scarlet smiled wickedly. "Oh, I didn't. I'm not wearing any."

The second the words left her mouth, his hands drifted down. He traced across her low back and onto her ass cheeks, pressing the thick material against her bare skin before trailing his fingers over her hips. Once he'd confirmed the lack of panty lines, his eyes drew back to hers. "You're torturing me with this. You know that, right?"

"Yes, I do know. What goes around comes around, Mr. Gregory."

Hunter groaned, dropping his forehead onto her belly. He wrapped both arms around her and pulled her closer, gripping tight to her body. Scarlet looked down at the top of his head, running her fingers through his hair, over his neck, and onto his shoulders, soothing him as best she could. Time passed while he hummed with her touch, the sounds he made lulling her as she glanced around his bedroom.

His furniture was all detailed and regal-looking, each matching in deep cherry wood. The window drapes were thick and floor length, blocking any light from the giant double windows. There was also a second ornate, cushioned chair – matching the one sitting beside the bathroom door – on the other side of his bed.

Scarlet envisioned herself placing her clothes on that chair each night as she prepared for sleep, while Hunter placed his clothes on the matching seat across the room. That image made her heart swell beyond reason, so she forced herself to look away. Focusing instead on the dresser by the far wall, she stared in wonder at the strange object laying on the surface. "Hunter? Is there a football helmet on your dresser?"

"Mm-hmm," he confirmed, nodding against her.

Scarlet studied the orange base and blue stripes. "What's it for?"

He raised his head, resting his chin against her stomach as he met her inquisitive eyes. "Well, when I made you come really hard up at Blue, sometimes you hit your head. And since the headboard I have is made of wood, and I intend to make you come over and over again in this bed, I worried you might hurt yourself. So, I got you a helmet."

"Oh my God. Really?"

Hunter chuckled, his shoulders rocking beneath her hands. "No, not really. That's my old football helmet. From high school."

Scarlet's fingers squeezed into his shoulders. "It is?"

"Yeah."

"Can I...can I see it?"

He reluctantly dropped his arms to his sides. "Of course."

Scarlet rubbed the scruff on his cheek before moving to the dresser. She stared at the helmet for a while, noting the little scratches and chips in the paint, before picking it up. "Is this always lying on your dresser?" she wondered aloud, familiarizing herself with the weight in her hands.

Hunter walked over to her. "No, it's not normally in my bedroom. I keep it in the far back of my closet, way up on a shelf behind some boxes. But today, I decided to dig it out."

Holding the helmet tight in her hands, she turned to him. "Why?"

He shrugged. "I wanted to show it to you. I haven't let anyone see it since high school, but it meant a lot to me. It was something I had for myself, independent of my family, and I really wanted you to see it. I don't know why. I just did."

Tears sprung to her eyes, since she knew how much this part of his life had meant to him. She knew he'd given it up because he felt like it wasn't important in the grand scheme of things. She also knew he'd lost a part of himself when he did.

Hunter stared at the smooth orange-and-blue surface while she held in it her hands, his face falling as his memories pulled him farther and farther away from her. Scarlet wanted nothing more than to bring him back, so she lifted the helmet and popped it onto her head. It was huge and it swallowed her completely, making her tilt her neck all the way back just to look up past the brim.

"What do you think?" she questioned. "Do I look sexy enough for you now? I could also pair this ensemble with some wooden shoes, if you like. All of that, on top of my gnome nightgown, would be quite the sight. I don't know how you could possibly resist me then."

Hunter laughed, although it was more of a half-laugh, half-cry. He reached out, drawing his hands down her arms to her lace-framed wrists before dropping them to his sides. "Actually, Scarlet, I know why I wanted you to see this helmet."

"Yeah? Why's that?"

"Because I love you. And I want to share everything with you."

Her lungs hitched with the sincerity in his eyes. Yanking the helmet off her head, she brushed back her disheveled hair and stared mutely up at him.

Hunter's shoulders fell. "Does it scare you when I say I love you?"

"No," she admitted, pushing the word past the lump in her throat. "It doesn't scare me at all. But that truth is frightening in itself, because it should scare me. It's not normal to fall in love so quickly."

"I agree. Nothing about this is normal. Honestly, I think that's why I trust it so much. I've never just gone with my emotions, not once in my entire adult life. I've always thought in practical terms and always tried to make sensible decisions. But all that ever made me was lonely and miserable. Now, I'm finally going to go with what *feels* right."

Those words soothed her as much as they concerned her, and Scarlet bit into her lip while matching his intent gaze.

Hunter slid his hand up her cheek, easing her lip from her teeth with his thumb. "Are you still worried that I suffer from erotic transference?"

"No. I don't doubt your love. I can see it in your eyes. I can hear it in your voice. I can feel it in your arms. I know you love me."

"I'm glad you know," he said, glancing down to watch her fingers squeeze around the helmet. "But you still seem worried."

"I am. I'm worried you're not the one suffering from a syndrome."

"What do you mean?"

Scarlet shook her head. "All of this just happened so fast. My feelings for you are gigantic and powerful and overwhelming, and that intensity makes me wonder if *I'm* the one with the syndrome."

"Wait a minute. You actually think you have a syndrome?"

"I do. After all, you gave me as much therapy at Blue as I gave you. You were there for me in a million ways, at a time when I needed someone so badly. So now, maybe I'm transferring my needs onto you."

She watched as he absorbed her words, unsure of how he would react. She studied his every move as he reached out, took the helmet from her grasp, and set it back on the dresser. The next instant, Hunter grabbed her face in both hands, tilted her chin up, and pinned her eyes.

"Honey, I don't think that's a syndrome. I think that's how two people in a relationship work together. They rely on each other. They fulfill each other's needs. They give each other strength. That's what being a partner means." He ran his hands into her hair, threading his fingers into her curls. "And you are, Scarlet...you're my partner."

His words settled her heart faster than she imagined possible. "Mmm. My Hunter is definitely a poet."

"Only when I'm with you," he said. "Will you come to bed now?"

When she nodded, his eyes lit up. Grasping her hand, he entwined their fingers to guide her to the side of the bed. He eased the covers down, revealing the fine ivory linens beneath. "Scarlet, do you remember that night at Blue when you fell asleep in my arms on your couch?"

She matched his questioning gaze. "I remember most of it. Right up until the point where I drooled on you."

Hunter chuckled. "Well, after you drooled on me, I carried you into your bedroom and laid you down on your comforter. I stood there for a minute, watching as you curled up on your side. At that moment, the only thing I wanted in the entire world was to curl up around you."

"Like a big spoon?"

"Yeah, just like that. So, if it's okay with you, I'd like to do it now."

"Oh, yes. It's more than okay."

He smiled with her agreement, stepping back to allow her room to crawl in. Scarlet immediately plopped down on her side, resting her head on the sinfully soft pillow. He covered her with the blankets before moving around the bed, shutting off the little lamp on his nightstand, and slipping under the sheets.

The mattress indented beneath his weight, pulling her backwards as Hunter aligned their bodies in the darkness. The moment his chest met her spine, he pressed a kiss to her hair. "Is this comfortable for you?"

"It's perfect," she admitted. "I'm glad I'm here."

"I'm glad you're here, too," he spoke beside her cheek. "Although I need to apologize again, for acting like a scoundrel these past few days."

She smiled into the pillow. "Thank you for the apology."

"And thank you for not calling security to remove me from your office yesterday. I wasn't positive what your choice was going to be there, but I had high hopes I wasn't going to get dragged away from you by two big, burly men. That didn't sound like it would be much fun."

"It didn't?"

"No, not at all," he said with a laugh, his hand slipping onto her hip, pressing the flannel fabric against her skin. "But I must admit, I'm relieved you have them in your building. I like knowing you're safe."

"Well, it is nice having two big, burly men at my beck and call."

"Hmm," Hunter grumbled, his fingers tightening on her hipbone. "What about me? Am I big and burly enough for you?"

He slid his chest up against her back, making her whimper into her pillow. "You most certainly are."

"Thank goodness for that."

Scarlet sighed when she felt him smile against her neck. "To be honest, Hunter, you are everything I could ever possibly need or want."

He froze in place with her admission. Resting his scratchy cheek on her soft one, he whispered, "I feel exactly the same way about you."

His cheek lingered against hers as his fingers ran a soothing path up and down her thigh. Eventually, his arm eased around her waist and his head settled onto the pillow. Scarlet exhaled, her body sinking further into the mattress.

Everything here felt soft and comfortable and safe. The house, the room, the bed, everything – it was all safe, because it was all his. In truth, this was the safest she'd felt in the last six months.

He placed his hand on her stomach, securing her to him. Her heart thumped steadily as his solid body supported her backbone, her mind returning to the thought she'd had earlier: *I want to heal. God, I want to heal so badly.*

Scarlet took deep breaths, fortifying her will. Her struggling inhales started his hand moving again, caressing up and down her thigh. She concentrated on that touch as she cleared her throat.

"You know, the security guards haven't always been there."

"They haven't?" he echoed. "How long has it been?"

"They've only been there for the past six m-months."

When her voice broke, his hand stilled. "The past six months?"

Scarlet focused on the feel of his strong chest lying flush against her back. "Yes. The manager of the building put in the security measures after it all happened."

"After what happened?"

"It's...it's the thing that happened," she said, not knowing exactly how to start. "I want to tell you everything about it. I really do. But I can't give you all the specifics, because he was a patient of mine."

Hunter raised his head. "I understand, Scarlet. I'm here to listen to whatever you want to say."

She nodded against the pillowcase, concentrating on the softness of her current environment. Then she closed her eyes and began. "I can't tell you his name, so I'm going to call him Simon. First and foremost, I want you to know he was a good person. Simon was a good man, but he'd had a lot of problems in his life, and they'd led him down a dark path. It was a path he struggled every day to come back from.

"He came to me at first because of a drug problem. He'd been to several other doctors, trying to break his pattern of addiction, but he couldn't resolve it. When he finally presented to me, he said he was at the end of his rope. I took his case, and I did my best to become the person he needed, the person he could rely on. And he did. He began to rely on me, and open up to me, and we started reaching into all the things that existed in his life to bring him to this place he was in.

"So much had happened to him as a child – horrible, unspeakable things. It took years for him to confide in me and work through his addictions, since it wasn't only drugs he contended with. He had many addictions, many needs that invaded his life in countless ways.

"I tried to help him with all of it, little by little, piece by piece. He made a lot of progress in the years we worked together. After a while, he managed to hold down a steady job, and get an apartment on his own. He even found a girlfriend. A woman he loved, even if he wasn't sure he deserved her love in return. But he was trying. He was really trying.

"He was doing so well, I thought we could take the next step. I thought I could push him to take a deep, searching look at the cold, hard truths in his life. Because sometimes, as a psychiatrist, you have to do that. Sometimes you have to push a person until they break, so you can help them rebuild, and you can guide them to a better life. So, I pushed him. I pushed him hard, because I believed he needed it. And he broke. He broke exactly the way I'd planned.

"I remember feeling relieved when it happened, because I knew I could help him finally put his life all the way back together. I stayed with him that day, long after our session was over, just to make sure he felt stable enough to go home. I also cleared my schedule the following morning, so I could see him again. I was actually really excited to see him again, and to start helping him rebuild."

Scarlet clutched the sheets beneath her hands, curling her fingers into fists. "I could tell something was off with him the moment he stepped into the room the next day, but I figured that was to be expected, since we were starting on a new path. We were starting a journey of healing together, and I was eager to do that. I stood from my desk and stepped toward him, wanting to sit with him on the couch. And that's...that's when he pulled out the gun he had in his coat pocket.

"I didn't even have time to react. I didn't have time to try to disarm him. I didn't have time for anything, because he didn't say a word. He just lifted the gun, pointed it to his temple, looked into my eyes, and pulled the trigger."

Scarlet drew her knees up to her chest, shrinking into a ball. She curled up as tight as she could, as small as she could, while the pain sliced through her body. The instant she caved inward, Hunter wrapped himself around her – his chest to her spine, his thighs against the backs of her legs, his arms banded around her chest – encasing her entirely.

"There was so much blood," she whimpered, choking on the words. "On the wall, floor, desk, and me. There were brains and blood spattered everywhere."

Tears streamed down her face. She pulled her knees higher and tucked her chin to her chest. "And then he just fell, Hunter. He just fell to the floor. Lifeless – instantly lifeless. And I had to take off my glasses, because I couldn't see through all the red on them, and I crouched down beside him, because I just wanted to help. I shook him. And I begged him. But he was gone. He was just gone."

Scarlet coiled up even tighter, desperate to keep the pain inside her from exploding. The stiffer she became, the firmer Hunter held her, enveloping her quaking body in his. "He trusted me. Simon *trusted* me, and I failed him. I failed him in every possible way."

"No, Scarlet, you didn't..."

"Yes, I did. I *did*. And the question I asked myself, again and again for months, was if I could fail that completely, then what was it all for? All the years of schooling and training and experience, all the hours and hours of sitting behind my office desk – what good did it do anybody, if I could lose someone right in front of my eyes?"

Sobs wracked her body as Hunter clung to her, his every muscle trembling from the effort of holding her without harm. Scarlet felt his struggles, but she also felt the security of his strength. She wasn't quite sure why he was still here, loving her, but she was so, so grateful for it.

"After Simon died, I lost all confidence in my abilities. I was certain my other patients would see that. I figured they'd see me as a fraud, and stop coming to my office. But they didn't. They continued trusting me with their problems, and allowing me to know their fears, and letting me hold their fragile hearts in my hands. And I wanted to help them. God knows I wanted to help.

"But I just couldn't do what needed to be done. Because sometimes, I need to poke a grizzly bear with a stick, or blow up a powder keg to see what's inside. Sometimes, I need to break someone, and I couldn't do it anymore. I couldn't push my patients the way they needed – not since that day with Simon. I knew I was failing them. They needed me to guide them, direct them, and push them. But I couldn't."

Scarlet swallowed hard against the acid in her throat. "I...I actually wasn't able to push anyone again. Not until that day I spent in the forest with you. I remember laying there, listening to you tell me everything that happened with Samantha, and realizing you'd abandoned the joy in your life in order to be what you thought she would want. That hurt me more than I can tell you. It absolutely ripped me in two. That's when I found the courage to push again – because you needed it. You were suffering, you were dying, and you needed me to push you. So, I did. And it was hard. It was so damn hard. But I did it because I wanted to be there for you. In every possible way."

She paused her words because she had to, because she needed air.

Hunter smoothed her hair back from her wet cheeks. "You *were* there for me, Scarlet, in every way. You still are. Every minute, every second, since the moment you laid eyes on me, you have been there for me. I know that without question. I just don't know if I deserve it."

"What do you mean, you don't deserve it? Didn't you hear what I just said? I'm a failure, Hunter. A *failure*."

"No. One loss doesn't make you a failure."

Scarlet shook her head, unsure if she could accept his understanding. "I went to Simon's funeral, you know. I went to the graveside, and stood in the back, while his friends and family mourned him. I felt like I needed to be there, but I didn't want to upset anyone, so I stayed on the outskirts. His girlfriend saw me, though. She knew who I was, and she walked over to me after the service was over.

"I expected her to scream at me. I expected her to call me a fraud, and say she planned to sue me for malpractice. I was ready to hear all of that. But instead, she threw her arms around me. She hugged me so tightly, and she thanked me. 'Thank you for getting him through the past few years.' That's what she said to me. Then she walked away and left me there, speechless.

"I didn't understand how she could do that. I didn't understand how she could grant me that forgiveness, when I knew I would never be able to forgive myself. I still don't know if I understand it."

She choked on a sob as Hunter dropped his forehead into her temple.

"A week passed before I could go back into my office," Scarlet continued, keeping her eyes shut tight. "They had to remodel the entire insides. They pulled up the carpet, put wood paneling on the walls, and brought in a new couch. They cleaned it all up, and when they were done, they asked me to come back to work. From the moment I walked into that office again, everyone treated me differently: the building manager who installed the security; the other doctors in my practice; and Marie, who just wanted me to feel better. God, poor Marie. She was right outside the door when it all happened, and she was the first person to run into the room. She saw me there, covered in blood, and she's never looked at me the same way since."

Hunter eased his hand over hers. "How do you think she looks at you now?"

"Like I'm breakable. They all looked at me the same way when I went back to work, like I'm made of glass. I didn't want that. I wanted to still be brave and strong, to give people what they needed. I wanted to be a doctor, because I'd devoted my life to it, and it was the only thing I knew how to do.

"So, I went to see Will. I went to your best friend and asked him to help me cope with the stress, because I had trouble sleeping. And I had trouble while awake. I had trouble understanding why my other patients came to see me, why I had a backlog of people waiting for my help, when I was obviously a fraud.

"Will helped me. He listened, and he gave me good advice, and he said all the right things. He said the things I knew he would say, since I'd studied PTSD and understood what I felt and how I was supposed to fix it. But knowing how to fix something and actually fixing it are two very different things, especially when I swore I could still see Simon's blood on the wall, day after day.

"That's when I started bringing the plants into my office," she confessed, the weary sound of her voice threading through the cool, dark air. "At first it was just a few, to cover up the phantom blood stains on the walls. The plants changed the color in the room, so it didn't all look red to me, and that made things better. After that, I kept buying more and more of them, until they filled half my office. Then one evening, while I sat alone at my desk, I stared at my wall of plants. I stared and stared, until I realized I'd created a makeshift forest, right there in my office. It was just like Blissful Blue, just like the forest I remembered from when I was a new doctor, wide-eyed and excited about treating my patients. It was the same forest I remembered as a child, as a Girl Scout.

"That was the moment I knew. I knew I had to go to Blue and get myself back into that forest. I knew I needed to return to my roots, to be the person who believed I could do anything I set my mind to. That's when I begged Abbott to let me turn part of my work time there into vacation time. I begged him until he finally agreed, and I accepted all his conditions, just for the opportunity to be in those woods. Because I realized, while sitting in my office that day, that I was dying. I felt like everything I'd created for my life was a lie, and I was dying just like my father did, right on his desk."

Scarlet shivered, the motion tightening Hunter's cocoon around her.

"I bided my time then, surviving as best I could, until the day I got to go to Blue. I still felt like a fraud for the first week, since so many patients had come to see me, and I didn't know what I could do for them. But I found a way to settle my mind. I wandered through the woods every afternoon, reminding myself of all the beauty I'd seen in the forest as a child. I brought my camera, and took pictures of the trees and the birds, and remembered how I'd dreamed about discovering my fantini, back when I was a believer. Then, the night before my vacation started, I sat down and wrote a lecture about appreciating all the little things in life. I wrote it from my heart, and I tried to wrap my brain around it.

"I gave that lecture the next day and the patients loved it. They thanked me, and told me how upset they were about not having any more sessions with me. I simply smiled and assured them I'd be back, since I hoped I would be. I hoped I *could* come back. I hoped I could be the person they all needed, even though I didn't know if I could ever be the strong and sure Dr. Tracey again."

She stilled, concentrating on the feel of his body surrounding hers. "At least, I didn't know until I met you, Hunter. I've told you many times how much you helped me when I was at Blue. I just hope you can see now why it's true. I don't think I could have come back home again, and believed in myself enough to walk into that office, if it weren't for you. I don't think I could have found a way to be Dr. Tracey without your help, and I can never truly thank you enough. For everything."

Scarlet stopped talking then. She stopped speaking and simply laid beneath his thick arm, with his warm body curled around hers. She listened to the air leave his lungs in short, labored exhales. Possibly because he was on the verge of tears. Or possibly because he was angry.

Part of her feared what he might say next. She feared he would acknowledge all of her faults and weaknesses, and finally realize she wasn't perfect, and ask her to leave. But the other part of her – the one that trusted in their love – believed he would stay with her, support her, and keep her safe. That was the part she decided to depend on.

After forever, Hunter pressed a kiss to her temple. His hand began a slow, steady path up and down her arm. "Scarlet, you once told me that intelligence comes with responsibility. Unfortunately, I don't think that's true. I wish it were. I wish all the intelligent people in the world would use their gifts to help others. That's not the case, though. Not for a lot of people. But you...you are like that. You took the mind your father fostered, and added it to the heart your mother nurtured, and became someone people can depend on. You use your gifts every day to help everyone else, and it's an incredible thing. People see that. They see your giving heart and your astonishing mind, so they keep coming back to you, because they know you deserve their trust."

Hunter ran his hand down to hers, threading their fingers together. "But that's not all you deserve," he whispered, his warm breath shifting across her ear. "You also deserve to be happy."

A sob snuck out of her throat, adding several more tears to the pillow beneath her cheek. "Are you sure about that?"

"I am. I'm absolutely, positively, completely sure."

She smiled even as the fresh wetness soaked into the linen. "That makes it sound like you're fairly certain."

"Unconditionally, unquestionably, undeniably certain," he insisted. "This thing that happened, it wasn't your fault. What Simon did wasn't your fault any more than what Samantha did was mine. I know you probably don't believe that, because you hold yourself accountable. But I hope one day you'll forgive yourself, since you deserve to be happy."

"I...I want to believe you."

"Then believe me. You deserve to be happy. I'll say it a million times if I need to, until I know you accept it. You deserve to be happy, and I just want the chance to show you how happy we can be together." His fingers tightened in hers. "Will you let me do that? Will you let me show you how happy we can be?"

Scarlet inhaled, breathing him into her lungs, and tucked his hand up under her chin. "Yes," she whispered, afraid to speak too loud. "I'd love to find out how happy we can be together."

He settled his head back onto the pillow beside her. "I'm going to show you. And it's going to be amazing, just like you are."

She hugged his arm to her chest, enjoying his slow exhales against her neck as he held her in a tight, perfect bubble. She felt a peace at this moment – a peace she honestly never imagined she could feel again. The reality of it gave her crystal clarity, and she knew beyond any doubt that this was where she belonged.

"Hunter?"

"Yes?"

Scarlet smiled into the darkness. "I love you, too."

He hummed in contentment. "Man, I really love hearing you say that out loud."

"Out loud?"

"Well, I already know you love me."

"I see. How long have you known?"

"For a while now."

"Did you know up at Blue?"

"Yes."

She nodded against the pillow. "Then you really do know me."

"I do," he confirmed, snuggling even closer. "Now go to sleep, please. I've got you. I'm right here, and I've always got you."

Scarlet closed her eyes. She allowed her body to sink fully into the mattress. Then she rested, truly rested, for the very first time.

16

THE MORNING AFTER

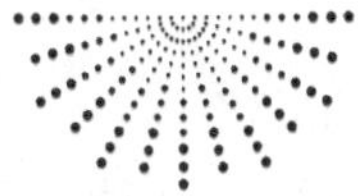

Scarlet woke to the feeling of warmth. For a moment, she thought she was back in the forest, basking in sunshine. But then she felt the movement of another person, and remembered exactly where she was.

She lay beside Hunter, in the comfort of his bed. His hand trailed up and down her arm, making her wish she could feel his skin directly on hers. Unfortunately, she still wore her long-sleeved nightgown. The thick material of the gnome outfit had twisted against her hips at some point during the night, whenever she'd turned over to snuggle into his chest.

"Mmm," she sighed, burrowing her face in the crook of his neck.

"'Morning," he whispered. "Did you sleep okay?"

"Yeah. Better than I've ever slept before."

"Good," he whispered, his fingers sliding down her arm and across the lace cuff at her wrist. She eased her hand onto his chest, flattening her palm over his heart. Prying her eyelids open, she registered a tiny ray of light in the room.

She dislodged herself from the nook of his shoulder in order to rest her check on the pillow beside him. "Hi."

Hunter's eyes fixed on hers in the pale morning sun. "Hi."

"Have you been awake for long?"

"Just for a bit."

Her fingers shifted over his heart. "Why didn't you wake me?"

"You looked peaceful. I wanted you to rest."

His soft, adoring gaze infused her with guilt. "I'm sorry, Hunter."

"Why are you sorry?"

"I'm sorry if you were worried that I might leave you alone in bed again, like I did our last night at Blue."

He gave her a gentle smile. "Well, I'd be lying if I said that wasn't a sore spot for me. But only because waking up without you the next morning felt tantamount to being drawn and quartered."

Scarlet cringed. "If it helps, leaving you tore me apart, too."

His fingers smoothed across her cheek. "Actually, that doesn't help at all. I never want you to hurt. Not ever. Although, in truth, I wasn't lying here worrying just now. I was lying here thinking."

"Thinking? About what?"

"About a million different things."

"Hmm. That's a lot of thinking. Care to share any of it?"

He slipped his hand down her neck and onto her shoulder. "Well, for one, I've thought a lot about what happened with you and Simon."

Her fingers balled up on Hunter's chest. Pain shot through her body, sharp and cold beneath her skin. "What did you think about it?"

"I think it's brave you shared it with me. Thank you."

Despite her pain, Scarlet found herself smiling. "You're welcome."

"I've also thought about Will. Did you know he's lost patients?"

She nodded against her pillow. "He told me when I spoke with him, although I don't know the specifics of his losses."

"There were at least two I'm aware of, since I remember the change in his personality afterward. I don't know if he's lost anyone in front of his eyes like you have, but I know how deeply they both affected him."

Hunter stroked her arm again, smooth, solid, and lulling. "When I think about it, Scarlet, I see just how difficult your work is. It's one of the hardest jobs ever. You place yourself inside the chaos of a person's life, and that is a damn scary place to be. Because ultimately, no matter how hard you try, you can't make anyone live if they don't want to."

She winced, searching Hunter's eyes for some evidence of his shame or disillusionment with her. She saw nothing of the sort.

He reached for her hand, winding their fingers together. "Honestly, I wouldn't have blamed you if you chose to give up after what happened. I wouldn't have blamed you if you never returned to your office again. But that wasn't your choice. You went back, and I can't even fathom the amount of courage it took for you to return to that room day after day, treating people in a place where something so horrible happened. I'm completely in awe of you."

"In awe of me? Really?"

"Absolutely. But I also feel guilty as hell."

"What on earth do you feel guilty about?"

"About how I acted in your office on Wednesday. If I'd had any idea of what happened there, I swear I wouldn't have done what I did."

She shook her head. "You don't need to feel guilty."

"I'm pretty sure I do. I blindfolded you, tied you up on your desk, and had my way with you. Right where you take care of your patients."

"Hunter, you really don't need to feel guilty. The moments I spent with you that day were the first good moments I'd had in my office in six long months. When you tied me up, I actually felt happy."

"Happy? Seriously?"

"Well, it was a sexually-induced happiness. But still happiness."

He squeezed onto her fingers. "I'm glad I could make you happy. Although nothing about it was happy for Marie, I imagine. She must have been terrified, seeing me barge into your office with a briefcase full of God-knows-what. That woman is never going to like me, is she?"

Scarlet offered him a reassuring smile. "I bet she will, once she sees how happy you make me. I think she's already starting to see that."

"You think so?"

"I do. And all the flowers you sent her yesterday didn't hurt, either."

"Oh, good. What else does she like? Maybe chocolate?"

"Yeah, I think chocolate might work out well."

Hunter reached to Scarlet's face, tracing a path across her jaw. "And what about you? How can I make amends for being so controlling and demanding with you that day? I feel pretty damn guilty. You could ask me for anything in the world right now, and I'd give it to you."

She covered his hand with hers. "But don't you see? What you gave me that day was just what I needed."

"What did I give you?"

"A good memory in place of a bad one."

"Do you truly feel that way?"

"I do. Oddly enough, the whole bondage thing seems to work well for me. When I tied you up, you gave me back the color red. And when you tied me up, you replaced a horrible memory with a happy one."

"Hmm. I guess good things do happen when we tie each other up," he considered, his serious expression giving way to a mischievous grin. "So...does this mean you'll let me tie you up again one day?"

"Do you *want* to tie me up again?"

"Well, I promised you last night that I would stop acting like a scoundrel, and I meant it. But if you'd still like me to be my demanding, controlling self – on occasion – I could certainly do that for you."

She bit her lip to keep from smiling. "I guess we'll have to see how I feel about that in the future."

He cocked an eyebrow. "Is that a maybe?"

"I suppose it is. I might even go so far as to say it's a probably."

"I'll take probably. Unless you want to change it to definitely?"

The smile she'd tried to suppress consumed her face. "Okay, then. I'll change it to definitely. But only when I say so, Mr. Gregory."

"Very well, Dr. Tracey. I will only be my demanding, controlling self when you desire it. I swear I'll wait for your approval. Although I think we should develop a code phrase, in case you ever want to use it."

"A code phrase?"

"Sure. You could tell me, 'Hunter, I want my scoundrel now,' or something to that effect."

Scarlet burst out laughing – a sound full of joy and promise – unsure of how he could make her feel this wonderful after the pain she'd relived with him last night. As her laughter subsided, he cupped her cheek in his palm. "What are you thinking now?" he asked.

She sighed, nestling further into his hand. "I'm thinking you are everything I could ever possibly need or want."

"Well, I certainly love hearing those words again."

"Good. I don't want you to forget them."

"I won't. And don't forget that I feel the same way about you."

"I won't," she vowed, her entire body pulling toward his. Every muscle she owned begged to reach for him, but she didn't give in to her desires, because he didn't reach for her. Instead, Hunter dropped his hand from her face and allowed it to fall back to the mattress, breaking all contact between them. Scarlet matched his intent gaze and stilled.

They lay mere inches apart, staring into each other. She licked her lips, drawing his attention to the motion of her tongue. He inhaled sharply, his body strung tight as a bow while focusing on her wet mouth. By the time his eyes drew back to hers, they were dark as night.

"What are you thinking now, Hunter?"

"I'm thinking how desperately I want to kiss you."

A whimper escaped her throat. "Then why don't you?"

He groaned with her question, yet held himself still as stone. "First of all, I'm trying very hard to not act like a scoundrel, since you haven't requested it yet. Second, if I start kissing you, I sure as hell am not going to want to stop there, and I know you have to go to work this morning."

"You did say you'd have me awake and alert for work," she sighed. "With croissants and orange juice and coffee, if I remember correctly."

"Yes, I promised you all of that. And I will keep my word."

"You're a good man," she praised, although she felt more than a little tempted to utter the phrase: *Hunter, I want my scoundrel now.*

He eased his hand out tentatively, tracing over the frumpy lace at the collar of her gnome nightgown. "So, I guess we're both in agreement, then? Absolutely no kissing this morning?"

"Lord, that is what I should say, isn't it? Absolutely no kissing."

Hunter tugged on the lace. "Yes, that is what you should say."

"You're right," Scarlet agreed, watching his eyes fall with her words. "On the other hand...we did wake up quite early, didn't we?"

"Did we?" he questioned, looking back to her with a gleam of hope.

"We did. And I should really go home this morning, to shower and change clothes, but I think I could modify my routine a little."

His fingers skirted beneath her collar. "Will that work for you?"

She swallowed hard. "Well, if I shower here, and wear yesterday's clothes to the office, then I won't have to go back to my apartment before I head in. Which means I'll have some extra time now."

His brow rose. "It'll be okay to go to work in yesterday's clothes?"

"Oh, no, it'll be weird as hell. But the only person who will notice is Marie, and she knows you're my boyfriend, so I can deal with that. Also, I have lots of fresh underwear in your bathroom to choose from."

"Damn, Scarlet. Are you sure about this?"

The rawness of his voice accelerated her pulse. "Pretty damn sure."

"Does this mean I can kiss you now?"

She curled her toes into the sheets. "God, that sounds amazing. But can I have a few minutes to brush my teeth first?"

Hunter chuckled. "If you have to."

"I think it would be best."

He dropped his hand away from the lace on her collar. "Be quick about it, please. I want the most time I can have with you this morning."

"I'll be lightning fast," she promised, grinning while throwing back the covers and jumping off the mattress.

His laughter trailed behind her as she bounded to the bathroom. Scarlet could still hear his chuckles even after she closed the door. Once she'd tended to nature's call and washed her hands, she grabbed her toothbrush and squeezed her favorite minty paste onto it. Her feet bounced while she brushed, her entire body bubbling with excitement, anticipating the first time she could be with Hunter here in his home. She was so anxious, she nearly forgot to brush her hair when she finished with her teeth.

After taming her bed-tousled curls, she splashed water on her face, ran a towel across her cheeks, and grinned at her reflection. She thought she looked quite presentable, except for the farcical flannel nightgown. Tearing open the door, she leapt back into his bedroom. She looked immediately to the disheveled ivory sheets, searching out his body in the meager light seeping through the heavy window drapes. When she saw his bed lay empty, she frowned.

Scarlet turned toward the door, intent to search the house for him. But then her eyes caught the ornate chair beside the bathroom and she stopped. Hunter's clothes lay across the cushion where he'd placed them last night. Reaching for his shirt, she drew the fabric up to her face and breathed in his lingering scent. *Damn*, he smelled so good – like the forest, and like happiness, and like home.

Without a second thought, she grabbed the hem of her gown to wrench off the gnome outfit. Once the flannel lay in a heap at her feet, and she stood utterly naked in the cool morning air, she pulled the shirt across her back. Pushing her arms through his sleeves, Scarlet moaned at the feel of the supple, scrumptious material. His shirt enveloped her, with the hem resting against her thighs, and a dreamy smile pulled at her lips while she began fastening the buttons.

"Holy hell, what are you doing?"

Hunter's voice came from the hallway, ceasing all her movements.

Her gaze darted up to his, her fingers stilling on the one button she'd managed to close over her stomach. "Um...I'm putting on your shirt."

He froze inside the doorframe. "Why?"

"Because that nightgown is hideous," she answered, motioning to the puddle of plaid on the floor. Her face heated before she added, "And because I want your scent all over me."

Hunter's lips parted, but he didn't say a word. He simply stood in the doorway of the bedroom, staring at her. His hands balled into fists.

"Is it okay that I put on your shirt?" she asked, her heart banging inside her chest. "If you have something against me wearing your clothes..."

"You are fucking gorgeous. You're so goddamn beautiful, standing in my bedroom, with my shirt on. And still no underwear."

She shifted her legs, pressing her thighs together to ease the ache he created. "Still no underwear," she echoed, letting her arms fall to her sides as she met his stark stare. "I missed you just now. Where did you go?"

He cleared his throat. "I went to the bathroom in my other bedroom, since I figured I should brush my teeth, too."

Scarlet pushed her hair back, the motion lifting his shirt higher on her bare thighs. "Well, that's good. Oral hygiene is important."

"Mmm," he growled in agreement, his jaw clenched tight.

Confusion settled deep in her chest as he remained in place on the other side of the room. She had no idea why Hunter didn't move toward her, to grab her and kiss her and touch her everywhere, since all she wanted was to feel his body slide against hers. His unearthly resistance to her state of undress frustrated her to the point of pain, so she drew her hand across the opening of his shirt, right between her breasts. "I guess that means you have another bedroom, then?"

His eyes followed the movement of her fingers with feral intent. "I have two other bedrooms, actually."

Scarlet flexed her toes into the carpet. "I see. And do you think we could have sex in every one of your bedrooms?"

Hunter swore beneath his breath. "To be perfectly honest, I fully intend to fuck the hell out of you in every room of this house."

She bit into her lip, nearly drawing blood. "In *every* room?"

His bare chest shifted on shallow breaths. "Yes."

"In the kitchen?"

"Absolutely."

"What about the shower?"

"God, yes."

"Even in the hallway?"

"Most definitely in the hallway."

Scarlet drew her hand down further, tracing the seam of his shirt from her chest to her thigh. She parted the material to the side as she smoothed her fingers across the top of her leg, giving him a very open view. "You know, I actually wanted you to fuck me in the hallway when I arrived yesterday, right there beside the elevator door."

Hunter nearly choked on his own tongue. He leaned toward her from across the room, his cock hardening rapidly in his sweatpants. But he didn't take a single step forward. "Holy hell, Scarlet. Did you really want me to fuck you in the hallway yesterday?"

"I did," she admitted, her palms dampening on her skin. "I still do."

His brow rose. "That's a dangerous place for us to be together, you know. Anyone could walk off the elevator at any time."

"Damn, that's true. I probably shouldn't want to have you out in the open like that, should I? I just want you anywhere and everywhere."

"Mmm. I feel the exact same way about you. You must know that."

Scarlet had more than a little trouble breathing, but that didn't stop her from shifting his shirttail up to her hipbone, revealing even more flesh. "Do you want us to go into the hallway now?"

His only response was a darkly growled, "No."

"Why not?" she questioned, her gaze dropping down to appreciate the blatantly obvious state of arousal now tenting his pants. "It seems to me, if we plan to have sex everywhere, we should probably get started."

"We're going to. But we're going to start here, in this bed."

She lifted her eyes back to his. "Yeah? Why the bed?"

"Because I've waited my whole, entire life to fuck you in my bed."

"Oh. Well, in that case, why don't you fuck me in your bed now?"

He groaned as he took his first step toward her. "Good God, I thought you'd never ask."

Hunter closed the distance between them with inhuman speed. He walked right into her, slamming his body up against hers, stumbling her backwards. He caught her to his chest, with one hand against her spine and the other hand under the hem of his shirt, cupping her ass. His mouth met hers that instant, fusing their lips and tongues.

Scarlet threw her arms around his neck and held on, barely conscious of the fact that her feet no longer touched the ground. He carried her to the bed, sunk her down onto the sheets, and dragged her to the center of the mattress, without ever taking his mouth from hers. She spread her legs wide as his taut, eager length pressed against her sex, sending impatient, demanding shocks throughout her body. His jutting shaft rubbed over her throbbing flesh, but he still had his sweatpants on, which meant she couldn't feel him the way she truly desired.

Grasping tight to his neck, she wrenched her mouth away only long enough to pant minimal instructions. "Inside me, Hunter. Now."

He didn't hesitate. Using one hand, he pushed his sweatpants down on his hips, just enough to free his erection. Lining up his swollen head with her soaking entrance, he plunged deep inside, stretching her inner walls to their limits.

"Oh, sweet heaven," she breathed, feeling him everywhere at once.

"Fuck, Scarlet. You feel absolutely incredible."

She gasped for air when he drove into her again. "Harder. *Harder.*"

Hunter did as instructed, fucking her hard and deep, over and over. His mouth ran from her lips to her neck, nipping and sucking her sensitive skin. She moaned as she wrapped her legs around him, linking her feet against his back like she'd wanted to do when he tied her up on her desk. This position opened her completely, allowing him to hit the tender nub at the top of her sex fully with each decisive thrust, bringing her to the brink faster than she could possibly imagine.

"No, wait," she whimpered. "Please stop."

He ceased his pounding movements immediately, raising his head to meet her eyes. "What's wrong? Am I hurting you?"

"God, no. Nothing hurts anywhere in my body. I'm just...I'm about to come."

A lopsided grin curved his lips. "Well, that is kind of the idea."

"I know, but it's – it's too fast. I don't want it to be over already."

Hunter shifted his hips, causing another electric current to pulse beneath her skin. "Then I'll give you a second orgasm after the first one."

"No, it's not...I just want to be on top. Can I be on top?"

"You can have anything you want, Scarlet. Always."

An instant later, he'd flipped over on his back and perched her above him. She wasn't exactly sure how he'd accomplished the change in position so quickly, but she felt grateful for her current dominance. After all, she had big plans for her man this morning.

Slipping her legs down beside his hips, she leaned forward to plant her mouth firmly on his. He ran his hands up and down her spine while they kissed, smoothing his fingers beneath her shirt as his tongue tangled with hers. Scarlet allowed that delicious distraction for several minutes before pushing up on her knees to ease his erection out of her body.

Hunter groaned at the lack of contact. "What are you doing? I need to be inside you."

"You will be," she promised.

Dragging his eyelids open, he looked up to her. "Then push yourself back onto me. Let me fuck you."

"Don't worry, I will. But I want you to fuck me the way you said you wanted to when we were in my office."

"Oh, hell. What did I say?"

"You...you said you wanted to fuck my mouth."

The air caught in Hunter's chest. He raised one hand to her face, smoothing his fingers across her lips, studying the movement intently. "No, I said I wanted to fuck your *gorgeous* mouth."

Scarlet nipped at his fingers, watching his eyes darken at the sight. Drawing her leg over his chest, she situated herself at the side of his body and sat back on her heels. "That's what I want you to do now."

He didn't respond, since his teeth were clenched too tightly. He just glared at her, his eyes on fire with raw hunger. Scarlet forced herself to calm down when she bent forward to place her lips on his chest.

She ran soft, slow kisses down the center of his body as Hunter dug his hand into her hair and buried his fingers deep inside her curls. He didn't hurt her. Not at all. But he did hold on for dear life.

While Scarlet eased her lips farther down his chest and onto his abs, she reached for his sweatpants and pushed them down his legs. By the time she traced her tongue around his bellybutton, the last of his clothing lay bunched on the floor. "Hmm. You're completely naked now."

Hunter propped his head up with one arm. "That I am."

She glanced up, trying not to obsess over the bulge of his bicep. "Do you want me to be naked, too? I can take your shirt off, if you like."

"No, please don't. I love seeing you in my clothes."

"Is that because it means I'm yours?"

"Exactly."

She didn't flinch at all. "I am yours, Hunter."

"I know," he said with a slow smile. "And I'm yours."

Scarlet returned his smile as his fingers tightened in her hair. Shifting over on her knees, she lined herself up with his very prominent erection. She didn't take her eyes off his when she grasped the base of his shaft in her hand, brought her lips down, and kissed his pulsing cock.

Hunter's pupils widened even as his eyes narrowed.

She licked him next, drawing her tongue from the base of his length all the way up to the tip, watching the pleasure move across his face. Then she closed her eyes, opened her mouth, and took as much of him inside as she could. He groaned, fingers fisting against her scalp.

Gripping his base, she worked her mouth up and down, again and again, flicking her tongue across his taut flesh. She felt his hips shift on the mattress, his fingers twitch in her hair, and his shaft throb against her tongue. She sucked harder, hollowing out her cheeks, making his entire body shudder. "Damn, honey. Do you...do you taste yourself on me?"

Scarlet pulled back only enough to see his face. "I do."

He licked his lips. "You taste amazing, don't you?"

Fire lit her face. She didn't respond. She just took him back inside her mouth, swirling her tongue and bobbing her head faster and faster. Her fingers shifted up and down, moving in time with her mouth.

"God, you feel incredible," Hunter gasped, his groans increasing in speed and tempo to match the pace of her movements. "Seeing your lips around me and my shirt on your body – you are so fucking beautiful. I could come right now. Right on your tongue."

"Do it," she panted against his flesh. "I want to taste you."

"I want you to. You have no idea how much. But not yet."

"Why not?"

"Because I want to taste you, too."

She turned her attention back to his face. "I'm sorry?"

A slow smile curved his lips. "I want to taste you."

"Well, that will be difficult at the moment. I'm rather busy."

"It won't be difficult at all, actually. Just shift your body up to me."

"Shift my body?"

"Yes. Bring your hips up this way."

"I'm not sure what you mean. Where do you want me?"

"I want you up here."

"But, I don't see how..."

"Please forgive me for putting this crudely, Scarlet. But for the sake of time, let me say it this way: I want you to sit on my face."

Her eyes widened. "What?" she questioned, holding firmly to his cock as he jerked inside her hand. "Do you...I mean...you want *that*?"

"Yes, I very much do. I want to be able to taste you at the same time you taste me. Does that sound like something you'd like?"

"I, um, I suppose so. I've just never tried that position before."

"Seriously?" he asked, the eager desire written in his eyes stealing the air from her lungs. "Holy fuck. Please let me be your first."

Scarlet nodded her agreement, although she wasn't entirely sure how to proceed. Releasing her grip on his shaft, she shifted up on the bed. Hunter dropped his head onto the mattress, obviously fully prepared for this. She stilled beside him, trying to work out the logistics in her mind.

"Just put your knees beside my shoulders," he coached, waiting patiently until she fully straddled his head. "That's perfect. Now put your hands down beside my hips, and lay your chest on mine."

She rested her hands cautiously on the mattress beside his hips. Settling slowly down onto his chest, she lined his erection up with her mouth, which seemed like the proper placement of body parts for this activity. "How is this, Hunter? Am I in a good position for y-*oh*..."

Scarlet didn't get to finish her question, since he wrapped both hands around her waist, flattened her belly against his chest, and licked his tongue straight up through the folds of her sex.

"Oh, damn," she moaned, "that is...*wow*."

He chuckled against her skin, his hot breath fanning over her slick, wet flesh. His lips glided across her skin and onto her sensitive nub of nerve endings, tasting that tender area quite thoroughly. Her eyes rolled back in her head as his tongue moved in perfect little circles.

"Why are you so incredible at this?" she wondered aloud, locking her elbows to keep from collapsing. "Did you take how-to classes? I never took any of those classes. I didn't know they were available."

His chest rumbled with laughter, but it only lasted a moment before latched onto her tender flesh, teasing her folds with the edge of his teeth.

"Oh! Yes, Hunter! That is just..."

Her voice failed her as he slipped his hands across her bottom, tracing the seam of her ass. When he pressed a finger deep inside her aching sex, Scarlet nearly bit through her tongue. He fucked her with that finger, in and out, before he added a second. Hunter continued, thrusting into her tight walls as his tongue found innumerable ways to set her nerve endings on fire. She fought the incorrigible urge to buck into him, to press down against his mouth and choose her own rhythm, even though the one he'd created for her was excellent.

Don't be greedy, Scarlet. You'll smother him. In truth, she was a bit concerned about smothering him now. But he didn't seem to mind in the least. He buried his entire face into her sex, licking and sucking and making wet, tempting noises against her flesh.

"Fuck, fuck, fuck," she breathed, her arms finally giving way. Her upper body collapsed onto his abdomen, the firm ridges of his stomach pressing her tight nipples into the softness of his shirt. She gasped in air, unable to focus on anything but Hunter's mouth and fingers.

Scarlet honestly forgot that she was supposed to be doing something else right now. But then his erection jerked hard against his abs, right beside her face. She zeroed in on the long length of his rigid cock, and on the thick drop of fluid collecting at the tip. Wrapping her fingers around his base, she ran her tongue across the tip, savoring her first taste of him. His hand grabbed onto her ass cheek, causing a wave of wetness to pool between her legs and into his mouth.

She took him completely inside of her, relaxing her jaw to feel the hard ridge of his shaft run all the way back along her palate. When she'd taken him nearly to her throat, she wrapped her lips around him and pulled back slowly, applying pressure the entire way. Hunter growled and moaned, arching up to press his face harder into her sex.

The next time, Scarlet tried to take him even deeper into her mouth. Her free hand fisted the sheets, giving her a modicum of support as her other hand rubbed his shaft and balls. She withdrew her lips, a little faster this time, before sucking him fully back inside once again.

Hunter's head thudded down against the mattress as he muttered something that sounded like, "Goddamn holy fucking shit." But she couldn't be sure, since her thighs muffled his voice. Scarlet hummed against his skin while his cock sat deep in her throat, making him utter a few more choice curses. Then he refocused entirely, diving back into her, his fingers stretching her slick inner walls, his tongue circling her tensed bundle of nerves, his lips suckling her tender flesh.

Bucking against his face, she fought the urge to bite down. She did add a scrape of her teeth as she pulled his cock from her mouth, which caused his fingers to grip onto her ass. She sucked him inside her, again and again, now able to concentrate on his pleasure even as she relished her own.

Scarlet found a sweet, tempting rhythm, one that matched the thrust of his fingers inside her sex, and breathed through her nose while he hit the roof of her mouth over and over. The wetness between her legs now trailed down her thighs, but Hunter certainly wasn't complaining. He only tasted her more thoroughly, holding her in place while humming his approval of her ridiculous state of arousal. His obvious desire for all things *her* made one thing perfectly clear: she was going to come hard and fast and strong, any goddamn second now.

Scarlet attacked him, wanting – no, needing – him to come with her. She sucked his stiff length into her mouth, grasped tight to his throbbing base, ran her fingers across his balls, and whimpered against his skin. His cock grew astonishingly harder as she worked his shaft between her lips and over her tongue, determined to taste him when he came.

Hunter finally began to fuck her mouth. He began fucking her *gorgeous* mouth, his hips thrusting up off the bed to push himself into her throat. His driving need made her thighs tremble, hurdling her to the edge. She couldn't help but grind her sex against his face, fucking his tongue and fingers in a purely uninhibited rhythm.

Scarlet cried out the instant she came, her unruly noises muted by his thick, stretched flesh in her mouth. Her fingers clenched onto his cock, hard and fierce, as her hips bucked against his face. Hunter's shaft swelled even further before he screamed his own release against her skin. She sighed with pleasure when his hot liquid finally surged down her throat.

Breathing hard through her nose, she worked to keep her lips clamped around him while his hips sputtered. His salty, tangy fluid pulsed out in waves, and she swallowed it down as every nerve ending in her body convulsed from her own unending orgasm. Hunter still slipped his tongue across her tender nerve bud, continuously tasting her in rhythm with her panted breaths, even when his erection began to relax in her mouth.

Once his cock finally ceased pulsing, and he dropped his head back onto the mattress, Scarlet released him from her lips with a little popping sound. She arched up, wanting to alleviate the pressure of her weight, but Hunter pressed his arm against her spine and pinned her down. Happy to admit defeat

– since her muscles were in no shape to move at this point, anyway – she allowed her body to collapse entirely onto his.

He chuckled when she flopped fully down on him, her arms falling limply onto the mattress. Scarlet sighed in contentment, resting her cheek against his abdomen as her hair fanned over his thighs. She couldn't drum up any concern over being spread eagle on top of him, and he didn't attempt to move her. He rested beneath her for the longest time, trailing his hands over her spine to soothe the skin he'd lit on fire just moments before.

She probably could have stayed like this forever, until she heard his very gentle request. "Um, Scarlet? Could you tilt on your side a bit?"

"Oh, yes, of course," she squeaked, swinging her leg over his head and scrambling to sit up beside him on the bed.

"You didn't have to move off of me entirely," he grumbled.

"No, no, I completely understand. I'm sorry I collapsed on you like that. I didn't mean to hurt you."

Hunter sat up, pushed her onto her back, and crawled on top of her. He lined their bodies up perfectly, pinning her beneath him on the mussed sheets, as a delectable smile curved his lips. "Do I look like I'm hurt?"

"Hmm. Not really," she admitted. In truth, he looked thoroughly satiated. And practically drunk. And definitively happy.

He gazed at her with his eyelids at half-mast. "Can I kiss you?"

"Hell, yes," Scarlet answered with giddy laughter. "You can put that mouth of yours anywhere you want to."

Hunter laughed along with her, right up until he pressed their lips together. His smooth, salty tongue wrapped over hers as he reached for her hands, pulling her arms above her head and entwining their fingers. She sighed into his kiss as he eased back and nudged her nose with his.

Scarlet still clung to his fingers, keeping her eyes shut. She didn't want to see or hear or think anything right now; she just wanted to feel. She wanted to revel in the sensation of his body, of his love surrounding her, knowing he was just as much at her mercy as she was at his.

"You're smiling," Hunter whispered. "That is the most beautiful sight in the entire world."

Her eyelids popped open. "You give me a lot of reasons to smile."

He looked into her with a wicked gleam in his eyes. "Does that mean you enjoyed our morning activity?"

"Oh, I don't think *enjoyed* is a strong enough word."

"I see. Then maybe we can do it again sometime?"

"Yes, please. Anytime you want."

Hunter groaned. "You might not want to give me carte blanche on that. I'd have my face between your legs all day long, if you let me."

Bravery surged through her as she gazed up at him. "And I'd let you fuck my mouth all day long, if you wanted to."

He shifted his hips with her words, his cock thickening against her thigh. "You'll let me fuck your *gorgeous* mouth all day long," he corrected.

"Y-yes. My gorgeous mouth."

Hunter stared into her with unapologetic desire. Leaning down, he kissed her again. The movement of his lips was slow and soft, even as he thrust his growing erection into her thigh.

She whimpered. "God, please stop. You're making me wet again."

"Am I? Well, I can certainly take care of that. I'll give you a second orgasm right now, if you want me to."

"Oh, I definitely want you to. But it's getting late, and I have to get ready to do something. I mean, I have to go to work. My goodness, I completely forgot about that. And I never forget about that." Scarlet exhaled. "It's just... it's you. You make the whole world slip away when we're together. You make me forget about everything but us."

He squeezed tight to her hands. "Is that a bad thing?"

"No, it's not. It's an amazingly good thing. You're like catnip, and I'm a tiger. I mean, if tigers like catnip. Do tigers like catnip? They're part of the feline family, so I assume they would. But tigers eat antelope and other such things, so maybe catnip doesn't mean all that much to them. The tiger-catnip thing might be a really poor analogy, but I think you know what I'm trying to say. At least I hope you do, because I'm obviously not speaking well right now."

"Come away with me."

Her eyes widened. "What?"

"I want you to come away with me this weekend. I only have a couple days left on vacation, and I want to spend them with you."

She lay beneath him, stunned into place. "Hunter, I..."

"Please, Scarlet. I promise I'll have you home by Sunday night. I know you have to work Monday morning. I do, too. We both have to return to reality, but until then, I want as much fantasy time with you as I can get."

"You want more fantasy time? I thought you said last night that you wanted everything between us now to be grounded in reality."

His fingers slipped into her hair. "This is still reality. It's simply a reality infused with magic. That's what you are to me – you're magic."

Scarlet melted into the mattress. "Where do you want to take me?"

"Can it be a surprise?"

"I love surprises."

"I know you do. Let me give you one. Say you'll come with me."

"Okay. I'll come."

Hunter smiled wildly with her consent. For several seconds, she didn't question her decision. Then she rolled her eyes and groaned.

His brow furrowed. "What's wrong?"

"Nothing. I'm just a little frustrated with myself."

"About what?"

She slid her fingers across his scratchy jaw. "Well, when I arrived here yesterday, I had every intention of taking things slow between us. I'd thought a lot about how to make our relationship work, and I decided it would be best to move at a snail's pace. I wanted our second date to be peaceful, and to end with a simple kiss, or three. After that, I planned to leave. I fully intended to go home alone last night, since I believe we both need to be cautious about all of this."

Hunter stared down into her for a long minute. Then he simply shook his head. "I don't want to take things slow."

"I know you don't. But I think we need that. I think..."

"Scarlet?"

"Yes?"

"I know you have a really big, wonderful brain, but have you ever considered that maybe sometimes you think too much?"

"Good heavens, I think that all the time."

"Then tell me what you'd do right now, if you didn't think about anything. What would you do if you just went with your feelings?"

"That's easy. I'd stay with you forever and never leave."

"That's the right answer," he insisted, his voice gentle yet firm. "You've got to know that's the right answer."

She smiled, even though she didn't know if it was the right answer. She couldn't know that for sure. But laying here with him now, and seeing the love in his eyes, it certainly felt like the best path to travel.

"When do we leave for our weekend trip, Hunter?"

His hand drifted over her skin. "Could you meet me back here tonight around six? Would that give you enough time to finish up at your office, pack a bag, and come back?"

"I think so. What kind of weather should I pack for?"

"It'll be warm where we're headed. Also, I definitely want to take you out for some nice dinners. Maybe you could pack a dress or two?"

"I can do that. Nice dresses it is."

"And, um, maybe..."

"Maybe what?"

"Maybe you could bring those shoes you wore to work Monday?"

"You mean my red high heels?"

"Fuck, yes. Those are the ones," he confirmed with a devilish grin.

Scarlet giggled. "I suppose I could bring those along."

He growled his approval, grinding his hips into hers, making his cock throb against her thigh.

"Damn it," she breathed, her pulse skyrocketing as wet heat pooled between her legs. "You're insatiable, aren't you?"

"No, I was quite satiated a few minutes ago. But it's been a while."

Scarlet shook her head. "Insatiable."

"Is that a complaint?"

"Nope. Not a complaint. I just have to go to work now."

Hunter settled down, steadying her face in his palm. "I know you do. I'm not happy about it, but I do understand that other people need you. They can only have you for a few hours, though, because I want you back here with me as soon as humanly possible."

"I'll be back as soon as I can."

"Then I guess I can let you go. For now."

He planted one more deep, salty kiss against her lips before he rolled off of her and onto his back. Scarlet forced herself to get up off of the mattress. She stood at the side of the bed, looking down at his naked, prone form, drinking in the hard length of his body and the depth of his loving gaze. Her entire body reacted to the sight of him, begging to have him back in her arms, and she couldn't bring herself to leave.

"God, I want you again," she sighed, blushing with her admission.

Hunter matched her blatant stare. She tracked his every movement as he stood and stepped toward her. He invaded her personal space, pressing their bodies together head to toe, and reached both hands to her face.

"You're so beautiful, Scarlet. Do you know that? Everything about you, inside and out, is simply breathtaking. I want to hold you against me forever, and never let you leave this bedroom. Hell, I would absorb you into my skin, if I could."

She whimpered, grasping onto his forearms.

He gave her a soft smile. "That's not a bad thing, honey. Maybe it feels that way, since it sounds desperate, but that doesn't make it bad. Not as long as we're still grounded in reality. You and I both know we have a physical need for each other, but this bond isn't just about sex. It's about knowing each other. It's about loving each other. So, no matter how fast things move between us, it's going to be okay. I swear."

Scarlet threw her arms around his neck. "I love you, Hunter."

"I love you," he breathed against her lips, just before kissing them. A moment later, he groaned and pulled away. "Now get in the shower and get ready for work. Before I can't control myself the way I should."

"Okay," she agreed, arching on tiptoes for one more kiss. She felt his eyes on her as she turned and stepped across the floor. When she reached the bathroom door, she stood beside his chair. Glancing over her shoulder, Scarlet held his potent stare as she slipped off his shirt, baring her backside fully before letting the fabric drape onto the cushion.

Hunter's greedy gaze dragged over her naked form, his breathing faltering when he fixated on her ass. She shuffled her feet, purposefully jiggling her exposed flesh. Then she brought her hands to her hips, just so she could slide them slowly down her bottom with a tempting moan.

His jaw dropped at the sight. Fisting his fingers, he looked back to her face. "You're playing with fire, Scarlet. You know that, right?"

"I do know," she said, certain he could see the sparkle in her eyes.

He lunged forward, erasing the space between them. She squealed and darted into the bathroom, slamming the door shut behind her. Giggles burst from her throat when she heard him growl at her from the other side. A moment later, he matched her laughter. "I'll meet you in the kitchen when you're done in there, my little bird."

Scarlet slumped against the door, smiling wildly at his pet name. Her mind drifted to the book he'd made and to the words he'd written beneath the photo of her yellow-crowned purple fantini. She could have stood here in his bathroom for hours, thinking about everything that had happened between them in the past weeks. In truth, she wanted nothing more than to do just that. But she didn't have time, so she urged herself away from the door and began her morning routine.

Pushing rapidly through the robotic actions, she worked to keep her mind from wandering too far. Once she'd showered, toweled off, and dried her hair, Scarlet stared at the rainbow assortment of panties he'd bought for her. She chose the green ones, appreciating the silky feel of the fabric as she pulled them on. After redressing in her shirt, skirt, and heels, she smiled contentedly at her reflection before opening the door.

Walking purposefully through his hallway and living room, she forged a path back to the kitchen and pushed through the swinging door. Her purse still lay on the granite countertop where she'd left it last night. Hunter stood in front of the sink, wearing his low-slung sweatpants and his glorious shirt – although she preferred to think of it as her shirt now.

He turned to her when she approached. "Croissants and orange juice," he announced, setting a plate and glass in front of her.

"Mmm. I love croissants."

Hunter erased the space between them with one long stride, pressing a quick kiss to her lips. "I know you do, although I can certainly make you something else. Eggs. Bacon. French toast. Whatever you like."

"You don't always have to cook for me, you know."

"But I want to. I also made you lunch."

"You made me lunch? Seriously?"

"I did," he said, gathering a brown paper bag from the counter.

Scarlet took the offering, feeling the weight of it before setting it down beside her purse. He grinned wildly as he stood in front of her. "My goodness, Hunter. Where have you been all my life?"

His smile fell. "I wish I knew," he said, drawing his hand down her arm. "I've been waiting for you this entire time, which is why I don't want to wait anymore. I want you with me from here on out."

She didn't know how to respond to that right now. She couldn't have responded in words anyway, so she wrapped her arms around his neck and kissed him instead. She meant for it to be a soft, tender kiss, but it didn't stay that way. He ran his hands from her arms to her waist, curling his fingers into her hips to pull her forward. Lodging her body against his, Hunter tasted her with a controlled, simmering intensity that slowly lost control, morphing into something needy and aching and hungry.

When her arms trembled and her knees gave way, Scarlet pulled back to rest her forehead onto his. "Damn," she sighed. "If I don't leave now, I'll never get to work on time."

"Then you should go," he groaned, even as his hold on her tightened.

"I'll be back before you know it."

"That's not true at all. I'll be highly aware of every moment you're gone, and I will loathe every single second of it."

"Wow. That's awfully dramatic."

He raised his head to look into her eyes. "Are you saying you're not going to loathe every single second you're away from me?"

"No, I'm definitely not saying that. I will absolutely loathe every single second. I'll despise them all with the fire of a thousand suns."

Hunter chuckled while finally releasing his hold on her. "Then just go already. So you can come back again."

"I'm going," she said, grabbing her purse, lunch, and croissant.

"Don't you want your orange juice? You'll be thirsty after eating that. I also have a ton of coffee."

The concern in his voice made her smile. "Thank you, but I'll grab a coffee at the office." Scarlet forced herself to leave, since turning away from him felt instantly wrong. She made it out his home and all the way to the elevator before meeting his eyes again. "I'll see you back here at six."

He reached around her to push the button on the elevator panel, his body leaning obscenely close to hers. "I can't wait. Although there's something I have to know first, before I let you leave."

"Yeah? What's that?"

"What color underwear do you have on?"

She grinned mischievously. "Oh, they're hunter green, of course. I chose them because it's your color, and I'm going to think about having you between my legs *all day long*."

"Goddamnit," he cursed, threading his hands into her hair. "You know I want to fuck you right here in this hallway, don't you?"

Scarlet swallowed hard. "I certainly hope you will, someday."

His fingers tightened against her scalp. "I definitely will. Although I'll have to ask Seth to turn off the security feed to this floor first."

Her brow jumped to her hairline. "Security feed?"

"Yeah," he said, nodding to the wall. "There's a camera right there."

"Oh my God! Do you think Seth saw us kissing here yesterday?"

Hunter shrugged. "Probably."

"I – I change my mind. I can't leave here. I can never look that man in the eyes again."

"It was just a kiss, Scarlet."

"It was one hell of a kiss."

"Well, imagine what would have happened if I'd known you wanted me to fuck you right then and there."

"Oh, hell. Now I definitely can never look Seth in the eyes again."

Hunter chuckled as the elevator door opened. "See you tonight."

She nodded while stepping into the shiny silver box. "See you tonight," she echoed, her gaze locked with his until the doors closed. He gave her a wink at the last second, and she held onto that image all the way down to the first floor. She did her best to remain calm and poised when she walked by Seth, giving him a sheepish wave goodbye.

17

FLIGHT

A million thoughts piled into Scarlet's head while she drove to work, roiling in the back of her brain. Except these thoughts weren't scary or painful, like so many she'd known in the past six months. The ones filling her mind now were of happiness, of peace, and of love.

A smile spread her lips when she pulled into the parking lot beneath her office building. That smile stayed with her through security, up the elevator, and to her floor. It stayed with her while she greeted Marie, whose brow rose when she noted the recycled outfit from the day before.

Scarlet smiled all the way to her desk and into her chair, which felt amazingly good. She'd spent so much of the past six months faking her smiles. She'd actually become an expert at it, plastering a carefree expression onto her face whenever she needed to demonstrate to a patient how promising life could be. But today, she didn't have to fake anything. Her smiles came easily and genuinely with each person who stepped through her door, and she knew they could feel the difference.

By the time she completed her final session of the day, Scarlet felt as happy as she could ever recall, even when she'd been a child frolicking in the woods with her mother. Dianna Tracey had always encouraged her to look for the happiness in life. She'd encouraged her to skip and bounce, to be free, and to love without restraint. When Scarlet was a little girl, she understood all of that. But she'd somehow grown out of it, or forgotten about it, or chosen to put it behind her.

Now, she didn't want to abandon her happiness anymore. And if the connection she felt with her patients today was any indication, there was a chance she could be happy and free and still be an effective physician. Just like Hunter had challenged her to be.

After completing her last annotation for the workweek, Scarlet rose from her chair, gathered her purse, and stepped purposefully toward her door. As she passed by her wall of plants, her footing faltered. She stopped beside the fern Hunter had touched the first time he came into her office, her body stilling as she studied the smooth, feathery leaves.

They grow well, even in low light: that's what she'd told him about this plant. It was definitely an ideal for her patients to strive toward, but it was also an ideal for her to strive for. Scarlet had brought these plants in here to help her see the light again. Now, thanks to Hunter, she could.

Reaching out to the fern, she curled the pot into the crook of her arm. She walked across her office and pulled open her thick door. The instant she stepped into the reception area, her jaw dropped.

"Is that the biggest thing you ever saw, or what?" Marie asked, her voice muffled by her full mouth.

Scarlet attempted to wrap her mind around the ten-foot-tall stuffed teddy bear sitting on the couch. "Yup. It's the biggest thing I ever saw."

"You want a chocolate?" Marie offered, lifting the large box of candies she held in her hand. "There are a dozen containers here, so if you want a different flavor, I'll open a new box."

"No, I'm okay, thanks," Scarlet replied, watching her receptionist swallow the candy. "I take it Hunter sent you a few more things today?"

"He sure did. All of this, plus a hefty gift certificate to a day spa. I already told Manny we're getting a couples' massage this weekend."

"I'm glad. But I am sorry if Hunter's being a bit overwhelming with the whole please-like-me thing. I can tell him to stop, if you want."

Marie popped another chocolate into her mouth. "Eh. I'll manage to power my way through it."

Scarlet giggled when her dear friend grinned. "I hope you and Manny enjoy your massages. I'll see you Monday morning, okay?"

"Okay," Marie agreed, straightening in her chair the moment Scarlet stepped around the desk. "Wait...what are you doing with that plant?"

She glanced at the fern. "Oh. I'm taking this to Hunter's place."

"You're actually taking a plant *out* of your office?"

"Yeah, I am. I think it's time."

Marie's eyes misted over. "You're...you're a very strong woman. You know that, right?"

Scarlet choked back a sob. "Thank you for that."

Marie closed the lid on her box of chocolates. "You know what? You can tell Mr. Gregory to stop sending me gifts now. You can tell him I like him just fine. In fact, you can tell him I adore him."

"I'm sure that will make him really happy."

"Well, he deserves it, since it's obvious he makes you happy."

"He does," Scarlet confirmed without question. "So happy."

"I hope you enjoy your weekend."

"I will. I'm going to spend it with Hunter."

"Good."

Scarlet smiled at her friend before taking her leave. After riding the elevator down to the lobby, strolling by security, and hopping into her car, she tuned in to the Elvis station and sang along with her favorite songs as she drove. When she arrived home, she rested the fern gently in the passenger's seat and scurried inside her apartment to get ready for her weekend away to someplace warm, trying not to think about anything but the fact that she would soon be back in Hunter's arms.

She changed her well-worn clothes first, yet kept her new green thong right where it was. Next, she donned a lilac sleeveless blouse and a tight black skirt which hugged her ass nicely, figuring he would appreciate that. Stepping to her closet, Scarlet pulled her suitcase from the top shelf and hurriedly filled it with clothes and toiletries. Hunter had asked her to bring nice dresses, so she grabbed a turquoise floor-length gown she'd worn to a wedding once. Then she stood in her closet for a minute, trying to decide what other clothes to bring. After perusing her modest collection, she caught sight of a dress she'd bought on a whim but had never found an occasion to wear – a scanty little red number with a gold zipper running the full length of the front.

She scooped the sultry outfit off the hanger and tossed it in her bag. As she grabbed the red high heels he'd requested, another million thoughts flooded her brain. Zipping up her suitcase, she shushed them all. She didn't have time to pay proper attention to her concerns right now. Hunter waited for her, and she was determined to go to him.

When she turned to leave her bedroom, Scarlet's eyes drew to her bedstand where his book had been sitting since the night she'd brought it home. She reached for it without thought, placing it into her purse before grasping the handle of her suitcase and exiting her apartment. She tossed her bags into the trunk of her car and sank down in the driver's seat next to the fern.

The trip to Hunter's building came naturally today and she arrived fifteen minutes early. Seth stood at the entrance to the parking garage, greeting her when she rolled down her window. "Hi, Scarlet."

"Hi, Seth."

"Hunter asked me to meet you, to direct you to your parking space."

"My parking space?"

"Yes, the spot marked one is now reserved for you."

"The first space is *mine*?"

He chuckled. "It is now. That's normally Hunter's space, but he moved his car to the second one. Also, he told me to tell you he's waiting for you upstairs, and you should just walk in when you arrive."

Her mouth hung before she could get out any words. "Thank you."

"Anytime. It's nice to see you again."

"You, too," she replied, returning Seth's gentle grin before easing her car into the parking spot next to the lobby doors. Hunter's silver Porsche sat in the space beside her. She giggled at the sight before grabbing her keys and fern and rushing into the building.

The trip through the lobby was quick. The trip up the elevator was quick. The trip down the hall to Hunter's door was quick.

But then Scarlet stood in front of his door with her feet frozen in place and her heart lodged in her throat. For a split second, she wondered if she should go in. Not because she didn't want to see him, but because she hadn't taken the time to think any of this through the way she should.

She knew she could stand in this hallway for days, debating the rationality of all this. But she also knew Hunter waited for her on the other side of this door, and she simply wanted to be with him. That desire felt like the most important thing in the world right now, so she tamped down the urge to reason everything out and stepped inside.

"Oh, good. You're here early," Hunter said, standing up from the couch in the living room the moment she entered his foyer.

"I'm here," she whispered, barely getting her words out for the wild flutter of her pulse. The man striding toward her remained as intimidating as ever, a wolf in expertly tailored sheep's clothing, his defined muscles moving with grace beneath his short sleeve shirt and fitted pants. She had to remind herself that he was indeed real, and that her heart couldn't actually explode just from looking at him.

"Did Seth show you to your new parking spot?" Hunter questioned as he stepped into her personal space.

Scarlet's gaze rose to his, her head bobbing in acknowledgement.

"Good." His bright blue eyes drifted down to the plant in her arms. "Is that the fern from your office?"

"Yes."

"Did you bring it so we could keep it here?"

"I did."

Hunter leaned forward, slid his lips onto hers for one gentle moment, and eased back. "That's wonderful. You can put it anywhere you like."

"Okay," she agreed, still feeling his warmth against her mouth as she stepped into the living room. She set the plant down on the end table beside one of the large sofas and stood back to admire it.

"Do you like the way it looks there?" he questioned from beside her.

"Yeah, I do."

"Perfect."

She turned her eyes up to his, watching as he grinned.

"Can I please see your car keys, Scarlet?"

"Um, sure." She opened her palm up to show him her keychain. Hunter took the small bundle from her hand. Reaching into his pocket, he pulled out another key and slipped it in place beside her others.

"I made a copy of my housekey for you," he explained as he set the chain back in her hand. "I don't ever want you to have to knock to enter here. I want you to be able to come in anytime you desire."

Gripping hard to the keys, Scarlet stared up into his eyes. She recalled all the times at Blue when he'd shown up at her door looking like a lost puppy and she'd grabbed him by the hand to tug him into her cabin. That's what this felt like now – like Hunter tugging her inside with him.

"Thank you for this," she whispered.

"Of course. And now, if you don't mind, we should really get going. There are a couple people waiting on us."

"People?"

"Yup. Come on."

Scarlet let him guide her out of his living room, through the front door, and down the hallway. "Can I ask who is waiting for us?" she questioned as he pushed the button for the elevator.

Hunter grinned. "I thought you wanted this trip to be a surprise."

"Oh, I do. I want all the surprises."

He leaned in to press a kiss to her hair. "Thank you for coming this weekend."

When the elevator door opened, he took her hand in his. Scarlet felt his large palm engulf her smaller one. "I'd go anywhere with you," she admitted.

Hunter sighed as he drew her forward. "Thank goodness for that."

Scarlet couldn't stop smiling while they rode down to the ground floor, or while they walked out to the garage, or while he opened the passenger door of his Porsche so she could sit inside. She waited impatiently as he transferred her bags from the trunk of her car to the trunk of his. She smiled again when he sank down beside her into the driver's seat, started the engine, and drove them out of the parking garage.

"So, how was your day?" Hunter asked while turning onto the road.

She stared out of the windshield at the beautiful pink and gold rays of the setting sun. "It was a really good day. But I missed you terribly."

"Did you despise every second you were away from me?"

"Of course."

He chuckled. "I had the same kind of day, then."

Scarlet turned toward him, drinking in the lines of his strong profile. His eyes met hers for the briefest moment before refocusing on the road. He grasped one of her hands, drawing it to his lips and pressing a kiss to the back, before resting their entwined fingers down onto her thigh.

"Did Marie like the gifts I sent over today?"

"Yeah, she loved them. Although she did say you can stop sending her things now, because she's decided she adores you."

"She *adores* me? Wow. It was the giant teddy bear, wasn't it?"

"In a way, I suppose. If you consider yourself the teddy bear."

"Hmm. I thought I was a grizzly bear in this scenario. Isn't that why you decided to poke me with a stick in the first place?"

"Yes, but you're not a grizzly anymore. You're definitely a teddy."

Hunter grinned. "Well, I'm okay with that, as long as you are."

"I'm absolutely okay with that," Scarlet assured, squeezing onto his hand. She looked back out of the windshield, watching the sun sink farther in the horizon while he drove them down the highway.

By the time the sun descended fully, morphing the sky to a soft grey with pale dots of starlight, Hunter pulled onto a long, single road. Scarlet read the sign at the entrance. "Is this a private airfield, Hunter?"

"It is," he acknowledged, slowing the Porsche when they approached the end of the path. "This is where our plane is."

A small airfield came into view just ahead, with two figures standing on a runway beside a moderately sized airplane with the letters GG printed on the side. "Is this your company's plane?"

"Yes. We use it mostly for trips overseas," he explained while parking the car and shutting off the engine. "I've never used it for pleasure before, but I figure I'm the CEO, and there's a first time for everything."

Scarlet watched as one of the two men standing by the aircraft walked over to them. "Wow. I've never been on a private plane."

"I hope you'll enjoy it," Hunter offered before stepping out of the car. She followed, standing by her door to wave at the person who approached.

"I take it you're Scarlet," the ginger-haired young man said when he arrived in front of her. "I'm Brett, the co-pilot for your flight tonight. I'll also be your steward." He grinned wildly while shaking her hand.

"Thank you so much, Brett. I appreciate it."

A rosy flush lit his freckled cheeks. "No problem."

Hunter walked over with their luggage. Brett dropped Scarlet's hand to lunge for the suitcases. "Let me get those for you, Mr. Gregory."

He stepped to her side while Brett grabbed their bags. Scarlet watched the gangly young man move swiftly back to the plane. "Brett is sweet," she said as Hunter reached for the small of her back, his fingers warming her skin.

"He is. And the captain is great. I'll introduce you."

An older man stood beside the aircraft steps, looking regal in his full uniform, smiling when they approached. "Good evening, Mr. Gregory."

Hunter shook the pilot's extended hand. "Good to see you, Rick."

"You too, Sir. And this must be Scarlet."

"It's a pleasure to meet you, Captain," she said, shaking his hand as well. "Thank you so much for taking us wherever we're going."

Captain Rick nodded. "You're welcome. Now come aboard and we'll get you there safe and sound."

Scarlet took her time ascending the stairs up into the plane, ducking through the door to where Brett waited for her. "Right this way," he offered.

She turned to her right, stepping into the main cabin of the aircraft. Six oversized leather chairs ran the length of the plane, three on each side, all with their own windows and copious amounts of legroom. Overhead lights illuminated the insides, along with two strips of tiny lights on the floorboards, twinkling like little stars. A plush blue carpet lay beneath the seats, making Scarlet feel as if she were walking on air.

"This is beautiful," she said, moving to the first chair. "Is it okay if I sit here?"

"You can sit anywhere you like. Although, probably not up there," Brett amended, hitching his thumb toward the front of the plane.

Scarlet glanced over Brett's shoulder, to the open door leading to the cockpit. "I guess you and Captain Rick sit up there?" she asked, sinking into the huge seat that swallowed her whole body with room to spare.

"Yes, but if you need anything, just scream and I'll come running. Well, don't actually scream, since that would be scary. But you can call for me anytime. I'll be listening out for you."

Hunter entered the cabin behind them. "Thank you for the attention, Brett. Are you comfortable, Scarlet?"

She dropped her purse beside her chair. "Definitely. Although I'll be more comfortable if I can take my shoes off."

"You can take off anything you want," Hunter offered with a wink.

Her eyes widened, darting to Brett. His pale skin flushed as he stepped away into the alcove beside the cockpit. Moments later, he returned with two glasses of red wine. "Here you are," he said, handing the first glass to her before offering the second to Hunter.

Scarlet clung to the glass stem while watching Hunter settle into the chair next to hers, which was still several feet away.

"I'll be serving dinner as soon as we're in the air," Brett told her.

"We're having dinner? How long is our flight?"

He didn't answer her question until he glanced to Hunter, silently asking permission. When Hunter nodded his consent, Brett exhaled and looked back to her. "Four and half hours, Ma'am."

"Oh. Okay. Thank you."

"It's no problem. Anything you need, just let me know."

"You don't have to wait on me, Brett. Although I appreciate it."

"Well, it's my job, so I'll just be right up here in the cockpit. You'll need to buckle up for takeoff now, but after we're in the air, you can move around a bit. The restroom is in the very back of the cabin."

"Thanks again."

Brett nodded and stepped away, joining Captain Rick in the front of the plane. Scarlet took a sip of wine before setting the glass down in the holder beside her. She slipped off her shoes, sinking her toes into the soft carpet as she buckled herself into her seat. Then she glanced out of her window, staring at the dark sky and illuminated runway.

"This is all so lovely, Hunter. Thank you for bringing me."

"Don't thank me yet. You don't even know where we're going."

"It doesn't matter," she said, turning to see him. "I'll be happy anywhere, as long as I'm with you."

He matched her attentive gaze. "I love you, Scarlet."

She grinned ear to ear. "I love you, Hunter."

He returned her smile, setting his wine glass down to reach for his seatbelt. His chair was just as huge as hers, and she wanted him to scoot over and let her sit beside him. But she didn't think Brett would approve, so she stayed where she was, listening to the muffled sounds of voices coming from the cockpit as the plane taxied down the runway.

Within moments, they were in the air. Brett returned with a cart full of food, and Scarlet chose the chicken salad with cheese and fruit. She sat happily in her seat, eating her dinner with Hunter across from her. They both enjoyed the meal, several glasses of wine, and talking to Brett, who told them how he'd just graduated flight school and was excited to sit beside an experienced ex-Air Force pilot like Captain Rick.

By the time they finished their food and drinks, Scarlet felt quite fond of the talkative, bubbly boy. She gave him a little wave when he stepped back into the cockpit and closed the door behind him. Then she sank further into the leather chair, which still felt entirely too big. "You know, Brett reminds me a bit of Colin."

"I could see that," Hunter agreed. "Speaking of which, I meant to tell you I asked Colin to come work for me when he finishes school."

"Oh. That's sweet of you, but I don't know if he's ready to leave Blue yet."

"He is, actually. He turned in his resignation the day I left."

"Really? I thought he was still saving up for his last year of school."

"Yeah, he was. But I wrote him a check so he could go back to school now."

She stared at the man across from her. "My goodness. You are truly amazing."

Hunter smiled softly as he leaned toward her, resting his forearms onto his thighs. "I just wanted to help him, since he helped me. You, Colin, Tyler, Abbott, Pete, Betsy – everyone up on that mountain helped me. I wanted the chance to help someone, too."

The few feet separating them now felt like a chasm. Scarlet pulled toward him, straining her seatbelt. "You know, we've talked so much about me in the past few days, and haven't talked nearly enough about you. How are you doing with everything since you left Blue?"

"I'm okay," Hunter assured. "Honestly, I'm better than okay, because I'm with you. But I know that's not what you're asking."

"Are you really doing okay?"

"I am. Truly. I went back into the woods again, the day before I left Blue. I sat in the forest like you taught me, and I talked to Samantha, and I felt like she heard me. It made all the difference in the world."

"Oh, that's wonderful," Scarlet breathed. "I'm so glad you found what you needed in that forest."

"Yes, I definitely did. Although I should probably stay in therapy, at least for a while. I told Abbott I would, and despite how angry I am with him for making you sign away your firstborn child for the chance to heal yourself, I still want to keep the promise I made." Hunter looked back to her eyes. "Maybe you can recommend a good therapist for me when we return home?"

"Yeah, I can do that."

"Good."

Scarlet kept her gaze glued to his. "You know, when we do return home, I think I'd like to talk to Will some more...as a patient."

Hunter's shoulders fell on a sigh. "I think that's wonderful. I know he'll appreciate you talking to him. He wants to help you heal."

"I'm sure he does. He's an incredible man."

Hunter nodded in agreement, and Scarlet spent the next few minutes just watching him, feeling the warmth and strength radiating from his body. His arms wrapped around her, tight and warm and secure, even though he didn't physically touch her at all. That sense of easy peace made her relax into her huge leather seat and allowed a yawn to sneak out.

"You didn't get enough sleep last night," he observed.

Scarlet shrugged. "I'm pretty sure I got more than you did."

"Do you want to take a nap? We're going to be in the air awhile."

"Will you nap, too?"

He unbuckled his seatbelt. "No, I'll go talk to Rick and Brett. They can keep me company while you sleep."

"Oh, yes, I nearly forgot. Hunter Gregory doesn't take naps."

"That's right," he confirmed as he stood. "Too much wasted time."

She watched as he turned off the overhead cabin lights, plunging the space into darkness, except for the tiny stars twinkling along the length of the floor. Pausing in front of her chair, he ran his fingers across her cheek. "Just rest for a while, Scarlet. I'll ask Rick and Brett to be extra quiet." Hunter leaned over, pressing a kiss to the top of her head.

"Thank you," she said, smiling up at him before he stepped away from her and disappeared on the other side of the cockpit door.

Scarlet stilled the moment he'd gone. She could hear Hunter's muffled voice, along with Rick's deep tone and Brett's softer one, while the men spoke to each other. She knew they were trying to be quiet so she could sleep, but she didn't really know if she could.

Laying her head back on her seat, she shut her eyes and concentrated on the sound of the plane's engine, hoping the hum would lull her. Hunter said he'd left so she could rest, but she suspected he'd also intended to give her a little time to herself. She appreciated having this space to breathe, although her chair was suddenly far too frigid, and she couldn't get comfortable no matter how much she wriggled and twisted.

"Too much wasted time," she whispered, echoing Hunter's parting words. She'd gone willingly to his home last night, for their second date. Willingly, but cautiously. She believed they needed to take their time with this relationship, yet she also knew he didn't believe that. He didn't want to be cautious. He didn't want to waste any more time apart.

I love you, Scarlet.

She'd heard those words a lot in the past day, and she didn't doubt his feelings. She didn't doubt her own, either. They hadn't even known each other for three weeks, yet they were unquestionably in love. God, that made no sense at all.

Scarlet shifted inside her seat again. Hunter had asked her just this morning what she would do if she didn't think and simply went with her feelings. Her answer had come quickly and easily: she would stay with him always. It wasn't a difficult conclusion, since she already knew how she felt. That wasn't the problem. The problem was her mind.

Sucking in a deep breath, she exhaled slowly, compelling her body to sit still in the engulfing seat. She could feel the physician inside her fighting to surface, begging her to be practical about these feelings. She did love Hunter, but she needed to decide what *kind* of love they shared, in order to meld her mind and heart together.

Dr. Tracey understood the psychology of love. She knew Lee's theories of Agape, Storge, Mania, Eros, Ludus and Pragma, as well as Sternberg's theories based on the three building blocks of love. She preferred Sternberg's model, with the pillars of intimacy, commitment, and passion forming the ideal triangle of a relationship. She knew love could exist based on just one of the pillars, but the ideal love consisted of all three, each in an equal and supportive relationship with the other two.

Scarlet also understood the kind of love she'd experienced in the past. With her ex-fiancé, Richard, she'd shared commitment and even some intimacy. But they'd never had passion. At the time, she was okay with that. She'd been concentrating on building her practice, and all she'd wanted was a simple, sturdy relationship to come home to. That's what Richard gave her. That's what they gave each other.

She and Richard made good companions, and she could have lived her entire life that way. But when her father died, it changed the way she saw her entire world. She didn't just want a companion to come home to, so she called off her engagement. The decision was painful, but right.

Scarlet didn't really think about having another relationship after that. She threw herself into her work, since that was all she really knew. Her mother didn't approve, of course. But at the time, she didn't want to hear her mother's thoughts on appreciating all the wonders of life. Work was Scarlet's stability and she needed it. Her single-mindedness about her job was one of the many reasons her mother had moved to Las Vegas. Dianna couldn't get through to her daughter the way she wanted to, so she left to start a new life for herself.

Scarlet had thought a lot about her parents' relationship during those long nights she'd spent alone after leaving Richard. She believed her parents had a fatuous love at first – they'd had passion, and had made a commitment based on that alone. But they were too different, and never truly had intimacy. When their passion diminished, all that remained between them was commitment. Dianna Tracey stayed committed to her husband until the day he died, and Scarlet didn't blame her for running off to start a new life when that commitment was over.

Commitment. Honestly, it was the only pillar of love Scarlet didn't fully have with Hunter right now. They definitely had intimacy. She'd shared more of her soul with him than she'd shared with anyone in her life, and he'd done the same with her, forming a bond between them that felt unbreakable. They also had passion. Their passion went without saying, since she simply didn't know what to say about it.

All that remained for them now was to be committed to each other. She knew they were already headed in that direction, and when they eventually crossed that bridge, they would have all three pillars of Sternberg's triangle. They would possess the ultimate, consummate love.

Scarlet hadn't seen much evidence of consummate love in her life. She and Richard didn't have it, her parents didn't have it, and only a rare few of her patients described anything like it. In truth, she'd been living inside her patients' lives for so long, trying to understand and help them, that she hadn't taken the time to understand herself.

She sighed as she thought about her last patient on Monday: Mrs. Sanderson, whose pain and addiction had manifested itself into nearly every aspect of her life. Mrs. Sanderson had trouble seeing the forest for the trees, and if Scarlet was being brutally honest with herself, she knew she'd traveled that same road. The pain over losing a patient in front of her eyes made Dr. Tracey question every single thing in her life, while clinging to her work as the only life raft in a raging ocean. And when that pain and addiction became too much to bear, she went to Blue.

She went to Blue in search of joy and wonder and magic. She went to take photos of trees and leaves and creatures, and to remember the love she held for nature. She went to be a child, and a fairy, and a bird, and to figure out if she could ever come back home as a doctor.

Sliding forward in her seat, Scarlet reached for her purse where it lay on the floor. She grasped the book Hunter had given her, along with her glasses. Switching on the reading lamp above her head, she watched the tiny spotlight illuminate the cover.

After slipping her glasses onto her nose, she turned to the page marked by the two leaves she'd brought home from her journey at Blue. Scarlet pulled both leaves out, set them in her lap, and focused on the picture of her yellow-crowned purple fantini. She smiled as she read over the words he'd written for her:

If you're fortunate enough to catch sight of this amazing bird, please don't attempt to lock it in a cage. The yellow-crowned purple fantini won't survive behind bars. This bird needs to be free to live and explore and dream. This bird needs to fly.

Scarlet drew a ragged breath in. Last night, when she finally told Hunter what had happened to take away the color red, he'd encompassed her with his entire body and grounded her to the earth. It was exactly what she'd needed, at that moment in time.

But today, they were inthe clouds. Today, he offered her surprises and magic. Today, he set her free. It was exactly what she needed at this moment in time.

Turning her gaze to the window beside her, Scarlet looked out to the dark night. She remembered how lost she felt when she got to Blue: weak and beaten and questioning of every decision she'd ever made. She remembered how strange it felt to get turned around in the woods the day she started her vacation, only to wander out on the road to find Hunter waiting for her. Making the decision to help him wasn't really a decision at all. Helping him felt as necessary and right as breathing, and by the end of their two weeks together, she could see so clearly how changing his world had changed her own. She came to the irrefutable conclusion that she needed to be a doctor again, because her time with Hunter proved she could still be brave and strong and helpful.

She returned to her office the following Monday morning, intent on being Dr. Tracey, because that's what she thought was right. She thought she needed to leave behind the freebird she'd discovered in the forest, and refocus her life on her work, just like before. She never expected Hunter to come barreling back into her world, challenging everything she thought was fixed and infallible.

Sitting here now, staring out at the vast sky with its twinkling stars and dotted clouds, Scarlet felt only gratitude for his actions. His challenges for her these past days had opened a thousand doors, showing her a world she'd long ago stopped believing in. *My little bird* – that's what he'd called her in his home this morning, and that's who she'd been with him – bouncy and bubbly, light and free.

Her gaze dropped back down to the two little leaves resting in her lap. She grasped onto their stems, twirling them together in her hand: green with red and red with green, bonded perfectly together. It was frightening to acknowledge how deeply bonded she and Hunter had become in such a short amount of time. She'd been independent for so long, and part of her feared letting that independence go. But the other part of her understood he wouldn't cage her. He would set her free.

Scarlet took a shaky breath as she looked back to the book, to the last words he'd written for her. *This bird needs to fly.* Brushing a tear from her cheek, she stared at the photo of her yellow-crowned purple fantini: the bird she'd found in that forest, with Hunter by her side. The bird she'd brought home with her. The freebird sitting here now, so deeply and happily entrenched in a new world.

Resting the leaves down inside the book, Scarlet closed the cover. She held his words in her heart and mind simultaneously. Then she stilled, and smiled, and breathed easy for the first time in a long time.

A few moments later, the door to the cockpit opened, drawing her gaze. Hunter stepped back into the main cabin and shut the door behind him. His eyes found hers instantly, making her smile grow wider.

"You're still awake?" he questioned.

She straightened in her seat. "Yeah. I couldn't sleep, so I read."

He glanced down to the book she held, grinning to himself as he walked back to his chair. Settling inside the soft leather, he looked to her. "You've just been sitting here reading this whole time?"

"Well, reading and thinking."

"Thinking," he echoed. "Anything you want to talk about?"

Scarlet shook her head. "No, thank you. I'm all good."

"Okay, well, I don't want to disturb you. Do you think you can still rest if I sit here beside you?"

"Honestly, I'd prefer it. I have trouble resting without you."

Hunter gave her a gentle nod. "I'll stay here and keep quiet then," he assured, settling against the backrest and turning his head to the window. His shoulders fell on exhale while he stared into the shifting clouds and distant lights.

Scarlet watched him for a long time, taking comfort in the easy strength of his solid body so close to hers. Everything about this man felt so certain and steady, grounded in every way. Yet he was still here in the clouds, right beside her, and she knew he would do anything to allow her to fly. That kind of love astonished and overwhelmed her. The magnitude of it was difficult to wrap her heart around, let alone her mind. But she wanted to do her damnedest to try.

Scarlet leaned forward, slipping her glasses off her nose, placing them into her purse alongside her book. She reached up to the reading lamp and switched it off, dimming the light in the cabin to just the tiny stars on the floor. Finally, she grasped her seatbelt and undid the clasp.

Hunter turned when he heard her unbuckle, watching as she rose from her chair. "What do you need?" he asked when she came to a stop in front of him.

"Can I sit with you?"

"Always."

The instant he agreed, she plopped down sideways into his lap and threw her arms around his neck. He banded his arms around her, pulling her onto his chest. His eyes closed as he rested his forehead on her temple.

"You feel incredibly good, Scarlet."

"So do you," she sighed.

He hummed in agreement, his breath flushing hot against her cheek, his fingertips pressing into her spine. She absorbed his warmth as she looked out of the darkened window. Scarlet watched the puffy clouds roll past the wings, feeling utterly weightless in his arms.

"Look," she said, nodding toward the window. "I'm flying."

He raised his head to see her face. "You are. You're flying."

"And you're right here, flying with me."

Hunter didn't take his eyes off of hers. "No place I'd rather be."

She smiled then. Scarlet smiled with all her heart and soul, with a depth of happiness she could never have imagined. All she could do was stare into him and say, "I love you."

His arms tightened around her. "I love you."

Her chest swelled, making it difficult to breathe. Angling her body toward his, she slid her arms around his neck and held him as close as she could. She just wanted him here with her. She just wanted them together.

Hunter gripped onto her, hard and strong, but it still wasn't enough. She twisted her hips so she could press her chest and lips fully onto his. The angle wasn't quite right, yet he kissed her perfectly, his mouth slanting over hers, his tongue seeking and insistent. Her fingers clamped onto his shoulders while her frustration built.

"Wait," she breathed when she managed to pull her lips away. "I...I need..."

"What do you need, honey? I'll give you anything. Just tell me."

"I need to be closer to you. Can I please be closer?"

He didn't take his eyes from hers when she straightened, but he did let his arms fall to his sides so she could stand and turn her body to face his. He watched intently as her fingers reached for the hem of her skirt, hiking the material to the tops of her thighs so she could spread her legs. She crawled back on top of him, straddling his hips, her knees meeting the back of the large chair as her body collapsed onto his.

Scarlet encircled his neck in her arms and pushed her breasts into his chest. She inhaled roughly, her muscles shaking with need. She kissed him again, eager for his taste, unable to hide her rising desperation.

Hunter's hands ran seamlessly up and down her spine as his lips melded with hers. She loved the feel of his mouth right now, but his kiss was so soft and gentle and tender. It matched hers, but it also didn't. She could feel him straining to stay under control and she didn't want that. She was free. She was flying. They were *both* flying.

She whimpered while pressing closer, shifting her hips into his. He'd already begun to harden for her. His growing erection pulsed between her thighs as she arched up and pressed back down, rubbing the edge of her panties against his zipper. She moaned deep in her throat, the sound as delirious as it was desirous.

He slipped his hand up to her face, holding her in place so he could search her eyes. "Scarlet? Are you doing okay right now?"

She dug her fingers into his hair. "I'm perfect, except that I can't get close enough. I can never be close enough to you."

His eyes narrowed. "God, I know that feeling."

Sitting bolt upright in the chair, Hunter pulled her closer, lodging her body fully against his. His thick arms spanned her back twice over, his hands fisting into the thin material of her shirt. Then he fell back on the leather, taking her even deeper into the seat with him.

Scarlet spread her legs when he yanked her forward. The motion pressed his stiffening length into the soft skin at the juncture of her thighs, and she let out a barely-stifled cry. He growled at the sound, his biceps tensing while his pupils widened disastrously in the dim light.

Hunter obviously wanted her. But Scarlet didn't want him to simply want her. She wanted him *desperate* for her.

Arching her hips into his body, she rubbed her sex up against his erection, over and over, pressing the silky material of her panties against the taut fabric of his pants. She gripped onto his hair, and ran her nose alongside his, their hot breaths mingling together as his cock thickened and pulsed with her rhythmic, needy thrusts. He cursed under his breath, his hips arching greedily to meet hers, his entire body responding to every urgent movement she made.

"I want you inside me," she panted. "I need to feel you. Now."

Hunter stilled, his eyes searching hers. An instant later, he nodded. "I want that, too. I need to be inside you. Always."

She whimpered with the words, shifting her hips again.

A groan escaped his throat. "Damn, Scarlet. If we're going to do this, we need to be quiet. We're not the only two people on this plane."

"I can be quiet," she breathed, easing back just enough to slide her hands down his chest. She trailed her fingers over his shirt and onto his pants, reaching for the button that strained tight over his swollen length.

Hunter's hands shifted across her low spine, tracing a path to her waist. He found the curves of her hipbones and squeezed onto them. Leaning in, he pressed his mouth to hers again, his tongue slipping softly past her lips. He tasted her with purpose and reverence, controlling his movements far better than she controlled hers.

Scarlet barely got his button undone for the trembling of her fingers, and took forever to undo his zipper. When she finally managed to free him, she took his rigid shaft into her hand. She slid her fingers up and down his hot, stretched skin as he throbbed into her palm.

He dug his hands into her skirt, pulling hard against the seams. "I need you now," he spoke against her lips, his voice gritty with urgency.

"Yes. Yes. It's just...my underwear..."

"I've got it," he insisted, gathering her bunched skirt roughly in his fingers to push the material up higher on her waist. Hunter steadied her body with one hand on her back while dragging his other hand down between her legs, reaching for her panties. He traced across the band of her thong before sliding his fingers down over her sex.

Scarlet knew she'd soaked through the silky green scrap of fabric. When Hunter felt the wetness, he growled his approval. Slipping his fingers beneath the edge of the material, he pulled it gently off to one side, opening her entirely up to him. She didn't hesitate to act. Tightening her grip on his cock, she arched up on her knees to direct his swollen tip down between her thighs.

The moment his thick erection lined up with her aching sex, Scarlet sank onto him. She slid down slowly, lodging herself on his length as her fingers flew to his hair, tightening against his scalp. They both sucked in a sharp breath with the descent, moaning when fully joined.

Her legs fell off the chair, dangling over either side, the tips of her toes barely reaching the carpet. Hunter wrapped both arms around her, splaying his hands across her back to band her chest to his. She sighed with the warm, fulfilled sensation, burying her face in his neck to muffle the noises she couldn't prevent. "Damn, this is perfect."

Hunter ran his hands up her spine, gripping one of her shoulders in each of his palms and pulling down, securing her in place. The action pushed his cock even further inside her, sending an arc of electricity throughout her body.

Scarlet whimpered as he pressed his lips to her ear. "It is. It's the most perfect thing in the entire world."

She looked to his eyes. "Have I told you recently that I love you?"

"Not recently enough," he answered, his hands drifting up into her loose hair. "You can always tell me again, and again."

Scarlet pressed her feet entirely into the carpet, so she could arch up a few inches before sinking back onto him. "I love you, Hunter. I love, love, love you."

He tightened his hands in her curls. "Say it again. Please."

She rose up and pushed down again. "I love you."

"God, I love you so much, Scarlet. I love you *so damn much*."

"I want to stay like this forever," she told him, blinking back the moisture from her eyes. "I never want to leave."

Hunter smiled softly while his gaze drifted across her face. "That sounds perfect to me. Although it might make things a bit awkward when we reach the ground again."

"But can't we just keep flying?"

"Absolutely. We'll just keep flying. We can do that as long as we're together. You know that, don't you?"

"I do know," she admitted, feeling his length pulse inside her.

He groaned, low and deep, the shade of his eyes darkening a hundredfold. He shifted his hips, inciting her slick flesh to throb around him. A pulse of energy ran beneath her skin and Scarlet had to bite her lip to keep from shouting at the top of her lungs.

Pressing her forehead onto his, she pinched her eyes shut. "I think I'm going to have trouble staying quiet, Hunter."

"Hmm. Just kiss me whenever you feel like screaming."

"I feel like screaming right now."

"Then kiss me right now."

Scarlet complied immediately. She fused her mouth with his as he pressed his feet down on the floor, leveraging himself to thrust up into her. They began a rhythmic dance, rocking into each other slowly and exactly, keeping their actions precise in order to keep them hushed. Their mouths stayed clamped together, their tongues tangling and tasting, their breaths mingling in hot, frantic little bursts.

The air around them turned fiery and hazy. They clung so hard to each other that Scarlet couldn't tell where she ended and he began. Right this minute, that was all she desired. She wanted to be one with this man, as much physically as emotionally. She wasn't certain it was possible, but she sure as hell wanted to try.

Banding her arms tighter around his neck, she fisted her hands into his hair. She gripped onto Hunter for dear life while she ground down against him and he pushed up inside her, over and over again. The leather chair groaned under the extra weight of their joined bodies, but that sound couldn't be helped. Honestly, Scarlet didn't really care who heard them. Not when he shifted his hips just so, pressing hard into the tender flesh of her sex, lighting all her nerve endings on fire.

His hands drifted down the length of her back to reach under her skirt and grab hold of her ass. He held one bare cheek in each palm, his fingers digging into her skin as he slid into her again and again. She felt the soft scrape of her panties pulling against his cock where he thrust inside her with pure, defined strokes. Wrenching her lips from his, she panted against his mouth. "I'm going to come. Are you with me?"

"God, yes, I'm right here. I need to feel you come. Please."

"Um-hmm," she mumbled in agreement, her ears filled with the sounds of squeaking leather and rapid breaths as he continued driving inside her. "You'll come, too?"

Hunter groaned, his fingers gripping mercilessly into the flesh of her bottom. "I swear I will. Just let go, honey. Just let go."

She nodded with her forehead against his. "Kiss me. Please."

Scarlet came the second his mouth landed on hers. She didn't know if it was the sensation of his soft lips, or the realization that her screams would be muffled against his skin, but she let herself go. Her orgasm hit full force, tightening every muscle in her body while she screamed into his mouth. Hunter kept his word, coming at the exact same time, his cock throbbing deep inside her walls.

He managed to keep his lips fused with hers when he cried out. She held onto him even harder, aware that neither of them could maintain complete silence at the moment, yet unable to bring herself to care. Hunter arched up into her a few more times, emptying himself fully inside her body while her inner muscles clamped down around him. She relished the feel of his stuttered pulsations deep in the walls of her sex, the feel of his body claiming hers in such a primal way.

"Fuck, that's incredible," he gasped when he finally managed to separate their mouths. "You are heavenly."

Scarlet pressed down against him one more time, pulling another shiver from each of them. She sighed with her final release, barely managing to keep her head up so she could see his eyes. Reaching for his face, she brushed her fingers over the damp, heated skin at his temples. "I'll take heavenly anytime."

A slow, satiated smile pulled at his lips. "You're always heavenly."

"Mmm. Thank you for this, Hunter. It's just what I needed."

"You don't ever have to say thank you for allowing me inside you."

"But it feels like I should, especially this time. I think I may have actually seduced you a bit."

He chuckled. "Well, maybe you did. A bit."

"I like the thought of that," she admitted, curling her fingers over the scruff of his jaw. "Although I'm afraid we weren't very quiet."

"It's probably fine," he assured. "The hum of the engine most likely drowned out the sound of us."

"And if it didn't?"

"Well, to be brutally honest, I don't really care. You wanted me and I wanted you. That's all the justification I need."

She remained perched on top of him while she laughed. The motion shifted their bodies, making him sigh. "Actually, Scarlet, you can stay right here on top of me for the rest of the trip, if you want."

"I do want that. But I need to run to the bathroom first, to clean up."

Hunter frowned. "If you have to."

She laughed again as she shifted her feet to the floor and rose up off of him, pushing her skirt down her thighs. "I'll be right back."

He didn't look happy about her leaving, but he did nod as he reached for his zipper to fix his state of undress. Scarlet scurried to the back of the plane with a wide grin planted firmly against her lips. She spent a few moments tidying up, and smoothing out her hair and clothes, before leaving the bathroom. When she returned to him, the cabin was still dark, with only the strips of safety lights on the floor illuminating her path.

Hunter remained seated in his thick leather chair. She knew she should probably sit back in her chair, to give him some space of his own. After all, they'd spent a lot of time together in the past day. They could both probably use some time apart, even if it was only a few feet.

But she didn't want that. God help her, she just wanted to be with him. She wanted to stay with him for every second she could.

"Hi," Scarlet whispered when she came to stand beside his chair.

Hunter looked up to her, his eyes brightening. "Hi."

"Did you really mean it when you said I could stay on top of you for the rest of the trip?"

He smiled. "I certainly did."

She returned his smile while plopping down on him again, sitting sideways on his lap with her face to the window. He wrapped her up immediately. She responded to that open invitation by snuggling into a ball on his chest, curling her bare feet against his thighs, digging her fingers into his shirt, and nuzzling her forehead into his neck. Hunter merely adjusted himself to better accommodate her, chuckling under his breath with her ardent, burrowing movements.

"I swear I'm not trying to seduce you again," Scarlet vowed as she wriggled in his lap. "I just like being really close to you."

He ran his hand down her arm, easing his fingers over her skin. "I promise I won't protest at all if you want to seduce me again."

"Does that mean you enjoyed our little dalliance on the plane?"

"I loved it, actually. It was my first time."

Scarlet's head popped up off of his shoulder, her eyes searching out his in the dim light. "What are you talking about?"

"I'm talking about having sex on a plane. That was my first time."

Her smile lit her entire body. "Seriously? I'm your first plane sex?"

"Yes, although I don't know why you look so happy about it."

"It's because I love being your first in something, Hunter. Especially since I feel like you're my first in everything. I mean, even if you don't count the joy that happened in your bed this morning, you're still my first sex on a counter, my first bondage experience, my first multiple orgasm, and my first mile-high-club partner. And even though I realize it's a silly thought, I still like knowing I'm your first in *something*."

He grabbed her face in both his hands. "Scarlet, you *are* my first. In every way that matters."

Tears sprang to her eyes. She sank onto his chest and pressed her mouth to his. He kissed her, soft and tender. When she finally managed to pull away from his lips, she murmured, "Love you."

"Love you."

Her hand fisted up tighter against his shirt, right over his heart. She dropped her head back onto Hunter's shoulder, letting herself sink into his embrace. Within seconds, a yawn popped out of her mouth. "Mmm. Sorry about that."

"You're so tired," he whispered into her hair. "I can feel it all over your body. Are you sure you wouldn't be more comfortable in your own chair right now?"

She shook her head. "That chair is too big and cold. And frankly, it's too far away from you."

"Then do you want to take a nap here on me?"

Her brow rose as she glanced up to his eyes. "Is that okay?"

Hunter's arms tightened around her. "Works out perfectly for me. As long as you're comfortable."

"Oh, Lord, I'm so comfortable," she sighed, reburying her face in his neck. Her brain thickened with fatigue, the exhaustion of the past days finally catching up with her. "You have the best arms ever, you know. I mean, you grew them perfectly. I don't know how you managed to do that. Maybe it was extra vitamins, or lots of steak. I can't know for sure. But it's as if you knew I'd need to be inside them someday."

He chuckled, the sound moving beneath her fingers as she stretched them over his heart. "I'm just happy I get to wrap them around you."

"Mmm," she hummed into his skin. "Arms good."

Hunter ran his hand up into her hair. "Yes, my little bird, arms are good. Now rest your eyes, please."

"'Kay," she agreed, already way ahead of him. The gentle stroke of his fingers against her scalp and the sweet darkness behind her eyelids lulled her into a happy trance, and she succumbed to sleep before she took another breath.

～

SCARLET WOKE to the feeling of warmth for the second time in one day. Hunter shifted slightly beneath her, his breaths deep and even against her body. His hand traced smoothly up and down her arm.

"You waking up?" he whispered.

"Do I have to?"

"Unfortunately, I think so. We're going to start descending soon."

She exhaled against his shoulder. "How long was I out?"

"A while. Long enough for us to arrive at our destination."

Scarlet blinked her eyes, struggling to reorient herself. She glanced out of the plane window, focusing on the glow she saw in the distance. "Hmm. I see lights. Lots of lights. Crazy, wild, boisterous lights."

The next second, she sat bolt upright on his thighs. "Good Lord, Hunter. I know those lights. Those are Las Vegas lights."

His hands grasped her hips, working to steady her as she started to topple off of his lap. She turned to face him, trying to maintain an upright position while searching for answers in his eyes. *You brought me here to meet my mother, didn't you? Did you already call her? Is she going to be waiting for us when the plane lands?*

Hunter shook his head. "I did not contact your mother."

"Did I just ask you that? I know I was thinking it, but I'm not sure if I said it out loud or not."

"You didn't say it out loud, but I can read your mind. The answer is no, I did not contact your mother. I promised you I wouldn't act like a scoundrel unless you desire it, so I'm not going to overstep my bounds."

Scarlet huffed. "Why is it that you want us to meet each other's families right away?"

His hands tightened, pulling her closer. "Honey, we don't have to do that. We don't have to meet with your mother at all while we're here. It's not my intention to pressure you. I just thought it would be nice for you to see her, since you told me it's been a year since the last time."

Hunter ran his hands up and down her arms. "I'm just happy to be with you, Scarlet. I brought you to Vegas so we could spend a fun, romantic weekend together, enjoying each other's company. But if you want to – since we're already here – you could choose to visit with your mother for a bit. And if you feel comfortable, you could bring me along to meet her. Only if you want to. I'll leave it completely up to you."

She stared into him forever, trying to wrap her thoughts around his. It amazed her, for the millionth time, how simply Hunter saw all of this. It amazed her how his unwavering certainty lent such a deep, profound credence to this cocoon he'd wrapped them in.

"Thank you," she offered. "I don't know if I want to see my mom on such short notice, but I appreciate you bringing me here and giving me the opportunity, just in case."

"Of course. I would do anything for you. You know that, right?"

Scarlet nodded. "I do."

He eased her hair away from her face. "As much as I love holding you, I think you need to go back to your seat for landing. For safety."

"I feel pretty safe here," she grumbled, having no desire to leave. "But I know I should comply with the rules, since I don't want to give Rick and Brett any more reasons to look at me funny."

"Why would they look at you funny?"

She rose from his lap. "If they heard what we did earlier."

"Scarlet, you don't have to worry about that. Even if they did hear, both pilots are company employees. They'll be discreet."

"Discretion is not what I'm worried about," she said, moving over to sit in her own chair. "Dying of embarrassment is another story."

Hunter chuckled. "No need to be embarrassed. These things happen."

"Not to me, they don't. At least, not until the day I met you."

"Hmm. That was a good day."

Scarlet shook her head at his satisfied grin. She buckled her seatbelt and turned to watch the lights out of her window grow brighter while the plane descended. The landing was impeccable, and she barely felt the bounce of the wheels against the runway. Yet her fingers still trembled as she anticipated all that awaited her in Vegas.

Once the plane stopped moving and Hunter unbuckled his seatbelt, Scarlet followed suit. She slipped on her shoes, gathered her purse, and stood beside him. By the time she'd readied herself to leave, the two pilots had already exited the staircase to the ground below.

She peered out of the window, to where Rick and Brett stood beside a large, sleek black town car. "Is that car for us?" she questioned.

"It is," Hunter answered, sweeping his arm out for her to exit.

"You can go first," she said, her cheeks already flushing.

"Okay, but you really don't have to be embarrassed. They probably didn't hear a thing."

She smiled with that lovely thought, but still tucked herself behind Hunter's back when they walked down the steps. The moment they reached the ground, she kept her eyes down and her ears open.

Captain Rick cleared his throat. "Your luggage is already in the car, Mr. Gregory, and the keys are in the ignition. We'll be here to take you back on Sunday afternoon."

"We'll see you then," Hunter replied.

Scarlet heard the easy cordiality of the men's words, so she raised her head to smile at the distinguished captain. Rick nodded to her, his kind eyes showing no signs of reproach. His calm demeanor made her breathe a bit easier, until she turned to the co-pilot.

Brett's pale skin was blotched red. He shifted his feet, twisted his fingers at his sides, and looked generally miserable. The young man stiffened his spine, obviously struggling to appear professional, as he averted his eyes. "I hope you both enjoyed your f-flight," he stammered.

Scarlet's heart leapt into her throat, making it difficult to respond.

"We did," Hunter answered, wrapping a protective arm around her shoulder. "Thank you for the smooth trip."

"Anytime, Mr. and Mrs. Gregory," Rick assured.

Hunter's muscles stiffened at the pilot's error, but Scarlet felt too flustered to correct the man. She was definitely *not* Mrs. Gregory, but Captain Rick mistaking her for Hunter's wife somehow made the circumstances of the flight seem more justifiable. She didn't bother to protest the title, not while Hunter pulled her toward the safety of the car.

The moment he opened the passenger door for her, allowing her to sink inside the safety of the vehicle, she breathed normally again. He sat beside her in the driver's seat, turned on the engine, and immediately reached for her hand. Pulling her fingers up to his lips, he kissed each one and smiled. She held tight to his hand as he drove, watching the city grow brighter while they made their way into the heart of Vegas.

Hunter eventually pulled the car in front of a gorgeous casino hotel that twinkled with reflective glass and vibrant lights. He stopped in front of the valet station, where a smartly dressed bellhop opened Scarlet's door and smiled broadly at her before grabbing their luggage. Hunter came to stand at her side, easing his hand onto her low back to guide her into the hotel behind the young man.

The sound of slot machines, cheering, and general raucousness accosted her ears the moment they stepped into the lobby. Scarlet blinked at the flashing lights and flashier clothes. She glanced around, hoping to catch sight of an Elvis, while they strode across the red carpet and over to the line of elevators. Once the gold doors opened and closed around the three of them, the noises dimmed.

"Your suite is ready, Mr. Gregory," the bellhop informed while they traveled up on the elevator. "The bed is turned down and there's champagne waiting."

"Thank you," Hunter replied, his voice deep beside her ear. She smiled with the warmth emanating from his skin, feeling the excitement of the city fill her body. She may not have seen an Elvis yet, but there was still time. Time to be here with Hunter. Time to simply be.

Once they stepped off the elevator, the young man led them down the hall to their room and opened the door. Scarlet thanked him while stepping across the threshold into the massive suite. Her eyes widened at the scope of it – the large sitting area with two couches, the adjacent dining table and chairs, and the separate bedroom in the distance.

Scarlet stepped toward the bedroom as Hunter tipped the bellboy and closed the door behind him. "Well, this place is huge," she marveled.

"You like it?"

She stopped inside the door and kicked her shoes off. Her toes squished into the plush carpet while her eyes drew to the king-sized bed nestled beside a massive window overlooking the city. "What's not to like?"

Hunter stepped into her from behind, his chest coming flush with her spine. "Would you like some champagne?"

She leaned back against him and sighed. "No, thank you. Honestly, I just want to get out of these clothes and get in bed with you. Just to sleep, I mean. Since we already did other things on the plane. Unless you want to do more other things, in which case I might not be that tired. Although I feel like that nap I took was just a hint at a whole night of sleep, and that bed looks so damn good."

He pressed a kiss into her hair. "Sleep sounds good to me, too. We should both get some rest. We have a big day tomorrow."

"A big day?"

"Well, yeah. I mean, we're in Vegas, so I figure we should do a lot of things. Maybe sightseeing. And shopping. And eating, since there are a thousand restaurants here. Not that we're going to hit them all in one weekend, of course. We can also spend time at the casino, if you like. We can do anything we want. The sky's the limit."

Scarlet faced him, wondering if her nervous speech had become contagious. "That all sounds wonderful. As long as we're together."

"We will definitely be together," he vowed, leaning in for a kiss.

"Hmm," she murmured against his lips. "Will you hold onto that thought until we get into bed? I'd like to get changed real quick."

"Sure. I'll grab your suitcase."

"Thanks."

He brought their luggage to the bedroom as Scarlet set her purse on the dresser. She dug into her bag for her toiletries and a nightie before darting into the bathroom. By the time she reemerged, Hunter stood by the bed wearing nothing but a pair of boxers.

His jaw dropped when he saw her. "Dear God, Scarlet, is that the same little slip you wore the first night we were together at Blue?"

She glanced down at the green satin chemise. "Yeah, I guess it is," she realized, smiling as she looked back to his face. "That was the first night you made love to me, right there on my kitchen counter."

"Made love to you?" he echoed. "Do you really think what we did that night can be considered making love?"

"I do. It all feels like making love. It always has."

Hunter stared at her as if she came from another planet entirely. Eventually, he huffed out a breath. "Damn, I just love you so much."

"I love you, too."

He pressed a quick kiss to her forehead before stepping into the bathroom. "I'll be right back and we'll go to bed. Sound good?"

"Very," she replied, holding his gaze until the door closed.

The moment he left her sight, Scarlet exhaled. She walked over to the lamp on the bedside table and switched it off, settling the bedroom into darkness, except for the illumination of the city sparkling through the wide window. She moved toward the glass, lured by the energy of a billion twinkling lights, staring out at the vivacious world around her.

If we're going to spend the rest of our lives together, I think we should get to know each other's families as soon as possible. I'm just making sure that happens.

The words Hunter spoke to her in his kitchen yesterday swam in her brain as she watched the distant lights. She knew his logic made sense, and even though he insisted they didn't have to see her mom while they were here, this would be the perfect time to introduce Hunter to Dianna. Scarlet stared at the lights for one more second before stepping from the window. Crossing the room to the dresser, she pulled her phone from her purse, dialed her mom's number, and waited.

"Scarlet, sweetie! Is that you?"

"Hey, Mom."

"My goodness, this is unexpected! How are you, darling?"

"I'm – I'm doing really well. How are you?"

"Oh, you know me. I'm still dressing fancy and singing Elvis in the City of Lights."

Scarlet paced on the lush carpet. "Yeah, about that...I'm here, too."

"What?"

"I'm in Vegas. With my new boyfriend."

"Oh my goodness, really? Will I get to see you? And meet this new man of yours?"

"Yes. Definitely. I mean, if you have the time. We're only going to be here for a couple nights, and I know it's short notice, but Hunter wanted this weekend to be a surprise. Do you remember how I always loved surprises when I was a kid? Like the Twinkies? Hunter bought me Twinkies just yesterday. He's really wonderful, Mom. Honestly, he's the best thing that's ever happened to me, and..."

"Baby?" Dianna interrupted.

Scarlet sucked in a breath. "Yeah?"

"You sound really happy. I can't wait to see you both."

"Oh. Okay. When?"

"Why don't you come to the lounge before my shift starts? If you get here around 10 a.m., we could do brunch."

"That sounds great. We'll see you tomorrow."

"Wonderful. See you both then."

"I love you, Mom."

"I love you, too, Scarlet."

"See you in the morning."

"In the morning. Bye, sweetie."

"Bye."

Scarlet held tight to the phone for another minute before setting it back inside her purse. Walking over to the bed, she slipped beneath the covers and rested her cheek against the soft, cool pillow. She tried to settle into the mattress, but her body didn't feel quite right being here alone. When the door to the bathroom finally opened, she sighed.

"How does the bed feel?" Hunter asked as he stepped toward her.

"It's terrible."

"Terrible?"

"Yup. I mean, don't get me wrong, it's soft and plush and delightfully delightful. Except it's not warm like you, and it doesn't have amazing arms like you, and it doesn't smell like you at all."

He laughed while pulling back the covers. "I think I can fix all that."

"Please do."

The mattress indented with the weight of his body, pulling her to him even before he wrapped his arms around her. She sank onto his chest, her muscles easing instantly with his heat. "God, you feel magnificent."

"You do, too," he said, urging her closer. "Absolutely magnificent."

Inhaling deeply, she filled her lungs with his scent. "Thank you."

"For what?"

"For all of this. For everything."

"You're welcome. Thank you for being here with me."

"No place I'd rather be," she echoed his sentiments from earlier. "You know, I made a phone call while you were in the bathroom."

His shoulders tensed. "Yeah? Who did you call?"

"My mother. We're meeting her for brunch tomorrow at 10 a.m."

He didn't say anything for a long minute.

Scarlet shifted closer to him. "Is that okay, Hunter?"

"It's better than okay. Are you sure about this?"

"I am. I want the two of you to meet."

"I want that, too. You have no idea how much. Only now, I'm a little nervous."

"There's no reason to be nervous. Mom is going to love you."

"You think?"

"I know. It'll be love at first sight."

"She'll fall in love with me faster than you did, then?"

Scarlet shook her head. "No, not faster than I fell in love with you."

"Does that mean you fell in love with me at first sight?"

"Well, you are very loveable. I think I've told you that before."

"You have. I don't know if I believed you the first time, but I do now."

"I'm glad you know."

"I do. I also know I'm going to love spending the rest of my life waking up with you in my arms every day."

Scarlet heard those words very clearly. She knew she should protest them.

She should formulate some sort of logical argument to counteract his brazen assumption, so they could have a reasonable conversation about the rest of their lives before he simply decided their fate. She should probably do all of that. But his body was so warm, his arms so strong, and his voice so certain. It all felt so damn amazing.

"*Every* day?" she questioned, figuring she should clarify his terms, at the very least.

"Yes. I want you with me every day and every night, from here on out. I think I've made that fact abundantly clear. Haven't I?"

She exhaled, closing her eyes and nestling her forehead into his shoulder. "Yeah, actually. You have."

"Good," Hunter said. "Now let's go to sleep, so we can start our lives waking up together."

Scarlet nodded against his skin, settled her hand over his heart, and smiled. "Sounds perfect to me."

18

THE NUMBER GAME

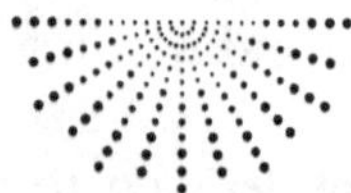

A smile. That's what Scarlet felt on her lips when she woke.

She knew she'd gone to sleep with a smile on her lips, but she didn't know she could smile during sleep. Apparently, she could. She sighed into Hunter's neck, where she'd buried her face yet again.

"Are you getting tired of me burrowing into you?" she wondered aloud, hushing her voice in case he was still asleep. Although the stiff erection pressed against her thigh implied otherwise.

"I'll never get tired of that," he insisted.

Scarlet ran her hand over his chest. "You sure?"

"Pretty damn sure."

Hunter shifted his hips, pushing his rigid length into her bare leg.

"Mmm, that feels so good," she hummed. "And I don't just mean *that*. It feels good that you like having me here, and I like being here."

"I know what you meant," he assured, reaching for her jaw to tilt her face toward his. He pressed a kiss to her mouth, the softness of his full lips rendering her mute about their unbrushed teeth.

When he eased back, she smiled into his eyes. "Do you realize we've known each other for three weeks today, Hunter?"

"I think that's tomorrow, isn't it?"

"Well, I met you on a Sunday, and tomorrow is Sunday, but today is the last day of the first three weeks, and tomorrow starts the fourth."

He chuckled. "Okay. We've known each other for three weeks."

"Sorry. I'm a bit of a numbers geek."

"You like numbers?"

"Yeah, numbers are fun."

A full, easy grin settled over his lips just before he sank his mouth onto hers. Scarlet flattened her fingers on his chest as his hand wandered up her leg and across her hip. The motion drew her silky slip to her waist while his heavy cock twitched against her. She pressed her thigh into that hard ridge, his thin boxers the only barrier to her skin.

Hunter groaned, digging his fingers into her hipbone. A moment later, he wrenched his lips away and clamped his eyes shut. "Damn it," he grumbled, tossing his head back against the pillow they shared.

"Is everything okay?"

"Everything is perfect, except I really want you. Right now."

She wriggled closer, drawing a moan from his throat. "I don't see a problem with that at all."

He refocused on her, his hands slipping through her mussed curls. "The problem is we slept in. We have to get up now, or we won't be on time to meet your mother."

"Eh. Mom thinks time is relative and flowing. She'll be okay if we're late."

"But we shouldn't be late. I want to make a good first impression."

Scarlet traced her fingers over the ridges of his abdomen. "Does that mean I can't entice you to join me in the shower this morning?"

"Holy hell, woman. Why on earth would you ask me that right now? You've put me in actual, physical pain."

"Well, you don't have to be in pain. I can take care of you with my hand, or mouth, or anything else." She slid her palm down over his prominent erection.

Hunter fisted her hair. "You're trying to torture me, aren't you?"

Scarlet wrapped her fingers around his shaft and squeezed, causing him to mumble a filthy stream of curse words. The next second, he released his hold on her, flipped over on his back, jumped up off the mattress, and stood by the side of the bed – all in one swift, continuous motion. "Wow. That certainly was acrobatic," she mused, too amazed by his rapid escape to be upset by his absence.

"Get in the shower, temptress," he griped, pointing to the bathroom.

She planted a frown on her lips as she drew herself up off the sheets and sauntered toward him. Reaching for his hips, she fit her body snugly against his. "But it's been almost *twelve hours* since I had you inside me."

"Sweet hell, Scarlet. What is happening with you this morning?"

"Mmm. I suppose I just woke up ravenous for you."

Hunter grabbed her face in both hands and planted a hard kiss on her lips.

"I'm ravenous for you, too. But I'm going to make myself wait to have you until we're done visiting your mother."

"Are you sure you want to do that?"

"Positive," he insisted, fixing her with a determined stare. "But when we get back to this hotel room later, all bets are off."

She giggled. "Nice gambling reference."

"Well, we are in Vegas."

"Okay, fine," she huffed. "If you can wait until later, then I can, too. I guess I'm going to hop in the shower now. Alone, apparently."

He stole one more kiss. "I swear we will take a shower together sometime this weekend. But for now, I'm going to wait out here until you're done. For safety."

Scarlet grinned into his vibrant eyes. She arched up on her toes, nipped at his jaw stubble, and skipped away to the bathroom. Hunter's laughter followed her into the room as she shut the door.

The shower stall was gigantic, with two showerheads that drenched her in soft warmth from separate directions. She stared at the cobalt wall tiles as she washed her hair, wishing Hunter were here to push her up against them now while his wet fingers slipped across her skin. The vivid image made her nipples harden despite the heat of the water.

"Damn, I am ravenous for him this morning," Scarlet sighed, curious if this was how she would feel every day she woke beside him. Which, according to him, would be every day from here on out.

She froze with her hair conditioner in hand, wrapping her mind around the words he'd said last night: *I'm going to love spending the rest of my life waking up with you in my arms every day.* She hadn't protested his declaration then and had no desire to protest it now. In truth, she felt perfectly happy waking up like this.

Shrugging off any remaining rational thought processes, Scarlet returned to her fantasy of him pressing her up against the shower wall. She used her conditioner, rinsed her slick curls clean, and exited the blue-tiled haven. After blow-drying her hair, she started to wrap her towel around her before stepping out of the bathroom. But then she changed her mind, dropped the towel, and stepped into the bedroom fully naked.

Hunter stood by the dresser in only his boxers, rifling through his suitcase. All of his movements ceased the instant she walked toward him. She forced herself to keep moving, even if the blatant desire written on his face made her legs wobbly. "The shower is all ready for you," she purred when she arrived in front of him. "I made sure it's extra hot and steamy in there."

Hunter clenched his fist around the shirt and pants he held, his biceps bulging as his eyes trailed down her bare body before dragging back up to her face. "Do you have any idea of what I'm going to do to you when we get back to this room, Scarlet?"

Her temptress façade faltered beneath his wicked stare. "I – I have some idea. At least, I thought I did. Before just now."

Hunter took one step forward, erasing the space between them. "You may be surprised," he promised, the words sounding deliciously ominous. Then he reached down and pinched her bare ass cheek.

"Ow!" she squealed, even though it didn't actually hurt. He simply smiled at her, and growled, and disappeared into the bathroom.

Scarlet broke into nervous giggles the moment he left. She focused on opening her suitcase, instantly catching sight of the slinky red dress she'd packed. "That's it," she breathed as she grabbed the soft, thin fabric. Holding the sleeveless dress by the shoulders, Scarlet let it drape down in front of her eyes. "I can't wait until he sees me in this."

She shimmied into a black lace bra and underwear before splitting the red fabric apart with the zipper running the full front. She pushed her arms through, wrapped the tight material around her body, and zipped it all the way back up before sliding her feet into the red heels Hunter had asked her to pack. Moving over to the full-length mirror on the wall, she studied her reflection.

Her flushed cheeks were framed with the loose black curls of her hair, her bright eyes highlighted by the smile she couldn't seem to lose. The scanty dress hugged every curve of her body, and even if she'd never considered herself a sexy woman, she had to admit she looked the part of a temptress right now. That thought made her smile even wider.

The door to the bathroom opened behind her and Scarlet pivoted on her heels to watch Hunter emerge fully clothed and perfectly preened. He looked like his dastardly handsome self, as he always did, only with a nervous tick to his clenched jaw. "You all ready?" she questioned.

The instant he saw her, his eyes bulged. "Good Lord! What are you wearing?"

"Oh, it's just a little something I had in my closet," she answered, bringing her hand up to the neckline to tug against the zipper pull, urging it down her chest an inch. "I've never actually worn it before. Did you notice how the zipper in the front goes all the way down?"

Hunter actually swayed on his feet. "Seriously, Scarlet. What are you trying to do to me this morning? I'm meeting your *mother* in a few minutes. How am I supposed to sit calmly beside you while you're wearing *that*?" His eyes drifted down. "Fuck me. You've got the red heels on, too."

"Well, you did ask me to bring them. And they do match the dress."

He pressed his fingers against his eyelids and groaned.

Scarlet wanted to celebrate having this powerful man at her mercy, but after watching him for a moment, she relented. Stepping across the floor, she placed her hands on his arms and pulled his fingers from his face. "Hey. Are you doing okay?"

Hunter blew out a shaky breath. "I'm just so nervous about meeting your mother. Holy hell, is this how you felt when you found out my whole family had come to our date to meet you?"

"Most definitely. Only times three."

His shoulders fell. "I'm sorry, again. I shouldn't have surprised you with all of them. If I'd had any clue of how nerve-wracking it feels, I would have...well, I can't say I would have done anything differently. But I am sorry it was diffi-cult for you."

She huffed out a laugh, finding it hard to stay mad about anything. "You'll be fine today," she assured, grasping his hand in hers. "Just be yourself. My mother will appreciate that."

"At least I know I've got a solid in with her. If I get into a tight spot in conversation, I can say it's unconstitutional to not like Elvis. But I'll try to hold onto that lifeline for as long as I can."

Scarlet squeezed his hand. "Honey, everything is going to be fine. Now come on, we don't want to be late."

Hunter followed faithfully as she led him to the door. She wasn't sure if he actually breathed, until he inhaled sharply. "Damn, Scarlet. You do realize how fucking edible your ass looks in that dress, right?"

"Edible?" she echoed, guiding him into the empty hallway.

He stepped beside her once they reached the elevator doors, leaning down to whisper in her ear. "Yes, edible. And I do mean that literally."

Her palm dampened against his. He only held her hand more firmly. Hunter kept her close by his side while they rode down to the first floor, walked through the casino lobby, and stepped out into the bright, bold Vegas sunshine. "Should I have the valet pull the car around?"

Scarlet shook her head. "Do you mind if we walk instead? I've always enjoyed walking here. There's so much to see."

"Sure," Hunter agreed, still clinging to her like a lifeline.

"The casino my mom works in is just a couple of blocks from here," she explained while they strode down the sidewalk, glancing at all the other people wandering the strip. "The lounge she works in is actually a karaoke bar. Her shift doesn't start for a few hours, but she likes to eat there beforehand. The chef's name is Philippe, which I always thought was funny, because the chef at Blue is Phil. Phil and Philippe. No relation, of course, because *first* names.

Anyway, Philippe makes the best breakfast, and hopefully he'll make it for us today, because I'm starving. Are you starving, too?"

"Yeah, I guess. A little."

Hunter's hesitant response wasn't what she'd hoped for. His anxiety fed her own, making her grip his hand harder as they walked. Knowing Dianna Tracey was just a few feet away from them churned up a tiny tornado in Scarlet's stomach, since her mother always made her feel like a child, no matter how old she got. She knew that was a fairly normal feeling, but it didn't make it any less daunting. Especially when she was about to introduce her mom to the man she'd come to love so completely in such a short amount of time.

When they arrived, Scarlet's feet drew to a stop. "Hunter, before we go in, I should warn you that my mother is a little, um, different."

He stilled beside her. "Different how?"

"For starters, she's going to be dressed a bit risqué."

"Really? From the way you described her, I thought she'd be a flower child."

"She is a flower child, at heart. But on the outside...well, let's just say she was the only Girl Scout Mom in our troop who didn't button her uniform shirt all the way to the top."

He chuckled. "It'll be fine."

"Are you sure? I thought you were nervous."

"I am nervous. But I'm with you, so everything will be okay."

Scarlet understood that feeling all too well. "Let's do this, then," she encouraged, leading him by the hand through the casino doors and down the purple-carpeted hallway, to the gaudy karaoke lounge beside the slot machine floor. A few tourists milled about, but since it was morning, the lounge was mostly deserted and not nearly as sparkly as usual. Except for the glittery, bleached-blond woman standing by the entrance.

Dianna began jumping up and down the moment they stepped inside the doorway. "My baby girl!" she shrieked, flinging her arms wide.

Scarlet smiled, both in relief that her mother's blue sequined dress covered her ample chest entirely, and also with excitement that she could have one of her ferocious hugs again after so long without them. Stepping up to her, Scarlet grabbed hold and squeezed.

Dianna sang beside her ear. "You're here! I'm so, so glad."

"I'm glad too, Mom. Truly."

"Oh, let me look at you," she fussed when she pulled back, grasping Scarlet by her bared shoulders and glancing down to her outfit. "Well, va-va-voom, sweetie! You look just spectacular in this dress!" Dianna turned her eyes to

Hunter's. "Doesn't she look spectacular in this dress? She looks absolutely *delicious*, right?"

Hunter coughed, blushing deeper than Scarlet had ever seen. "Yeah, um... yes. She's beautiful. She's always beautiful."

"You know that's right," Dianna confirmed, sighing as she turned back to her daughter. "So, introduce me to your new man, please."

Scarlet couldn't help the grin spreading her lips when she stepped back to his side. "Mom, this is Hunter. Hunter, Dianna Tracey."

"Hello, Hunter. It's a pleasure to meet you."

"You too, Mrs. Tracey. An honest pleasure."

"Oh, call me Dianna, please," she offered, pinning him with her heavily-lined doe eyes. "Now tell me something about yourself, Hunter! I want to hear something amazing! Something magical and fantastic! Something that will simply knock my socks off!"

He made a strangled noise in the back of his throat. "I think not liking Elvis is unconstitutional," he blurted.

Dianna stilled, staring at him. A moment later, she turned back to Scarlet with a cheeky grin. "You've done well, sweetie. Beauty *and* brains on this one. Where on earth did you find him?"

Scarlet shrugged. "He tripped over a squirrel and fell into my lap."

Dianna didn't bat an eyelash. "So, it was just meant to be, then?"

"Yup. Meant to be."

"Perfect," she gushed, nodding at her daughter before turning her attention back to him. "Welcome to the family, Hunter."

His eyes widened. "Thank you."

"Of course. Now come over here, both of you! I had Philippe fix us a meal to die for!"

Scarlet re-entangled her hand with his while Dianna led them to a deep booth in the corner of the lounge. The curved seats were lavender velvet, the round table filled with plates of French toast, bacon, crepes, omelets, and fruit. "This – this is amazing," Hunter said.

Dianna grinned. "Philippe makes the best brunch around. And believe me, I have *definitely* been around."

"*Mom*," Scarlet groaned.

"Oh, I'm only joking, dear. Just trying to lighten the mood a bit. Honestly, I've seen nut crackers with more relaxed jaws than Hunter's."

He huffed out a laugh. "I'm sorry, Dianna. I'll admit I was a bit nervous to meet you."

"Well, that's okay, sunshine. Meeting your girlfriend's mother can be a daunting experience. But you flew my baby all the way across the country to see me, so I'm already madly in love with you."

Scarlet leaned into him. "Told you she'd love you," she whispered beside his ear, although it wasn't much of a whisper at all.

He pressed a kiss to her temple. "You did."

Dianna's gaze shifted between the two of them before her hands flourished over the table. "Dig in, please!"

They all piled food onto their plates, humming in pleasure as they ate. Scarlet loved watching Hunter shovel forkfuls into his mouth, with his jaw finally relaxed. His entire body settled in easily beside hers, so she didn't resist her impulse to caress his leg under the table.

"Do you still enjoy living above the casino here, Mom?" Scarlet asked between mouthfuls, her fingers alternately rubbing and squeezing Hunter's knee. He shifted closer, draping his arm around her shoulders.

"I do," Dianna answered. "I have my art supplies upstairs in my apartment. I love painting and sculpting, when I'm not working or out seeing the sights. It's a good life."

"Wonderful," Scarlet sighed, easing her hand up Hunter's thigh.

"And how is your work going, sweetie? The last time we spoke on the phone, I was a little worried about you."

Scarlet's hand stilled on his leg. He smoothed his fingers across her upper arm, his touch strong and certain, helping her relax again. "Things are better now, Mom. Much better."

Dianna smiled between bites. "I'm so glad. You know how much I want you to be happy."

"I do know."

"And what about you, Hunter? What do you do for a living?"

When Hunter responded, Scarlet giddily observed the look on her mother's face as she realized he was Hunter Gregory. Not that her mother placed much emphasis on wealth, but it was amusing to see her process the information. Scarlet ran her fingers firmly across his thigh, absorbing the heat of his skin through the fabric of his pants. His hand drifted across her back, from her shoulders to the low slope of her spine, while he chatted easily with the woman across the table.

The lounge filled with patrons as the three of them spoke, but Scarlet barely noticed the change in scenery while watching her two favorite people interact. Unfortunately, her bubble of peace was shattered far too soon. A shrill voice began mutilating a beloved Elvis song from the karaoke stage in the far corner of the room, making Scarlet cringe. She turned to gauge her mother's reaction.

"Oh, sweet heavens, I hope the King isn't hearing this right now," Dianna sighed in response to the attempted crooning. Seconds later, she sprang up from the table and held her hands out to Hunter and Scarlet. "Come on, you two! There's only one way to reverse this agony! We have to dance along – it's what Elvis would want!"

Scarlet glanced over in time to watch Hunter's brow rise.

"Don't you dance?" Dianna questioned him in their silence.

"He dances on the inside," Scarlet defended, not wanting him to feel pressured. He gave her an appreciative smile, so she pressed a quick kiss to his cheek before leaping up to join her mother.

Scarlet shimmied as best she could on the dance floor, given the tightness of her dress and the painful butchering of more than one Elvis song by a tourist in black pleather who'd had way too much to drink before noon. But she still enjoyed herself, because her mother danced beside her with joy in her eyes, and Hunter watched her with a sweet smile plastered to his lips – a smile that turned more and more wicked the longer she wriggled her hips. By the time the dreadful singing finally ceased, allowing them to head back to their booth, Hunter's gaze had fastened solely on her.

Scarlet nearly tripped in her red heels with the ravenous look in his eyes. She honestly forgot her mother was in the same room, let alone everyone else. Instead of playing the part of a dutiful daughter or an upstanding physician, she walked straight into his arms, plopped down on his lap, pushed her fingers in his hair, and planted a hard kiss on his lips.

Hunter wrapped her up in an instant, his hands flattening against her spine to plaster her chest against his. He groaned into her mouth, his tongue wrapping around hers the moment she ventured to taste him. Scarlet wriggled her bottom against his thighs, burrowing into his body, gratefully losing herself in their cocoon. She would have stayed here forever, if it weren't for the incessant ringing coming from his pants.

"Is...is that your...your cell phone?"

"Sorry," he breathed over her lips. "I should've turned it off."

She forced herself to pull back, although Hunter kept one hand firm against her spine. "You should probably see who it is."

He frowned before reaching into his pocket and glancing down at the screen. "It's Maxine. Do you mind if I talk to her for a minute?"

"No, of course not."

"I should step outside. It's a bit noisy in here."

Scarlet nodded as she climbed off of his lap and onto the seat beside him. Hunter stood and took her hand, squeezing her fingers while he looked over to Dianna. "Please excuse me for a moment."

"Certainly," Dianna obliged.

He leaned down to press a quick kiss to Scarlet's lips before stepping away, holding her hand for as long as he could until their fingertips fell apart. She watched him disappear from the crowded room. Her head shook with the realization that she missed him already.

"So, who's Maxine?" Dianna questioned when he'd gone.

Scarlet settled back into the booth, trying not to feel guilty about her very recent, very public, display of affection. "She's his little sister."

Her mother observed her from across the table. "You know, I realize we don't talk often, sweetie, but I'm surprised I've never heard you mention Hunter before. Especially with as close as you two obviously are. When did you meet him?"

She froze, petrified to say the words. "Um, three weeks ago?"

"Three weeks?" Dianna repeated, her jaw hanging for a moment. "I guess it's been a pretty fantastic three weeks, then."

Scarlet's brow lodged into her hairline. "Seriously, Mom? Is that all you're going to say? Doesn't it bother you that you welcomed a man into our family who I've just met?"

"No, it doesn't. The way you feel about each other is very apparent. You've barely kept your hands to yourself this entire time, and frankly, I'm relieved you finally found someone you're passionate about. You know, that's what brought your father and I together at first, back in the day. And let me tell you, that man could go *all night*."

Scarlet grimaced with her mother's words, for more reasons than one. "But...but that faded, right?" she whispered, clasping her hands together on the table as the hold she'd had on her nerves since yesterday began to unravel. The future was just so uncertain, despite Hunter's determination to barrel full force into it together, consequences be damned.

Her fingers worked against each other while she looked to her mother's eyes. "The passion between you and Dad faded over time, didn't it? Do you think that's simply inevitable?"

Dianna leaned toward her. "You shouldn't compare me and your father to you and Hunter. The two of you are entirely different. And yes, all passion settles down to some degree as time goes on. But honestly, I think it can settle into something even deeper, and better."

"I – I suppose that's true."

Dianna reached out to take her daughter's hands, stopping their anxious movements. "Sweetie, you're thinking about this too hard. You've always done this. You think and think, and you forget to feel."

Scarlet's shoulders sagged. "But I'm doing better now. I promise I am. I'm trying to let myself feel everything I can with Hunter."

"I know that. When you see him, you light up like a Christmas tree."

"Don't you mean I light up like a menorah? Since we're Jewish?"

Her mother laughed, but Scarlet's stomach churned anew. "Oh, hell, Mom. Hunter doesn't even know I'm Jewish."

"Well, you have plenty of time to talk about those things."

Scarlet shook her head. "No, you don't understand. Everything happens so fast between us. He gave me the key to his home yesterday, and last night he told me we'd be waking up together every morning from here on out, and I didn't argue. I mean, we've basically decided to move in together, when we've only known each other for a handful of days. And last week, he told me I would look beautiful pregnant – *pregnant* – and asked how many kids I wanted and I said two and he said that was a nice number. Good Lord, we'd only known each other for *two weeks* at that point, yet we still talked about having a family together, because Hunter doesn't want to waste any more time without each other, and I don't either, but what if we're wrong, what if we're *both* wrong, and..."

"Scarlet!"

Her ramble ceased with her mother's firm voice.

Dianna stiffened her spine. "I want you to listen to me right now, baby. You aren't doing yourself any favors by thinking all of this to death. Just *enjoy* it – enjoy that passion between you and Hunter. Try not to think about every little moment the future might hold. Try to just be present, here and now, and appreciate all the beauty life has to offer."

A laugh bubbled up from Scarlet's chest. "You know, I gave a lecture on appreciation at Blissful Blue just two weeks ago. I really want to heed your advice, as well as my own. But I have so many questions about all of this, and I wish I had even one answer."

"Then let me ask you something. How do you feel about Hunter?"

"I love him," Scarlet answered without hesitation. "God, I love him so much, it borders on ridiculous."

"And how do you feel when you're with him?"

"I feel perfect, Mom. I feel like I've found peace. I feel like I'm home. And I feel happy. So incredibly happy."

"Well, sweetie, that sounds an awful lot like an answer to me."

Scarlet smiled despite the tears in her eyes. "Thank you."

Dianna matched her smile and her tears. "Of course. I'm always here. You know that, right?"

"Yeah, I know. I love you."

"I love you, too."

Scarlet leaned over the table to wrap her mother in a bear hug. She held on tight, breathing in her sweet perfume and sighing. Dianna stroked her hair and pressed a kiss to her cheek before settling back down in her seat. They each swiped at the moisture in their eyes as Hunter walked back into the lounge.

"Everything okay with Maxine?" Scarlet asked when he arrived at their table.

Hunter grasped her hand while slipping into the booth beside her. "Yeah, she's good. She just wanted to chat before she heads back overseas tomorrow."

"But she's coming home soon, right?"

"Yes. She only needs to settle her affairs at Gregory Global Paris."

"You know," Dianna interrupted, "I think you two probably have a lot to talk about, and I actually have to get ready for work now, so I'm going to say goodbye for the time being." When she stood from the table, they both followed suit. "It's been a true pleasure meeting you, Hunter," she said, throwing her arms around his shoulders for a hug. "I hope to see a lot more of you in the future."

"I hope you will, too," he replied when she pulled away. "Thank you so much for the meal today, and for the welcome into your family."

"Happy to give it," she assured with a sparkly grin before turning to Scarlet. "Love you, sweetheart. Have a safe trip home."

"Love you, too, Mom. Thanks for everything."

Dianna nodded, giving her another hug. Scarlet held her mother's tender gaze as long as she could before Hunter slipped his arm around her waist and led her from the lounge. Scarlet reached for the back of his shirt, clinging fiercely to him while they walked out of the casino and back into the Vegas sunshine.

"That was wonderful, Hunter. Thank you for bringing me here."

"Thanks for letting me meet your mother. I really enjoyed that."

"I'm glad. She adores you, of course. Because you're adorable."

He chuckled. "Thank goodness for that. What would you like to do now? We can head straight back to the hotel, or do some sightseeing."

"Hmm. Why don't we wander slowly back to the hotel, and stop wherever we like along the way?"

"Sounds great," he agreed, curling his fingers into her hip to secure her beside him. The next step they took fell perfectly in sync, along with the next and the next, and Scarlet simply smiled and held on.

They spent the afternoon drifting down the sidewalk, admiring the sparkling displays of dancing fountains and pirate ships and Elvis costumes, sampling morsels of food from different vendors, and even stopping to play a few hands of blackjack in one of the countless casinos. Hunter hovered close to her, with his hand on her arm, back, or hip the entire time, and with his lips pressing against her shoulder, hair, and mouth at random intervals. He talked with her, laughed with her, and stared at her like she'd hung the moon.

Scarlet reminded herself of her mom's words as they wandered. She reminded herself to simply appreciate this moment in time, and to let herself feel all these wondrous emotions. Honestly, it wasn't difficult. Her entire body felt at peace beside him, and her whole heart filled with love, and she knew she belonged here.

Hunter remained a perfect gentleman with her throughout the day, although his hand grew restless, exploring her dress more intently the closer they came to their hotel. As the sun began to sink behind the flashy buildings on the Vegas strip, his fingers dragged down the back of the thin red material. He didn't stop his exploration until he reached the indentation at the base of her spine, his hand fisting into the fabric. Scarlet knew he would have reached down to grab hold of her backside, if not for the hundreds of other people wandering the sidewalks.

When the entrance to their hotel finally came into view, he leaned over to whisper in her ear. "You know, this dress has been driving me crazy all day long. I'm so goddamn jealous of it."

She met his eyes. "Why are you jealous of my dress?"

"Because of the way it squeezes your ass. Not that I can blame it."

Scarlet managed to hold his blistering gaze as they walked through the front door. She remained glued to Hunter's side while he guided her into their hotel, urging her swiftly past the raucous casino floor and the multiple shops, toward the waiting elevators. She trotted happily beside him, until her eyes caught on something shimmery and splendid.

"Honey?" he questioned when she froze in her tracks. "What is it?"

"Oh, sorry," she offered, staring through the window of one of the hotel's clothing stores. "I've just never seen a dress quite this stunning."

Her eyes feasted on the empire-waist gown on display. Every shade of the rainbow wove through the intricately detailed fabric of the dress, with a sparkling gold inlay hemming the edges, making it even more beautiful. "Nope, don't need it," she admonished herself aloud.

Hunter pressed a kiss into her hair. "If you want it, it's yours."

"What? No, it's..." Scarlet protested as he tugged her into the store. "The dress doesn't even have a price tag. That's never a good sign."

"I don't care what it costs. If you want it, it's yours."

"But I don't need you to buy me things."

He stopped moving in the middle of the clothing racks and pulled her up against him. "I know you don't, but you can *let* me buy you things. After all, you've let me buy you underwear before."

"Yes, but only because you tore my other underwear."

"Okay, then. The minute we get upstairs, I'll tear this dress off of you, which will justify the purchasing of a new dress."

"Hunter! You don't need to tear this dress! If you want it off of me, you can just use the zipper!"

He chuckled. "Very well, then. I promise I will use the zipper on this dress, if you agree to let me buy you the new dress."

Her eyes narrowed. "That's darn close to blackmail, Mr. Gregory."

"Hmm. I suppose it is," he admitted, his eyes twinkling despite his look of contrition. "I'm sorry about that. I know I'm not supposed to act like a scoundrel again until you tell me you desire it."

The assumption that she would want Scoundrel Hunter back at some point did funny things to her innards, and she forced herself to shake her head. "It's not necessary to buy me the dress. I don't need it."

"You may not *need* it, but you *want* it. I'd like this weekend to be about us doing the things we want to do. Let me buy you the dress, please. I want you to have it."

She stared up into him for a minute before finally letting herself relax. "Okay. Thank you for this. I really do love the dress."

He grinned, pressing a quick kiss to her lips as he pulled her to the front counter. A short time later, they emerged from the store with her fingers curled around the handle of a shopping bag. She giggled in sheer giddiness all the way down the hall. "My goodness, this dress and I are going to be such good friends."

Hunter ran his hand up her spine. "I'm your friend, too, right?"

"Oh, yes. You're my best friend, and my lover, and my everything," she admitted. "Wow. That sounded really cheesy, didn't it?"

He chuckled when they stopped in front of the elevators. "I'm okay with cheesy," he said, lowering his voice when several people joined them by the doors. "What I'm not okay with is this damn dress you're still wearing. I think my jealousy has transformed to actual anger."

She met his fearsome stare. "You're angry with my dress now?"

His fingers fisted on her spine. "Fuck, yes. I want to tear if off you with my bare hands. Or maybe my teeth. Are you sure I can't?"

The air caught in her lungs as the question he'd asked her this morning rang in her ears: *Do you have any idea of what I'm going to do to you when we get back to this room, Scarlet?*

She didn't have a chance to answer, or relent to him entirely, before the shiny doors opened in front of them. She wasn't sure how she managed to walk into the elevator of her own accord, given her threaded pulse and weakened knees. Hunter kept his hand on her low back as they moved to the rear of the elevator. They stood against the wall in the far corner, looking innocently up at the ascending numbers above the elevator door, surrounded by a dozen other people.

Scarlet pressed her body against his, wanting him close even in this tiny space. His hand drifted down onto her ass, his fingers curving into her flesh through the thin material. She swallowed the groan in her throat.

The elevator doors opened and shut on various floors while Hunter constantly caressed her. When they finally arrived at their floor, only two other people remained. Scarlet offered a polite, "Good evening," while they stepped out and turned to walk in the opposite direction down the hall. Hunter didn't bother speaking. He just leaned down and bit into her earlobe, pulling it in his mouth before running his tongue along the edge.

Her nipples tightened, making her stumble in her heels when he guided her out of the elevator toward their room. She white-knuckled her bag as he used the key card to gain entry to the suite. The second he pulled her inside, she dropped the bag and reached for him. Hunter shut the door by pressing her up against it, protecting the back of her head with his hand as he fastened her spine to the wood and sank his mouth onto hers.

Scarlet's fingers gripped his shirt, fisting the crisp fabric and yanking on the buttons, while his tongue wrapped around hers. His hands slid down her sides and over the curves of her hips before slipping around to grab hold of her ass. They each moaned into the other when he palmed her cheeks and wrenched her up onto him.

His cell phone rang again, vibrating over her leg through his pants. Hunter ignored the sound, pulled her closer, and kissed her harder. While his masterful tongue drove her mad with need, the ringing stopped. Yet it restarted mere seconds later, the unruly noise breaking through the haze in Scarlet's brain. She wrenched her lips from his with a pained whimper. "Just... just see who it is, honey."

He cursed against her mouth, his hands still kneading her backside even as he straightened. Reaching into his pocket, he pulled out his phone and stared at the screen. "Goddamnit, Maxine," he grumbled, pressing the phone to his ear. "What in the hell do you want now?"

Scarlet cringed with his ferocious greeting, shifting her spine against the door he kept her pinned to. Hunter's hand tightened around her waist, holding her in place, while Maxine shrieked at him across the phone. "I'm sorry," he offered his sister, looking into Scarlet's eyes as he spoke to the other woman. "I didn't mean to snap at you. I'm just right in the middle of something incredibly important."

Patting his hand, Scarlet whispered, "It's okay. Talk to your sister. I'll wait for you in the bedroom."

Hunter dropped his arm to his side, allowing her to step away from him. "Scarlet," he called, waiting until she turned back. He pressed the phone flat against his chest to muffle his next words. "Don't you dare take that dress off yet. *I* want to do it."

He stared the words into her eyes before bringing the cell back up to his ear. She heard his sister yelp at him from the other end. His brow furrowed as he barked, "Well, if you don't want to hear things like that, Maxine, then stop calling me when I'm in Vegas with my girlfriend!"

Scarlet laughed while walking into the bedroom. Her first instinct was to kick off her heels, but then she remembered how much Hunter liked the shoes and kept them in place. Crossing over to the lengthy window on the other side of the bed, she looked out on the bustling city. The sun was just beginning to set on the horizon, turning a molten orange with streaks of pink and red streaming out across the sky.

She sighed as she watched the infinite lights from other hotels twinkle brighter with the dimming sun. She felt so grateful for this day, having had a few precious moments with her mother after a year apart. She hadn't realized how much she needed to see her, to talk about her fears and hear her advice. Dianna had always encouraged her to follow her heart, just as she had this morning.

Being here with Hunter was exactly what Scarlet's heart wanted. She wanted to believe in the reality he believed in – the one where the two of them could be together always – while still experiencing magic along the way. She wanted to believe that if the passion between them eventually faded, the intimacy and peace they knew in each other's arms would be enough to sustain them both. She wanted to believe all of it, because as frightening as her thoughts of the future could be, she had no doubt she wanted to spend that future with him.

Wrapping both arms around her waist, Scarlet hugged her body while staring out at the sunset. She told herself not to worry so much about their future. It had only been three weeks, after all, and she needed to just breathe and relax and appreciate the here and now. But she couldn't accomplish any of that...not until she heard him.

"Hey," Hunter spoke from behind her, his approaching footsteps soft on the carpet. "You doing okay?"

The sound of his voice soothed her in an instant, allowing her arms to fall back to her sides. "I'm doing great, now that you're here. Is everything still okay with Maxine?"

"It's fine. She's just particularly chatty today." He stopped walking when he arrived behind her, warming her body without a single touch. "But I don't really want to talk about my sister right now, if that's okay."

Scarlet turned around, pressing her spine against the window to match his intent stare. "What would you like to do instead?"

Hunter's eyes sparked sinfully, making her shift in her heels. "Actually, I thought you might like to play a game with me."

"Yeah? What kind of game?"

"It's something I thought up this morning, when you were in the shower. I figure we can call it the Number Game."

"The Number Game?"

"Well, you did tell me you're a numbers geek," he teased.

Scarlet grinned. "That I am. So, how do you play this game?"

"It's easy. You just need to pick a number."

"Can it be any number in the entire world?"

"Um, let's go with any number between two and ten."

"Okay, then. How about pi?"

"Pi?"

"You know, 3.1415926...I could go on."

"You really are a numbers geek, aren't you?"

"Mm-hmm."

He reached to her face, sliding his fingers across her cheek. "And that is wonderful, but choosing pi will make this game a bit difficult to play. I need you to pick a whole number, please."

"In that case, I'll round pi down to three."

"Or you could round it up to four."

"Do you want me to round it up to four?"

"I'm just saying you can pick a higher number, if you want to."

She huffed out a laugh. "What number do you want me to pick?"

"Oh, no, four is good," he assured. "We can certainly go with four."

"Four it is, then."

Hunter watched her for a long minute, a playful smile curving his lips before he straightened his spine. He dropped his hand from her face to her shoulder, his eyes tracking the movement as he traced across the high neckline of her dress. Scarlet swallowed hard.

"Are you going to tell me the rules of the game, Hunter?"

His fingers sought out the zipper at the top of the red fabric, grasping hold of the little gold pull. He tugged down smoothly, parting the dress slowly over her chest. "I'll tell you the rules later. Right now, I have other things I want to do."

Scarlet bit her lip while he dragged the gold pull down farther and farther, until he reached the lower hem. The zipper fell apart, opening the dress completely. The taut material still clung to her hips and backside as the cool air slid across her heated skin.

Hunter slipped his hands into the opening of the dress just above her knees, drawing his fingers all the way up her body – tracing slowly over her thighs and her panties, across her belly and over her bra, up her chest and neck – until his fingers edged into her hair. He fisted them inside her curls, holding her steady as his mouth hovered over hers.

"Is this where I was before we were so rudely interrupted?" he asked, his warm breath fanning over her face.

"I...I do believe so."

He smiled against her lips. "Actually, I don't think that's entirely accurate." His fingers uncurled from her hair to run across her arms, over her hips, and onto her back. He reached down, palming her ass in both hands, securing her body onto his as his cock jutted into her belly.

"*This* is where I was," he insisted with a full squeeze of her flesh.

She circled her arms around his neck. "You're so, so right."

Hunter's lips skimmed over hers while he ran his fingers up and down the clothed seam of her bottom. "Fuck, I love your ass. I mean, it's just one of the numerous parts of you that I love. Honestly, I love every part of you. But, damn, this is a magnificent ass."

His hands cupped her flesh before dragging across her waist and onto her belly. He nipped at her lower lip, pulling it into his teeth and soothing it with his tongue, as his fingers hooked into the sides of her thong panties. "May I tear these off of you?"

Scarlet pushed her hands up into his hair. "Of course."

He snapped the strings easily, growling his approval when the ripped fabric fell to the floor. "Will you do me a favor now?"

"What's that?"

"Will you spread your legs for me?"

A little whimper escaped her throat. "Right here?"

"Yes. Right here."

"Um, it's...yeah," she fumbled, having difficulty forming a proper sentence beneath his devouring stare. Using the window for support, she shifted her heels apart on the carpet. Hunter's fingers drifted up to cup her breasts, his thumbs raking across her lace bra, enticing her nipples to eager peaks. He pressed his mouth to hers, edging his tongue between her lips.

Tightening her calf muscles, she pressed her back into the glass to keep herself upright while he explored her with his fingers and his tongue. When he finally pulled his mouth away, she pinned his darkened eyes. "I want you so damn much," he confessed, the words rushing out as he dragged his hand down her stomach to slip between her parted thighs.

Scarlet cried out when he pressed one finger through her soft folds and up into her sex, all in one smooth motion. "God, you're so wet, honey. I love how wet you are for me."

She shifted her hips to rub against his hand. "I need you, Hunter."

"I know you do. I need you, too. But first, I need to taste you."

"Taste me?" she questioned, barely getting the words out before he sank to the ground in front of her. Her hands flattened against the window, giving her a small means of support while he settled on his knees. He pulled his finger out of her sex, licking her wetness off of his skin, before he pressed his face between her thighs.

Hunter grabbed her hips in both hands as his tongue moved decisively up through her soft folds and onto the little nerve bud at the top of her sex. Scarlet bent her knees, rather involuntarily, when his chin parted her legs farther. The scrape of his jaw stubble against her soft inner flesh sent bolts of electricity coursing through her body.

She dropped her head back on the glass. "Damn, that is...damn," she breathed, failing to recall any other curse word. "Damn, damn, *damn*."

He moaned into her skin, as if he'd never tasted anything better in his life, and the thought made her eyes roll back in her head. His tongue pressed up into the tight walls of her sex, licked through her folds, and ran in circles against her taut little nub. Her legs shook with the effort of standing in her heels without clamping her thighs around his face.

Hunter's fingers held tighter to her hips when she trembled. She wanted to thank him for the support, but didn't have the words. Instead, she wrenched a hand into his hair and twisted her fingers against his scalp, hearing him growl his approval of her ferocious grip. His hot breath fanned over her sensitive skin as he began tonguing her in a more regular rhythm, working her tender flesh over and over again.

Scarlet honestly tried to remain still and steady, but eventually she had no choice but to fuck his tongue. She shifted her legs, arching her hips up and then down, rubbing her still-clothed ass against the window. The movement gave her some sense of control, even while knowing she truly had none. Hunter simply owned her at this moment, and that foggy realization was more erotic than she wanted to admit.

"Oh, oh, *oh*," she moaned, pressing harder into his face while he worshipped her with his mouth. Every muscle in her body tightened at once, her thighs shaking ferociously, seconds before the illicit waves crashed over her. She screamed when her orgasm hit, not even trying to censor the formidable sound. Her fingers gripped hard to his hair as she did her best to not collapse on top of him.

Hunter didn't move for the longest time. He simply held her hips steady while his mouth dwelled against her skin, running kisses over her thighs and belly in between long, slow licks up her sex. Scarlet shivered and whimpered, wanting nothing else in the world except him.

Time stopped until he rose to stand. The moment his body leaned into hers, pushing her onto the glass at her back, she draped her hands over his shoulders. "Sweet hell, that was incredible."

Hunter hummed his agreement as he pressed a kiss to her lips, his tongue slipping inside to share the salty taste of her sex. He kissed her long and deep, and then pressed another kiss to her cheek, and another to the shell of her ear. "That was number one," he whispered.

Scarlet gripped the back of his shirt. "What?"

"The Number Game. You picked four. That was one."

"You – you mean *orgasms*?"

He straightened, smiling into her eyes. "That's exactly what I mean."

"Oh my God! The Number Game is how many orgasms you plan to give me? Are you *serious*? What if I'd picked *ten*?"

"Then I imagine we'd both be walking funny by morning," he answered with a chuckle. "Honestly, I don't mind if you want to pick a bigger number now, after hearing what the game entails."

"No, that's...that's okay. I don't even know if I'm capable of four."

Hunter stopped everything to stare straight into her. "We're definitely capable of four, Scarlet. Trust me."

With that promise, he stepped back. She instantly reached for him, until she realized he'd only moved far enough away to allow room for stripping off his clothes. Standing frozen against the window, her thighs still trembling from her first orgasm, she attempted to wrap her mind around the thought of having three *more*. Once his shirt fell to the floor, and his fingers popped open the button on his pants, Scarlet felt her knees start to give.

"You okay?" Hunter asked as he reached for his zipper.

"Um, yeah. My legs are just a little shaky. Or maybe a lot shaky."

He pushed his pants down his thighs, freeing his thick cock to the view of her widening eyes. "I promise I'll help out with that in just a second," he vowed before peeling away the last of his clothes and kicking them all into a pile.

Hunter straightened before her, wearing nothing but a sinful smile, although his gigantic erection stood like a third person in the room. Closing the space between them in an instant, he reached both his hands to her ass and wedged her body onto his. "I'm going to lift you up and pin you against this window now," he informed her. "And you're going to wrap your legs around me, and take me inside you, and then I'm going to fuck you right here, up against the glass."

She couldn't respond with anything but a whimpered squeak.

He softened his voice. "Is that okay with you?"

Her head bobbed even as she attempted to keep her eyes glued to his.

"Good," Hunter said, his hands drawing up across the red fabric still clinging to her hips. He eased his grip on her in order to smooth his fingers over the skin of her belly, and slowly up the center of her chest, all the way to her neck. She groaned and locked her knees.

"I'm going to take this gorgeous dress off of you now, Scarlet. For two reasons. First, because I'm still angry as hell at it. Second, because I want you completely naked for the rest of this. Is that okay, too?"

She nodded over and over, enough to feel dizzy.

Hunter's hands eased across her shoulders, slipping the dress from her skin. She dropped her arms to her sides, allowing the material to fall to the floor. Standing still as stone, Scarlet concentrated on the aching need in his eyes while he unclasped her bra and drew it down to fall on the ground.

His actions left her standing before him in nothing but red high heels, and he didn't waste another second. Grabbing her ass in both hands, he lifted her up off the ground and entered her quickly and seamlessly. She wrapped her legs around his hips as he drove her bare spine into the window, sealing their bodies together.

When his cock settled deep inside the walls of her sex, they both exhaled. Hunter's fingers dug into her flesh as his lips melded with hers. Scarlet simply banded her arms around his shoulders and held on.

The glass shook behind her when he began moving, running his thick length up inside her again and again. She whimpered with every lunge, feeling her heels slip slowly off of her feet, curling her toes in a futile attempt to hold the shoes in place. When he thrust even harder, enough to steal the air from her lungs, her heels finally hit the floor.

Hunter's entire body stilled with the sound. "Holy hell, Scarlet. Did your shoes just fall off?"

"Y-yes."

"Damn, that's fantastic."

Her brow arched. "You're happy my shoes fell off?"

"Are you kidding? I'm *ecstatic* about it. I've wanted to fuck you out of these red heels from the second I saw you in them."

"But that was in my office on Monday."

"Yes. Yes, it was."

Scarlet moaned. "You wanted to fuck me that day?"

He shifted his hips, sliding his cock out and back into her soaking sheath, pinning her in place against the window. "I did. I wanted to have my way with you right there in your chair. Or on the floor. Or the couch. Or your desk. Anywhere and everywhere, really."

She tightened her legs around his waist. "Mmm. You did have your way with me on my desk when you came back Wednesday."

Hunter drove into her, causing a shock of electricity to flit down her spine. "I did. But I won't ever do it again, if you don't want me to."

Her fingers dove into his hair. "I do want you to."

"Are you sure?" he asked, searching her eyes.

"Of course. Why wouldn't I?"

"Because that's where you see your patients. And it's where..."

"No, Hunter. I'm not going to think that way anymore. I told you yesterday, being with you in my office was a happy memory. I'm so tired of having to fake my feelings there. I want to smile when I walk into that office, and have my patients see how genuinely happy I am, so they'll know it's possible to have happiness in their lives, too."

He stared into her for a long minute before resting his forehead against hers. He held onto her tight, so tight that his arms trembled with the effort, before looking back to her eyes. Scarlet absorbed the depth of emotion in his brilliant blue as he struggled to compose himself.

Lengthy seconds later, he edged his thick shaft farther inside her slick walls, drawing a moan from her throat. His eyes narrowed with the sound. "Tell me more, honey. Tell me about how you want me to fuck you in your office. Tell me how often you want me there."

She whimpered. "I want you whenever I can have you."

He slid out and back in. "Do you mean that? Because I could walk across the street for lunch every day."

Her eyes widened. "*Every* day?"

"Yes. I'll bring your lunch over and fuck you right on your desk."

"Mmm. But what on earth will you eat for lunch?"

"Good God, Scarlet. Please tell me you're offering to be my lunch."

She bit into her lip, watching his eyes track the movement. "I'd love to be your lunch. And I'd love for you to be my lunch, too."

"Sweet hell," Hunter breathed, arching out and back inside her. "You drive me mad, I swear. The things you do to me are unreal."

He began pounding into her, gripping her ass in both hands as he rammed her repeatedly into the window. The glass at her spine rattled while she held on, digging her fingers into his hair. A sheen of sweat sprung up between them, sliding their heated flesh together, awakening every nerve in her body.

"I'm going to walk across the street for lunch every day," he panted into her neck, "and I'm going to spread you out on your desk, and sink my mouth down between your legs, and feast on you."

"Yes, yes," she whimpered as he plunged inside her, over and over, sending a thousand surges of electricity shooting through her skin.

"I'm going to make you come so hard. I'm going to make you come so fucking hard, right on my tongue, and then..."

"Hunter!" she screamed, her orgasm hitting her with the force of a truck as he crashed her into the glass. She shouted and moaned and cursed, the shocks going on and on while she clung to his slick skin. His stiff cock pumped deep inside her, pulling several more mewls from her lips as the unending waves washed over her skin.

Scarlet didn't want him to stop moving. She wanted him to fuck her for as long as it took until he came, too. But he slowed his actions as soon as her inner muscles stopped contracting, holding her in place as her forehead collapsed onto his damp hair. "Damn, you're good," she sighed.

Hunter smiled against her cheek. "That's number two."

"That's number two. And I don't even care if the things you said about office lunches were true, because I just like hearing about them."

"Well, I am very aware that my little bird likes dirty talk. But I'll be more than happy to discuss our lunches further when we get back home."

She hummed her consent, loving the thought of future lunch dates, although not as much as she loved the word *home*. Easing her lips onto his jaw, Scarlet ran her tongue over his stubble to taste the salt on his skin. He groaned and tugged her more solidly onto his chest, pulling her away from the window and balancing her body against his.

"You know," she mused, "half of Las Vegas probably just saw my bare ass cheeks pressed up against that window."

Hunter growled. "Lucky bastards."

Scarlet giggled while he walked them over to the bed. He kept her body clamped to his with both arms around her back, his biceps bulging as he crawled onto the mattress and lowered her down in the center of the soft comforter. His hips jostled against hers, yet his rigid length still remained buried deep inside the walls of her sex.

"My goodness, how have you not had an orgasm yet?" she questioned, matching his devoted stare. "I mean, I know you're controlling yourself for my benefit, but I don't know how you're managing it. Do you have some sort of superpower to maintain an erection?"

He laughed, which moved his cock deliciously inside her. "I don't have a superpower, unless you count the overwhelming desire to give you multiple orgasms, which is the only thing preventing me from coming inside you this instant. Also, it helps that we had sex twice yesterday, even though I don't know how much longer I can last now."

"I want you to come with me this time. I don't want to have three orgasms while you have none. Will you come with me? Please?"

"If it'll make you happy, I'll come when you do. Although I think you need to be on top for this one, so you can control it."

Scarlet nodded vehemently, excited by the idea of him giving her full control. Hunter grabbed hold of her and flipped them over effortlessly. As soon as she lay on top of him, she slipped her knees down to the comforter and pinned his waist between her thighs. Pushing up on her arms, she slid his cock slowly out and back inside her clenched walls, watching his eyes spark with raw need.

His hands moved to her hips, curling firmly into her flesh, yet he didn't attempt to control her movements. He simply held on while she directed the friction of their bodies. Her breasts bounced each time her ass landed against his thighs, drawing his attention to the tightly peaked buds. He licked his lips, which felt very much like an invitation, so she bent forward.

Hunter arched his head off the bed the moment she came close, his mouth latching onto one breast, his tongue circling her nipple. She shuddered, digging her fingers into the bedding beside his shoulders while grinding her bottom down harder into his flesh. He tightened his hold on her hipbones as he feasted on her skin, but he still didn't direct the stuttered movements of her body.

Scarlet's thighs trembled and tensed. She closed her eyes, absorbing the feel of his rigid length moving deep inside her while his tongue worked magic on her aching breasts. He shifted his attentions from one firm peak to the other, never losing contact with her skin, causing her to mewl and purr and make other sounds that weren't quite human.

Eventually, Hunter rested his head back on the mattress. His entire body stilled, except for his fingers, which moved slowly and gently across her legs. Scarlet loved being able to direct their lovemaking right now, although she couldn't prevent other devilish thoughts from springing to mind. She kept her eyes shut tight as she fantasized about her scoundrel taking control of her, bringing them both to completion with his supremely skilled body while she gave herself over to that pleasure.

She whimpered with images of ropes and scarves and duct tape, impaling herself on his stiff cock over and over, relishing the swelling waves of electricity reawakening beneath her skin. She'd never experienced three orgasms in a row before, but since Hunter believed she could do it, she wanted to believe it, too. That energy built inside her, not as hard-and-fast as the first two, but steady and driven and purposeful.

Excited about the possibility of actually having a third, Scarlet reopened her eyes. She wanted to see Hunter, to make sure he was close to his own completion, so she could enjoy this moment fully. But when she zeroed in on his eyes, she didn't see the lustful, wanton need she expected to see. Instead, he stared up at her with earnest, loving intent.

She ceased moving in order to concentrate solely on him. The fading glow of sunset filtering through the window lit his face in soft, perfect shades of gold. "Have you been watching me, Hunter?"

He gave her a tender smile. "I have."

"Do you like watching me?"

"I love watching you. I could watch you forever."

His words were gentle, caressing her skin as surely as his hands. Scarlet sank her chest against his. "You look like you're deep in thought."

"I am," he admitted. "I mean, not too deep, but I am thinking."

"Care to share your thoughts with me?"

"I was just thinking about what you said to Dr. Abbott."

"Good Lord! Please don't tell me you're thinking about Adrien Abbott while we're having sex!"

Hunter chuckled, his hands tightening on her hips. "Well, I'm not *actively* thinking about him – you can trust me wholeheartedly on that. Although I'd like to point out that this isn't much worse than you thinking about *Star Wars* during our first time together."

Scarlet paused to consider his point. "Touché," she said, easing her fingers up into his hair. "Why are you thinking about Abbott?"

"I'm wondering if you actually promised him our firstborn."

"What?"

"You told me you had to promise Abbott all sorts of things in order to take your vacation at Blue. But I want to make sure you didn't really offer him our firstborn child, since I want to keep our firstborn. And all the others, for that matter."

"*All* the others? I thought we already covered this topic in the underwear honor store. We talked about having *two*."

Hunter's serene smile transformed into a self-satisfied grin. "You're right. We did agree to have two kids, didn't we?"

Scarlet's lips parted, yet she fell mute. He'd been contemplating their future children, right in the middle of sex, and she didn't know what to think about that. She could only sit and ogle him as a thousand thoughts fired simultaneously inside her brain.

She probably wouldn't have ever moved again, if he hadn't moved her. Hunter used his firm grip on her hips to shift her body up, just enough to run his cock out and back inside her sex. The perfectly sinful gliding sensation took her breath away, reminding her that they were involved in something other than spoken conversation. He groaned when she settled all the way down again, his fingers clenching her skin, but he didn't attempt to control her movements any further.

Scarlet worked to refocus. She told her brain that her body was quite engaged at the moment, and she had things to do. Yet her mind simply wouldn't relent. Placing her hands to either side of his head, she fixed his eyes. "Hunter, I realize now may not be the best time to have this discussion, but there's something I really need to tell you."

"What is it?"

"It's just that I'm...I'm Jewish."

His brow rose. "Okay. Well, I'm not. Is that going to be a problem?"

"Oh, no, I don't expect you to convert, or anything. I'd just like to put up a menorah, along with a Christmas tree, for the winter holidays."

"That sounds good to me."

"Also, I would like to teach the kids about both religions."

He gave her a lopsided grin. "You mean *all* the kids?"

She huffed out a laugh. "Yes, *all* the kids."

"Then all of our kids are lucky they're going to have a mother as wonderful as you." His eyes glided over her face as his voice softened. "I'm going to love spending the holidays with you, Scarlet. I'm going to love every day I'm with you. And I'm especially going to love raising a family with you."

Her heart stopped for a few seconds, banging ferociously in her chest when it restarted. "I'm...I'm going to love all of that, too."

Another sweet smile curved his lips, just before he ran his hand up her jaw and tugged her down to him. The moment their lips touched, he released his hold on her. He allowed her the freedom to pull away from him, should she desire it. But Scarlet didn't pull back, since this was exactly where she wanted to be.

Hunter kissed her softly, lovingly. It was a kiss of promise and fulfillment more than passion, yet it was still passionate. She gave in to his desires as well as her own, cradling his face in her hands, kissing him back with all she had to give.

Raising her hips, she slid his rigid erection from her body before running herself back onto him. Waves of electricity raced through her skin as she worked her hips up and down, over and over. Hunter held entirely still beneath her for the longest time, letting her ride him the way she desired, until she found a smooth, solid rhythm that brought her entire body to boiling. A moan forced its way from her throat, drawing a responding groan from his. He shifted his hips then, meeting hers thrust for thrust. He still let her control their pace, but he worked with her now, pushing his length deeper inside her body each time she ground down.

Her loose hair fell in waves beside his face, but Scarlet didn't bother to pull the curls back. She just held tighter to him as her hair veiled their faces, heating the air around them with their rapid, warm breaths. His hands roamed freely over her skin, trailing down her spine and across her waist as they whimpered into each other with every matching movement.

Scarlet's orgasm started slowly, deep in the center of her body, her pulse sputtering with the aching, deliberate build. Her muscles tightened and wound, her fingers fisting into his hair as she drove down onto his shaft again and again, bringing that far-off sensation closer every second. His hands gripped onto her thighs as she mewled against his lips, his arm muscles bulging with the effort of holding her to him.

Hunter came first. He came hard, dropping his head back on the mattress with a roar, his hips driving up in stuttered beats. His cock pulsed hot and heavy inside her sex as Scarlet clamped her inner muscles around him. The instant she milked his erection, her own orgasm hit. It wasn't the wildly fierce sensation she'd experienced twice earlier. This orgasm was smooth and soft, washing through her body with quiet satiation.

Only a tiny moan escaped her throat when she slumped down onto him, burying her face in his neck and filling her lungs with his scent. Hunter's heart pounded in his chest, so rapid and strong that she could barely hear her own pulse as it rushed through her ears. She kept pace with his movements as his hips jerked a few more times, trying to ensure his enjoyment of the one orgasm he'd allowed himself.

When his arms finally loosened around her, and his panting breaths began to slow, she stretched her body out on top of his. Relaxing fully into his warmth, she fell nearly unconscious within seconds. Hunter's voice actually scared her when it rumbled beneath her.

"Um, Scarlet?"

"What? I'm so sorry. Did I drool on you already?"

"No, no, I just...was that number three?"

"Oh my goodness, yes. That was definitely number three."

Hunter let his arms drop onto the bed. "Wonderful," he sighed. "I wasn't exactly sure, since you didn't make a lot of noise with that one. At least, not like you normally do, which I've grown really used to."

She drew herself up to sit on his lap. "That's because this one was softer and deeper," she assured, tracing her fingers over his damp chest. "Yet still amazing."

He ran his hands over her legs. "Good. There's just one more to go."

Scarlet giggled wildly. She couldn't help it, since she truly couldn't fathom the concept of having another one. She laughed even harder when Hunter frowned up at her.

"I don't know what you find so funny about this," he grumbled.

"Nothing. I'm just a little punch drunk after the first three. I think I need to take a short break before trying again."

"Okay, then. You can take a short break, if you really need it."

She lifted herself off of him, tipping over to land on her side against the fluffy comforter. Hunter rolled toward her immediately. He reached to her waist, pulling her into the cocoon of his body once again.

"Hmm. Can I close my eyes for just a minute?" she asked, her lids already drooping as she snuggled into his shoulder.

"Of course."

"I'll only close them for a mimut...a...a minute."

"Yeah, honey. Only a minute," he repeated, his heat surrounding her in the softly lit room as his fingers drew circles across her back, soft and gentle and so very, very soothing.

19

MAGIC

When Scarlet reopened her eyes, the first thing she noticed was how dark the room had gotten. No more golden glow of sunset surrounded them on the bed. Now, only the dim illumination of distant Vegas lights seeped through their tall bedroom window. Her eyes sought Hunter's face, which rested just inches from hers.

"Oh, damn it. I fell asleep again, didn't I?"

He smiled softly, his fingers tracing a path up and down her arm. "It wasn't for long. Less than an hour."

"You probably think I'm narcoleptic at this point."

Hunter laughed. "I don't think you're narcoleptic."

"Well, good. I swear I'm not. You're just so warm and comforting and loving and I'm just...I'm at peace when I'm with you."

"Perfect," he whispered, leaning in to press a soft kiss to her lips. "That's what I want for you."

Her fingers settled on his chest. "I wish you felt that peace, too."

"I do. I'm completely at peace when I'm with you. Believe me."

"Then why didn't you nap with me? I mean, I know you never nap. But today seems like the perfect day for it, if you were ever going to."

"You're right; it is the perfect day. I guess I just have a lot on my mind. It helps me to lie here beside you and think."

"Yeah? What are you thinking about?"

"Well..." he hesitated, trailing his hand down her arm and onto her waist. "For one, I'm thinking about the fourth orgasm I owe you."

"Seriously? I really don't think that's necessary. The first three were amazing, and I'm content to leave it at that."

"But I'm not. I promised you four. I have one more to go."

Scarlet nibbled against her lip, her body already responding to the thought of being with him again, especially as his firm fingers drifted over her skin. "Are we really going to try for a fourth?"

"We're not just going to try, Scarlet. We're going to succeed."

She sighed with that promise, easing her fingers down his chest and onto his abs, watching the spark in his eyes while she slowly traced the indentations of his muscles. When she moved lower still, to wrap her hand around his hardening cock, Hunter moaned. "I'll only agree to finish this game of ours if you'll come again, too," she told him, working her hand up and down his swelling length.

His eyes narrowed as his fingers closed around her thigh. "I don't think that will be a problem," he assured, his shaft pulsing inside her palm, growing harder and heavier with her attentions.

"Then can we get into the shower for this one? I wanted you with me in the shower so badly this morning, I could hardly stand it."

Hunter grinned deliciously. "The shower it is," he agreed, thrusting his erection into her palm before withdrawing himself from her entirely.

He rolled over, rose up off the mattress, and looked to her in the darkened room. Scarlet took the hand he offered, using his support to shift across the sheets and stand beside him. He entwined their fingers as he walked them to the bathroom, guiding her inside the door. He flipped on the light, making her blink with the brightness.

"Is the light okay?" he asked.

"Sure, if you want it on."

"I do. I want to see you."

Her face heated, which surprised her, given everything she'd already done with this man. "I want to see you, too," she admitted.

Hunter smiled as he opened the glass shower door, turning on both showerheads and testing the water temperature. "Ladies first."

Scarlet stepped into the blue-tiled haven and moved under the spray, letting the warmth run over her face and across her body. She heard the door close just before his chest came flush with her back. His arms encircled her waist as she smoothed her wet hair away from her face.

Leaning back against him, she rested her head on his shoulder. He kissed her temple, his rough beard sliding over her soft skin while he flattened his hands onto her stomach. The hot water droplets slid over their bodies, soaking them through as steam rose into the air.

Scarlet shifted her feet, wanting to experience the sensation of his slippery flesh on hers. "You feel really good when you're wet, Hunter."

"Hmm. You always feel good when you're wet."

"Well, you certainly do a fantastic job of making me wet."

His erection pulsed with her words, twitching into the flesh of her bottom, catching her breath in her chest. Her mind leapt back to Blue, to the night he'd eaten his steak dinner off her skin, when he confessed to wanting to fuck the seam of her ass cheeks. Scarlet shivered with that memory, regretting the fact that he'd refused to grant himself the fantasy then, since he feared she wouldn't enjoy it. She didn't want either of them to have that regret any longer. She wanted to take care of him tonight, knowing for certain that he would take care of her.

Reaching her arms up, she stretched them overhead so she could thread her fingers into his hair. She held him in place behind her while pressing her bottom firmly onto his erection and rocking her hips up and down. Hunter inhaled sharply, gripping hard to her waist as she rubbed her backside against him.

The more Scarlet ran her slippery flesh over his, the tighter he held her, his fingers digging into her hipbones. His cock grew more rigid and full each time she ran her ass against it, making him growl and curse beside her ear. Those desperate, heady noises only enticed her further.

Her fingers tightened in his hair while she moaned in response, taking pleasure in the feel of his thick shaft and tense muscles. She would have been quite content to finish him off just like this, but Hunter eventually groaned and pushed her forward, forcing her to drop her hands back to her sides. He held her at arms' length for a moment, just long enough to curse several more times and suck in a few deep breaths. Then he grabbed her by the hips and spun her around.

The moment she faced him, he pressed her back against the tiled wall and planted his mouth on hers. His kiss was hungry, his tongue insistent, his lips firm and demanding. Yet he still wrenched himself away seconds later. "I think we need to slow this down, Scarlet."

"Hmm," she whimpered. "Do we have to?"

He shifted his feet, jutting his lengthy, eager erection into her belly. "Yes, we have to. I am obviously more than ready to do this, but I need to make sure you're ready, too."

"I think I feel pretty ready."

"Well, that's not good enough. I need you to have a fourth orgasm, so I need to make sure you're absolutely ready for me again."

Scarlet couldn't help smiling. "What can I do to help?"

He nudged the tip of her nose with his. "Why don't you just wrap your arms around my neck and hold onto me while I touch you?"

"'Kay," she breathed, not currently capable of forming a full reply.

She encircled his shoulders, lacing her fingers against his neck, while Hunter pressed his lips high on her cheek, then low on her ear, then under her jawline. His mouth explored her skin while his hands smoothed over her thighs and stomach before easing up to her breasts. Scarlet whimpered when he ran his fingers over her nipples, the peaks tightening with furious intent. Wetness pooled between her legs – wetness that had nothing to do with the water pulsing over their bodies – and she closed her eyes and dropped her head back against the wall, allowing herself to simply feel.

Hunter continued to kiss her neck and face and mouth, his soft lips caressing her skin while his strong hands gently kneaded her breasts. Eventually, he eased his skilled fingers around her body and onto her back, tracing the straight line of her spine up and down, over and over. His hands slid lower on her back each time, until he finally allowed them to smooth down entirely. He groaned when his palms flattened against her ass cheeks, his fingers edging near the soft center seam.

He had the same feral reaction as always to touching her this way, desperate and desirous and sinful. He gripped her fiercely with both hands, growling as he pulled her up onto him, jutting his stiff cock into the rounded swell of her tummy. Scarlet whimpered, peeling her eyelids open to half-mast. "I – I think I'm ready for you now."

Hunter matched her lustful gaze, but still shook his head. "No, not yet," he said, releasing his grip on her. "I need to do more for you."

"More?"

"More," he verified, smoothing his hands over her stomach and down her legs, moving closer and closer to the juncture of her thighs.

She knew what he had planned. He would touch her with his magic hands, stroking her sex with merciless precision. He would light her entire body on fire, and she would come apart from merely the touch of his fingers. But that wasn't what she wanted, for her or for him.

When his hand moved between her legs, Scarlet grabbed his wrist. He ceased moving immediately and looked to her eyes. "Everything okay?"

"Yeah," she breathed, slipping her fingers over his. "I just want to talk about something."

"What do you want to talk about?"

She took a deep breath. "Do you remember that night up at the cabin, when you ate your steak dinner off my back?"

Hunter entwined their fingers. "It's not something I'll ever forget."

Her lips pulled up in a shy smile. "I'll never forget, either. Especially that moment when you said...you said, um..."

"What did I say?"

Scarlet pressed her shoulders back against the wall. "You said you wanted to fuck the seam of my ass."

His eyes widened, glancing down to her lips as if he'd never imagined those words coming from them. "I did say that, didn't I? That was an unusual night for me. I let my mind wander to all sorts of places. I hope I didn't offend you."

"Offend me?" she echoed, drawing his heated gaze back to her face. "I wasn't offended. Not at all. I love that you want me in that way."

"God, I want you in every way," he groaned, staring her down. "You should know that by now."

She had trouble taking an even breath. "Then I want you to have me this way. I want you to fuck the seam of my ass. Right here and now."

Hunter instantly shook his head. "I appreciate the thought, but..."

"But nothing. Like you said earlier, this weekend should be about us doing the things we want to do. I know this is something you want."

Their eyes locked for a long minute. He reached for her face, his fingers easing over her jaw and into her drenched hair. "I love that you're willing to give me this. But there are a few obstacles to it now."

"What obstacles?"

"Well, water isn't the best lubricant, and I don't know if I could get your skin as slick as I would need. More importantly, I'm still not sure you'd enjoy it, and I very much want you to have another orgasm."

"Actually," she hemmed, not wanting to appear too eager, "I think we could solve the lubrication problem pretty easily."

"Yeah? How so?"

"It's just that we're in the shower, and there's a particularly slick thing in here that I use every day. Although maybe you don't use it, because you don't need to, since your hair is perfect and you probably don't need to do anything to keep it that way. You probably wake up gorgeous and stay gorgeous all day. And I don't even need to say probably, since I've seen that fascinating truth in real life."

Hunter grinned. "What slick thing are you talking about?"

"Hair conditioner. It's very slick, so we could probably use it as a lubricant. I mean, if you think it would work."

"Wow. That's certainly creative."

"Um, thank you? Although I don't know why our room didn't just come with a supply of lubricants. I mean, really, this is Vegas. They should have sex toy vending machines at the bedside, or something."

Hunter chuckled. "Would you like that?"

"Like what?"

"For us to have sex toys to play with?"

Her throat ran dry. "Well, I guess I wouldn't say *no*."

He pushed both hands into her hair, his pupils dilating as he held her in place. "Damn, honey. You can't even imagine all the things I'm going to make you feel when I have toys at my disposal."

Scarlet's mouth fell open. "Yes, well, I, uh...I think that's a great discussion to have. But on a different day. Right now, I want to talk more about the lubricated-ass-seam thing."

Another chuckle rumbled through his chest. He leaned down to press his lips to hers. "You're wonderful, you know that? You're so incredibly wonderful, and that's why I still don't think we should do this now."

"Why not?"

"Because I want today to be amazing for you. I want everything you experience to be perfect. I want you to feel happy and loved, and I definitely want to give you another orgasm. And I don't know if I can accomplish all of that while fucking you in this particular way."

Her hand settled over his heart. "I already feel wildly happy and blissfully loved. Today will only get better if we do this, since I'm going to be even happier knowing I'm giving you something you want."

Hunter's shoulders fell on a sigh. "I don't know what I ever did to deserve you. I honestly don't."

Scarlet whimpered at the look in his eyes. The level of adoration in that perfect blue had reached ridiculous proportions, making her come to a sad conclusion. "You're not going to do this, are you? You're not going to let yourself have this fantasy."

He shook his head slowly. "Only because I want you to be happy."

But this will make me happy, she thought, although she didn't bother to say it out loud. She knew he had no intention of focusing on his own desires right now – only hers. He'd been nothing but sweet and tender and caring with her all day, and this teddy bear standing before her now wouldn't dare do anything she might consider remotely untoward.

Scarlet huffed out a breath, currently frustrated as hell by Teddy Bear Hunter. This side of him was wonderful under normal circumstances. But right this minute, she really missed Grizzly Bear Hunter.

Curling her fingers up on his chest, she absorbed the determination written on his face. She knew there was only one way she could have her grizzly bear back now. After all, he'd told her what she needed to say when they were in his bed yesterday morning. The words danced on the tip of her tongue, making her blood bound ferociously through her veins.

Lifting her chin, she matched his frank stare head-on. "Hunter?"

"Yes?"

"I want my scoundrel now."

His jaw unhinged the instant the phrase left her mouth. He blinked repeatedly, searching her eyes for torturous seconds. Finally, he dragged his hand onto her jaw, cupping it in his palm to ground her gaze to his. "Are you sure about this, Scarlet?"

"I am. I'm sure."

"And just so you and I are both clear about what we're going to do now, this means you want me to be my demanding, controlling self with you during sex. Is that right?"

Her breath hitched. "Yes."

"Mmm. I like the sound of that," he hummed, running his tongue across the seam of her lips before melding them together, kissing her so thoroughly that she had to lock her knees to keep from collapsing. His hand still cradled her face when he eased back to rest his forehead on hers. "You know, while I'm being a scoundrel, you can always tell me to stop what I'm doing at any time."

"I know. I trust you implicitly. And I want my fourth orgasm."

"You'll have it," he vowed, capturing her gaze. "You do understand that I'm going to tell you what I want from you, right? And that I expect you to do everything I say, the moment I say it?"

Her nipples hardened with the deep scrape of his voice. "I understand. I'm at your mercy."

"I'm also at yours."

"I love you, Hunter."

"I know you do. But I love you more."

"*More*? I don't think so. You can't possibly love me more."

"Damn it, woman. Do *not* correct me."

Scarlet scoffed at his command. Every muscle in her body stiffened, her entire being screaming at her to correct his ass right this instant, in her loudest voice ever. She opened her mouth to do just that, when she witnessed the teasing curve of his lips and daring rise of his brow.

"Sweet hell," she breathed, realizing Hunter was testing her now. He wanted to see how far he could push her with this whole scoundrel-thing, and she had to decide what she would allow. She could stop him this instant, of course, if she wanted to. In truth, he probably expected her to fight tooth and nail against his controlling, demanding side – even though she'd been the one to request it.

Pursing her lips, Scarlet grappled with her decision. She could either call off this game of theirs this minute, or she could give up her control for a little while. She could allow them both these moments to play together, trusting him to keep her safe and ensure her pleasure.

Hunter stood in silence, awaiting her decision. She soaked in every emotion on display in his eyes before inhaling steeply and squaring her shoulders. "I'm sorry," she said, barely recognizing her own voice for its breathiness. "I promise I won't correct you again."

If he was surprised by her submission, he didn't show it. The teasing grin on his lips transformed into something dark and desirous as he let his hands fall to his sides and cleared his throat. "Excellent," he praised. "Now that we have that settled, I want you to put a good amount of hair conditioner into your hands."

Scarlet complied without hesitation, reaching to the shelf, opening the bottle, and pouring the thick white cream into her palm. Hunter adjusted the angles of the showerheads down to their feet, so the heat from the water still rose around them, even if the droplets no longer landed directly on their bodies. After setting the bottle back on the shelf, she stood with her spine against the cool surface of the wall and breathed in the flowery scent of the conditioner in her hand.

Hunter watched her closely. "I'd like you to rub that between your palms now, to warm it to the temperature of your skin."

She did as instructed, running the smooth cream against her fingers.

"Very good, Scarlet. Now I want you to put it on me."

Reaching down, she wrapped both hands around his jutting cock. Her warm fingers still felt cool compared to the heat of his skin, and he sucked in a sharp breath the moment she touched him. But he didn't move, or flinch, or even blink, as he held her eyes.

She slid her hands up and down his long length, slathering the cream over his taut skin. The muscle in Hunter's jaw twitched as she worked, his powerful stare making her nipples harden further even in the hot, steamy air. Biting her lip to keep from moaning, Scarlet squeezed tight to his shaft, rubbing him over and over, until he eventually groaned and reached for her wrists, grasping one of them in each of his hands.

"That's enough," he told her, his voice strained as he lifted her arms to the sides, placing her hands beneath the showerheads.

Hunter held her fingers under the water, rinsing them clean. The moment the thick cream washed away, he brought her hands to his face, gathering them close to press a kiss into each of her palms. When she giggled with the ticklish sensation of his jaw stubble, he nipped her skin.

"Ouch!" she squealed.

His brow rose. "Did that hurt?"

"Well, you did just *bite* me."

"Yes, I did. And I intend to bite you a lot more, so I need to know if it really hurt, or if it actually felt good."

She took a shaky breath in. "It – it felt good."

Hunter smiled before bringing her hand back to his mouth and biting her again. She didn't protest this time. She just relished the way his teeth felt against her flesh, and how his tongue soothed over the little indentations he'd left on her skin. By the time he pinned her eyes again, goose bumps rose all over her body.

"I want you to turn around now, Scarlet. Turn to face the wall, and place your hands flat against the tile."

She could barely drag her eyes away from his to do as he'd ordered. But she finally managed it, pivoting toward the dark tiles. She flattened her palms against the cool wall and stretched her fingers out.

Scarlet stilled, sensing his body behind hers. He didn't touch her anywhere, at least not physically. Yet she could still feel the heat of his skin moving across the inches that separated them, and the warmth of his breath brushing over her shoulder, as he stepped closer. Her air came in short, stuttered bursts to her lungs while she waited for him to do something. Then she felt his hands in her hair, brushing her curls over one shoulder, pushing the soaked strands forward onto her chest.

Hunter pressed his mouth to the back of her neck, his lips caressing the skin he'd exposed. He spent a thorough minute loving that particular spot, until he kissed his way down to her shoulder. He hovered there, his breathing rough and strained. Scarlet tensed in anticipation until the moment his teeth sank into her.

She knew it was coming, but the instant he bit her flesh, she groaned. Her fingers fisted against the tiles as wetness pooled between her thighs. She let her head fall back, dropping it onto his shoulder while he stroked his tongue across her freshly marked skin. Her hips arched backwards, aching for more contact.

Hunter didn't allow it. He reached down the moment she tried to press her bottom onto his cock, grasping her waist in his hands. When he steadied her in place, she whimpered. "I – I want to touch you."

He nipped at her shoulder again. "I know. But not yet."

"Why not?"

"Because I want to touch more of you," he whispered beside her ear. "I want to touch you all over, so I can feel your smooth, perfect skin under my fingers. And I fully intend to do what I want right now."

He released his hold on her, dragging his hands onto her back, smoothing his palms up the line of her spine. Scarlet's head fell forward against the shower wall. She stared at the floor, focusing on the sight of her pink painted toenails in the swirling water, attempting to ground herself so she wouldn't dissolve entirely while he worshipped her body.

Hunter ran his fingers everywhere, from the nape of her neck to the lines of her shoulders, across her arms, back, waist, and thighs. He didn't touch her bottom, though. He ignored that part conspicuously enough to be intentional, coming to a halt when his hands reached her low spine and curving his fingers around her hips instead, before continuing his exploration down her legs.

Scarlet felt him sink to the ground behind her. She felt his hands move down her thighs and onto her calves, felt his fingers massage all of her tensed muscles. She could only moan and whimper, knowing he knelt behind her, his face now flush with her bottom.

He continued to kneel on the ground even when his hands stopped their exploration and settled onto the backs of her thighs. She heard nothing but the sound of the water falling, and the voracious pounding of her heart in her ears, while Hunter shifted closer. She felt the heat of his breath on her skin, right over the curve of one ass cheek. She gasped when he kissed her there. She gasped even louder when he bit down. He held her flesh between his teeth, his tongue tasting her skin with tiny, deliberate licks, until he soothed the spot with a kiss.

His jaw stubble scraped across her when he moved over an inch to bite and kiss another spot. He repeated his actions again and again, growling from deep in his chest as he tasted her flesh. Scarlet whimpered with each graze of his teeth, not because it hurt, but because of how attentive he was to every single part of her. She had no idea how much time passed while he explored her skin, but it was long enough for the wetness seeping from her sex to dampen her thighs.

When Hunter eventually stood back up, he dragged his hands along with him, never breaking contact with her skin as his fingers traced a path up her legs and onto her belly. He pressed his chest flush with her spine, lowered his mouth, and bit into her earlobe. "I was right about what I said this morning, Scarlet. Your ass is quite edible. And just so you're aware, I'll definitely be tasting more of it in the future."

She could only whimper in response to that promise, although she did manage to nod her head. He hummed his contentment with her agreement while his fingertips circled her bellybutton. She waited in pained anticipation to see what he would do next, holding her breath as he moved his touch up slowly, skimming over her hot skin with his even hotter hands, until he grasped her breasts in both palms.

She squeezed her eyes shut, muttering several choice curse words when his fingers edged across her nipples. Then he rolled and pinched them, just hard enough to be painful. "Damn, Hunter, that is…"

"Too rough?"

"No. Not. At all. Not."

He huffed out a laugh against her shoulder. "You're so beautiful. Do you know that?" he asked, cupping the weight of her breasts in his hands. "Do you know how beautiful you are?"

She didn't answer him.

"Tell me you know that," he urged in her silence, his voice deep and lulling, traveling beneath her skin. "Tell me you're beautiful."

"I'm…I'm beautiful."

He pressed his cheek to hers. "Say it again. Like you mean it."

A soft smile pulled up her lips. "I'm *beautiful*."

Hunter sighed into her hair. "You are. You're so incredibly beautiful. Honestly, I can't believe you're mine. It's unreal."

"I am yours."

"I know. And I love it. I love you. Always."

"Always," she echoed.

He ran his fingers over her nipples again, smoothing across her wet skin with deliciously sure strokes, sending tiny bolts of electricity straight to her sex. Scarlet stretched her hands out against the tiles, trying and failing to grasp onto something. She shifted her legs, repeating the motion more and more forcefully, attempting to soothe the pulsing ache between her thighs.

Hunter growled beside her ear. "Stop. Moving. Your. Legs."

"Why?"

"Because it's driving me mad. I want to fuck you so badly."

"Then why don't you?"

He inhaled steeply. "Actually, I think I will."

She pressed her forehead harder into the wall, her entire body tensed in expectation. He pinched her nipples one more time, pulling a moan from her parted lips, before easing his fingers down to her waist. He dragged his hands across her hips and around to her ass, touching her there for the first time with his hands, pressing both palms flat to her cheeks and curling his fingers into her flesh. "Damn, honey. Do you know what I'm thinking right now?"

Scarlet smiled. "Are you thinking you love my ass?"

"That's exactly right. I'm thinking how much I fucking love your ass. And how much I'm going to love fucking your ass."

Her breath hitched with those words.

"Just the outside," Hunter amended, pressing his lips to her shoulder. "I'm only going to fuck the outside of your ass right now. I'm going to fuck the perfect seam between your cheeks, and come into this gorgeous little indentation at the bottom of your spine."

He moved one of his hands up, tracing across the dimple at the base of her back. He touched her softly and reverently, caressing that tiny spot with the tips of his fingers. His mouth latched onto her neck, his tongue forging a wet path against her damp skin.

Scarlet balled her fists into the wall as she concentrated on the feel of his lips and fingers. She held her breath to hear his, relishing the shallow pants that left his chest as he edged his body closer. When his cock finally pressed into her flesh, easing up against her soft center seam, she shuddered. He pushed in a little farther, settling his full length between her cheeks, until his hips made contact with her skin. She groaned when the head of his shaft bobbed against her spine.

"You okay?" Hunter questioned, his voice rough as sandpaper.

"Yes, it's just...it's a little different."

"What does it feel like?"

Scarlet chewed on her lip when his cock twitched between her cheeks. "It feels soft, since the conditioner is slick. But it also feels hard, like you. Which I love."

He slipped his hands over her waist. "I want to move. Is that okay?"

"Mm-hmm."

Pressing another kiss to her neck, Hunter curled his fingers into her hipbones to steady her. He slid back a bit before arching into her, running the hard ridge of his erection up the center of her ass. The pressure pushed Scarlet forward against the tiled wall.

"Oh," she squeaked.

Hunter stilled instantly. "Are you doing okay with this?"

"I am. I'm doing great, it's just..."

"Just what?"

"When you pushed into me, I hit the cold tile."

"You mean your breasts hit the tile?"

"Yes."

"And did that feel good?"

"I – I don't know."

"Then let's try it again," he encouraged, holding tight to her flesh as he thrust into her. Scarlet moaned with the sensation of his slick, hard length rubbing into her sensitive skin, but could barely focus before her breasts hit the tile, the cold surface pulling against her tight peaks. She made a sound somewhere between a gasp and a curse as she attempted to reconcile each unique sensation.

Hunter uncurled one hand from her hip, trailing it slowly up her body all the way to her fist. He rubbed her knotted hand over and over, until she finally relaxed and rested her palm flat on the wall. He wound their fingers together to hold her steady.

"Scarlet, if this is too much for you, we'll stop."

She shook her head. "No, don't stop. Please don't stop. But do keep holding my hand. I love that."

His fingers tightened in hers. "I love it, too," he said, placing a kiss on the shell of her ear.

He thrust his cock up inside her soft ridge again, rubbing her nipples deliberately into the tile. The motion sent a spike of lightning from her breasts to her sex, and she gripped his fingers and groaned. Scarlet shifted forward again, pressing her nipples against the tile of her own volition, sending another shock wave through her body.

His lips pulled into a smile against her shoulder. "You like the way the wall feels when your nipples rub against it, don't you?"

"God, yes," she admitted.

"Then keep doing it. I want you to rub yourself against the wall every time I thrust into you, since I don't have enough hands right now."

"You don't have enough hands for what?"

"To touch you in every way I want to," he explained, dragging his free hand down from her hip, across her thigh, and between her legs.

Scarlet shifted her knees apart the moment his fingers roamed close to her sex. He touched her slowly, tracing over her inner thighs and around that tender area without entering her at all. His teasing motions made her huff in anticipation – and more than a little frustration.

He shifted his cock back up the seam of her ass, pushing her nipples into the wall again. "Goddamnit, Hunter. Just do it already."

He nipped at her shoulder. "Does that mean you'd like me to put my finger inside of you now?"

"Yes. Please. *Please*."

"Hmm. You first."

"What?"

"I want you to touch yourself. I need to see that."

Flames of heat flushed her face, a surprising accomplishment given the level of steam building in the shower around them.

"Slide your finger up inside your sex, Scarlet. Do it for me."

She complied without thought, slipping her hand onto her belly first, warming her skin to the temperature of her body. Hunter's chin pressed into her shoulder as he looked over it, watching her every movement. When she finally pushed her hand down between her legs, and slid one finger up inside her sheath, they both groaned.

He bit into her neck, making her eyes roll back in her head. "Tell me how it feels," he urged. "Tell me what you feel when you touch yourself."

"It feels...it feels soft. Soft and smooth and so, so wet."

Hunter pressed his hips forward, gliding his stiff length up between her ass cheeks. "You feel amazing, don't you?"

She shifted her finger inside her throbbing flesh. "Y-yes."

"I already know that. I just want to make sure you know it, too." He kept one hand tangled up with hers against the wall. With his other hand, he trailed a path down her arm and over her wrist, pressing into her palm in order to push her finger deeper inside her body.

"God, Hunter, that is..."

"It's incredible, isn't it? Feeling you is so fucking incredible. I can't wait to feel how soft and wet you are for myself. In fact, I'm not going to wait anylonger."

Scarlet didn't have time to react. Not before his palm slid down and his middle finger eased swiftly and seamlessly into her. She gasped as both their fingers came to rest side-by-side within the walls of her sex.

Hunter pushed the head of his cock into her lower back. "You're right. You feel amazing inside. Simply amazing."

She exhaled shakily. "I don't know why this should surprise me, because you've certainly had two fingers inside me before, but having one of those fingers be mine is a bit different."

"Different in a good way?"

"Very good."

"Perfect," he growled, squeezing onto her other hand to stabilize it against the wall. He pressed his chest fully into her spine and lodged his finger deep inside her sex, fusing their bodies together. "I'm going to fuck you now, Scarlet. I'm going to fuck you with my cock in the seam of your ass and with our fingers inside your sex, while your nipples drag against this wall. And you're going to come for me. You're going to come *so goddamn hard* for me. Do you understand?"

"I do," she said, her forehead bobbing on the tile. "I understand."

Hunter curled his finger up inside her body. "You ready?"

"Mm-hmm. Ready."

He did what he promised then. He rubbed his cock inside her ass cheeks, and pushed her nipples against the wall, and slid his finger against hers so they could stroke her inner muscles together. At first, there were too many sensations for her to take all at once. The feel of his hard length against her tender skin, of her peaked nipples dragging over the cold tile, of their fingers pressing inside her wet heat – it overwhelmed her, making it difficult to focus. Scarlet told herself to breathe, to feel, to enjoy the undulating waves of electricity surging through her body.

Steam rose around them, filling her lungs with warmth, surrounding them in a tight cocoon. Hunter rested his face beside hers, his breaths coming in short, staccato pants as he controlled every movement. She worked to absorb each sensation while her hand gripped onto his for dear life. He moaned deep in his chest, the sound rumbling against her spine, bringing a smile to her lips.

"Do you – do you like this?" she asked, not because she questioned it, but because she wanted to hear him say the words.

He squeezed hard to her fingers. "God, yes."

"Is it everything you wanted?"

"*You* are what I want. *All* of you."

His hips shifted again, pressing her into the wall while his finger drove in and out of her sex, urging her finger to do the same. When he rested his forehead against the back of her hair, Scarlet knew he looked down to watch his cock slide up through her seam. She envisioned the sight of his rigid erection between her ass cheeks, the image causing a fresh wave of wetness from inside her sheath to bathe their fingers. "Do you like what you see, Hunter?"

"Yes," he breathed, pumping his hips faster.

She bit into her lip when he pressed the palm of her hand flush against the throbbing folds of her sex, shooting a frisson of lightning through her body. "You like watching yourself move inside me like this?"

"Yes. Hell, yes. I love it."

Scarlet whimpered with the driving sensation of their fingers in front of her and his cock behind her. "I love it, too. I love feeling your skin slip across mine. I love it when you fuck my ass."

"Goddamnit. Stop talking. Now."

"Why? Because the sound of my voice makes you want to come?"

"Yes."

"I want that," she insisted, pressing her palm down against her tiny bundle of nerves, feeling the crackles of energy radiating out from her aching flesh. "I want you to come now, right on my back."

"Fuck, honey. I'm going to. I can't last much longer."

"Then let go."

"I want you with me."

"I will be. When I feel you come, I will, too."

He ran his finger even deeper inside her walls. "Swear it, Scarlet."

"I swear it."

Hunter muttered beneath his breath, something that sounded like a grateful curse. He pumped his hips a few more times, running his cock hard and steady between her ass cheeks, until his entire body tensed at once. He bit into her shoulder the moment he came, muffling the sound of his screams as his liquid spurted, hot and thick, onto her back.

The second she felt that wetness pulsing on the base of her spine, Scarlet pressed her hand into her sex and pushed her nipples against the wall. She came instantly, her mouth dropping open so her screams rang out loud and clear, reverberating off the shower walls.

Hunter unwound their fingers to wrap his arm across her chest. He clamped them together while his tongue soothed the teeth marks he'd made on her shoulder, his muscles still contracting with the last few pulsations of his cock inside her seam. Scarlet braced her hand on the tile as she basked in the arcs of lightning still firing throughout her body.

He pressed hot, languid kisses over her neck, his lips dragging all the way up to her ear, as the last explosions of her nerve endings subsided. Exhaling entirely, she allowed her body to sag back against his. Hunter eased their fingers out of her sex to grab onto her hand and wind it with his, bringing them both to her waist so he could band her tighter to his chest. When her legs swayed, he pressed his knee between hers, creating a makeshift chair for her on his thigh.

Scarlet slumped down onto him. "Mmm. That's number four."

"That's number four," he echoed, pressing a kiss to the curve of her ear. Steadying her body with one hand, he reached the other up to a showerhead. Hunter directed the water onto her spine, washing his thick liquid from her skin. Once he'd rinsed her clean, he wrapped her back up in both arms.

All she could do was giggle in drunken delight. "You know, four orgasms for me and two for you makes a total of six in just a couple hours. I wonder if that's some sort of world record."

He laughed, shifting his body delightfully beneath hers.

"I'd really love to see your smile," she sighed. "Can I turn around?"

"I don't know. Can you stand?"

"Probably. If I make myself."

"Okay, we'll try it," he said, grasping her hips as she pivoted.

The instant Scarlet faced him, she threw her arms around his neck and plastered her mouth to his. Hunter returned her eager kisses, his hands snaking around her back to slide across her wet skin. After lengthy, unhurried moments with her lips pressed to his, she pulled back to see his face. "I have to say, I really like the Number Game."

His eyes sparked. "In that case, we can play it whenever you like."

"You certainly are willing to put in any effort to make me happy."

"I'd do anything to make you happy. You know that, right?"

"I do know. I just hope the Number Game made you happy, too."

"It did. Very happy."

"Does that mean I actually managed to fulfill your fantasy? The one I still owe you from when we were at Blue? I thought maybe the ass-seam-sex thing would be the one you'd want."

A slow smile curved his lips. "I'm sorry, but no. I loved everything about this fantasy, obviously. But you do still owe me one."

"Really? There's still another fantasy you want me to give you?"

Hunter huffed out a laugh. "I suppose, in a way. Honestly, I don't know how to answer that question, since the truth sounds really bad."

"That's...that's okay. Just tell me."

He shifted his feet on the wet floor. "The truth is that I have no intention of asking you to fulfill that fantasy. Not ever. I don't want you to fulfill it because I want you to owe it to me always. You see, as long as you owe me that, I figure you'll stay with me. And that's what I want more than anything. I just want you to stay with me."

His confession clamped her heart in a vice. "Hunter, I'm not going anywhere. Not as long as you want me with you."

"Promise?"

"Promise."

He relaxed then. He exhaled, rested his forehead onto hers, and eased the tight bands of his arms. "Thank God," he breathed.

Scarlet closed her eyes with his words, smoothing her fingers into his hair. Water rained down around them, making their entire world warm, soft, and enveloping. She could have fallen asleep again right here, holding onto him inside their bubble. But then her stomach grumbled.

"Apparently, I need to get you something to eat," he responded to the ominous sound. "Is it okay if I take you out to dinner now?"

"Gosh, I don't know," she answered with a grin. "Having dinner is such a big step in our relationship. I'm not sure if I'm ready for it."

He met her playful gaze with his own. "Is it too much, too soon?"

"Well, I guess it'll be fine. It's a bit late for me to play hard-to-get."

He laughed, deep and full, before pressing his lips to hers. By the time he eased away, her innards felt downright squishy. "I'm going to wash up really quickly, and then you'll have the place to yourself," he assured.

Scarlet gave him a leisurely smile, propping against the wall to watch him run a bar of soap across his skin. She shook her head, silently admonishing herself for envying a bar of soap. The moment Hunter finished, he leaned in for another kiss. "Take your time in here, and I'll meet you outside when you're done."

"'Kay," she agreed, still grinning even after he left the bathroom. Smiling actually felt like a permanent affliction at this point, so she decided to simply enjoy that sensation as she washed up. Her smile only grew wider when she reached for her hair conditioner.

When Scarlet eventually left the shower and began toweling off, she saw the dress Hunter had bought her earlier today resting on the counter by the sink, along with her red high heels. He'd set the outfit here for her, and she couldn't wait for the look on his face when he saw her wearing it. After drying her hair, she fixed it into a soft up-do. Then she fussed over her gorgeous new dress, just because she could.

The moment Scarlet finished slipping on the deliciously soft fabric and stepping into her heels, she walked out of the bathroom. Instantly, her eyes locked in on him across the room. He'd dressed in a tailored black suit with a crisp white shirt beneath it, and he now stood by the window, staring out over the city.

"God, you look so handsome," she breathed.

Hunter turned at the sound of her voice, striding around the bed to appear before her with lightning speed. His hands found her face, his lips found her mouth, and she wrapped her fingers around his forearms and simply held on. When the kiss ended, he whispered, "You look absolutely gorgeous."

"Thank you. For the dress. For everything."

"Thank you for coming to dinner with me."

When he held out his arm, Scarlet laced her hand around his sleeve, allowing him to guide them both out of the hotel room, into the elevator, down to the first floor, and through the lobby. As soon as they stepped from the building and onto the sidewalk, the sights of Vegas surrounded them – glitter and gloss, raucous noises and joyful laughter, happiness and smiles. She held tight to his arm while they strolled together for several blocks, until he led her through the doors to an elegant restaurant close to a magnificent display of jumping fountains.

Hunter pulled her chair out for her when the hostess brought them to their table, seating himself by her side. He touched Scarlet often as they ate, caressing her hand or shoulder, or running his fingers over her thigh. They shared a scrumptious meal, and enjoyed easy conversation, and exchanged so many adoring, loving looks that she feared the other restaurant patrons might have difficulty keeping their food down.

He maintained constant contact with her, even when he led her out of the restaurant sometime later. He took her hand securely in his while they ventured onto the sidewalk, blending in with the throngs of tourists still wandering the strip at night. Small gatherings of people punctuated the sidewalk at intervals where onlookers gathered to watch various street performers. The makeshift circles formed around musicians, living statues, and oddly dressed men and women of all shapes and sizes. Hunter steered her around the crowds, keeping them on course to return to their hotel, even as she tried to see everything at once. Scarlet tugged on him occasionally, eager to watch all the shows on the side streets, but he held her steady and kept her moving forward.

His footing never faltered once.

Not until they reached the chapel.

It was a little white chapel, right on the corner, with a purple door and purple glass windows looking out to the street. She probably wouldn't have glanced at it twice, except for the fact that Hunter paused. He slowed them both down in front of it and looked to the door, his hesitation drawing her attention to the quaint building.

Scarlet's entire body stiffened that instant. For one minute, she thought he might guide her straight to the chapel door. She thought he might ask her to marry him, here and now. All of this just felt too perfect – how lovely their day had progressed, how intimately connected they'd been, how beautifully dressed they now were – it all felt damn near flawless, and she feared his intentions.

Her body remained wound like a knot next to his. She held as still as the human statues they'd seen on the street, frozen beside him. Right up until the moment he began walking again.

Hunter didn't mention anything about the chapel when he resumed his footsteps. He just pulled her by the hand, guiding them both down the sidewalk. Scarlet decided not to ask any questions about the chapel, since she knew it should be a relief to her that he didn't intend to travel that road. After all, an impromptu Vegas wedding shouldn't be something either of them desired.

Once they made their way safely past the chapel with the purple door, she allowed herself to resume a gawking fascination at the world around them.

Hunter listened to every excited word that left her lips, yet he remained quiet as they strolled. He kept their fingers interwoven while maneuvering her deftly through the crowds, winding them around a street magician performing card tricks and pulling her close when a group of young women rushed past them on the sidewalk.

"I do believe that is a bachelorette party," Scarlet informed him as the squealing ladies zipped by in their festive dresses and high heels.

He chuckled. "What was your first clue?"

"I think it was the woman wearing the sash that says, 'Bride-to-be' and sporting a huge foam penis on the top of her head."

"Yeah, that was my first clue, too."

"Well, I hope whoever she's marrying will give her lots of orgasms."

Hunter choked on his tongue.

Scarlet glanced up to his face. "Oh, sorry, I guess that sounded a little funny. I'm just feeling incredibly satiated from all the orgasms you gave me earlier, and I'm wishing the best for that young woman."

His tensed shoulders settled. "All I took from that sentence is you think I'm the best."

She giggled, holding tighter to his hand as they walked. "You are definitely the best. In every way, shape, and form."

Another wedding chapel appeared beside them, this one twice the size of the last, with large pink neon palm trees glowing brightly in the front yard. Hunter's footing didn't falter at all as they strolled by it, so Scarlet allowed herself to marvel at the curious sight. They passed a third chapel on the next block, this one painted in gold and silver stripes, and she remembered that wedding chapels were a dime a dozen in Vegas. That realization made her acknowledge how silly it was to even consider that he might propose to her tonight, when they'd only known each other for three weeks.

Scarlet settled her mind, content to simply enjoy the solid feel of his body beside hers as he led her down the street. Eventually, she spotted their hotel in the distance, just as the sound of music filled her ears. She turned her head to see another street performer – an older gentleman strumming on a guitar – and she hummed along with the familiar tune while Hunter guided her around the crowd of people gathered to watch him play. Just a few steps later, she saw another chapel on their right, this one white like the first one but with colorful stained glass windows.

She didn't realize she still hummed in time with the guitar music until Hunter started humming with her. The sound of his voice made her smile, until he dropped his hand from hers for the first time tonight. She frowned when he took a step away, but smiled again when he grabbed hold of her waist and pulled her fully against him. He lifted her straight off the ground, holding her tight to his chest and spinning them both in a circle.

Scarlet threw her arms around his neck, squealing as he twirled them together on the sidewalk. The instant Hunter set her down, he took one of her hands in his own while wrapping his other arm around her back. Then he started dancing, swaying her side-to-side, right here in the middle of all these people.

She didn't know how to respond, so she just held tight to his fingers and grinned up at him. His eyes gleamed in the glow of the streetlights, his chest rumbling against hers with the new song he hummed. Scarlet recognized this tune, since it was the same Elvis song she'd hummed to him after they'd made love in her bed at Blue.

Hunter stepped away from her again, only to spin her out in a circle before tugging her back onto his chest. The moment he had her in his arms, he dipped her down nearly to the ground. Once he brought her slowly up to standing again, he kissed her lips. "Hmm. This is nice."

Scarlet pinned his eyes. "It is. But I thought you didn't dance."

He came to a standstill, steadying her in front of him. "I don't, normally. But I also don't want to have any more regrets."

She tilted her head. "What are you talking about?"

"I'm talking about the last night we spent together at Blue, when we made love in your bed, and you hummed that Elvis song to me. I'm talking about how you asked me if I had any regrets about our time together, and I said I didn't. I'm talking about how I realized, from the moment I woke up without you the next morning, I did have regrets."

Scarlet whimpered with his confession. Hunter reached one of his hands to hers, entwining their fingers together. "Not about our time together," he assured. "I don't regret anything I ever did with you up on that mountain. But I do regret the things I *didn't* do."

"Like what?"

"I regret not curling around you like a big spoon the night you fell asleep on me and I carried you into your bedroom. And I regret not dancing with you in the forest when you asked me to. But mostly, I regret letting you go that last night. I regret letting you walk out of my life at all, even if it was only for a few days."

He pulled her hand up to press her palm flat over his chest. "I've lived with so many regrets in my life, Scarlet. I've lived in regret for the last sixteen years. I don't want to live that way anymore."

Hunter's heart pounded beneath her fingers, quickening her own pulse. "Well, I – I think that's a wonderful creed to live by."

"I think it is, too. Which is why I have a confession to make."

"What confession is that?"

"You remember the Number Game we played earlier this evening?"

"Yeah," she laughed. "I vaguely recall it."

"Well, that game was actually meant as a positive reinforcement."

"A positive reinforcement? Does that mean you gave me all those orgasms as a reward for something?"

"I did."

"Were you rewarding me for getting to spend time with my mother? Because if that's the case, I'm sure she'd be available for brunch again tomorrow. I can call her right now."

He grinned. "No, it wasn't for that. I mean, I'm glad I met Dianna, but the Number Game was actually a *preemptive* positive reinforcement."

Scarlet's brow rose. "Preemptive? I guess that means you rewarded me for something I haven't done yet?"

"Exactly."

"Then I suppose you want something from me now."

"Yes. I do want something from you."

"What do you want?"

Hunter gave her a soft smile while pressing her palm down over his heart. "I want your hand, Scarlet."

"My *hand*?"

He inched closer, fastening her beneath his focused gaze. "Do you remember two weeks ago, when we stood in your cabin, and I told you that as close as we'd become in one week, I figured in another two weeks we'd be married?"

"I remember."

"And do you remember how I said I was joking about the marriage thing?"

"I do."

"Well, I...I wasn't joking."

Scarlet opened her mouth to reply, but nothing came out.

Hunter stilled himself in the midst of her silence. Then he glanced down, reached into his coat pocket, and pulled out three rings. They lay inside his palm for a moment before he held his hand out to show them to her: two platinum wedding bands, and a diamond engagement ring.

Her fingers curled up over his heart, her nails digging into her palm as she focused on the obscenely large gemstone. "Dear God, Hunter. Please tell me that diamond is an age-old family heirloom."

"Do you want it to be a family heirloom?"

"Kind of," she said, her eyes searching his. "That would mean you didn't buy it this week, at least. Did you buy it this week?"

"I bought it Tuesday afternoon."

She groaned. "You bought me an engagement ring Tuesday, before I'd even agreed to go on a second date with you?"

"Yes. I bought an engagement ring for you, and wedding bands for both of us. Right before I bought you the silly putty, if that matters."

"So you knew, from the moment you walked into my office Wednesday with a briefcase full of scarves and duct tape, that you were going to ask me to marry you this weekend?"

Hunter nodded. "That was my intention."

"I...I just...oh my God."

He raised one of his hands – the one not holding three rings – to her face, brushing his fingers across her jaw. "I know how fast this seems. I know we only met each other very recently, and I know three weeks isn't a very long time..."

"It's twenty-one *days*."

"You're right. It's been twenty-one days since I first laid eyes on you. And now, I don't want to go another day without you. Because when you realize you want to spend the rest of your life with someone, you want the rest of your life to start as soon as possible."

Her mouth fell open. "Did you just quote *When Harry Met Sally*?"

"I did. I know how much you love movies, and I thought that was a particularly good scene."

"It's like...the best scene ever."

"Well, you know me. I quote movies *all* the time."

Hunter stood before her, holding the rings in his hand as he smiled into her eyes. He smiled at her with happiness and love and sheer, utter joy. Scarlet had to lock her knees.

"Mrs. Gregory," she whispered, trying to wrap her mind around this.

"I would love it if you took my last name," he told her, his thumb tracing the lower edge of her lip. "Or you could keep your own, if you prefer. Although I do remember you telling me you didn't care for the name Tracey. But we can do that any way you want."

"Mrs. Gregory," Scarlet repeated, not because she was making a choice in the matter, but because she couldn't quite get over the sound of it. "Oh, dear Lord, did Rick know?"

"Who?"

"Captain Rick, the pilot on our flight yesterday. He called me 'Mrs. Gregory.' Did he know you were bringing me to Vegas to get married?"

Hunter's hand dropped from her face. "Well, I may have let my plans slip when I was talking to him in the cockpit."

"So, Captain Rick knew before I did?"

"I'm sorry about that. I hadn't told anyone and I was damn near bursting. Also, since we're on the subject, Maxine knows, too."

"You told Maxine? Really?"

"Well, when she called this morning, I told her we were in Vegas to see your mom. When she called back later, she asked if we were only in Vegas to see your mom or if we came to get married. She asked me pointblank if I was going to propose to you, and I didn't want to lie."

"Wh-what did she think about it?"

"She screamed in my ear, giggled a lot, and said we'd better wait until she came home from Paris next month to throw a big reception."

Scarlet stared at him for a long minute. "So, then...did we come to Vegas to meet my mother? Or did we come to get married?"

"Both, really. I felt strongly about us meeting each other's parents before we got married, which is why I arranged that surprise family dinner two nights ago. And I definitely wanted to meet your mother beforehand, although the fact that she lives here in Vegas, where there's a wedding chapel on nearly every street corner, just happened to be incredibly convenient. I mean, really, what are the chances of her living here? I figure they're about as high as me tripping over a squirrel on the side of a mountain and falling into your lap. Honestly, the way I see it, this was all just meant to be."

Her heart pounded a thousand times a minute as she watched him grin with delight. The only noise she managed to make was a strangled whimper. Hunter sighed when he heard her.

"I'm sorry Maxine knew before you did, Scarlet. And I'm sorry Captain Rick knew first. Although you didn't correct him when he called you Mrs. Gregory."

"No, I didn't," she defended, "but that's only because it seemed better, after what we did on that plane, if he thought we were married."

"Then are you saying it's justifiable for us to make love anywhere we want to, as long as we're married?"

"Well, I think it's *more* justifiable, certainly."

He smiled down into her eyes. "Hmm. I'd say that's yet another good reason for us to get married tonight."

Scarlet couldn't move. And the smile on Hunter's face was so damn endearing that she could hardly speak, either. "But why...why tonight?"

"Why not tonight?"

She opened her mouth, trying to formulate an answer, as her fingers curled tighter against his chest. The rings sparkled in his hand, practically blinding her. She turned her head away, glancing at all the people walking and skipping and dancing on the sidewalk. Her eyes drew to the chapel beside them, the pretty little white one with the colorful stained glass windows. "We passed three other chapels on the way here, Hunter. Did you bring us to this one for a reason?"

"I did."

Scarlet turned back to him. "Is it because it's the closest chapel to the hotel we're staying in?"

"No. We're staying in that hotel because it's the closest one to this chapel. It's the only one I found that has Elvis impersonators on staff."

She whimpered. "I guess you researched that ahead of time?"

"Yes."

"On Tuesday?"

"Monday night."

Scarlet's lip quivered as tears gathered in her eyes. She pulled her hand away from his heart, dropping her arm to her side. "This is too much. You know that, right? These past three weeks we've spent together have been a whirlwind. They've been wild and insane and we've only seen the best of each other."

Hunter's brow shot to his hairline.

She shook her head immediately. "Okay, okay, I know that's not true. We've seen the worst of each other, too. I'm aware of that. But still, it's been a fantasy. There's been a little reality in the past few days, but it's mostly been a fantasy. And the thing is," she added, barely getting her words out for the ache digging at her heart, "what if all of this fades? What if the passion we have fades, and you get bored with me?"

"*Bored*? What on earth are you talking about?"

"Up at Blue, you told me I would never bore you. But that won't be true forever. I'm going to bore you at some point."

He laughed. "Scarlet, do you know what I was doing earlier tonight, when you fell asleep between numbers three and four?"

"You told me you were thinking."

"And I was, some. But mostly, I just watched you. Did you know you smile in your sleep? You smiled in your sleep this morning, and again when you napped this evening, and it's the best thing I've ever seen. So, I can pretty much guarantee you're never going to bore me, since you fascinate me even when you're unconscious."

She whimpered with his words. All she wanted to do was to touch him again, to feel his strength. Yet she feared letting herself right now. "But what if none of this lasts forever? The passion we share probably can't, and the world is definitely going to change all around us, and everything can be different in the blink of an eye. Real life isn't anything like what we've experienced in the past three weeks."

Hunter stared into her for a long minute before inching forward. "Do you honestly think I don't know what real life looks like, honey? I've been surviving in the real world for a long time, and I know what it is. I also know things between us aren't always going to be the way they've been for the past three weeks. Our future will be an entirely new journey. Sometimes we're going to laugh with each other, and sometimes we're going to cry. Sometimes I'll be frustrated as hell with you, and sometimes you'll want to strangle me with your bare hands. Sometimes we'll be adventurous and climb mountains, and sometimes we'll be content to just sit and watch movies. Sometimes we'll have wild sex up against a window, and sometimes we'll make love slowly in a warm bed and fall asleep in each other's arms. And sometimes *life* and *work* and, God willing, *kids* will have us so damn tired that we'll go for weeks without being physically intimate at all. But through it all, I'll be there with you, and you'll be there with me, and we'll feel everything together. And that will be more exciting and more fulfilling than anything else on this earth."

Tears streamed freely down Scarlet's face. "Oh, hell. You're perfect, aren't you? You're so goddamn perfect."

"No, I'm not. I'm not perfect at all. But I'm a thousand percent sure I'm perfect for you."

She stood, trembling and crying, staring into his brilliant blue while Hunter continued to hold the rings in his open palm.

"Scarlet, I want to marry you. Tonight. And I'm going to ask you to marry me in just a minute. But first, I have a different question for you."

She swiped at the tears on her face. "What is it?"

"Do you doubt the fact that I'm your husband? Do you have any doubt in your mind that it's going to be me, eventually?"

Her head shook before her brain even caught up to answer. "No, I don't doubt it."

"You have no doubts at all?"

"None."

Hunter exhaled. "Well then, if you don't doubt that I'm your husband, and I sure as hell don't doubt that you're my wife, why should we have to wait to make it official? Are we supposed to delay our lives for the passing of some unspecified amount of time society approves of? And if so, how long will that be? Three weeks? Three months? Three years? Because the way I see it, three years didn't make anything right for either of us when we were with other people. But three weeks was more than enough time for you and I to fall madly in love with each other."

A laugh bubbled up from Scarlet's throat.

He shifted his feet. "Would you rather have a big wedding?"

"No, no. I don't need that."

"I'll understand if you want a big wedding. We can do it. I'll slip this diamond on your finger now, and we'll start planning a massive ceremony the moment we get home. We can be engaged as long as you like, if that makes you happy. Or, if you decide you want to do this with me now, we can bypass the engagement and get married in this chapel. We can say our vows tonight, and have Elvis sing us songs, and go home tomorrow and make plans to get married again with a ton of people around us. Hell, we can get married as often as you like. Two or three times a year. Maybe even once a month, or twice a month, or..."

"Hunter."

"Sorry," he relented. "I know my nerves are getting to me. It's just that I've spent my entire adult life searching. Searching for love, and happiness, and peace. Then one day, quite literally out of the blue, I found everything I ever wanted. I found it up on a mountain. I found it with you. And I'm done searching now. I'm done, and I know the truth of that fact deep in my soul. I *know* it, and time isn't going to change it. Time doesn't have a goddamn thing to do with this. This just *is*."

He looked into her eyes and sighed. "But I'll wait if you want to, my little bird. I'll wait until you're ready. I'll wait forever for you, because you're my best friend, and my lover, and my everything."

Several more tears flowed down Scarlet's face. She used both hands to brush them away, so she could focus on the man in front of her. "Do you think the Elvis in this chapel does more than just sing?"

Hunter's brow quirked. "What more do you want him to do?"

"I just wonder if he can legally perform the ceremony. I figure we're in Vegas, so it's possible an Elvis impersonator can also be an ordained minister. I've always wanted Elvis to marry me, ever since I was a kid. I mean, not marry me as in become my husband, but marry me as in legally bind me to the man I want to become my husband."

"Does that mean you want *me* to become your husband?"

Scarlet reached out, grasping tight to his hand. The three rings pressed between their palms. "Hunter Gregory, will you marry me?"

"Good God, I thought you'd never ask."

She laughed and he joined her, the sounds so bright and sparkling to her ears. He stood, just looking at her, with his fingers trembling under hers. Scarlet dropped her arms to her sides and waited.

Hunter looked down to the rings the moment she released his hand. "I – I guess I'll put these two in my pocket for now, until we get inside the chapel," he said, slipping the wedding bands back into his jacket.

He took the diamond between his fingers, staring at it before looking to her eyes. "I'm going to kneel down now. Because I really want to."

"Okay," she said, her mind barely registering the group of people on the sidewalk who'd stopped everything to surround the two of them.

A collective gasp moved through the gathered crowd when Hunter sank to his knees before her and held the ring up in his fingers. "Scarlet," he breathed. "Will you please make me the happiest man on earth?"

She clasped her hands in front of her, and giggled, and nodded.

Hunter grinned up at her. "Yes?"

"Yes," she said, sinking down to join him on the ground.

He grabbed hold of her just as she threw her arms around his neck. The crowd went wild, yet she barely heard anything but the pounding of her heart. She didn't release her fierce grip on him until he started peppering kisses across her face and lips.

"I love you," he whispered, the warm words fanning over her skin.

"I love you, Hunter. I love, love, love you."

His arms banded around her back to pull them both to standing. He lifted her feet straight off the ground, making her feel like she was flying. The crowd continued cheering even when he finally set her back down.

Hunter slipped the diamond ring on her finger. "You ready, honey?"

"Yes. Definitely yes."

They smiled, and laughed, and flew up the chapel steps together.

20

TIME

Hunter woke in his bed at 7 o'clock on Saturday morning, his internal alarm not allowing him another second of sleep. Careful to exit the mattress quietly, he snuck out of the bedroom, used the bathroom at the end of the hallway, and then proceeded into his home gym. He did his usual hundred sit-ups and push-ups, then turned on the television to watch the news as he stepped onto the treadmill. His eyes scanned the stock market data while he ran, his mind reviewing any impact the figures might have on Gregory Global.

An hour later, he stepped off the treadmill just as his phone rang. When Hunter saw the number, he smiled. "Hey, Tyler," he spoke into the receiver, grabbing a towel to wipe his brow.

"Hunter, buddy! You ready for tomorrow? I don't think you could possibly be ready, quite frankly."

"I'm ready," he insisted, unable to scrub the grin off his face while listening to the ribbings of the man who'd become such a close friend in the past three years. "Are you?"

"More than ready. Hensen Incorporated is finally going to take down Gregory Global."

Hunter huffed. "In your dreams."

"Nope, not this time. We are done being defeated by you."

"What makes you so sure?"

"Because your star player is benched. She told me yesterday."

"You know, I can hit the ball fairly well myself," Hunter defended, even though he knew Tyler made a fair point. Without Scarlet on the team, the chances that GG would win the quarterly softball game against the Richmond branch of Hensen Incorporated were slim to none.

"You're a fine player, Hunter, but you're nowhere near as good as your wife. Besides, I've got Natalie playing tomorrow, too."

"Natalie? You know she's not allowed to play. Only employees and their family, remember?"

Tyler fell silent for a split second, which was a long time for him to be silent. "Well, actually, that brings up a question I have for you."

"Yeah? What's the question?"

"I don't suppose you'd consider being my best man?"

Hunter took a moment to absorb that news. "God, really? Did you finally ask Natalie to marry you?"

"I did. And she said yes, for some odd reason. So, I'm asking you to stand up with me."

"Of course, buddy. I'd be honored."

"Then you're officially my best man. Although I'm still going to wipe the softball field with your ass tomorrow."

"Damn, you probably will. Honestly, with Scarlet on the bench, we don't stand a chance against you. I won't beg for softball mercy, but if I could maintain some dignity in front of my wife, that would be very kind of you."

"Ugh. Are you really playing the sympathy card right now? You know I'd do anything for the two of you."

"I do know, because you're a great friend. I sure as hell am happy for you and Natalie. You'll have to come over for dinner to celebrate."

"We'd love to, whenever Scarlet feels up to it. How is she today?"

"She's still sleeping, but I'll tell her you asked about her."

"Please do. And be sure to rest up for tomorrow."

"Will do. Congratulations, Tyler."

"Thanks, buddy. Who'd have thought I would ever make it this far, right? You know it's all because of your wife."

A smile curved Hunter's lips. "Yeah. She is amazing, isn't she?"

"She is. See you tomorrow."

"Tomorrow."

"Bye."

Hunter still smiled after he hung up the phone. He walked back down the hallway and snuck into the bedroom, careful not to wake his sleeping beauty. Creeping softly into the bathroom, he took a quick shower and came out to get dressed. Scarlet still didn't stir, even when he'd finished throwing on his clothes, so he left to head to the kitchen.

He walked purposefully through the living room, determined to fix a presentable breakfast for his wife, but his footsteps faltered when his toes landed on a squeaky toy. Hunter grumbled with the discomfort, as well as the jolting sound, but found himself smiling again when he picked up the bright object and held it in his hands.

"Connor is probably missing this," he realized, picturing the elder of Will and Maggie's twin boys. The Rands had been over for dinner last night, and Connor had apparently chucked his favorite toy onto the floor and forgotten about it.

Hunter reached up to set the toy on the fireplace mantle. When he laid the squeaker down on the brick, his eyes drew to the row of picture frames lined across the ledge. Scarlet had placed several photos here over the past three years, and he loved seeing the story of their lives in these frozen moments of time.

The first frame on the ledge was the photo she'd taken up at Blue, the blurry green-and-yellow image of the tree that may have held a fantastical bird. She'd been shy about leaving the photo out, but Hunter insisted on it. They'd been asked about the picture several times over the years. His answer was simply that Scarlet was a nature reporter at heart. After all, the picture was just for the two of them. No one else needed to know what it meant, or why it meant so much.

His eyes drew to the next frame, which held an image of her and him and the Elvis who married them that night in Vegas, three weeks after they'd met. Hunter loved seeing Scarlet's eyes in this photo, because they were so happy and sparkling. He remembered them filling with joy as she promised to love and cherish him for their rest of their lives. He remembered them filling with tears as he vowed the same to her. And he remembered looking into them when they woke in their hotel bedroom the next day, naked and tangled up with each other. He remembered spending that lazy Sunday morning in bed with his wife, and never feeling happier in his entire life than he did right then.

The next photo on the ledge was of the two of them a month later, surrounded by family and friends here in their home, when they'd hosted a reception to celebrate their marriage. They'd waited until Maxine got back from Paris to have the party, although Maxine wasn't actually in this photo, because she'd been the one to take it. She was, however, in the next picture on the mantle: a panoramic view of the entire Gregory family up on a mountain together. Maxine had insisted on going along with everyone on their mountain climbing vacation, since she wanted to see how Hunter coped with the great outdoors. He was happy to say he'd done remarkably well, especially with Scarlet beside him. He was even happier to know he'd made his sister proud.

Hunter enjoyed that vacation, but not as much as the one represented by the next frame. This picture was of him and Scarlet on the beach in Bali, where they'd gone to celebrate their second anniversary. They'd renewed their vows while standing together on that white sand, just because they could. He absorbed the sight of his wife in the photo: her wind-tousled hair and sun-kissed skin and her bright, beautiful smile. He remembered how he'd worshipped every inch of her body later that night, and how they'd decided in their satiated aftermath that they were ready to start trying for a family when they got back home.

The next photo on the mantle was of the Rand family, with Will and Maggie standing behind Hunter and Scarlet as they each held one of the twin boys in their arms. The Rands had made Hunter and Scarlet the twins' godparents, and the christening ceremony was full of joy and hugs and tears. His chest swelled as he thought about that moment, and with the knowledge that Will and Maggie would be the godparents to the new life Scarlet carried inside her now.

Hunter shifted Connor's squeaky toy over toward the last picture on the mantle ledge. This frame held Scarlet's ultrasound photo from a few months ago, when they'd found out they were having a baby girl. He could see their daughter's tiny, sweet face in the black and white image. He swore she smiled.

"You've got so many toys waiting for you to play with," he spoke to the photo. "And so many people who can't wait to see you."

He touched the edge of the frame, smiling back at his daughter, just before he turned toward the kitchen. Pushing through the swinging door, he hurried to fill a breakfast tray with croissants, jelly, orange juice, and milk. Then he added a Twinkie in the middle.

Carrying the tray back through the living room and across the hall, he stepped gingerly into the bedroom, careful not to rattle the dishes. He moved over to the mattress and set the tray on the nightstand closest to Scarlet. Hunter gazed down at her ebony hair spread wildly across her pillow, and her mouth hanging slightly open, as she snored softly in the cool air. His eyes drifted down to her left hand, where it lay against her belly – her very big, very pregnant belly. The wedding rings on her finger glistened in the light seeping through the curtains.

Scarlet wore one of his shirts, the sight of her in his oversized button-down reminding him of the first morning they'd spent in this room together. From the moment they'd come home from Vegas as husband and wife, Scarlet often wore his shirts around the house. But she'd only recently started wearing them to bed, since they fit better around the baby. Although her belly had gotten so big now that she left the bottom half of the shirt unbuttoned, which allowed him a perfect view of her bare skin.

He reached to touch his wife's face, drawing his fingers down her cheek and watching as her lips twitched. Moving around to the other side of the bed, he edged beneath the sheets until his chest met her back. Hunter draped his arm across her hip and smoothed his hand onto her rounded stomach, feeling an instant, firm kick beneath his fingers.

"Did you bring it?" Scarlet's sleepy voice floated into the air.

"Of course. I know better than to keep my pregnant wife away from her Twinkie first thing in the morning."

"You're the best husband ever," she declared, stretching her limbs out before snuggling back into his chest again.

He pressed a kiss to her hair. "Guess who called me this morning."

"Mmm...Tyler?"

"How did you know?"

"He told me yesterday in his session that he was going to call you. I wanted to tell you about it last night, but I couldn't, especially since he reminded me that I couldn't say anything, due to doctor-patient confidentiality. Which was frustrating, believe me."

Hunter chuckled. "I suppose you know he proposed to Natalie?"

"Yeah, I do. It's wonderful, isn't it?"

"It is, and it's all because of you. I remember him telling me up at Blue that he would probably get better if he could see you all the time. The moment Hensen Incorporated opened their branch here, and he started coming to you regularly, I could see him improving."

Scarlet smiled sleepily up at him. "You give me too much credit."

"No, I don't. You're a miracle worker. Always have been."

"Well, I assure you it's not a miracle. Tyler is just finally willing to put in the effort to work on his issues. And it doesn't hurt that Natalie loves him to pieces and is willing to help."

"It still sounds like a miracle to me," Hunter insisted, leaning down to rub his nose against hers. "And even if you're not a miracle worker, you're *my* miracle."

"Wow. You sure are mushy this morning, Mr. Gregory."

"I have a lot of reasons to be, Mrs. Gregory," he said, watching his hand as it slipped across her bare belly. "How is our little prizefighter doing today?"

"Mmm, she practiced really hard last night. Kept me up for two hours. She likes to try out her kickboxing moves on my bladder."

"You were up for two hours? You should have woken me."

"No, you need your rest. Besides, I like watching you sleep."

"Okay, but you'll wake me in the middle of the night after she's born, right? You know I'm really good at changing diapers now. I can't even remember the last time I dry-heaved. I daresay I'm an expert."

Scarlet grinned. "Remind me to thank the Rands again, the next time I see them, for having three kids for you to practice on."

"Definitely," Hunter agreed, remembering how full the house felt when they were here last night and knowing how much fuller it would be soon. "I guess I'll also have another kid to practice on in six months."

Her face scrunched. "Six months? I'm due in *three weeks*."

"Yes, I know that. I'm just thinking about the *other* kid."

"Oh, right. Sorry. I'm half asleep." She worked open her eyelids to focus on him. "You're still upset about Maxine being pregnant?"

"No, I'm not upset, I'm just..."

Scarlet skimmed her fingers across his jaw. "I know you're upset. It's okay. You can always talk to me."

Hunter exhaled, resting into the warmth of her touch. "You're right. I'm still upset. I just don't see why they didn't get married first."

"Colin adores Maxine, Hunter. And she has an engagement ring on now."

"Yeah, a little *late*."

Scarlet huffed out a laugh. "You know you love Colin."

"I do. I absolutely do. I just didn't think, when I brought him to Richmond to work for me, that he would knock up my baby sister."

"Well, you are the one who introduced them. Besides, accidents happen. You and I certainly didn't wait until marriage to have sex."

"No, but I had these rings on your finger less than three weeks later."

She patted his hand. "You did do that, didn't you?"

"Yes, I did."

Scarlet squeezed onto his fingers. "Just try to be happy for them, honey. Colin loves Maxine more than anything in the world."

"I know he does, and I'm trying to let Maxine lead her own life. In fact, I think I've been really good about not interfering. But it's hard for me to let go of the brotherly protectiveness."

"You're a wonderful brother, and you're going to be a fantastic uncle. You'll also have five months of Dad-experience before Colin becomes a father, so he'll need you for guidance and support. You know how he looks up to you."

A smile crept onto Hunter's lips. "I know. Colin is family. I've never been upset about that. But sometimes my growly grizzly bear side still comes out."

Scarlet quirked her brow. "Only sometimes?"

Hunter narrowed his eyes at her, running his hand up the inside of her arm where she was most ticklish. "You take that back," he insisted as she giggled and squirmed beneath his touch. "You know you call me your teddy bear a lot more than you call me your grizzly bear."

"Okay, okay...I take it back," she panted, trying to catch her breath between laughs. "You can't tickle me first thing in the morning. It makes me hungry. God, where is that Twinkie?"

He ceased his torture to reach over her head to the tray on the nightstand. Gathering the spongy dessert in his hand, he barely got it off the plate before she grabbed hold of it and shoved a huge bite into her mouth. She groaned in bliss while she chewed.

Hunter couldn't help chuckling as he watched her. "You know, I talked to my mom yesterday. She asked how you're doing and I told her your Twinkie craving has reached maniacal proportions. She said she's going to have a case of them delivered here this weekend."

"A *case*?" Scarlet protested with a half-full mouth. "There's no way I'll eat a case in three weeks! Good Lord, I'm already huge! I can't even play softball!"

"You're not huge," he assured, easing his hand across her belly. "You're busy growing a new human inside you. Besides, whatever Twinkies are left we can send back to my mother. She'll tell us she's returning them, then she'll secretly stash them and eat them herself."

Scarlet burst out laughing, shaking her whole body against his. He shifted closer, bringing his legs up to spoon her fully. As the tiny beams of sun caressed her face, he dragged his hand across her waist and up to her hip, curling his fingers into her skin.

Her giggles ceased the moment he gripped her hipbone, her lips parting on a breathy moan. Dipping his head, Hunter pressed a kiss to her mouth. He hovered there, running his tongue across her lips. "Mmm. You taste like frosting."

"Sorry about that."

"Don't be sorry. You know I love it."

Scarlet smiled up at him with her eyes closed. He let his gaze roam over the curves of her body, from her lush pink lips all the way down. The pregnancy had made her breasts fuller, and increased her belly size exponentially, and also made the smooth curves of her ass even rounder. She was just so damn beautiful, even more than ever before.

Her hips shifted beneath his hands, rubbing her bottom into his lower abs, making him groan. His fingers drifted onto her thigh while he leaned down to nuzzle his nose into her hair. "Scarlet?"

"Mmm?"

"I think you should pick a number for me."

"Ooh. Do we get to play the Number Game today?"

"Definitely."

"Any number between two and ten?"

He smoothed his hand across her leg, moving slowly closer to the juncture of her thighs. "Actually, since you had such a rough night, I think you should pick any number between two and a hundred."

"*A hundred*? My goodness. That's bold, even for you."

"A bit bold, perhaps, but certainly justified. It's only right that I offer rewards to the amazing, miraculous, gorgeous mother of my child."

A wicked grin tugged at her lips. "In that case, I pick ninety-nine."

"Ninety-nine? Seriously?"

"Well, picking a hundred sounds greedy, so…"

Hunter chuckled, slipping his hand between her legs. "I suppose we should get started then, if we're going to accomplish all of them by the end of the day."

Scarlet reached for him, threading their fingers together. "Honey, I don't doubt for one second that you can give me ninety-nine orgasms. But I'm pretty sure if you do, I will go into labor."

"That's okay by me. I'm so ready to see our little girl."

She tugged his hand up, bringing it to rest over her belly again. "I am, too, but I think she could use a couple more weeks to bake in here."

His fingers eased across the roundness beneath his palm. "Well then, maybe not ninety-nine. But you'll have to pick another number."

"Okay. I'll pick another number," Scarlet agreed, a drowsy yawn sneaking out of her mouth while her shoulders slumped against the mattress. "Just as soon as I wake up."

"As soon as you wake up? But aren't you awake now? I've been waiting for you for *hours*."

"Do you think I can have one little extra nap? Please? It's very tiring growing a world-renowned boxer inside you."

He huffed, curling his body up even tighter around hers. "Okay, you can nap for a bit. But I'm staying here with you."

"I'm certainly not going to argue with that," she said, her voice already thickening as her body settled farther into the sheets.

Hunter observed her amusedly, shaking his head when he saw her breathing even out almost immediately. He wouldn't have believed she could be this sleepy right after eating that much sugar if he hadn't seen it a dozen other times during the pregnancy.

"Mmm. I love you so much," she sighed.

He leaned down to kiss her shoulder. "I love you more."

Scarlet's nose crinkled at the statement, but apparently she didn't have the energy to correct him now. Instead, she snuggled her back into his chest and ran her fingers over his hand. A moment later, her soft snores drifted into the air.

Hunter smiled with that calming sound. He settled his head onto the pillow beside her, staring at her loose curls for a moment before he closed his eyes. Threading their fingers more intricately together, he held both of their hands in place over her belly.

He took a deep breath in and released it slowly. He let his body relax into hers, let himself absorb the comfort of them, together here in their soft, warm bed. Hunter let himself be at peace.

Then he fell asleep.

Tina is the author of multiple books and the owner of the publishing company Day and Knight Romance Publications. Writing as Day for her young adult novels and Knight for her adult novels, she offers a wide variety of journeys to satisfy your appetite for romance, love, and passion. Tina enjoys couch surfing, movie theaters, steamy reads, and bonding with fellow obsessive romantics who 'ship all the 'ships there are. Fortunate enough to have stumbled onto her soulmate back in the 1990s, she has been married for over a quarter century to a man who still tells her she's beautiful, no matter how many wrinkles she grows or cupcakes she eats. They live in Virginia with their two children, multiple fish, a fuzzy kitten, and a silly puppy, who are all frankly just too darn cute.

~

Visit Tina Online:
    Facebook.com/TinaKnightBooks
    Instagram.com/TinaKnightBooks
    Twitter @TinaKnightBooks